Mary Larkin was born in Belfast and, after 40 happy years there, now lives in the north-east of England.

Praise for *Best Laid Plans*:

'Working class gritty reality set against a romantic backdrop'
Belfast Telegraph

'Belfast's answer to Catherine Cookson'
Sunday World

Praise for *Sworn to Secrecy*:

'A real chick-lit indulgence'
Woman's Way

MARY LARKIN OMNIBUS

Best Laid Plans
Sworn to Secrecy

SPHERE

This omnibus edition first published in Great Britain by Sphere in 2009
Mary Larkin Omnibus copyright © Mary Larkin 2009

Previously published separately:
Best Laid Plans first published in Great Britain by
Time Warner Books in 2003
Copyright © Mary Larkin, 2004

Sworn to Secrecy first published in Great Britain by
Time Warner Paperbacks in 2005
Copyright © Mary Larkin, 2005

A CIP catalogue for this book is available from the British Library.

ISBN 978-0-7515-4157-1

Printed and bound in Great Britain by
Mackays of Chatham Ltd, Chatham, Kent

Sphere
An imprint of
Little, Brown Book Group
100 Victoria Embankment
London EC4Y 0DY

An Hachette UK Company
www.hachette.co.uk

www.littlebrown.co.uk

Best Laid Plans

I dedicate this book to my late dear father
Tommy McAnulty.

Acknowledgement

Grateful thanks to my son, Con, for designing and maintaining my web site, and to his wife, Debbie, for her constant support.

Author's Note

The geographical areas portrayed in *Best Laid Plans* actually exist and historical events referred to in the course of the story are, to the best of my knowledge, authentic. However, I would like to emphasise that the story is fictional, all characters fictitious and any resemblance to real persons, living or dead, purely coincidental.

Chapter One

'I forbid you to go! And that's the end of it!'

They glared at each other across the kitchen table, like arch enemies ready for martial combat. Grim-faced, Alice Maguire thumped the wooden surface with her clenched fist for the second time, to emphasise her words or to try to scare the living daylights out of her daughter, and ground out between clenched teeth: 'Do you hear me?'

'Hear you? I'm sure they can hear you at the top of Springfield Road. You're screaming like a banshee, so you are. But you listen to me, Mam! I'm going, with or without your permission. Only an idiot would pass up the chance to see the Rolling Stones live on stage. It was only by sheer good luck that Agnes got the complimentary tickets in the first place. If her sister's boyfriend hadn't been suddenly taken into hospital with appendicitis this morning we'd be going to the Broadway or the Windsor as usual.'

Alice was now gnawing worriedly at her lower lip. Since threats didn't appear to be having any effect, perhaps an appeal to her daughter's better nature would do the trick. 'Please don't go, Tess. I didn't want to tell you, but I had one of my bad turns today when you were at the wholesaler's.'

Tess had heard these very same words all too often in the past, when her mother wanted to put pressure on her to get her own way. Usually the ploy worked and Tess gave in for the sake of peace. Not today, though. This was the chance of a lifetime and Tess was not to be swayed. However, she did walk round the table and put a sympathetic hand on Alice's shoulder, and the tone of her voice was caring. 'Mam, tell me the truth, now. Did you really have an asthma attack?'

Shamefaced, Alice admitted, 'No. But I'll be worried to death about you going to see the Rolling Stones. And you know that could be enough to bring one on. Remember last year when the Beatles were here? There was near riots that night. The police had to send for reinforcements. Some young girls even finished up in the Royal.'

'That concert was held in the Ritz picture house, Mam. We're going to the Ulster Hall. They're used to live shows there. Think of all the boxing and wrestling tournaments that have been held there and no sign of crowd trouble. Everything will be fine, so it will.'

'Hah! How do *you* know there was no trouble? You've never been to the Ulster Hall before.'

'It would have been in the newspapers, Mam.'

'How often do you read the papers, eh? Your nose is always stuck in those silly romantic magazines you waste your money on.'

'See, Mam? As far as you're concerned, I can do no right. All my friends read magazines. Why should I be different?'

'Because I brought you up to be sensible, that's why! There'll be trouble, you mark my words. Young people today get carried away where these long-haired lads are concerned. Don't go, Tess. Please don't go.'

[2]

Aware that her mother could have an attack when it suited her, Tess was urged to action by the peal of the doorbell. 'That'll be Agnes now, Mam,' she said gently. 'I'll have to go, but I'll try not to be too late. And I promise to be careful and stay away from any trouble.' Giving Alice an affectionate hug, she quickly left the room.

Alice heard the outer door slam and hurried to the room at the front of the house they used as a workshop. She stood at the bay window and watched her daughter and Agnes Quinn, heads close together, striding arm in arm down Springfield Road until they were out of sight. Young ones were so independent nowadays, thinking they knew it all. With a swift glance upwards she asked God to look after them, and returned to her chores in the kitchen.

Bubbling with excitement the two girls jumped off the bus at the bottom of Grosvenor Road and turned to gaze at each other in amazement at the sight that met their eyes. Throngs of people were hurrying along Howard Street towards Bedford Street.

Quickening her steps, Agnes cried, 'Do you think they're all going to the Ulster Hall?'

'Where else?'

'We'd better get a move on, then.' Grabbing Tess by the elbow, Agnes almost dragged her friend along. 'Come on, hurry up or we mightn't get in.'

'But we've got passes!'

'If this crowd has its way it will be first come first served, no matter about passes or what not. I've never seen the likes of this in my whole life.' Since Agnes's life, like Tess's own, spanned a mere twenty years, Tess smiled mockingly at her. 'What on earth are you grinning at?'

'Nothing. Nothing at all. But you're right, we'd better get a move on.'

It was absolute bedlam outside the Ulster Hall, the crowd a heaving mass of bodies surging towards the building and then being pushed back. Tess laughed delightedly, her eyes dancing with excitement. This was indeed a new experience for them. Why, if they were on a boat they would be seasick with all this motion. A glance around showed her that some girls nearby did indeed look a bit under the weather.

Clutching their precious passes tightly they slowly elbowed their way towards where the stewards were trying to force the crowd into some kind of order and ensure that all paid their money at the kiosk before being allowed through the doors. After a lot of pushing and shoving, and rejecting extravagant offers of money for their tickets, Tess and Agnes reached a uniformed steward. He gave a quick glance at the passes and pushed the girls none too gently through a door and into the hall, pulling it shut after them.

Inside they came to a breathless halt and gazed around them in awe. There was little order as harassed staff strived in vain to keep control of the ever increasing crowds, amidst loud shouts and whistles. Another steward relieved them of their passes and, tearing them in two, waved the girls into the concert hall. Without further encouragement they pushed their way as close to the stage as they could manage.

Agnes turned to Tess with a rueful smile. 'I feel so guilty, being here, in all this excitement, about to see the Rolling Stones, and our poor Marie sitting in the Royal holding Dennis Sullivan's hand.'

'Why did she not come with you?'

'Well, you know what our Marie's like. She didn't like

to leave poor Dennis. I could see she was tempted, mind you, but she was afraid of something dreadful happening to him. You can die, you know, if the appendix bursts.'

'I know that. You can get some kind of blood poisoning, can't you? Poor Marie. But her bad luck is my good fortune.' Tess gripped Agnes's arm. 'Thanks for asking me along. I'll never forget this! Never!' She gazed around her in awe. 'It's an honour to be here, so it is.'

'Who else would I ask, eh? You're my best friend. Did you ever see so many girls in your life before? They certainly outnumber the men.' Standing on tiptoe she peered down towards the stage. 'I wish we were down there at the very front. Those girls might even get to touch the Stones. Imagine being that close to Mick Jagger.'

'Don't be so ungrateful. We're lucky to be here at all.'

'I know. I'm never satisfied,' Agnes admitted with a wry grimace.

'Anyway,' Tess continued, 'I'd prefer to touch Keith Richards. I think he's gorgeous. That is, if he has turned up. I heard on the news at lunch time that he wasn't on the same flight as the others. There might only be four Rolling Stones here tonight.'

The lights dimmed and Agnes stated the obvious. 'It's about to start.'

Rolling her eyes in exasperation, Tess exclaimed, 'I'm not stupid, Agnes. I can see it is.'

An expectant hush fell as order was called for, the curtain lifted, and the show began.

During the acts that preceded the Rolling Stones, the heat built up and the excitement mounted towards fever pitch, the dancers going into a frenzy as they jumped and twirled on the floor. When at long last it was time

[5]

for the Rolling Stones to appear, everyone was already in a lather. Sweat rolled down Tess's face and she could see that those around her were also sweltering.

The curtain rose and the crowds were jumping with joy and screaming at the tops of their voices. And there they were, five very ordinary young men – obviously Keith Richards had turned up – that the audience was idolising as if they were some sort of gods. In spite of having warned herself not to go overboard about them, Tess was jumping up and down with the rest of the crowd, screaming and hysterical. The group paid very little attention to their fans and concentrated on their musical instruments, Mick Jagger prancing about the stage singing his heart out.

Near the beginning of the act there was some disruption at the front but Tess and Agnes were too far from the stage to see what the trouble was. The police were there in numbers and managed to keep some sort of control. At one time there were more police and St John's Ambulance men on the stage than musicians, as they tried to remove fans who had managed to climb up from the floor. As time passed, to her amazement, Tess saw girls dropping like flies. The St John's Ambulance crew was working flat out trying to revive them but most were being carried out on stretchers. Some hysterical fans were in such a frenzy they had to be put in straitjackets before being removed from the hall.

Her mother had been right after all. Alice would have a field day tomorrow when she saw the newspapers. Tess glanced at Agnes and saw she was white as a sheet, as if alabaster had replaced the blood in her veins.

'Are you all right?' she shouted above the din.

Agnes nodded but confessed, 'I just feel a bit faint.'

'Well for goodness' sake take it easy. If either of us

gets carried out of here, I'll never hear the end of it. My mam will make sure of that.'

All too soon it was over. They were hoarse, and limp as wet rags, when after many encores the curtain finally fell for the last time and the group could be seen no more. It had truly been a wonderful experience for the girls.

Tess and Agnes hung back as the crowd now turned its attention to leaving the hall. Most of them, carrying souvenir programmes, were intent on getting to the stage door to try to get the group's autographs. The two girls had no such intention, so they dallied to let the eager ones get ahead. Even so, they were pushed and buffeted as they tried to make their way out of the hall, and eventually in all the confusion they became separated.

Tess stumbled, keeping her feet with difficulty in the crush and looking around vainly for her friend. When a tall young man placed an arm across her shoulders, cushioning her from some of the mad confusion, Tess quickly glanced up at him, decided he was harmless and allowed herself to be propelled in the direction of the exit.

It was a great relief to get outside and she stood for some moments, hands on hips, gulping in great mouthfuls of warm night air. It was far from fresh, but better than the smog and stench of body odours inside the concert hall.

The lad looked at her in some concern. 'Will you be all right, now?' Tess shot him a tremulous smile and nodded. Still looking concerned he said tentatively, 'I'll have to go and look for my mate.'

Tess gazed around her in dismay. 'I'll never find my friend in this crowd,' she wailed. Afraid he might think she wanted him to remain with her, she hastened to add, 'But don't let me keep you any longer. I'll manage. And thanks! I'd be still in there if you hadn't rescued me.'

'Where do you live?'

'Up the Springfield Road.'

He laughed. 'Well, that settles it! I live off the Falls Road, so I suggest we make our way round to the bottom of the Grosvenor Road. If we do that we can't possibly miss our friends, unless they decide to take a short cut and I can't see them doing that.' Struck by a thought, he inquired, 'That is, assuming your friend lives up there too.'

'Tess! Where on earth did you get to?' Breathless, Agnes arrived at her side and cast a suspicious look at her companion. 'Is he annoying you?' she asked protectively.

'On the contrary, when we got separated, this young man . . . excuse me, I don't know your name? . . . helped me to get out of that mad house.'

With a slight bow he introduced himself. 'I'm Jack Thompson.'

'I'm Tess Maguire and this is Agnes Quinn.'

Just then another figure approached them and Jack said, 'And here is my best friend Tony Burke.'

Since they were all going in the same direction it seemed only natural that they walk home together. Tess found herself paired off with Jack.

They got on like a house on fire, debating the state of the country, unemployment and sport, and giving their versions of how the world could be put to rights if they were in charge. All too soon they arrived at the junction of the Falls and Springfield roads.

Tess's heart missed a beat as Jack smiled down at her. 'I've really enjoyed your company. Would you care to come out with me some time?' he asked tentatively.

Unable to hide her delight, she beamed up at him and readily agreed to meet him the following Wednesday. After good nights were exchanged, Jack and Tony made off down the Falls Road and Tess and Agnes continued on their way.

With a sideways glance, Agnes said, 'You look pleased with yourself.'

'Jack has asked me to go out with him,' Tess confessed.

'And are you going?'

'Yes.' Suddenly doubtful, Tess asked anxiously, 'Didn't you like him?'

'Come off it, Tess. I hardly exchanged two words with him. But he's nothing to write home about, is he?'

Tess shrugged. 'Well now, Agnes, I'm no oil painting myself, am I?'

'You're a businesswoman, Tess! You could do well for yourself if you put your mind to it.'

'Hah! I'm only a glorified dressmaker.'

'You know you and your mam are very good at what you do and are doing very well in your little business. I only wish I was in your shoes. I can assure you, I wouldn't go jumping at the first guy that came along. I'd pick and choose, so I would.'

Tess looked at her friend's blonde curls, big blue eyes and pretty elfin face. 'You'll have no bother making a good match. I'm surprised Tony didn't ask you out.'

'He did. But I'm not exactly over the moon about it, like you. They're just two ordinary lads, after all. And remember, we know nothing about them. They could both be married for all we know.'

Tess laughed at the idea. 'Don't be silly. Are you going out with him?'

Agnes shrugged. 'I might.'

'When?'

'I'm supposed to meet him on Tuesday night.'

The thought of what might happen if Agnes stood Tony Burke up hit Tess like an icy blast. 'But you've got to meet him! You've just got to,' she wailed.

A bewildered frown was bestowed on her. 'I don't have to do anything of the sort, Tess Maguire!'

Tess gripped her arm. 'Don't you see? If you don't turn up he will probably tell Jack and maybe Jack won't come to meet me, in case I'm as fickle as you. Please, Agnes, go out with him at least this once. Do it for me, please.'

Seeing her friend was in a really agitated state, Agnes reluctantly gave in. 'All right. All right. Don't get your knickers in a twist. I'll meet him this one time, but I'm not making any promises further than that.'

The next six weeks were heaven to Tess. Jack took her out at least once a week, sometimes twice, and she was in her glory. How her mother never guessed she was seeing a bloke was a mystery to her, as she worked alongside her in a happy haze. But alas, it ended all too soon.

It wasn't hard to remember their last date. It coincided with the riots that flared up that particular night in September and would be for ever etched in her mind. They had been to the pictures on Royal Avenue and were waiting at the bottom of Castle Street for a bus when the news came, via word of mouth, that no more buses would travel up the Falls Road that night as there was rioting in Divis Street. They were advised to take an alternative route home.

Nodding her head wisely, Tess said, 'We'd better go up the Grosvenor Road.'

'Are you not in the least bit curious to see what's going

on?' Jack gasped, disbelief written all over his face.

'It could be dangerous. We might get caught up in it.' Tess was apprehensive; if people had any sense at all they didn't go anywhere near situations like this, she thought.

Gripping her by the shoulders Jack shook her gently and urged, 'Let's live dangerously for a change, eh, Tess? Just this once, let's take a chance.'

As she gazed up into eyes alight with excitement, some of his fever rubbed off on her and, pushing away thoughts of how her mother would react if she ever found out about her daughter's stupidity, Tess eagerly agreed. 'All right. Let's go for it!'

'Good girl! Don't worry, I'll look after you.' Tucking her hand under his elbow Jack pressed it close to his body and started walking briskly up Castle Street, Tess skipping and running alongside to keep up with him.

Long before they arrived at Divis Street they were aware that things were bad. The RUC seemed to be out in force and they were being attacked with stones and bottles. Why? What on earth had started all this? Determined to find out, Tess and Jack stayed on the fringe of the mob. After a conversation with a young man who he thought might be a reporter, Jack explained to her the apparent reason for the riots. It appeared that the RUC had forcibly removed a tricolour from the window of the Republican office and had actually broken down a door to do so. Word of this had quickly spread around the adjoining streets and a small crowd of stone-throwing youths had soon snowballed into a full scale mob.

'I'm sorry now I talked you into coming up here, Tess. It was irresponsible of me. This could be very nasty. Let's make a detour and get you home.'

They backtracked to Hamill Street and cut across to Durham Street and eventually reached the Grosvenor Road.

Glancing at Tess, Jack saw how white she was and placing an arm across her shoulders hugged her close to his side. 'Are you all right?'

'I am now, but I was really frightened back there, so I was,' Tess confessed. 'It's hard to believe the removal of a silly flag could cause such anger.'

'It's not actually the removal of the flag that's the trouble, Tess. That flag has been in the window since the Republicans took over that shop as offices, to prepare for the elections, weeks ago. So why target it now? Believe me, there's more to this than meets the eye. Who sent the RUC in to get it? They certainly didn't take it down off their own bat! You wait and see. All will be revealed. It'll be in the papers tomorrow morning.'

Tess could tell Jack was agitated and restless and respected his silence for the rest of the journey until they arrived at the corner of Malcomson Street. There she stood on tiptoe to kiss him on the cheek, her usual form of good night. 'Don't you worry about it, Jack. It will probably be all over tomorrow.'

To her amazement and joy, he drew her into his arms and pressed her close. 'Tess, I'm in a bit of a quandary. I need someone to talk to.'

'Well, I'm here. Talk to me,' she urged.

Whether or not it was the emotional state the riots had raised in him Tess didn't know, but there, on the corner of Malcomson Street, for the first time ever Jack had cradled her in his arms and held her clasped to his chest. Overcome with joy she had nestled against him. They cuddled and kissed and it all came pouring out, punctuated by dry sobs, and urgent kisses: his distress that he was secretly meeting his mother without his father's knowledge.

Bemused, and not really understanding what he was going on about, aware only of the pressure of his body crushed against hers, she had gripped him tighter still, whispering words of encouragement and comfort, her arms willingly enfolding him, her lips feverishly returning his kisses. Even when his kisses became fierce and demanding and his hands explored her body she had not rebuffed him as a decent girl should. No, she, fool that she was, had exulted in the emotions that were carrying them along on a wave of passion such as she had never dreamed existed and allowed him to touch her up.

With hindsight she was mortified at her actions that night, in plain view should anyone pass by. Oh, it was quite dark in the shadows where they stood. But still . . . to behave like that in public. At the time all she knew was that she wanted him to kiss and touch her; wanted the moment to last for ever. It was her first encounter with sexual pleasure and she revelled in it.

He was the first to recover some composure and had gently put her from him, apologies tumbling from his lips. 'I'm sorry. So very sorry, Tess. I had no right to do that. I don't know what on earth I was thinking of. I'm afraid I got carried away. Can you ever forgive me?'

Believing that this was the beginning of their love affair she had waved his apologies aside and tried to draw him close once more. He had resisted her efforts and, saying he would be in touch soon, had hurried down Malcomson Street, head lowered, a shamed hunch to his shoulders. Although she wasn't aware of it, he was walking out of her life.

*   *   *

The Republicans had pledged that if the tricolour, removed on Monday night, were not returned, another one would take its place on Wednesday. Tuesday passed without incident but with no flag. On Wednesday, true to their word, the office staff displayed another tricolour in the shop window, and young people who a week ago hadn't even noticed there was a flag there gathered in Divis Street to admire and if necessary defend it.

Tess and Agnes met on Wednesday evening and, worried that Jack had not contacted her on Tuesday, Tess surprised her friend by suggesting that they take a walk down to Divis Street and see if everything was quiet.

'Why shouldn't it be?'

'You amaze me, Agnes. Do you not know about the riots on Divis Street on Monday night?'

'Of course I know all about them. They've talked about nothing else in work these past two days. The RUC removed a tricolour from a wee shop in Divis Street and were pelted for their trouble. They're hardly likely to make the same mistake again. Now are they?'

'I don't know about that, now. I was there. It was an awful experience, so it was. I was terrified. We had to make a detour to get to the Grosvenor Road because we couldn't get past the rioters in Divis Street.'

Agnes's eyes widened and she gasped at the glow in her friend's eyes. 'Let me get this straight. You say you were terrified, yet you want to go back? Are you daft? You're better staying away from anything like that, unless you want to end up in hospital, or even jail. Your mam would just love that, wouldn't she?'

'I know, but it was also exciting, Agnes,' Tess confessed earnestly. 'Besides, we don't have to go right down. We can go as far as Albert Street and see how things are. We needn't go any further if you don't want to.'

Agnes dithered. It didn't seem right to her to go seeking trouble; she had been brought up to avoid it, if possible. So to appease her conscience she compromised. 'Tell you what . . . we'll dander down to Victor's for an ice-cream, but if there is any sign of trouble whatsoever, we turn back immediately. Okay?'

'That's fine by me,' Tess eagerly agreed. She was secretly hoping to see Jack. He had been enthralled by the riots on Monday night and she had a gut feeling he would be down again tonight. She had been uneasy about the abrupt way he had left her. Had she disgusted him with her display of passion? Was that why he hadn't been in touch the night before?

They arrived at Albert Street and from there onwards as far as the eye could see the road was black with people. The rioting was intense. Police were being driven back by a barrage of bottles and stones and anything else the mob could lay their hands on. Some petrol bombs were also being thrown, the fumes and smoke permeating the air and catching one's throat. In the distance a trolley bus was blazing furiously.

In spite of their good intentions, curiosity got the better of Tess and Agnes, and in no time they were caught up in the midst of it. They were flung this way and that and would have fallen had there been room to do so. Frightened, and gasping for air, Agnes cried in alarm, 'This is awful! Let's get the hell out of here.'

They had left it too late. They had been dragged into the centre of the crowd and now all possible avenues of escape were cut off by armoured cars parked at the entrances to the narrow streets, their headlights picking out the dense mass of rioters. Rain spattered over them and Tess was thankful, hoping it would cool down the tempers. Only when the water lashed against her, almost lifting her off her feet, did she realise that it wasn't rain but a water cannon the police were using to quell the mob. The sound of breaking glass and sirens was deafening yet some of the mob were trying to make their voices heard above it all as they sang Republican songs, and swore and jeered at the police.

The RUC, wearing steel helmets and using bin lids as body shields, battled their way to the front of the shop that held the offending tricolour. This time the Republican offices were barricaded against them and resisted their efforts at entry with crowbars, so they smashed the window to remove the flag. The crowds were enraged at their audacity and all hell broke loose as emotions soared completely out of control. More stones and bottles were thrown at the RUC. They retaliated with baton charges and the fighting intensified. The girls were in tears and shaking with fright when at last they managed to struggle free from the angry mob.

Looking down at her sodden clothes Agnes cried wrathfully, 'I hope you're satisfied now, Tess Maguire! Look at the state of us. This new skirt of mine is ruined and it's all your fault. The next time you want to go chasing after a cheap thrill, do it on your own. I've had enough to last me a lifetime. My mam bought me this skirt for my birthday. It cost a wee fortune, so it did. She'll kill me when she sees it.'

Mournfully Tess agreed with her. 'I'm sorry. You're right, it's all my fault for encouraging you to come down here and I'm sorry about your skirt, Agnes. Come home with me and maybe my mam will be able to sort something out.'

'I doubt it. Your mam will be angry too. She'll be too

busy venting her wrath on you to be bothered with the likes of me.'

'She will help you. I know she will,' Tess replied with more confidence than she felt.

Alice went berserk when Tess eventually arrived home, hair plastered to her head and clothes soaked. She surmised that somehow her daughter had been involved in the rioting she had heard about on the radio. 'In the name of God, have you no sense at all, girl?' Seeing Agnes was in a similar condition, Alice urged, 'Get you two up the stairs and out of those wet clothes before you catch your end. You did right to come here, Agnes. Your mam would hit the roof if she saw you like this.'

Agnes wholeheartedly agreed with her. Her mother was a bit of a snob and she would be furious if their neighbours saw her daughter come home in this condition. Agnes was glad of the opportunity to make herself presentable before going home. 'Thanks, Mrs Maguire. I appreciate this.'

In the bathroom the two girls gazed at each other and burst out laughing. 'You'd think we'd been through the wars,' cried Agnes.

'In a way, I suppose we have,' Tess agreed ruefully and threw her friend a towel. 'Let's get our hair dried and into some dry clothes. It's just as well we take the same size.' She lifted Agnes's wet skirt and grimaced sightly. 'Then I'll get Mam to take a look at this. Actually, I think a good pressing just might do the trick.'

Alice had pulled a small table close to the fire and a tray containing a pot of tea and a plate of sandwiches awaited the girls when they descended the stairs.

'Oh, how lovely, Mrs Maguire,' Agnes cried. 'You're an angel.'

'I don't feel like an angel, believe me, Agnes. I feel like banging your two heads together. When I heard on the radio that there was trouble in Divis Street I was sure you would have enough sense to steer clear of it. This could become very nasty, you know, if it's not nipped in the bud.'

'We realise that, Mrs Maguire, but I can't see it continuing. People are too sensible to go on fighting over a wee flag. It will blow over. You'll see.'

Alice sighed. She wasn't so sure about that. But then, how could she expect them to understand? They had grown up during the forties and fifties when, although after the war there had been rationing and a shortage of material things, everything in Northern Ireland was relatively peaceful. She herself remembered her own young days when things hadn't been so good.

Taking the offending skirt from her daughter, she said, 'This is wool. Hard to work with. See . . .' She pointed to the label inside the waist band and read, 'Dry clean only. But I'll do my best.'

In the kitchen, spreading the pleats on the ironing board, she covered them with a damp cloth and carefully pressed the skirt. As she did so, the past came back to haunt her. When she was a young schoolgirl her mother and father had taken her down to Royal Avenue one Twelfth of July to watch the Orange parades. The footpaths had been crowded and they had had to walk some distance along the road before they found a gap near North Street and settled down to watch the marchers go by. To her young eyes it had been a wonderful spectacle.

Each lodge was heralded by a large banner followed by a band dressed in colourful uniforms and there were all kinds of instruments: bagpipes, accordions and flutes.

Her favourite had been the drums. She had been mesmerised by the way the drummers swung the drum sticks, throwing them in the air and catching them without missing a step. The Orangemen looked grand in their fine bowler hats and orange sashes as they marched proudly in step with each other, but it was the young boys striding in front that caught her attention; boys no older than herself, twirling their long staffs into the air and catching them with little effort.

Alice was enchanted, and sighed when the end of the procession came in sight and she knew that soon they must return home. Suddenly loud cracks rent the air and she had thought it was fireworks going off, but to her amazement the marchers scattered in all directions and the next thing she knew her father had swung her up in his arms and grabbing her mother by the arm had sought shelter in a shop doorway, protectively shielding their bodies with his own.

Somehow her father had managed, by taking them into Smithfield Market and cutting up side streets across to Townsend Street, to get them away from the trouble. Eventually they reached the safety of their own home. Although her mother was tearful and shaking like a leaf, her parents had played down the severity of the incident for her benefit. However, for weeks afterwards nightmares about the event had caused her many sleepless nights.

That was the start of the rioting in July 1935 and it had continued for some time. Was the same thing about to happen again? Carefully spreading the skirt over a chair she went to tell Agnes the good news that her birthday present was as good as new and she could face her mother without fear, but her thoughts were still troubled.

The next week showed that her anxiety was unfounded. To everyone's relief the rioting in Divis Street was quickly over and somehow or other there were no apparent consequences. An uneasy peace returned to the city.

Tess paused, breathless, at the top of Spinner Street and chastised herself. Why was she in such a big hurry? Probably only bad news awaited her anyway. She stood for some moments outside the Dolphin chip shop until her breath had settled to a steady rhythm before turning the corner and slowly walking down past the row of terrace houses, some of them still with just the basic kitchen, scullery, and small room downstairs and two bedrooms upstairs. She had been in Jack's home once before and was aware that he and his father lived in just such a house. You couldn't blame them. Two men living together wouldn't worry too much about the latest mod cons.

The terraces had been built years earlier to lure workers from rural areas to seek employment in the nearby linen mills. Her eyes scanned the red brick walls and high narrow windows. She smiled as she observed, by the light of the street lamps, the well-looked-after front steps and scrubbed semicircles of pavement outside a lot of the front doors. Caring women must surely live in these particular houses. They were obviously their owners' pride and joy.

Would Jack Thompson be annoyed at her for coming, uninvited, to his home? No matter. She had to know where she stood. It was almost two weeks since he had been in touch; long days of yearning for the sight of him. What if he was ill and unable to get word to her? In her heart she knew she was deluding herself.

Although private telephones were, as yet, rare in this district, there was a public pay phone in the Clock Bar at the top of Lower Clonard Street. If Jack was unable to get out at all, surely his father, if asked, would have phoned on his behalf.

She was halfway down the street when she was startled from her musing. To her dismay she saw Jack coming out of his house at the bottom of the street, ushering a young girl before him and turning to lock the door. In a panic, she stepped into the nearest hall, thankful that, unlike the road where she lived, the occupants of these houses when at home left their outer doors open. What if Jack and his companion came up the street and saw her? It didn't bear thinking about. He would know, only too well, that he was the only reason she was likely to be in Spinner Street. She whispered a short prayer that God would not let the owner of the house where she now stood, shaking with nerves, become aware of her and open the door into the hall.

Tess prayed in vain. First the net curtain on the half-glass vestibule door leading to the kitchen was twitched aside and then the door itself was pulled open. A small, dark-haired woman suspiciously eyed the stranger standing in her hall. What would she be wanting here? She didn't know her from Adam. 'Can I help you?' she asked, in a not too friendly tone, looking as if she was ready to slam the door in Tess's face and retreat for assistance if need be.

The name of an acquaintance came to Tess's mind. Stella Mullen lived in one of these streets. 'Does Stella Mullen live here?' she asked in a trembling voice.

The woman's demeanour softened. 'Oh! You've got the wrong street, love. Stella lives in Lower Clonard Street.' Stepping into the hall, the woman forced Tess to retreat backwards before her and move out on to the pavement. The woman pointed down the street. 'Just go to the bottom of the street here, and turn the corner. It's one of the houses facing you on Lower Clonard Street.'

Thankfully aware that Jack and his companion had, before her forced exit, passed by without so much as a sideways glance in her direction, Tess, with a sigh of relief, thanked the woman and continued on down Spinner Street, anxious to put as much distance as possible between herself and Jack Thompson.

Blinded by tears she turned the corner at the bottom of the street and walked quickly up Lower Clonard Street. Near the corner, passing the Clock Bar, she was brought to an abrupt halt when the tall figure of a man suddenly exited the pub, causing her to collide with him. He gripped her arms to prevent her falling and when he spoke she recognised Dan Thompson's voice.

'Whoa, there.' Jack's father peered into her face and she smelt the whiskey on his breath. 'Why, it's young Tess! Why the big hurry, love?'

She tried to smile through her tears but failed miserably.

Putting a comforting arm round her shoulders, he said, 'I was trying to coax myself to go into the Dolphin for a fish supper, but I hate eating alone. Will you join me?'

She sniffed. Was he blind? Couldn't he see she was upset? How could she go anywhere the state she was in? 'It's very kind of you, Mr Thompson, but I'm not in the least bit hungry.'

'Have a Coke, then, Tess. Go on, keep me company. I really do hate eating alone.' He was not hungry either, but this young girl was obviously upset about something. He had an idea that his son was the cause of her distress and felt compelled to help her.

'No. I'm sorry . . .'

'Please? I'm feeling a bit down and I don't want to go home yet. I'd be glad if you'd come,' he said persuasively.

She was about to refuse again, but realised that in the circumstances she might just perhaps find out who the girl with Jack was. After all, she might be a cousin or a family friend. Against her better judgement she found herself agreeing to accompany Dan. 'All right. If you're really that hard up for company, I'll join you.'

They crossed the street and walked the short distance to the Dolphin. It was too early for the second show in the Clonard picture house to be over and the shop was practically empty.

The proprietor, Johnny Reid, gave them a friendly wave and continued shaking the chips in the wire basket, whistling cheerfully away as usual. Johnny was well liked and his fish suppers were delicious. According to Johnny the batter on the fish was prepared from a closely guarded family recipe handed down through the years, and it was certainly always light and crunchy. Dan escorted Tess to one of the boxes along the far wall and when they were seated he leaned across the table towards her. 'Tess, I insist you have something to eat.'

The strong aroma of the fish and chips teased her nostrils, making her aware that she had eaten very little since lunch time. 'I'll have a fish, then, if you don't mind. No chips, thank you.'

'Mind? I'm delighted. You're getting far too thin, you know. A few chips wouldn't do you any harm either. Are you sure you won't have some?'

'Just a fish, thank you,' she reiterated.

Dan went up to the counter to place his order and his heart was heavy. Hadn't he warned his son that Tess might be reading much more into their friendship than he intended? But Jack had laughed at the idea, saying, 'Come on now, Dad, Tess is a big girl. Me and her are just good friends. Nothing more. And she knows it. She's great to talk to, discuss current affairs with, and she even knows a fair bit about sport too, but I'm just not attracted to her in the other way. That's why I stopped seeing her. I didn't want her getting the wrong idea.' Colour had burned in his cheeks as he recalled his last meeting with Tess. He felt a cad. She had every right to think he was interested in her, the way he had behaved that night. What on earth had got into him? He had ruined a good friendship with his carry-on. And who knows how things would have gone if Colette Burns hadn't come into his life? But she had, and he had fallen for her, hook, line and sinker.

At Dan's look of contempt his voice had trailed off. His dad was no fool. He'd be well aware that Colette had changed things as far as his son was concerned. Colette with her thick black hair and sultry brown eyes.

Dan stole a sideways glance towards where Tess sat. By the look of that poor soul she had expected better from his son.

However, when he returned to the box he found Tess more composed. 'What upset you, lass?' he asked tentatively, not wanting to become too involved but feeling the need to show some concern.

Wearily she ran her fingers through her bright auburn curls and confessed, 'Oh, this and that. You know how it is? Some days nothing seems to go right no matter how hard you try.'

'You can say that again. I've had plenty of those days myself. But, believe me, they do pass, love. Can I be of any help?' His look took in the big green eyes that would put emeralds to shame, and her hair was lovely, a mass of red highlights. Could his son not see she had her share of beauty? With that hair and those eyes she would soon be snapped up.

Tess gazed back at him, seeing only compassion and caring in his dark eyes, and longed to question him about Jack. Her mouth contorted into words that would not emerge. 'Not really,' was all she could manage.

Johnny gave a shout to let them know their order was ready and Dan went to the counter to collect it. When he returned Tess saw that Dan also had only a fish on his plate. 'I thought you said you were hungry? Or are the chips not ready yet?'

'They are ready and I am hungry, but I must watch my weight.' He patted a non-existent tummy and dared to bring his son's name into the conversation. 'My Jack had better watch his weight as well. He's drinking far too much these days if you ask me.'

'He misses his mam,' Tess said softly, remembering the feel of Jack in her arms when she had consoled him.

'It's time he put all that behind him,' Dan said abruptly.

A hand reached across and patted his in sympathy. 'Have you heard from her at all?' she dared to ask quietly, thinking that perhaps, unknown to Jack, Anne Thompson had also been in touch with her husband. Jack was in such a state because she had contacted him and not his father. She must be a cruel woman, making Jack promise not to tell his father that she was back on the Falls Road. But at least it had brought Jack into Tess's arms for comfort and for that she was grateful. On the other hand, by returning his affection that night, letting him see how much she cared, had she scared him off? She dragged her attention back to what Dan was saying.

'No. Not a single dicky bird. I suppose our Jack has told you all about it. If she'd told me just how unhappy she was, we might have sorted something out. But no, she just upped and packed a few things and went off with some guy from work. The coward's way out,' he said bitterly.

Since meeting Jack, Tess had, from different sources, heard various accounts of why Anne Thompson had left her husband and son but it was none of her business, so she held her tongue. He had yet to touch his fish, and Tess felt the need to apologise. 'Look, I'm sorry I brought the subject up. Please eat up. Don't let me put you off your meal.'

He smiled grimly. 'I will, lass, if you'll eat yours.'

She forced herself to take a forkful of fish and place it in her mouth. It was delicious and she savoured the fine-textured cod and crispy batter. After a short pause, Dan followed her example. They ate in silence, Tess trying to think of some way to inquire about Jack's companion, and Dan trying to avoid opening a floodgate of tears. Her back was to the door and she didn't see Jack enter. Dan did and, with a glance at her bent head, gestured to try to warn his son off.

Apparently not understanding, and looking apprehensive, Jack approached their box. 'Hello, Tess. Are you keeping my old man company tonight?' he asked tentatively.

Her cheeks coloured slightly as a young girl joined Jack and smiled at them in a friendly fashion. The second house in the Clonard picture house must have recently finished because a surge of noisy teenagers at that

[26]

moment entered the shop, saving her from having to answer him.

Jack glanced over his shoulder as the boxes filled up. 'Can we join you?' he asked his father.

Knowing that Johnny Reid, understandably, would expect every available space to be filled now the picture house was out, and aware that someone would eventually be sharing their box, Dan nodded reluctantly. Rising to his feet he politely gestured for the girl to sit down facing Tess.

'Tess, this is Colette Burns, a friend of Jack's. Colette, this is Tess Maguire.'

'Hello.' White teeth flashed in a Mona Lisa face and a hand was thrust in Tess's direction. 'Jack has told me all about you.'

Tess shook the proffered hand and nodded a greeting. She felt betrayed that Jack had discussed her with this stranger. Just what had he told her? She picked at her fish now, afraid each morsel would choke her as she forced it down a throat constricted with nerves. A glance at Dan revealed the pity in his eyes and unable to bear it she rose abruptly to her feet. Why should she sit here being patronised?

'Forgive me, Dan, but I did warn you I wasn't hungry.' She glanced across at the girl. 'Excuse me, Colette, but I must go. My mother will be wondering where I've got to. Nice to meet you.'

Jack was leaving the counter after placing his order and he gazed in bewilderment at Tess's back disappearing through the door. He looked askance at his father. Muttering angrily that he would speak to him later, Dan excused himself and, bidding Colette good night, followed Tess. He caught up with her at Dunville Park and grabbing her arm brought her to a standstill.

'Here now, slow down, girl.' He was dismayed to see tears pouring down her face. 'You mustn't upset yourself like this, Tess. No man's worth it.' He thrust a clean white handkerchief into her hand.

She mopped the tears away and blew her nose. Grimacing at him, she said apologetically, 'I'll wash this and get it back to you,' before pushing the handkerchief into her coat pocket.

He wagged a hand to show it didn't matter. 'Don't worry about it. Come on, I'll walk you home.'

He turned to walk up the Falls Road and she cried in dismay, 'There's no need. I'll be all right.'

'I want to see you safely home,' he said stubbornly, and reluctantly she fell into step beside him.

They walked in silence until they reached Springfield Road. For the life of him, Dan couldn't think of anything to say that wasn't an inane cliché.

Tess was ashamed of her behaviour. She should have stayed and put on a brave face; tried to show she didn't care that Jack had dumped her for a new girlfriend. But she had been too upset to put on an act and now here she was completely tongue-tied. Mr Thompson would think her a fool.

She stopped and faced Dan. 'There is really no need for you to come any further, Mr Thompson.' She nodded up the Springfield Road. 'This is a well-lit road. Besides, it's still early and there's plenty of people about.'

'I'll see you to your door.' She tut-tutted in frustration and he reiterated firmly, 'I'll see you to your door.'

To her dismay, when they arrived at her home her mother was watching from the big bay window, and before Tess could say good night to Dan and send him on his way the door was thrown open.

'I've been worried sick about you, so I have,' her

mother cried shrilly, her eyes taking in the big feller from his thick dark hair and rugged face to his well-polished brogue shoes. What on earth was her daughter doing out with this middle-aged man?

She intended finding out. 'Come in, the pair of you. I'll put the kettle on.'

Dan flashed Tess a glance to gauge her reaction to this request but she was staring abjectly down at her feet and failed to notice.

Having recognised the woman standing in the doorway, he said tentatively, 'If you're sure it's no bother?'

'None at all. Come on in.'

Resigned, Tess climbed the steps to the door and Dan followed. Now her mother would find out she had been dating a young man and would want to know why Tess hadn't mentioned it to her. An inquest would be held.

In the hall, Tess introduced them. 'Mam, this is Mr Thompson, a friend of mine.'

Seeing a puzzled frown gather on Alice Maguire's brow, Dan was quick to intervene.

'Your daughter is a friend of my son's, Mrs Maguire.'

'Oh, I see.' But she didn't. If that was the case where was the son and how come she'd never heard tell of him? 'Show Mr Thompson into the living room, Tess. I won't be five minutes.' Alice headed towards the kitchen at the back of the house. Slipping out of her coat, Tess hung it on a rack in the hall.

'Would you like to take off your coat, Mr Thompson?'

He eyed her apprehensively. 'I realise now that I shouldn't have come in. Would you like me to beat a hasty retreat?'

In spite of her misery she laughed at the idea. 'Too late for that now, I'm afraid. Here, give me your coat and prepare yourself for the third degree.'

Alice was deep in thought as she put the kettle on for the tea. There was something familiar about this man, but then she had probably seen him about the road. It was a busy thoroughfare and he was handsome enough to catch any woman's eye. She carried the tray into the living room and Dan was quickly on his feet to relieve her of it.

Alice was using her best china. Pouring the tea, she handed Dan a cup on a matching saucer, and inquired with a reproachful glance in Tess's direction, 'I'm surprised my daughter hasn't mentioned you, or indeed your son, to me. Have you known Tess very long, Mr Thompson?'

'Dan. Please call me Dan. You too, Tess. We've just known each other a matter of weeks.' Then Dan dropped a bombshell. 'I recognise you from way back, Mrs Maguire. Me and your husband were mates for a time before he left Ross's mill. I even remember dancing with you a few times at the Gig.'

Alice was gazing at him open-mouthed, loath to admit that she had ever frequented such a lowly place as the Gig, and had apparently been held in this man's arms; not just in his arms but probably crushed against his body, the Gig being so small and always packed to capacity, she recalled. 'I'm afraid I don't recognise you at all,' she admitted weakly.

Wide eyed, Tess sat taking all this in. He had never mentioned knowing her mother. But then she had only met him briefly when Jack had forgotten his keys one night and they had returned to his home to collect them.

Dan winked at her while Alice poured another cup of tea. 'Probably not. I was run of the mill, but you . . . well.' He shrugged, not willing to imply that she had thought herself better than the rest of them, a bit of a snob in fact. 'You had class,' he finished lamely.

Mollified to learn that he had apparently recognised her worth even back then, Alice asked, 'Where did you live in those days, Mr . . .' At his raised brow she quickly said, 'Dan?'

'Not far from here. I lived on Cavendish Street.'

'My, but isn't it a small world?'

'Indeed it is.' His face became solemn and he said gravely, 'I was very sorry to hear about Tommy's death. I attended the Requiem Mass, but I didn't go to the cemetery. It was a shame he died so young. Is Tess your only child?'

'Yes, and a great comfort she's been to me.' Alice looked fondly at her daughter who sat gazing into her cup, anxiously awaiting her mother's interrogation of Dan Thompson. 'I don't know what I'd have done without her.'

Relieved that his cup was almost empty and if he made a quick exit there would be no time for questions, Dan drained it and rose to his feet. 'I'll have to be going now.' She hadn't given him permission to call her Alice but he did so nevertheless. 'Good night, Alice, Tess.'

To Tess's relief, before her mother could gather her wits about her, he was in the hall and shrugging into his overcoat, and then he disappeared out the door.

Chapter Two

Dan slowly retraced his steps down Springfield Road, his mind alive with long-forgotten scenes from the past. It had never dawned on him that Tess might be Tommy Maguire's daughter. She didn't resemble either of them. Her mother had been a beauty in her day and half the men in town had chased after her, himself included. Everybody had been surprised when she had chosen brash, loud Tommy Maguire to be her beau.

Of course his job as a buyer in Ross's mill had appealed to her, and soon she had got rid of his rough edges. She also had him speaking properly in no time.

Dan remembered ribbing Tommy about his new posh Belfast accent, but he also recalled feeling a bit jealous. Tommy was an only child, and his parents had insisted on his staying on at school. He had achieved good qualifications, too good for working in the mill, really, albeit in the office, and Alice had great plans for him. He had stayed in the mill because he wanted to remain one of the lads, didn't want to outclass his mates too much. Alice had soon convinced him otherwise. Without any bother he had acquired a position more appropriate to his qualifications, as a quantity surveyor in Farrans of Dunmurry.

For a time Tommy and Dan still had the odd night

out but Alice never deigned to meet Dan socially. Then when she and Tommy got married they bought a house on the outskirts of Belfast to be near his work and the two friends had eventually lost touch with each other. A shame that, but Alice had still thought herself a cut above Tommy's mates and had put a stop to his going out for a drink with them. Dan had often wondered if she had allowed Tommy to keep in touch with his parents, who had since died.

Dan's house at the bottom of Spinner Street was on the bend and faced the Falls Road. Even from the top of the street he could see that his son was at home. The blind was down and the light was on. The question was, was he alone? When Colette Burns had come to stay with her grannie in the house next door to them, Dan had encouraged his son to show her around, little thinking he would drop Tess in the process. But Colette was a pretty little thing and had apparently won his son's heart. Tess would really be a far better match for Jack but young ones wouldn't be told; they thought they knew best. Colette lived with her mother and stepfather in Omagh and worked in one of the banks there. She had been just on a visit to Belfast, but now had apparently got herself a job in the Northern Bank in Belfast city centre and intended staying here. Her and Jack were very close. It looked serious between them.

The outer door was locked and Dan rattled his key with unnecessary force before he entered the small hall. He heard shuffling in the kitchen and delayed a few seconds before opening the vestibule door and entering the room. Jack and Colette were sitting suspiciously far apart on the settee.

'Hiya,' he greeted them and continued on into the

scullery, saying over his shoulder, 'Who's all for tea?'

'Not for me, Mr Thompson. I'd better get in next door before my grannie comes looking for me.'

He turned in the doorway and appraised her. Her hair was tousled and the buttons of her blouse were wrongly fastened. 'I think I'd be worried too, if my seventeen-year-old granddaughter was out this late.'

Colette followed his gaze and quickly adjusted the buttons. With a wry grimace at Jack, she bid them both good night and quietly left the house. The two men were silent until they heard Mrs Burns's door open and close.

Jack rose to his feet and faced his father. 'What was that all about?'

'It's twelve o'clock! That young girl should have been in bed an hour ago.'

'Says who?'

Dan stabbed a finger in his chest. 'Me! This is my home and there'll be no hanky-panky in it while I'm about. Okay?'

Tight lipped, Jack said tersely, 'We were doing no wrong. Just a few kisses.'

'Look, son, I'm not over the hill yet. I'm still young enough to remember where a few kisses can lead.'

'Pity you didn't give Mam some more then and keep her at home.' The words came out on a sneer.

Dan's jaw dropped and he stepped threateningly towards his son. 'You'd better watch your tongue, young fellow!' he growled.

Jack straightened to his full six feet and eye to eye with his father glared at him. 'Or?' His voice was softly dangerous.

Resisting the urge to punch his sneering face, Dan turned his back and entered the scullery.

A few minutes later Jack passed him in the narrow space and opened the back door. 'You could at least have got an inside toilet built. That might have helped.'

Because there was truth in what he said, these words rankled and when Jack returned from the yard Dan rounded on him.

'Look you, when we were lucky enough to get the key to this house, your mother and I were over the moon. Granted, it was far from perfect, but we were living in rooms at the time and glad to get a place of our own. You were a baby in your mother's arms and I was determined to make it into a home your mother would be proud of. You think this is bad?' A wide sweep of an arm embraced the kitchen. 'You should have seen it then. At that time, it was lit by gas mantles. There was an ugly big cast-iron range along that wall' – he motioned to the kitchen wall where a Devon grate now held pride of place – 'for cooking, and the floor was rough flagstones. Your mother near died at her first sight of it, but it was ours and we were enough in love to overcome all the hardships. I worked my fingers to the bone to have it as nice as it is today. It wasn't easy, you know. These things take time but she got fed up meanwhile. Everything else would have followed, but she couldn't wait any longer. There was no pleasing her. No one could have worked harder or done better. Even if I do say so myself.'

'Huh! You call this nice? Well, obviously your best wasn't good enough or she wouldn't have left us.'

Wanting to wound his tormentor, Dan cried, 'I don't know why you're defending her. After all, she left *you* behind.'

He had touched a sore point. How many times had Jack wondered about that selfsame thing? Why had his mother left him behind? Was he so unlovable? Now he cried defensively, 'Only because she couldn't afford to take me with her.'

'Hah, that's a gag! The only reason she didn't take you with her was because she didn't care enough.'

'No, you're wrong. She wanted to! But I was only twelve at the time, remember, and this guy she run off with wouldn't allow her to take me with them.'

A puzzled frown gathered on Dan's brow. 'What makes you think that?'

'She told me. So there!' The words spewed out before Jack could stop them. He was behaving like a wee child. Head bowed with shame, he awaited his father's wrath.

Dan stared, uncomprehending, for some moments then gasped, 'You've seen her! Haven't you?'

Jack wished he hadn't opened his mouth. In his heart he knew his dad had made the best of a bad job and had looked after him well. Until he himself reached seventeen, his father had had no social life worth talking about to call his own. 'A few times,' he admitted.

'And you never said?'

'She asked me not to.'

'Why, you ungrateful bastard . . .'

'Don't you dare call me that.'

'Why not? You would have been one if I hadn't married your mother.' Then, at the horrified look on his son's face, Dan cried in anguish, 'Ah, son, I'm sorry. I'd no right to call you that.'

'Hadn't you?'

'There was no need for you to know and I'm sorry I opened my big mouth. You took me unawares, son.' He reached out a hand pleadingly.

Pushing it roughly aside Jack snarled back, 'Go to hell.' He thumped up the stairs two at a time, and his bedroom door slammed with a resounding bang.

Dan stood still, his thoughts in turmoil. His son had always blamed him for his mother's leaving them and perhaps he was right. Dan and Anne had drifted so far apart he hadn't realised how unhappy she was. Heaven knows, he had worked hard to make this house into the kind of home she wanted and he was getting there. He'd given up smoking and spent the money on things she wanted done. He'd thought he was succeeding; had been gobsmacked when he arrived home from work one night and found a letter telling him Jack was with a neighbour and that she had gone to live with someone else.

To be truthful, his first emotion had been one of relief. No more coming home to bickering and unrest. No more listening to her gripes and jealous comments. Then anger had consumed him when he realised she had taken the brand new TV set. They were so expensive they couldn't really afford one but she had plagued him and he had bought one on the never never to please her, had still owed a lot of money on it when she had upped and gone. Tearing the letter to pieces he muttered, 'Good riddance at any price.' Whoever the guy was, he was welcome to her.

It was only when he collected his son from the neighbour's house that the whole sorry mess really hit home. Jack, through no fault of his own, was the one who would suffer most. How could any woman do that to her son? Why was it always the innocent children who suffered?

Alice Maguire was also remembering the past as she washed and dried, and carefully put her precious tea set back in the china cabinet. She could not really recall dancing with Dan Thompson, but then there were so many lads wanting to dance with her in those days and, to be truthful, she had cultivated only the company of a chosen few.

Oh yes, she had been very particular in her day. Only lads whose fathers owned pubs or shops or who were businessmen of some kind or other got her attention.

Then Tommy Maguire had captured her heart. Not quite what she had hoped for but she had been unable to resist the magnetic pull that was constantly there between them; the need to be with him, to hold his hand and gaze into his eyes. No other man had been able to capture her imagination the way Tommy did.

He had been putty in her hands; her wish was his command. Tears filled her eyes when she recalled how handsome he had been. She had been so proud to be seen out with him. The big house outside town that she had set her heart on was quickly acquired and her cup was full to overflowing. Their marriage had been blissfully happy, and when they were blessed with a beautiful baby girl their happiness was complete.

The tragic accident that had taken his life at the early age of twenty-nine had almost destroyed Alice as well. She knew in her heart that Tommy's parents, although they had tried to hide it, blamed her. If she had left well alone and let him stay in Ross's mill he might be alive today. But no! There was no prestige working in the mill and Alice had felt that it was in their best interests to talk him into seeking a better appointment. Unfortunately, Tommy had died in a freak accident, struck by falling masonry while crossing from the offices to the work site. He had neglected to wear a safety helmet and compensation was reduced accordingly.

Alice was inconsolable, and wanted to die herself. Only the thought of her daughter had kept her going. Now she went in search of that daughter. She must get to the bottom of this affair. She found Tess in the workshop at the front of the house. Alice had been trained as a milliner and the bay window was used to display her handiwork. She was very good at her trade and her creations were soon snapped up. Coloured posters also advertised her daughter's dressmaking designs, and between them they had built up a small but prosperous business.

They had worked hard and, with the little money left over after purchasing their house, had built up the business from scratch. Now people came from near and far to get wedding dresses and ballroom gowns and suits made to order.

Alice designed hats to match the outfits her daughter made and the clients were so impressed that the Maguires were seldom left with any spare articles on their hands. All in all they were a good team. When she left school at fourteen Tess had started work in the Belart stitching factory, renowned for its beautiful children's clothes. It was there she discovered that she had a flair for dressmaking. She loved Belart's exquisite children's designs and had, in time, created some patterns of her own. Now she designed exquisite flower girl dresses and page boy outfits for weddings.

The door was open and Alice stood for some moments unobserved, contemplating her daughter at work. Rich auburn hair fell forward like a curtain and the bright electric light picked out the highlights. Alice knew better than to speak while the scissors were sliding across the table, but when Tess stopped to adjust the material she warned, 'It's too late to start cutting now. The skirt of that wedding dress is on the bias. One wrong snip and the lot will be ruined.'

Tess turned wearily from the table. 'Mam, go to bed

and let me get on with it. I haven't made a mess of anything yet, have I?'

'No. But there's a first time for everything and I can see you're not yourself at the moment.'

'Please, Mam. I'm all right. I just don't feel like sleeping. Leave me alone.'

Sensing her daughter's misery, Alice said softly, 'Would you like to talk about it, love?'

'There's nothing to talk about. Jack Thompson and I went out together a few times. That's all there is to it. It was nice while it lasted. Short and sweet.'

'How come you never mentioned him to me?'

Tess smiled grimly. 'Because you would have been hearing wedding bells, frightening him away before it got off the ground.'

Annoyed at her daughter's tone, Alice thoughtlessly retaliated. 'So somehow or other you managed to do that yourself.' Then sadness engulfed her at the stricken look her daughter turned on her.

'That's right. I didn't need any help from you.'

What had gone wrong, Alice wondered. 'But you had hopes, didn't you?' she queried gently. Tight-lipped silence greeted this remark and Alice continued. 'Did you like him very much?'

'Quite a lot,' Tess said curtly. 'But now he has a new girlfriend, a very pretty girl, and he hadn't the decency to tell me to my face. So what does that tell you? Whoever said looks don't count didn't know what they were talking about.'

'Look, Tess, love, you're gifted and talented and there's plenty of time to meet someone who'll appreciate your worth.'

Tess had heard all this before. 'All right! No need to go on about it!'

'It's true, love. Just wait and see.'

Placing the scissors to one side Tess brushed roughly past her mother, and headed for the stairs. 'I'm away to bed. You've put me right off the notion of working. Good night.'

Alice watched her climb the stairs and her heart was heavy. Why had this to happen to her daughter? If only Tommy had lived things might have been different. Had she done the wrong thing selling her beautiful house and moving back to the city? She had bought this house to be near her mother, so that Tess could at least have one living grandparent to visit. Unfortunately her mother had died shortly after their moving to Springfield Road and the only relative Alice now had in the world was her brother Malachy, who lived in Carlingford. Some years ago he had bought a small farm-holding and now he worked hard to make a living out of the land, and they rarely saw him.

What if she died? Tess would be alone in the world. Sometimes Alice wondered if she should make an effort to remarry. Give Tess someone to turn to if in need, but the idea didn't appeal to her. Besides, who would have her? She was no young beauty any more and the only man to have shown any interest in her lately was a widower, the owner of a shop further up Springfield Road. He was enormously fat and the very idea of being held against his body filled her with revulsion.

Finding no solution to her immediate problems she sighed and, covering the satin material with a dust sheet, left the room and began to lock the doors and windows. It was as she climbed the stairs that the memory of Dan Thompson's handsome face entered her mind. Now, what made her think of him? Wasn't he a married man?

*   *   *

Alone at last, Tess lay on top of the bed, tears streaming down her face. She had thought that Jack cared for her. Obviously he didn't. And why would he? In spite of what anyone else said she knew she was as plain as a pikestaff. And didn't this prove it? Still, she really had thought Jack cared and now she felt betrayed. They had been getting along so well! Not that he had made any promises. Ah no, she couldn't say he had encouraged her. Why, the evening he had broken down and confided in her that his mother had come back was the only time he had shown any physical attraction to her, and he hadn't backed his actions up with any reassuring words. Still, didn't they say actions spoke louder than words? And that night his kisses and hands had implied that he cared.

Tess rose from the bed and went to the long mirror on the door of the wardrobe. Examining her reflection, she decided she wasn't all that bad. She was passable; thick auburn hair, bright green eyes and slim figure. After all, everyone couldn't look as lovely as her mother, or Colette Burns, for that matter! And besides, Jack Thompson was no Errol Flynn; he was just an ordinary run of the mill lad who had managed to arouse passion within her. She realised she wasn't anywhere near as attractive as Colette, of course, but passable. Her mother said when she met a man who really cared for her things would be different.

But would they? She had thought Jack cared but now he had a new girlfriend, which proved her wrong. A very pretty girl, Tess reminded herself, and felt bereft. Slowly she undressed and without looking at her image again returned to her bed. Burying her face in the pillow, she sobbed soundlessly. Would any man ever want her? Indeed, would any other man do, the way she now felt about Jack? She very much doubted it.

* * *

The atmosphere was strained as father and son ate breakfast next morning. Jack worked in the Silk & Rayon factory in Waterford Street and when on the late shift, as he was today, it was his duty to clear the breakfast dishes away. He gathered the plates up and headed for the scullery where a kettle was already bubbling away on the stove ready to wash them.

Returning for the rest of the dishes he hesitated beside the table and apologised for his behaviour the night before. 'Dad, I'm sorry if I upset you. I didn't mean half the things I said. You know that, don't you?'

Glad to receive the olive branch, Dan said, 'Likewise, son. We were both out of order. Still, I do wish you had told me about meeting your mother.'

'To be truthful, Dad, I didn't think you'd be interested. You don't seem to care one way or the other about her.'

Dan turned these words over in his mind. He mustn't give Jack false hope by letting him think he might take his mother back. Too much water had passed under the bridge for that to happen. 'I don't care, if by that you mean wanting her back. Not any more,' he admitted. 'For your sake, I would have considered letting her return at the beginning, but as the months passed and she made no effort to even see you, not even when she wrote asking for a divorce, I realised how heartless she was.'

'I explained why she couldn't do that.'

'And you believe her? Come off it. Surely you aren't that naive, eh, son?'

Jack sank back down on to his chair. 'It was better than believing she didn't love me,' he confessed sadly. His father's words belatedly penetrated his misery. 'I didn't know you were divorced,' he gasped, seeing any hope of a reconciliation fading.

'We aren't. As you well know, Catholics can't get divorced. I warned her anything she achieved would be under her own steam. I heard no more about it, so I assumed she didn't pursue it further.' Dan's heart was wrung with pity at his son's unhappiness and he warned himself to go carefully and not shatter the lad's fragile pride. 'You know, she did love you, Jack. She loved you very much. It was me she couldn't abide. But we did manage to get along fine without her, didn't we, son?'

Jack's shoulders rose in a negative shrug. Who knew how things would have been had his mam stayed? Seeing his father's face fall, he hastened to reassure him. 'Of course we did, Dad. You've been a great father to me.'

Aware it would be better not to know, Dan found he could not let the matter drop, and asked tentatively, 'Tell me, son. Did you just bump into her in town or something?'

'She was waiting for me outside the factory one night.'

Dan jerked to attention. 'Outside the Silk & Rayon? When was this?'

'A few months ago.'

'How did she know you worked there?' Jack shrugged and Dan continued, 'What reason did she give for being there?'

'At first she just wanted to talk to me. It was a bit awkward, you know – we were like strangers. But later she suggested we should share a flat.'

Dan was dumbstruck. 'I can't take this in. What about "his nibs" – the guy she couldn't live without?'

'It seems he moved on some time ago.'

'Hah, I see! And she thinks she can just come back into your life as if nothing had ever happened?'

'She is my mother, Dad, and I must say I'm tempted.

A flat or even a house with all mod cons? It would be a dream come true.'

'You can have all those things without joining ranks with your mother, son,' Dan cried in frustration. 'If you had said you wanted to live away from home I'd have helped you.'

'That's just it. I don't fancy living alone, Dad. Besides I couldn't afford to. Not on the money I earn.'

'Well, you've no one to blame but yourself about that. I tried to get you to stay on at school, but you wouldn't listen to me. If you had you'd be earning good money today.'

'I know, Dad. I know you did. And to be truthful I was content enough here until she put these ideas into my head. You've got to admit, it would be nice to come home to a warm house and a hot bath at night. Especially you, working out in all kinds of weather. Does that idea not appeal to you at all? It's all right during the summer months, but in winter, to tell you the truth, I dread getting up to a cold house every morning.'

Dan, hardened from boyhood to getting up to a freezing house and, when young, having to fetch water in from outside to see his mother through the day, was staring at his son in amazement. 'Why didn't you say?'

'I didn't realise what I was missing until Mam pointed it out to me. We are quite primitive here, with an outside toilet and no hot water. Mam says a lot of our neighbours already have these basic mod cons.'

It was the gentle way his son said 'Mam' that made Dan aware his estranged wife was using her wiles to win back Jack's affection.

'How would she know?' he cried furiously.

'She visits Lily Brady, so she does. She knows more about our neighbours than we do.'

Dan couldn't believe his ears. To think Anne was so close at times, just a few doors away. She was probably checking up on him and he hadn't even known. 'Do you see her often?' he asked fearfully.

'Not really. Every now and again she'll be there, waiting outside work.'

A glance at the clock brought Dan to his feet. 'Good God, look at the time. I'll have to run or I'll miss my lift. Can we talk about this tonight, son?'

'Sure, Dad. See you then.'

On the building site, Dan found himself working like someone possessed. He was a dedicated craftsman and was given all the important brickwork to do. At the present time he was working on an ornate surround that would house a huge door to a luxurious office block. Small coloured bricks of odd shapes intertwined in a beautiful pattern. No matter how tricky a job might prove he could practically do the work with his eyes shut. Today, however, he had to stop every now and again, step back and take note of how his work was going; once he even had to rectify a mistake.

Lunch-break was a happy release for him. It was a cool dry day and, declining to join his mates in the Portakabin used as a site canteen, he sat outside.

Anne's face was haunting him. Not yet ready for marriage, he had been shocked beyond belief to find out that she was pregnant. Anne had been annoyed at his reaction, had wanted to know if he doubted it was his. That had been a bad time in his life: the rushed wedding leaving them skint, honeymoon put off till another day. A honeymoon that had never taken place. How could it, when there was always something or other needed for the baby or the house? Still, Anne had held it against him; she had expected miracles. When she had talked about getting a job he had encouraged her, thinking the extra money would keep her happy. Look where that had led! To the break-up of their marriage.

He was also remembering the good times when they had worked together to make the house a worthy home for their young son. The times when they lay in bed locked in each other's arms and planned the future. If only she had been patient; given him more time. To be truthful, he had to admit that he had slacked off a bit. Eleven years should have seen this house looking like a wee palace but things had gone wrong. Anne had met someone through her job who could give her more than he could.

Still, they had been happy together once. Could Anne possibly be hoping he'd take her back? Had she discovered the grass was by no means greener on the other side? He shook his head in despair. There was no way he could ever forgive her betrayal of him and especially Jack. Besides, she would have approached him, not Jack, if that were the case. No, it was only her son she wanted. He would just have to make sure that she didn't succeed in winning Jack over.

Chapter Three

Life did go on, Tess found, even with a broken heart. Admittedly, some days she was surprised to find that she was too busy with her work to even think of Jack Thompson and other days she found it hard to cope with the sense of loss that threatened to overwhelm her. She thought it strange how things had worked out. There was Agnes, who hadn't wanted to date Tony Burke in the first instance, yet she was still going out with him, and although she insisted he wasn't Mr Right she seemed to enjoy his company, and here was Tess, nursing a broken heart over the loss of Jack.

When Agnes heard that Tess's romance, if you could call it that, was over, it bothered her to see her friend so unhappy. Unknown to Tess, she tried to coax Tony into arranging a foursome, to try to patch things up between Tess and Jack. Tony wouldn't hear tell of it, saying that if he did so it would probably be Colette Burns that Jack would bring along and then what would Tess think of them? He knew Colette was now the one in Jack's life and he would not be swayed in spite of his own deep feelings for Agnes and his desire to please her. Agnes saw his point of view right away and agreed with him, although her heart was sad for her best friend.

Tess hadn't set an eye on Jack since that night in the

Dolphin chip shop. She had however met Dan a few times; had even joined him once, on the spur of the moment, for a drink in the lounge of the Clock Bar. What an experience that had been!

One of her regular customers who was poorly and temporarily confined to her home had received an unexpected invitation to a wedding in two weeks' time. She had phoned Tess in desperation, asking if she could possibly make her a suit for the occasion at such short notice. Tess had assured her that, as a valued customer, she certainly would somehow be fitted into her busy schedule. That very same evening, armed with samples of material and tape and pins, the tools of her trade, she ventured forth.

It was a bad night to be outdoors, the November weather being atrocious, but Tess wanted to show Nell Montgomery some patterns and discuss the choice of fabric for the suit as soon as possible. On her way home, cowering under her umbrella against the elements, she had been unaware of Dan until he fell into step beside her at the top of Albert Street where it joined the Falls Road.

Peering in under the umbrella, he said, 'I thought it was you, Tess! What on earth brings you out on an night like this?'

She raised the umbrella to cover them both and, smiling up into his face, said, 'Work has me out tonight, that's what. There's no rest for the wicked, you know. Mind you, only something worthwhile would tempt me out in this awful weather. I was measuring up one of my special customers for a suit. What about you? What's your excuse for being out on an awful night like this?'

Glad to see she didn't, outwardly at least, appear to be pining away because of Jack, Dan suited his step to hers and gestured to the umbrella. 'Protect yourself with that. I'm already soaked through. I've been down to Cullingtree Road to see an old work mate who's a bit poorly. It beats sitting in the house alone. Anyway, how are you keeping these days?'

'I can't complain. I've plenty of work in hand to keep me busy for the next two months. In fact we're thinking of taking on a machinist to help out. Someone to train in our ways of working.'

'Expanding the business, eh? That's wonderful news. It's nice to hear someone is doing well.'

She laughed. 'Well now . . . there's well and there's well, but every little counts. What about yourself? Anything different since I last saw you?'

Realising it was really Jack she wanted to know about he shook his head and said gently, 'No. My wife has yet to persuade Jack to leave home and he is still dating Colette Burns.' They were approaching Spinner Street and he turned to leave her, a farewell on his lips, then paused. 'I don't suppose you'd care to come into the Clock Bar with me and let me buy you a wee hot whiskey to warm the cockles of your heart?' he asked tentatively. 'It would do you a world of good, on a foul night like this.'

Tess couldn't believe her ears. Her cheeks reddened with mortification. He was inviting her to go into a *public house* with him! What kind of girl did he think she was? According to her mother only loose women went into those places of ill repute, as she called them. Did Dan think her loose? Of course he didn't, she quickly assured herself. It was just that her mother was old-fashioned. Dan was only being kind to her. She had once questioned Alice as to what the inside of a pub looked like, only to be informed that her mother had no idea whatsoever, as she had never been inside a public house and had no intention of ever doing so. But, she warned her daughter, she had heard all about those dens of iniquity; even knew some hussies who frequented them. They were most certainly no place for a Christian girl to be seen in.

Curiosity aroused, Tess had questioned her mother. 'What! You mean to tell me that you know some scarlet women, then?' she asked, her hands clutched at her breast in feigned amazement, and wasn't surprised when her mother couldn't come up with any names.

'Well now, not exactly,' Alice blustered. 'But I did once hear that Molly Connelly, for instance, a girl about the same age as yourself, goes into different pubs every weekend. Her mother should put a stop to it. And furthermore she drinks *gin and tonic!*' The horror of this revelation made Alice's voice quite shrill. How did she know all this, Tess wanted to know, only to get a vague 'I heard talk about it' for an answer. Tess warned her mother in no uncertain terms to be careful about repeating such things outside or she could be up for slander. Alice had laughed and pooh-poohed the idea. Dan watched Tess closely as all these thoughts passed quickly through her mind and from her expression wasn't surprised when she refused his offer.

'Mam would be scandalised if she ever heard I went into a pub,' she explained. 'Besides, ugh!' A grimace distorted her mouth. 'I wouldn't thank you for a whiskey. It's horrible. Even the smell of it turns my stomach. But thanks all the same for asking me, Dan. It's very kind of you.'

'I wish I felt as you do about whiskey, but unfortunately I don't. It's one of my few vices. You, my dear, can have a brandy and lemonade if you like.'

Sensing his loneliness she hesitated, tempted. After all, why not see for herself what it was like inside a pub? Not that she would have a brandy, oh no, but it would be nice to get in out of this rain for a while and get a bit of warmth. Still, it didn't seem right to go into a public house, especially with this man who was old enough to be her father, but she knew that Dan had no ulterior motive for inviting her; she trusted him.

He smiled wryly as he observed the mixed emotions flitting across her face again. 'There is a small lounge, you know. There will probably be other women present at this time of night,' he assured her. He gave a slight laugh as with hands spread wide he acknowledged the elements. 'Although, mind you, on a night like this we could very well have the place to ourselves.'

The rain seemed at that moment to get heavier, bouncing off the umbrella with a loud staccato rhythm and splattering to the ground, soaking her feet. As far as Tess was concerned that settled the matter. 'Right! Let's go in.'

With a delighted chuckle Dan took her by the elbow and escorted her along to Lower Clonard Street. What a girl Tess Maguire was. His son needed his head examined. Colette Burns seemed like a wee child in comparison.

Leading her to the side door of the pub, Dan took the umbrella from her and shook it free of excess water before he closed it. Then he thrust the door open and ushered her inside. He was wrong. The lounge was full and a hush fell as all eyes took in the newcomer accompanying Dan Thompson. A girl young enough to be his daughter, no less. Most of the people greeted him by name and it was obvious he was a popular figure in here. They were probably wondering who she was, Tess thought, as eyes full of speculation examined her from head to foot. Uncomfortable under their scrutiny, she glanced around, surprised at how small the lounge was. Why, you couldn't swing a cat in here. There were already three couples seated around the walls on benches, facing small round tables on which their drinks rested, which took up most of the floor space.

The occupants, whilst smiling knowingly from her to Dan, obligingly moved round and made room for Tess to sit down. Not wanting to drink in close proximity with these strangers Tess turned to suggest to Dan that they go elsewhere. To her dismay he was ignoring her, his attention focused on one of the women. A very attractive woman, with natural blonde hair worn shoulder length in soft curls. With a vague wave of the hand Dan indicated that Tess should sit down and went to the small hatch that served the lounge from the bar. She heard him order a double Black Bush and a brandy and lemonade.

Conversation had started up again and the woman Dan had shown interest in turned to Tess in a friendly manner. 'It's a terrible night out there, isn't it, dear?'

'It sure is,' Tess agreed. 'It's really pelting down now.' She was relieved when Dan's arrival with the drinks saved her from further conversation. She moved along so that Dan could sit down between her and the woman, but he chose to remain standing, elbow propped against the wall.

An amused laugh escaped the pale pink lips of the blonde and, tossing her head, with a mischievous look in her eye, she asked innocently, 'Are you not going to introduce me to your friend then, Dan?'

Aware that they were being covertly watched by the others and that sly smiles tugged at the mouths of the women, he turned a glare on her and said abruptly, 'I don't think that will be necessary.'

Her mouth opened to protest but her companion, a man much younger than herself, placed a hand warningly on her arm. Light blue eyes framed with thick, dark lashes met his and an unspoken message passed between them. She patted his hand knowingly where it still lay on her arm and his fingers turned and entwined with hers. She apparently forgot all about Dan's existence as she leaned closer to her companion, giving him all her attention.

Tess watched closely. The woman was quite young – late thirties, maybe early forties, Tess surmised – and she obviously took care of her looks. Carefully applied make-up emphasised a smooth forehead with darkened arched brows, and pink rouge threw high cheekbones into relief. The only noticeable lines were faintly etched around a wide sensuous mouth.

Sipping at the brandy Tess grimaced in distaste and decided she didn't like it; not one little bit. It was her first and, she vowed, her last taste of alcohol. She hadn't had a chance to tell Dan that she would prefer a soft drink. He should have asked me what I wanted anyway, she thought indignantly, but he had been preoccupied. In dismay she watched Dan down his whiskey in a couple of gulps and returning to the hatch order the same again.

When he placed another brandy and lemonade in front of her he caught her look of reproof and, leaning forward, whispered, 'Sorry about this, Tess. We'll leave after this one. Drink up, lass.' Dan was annoyed at himself for letting his estranged wife get to him. It was just so unexpected seeing her sitting there with a lad young enough to be her son.

Another few tentative sips of brandy and Tess was surprised at how the liquid really did warm her all the way down to her stomach, sending a glow throughout her body. But she'd never be able to drink two of them. Never in this wide world, she told herself. How wrong she was. When one glass was empty she reached, without hesitation, for the second glass and started sipping away.

There was nothing else to do. She was disappointed in Dan. He stood silent and sombre, dark head bent, not even meeting her eye, let alone engaging her in conversation. She got the impression that he was watching, and eavesdropping on, the blonde and her companion. And here was she, sitting like a fool in the midst of all these strangers, sipping brandy as if it were a regular occurrence. None of them seemed inclined to start up a conversation with her, except the one she thought Dan wouldn't want her to talk to, and even she was now preoccupied.

The minutes dragged and eventually the other two couples, who had been talking quietly among themselves, drained their glasses, bade the rest of them good night and left the pub. Dan motioned Tess along the bench and, sitting down beside her, deliberately turned his back on the other two, who were getting quite amorous.

His glass was empty again and he gestured towards hers. 'Another one?'

'Oh, no! I've had more than enough already.' Her glass was still more than half full but, not wanting to delay any longer, she quickly drained it and stood up with a shudder of distaste, the sudden movement sending sharp pains to her head. 'Let's go,' she said in a voice that shook.

The woman, although her friend strongly objected, followed them outside to the covered doorway. Placing a hand on Dan's arm she said urgently, 'We've got to talk, Dan.'

He roughly threw her hand off and growled, 'Away back to your toy boy.'

She smiled triumphantly. 'I do believe you're jealous, Dan Thompson.'

'Of that wee whipper-snapper in there? Don't flatter yourself. I would have thought you'd have done better than that.'

Tess felt invisible standing there. They were so engrossed they appeared to have forgotten that she existed. Well, she vowed, she would soon put an end to that nonsense! Whether it was inconvenient or otherwise they would just have to remember her presence.

'Dan!' Her voice came out loud and high pitched and she covered her mouth in confusion for a few seconds before finishing lamely, 'If you'll be so good as to put that umbrella up for me, I'll be on my way and leave you two to it.' Instantly she had his attention.

'Tess, forgive me, dear.' He struggled with the catch of the umbrella and at last had it open. Placing an arm across her shoulders he held the umbrella aloft and, ignoring the woman, said, 'Come on, let's get you home, lass.'

Aware that they were still being watched, Tess waited until they were round the corner out of view before angrily shrugging off his arm and striding ahead. At least that's what she intended to do, but, to her dismay, without his support she began to weave back and forth across the pavement. What on earth was wrong with her? Her legs were behaving as if they didn't belong to her. She felt light-headed.

Once again Dan's arm was around her, gathering her close to his side and piloting her in a straight line. 'You're tipsy, love. I'm sorry. It's all my fault entirely. Brandy should be sipped, not gulped, and to crown it all you get good measures in the Clock. To be honest, I shouldn't have got you that second drink. I just wasn't thinking straight. Will you come down to the house with me and have a cup of strong tea to help you sober up before you go home? Alice will never forgive me if you arrive back in this state.'

'It's late, Dan. Mam will be worried about me as it is, without me being any later. Besides, I don't want Jack to see me like this.'

'Just as you wish, Tess, though you needn't worry about Jack. He won't be there. He's gone to Omagh for a couple of days with Colette to meet her folk and collect some of her belongings.' She swayed unsteadily and he argued, 'Mind you, a cup of tea will make a big difference.'

Thinking of her mother's face if she were to see her now, Tess agreed, if somewhat ungraciously. 'Oh, all right, then. But it had better be a quick one.'

Her legs felt rubbery and she clung tightly to Dan's arm for support as they retraced their steps and walked the length of the street. Once inside the house Dan led her to the table and she sat clasping her throbbing head while he busied himself in the scullery brewing tea. After what seemed like an eternity, a mug was placed in front of her. The house was freezing and she curled her hands gratefully around the welcome heat of the steaming mug. 'Thank you.'

One mouthful of the brown liquid, however, and her stomach turned over. 'I don't take sugar,' she gasped. She tried to control her heaving stomach but the strong sweet tea going down on top of the brandy proved too much for her. She rose abruptly to her feet, hands pressed tightly against her mouth.

'Here, this way.' Dan motioned her into the scullery. She reached the sink just in time and retched and retched. Where on earth was all this water and bile coming from? An empty stomach, she lamented inwardly. In her hurry to go and see Nell Montgomery she had neglected to eat anything, assuring her mother she would get something when she returned. Now look at her! She was ashamed of herself; ashamed that Dan was seeing her in this drunken state.

Dan turned on the tap and pushing her cuffs up her arms made her hold her wrists under the freezing water. Then he gently dried her hands and wiped her face with a towel. 'You'll feel a lot better now.'

Pushing roughly past him she returned to the kitchen and sank down on the end of the settee. 'Better! I feel worse.'

'Have you never drunk spirits before, Tess?'

'Never! Just a sip of whiskey once when I had a bad cold and it was enough to put me right off, I can tell you. You should have asked me what I wanted to drink,' she cried accusingly, putting the blame at his door. She started to shiver uncontrollably. 'It's awfully cold in here. Or is it just me?'

'A bit of both. It is cold but you feel it more because you've been sick.'

'Sick! I think I'm going to die,' she wailed.

He sank down on to the settee beside her and taking her hands in his tried to rub some warmth into them. Shame was eating away at his conscience. What in the name of God had he been thinking of? He should have realised that a young girl like her didn't drink spirits.

And she was right. He should have asked her her preference. The sight of his estranged wife with that young lad – why, he was no older than Jack – had driven everything else from his mind.

'I'll have to get you home, love.'

'My mam will kill me.' Tears overflowed at the very thought of facing her mother. She would never be able to explain it to her. What excuse could she offer? What's more, her mother would never trust her again.

To her relief, Dan assured her, 'Don't you worry, I'll explain everything to Alice. You see, Tess, that was my wife in the pub. She has never been in before and I was gobsmacked when I saw her there tonight.' He shrugged. 'On the other hand maybe she's a regular. You see, I hardly ever go into the lounge, so I don't know how the land lies. I know Jack and Colette go in there now and again but he has never mentioned seeing his mother there. Not that he'd tell me anyhow. In fact, maybe that's where they meet,' he confessed bitterly. 'She's a sore point between us at the moment.'

A loud knock on the door brought him to his feet. 'Who the blazes . . .' He was amazed to see Anne standing outside on the pavement. 'What do you want?' he asked abruptly.

Holding out a handbag towards him she said drily, 'Your friend left this behind in the pub.'

'Oh. Thank you.' At a loss for words, he gazed bleakly at her in silence.

'Can I come in? It's wet out here, you know.'

He pulled the vestibule door closed as she stepped into the hall. 'You can't come any further. Tess isn't feeling too good. She'd only be embarrassed.'

Her brows rose in surprise 'She's still here? I thought you were seeing her home. Surely you're not taking advantage of that young girl, Dan Thompson.'

'Don't be silly! Even so, it's none of your business what I do. Where's the toy boy?'

Pleased that he sounded jealous, Anne smiled. 'I sent him home to his mam.'

She moved closer and he smelt her perfume, and was surprised to find her proximity stirring emotions he had thought long dead. He tried to put some distance between them but the hall was too small to do much manoeuvring. She swayed towards him, her lips parted invitingly. Abruptly he turned his head aside to avoid them. There would be none of that nonsense here. She could save her favours for the others. Her face was a study of hurt bewilderment. He gaped at her. What did she expect? That he would take her in his arms and smother her in passionate kisses, and all would be forgiven? Some hope!

The inner door was pulled open and Tess stared at them open mouthed. What was that woman doing here? How come she was standing so close to Dan? And why was Dan encouraging her? Hadn't Jack said that his father hated his mother? So why didn't he tell her where to get off?

Shamefaced, but glad of the respite, Dan at last made the overdue introductions. 'Tess, this is my wife. Anne, meet Tess Maguire.' He held the bag up. 'You left this in the Clock Bar. Anne was good enough to bring it down here.'

Tess stared at the bag, then, in confusion, at him, shaking her head in disbelief. Forgot her bag? It was unheard of. Oh, how she wished she was at home in her comfortable, warm bed; just to get this day over and done with. One thing was for sure, she would never enter a pub again. 'I didn't even miss it,' she admitted.

With difficulty she focused her attention on Anne. 'Thank you very much.' Turning to Dan in despair, she cried, 'Dan, I must go home now. My mam will be off her head with worry.'

'How do you feel?'

'Awful! But I can't see me feeling any better for some time to come, so I'm going home now,' she added defiantly, almost in tears in her anxiety to get away.

'Right! Don't worry, Tess. We'll go now. Will you excuse us, please, Anne? I must see Tess safely home.'

These words produced a harsh laugh from his wife. 'Safely? I wonder what her mother will think about that when she sees the state she's in?'

'Will you two stop talking as if I'm not here!' Tess bellowed, increasing the throbbing in her head. Clutching a hand to her brow she muttered through clenched teeth, 'Dan, thank you all the same, but I'd rather go home alone. Besides, the rain seems to have stopped and the cold air should help clear my head.'

'Tess, much as I dread your mother's reaction when she sees you like this, I insist on seeing you home.'

'Mam will be worse if you're with me. She'll hit the roof, Dan. There's no telling what she'll say or do. I've never been drunk before, you know, so she's sure to blame you.'

'Can I make a suggestion?' Anne ventured.

Dan turned warily to her and growled, 'Are you still here?' although he had been very much aware of her presence.

She just smiled and said, 'Why don't I come with you? It won't look so bad, so it won't, if the two of us take her home. Mm?'

Dan pondered her words. She was right, of course. Alice wouldn't react so badly if Anne came with them,

[61]

especially if she thought they had been together all evening. With a slight shrug, he agreed. 'All right, let's go.'

'Before we go, let's tidy you up a bit, Tess.'

Without further ado, Anne brushed past Dan and entered the house she had called home for twelve years. A quick glance round showed her it looked exactly the same. She grimaced. It shouldn't be too hard to coax her son to leave these surroundings. But did she really want to come between father and son?

With a sigh she turned her attention to Tess. 'Have you a comb with you, Tess?'

Tess motioned to the bag Dan still held. 'In there.'

Since Tess was no different from most other women her large handbag held just about everything except the kitchen sink. After some rummaging, Anne produced a comb and proceeded to tidy Tess's hair, remarking on its lovely colour and texture. Next she produced Tess's compact from her bag so the girl could powder her face, and at last she seemed satisfied by the result. Standing back, she eyed her charge. 'There now, you look much better already.'

Dan had to agree. Having got rid of the booze and with her hair combed and nose powdered, Tess looked more like her old self.

'Thanks,' he acknowledged, with a nod in his wife's direction. Extending a helping hand to Tess, he said, 'Let's go, lass.' He ushered the two women out into the street and locked the front door.

Miraculously the rain had stopped and an icy breeze fanned their faces. They walked three abreast, arms linked, Tess in the middle, grateful for their support and the cold air on her face. The dark grey clouds were thinning out and a moon was trying to lighten the shadows.

The air was soothing on her hot eyelids but did little to ease the pain in her head. They all remained locked in their own thoughts until Tess's home was reached.

They had no sooner arrived at the steps than the door was thrown open and Alice bounded out. Frantic wasn't the word to describe the state she was in. She was beside herself with worry, her hair standing on end where she had obviously dragged her hands through it more than once.

'Where on earth have you been, Tess?' she cried, tears spurting from her eyes in relief at seeing her daughter safely home. 'I've been at my wits' end with worry. I was just about to go down to the police station, so I was.'

'Alice, it's my fault she's so late. Anne – my wife here – and I invited her into the Clock Bar for a drink and then she came down to the house with us for a cup of tea.'

Alice glared at him suspiciously, then as his words penetrated her brain she rounded on her daughter. 'I don't believe it! After all the warnings I gave you, you went into a public house? How could you be so foolish, girl?'

Glad that Anne had made her look at least half presentable, Tess heard her mother out in silence and hung her head in shame. After all was said and done, her mother had been proved right. Look how wretched and sick she felt through entering a pub. If only she had obeyed her mother and steered clear of that 'den of iniquity' she wouldn't be feeling as if she were about to die.

Getting no response from her daughter, Alice turned her wrath on Dan. 'As for you . . . what were you thinking of? You're old and ugly enough to know better. You ought to be ashamed of yourself . . .'

Moving closer to Alice, Anne interrupted softly. 'It

was all my fault, Mrs Maguire. Dan and I met Tess just outside the pub and I wanted so much to meet your daughter that I suggested we go into the lounge for a drink. It was pouring out of the heavens and it seemed like a good idea at the time. I'm sorry. I didn't mean any harm. It was all quite respectable, I can assure you.'

'Huh! That's as may be, but you had no right to take Tess with you. She's far too young to go into places like that.' Her eyes raked Anne from head to toe. 'If you don't mind my saying so, you don't look like someone who would frequent pubs.'

'You're right, I don't often go into them,' Anne lied through her teeth. 'But as I said, it was pouring down and I knew my son used to date Tess. Jack has spoken often of her and I did so want to meet her. I'm sorry about the pub. It won't happen again. I can assure you it was a one-off and she was quite safe with us.' Big limpid blue eyes asked for understanding.

Mollified, Alice allowed her demeanour to change. 'Oh well, since she doesn't seem to have come to any harm I'll overlook it this time. Would you like to come in for a cup of tea?'

'No, thank you, Mrs Maguire. It's not long since we had one.'

Having made a few attempts to speak and been ignored, and feeling that her legs wouldn't hold her up much longer, Tess at last made her voice heard. 'If you'll excuse me, Anne, Dan, I'll go on in. And thanks for everything.'

'You do that, Tess. We'll be getting back now. Good night.' Dan watched, breathless, as Tess carefully picked her way up the steps. She entered the house safely and, relieved that everything had gone so well, he smiled at Alice. 'Good night, Alice.'

'Good night, Dan. It was lovely meeting you, Mrs Thompson. Good night.'

'Likewise, Mrs Maguire. Good night.'

Dan smiled wryly at his estranged wife as they retraced their steps down the Springfield Road. 'Man, but you can certainly spin a good yarn. You almost had me believing you back there.'

She smiled slyly at him through lowered lashes. 'I thought you wanted to keep Tess in her mother's good books.'

'That's true.'

'Well then, stop complaining.'

'I wasn't complaining. Just the opposite if you must know. So Jack told you all about Tess, did he?'

'Yes. He was dating her when I first approached him.'

All the old rancour came to the fore at these words and he glowered at her. 'What do you hope to gain from pestering him? Eh? He'll never leave home for you!'

'Tell me something, Dan,' she asked. 'What have you done to make that house a better place to live in since I left eight years ago?'

Thrusting his face towards her, he growled, 'Forget the house for a minute! I fed and clothed our son. I wiped his tears and consoled him each time he cried for want of you. I saw he went to school and helped him with his homework. All that was far more impor-tant to me than decorating the house.'

This was something she felt guilty about, her son not furthering his education, and she was glad Dan was giving her the chance to gripe at him about it. 'You should have made him stay on at school,' she cried indignantly. Then she backed away from him, such was the anger radiating from him as he glowered at her.

Was the woman daft? 'I tried. God knows I tried! But he wouldn't listen. He wanted to earn money right away.'

'But why the Silk & Rayon, of all places?'

'It was either that or the mill.'

'Don't be silly! You're well known in the building trade. Surely you could have at least got him an apprenticeship?'

'Again, I tried. I set up interviews for him but he didn't want to know. He just didn't bother turning up. If he had listened to me he'd be an electrician or a joiner today.'

'You should have made him go to those interviews! I would have.' Her anger matched his now.

He eyed her through narrowed lids and replied in a low, menacing voice. 'Ah, but you weren't at home, were you? No! You were away flying your kite. Gallivanting about all over the place with your fancy man!'

'If I had only known,' she lamented. 'I wasn't all that far away. I might have influenced him. Talked him into seeking an apprenticeship.'

'You should have kept in touch with him. You broke the lad's heart. We'd no idea where you were, what you were up to, until you asked for a divorce. Then, although I didn't mention divorce to him, I could at least tell him that you were still in Ireland. As far as we were concerned, until then you could have been in America or Australia. Anywhere in the world.'

'I thought a complete break was for the best all round. I didn't want to upset him more than was necessary.' She laughed ruefully. 'Do you know where I was living? Whitehouse!'

'Down the Shore Road?' he cried in disbelief. 'I don't believe it! I passed through there every day for a couple of years when I was working in Jordanstown. Where did you work?'

She sighed deeply. 'I didn't have to work. Jimmy is high up in Greeves mill, and isn't short of a bob or two. I thought it would be great to be a woman of leisure for a change.'

'What went wrong, then?'

'I got bored. Jimmy didn't want any children, said he was too old and I suppose he was right. I didn't realise he was so set in his ways.'

'The story of your life, eh, Anne? Never satisfied with what you've got.' They had reached the top of Spinner Street and he came to a halt. This was as far as he wanted her to come. 'I'll bid you good night. And thanks for your help with Tess. I really do appreciate it.'

A hand on his arm stayed him and she moved closer. 'Dan, I made a terrible mistake when I left you.'

He snatched his arm away. 'Here, pull the other one. You're just one selfish, discontented bitch that no one could ever please no matter how hard they tried.'

'That's not fair! I tried. You don't know how hard I tried. But you'd lost interest in everything. Your efforts on the house had come to a standstill and Jimmy was filling my head with talk of this big house he owned in Whitehouse. He even took me to see it one day at lunch time and I couldn't get over the grandeur of it. You could even see Belfast Lough from the upstairs windows.'

All this had been going on and he had been unaware of it. He must have been blind! The disgust he felt came to the fore. Disgust at himself for not noticing and at her for being so easily tempted. 'And you left a wee twelve-year-old boy because of a big house?' He sounded every bit as flabbergasted as he felt.

Her head was bowed in shame. 'I admit I was weak, but don't make me pay for the rest of my life . . . please.'

He gazed down at her and, in his opinion, her crocodile tears. 'As far as I'm concerned you can go and rot in hell.' With these words he strode off down the street.

Her pleading voice followed him. 'Dan, wait, hold on a minute.' When he kept walking, she shouted, 'I'll take Jack away from you, so I will.'

'Just you try!' he threw over his shoulder, defiantly, but kept on walking.

She followed him down the street and he swung round and stepped threateningly towards her. 'Get away home! Or wherever you're staying at the moment. You're not wanted here.'

She glared at him. 'You watch yourself, Dan Thompson. I've every right to be here. I'm staying with Lily Brady, if you must know.'

He was bewildered. How had he missed her coming and going if she was lodging in the same street?

She read his mind and said, 'I just moved in today. It's only until I get a place of my own. A place for me and Jack,' she added daringly.

'Stay out of my way, Anne! And leave our Jack alone,' he warned. 'Or I won't be responsible for my actions.'

He strode off and she watched him, anger eating away at her. She shouldn't let him get to her like this. After all, she didn't care one way or the other what he thought. Or did she? Wasn't the old attraction trying to raise its head? Did he feel it too? Is that why he was so objectionable? Was there a chance that he might take her back? Would she be willing to go? Nothing was any different from the way it was before, after all was said and done. Still, perhaps it was worth giving it a try. According to Lily Brady, there hadn't been any other woman on the scene since she had left him and with his handsome looks he must have had his chances. Perhaps he did still care a little.

Alice was dismayed to find Tess had retired for the night when she entered the house. That was quick. Had that woman upset her in any way? It had come as a surprise to find that Dan and his wife were still together. She hadn't liked to show any interest in his affairs by questioning her daughter about him, but somehow or other she had got the impression that they were separated. Now what had given her that idea? And why did she feel sad about their reconciliation, if that was what it was? Had she actually fancied him? Surely not!

Tapping on the bedroom door she asked softly, 'Tess, are you awake? Can I come in for a minute, love?'

Tess pulled the bedclothes tighter around her ears and willed her mother to go away. There was no way she could hold a rational conversation tonight. So far her mother had been duped, but once she got close enough and smelt the brandy on her breath all hell would be let loose. Her mother would be assuming that she had been on soft drinks. Any whiff of alcohol she might have noticed at the door would have been put down to Anne and Dan. Dear God, make her leave me alone!

After what seemed an eternity, she heard the squeak of a couple of loose treads as her mother descended the stairs, and blew out a long sigh of relief. She admitted that she had got off very lightly. All thanks to Anne!

Would Anne and Dan get back together again now the ice was broken? It would please Jack so much if they were to be reconciled. But then, why should she care whether or not Jack was pleased? Look at the way he had treated her! What was it Dan had said about his son and Colette? Tess delved into her mind but everything was fuzzy. She would never get drunk again if this was the condition it left you in.

Ah! Dan's words came back to her. He had said they were away to Omagh to collect some of Colette's things. It looked as if it was serious between the two of them. Hot tears escaped from her eyes and she let them flow freely. She hoped it would make her feel better. It hadn't before, but perhaps this time they would ease the pain of rejection.

She fell into a troubled sleep and in her dreams Jack was running away from her. At last she caught up with him and grasped his arm. He turned and to her dismay it was a stranger's arm she was clinging to. The man tugged his arm free and she was left feeling desolate. Next morning she awoke with smarting eyes and cheeks still wet with tears.

Christmas was fast approaching and Tess and her mother were kept very busy. Christmas Day was on a Friday this year and they wanted all their work squared up and out of the way at least a week beforehand.

At breakfast one morning Alice squinted at a letter with an Irish postage stamp and recognised the handwriting. 'Huh, imagine that! It's from your Uncle Malachy,' she gasped in surprise and quickly knifed it open. 'What do you think? He wants to join us for a few days over Christmas.'

They usually spent Christmas and the New Year alone and a wide smile split Tess's face at this news. 'That's wonderful! It will be great to have some company for a change, especially family.'

'There's a snag. He wants to bring a friend along.'

'That's even better! The more the merrier. We've plenty of rooms.'

'It's a woman friend.'

'Well, I'm glad he's met someone at last. Perhaps they'll get engaged while they're up here.'

'I hope he doesn't expect me to let them share a room, that's all I can say,' Alice said piously. 'There'll be no hanky-panky under my roof while I'm alive.'

Tess tut-tutted in disgust. 'Oh, Mam! Stop being so sanctimonious and stop taking all the pleasure out of them coming. I'm delighted, so I am. And it's none of your business, or mine for that matter, what they get up to while they're here.'

'In my house it is!'

Resisting the urge to start an argument, Tess rose, pushed her chair away from the table and started to noisily clear the breakfast dishes. Her mother's holier than thou attitude annoyed her at times. She could take the joy out of everything without even trying. You would think she was the only one that mattered; the only one without sin. As if!

'Malachy's taking it for granted he can come. He says we're not to buy a turkey as he will bring one with him and a leg of lamb as well. Isn't that great? That wee farm of his must be doing well at last. All that snow last year nearly ruined him, you know. It was well he was insured. But just think, all we'll have to buy is a roast of pork and all the other smaller bits and pieces.' Alice lifted the remaining dishes and followed Tess into the kitchen. 'I'll have to buy a fruit cake,' she said mournfully. 'I know it won't be nearly as nice as my own, but it's too late now to bake one. Oh, I wish he'd given us a bit more notice. We could have been better prepared.'

'You can bake some of your lovely mince pies and

make a big trifle,' Tess consoled her. 'You know every-one loves your trifles.'

Alice relaxed. 'You're right, of course. I don't suppose he'll notice. After all, one fruit cake doesn't make a Christmas.'

Tess put her arms round her mother and twirled her around the kitchen. 'I've a feeling this is going to be the best Christmas ever, Mam.'

Alice looked at her daughter's laughing eyes and smiling face and vowed it would indeed be a happy time if she had anything to do with it. She would turn a blind eye to her brother's shenanigans if his stay enabled her daughter to put her troubles behind her. She would do all in her power to make this festive time a happy one.

Chapter Four

Malachy and his friend arrived on Christmas Eve. Early in the afternoon a Land-Rover pulled up at the front of the house and Tess, who had been eagerly watching for them on and off since morning, rushed out to help them disembark, shouting a warning over her shoulder to her mother that they had arrived.

Malachy gripped her close. 'My, but you've grown!' He then held her at arm's length and cried, 'You look a picture! Doesn't she, Rose?'

'She does indeed,' his companion agreed, with a slow appraising look.

Tess was flustered; but they did sound so sincere. 'Ah well, now, I don't know about that.'

'Take my word for it.' Her uncle drew the woman forward. 'Tess, this is my dear friend Rose Donaghy, and Rose, you'll have guessed that this is my lovely niece, Tess.'

As they shook hands, Alice came down the steps in a rush, almost tripping in her haste. Malachy reached forward and stopped her headlong progress. 'Hey, steady on there. We don't want to spend Christmas visiting you in hospital, do we?'

Lifting her face for his kiss, Alice apologised. 'I'm sorry about this. I was checking that everything was all right in the kitchen. I don't want to give you a burnt offering on your first day here.' Her eyes were on the woman as she spoke. Malachy made the introductions and his sister said, 'You're more than welcome in our home, Rose. Come inside. It's cold out here.'

The two women climbed the steps and Tess smiled at her uncle. 'I can't tell you how pleased I am to see you, Uncle Mal.'

'And I you! I've a lad working for me now and he offered to look after the stock till I get back. Never one to look a gift horse in the mouth, I accepted right away. Mind you, there was motive in his madness. His girlfriend will be staying with him while I'm away.' He gave Tess a knowing wink and a nudge with his elbow and she burst out laughing.

'I hope you have the good sense not to tell Mam all that or she won't be able to enjoy Christmas for worrying about what they might get up to.'

'I know my sister better than you think, Tess. I know where to draw the line. I only hope she can see her way to letting Rose and me share a room.'

They had emptied the Land-Rover and were lifting cases and boxes up the steps and into the hall. Tess stopped in her tracks and eyed him with something akin to horror.

Malachy threw back his head and laughed at the expression on her face. 'Do you think I'd be that daft, Tess? No. Besides, there's nothing like that between Rose and me. She lost her husband a few months ago and I persuaded her the break would do her a world of good.'

'How sad.'

'Well now, he wasn't the best of husbands, mind you. Not by any means. But of course now he's gone she can only remember his good points.'

'As far as I can make out that's always the way. They're all saints once they go. What about you, Uncle Malachy? Is there any woman in your life yet?'

'Nobody would have me, Tess.'

Tess examined him and silently disagreed. A bit portly in build, he was nevertheless tall enough to carry the weight. He still had a good thick head of brown hair and mischievous brown eyes laughed at her as he returned her look.

'I find that hard to believe, Uncle Malachy.'

The laughter left his face. 'Although my farm is at last paying its way and I'm quite comfortable, it's no life for a woman, Tess. I couldn't expect anyone to share it. It's all hard graft, especially in the dark winter months.'

'But if she loved you?'

He shook his head. 'To be truthful, I don't even get the chance to meet any eligible women. All my friends and acquaintances are already married to each other.'

Big sad eyes regarded him. 'I'm so sorry,' Tess whispered.

'Hey! Don't get me wrong, I'm not complaining. I'm very contented with my lot. Now, let's get these things inside before your mother comes looking for us.'

They all went to midnight Mass in Clonard Monastery and Rose was enthralled at the beauty of the church and the Christmas service, especially the choral singing.

Back at the house they had a glass of ginger wine and some of Alice's delicious mince pies. Thus fortified, Rose and Tess settled back in comfortable easy chairs and listened raptly as Alice and her brother reminisced over their early years. Alice had never complained about her childhood and Tess was surprised at just how hard a beginning she had apparently had. According to Malachy, their father had been a tyrant who had ruled his home with a rod of iron. He had expected his daughter to pull her weight and quite literally work like a man.

Looking fondly at her brother, Alice confessed, 'Malachy did most of my work as well as his own and many a time took a blow that was meant for me.'

Embarrassed, her brother was quick to deny it. 'Here now, sis, we'll have less of that. Don't you try to make me out to be some kind of Sir Galahad. If I ever took a blow meant for you it was because I deserved it in the first place.'

Sadly Alice shook her head. 'Hark at him! I suppose it was your fault the day Dad discovered me behind the shed with Tom Mitchell? Remember him?'

'Yes, that was my fault! If I hadn't brought him home from school with me you'd never have been tempted. Besides, you were doing nothing wrong. I'm sure it was just an innocent peck on the cheek. You were too good-living even then to commit a sin. You know, you're very like me dad in some ways, Alice. There are no grey areas in your mind. Everything is in black and white.'

Alice laughed aloud. 'Don't you believe it! I was just a curious schoolgirl, and like my friends I was tempted. We never did anything really bad but we felt we were being daring if we egged the boys on. Anyhow, you must have been worried, because you never brought any of your schoolmates home after that. But it did give me an idea of what it felt like to be admired and desired and after that I longed for the company of the opposite sex.'

'Admiration was something you always had plenty of, Alice. Everybody who came to the house thought you were beautiful. You still are,' Malachy gallantly assured her.

Flushed with pleasure at all these compliments, Alice's eyes sought her daughter's face. If only . . .

From past experience, Tess could guess the drift of her mother's thoughts. Why couldn't her daughter have inherited her good looks? Well, she hadn't. So, tough! She rose abruptly to her feet. 'If you'll excuse me, I'll go on up to bed now.' She kissed both visitors on the cheek. 'I'm so glad you're here. See you in the morning. Good night, Mam.'

There was silence for some moments when she left the room. It was Malachy who broke it. Shifting uncomfortably in his chair, he asked tentatively, 'Did I say something to offend Tess?'

With a sad shake of the head, Alice admitted, 'I'm afraid Tess has never come to terms with the fact that she didn't inherit my good looks.'

Malachy's mouth dropped open. 'But she's lovely,' he cried. 'Oh, she hasn't got the conventional Irish rose beauty, but with those eyes and that hair, she's beautiful. She would put Greer Garson to shame, so she would.'

'Do you really think so?'

He could see Alice was taken aback at his outburst and said, 'I hope you haven't been putting the wrong ideas into her head by making her think she's plain, just because she doesn't have your looks?'

'No, no,' she hastened to reply. 'I've always assured her that one day a man will come into her life who will realise her worth.'

That said it all as far as Malachy was concerned. Poor Tess, he thought.

Rose had taken all this in in silence. Now, not wanting Malachy to say something he might later regret, she pretended to smother a yawn. 'If you'll excuse me, it is getting late, so I think I'll also retire for the night. It's been a long day. Good night, Alice, and thanks for having me.'

Malachy rose to his feet, stretched his tired muscles and groaned. 'Me too.'

He stifled a laugh as his sister hurriedly assured them, 'I'll be right behind you. I've just to check the windows and doors.'

On the landing, outside the room allocated to Rose, Malachy turned her round to face him and placed a hand on each of her shoulders. 'Will you be all right?'

'Of course I will. The room is lovely and comfortable, and I'm so tired that I'll probably drop off the minute my head hits the pillow.'

He smiled at her and stretched his neck to look up the second flight of stairs. 'It's as well we're just good friends. Alice certainly intends keeping us apart.'

With a slight push and a laugh Rose sent him on his way. 'Away you go and don't give your sister any cause for concern. Good night, and happy Christmas, Malachy.'

He turned towards the other stairs. 'Good night, Rose, and a happy Christmas to you too.'

She watched him for some moments before entering the bedroom. Chance would be a fine thing, if a man like Malachy could ever take a fancy to her. She certainly wouldn't be holding her breath on the off chance.

Christmas Day for Tess was like a fairy tale come true. After a late breakfast, they gathered in the sitting room to open their gifts. Malachy had bought his niece an exquisite gold bracelet, studded with tiny diamonds.

Open mouthed, she gazed from the bracelet to him and back to the bracelet, then threw herself into his arms. 'Oh! It's beautiful, Uncle Malachy. But far too expensive. You shouldn't have!'

'It's not quite as expensive as it looks, but it is a good one nevertheless. I haven't bought you much over the years, Tess. To be truthful, I couldn't afford to. But from now on I intend spoiling you with nice presents. After all, you're my only niece.' He opened his parcel and exclaimed in delight at the thick Aran pullover she had bought him. 'Wow! Just what I need, love. Thank you very much.'

He had bought his sister a beautiful stole in soft cashmere wool. Crocheted, it was like a mass of cobwebs. She was so quiet when she opened it that he asked tentatively, 'Don't you like it, Alice?'

She pressed its softness to her cheek and assured him, 'It's lovely. Thank you.'

However, he saw her eyes returning to the bracelet that Tess had by now put admiringly on her wrist, and frowned. Surely his sister wasn't jealous of her own daughter?

Rose had bought perfume for the two women and received gloves and a scarf in return. She was embarrassed when they apologised for not buying something more original, saying the gifts were lovely and would come in useful. And sure, hadn't she been in the same boat, not knowing what to buy them?

Malachy was then persuaded to take Rose out for a drive, to show her some of Belfast's famous landmarks, while Alice and Tess put the finishing touches to the Christmas dinner.

As Alice fussed about making sure everything was just perfect, Tess set the table with their best linen tablecloth and napkins. The Waterford crystal glasses sparkled against the pure white of the linen and their best cutlery reflected the glow from the overhead chandelier. It was great to have someone to go to all this bother over. Alice was in her glory that all her precious things were on show at long last.

Tess smiled at her fondly. 'Mam?'

'Mm?'

'Were you annoyed at Uncle Malachy giving me such a valuable present?'

Alice kept her attention fixed on the floral display she was preparing for the centre of the table. 'Why should I be annoyed?'

'Maybe you think he should have given it to you.'

'And when would I ever get the chance to wear something as grand as that, tell me, eh? It would probably end up like everything else I have of any value. Hidden away in my bedroom dresser never to see the light of day again.'

Tess shrugged. 'You'd have as much chance as me. But that's not the point. Do you mind Uncle Malachy giving it to me?'

Slowly Alice lifted her gaze to meet her daughter's eyes. She grimaced slightly and confessed, 'I suppose I was a little bit jealous. No one ever bought me anything as expensive as that. Not even your father. He promised me the world but he died before he was in a position to spoil me.' A tear trickled down her cheek and she brushed it roughly away with the back of her hand. 'But he would have, you know. If only he'd lived longer. But give over! I'm glad my brother intends spoiling you. He couldn't spoil a nicer person.' Alice fondly gathered her daughter close. 'I just wish I could afford to shower gifts on you.'

'Oh, Mam, you know I want for nothing. Thanks to you, I've all my needs.'

They smiled tearfully at each other, then Alice pushed her gently away. 'Doesn't the table look wonderful?'

'It sure does. You'd think it was the queen coming for dinner instead of Malachy and Rose,' Tess replied with a smile. 'We should use all these grand things more often, not keep them locked away, gathering dust.'

'I was just thinking along those very same lines myself. Meanwhile, let's get this meal ready before they return, and remember, Tess, I love you dearly.'

The day passed in a cheerful atmosphere and they were relaxing in the evening, drinks in hand, when there was a knock on the door.

'Are you expecting anyone, Mam?' Tess asked with a frown as she rose slowly to her feet to answer it.

'No. Maybe it's that boy you know, or his father.'

'No chance,' Tess threw over her shoulder with a baleful glare as she left the room. She was surprised when she threw the door open to see Agnes and Tony standing on the top step. They cried in unison, 'Happy Christmas,' and holding high a sprig of mistletoe Tony stepped forward and planted a kiss on Tess's lips. 'Happy Christmas,' she replied.

They had been invited to come up on Boxing Night to meet Malachy and Rose and now Tess cried in disappointment, 'Does this mean you can't come tomorrow night? It's all arranged.'

'No, never you fear, we'll be here tomorrow night,' Agnes said. 'I just couldn't wait to show you this.' She pulled the glove off her left hand and extended it for Tess to view.

There, on the third finger, glistened a solitaire diamond ring. A bit put out, Tess grabbed her friend's hand and pulled her into the hall. 'What am I thinking of, keeping you standing out there in the cold.' She beckoned to Tony. 'Come in, Tony, and close the door while I get a good gander at this rock.'

Her mind was in a turmoil as she examined the ring. 'It's beautiful, Agnes. Congratulations. You too, Tony. I hope you will both be very happy together.' There was a questioning look in her eyes as she grabbed her friend to hug her close. 'This is a surprise. You never let on,' she whispered.

'I was surprised and all,' Agnes admitted. She gave Tony a wide smile. 'He just produced this ring out of the blue earlier today, and asked me to marry him.'

'Come on in and show it to Mam. And you can meet Uncle Malachy and his friend while you're here.'

As a result of the big meal and a couple of glasses of sherry, Alice was heavy-eyed as she rose unsteadily to greet them. 'I thought it was tomorrow night you two were coming?'

'It is, Mrs Maguire. I just wanted Tess to know I got engaged today.'

Tess introduced her uncle and Rose and they all gathered round to admire the ring.

'Have you time for a drink?' Malachy asked. 'You can't go without a toast to celebrate the big occasion.'

Tony nodded his approval. 'Just one, mind. We have other people to visit and break the news to.'

'I'll just nip up to the loo,' Agnes said with a glance in her friend's direction.

Tess followed her up the stairs into the bathroom. Making sure the door was closed and they couldn't be overheard, Agnes said, 'Well, what do you think?'

'I don't know what to think, Agnes. You always said he wasn't Mr Right and I believed you. Now you land in here telling us you're engaged. I'm gobsmacked, so I am.'

[82]

'To tell you the truth, so am I. Tony just landed into our living room earlier on today, and getting down on one knee he produced this ring and asked me to marry him. Right there in front of everybody. I could see that they all thought we'd planned it that way. What could I do but say yes?'

'How did your mam take it?'

'Oh, she smiled and pretended to be pleased but I could see she wasn't too happy at the idea. But what else could she do? Marie and Dennis have set the date. They're getting married at Easter and Dennis's parents are at our house at the moment. They've been invited over to celebrate and discuss the wedding arrangements. I had to get away from all the questions. Sorry for bursting in on you like this.'

'Don't be silly! I'm glad you came. I just don't understand. What are you going to do? You can't just marry him because he bought a ring. He should have asked you first.'

'Tony says if he had asked me first I'd have made all kinds of excuses. This way I had to give him an answer one way or the other.'

'He took a chance, didn't he? What if you had said no?'

Agnes shrugged and spread her hands wide. 'I suppose he knew I wouldn't embarrass him in front of everybody.'

'Still, it wasn't fair of him to put you on the spot like that.' Tess eyed her friend closely. 'Do you love him, Agnes?'

'That's just it. I don't know. What is love? As you know, he's my first real boyfriend. I admit we get on great but I've no one else to compare him with.' She sighed. 'Anyhow, for the time being I'm engaged. Now let's get back downstairs. We're going over now to break the news to his family.'

She sounded so despondent, Tess put her arms round her and hugged her in sympathy. 'Never mind. Engagements can be broken.'

'Do you think this one will?'

A slight uplift of the shoulders accompanied Tess's reply. 'How can I tell? Come on, Tony's waiting. We can talk about it another time.'

Amidst more congratulations and best wishes the couple left. As they settled back in their chairs and reached once more for their drinks, Alice admonished her daughter. 'You never said it was serious between Agnes and that young lad.'

'I didn't know anything about it. Agnes always maintained that they were just good friends. He just landed in with the ring and proposed to her in front of her family. She said yes to save him any embarrassment.'

'Not a good recipe for a happy marriage,' Rose said softly. 'What kind of work do they do?'

'He's a plumber and Agnes works in a typing pool.'

'Well, those are two good jobs so they should be all right moneywise, and that always helps.'

'But surely there should be some magic there as well?' Tess queried.

'I've found that's not always the case, but if a marriage is worked at it will probably last. Mine did,' Rose added absentmindedly and then turned bright red at the realisation of her admission.

Malachy jumped to her rescue. 'But then, Rose, you're an exceptional person.' He then changed the subject, to Rose's obvious relief.

The following evening Agnes seemed totally resigned to the idea of becoming Mrs Burke and Tess looked at her in wonder. Twenty-four hours had certainly changed her attitude. Could an engagement ring, even a beautiful solitaire, really make so much difference? Getting her friend alone in the kitchen for a few minutes, she questioned her.

'So you've decided it's all for the best, then?'

Agnes shrugged. 'Who knows? Only time will tell. We're having a bit of a do in our house on New Year's Eve to celebrate. Just a small gathering. You will come, won't you?'

Tess's thoughts immediately turned to Jack. 'Will Jack be there?'

'Nothing's been said, but he is Tony's best friend, after all, so I imagine he will be.'

'You'll have to excuse me then, Agnes, but I couldn't bear to be in the same room as him and Colette.'

'You're my best friend, Tess Maguire! You must come. There won't be many there. Just family and a few close friends. I'm going to ask your mam to come along as well, so you'll have to accompany her.'

'That's blackmail, so it is!' Tess gasped.

'Ah, come on now, Tess. You'll have to get used to seeing them together sometime.'

'Why? Tell me why? I haven't set eyes on Jack for months. Belfast is big enough for both of us.'

Tears glistened in Agnes's big blue eyes. 'I thought I could depend on your support. I thought we were best friends.' A tear escaped and slid down her cheek.

'Okay, okay. For heaven's sake give over. I'll come.'

'Thank you. I owe you one.'

'Oh, Agnes, I hope you're doing the right thing.'

'So do I, Tess. So do I.'

'Promise me you won't rush into marriage, sure you won't?'

'No fear.'

'And you'll be careful, won't you?'

A bewildered frown plucked at Agnes's pale eyebrows. 'I don't know what you mean.'

'I'll spell it out for you, then. Make sure you don't get pregnant or then you'll have to get married, like it or not.'

Agnes's mouth fell open at the insinuation. She quickly snapped it shut. 'That's not likely to happen. We don't do things like that. Tony respects me too much for any of that kind of caper, so he does. Why, we hardly even kiss, just in case we get carried away. A ring isn't going to change our morals overnight, I can assure you.'

Somehow, instead of reassuring Tess, this dismayed her. Surely if two people were planning to marry they should at least feel the urge to show each other affection? Look how she had responded to Jack Thompson. Who would have believed she could be so blatant? But she had cared deeply for him. Would it be the same with every man she dated? Was everyone different?

The appearance of her mother curtailed further conversation. 'Are you two going to stay in here all evening or are you going to join us in the living room?'

Agnes gave her an apologetic look. 'We're coming in now, Mrs Maguire.' She was glad to escape her friend's interrogation and gladly left the kitchen.

To the surprise of all concerned, Alice and Rose got on like a house on fire over the Christmas period. After cautiously sizing each other up on that first day, they discovered that they had all sorts of things in common and chatted to each other for hours on end. Alice, not being too fond of animals, and with a great dislike of farmyard smells and muddy fields, had only occasionally ventured to her brother's farm for a few days at a time during the summer months. Now she was actually promising Rose that she would visit him at Easter so that she and her new friend could renew their acquaintance. And perhaps, if they hadn't too much work on, she might stay a few weeks if Tess was able to manage without her.

It was Monday morning and they were loading the Land-Rover for the couple's return to Carlingford when this conversation took place. Malachy and Tess exchanged startled glances at Alice's promise. Tess was quick to intervene. 'You know we always have a quiet spell after Easter, Mam. Of course you must go! You deserve a wee break. It will do you good to get away for a while.'

'Well, if that's the case . . . then why not?'

'Why don't you both come?' Malachy suggested.

'Well now, Uncle Malachy, we don't close down completely at Easter. You see, some customers get their orders on credit. It's the only way to do business these days and it works out fine for us. However, it does mean that Mam or myself has to be here every Friday and Saturday to collect the money.'

'Ah, I understand perfectly. But you will come later in the year, won't you?'

Tess laughed aloud. 'Do you want me to put the blink on you again? Remember last year when I promised to visit? It snowed fast and furious. It was like living in Siberia. Why, we were up to our knees in snow and slush for many a long day. Would you like that to happen again?'

He joined in her laughter. 'I would not! Nor will I ever forget it. It almost wiped me out, so it did. It was lucky that I was insured. Some of the other farmers weren't so lucky when the thaw came and with it the floods. Some of my fields never fully recovered their true richness, either. They're still unsuitable for most crops, but I'm working at it. But do you know something, Tess? Somehow or other, I don't think it was your fault.'

'Even so, let's play it by ear, eh? Just to be on the safe side. I'll not make any promises. We'll wait and see what the weather is like. Okay?'

'Whatever you say. But I would really like you to come down. Bring a friend along and then you won't be bored.'

'I'd never be bored in Carlingford. There's too much to explore, what with the lough and the Cooley Hills. Your farm is situated in a lovely spot, Uncle Malachy, the way it overlooks the water.'

'I couldn't agree with you more. I never tire of the views. Especially in the spring and summer months. So, I can expect to see you sometime next year?'

'You can count on it. I just wish you and Rose could stay to see in the New Year with us. Is there no chance?'

'I'm afraid not. Duty calls. A working farmer can't afford to take much time off, you know, Tess.'

Impulsively, Tess gave him a quick hug. 'Thanks for coming. I can't recall a better Christmas, and I promise to visit you sometime in the summer.'

Chapter Five

New Year's Eve had arrived and it was with trepidation that Tess accompanied her mother along Violet Street to the big parlour house where Agnes lived. She dreaded the evening lying in wait for her; dreaded having to watch Jack and Colette together as a couple. What if they took this opportunity to announce their own engagement? How would she be able to face that? Worse still, how would she react in front of everyone?

She was glad when her mother broke into her troubled thoughts. 'It was nice of Agnes to invite us along. Do you think she will like the wee present I've bought her?' Alice whispered as they came up to the door and awaited a reply to their knock.

'I think most people are grateful for any kind of gift for their bottom drawer. Not that yours is *wee* by any standards.' Tess repressed a grimace at the size of the parcel her mother clutched in her arms. A bedside lamp! It would be some bottom drawer that that fitted into. At least her Irish linen tablecloth wouldn't take up much room.

The door was thrown open and Ted Quinn thrust out his hand in welcome. 'Come in, come in. My daughter will be down in a minute, Tess. I hope you are well, Alice,' he said cordially.

'Is Tony upstairs with Agnes, Mr Quinn? Or can I go up to her?'

'Oh, no. She's alone all right. There'll be none of that carry-on in this house just because she's got a ring on her finger. His place will be down here. *You* can certainly go up to her. Here, Alice, let me take your coat. You too, Tess. You go on into the sitting room, Alice, and my wife will look after you.'

The first person Alice saw when she entered the room was Dan Thompson, looking very handsome in a cream pullover over an open-necked shirt and brown trousers. A quick glance round showed no sign of his wife, though that didn't necessarily mean Anne wasn't there. She could be in one of the other rooms.

Dan caught her eye and advanced to meet her. 'I'm sure you were as surprised as I was to get an invitation here tonight?'

'I was indeed, and what's more, I was told it was a small gathering of friends.' Alice gazed around the crowded room in bewilderment.

Dan laughed. 'These things are inclined to run out of control. Still, as far as I can make out, bar the prospective groom and his parents, I think you and Tess are the last to arrive.'

'You know something? I thought Tess was going to renege. I don't know what's got into her. She made all kinds of excuses not to come. She's here under duress, mind you, because I wouldn't come on my own.'

Dan looked uncomfortable; he could well imagine what was wrong with Tess. His son had a lot to answer for. 'Can I relieve you of that parcel, Alice? All the gifts are in the dining room.'

Gratefully Alice relinquished her hold on the lamp. 'Thank you very much, Dan.'

He made his way from the room with the parcel and May Quinn arrived at Alice's elbow. 'Can I get you a drink, Alice?'

Alice eyed her closely and decided she looked far from being the happy hostess. 'That would be very nice, May. I suppose you're overjoyed at the idea of having two weddings in the family?'

'Far from it, I can assure you. I've warned Agnes that she will have to wait a year or two until we get over Marie's wedding. Everything is so expensive these days. Why Agnes had to rush and get engaged just as Marie and Dennis finally set the date, I'll never know. Still, that's all in the future. What will you have to drink, Alice? Gin, wine, sherry?'

'A glass of white wine would be lovely, thank you.'

It was Dan who returned with her drink, a tall lad and a small dark-haired girl in tow. 'This is my son Jack and his girlfriend Colette.'

So this was the young man Tess was breaking her heart over. The reason for her reluctance to come here tonight. Alice's eyes ranged over the tall gangly lad and found him wanting. Tess could do a lot better than this, surely!

'Pleased to meet you, Jack. Tess has spoken of you.' She nodded at his companion. 'You too, love.'

Sensing he had been found wanting, Jack teased, 'Not all bad, I hope.'

'No . . . but could you blame her if it was?' Alice's gaze rested on his companion.

A slight frown puckered Colette's brow as she gazed back. 'I don't understand.'

Quickly Jack interrupted. 'Dad, a friend of mine has just arrived and I promised to introduce him to Colette. Will you excuse us, Mrs Maguire?'

Dan quirked a brow at Alice. 'I think Jack did the

right thing there, don't you, Alice? Tess wouldn't have liked you intervening on her behalf. Now, would she?'

'Mm . . . I suppose you're right.' She raised her glass. 'Cheers.'

Upstairs Tess sat on the bed and watched Agnes put the finishing touches to her make-up. When at last she turned from the mirror and faced her friend, Tess said sincerely, 'You look lovely.'

'Thanks. Has Tony arrived yet?'

'I didn't see him. But then, I came straight up here. Is Jack coming?'

'I'm afraid so.' Putting her hand on Tess's arm, Agnes said earnestly, 'Colette's nice. You'll like her.'

'Huh! That's a great comfort to me, so it is.'

A sad smile puckered Agnes's lips. 'Shall we go down and face them all?'

'I don't know what you're so worried about, for heaven's sake. It's *your* engagement party! You should be full of beans.'

'Ah, but I'm not. That's why I'm worried,' Agnes confessed with a rueful grin. Nevertheless, there was a bright smile on her face as she trooped down the stairs with Tess trailing behind her.

Alice hailed her daughter. 'Tess, look who's here.' She indicated Jack and Colette, who had returned for their drinks.

Reluctantly, Tess joined the group in the corner. How could her mother be so insensitive? 'Hi, Jack, hi, Colette. Did you have a nice Christmas?'

'Very nice. Very nice indeed.' Jack bestowed a fond smile on Colette. 'Colette cooked the dinner and her grannie joined us. The meal was delicious and the four of us had a lovely, lazy day.'

'Your mother wasn't with you, then?' Alice was quick to note.

A wry smile twisted Jack's lips. 'No, she had already made other plans.' He had no intention of letting anyone know that his father had refused to let his wife join them.

'Oh? How odd,' Alice said softly.

Afraid she would pursue the matter, and push her nose in where it wasn't wanted, Tess flailed about in her mind for something to change the subject. To her relief the young man in charge of the record player suggested that it was time to take partners for a dance. The music that had been playing softly in the background intensified and Jack excused himself to gather Colette close and shuffle across the floor with her.

At that instant Tony and his parents arrived, obviously flustered and full of apologies. 'Sorry we're late. We couldn't get a taxi. They're like gold dust tonight and Mam refused to walk in her new shoes,' Tony explained.

The small plump woman who was Tony's mother indicated her husband and son. 'They were mad at me, but I'd have been crippled, so I would, and it would have spoilt my night.'

May Quinn was quick to accept the excuse. 'You did right, Maeve, not to walk here in new shoes. We understand perfectly. Here, let me take your coats and Ted will get you all a drink.'

Tess, being without a partner, found herself alone during some of the dances. Dan Thompson was paying a lot of attention to her mother and danced with her every chance he got. He also danced with Tess a couple of times and Tony and Ted Quinn gave her duty dances.

Covertly watching Jack and Colette, Tess could see

they were very much in love by the way they obviously savoured each other's closeness, kissing each other's cheeks and necks at every opportunity. On the other hand Agnes and Tony danced with daylight between them. Fears for her friend rose in Tess's breast and she felt fiercely protective of her.

It was almost midnight when Jack approached Tess and asked her to dance with him. She wanted to refuse but pride made her smile and join him on the floor. After all, she surmised, he probably was just as averse to dancing with her but had been sent over by Colette to do his duty.

He smiled down at her, a strained, embarrassed smile, and she thought perhaps he had read her mind. 'Don't look so worried, Jack. I won't bite.'

He laughed and relaxed a little. 'Tony's a dark horse. He never even dropped a hint that he was thinking of getting married,' he declared.

'He was playing it safe in case she turned him down. Which she might have done, if he hadn't put her on the spot by asking her to marry him in front of every-one.'

Jack looked surprised. 'You can't seriously mean that. Surely she must love him to have agreed to marry him, no matter what the circumstances.'

Hastily Tess agreed with him. 'You're probably right, Jack. I don't know when to keep my big trap shut. What about you? Are you planning any surprises?'

'No. At least not for some time to come.'

She felt as if a hand had squeezed her heart. *Not for some time to come.* So marriage was on the cards, then. Well, hadn't she guessed as much from the antics of the pair of them on the floor?

A quick glance at her watch told Tess it was a few

minutes to twelve. Soon the New Year would be welcomed in. 'Good gracious! It's almost twelve.' She gave him a gentle push. 'Away you go, Jack, and greet the New Year in with your girlfriend.'

'I didn't realise it was that time.' He was uneasy, not wanting to leave her coming up to midnight. 'Where's your mother?'

'Don't worry, I'll find her. The house isn't all that big. Away you go.'

She watched him thread his way to where Colette was standing. Saw Jack take the girl in his arms and glance in Tess's direction. Felt the pity radiating from Colette.

Blinded by tears she turned away. If only things had worked out differently and she was the one in Jack's arms tonight, how wonderful life would be. Her dance with him had made her aware that she was still very much attracted to him. Her mother and Dan sought her out just as the doors, front and back, were thrown wide to the peal of church bells and the blare of sirens as Belfast welcomed in 1965. 'Happy New Year' was on everyone's lips and neighbours first-footed with their pieces of coal, bread and small silver coins to bring happiness and prosperity to the household.

After the wave of excitement had died down and everyone was exchanging kisses and good wishes, Tess whispered to her mother, 'Mam, I'm going to slip away. I'm sure Dan Thompson will walk you home.'

'What?' Still tingling from the feel of Dan's New Year kiss on her lips, Alice blinked at her daughter in bewilderment. 'You can't go home alone! I won't hear tell of it. I'm coming with you.'

'You'll do nothing of the sort.'

Arms encircled Tess and she twisted round to find it

was Dan. 'Happy New Year, Tess. I hope you get your heart's desire.'

His lips were gentle on hers and she gazed at him pleadingly. 'Dan, I want to leave now. Will you see Mam safely home?'

'Of course I will. But must you go? What about the buffet?'

'I couldn't eat a thing. I just want to get away from here.'

'If that's what you want, love. I'll look after your mother.' When Alice would have insisted, Dan said, 'Let her go, Alice. She knows what she's doing.'

Throwing him a grateful glance Tess went to seek out Agnes and Tony, to bid them good night. She wished them all the very best in the New Year and made her way upstairs to retrieve her coat. As she left the bedroom she came face to face with Jack coming from the bathroom.

Plastering a smile across her face, she cried gaily, 'Happy New Year, Jack,' and proffered her cheek for his kiss.

Roughly gripping her jaw, he turned her face up to his and claimed her lips. To her shame, all the longing of the past months surfaced and she hungrily returned his kiss, all the while reminding herself that he was drunk and didn't know what he was doing. She, on the other hand, was quite sober and knew very well that she was making a fool of herself. He gripped her closer still and how she wanted to give in to his silent demands. There was no one about. She might never get another chance. However, good sense prevailed and she pushed him away. 'Colette will be wondering what's keeping you.'

'Tess, I'm sorry things couldn't be different. I honestly didn't mean to hurt you.'

Pride lifted her chin high. 'And what makes you think you have? After all, what do a few kisses matter? Nobody got hurt. It was a pleasant interlude, that's all.'

With these words she left him and literally ran down the stairs and out into the cold night, glad of the breeze that fanned her burning cheeks.

'How dare he!' she fumed. 'How dare he patronise me like that. Who the bloody hell does he think he is anyway?'

Her mind retaliated. 'What did you expect? Didn't you nearly eat the bake of him back there? You'll have to learn to control your emotions, girl.'

As she walked up the road to her home tears of self-pity rolled down her face. Some Happy New Year this was! Would she ever have a man of her own?

The Maguires were always glad of the quiet spell after Christmas and the New Year. It gave them time to give the work room a good clearing out and pay attention to those things that needed doing, like painting and decorating. It was also at this time of year that the wholesalers were making room for new stock and Tess haunted the warehouses and factories looking for quality remnants at bargain prices to renew her own supplies.

Tess had all her materials in when in the middle of January there was a ferocious storm. Gale force winds, gusting up to almost eighty miles an hour and accompanied by torrential rain, swept across Belfast, lifting slates off roofs and causing a lot of structural damage to many buildings.

Tess and Alice stood by the window of the workshop as the rain lashed against it in a cold fury. Abating and then intensifying, and all the while howling like a banshee, it threatened to break into the house. They watched in awe as the road outside took on the appearance of a river, sweeping all debris before it.

Alice almost wept as she thought of the vagrants out on a night like this. 'God help anyone without a roof over their heads tonight. It must be dreadful to be out there and have nowhere to go.'

Tess was more practical, however. 'I'll tell you this, Mam. There's bound to be floods after all this rain. In the morning I'm going shopping again to see if there is any water-damaged material around. One shouldn't look a gift horse in the mouth, you know.'

Alice bestowed a reproachful look on her daughter. 'It seems wrong to benefit from someone else's misfortune.'

'Don't be silly, Mam. Someone *will* benefit and it may as well be us as the next one. They'll all be well insured against storm damage, and some will be claiming for a lot more than they're entitled to. They'll be jumping on the bandwagon, if I'm not mistaken.'

'You've very little faith in human nature, Tess.' Struck by a sudden thought, she said, 'I wonder what it's like in Carlingford? I hope your Uncle Malachy isn't getting it as bad as this.'

This did cause Tess some concern. 'I sincerely hope not,' she exclaimed. 'After all that carry-on last year, he could certainly do without any more flooding. Maybe we should get in touch with him and find out.'

'That's a good idea, love.'

Next morning they learnt on Radio Ulster the full extent of the damage caused by the storm. Among other things, the newsreader reported that St Brendan's Church on Connsbrook Avenue had collapsed and the *Royal Ulsterman*, a steamer, had struck an oil tanker at

Sydenham oil refinery causing untold damage.

Undaunted, but pausing long enough to say a wee prayer for those in need, Tess ventured out next morning. It was still raining but nothing like the night before and the winds had abated a great deal. There were plenty of signs of the destruction caused by the storm, she noted as she made her way down to the city centre, but it was not as bad as she had anticipated, after the ferocity of the winds and rain the previous night.

Broken slates were strewn across footpaths with warning notices to take care pasted in prominent positions. Some areas were cordoned off to protect pedestrians and Tess felt quite safe as she made her way to her favourite haunts in search of bargains. Her quest was not in vain. About lunch time a jubilant Tess returned home in a taxi, two bolts of material wedged between the seats and a box with buttons and zips and fancy dress trimmings on her knee. She had purchased them at rock-bottom price and knew that they could be easily salvaged. The old saying was indeed true; it was an ill wind that didn't blow somebody good. There was no angering her the rest of the day.

'I'm home, Mam.' Alice came to the top of the stairs and Tess paused at the bottom to impart her news. 'What do you think, Mam? The taxi driver told me that Sean Lemass – you know, the Republic's premier – arrived at Stormont to meet Terence O'Neill a short time ago.'

Slowly descending the stairs, Alice gazed at her daughter, eyes wide with surprise. 'I don't believe it!' she gasped. 'I never heard a word about it on the news. Just imagine! The Taoiseach up here in Ulster. Whatever next?'

Not so sure now, Tess said, 'Well now, it was the taxi driver who told me and he sounded pretty sure of his facts. Of course I can't swear to it being the truth.'

'If it is true, it could do a lot of good, but O'Neill is taking a big chance. There'll be those who won't like it one wee bit, you know.'

'You're right. Come to think of it, it doesn't sound possible. Terence O'Neill wouldn't take a chance like that. The driver must have been talking a load of rubbish.'

Alice reached for her coat and headed for the door.

'Where are you going, Mam? I want to show you the bargains I got.'

'They can wait. I'll see them later. I'm away up to the monastery to light a candle that everything will be okay. This could be history in the making.'

'Mam . . .' Tess was talking to herself. Alice was already out of the house.

As it turned out, the historic meeting between O'Neill and Lemass did indeed take place at Stormont and had been so secret that even cabinet ministers had not been made aware of it until that morning. The meeting was held in an effort to promote better community relations and economic strategy between north and south. Whether or not it would do any good remained to be seen.

Tess and her mother turned their attention to the orders in their books. If any wedding outfits had to be made between now and Easter they were to be given priority over everything else. This year there were three wedding dresses and bridesmaids' outfits on order for Easter weddings. The Maguires toiled over them for long hours each day and had them ready for final fittings in record time. Then, before they knew it, the Easter rush was on. It was late this year, Easter Sunday falling on 18th April. A few mothers, hoping for good weather, wanted suits for themselves and pretty dresses for their daughters with matching Easter bonnets.

The orders came rolling in. Careful of her mother's health, once the wedding outfits were ready, Tess insisted that Alice worked no more than six hours a day, but she herself worked far longer. It was late one evening in March when a knock caused her to lay aside the flower girl dress she was hand-hemming and go to the bay window to ease the heavy curtain aside and peer out into the night. To her surprise Jack and Colette stood on the top step peering back at her. She acknowledged them with a nod and, pulling the curtain back into place, went to open the door.

What on earth did they want here at this time of night? What else but a wedding dress, she fumed inwardly. They must have decided to get married after all. Well, there was no way she would make this girl's wedding dress. How tactless of them to even consider asking her. Successfully hiding her emotions behind a bland exterior, she opened the big outer door and stood aside to admit them, along with a great blast of cold air.

'My, but it's bitter out there,' Jack declared and gave her a timid smile as he sidled past her and entered the hall behind Colette. Guilty conscience there, Tess surmised, and closing the door she ushered them into the sitting room.

'This is a surprise,' she managed to utter pleasantly enough, then, without inviting them to sit down, waited to hear what had brought them up here on such a bitter cold night. After all she could be wrong; not everyone wanted Tess Maguire to make their wedding dresses.

Marie Quinn, for instance, was going to a top designer in the city centre, according to Agnes.

She looked inquiringly at them until Colette broke the silence. 'I'm sorry for disturbing you so late, Tess, but I was wondering if you would consider making my wedding dress?'

The silence stretched as Tess digested these words. At last she managed to find her tongue, excuses dripping from her lips. She was glad she could voice them truthfully. 'I'm very sorry, Colette, but we're swamped with orders at the minute. We couldn't possibly take on anything else until after Easter . . .'

Colette interrupted her. 'Oh, not for Easter. It will be August before we marry. We were just passing by and saw your light on, and knowing how popular your dresses are, and how busy you always are, I suggested to Jack that we call in and book early so as to avoid disappointment. Jack thought that in the circumstances you might not want to make my dress, but I said business is business. No one turns good money away these days. Please say you'll make it, Tess.'

Resigned, Tess casually waved towards the settee. 'Please sit down and I'll fetch the order book.'

She was leafing through a big, well-thumbed register when she returned. 'August, you say?'

'Yes,' Colette said enthusiastically.

'We can fit you in, but, mind you, I would want to start on it early. No last minute rush. I like to get everything just right and that means at least two fittings before the final sewing.'

At these words Colette dived into her handbag and withdrew a pattern. 'It's just a simple design. I've been carrying it about with me ever since I discovered it on a stall in Smithfield market.'

Tess grunted as she took the pattern and examined it. In her experience simple designs were usually the trickiest to follow. However, one glance at it and she said, 'I've made this dress before. Last year, in fact. It's tricky, all hidden lines, you know, but beautiful. Well worth the bother. What kind of material have you in mind?'

'I was hoping you would advise me.'

Tess sat back in her chair and examined the girl who had stolen Jack from her. For the moment, all animosity was gone. All she saw was a new customer with exceptional looks, and she knew just the material that would best suit her.

Getting to her feet she said, 'Come with me, please.'

Jack remained seated but Colette rose eagerly and followed her from the room. In the workshop Tess walked along a row of material piled almost ceiling high against one wall. At last she stopped and turned to Colette in frustration.

'Just my luck. Wouldn't it have to be one of the top ones?'

'I'll fetch Jack to give us a hand.' Colette turned and made to leave the room, but with a raised hand Tess stopped her.

'That won't be necessary. I'm used to managing on my own.' She pulled a stepladder forward and proceeded to climb. 'They're not heavy. I'll ease it out and hand it down to you.' She carefully lowered the bolt of material to the floor and Colette grasped it. 'Just stand it upright against the others.'

Tess descended the ladder and gently caressed the soft ivory material with the back of her hand. 'Feel that,' she suggested. 'Isn't it beautiful? So different from anything else I have. I was lucky to get it. It's from a top designer house. Excess to requirements, according to the manager. I jumped at the chance to buy it on the cheap.'

Tentatively Colette stroked the fabric. She looked a bit put out. 'It's beautiful but . . . I hope you don't mind . . . I had white in mind.'

It was Tess's favourite material and she thought it just right for Colette's colouring. If only this girl knew how honoured she was. A bit disappointed, she nevertheless assured Colette, 'Everybody to their own taste. I've plenty of white material. Silk, brocade, satin, et cetera. You name it, I have it.' She reached for a bundle of material squares. 'Here, there's plenty of samples to choose from. In fact you don't have to make up your mind right now. So long as your name is down in my book you can take those samples home with you and bring them back another time. After Easter will do fine. Of course, you can buy your own material if you wish and bring it to me. I don't mind one way or the other.'

'Thank you very much, Tess. My grannie will be delighted to browse through these with me. It will make her feel important. As if she's part of the show.'

'What about your mother? Won't she want to help you choose?'

'Well, you see . . .'

Tess tensed. She sensed that she was about to hear confidences and this she wanted to avoid; the less she knew about Colette Burns the better it suited her. 'I expect with your mother being so far away it will be difficult to let her see them,' she said hurriedly. 'But you can borrow those samples again any time you like.'

'Thank you, I'll remember that. However, I may as well tell you. Jack and Mam didn't exactly hit it off. You see, she had big plans for me. She worked hard to put me through school and she thinks I'm wasting my time on the likes of Jack. That's one reason I want to be married in white. Mam always thinks the worst. She thinks Jack and I are practically living together and nothing I say convinces her otherwise. If I choose ivory she would be convinced that she is right and I'm not a virgin any more.'

Tess nodded in understanding. 'I'm sorry to hear that. Jack is a fine lad.' She led the way from the work room.

When they were leaving, at the outer door Colette offered Tess her hand in farewell. 'Thank you for agreeing to make my dress.' She held up the bag now holding the samples. 'I'll bring these back as soon as me and Grannie agree on which material I should go for.'

Tess sat for some time after they had gone, fingers entwined in her lap, thoughts working overtime. So much for her determination not to make Colette's wedding dress, but somehow it hadn't mattered. She had suddenly realised that being in Jack's company no longer set her pulse racing. It was the memory of her antics towards him that one night at the corner of Malcomson Street that filled her with shame and made her want to avoid his company. How she wished it had never happened; then she could look him straight in the eye. If only she hadn't been so stupid!

She was glad that she now saw Colette as just another customer and not a rival in love and hoped that Jack would not accompany her to the fitting sessions. And, by the sound of it, if Mrs Burns had her way the wedding might never take place, Tess mused. Now there was food for thought! A few weeks ago she would have been over the moon at the idea that Jack and Colette might part. Now the notion left her completely unmoved. She couldn't care less, one way or the other.

Tess had offered them tea but they had declined and she was glad. She wanted them long gone before her mother arrived back from visiting a friend, knowing Alice would be far from pleased at her agreeing to make the dress in the first place. Hearing the outer door open, Tess quickly gathered the flower girl dress on to her lap and proceeded to sew as if she had been at it all night.

Alice stopped at the work room door and eyed her daughter in dismay. 'Are you still at it, love? You make me feel ashamed. Here's me gallivanting about and you sitting there toiling away.' She entered the room and shrugged out of her winter coat. 'It would skin a fairy out there tonight, so it would. I wouldn't be a bit surprised if we wake up to snow in the morning.'

'Surely it's too cold for snow?'

'You're probably right.' Alice returned to the hall and hung her coat on the stand. She appeared nervous, her eyes darting about until they caught sight of the ivory material. 'What's that doing down?'

Tess gave a start of surprise. So much for wanting to keep quiet, for the time being, about Colette's visit. She had completely forgotten about the material. Her mother was no dozer. Better to tell the truth and get it over with.

'I was showing it to a prospective customer.'

'Your favourite material?' Alice sounded scandalised, bringing a smile to Tess's face. 'Who? Must be someone special. Has Marie Quinn changed her mind, then?'

'Afraid not, Mam. There's no chance of Marie changing her mind. Mrs Quinn wants only the very best for her daughter.'

'Our dresses can hold their own against the best in town,' Alice cried indignantly.

Tess shrugged indifferently. It was no skin off her nose

where Marie chose to go. After all, it was the bride's prerogative. Just because Tess and Agnes were close friends didn't mean Agnes's sister was obliged to ask Tess to make her wedding dress. She was kept busy enough as it was, and certainly didn't need or indeed want Marie's custom. If she had been chosen to make Marie's dress, Mrs Quinn would have been breathing down her neck every chance she got. May Quinn was one of those people who looked for faults where there weren't any. If there was such a thing as a professional nitpicker, she'd fit the bill perfectly. That was something Tess could definitely do without. 'If you must know I was showing that material to Colette Burns.'

She smiled as she watched her mother swallow convulsively before gasping, 'Colette Burns? The cheeky bitch! Did she ask you to make her dress? I hope you told her we were too busy?'

'I certainly did. However, she doesn't want it until August. So what could I do but agree?'

Alice ducked her head to peer into Tess's face. 'I can always tell her to take her custom elsewhere if you like. How do you feel about it, love?' she asked quietly.

'What do you mean?'

'You know very well what I mean!'

'Funnily enough, I didn't think of her as Jack's future wife. Simply as a customer. So much so that I showed her my favourite material. What do you think of that? But she wasn't in the least bit impressed with the ivory. She took away the white samples to pick from.'

'Mm . . . I must admit she would look good in that ivory shade. She's got the right colouring for it.'

'That's what I thought, but everyone to their own taste.' Tess looked thoughtfully at her mother. There was something different about her. A slight smile played about her lips and there was a dreamy cast in her eyes. 'What are you looking so pleased about?'

'What? . . . I don't know what you mean.'

'Mam, I can read you like a book, so out with it. Why all this suppressed excitement?'

'Don't be silly. I'm not in the least bit excited.' Alice drifted about the room and, sensing there was more to come, Tess maintained an expectant silence. After a short pause, Alice casually continued, 'Dan Thompson was at the confraternity in Clonard tonight and we just happened to bump into each other, so he walked down the road with me. Hardly anything to get excited about, is it?'

Uneasy now, Tess muttered, 'Well, well!'

Colour brightened Alice's cheeks and she confessed shyly, 'He has asked me out for a meal next week.'

Tess set her sewing to one side and, rising to her feet, led the way from the room. She would have to tread very carefully here; not get her mam's back up. 'Come on. Let's have a cup of tea and you can tell me all about it.'

Alice fluttered aimlessly about the kitchen, stopping to gaze vacantly into space, getting in Tess's way and generally acting like a teenager in love. Really perturbed now, Tess gave her a gentle push in the direction of the door. 'Look, Mam, you're not much good in here, so you may as well go and sit down and I'll bring the tea in to you. Poke the fire and get a bit of heat into the house.'

By the time Tess carried the tea into the sitting room, Alice had put some more coals on the fire and it was burning brightly, throwing a warm glow around the room. They sat side by side on the settee and, clasping her mug in her hands, Tess challenged her mother. 'Come on, now. Tell me all about it.'

'I've already explained. He asked me out.'

'And you, of course, knowing he is a married man turned him down.'

'Well . . . not exactly.'

'What do you mean, not exactly? Surely you can see there is no alternative, Mam?'

'He was so nice I didn't want to appear too prudish with him, so I told him I would think about it.'

'Mam!' Tess cried in exasperation. 'I'm surprised at you, so I am. You, of all people, contemplating going out with another woman's husband. I just can't believe my ears.'

'Ah now, hold on a minute . . . it's not as if they're living together. He says they're separated.'

'What difference does that make? Eh? There can never be a divorce. You know that. And you, Mam, of all people are not the kind of person to live in sin. Or even, for that matter, have a fling with a married man.'

'Oh, for heaven's sake, Tess, we would be just going out for a meal! He hasn't asked me to move in with him.'

'And what if you get to like each other and he does suggest something like that? What will you do then?'

Alice's nose wrinkled in distaste. 'Live in Spinner Street? You've got to be joking.'

'So you'd invite him to move in here, then? Is that the idea?'

'He knows better than to suggest that. You're way off the mark, girl. It would be purely a platonic relationship. He's lonely and you have to admit it will keep me out of your hair. Give you a chance to meet some suitable young men.'

Tess frowned. 'Why are you suddenly worried about me meeting suitable young men, eh? You were never bothered about it before. Was that Dan's excuse, then? Did he play on your sympathy?' Distressed now at the idea of someone feeling sorry for her, Tess wailed, 'How dare he pity me! And tell me this, how is you going out for a meal with Dan Thompson suddenly going to change my way of life? Eh?'

'Ah, Tess, now, don't get yourself all upset. Of course Dan doesn't pity you. He thinks the world of you.' Realising she was fighting a losing battle, and her daughter would not be swayed, Alice cried in frustration, 'Anyway, why do you always have to go and put a damper on everything I do?'

Tess gaped at her open-mouthed. '*Me*, put a damper on *you*? I'm afraid you've got that arse about face!' she cried angrily. 'I'm only trying to save you from making a laughing stock of yourself. There's no future in what you're contemplating.'

'All right, all right! Let's not make a song and dance about it. I've got the message loud and clear. When he phones I'll make some excuse to say I can't make it. Will that satisfy you? Are you happy now? And another thing, madam. Don't you ever use that kind of language in this house again. Now, I'm off to bed. Good night.' Lifting her empty mug, Alice left the room with an exaggerated flounce. In the kitchen she rinsed the mug under the tap before thumping upstairs in a temper.

To say that Tess was amazed at her mother's attitude would be an understatement. Alice was so good-living she considered it a sin to stay in the company of anyone who made rude remarks. And remembering the way Dan had danced attendance on her at Agnes's engagement do, Tess was sceptical of the outcome. Alice was deluding herself if she thought Dan Thompson could just be her friend. That he fancied her, there could be no doubt . . . and what about her mother? Didn't the signs all point to her liking Dan more than just a little?

As she locked up for the night, Tess vowed to do all in her power to persuade her mother not to become involved with Dan Thompson; it could cause nothing but unhappiness. And . . . God forbid, it could throw herself and Jack together and she didn't want that any more. She preferred to bury the past, get on with her life, and forget her wanton actions towards him. How could she do that if her mother and Dan became close friends? Or . . . lovers? It didn't bear thinking about.

Alice sat at her dressing table and examined her image in the mirror. Turning her head this way and that she had to admit that she found it easy to agree with Dan. She was still an attractive woman, she mused. Dan had taken her hand when he had paid her this compliment earlier that evening and a shiver of excitement had run down her spine at his touch.

She recalled how flattered she had been when he had shown so much interest in her on New Year's Eve, but when he had failed to follow it up by getting in touch with her she had suppressed her disappointment and put all thoughts of him from her mind. After all, she reminded herself, he was a married man and she would be foolish to let her thoughts dwell on him.

Tonight was their first meeting since the New Year. He had been approaching the corner of Dunmore Street as she walked past and had called out to her.

She had been completely unaware of him but the very sound of his voice sent a tremor through her body. She stopped and waited until he joined her on the Springfield Road.

Gazing down into her eyes, his expression was warm and welcoming. 'Long time no see, Alice.'

'Hmm.'

Her look of reproof brought a hurt look to his face and he replied to the implied criticism. Reaching for her hand he had said, 'You're a very attractive woman, Alice Maguire, and I thought it better to give you a wide berth.'

She was aware that her hand was trembling in his grip and tugged to remove it. 'Oh, indeed?'

He gripped her hand tighter and, smiling, leaned closer. 'Yes, indeed. You know why that must be, don't you? I'm not a free man.'

She managed to release her hand and started to walk slowly down the road. He fell into step beside her. 'Of course, I can't see it doing any harm, us going out now and again.' He slanted a sideways glance at her. 'Can you?'

'What about your wife? Is she still in Belfast?'

'Unfortunately, she is, but we've been separated a long, long time now and, believe me, there is no chance of us getting back together.' His lips tightened on these words. Anne was proving to be a right thorn in the flesh.

'Are you sure there is no chance of a reconciliation?' Alice countered.

'Quite sure. Too much water has passed under the bridge for that. So how about coming out for a meal with me?'

'It would give rise to unnecessary gossip if we were seen out together,' she replied with a grimace. 'You know what people are like round here. They can't mind their own business.'

They were passing the Blackstaff factory and he drew her into the gateway. Talk or no talk he wanted her to go out with him more than ever now. He enjoyed her company; admired her good looks; was aroused and excited in her presence. It was now or never. He needed to convince her before they arrived at her door and, maybe, find Tess at the window watching out for her. He was aware that mother and daughter were very protective of each other.

'Listen, Alice, let's give it a try, eh? I'm sure we can be friends. It would be nice to have someone attractive to go out and about with.'

Inwardly she agreed wholeheartedly with him. It would be nice to have a male companion to share outings with. But could they be just friends? She dithered and he urged, 'No strings attached. Honest!'

'Well, I suppose we could at least give it a try . . .' she ventured.

Relief flooded through him. 'You'll come for a meal with me at the weekend, then?'

'Oh, no! Not the weekend. Give me a ring and we'll arrange something for during the week. Okay?'

He knew not to push his luck; she would only run off and it would be over before it had begun. 'All right. I'll phone you.'

They continued down the road to her home and seeing that the curtains were drawn across the bay window he risked a kiss on her soft cheek. 'See you soon, I hope.'

Breathless, she had watched him stride off down the road and out of sight, thinking what a handsome man he was. I'd be a fool not to take him up on his offer. Just for companionship, she assured herself.

Now, after Tess's reaction, she considered the wisdom of her plans. Her daughter was right, of course; she was treading on forbidden ground. It was so long since she had felt these emotions, they were frightening her. Why, she was behaving like a lovestruck young girl, but she must not let her emotions rule her head. It would be better if she didn't start something that she couldn't finish. When he phoned she would tell him it would not be in their best interests for them to meet.

It was the following Monday when Tess answered the phone to find Dan Thompson on the other end of the line. He greeted her cordially. 'Hello there, Tess. I trust you are well?'

'Yes, very well, thanks. How can I help you?'

Her voice was clipped with disapproval and he grimaced but dared to continue. 'May I speak to your mother, please?'

Dan heard Tess's frustrated, if not exaggerated, sigh and then, 'Hold on, I'll give her a shout.'

A shout was unnecessary; Alice came from the living room like a greyhound out of the starting trap, asking breathlessly, 'Is it for me, Tess?'

'As if you didn't know.' A hand covering the mouthpiece, Tess whispered, 'Please be careful, Mam.'

With an angry toss of the head, Alice took the receiver and stood silent, waiting for her daughter to make herself scarce, although she doubted she would go out of earshot.

Tess didn't move too far away. From just inside the living room door she strained her ears, unashamed, to catch her mother's side of the conversation.

'Hello, Dan.'

A pause and then, 'Well now, I've been giving your suggestion a lot of thought, Dan, and I'm having my doubts. Do you think it would be wise for us to see each other?'

Another pause, 'I'm inclined to agree with you but Tess thinks it would be foolish of me to put myself in a compromising situation.'

After another short silence Alice cried indignantly, 'Of course I don't let Tess or anyone else for that matter tell me what to do, but you are a married man and it could start a lot of tongues wagging.'

A longer pause this time and Tess guessed that Dan was pleading his case.

'I suppose you're right. One date can't do any harm. Yes, Thursday night would be lovely. Seven o'clock? I'll be ready and waiting.' Replacing the receiver, Alice said resignedly, 'You can come out now, Tess.'

When her daughter slowly entered the hall Alice eyed her defiantly. 'Well, did you hear all that?'

'Enough to know you intend seeing him on Thursday night.'

'Oh, don't look so disapproving! We're only going out for a meal, for heaven's sake!'

With a shrug, Tess said, 'On your own head be it then. Just don't expect any sympathy from me when things start to go wrong. And they will, Mam. You mark my words.'

'Tess, please don't take all the pleasure out of this for me,' Alice said wistfully. 'It will probably only be the one date, you know.'

To her consternation Tess saw a tear ripple down her mother's cheek. Alice turned away and hurried towards the stairs, unwilling to let her daughter see how much this date with Dan Thompson meant to her.

Tess beat her to the staircase and barred her escape. Taking her in her arms she said, 'Mam, I don't mean to spoil things for you. Surely you know I'm only concerned because I don't want you to get hurt.'

'Can't you see, Tess?' Alice pleaded. 'If I don't go out with him, I'll regret it for the rest of my life. I'll always feel that I've missed out on something.' She was silent for some moments then added, 'I do think it will peter out. I'm getting far too old for all that old nonsense. You know what I mean? So if Dan should have anything other than friendship in mind he's in for a big disappointment.'

'You're far from being too old, Mam, but I know what you mean. You've missed out on so much with Dad dying so young. I only wish that Dan Thompson was a free man and then there wouldn't be any problem.'

Alice eyed her daughter hopefully. 'Does that mean I have your blessing for just one date with him?'

Hugging her mother, Tess smiled. 'Oh, I suppose so.'

Alice's radiant smile was reward enough for her daughter.

Chapter Six

Thursday dawned frosty with a weak sun painting the sky a pale shade of pink. As they worked side by side Tess couldn't help but notice her mother's suppressed excitement and worry gnawed at her. God knows, not for one minute did she begrudge her mother any pleasure she might be lucky enough to find in life. She deserved all the happiness she could get. But . . . where would it all end?

She was brought out of her reverie by a hand placed lightly on her arm. 'I know what's going through that mind of yours, Tess, but believe me, I know what I'm doing. I'm a big girl after all,' Alice chided.

Covering the hand with her own, Tess squeezed it. 'Just be careful, Mam. I don't want to see you getting hurt.'

'I'll take care, Tess. I promise. Now stop worrying about me.'

Easier said than done. Some hours later Tess rose from the big factory sewing machine, and stretched her aching back. 'I'll have to try and learn to sit more upright in front of that machine before I give myself a bad back,' she groaned. 'Anyway, since you will be eating out tonight let's have a snack now. I might even go out myself to the pictures tonight. There's a good film on at the Broadway. Agnes couldn't get away last night so perhaps she'll come with me tonight.'

Marie Quinn's forthcoming wedding was putting a lot of pressure on her family. The preparations for it seemed far-reaching and had already eroded the few hours Agnes shared with Tess. Her friend saw very little of her these days. She was overjoyed when Agnes agreed to accompany her to the cinema, saying that the wedding plans were on hold at the minute as far as she was concerned and Tony was putting in some overtime while it was available, so she was free to go out on her own for a change.

Delighted to have something to look forward to, Tess prepared a snack for herself and her mother with a light heart. After all, as her mother had pointed out, she was a big girl and could look after herself.

Promptly at seven o'clock, Dan arrived at the door. Alice took a final look at her reflection in the hall mirror, making final adjustments to her hair that were totally unnecessary, and hastened to admit him.

His eyes took in her appearance with a sweeping glance and he said sincerely, 'You look lovely, Alice.' A taxi was parked at the kerb, its engine idling away. 'I told the driver to wait, so if you're ready, let's go.'

Tess, who had followed her mother into the hall, sighed and looked from one to the other of them. It was obvious they were very attracted to each other. 'See and enjoy yourselves.' Her voice was sincere and Dan flashed her a grateful smile.

'I'll see no harm comes to your mother while she's with me, Tess.'

'Good night, Dan.'

Tess watched as Dan handed her mother into the taxi

and then climbed the stairs to finish her own preparations to go out. She was calling for Agnes at half past seven and needed to get a move on.

Agnes must have been on the look-out for her. Before Tess could knock, the door opened and her friend joined her on the pavement.

Slipping her arm through Tess's, Agnes hugged it close. 'I can't tell you how pleased I was when you phoned. It's great to be going out with you again. I've been so bored lately I could scream my head off.'

Tess flashed her a worried look. 'That sounds ominous. Are you and Tony not getting on, then?'

'Oh, we get on fine. It's just that there's so much to do for Marie's wedding, and to crown it all Tony is planning ahead for ours and is taking all the overtime he can get.'

They left Violet Street and hurried along Cavendish Street. 'Tell me all about it,' Tess urged. 'How many bridesmaids will there be?'

'Just me and Dennis's sister Joan, and her three-year-old daughter will be a flower girl.'

'Come on, Agnes, for heaven's sake. Out with it. Anyone would think it was a hush hush affair the way you're getting on. Don't have me dragging every wee detail out of you.'

Agnes laughed. 'I forgot. It's been a while since we've been out together. Well . . . Joan and I will be in primrose and young Amy will be in white. What else do you want to know?'

'The last time we were talking you said Tony might be best man. Is he?'

'I'm afraid that fell by the wayside and he's very disappointed. Remember I told you Dennis had a brother in Florida?'

Tess nodded. 'You said he hadn't been home for about ten years and was a kind of black sheep of the family.'

'That's right! Well, he has decided to grace us with his presence and has agreed to come home and be best man. What do you think of that?'

'The question is, what do *you* think?'

Agnes shrugged. 'It makes no difference to me. He's to arrive a week before the wedding in time for the church rehearsal. He will be home for two months but once Dennis and Marie are married I imagine our family will see very little of the Sullivans. They're not like Dennis at all. Whereas he's friendly and down to earth, the rest of them are inclined to be a bit on the snooty side. To be truthful, I don't envy our Marie her in-laws.'

'But . . . I thought they lived on Mackie's Height?'

'They do.'

'Hah!' Tess showed her disdain. 'I wouldn't have thought anybody up there had anything to be snooty about. Why, they're no better off than we are.'

Agnes shrugged. 'I know, but Mr Sullivan has a good job. He's high up on the council and he and his wife seem to think that puts them a cut above everyone else.'

They had passed down Oakman Street and along Beechmount Avenue out on to the Falls Road. The queue for the Broadway picture house was slowly shuffling into the foyer and they hurried across the Falls Road to join it. Soon they were settled in the back stalls and all further information about the Sullivans was shelved as the lights went out and the big picture started.

Blowing her nose noisily into her handkerchief as they left the cinema, Tess admitted, 'I really enjoyed that! I love a good old cry at a film, and *An Affair to Remember* was certainly a weepy.'

'Actually I didn't realise that was the film on tonight. I saw it in the Windsor some time ago,' Agnes admitted, 'but I enjoyed it again. I thought he was never going to discover that Deborah Kerr was crippled.'

'So did I. Isn't Cary Grant a real smasher?'

'He sure is. You know, I think Dan Thompson looks very like him.'

'Don't be daft,' Tess retorted. 'Did I tell you me mam is out with Dan at this very minute?' A quick glance at her watch and Tess amended her words. 'I'm sure they're home by now.' She could feel Agnes gaping at her but pretended not to notice her surprise.

'You know damned well you haven't said a word about your mam and Dan,' Agnes said reproachfully. 'When did this all start, then?'

'Tonight is their very first and, I hope, their only date. I think he bulldozed Mam into going out with him.' They were crossing the Falls Road and Tess asked hopefully, 'I suppose you wouldn't fancy catching the bus down to the Dolphin for a fish supper?'

'Oh, I'd love one,' Agnes cried enthusiastically. 'Tony would consider it a waste of good money to go into a chippie. To tell you the truth he gets on my nerves at times the way he keeps on counting the pennies.'

'Great! We'd better put a spurt on. That bus is ready to go.'

The bus was packed and they caught it by the skin of their teeth, hanging on to the platform pole for grim life. There was an exodus at the stop at the bottom of Clonard Street and the girls discovered that everybody seemed to be in the same frame of mind and intent on visiting Johnny Reid's chippie.

They joined the growing queue and as they waited Agnes whispered in her friend's ear. 'How do you feel about your mam going out with Dan Thompson, then?'

With a furtive glance over her shoulder, Tess hissed back, 'Hush, for heaven's sake! This is not the place to talk about it. You never know who might be listening. Look.' She nodded towards the far end of the counter. 'Johnny has a helper on tonight doing the takeaways and that queue is moving quicker. Shall we join it and eat ours on the way home?'

'Yes, that's a good idea,' Agnes agreed and in no time they were outside and heading for the Springfield Road, digging into a feast of crispy cod and chips.

'Do you know something, Agnes? I didn't realise how hungry I was. We didn't have a proper dinner today, just a snack, because Mam was eating out. This fish is delicious.'

Stuffing a chip into her mouth, Agnes mumbled, 'So are the chips.' Then silence reigned as they did justice to their food.

As she screwed up her greasy paper into a ball to take home, Tess confessed, 'Now that's given me a thirst. Come up to our house for a cup of tea, Agnes.'

'I can't. Tony said he would call in after work and he'll be fuming if I'm not there. After all, I didn't even know I was going out. He'll probably be sitting there twiddling his thumbs trying to keep a conversation going with my dad. They haven't got very much in common, you know.'

'You may as well be killed for a sheep as a lamb. Go on, coax yourself. God knows when I'll see you again.'

Agnes didn't need much coaxing. She gave in straight away. 'Okay, you've twisted my arm. Let's go.'

The light was on in the kitchen, casting a faint glow

into the hall, and Tess stopped at the foot of the steps in dismay as she saw it shining through the fanlight above the front door. For a short time she had completely forgotten about her mam and Dan. It was obvious her mother was home, but was Dan with her? She fervently hoped not.

Dashing up the steps, Agnes cried impatiently, 'Hurry up, for heaven's sake, and open the door. I haven't all night, remember.'

Sorry now that she had invited Agnes back, Tess reluctantly unlocked the front door and stepped into the hall. The house was very quiet. Had her mother forgotten to switch off the kitchen light and retired for the night? Removing her coat she hung it on the hall stand and invited Agnes to do likewise, all the while straining her ears for the sound of voices.

'It's not worthwhile me taking my coat off. I'll have to run as soon as I finish my tea. That's if you ever get round to making it.' Agnes gave Tess a slight push in the direction of the kitchen just as Alice came through the door.

'I thought I heard voices out here. Hello, Agnes. I've a pot of tea ready, but you'll enjoy it better if you take your coat off and sit down.'

'Thanks, Mrs Maguire.' Agnes pushed open the living room door and stopped abruptly. Over her shoulder Tess could see the reason for her surprise. Stretched out in the armchair close to the fireside, toasting his stocking feet, Dan Thompson looked very much at home. Very much at home, indeed!

He had obviously been unaware of their arrival and quickly rose from his seat in embarrassment. 'Hello, Agnes. Hi, Tess. I didn't realise you were home. Was the film any good?'

'It was smashing, Mr Thompson. A real weepy.'

'It wouldn't have suited me at all then, Agnes. I've enough to cry about in real life. I'd rather have a good old western any day.' Seeing Alice hovering in the hall with a loaded tray, he hastened over to relieve her of her burden. 'Here, let me take that.'

Tess stood speechless; the shock of seeing Dan so much at home had stunned her. Alice looked at her daughter anxiously. What on earth was the matter with her? Surely she hadn't expected her to say good night to Dan at the door? If so she was being rather childish.

Not in any hurry at all to leave now, Agnes removed her coat and placed it over the arm of the settee.

'You sit down, Mam. I'll pour the tea.'

When she handed her mother a cup, Tess received a reproachful look. Agnes was perched on the edge of the settee, eyes agog, not missing a single thing. Why on earth had Tess asked her back? She might have guessed Dan Thompson would be here. The conversation was general and when Agnes could delay no longer she rose reluctantly to her feet.

'I'll have to be going now,' she said regretfully. 'They'll all be wondering what's happened to me.'

Dan slipped his feet into his shoes and quickly tied the laces. He could see that Tess was sitting tight lipped and sullen, looking down into her cup. Alice and he had had a wonderful time and he didn't want to spoil it by a confrontation with her daughter, the mood *she* was in. It was time to leave while he was still ahead. 'I'll walk down with you, Agnes.'

Leaning close to Alice he said softly, for her ears only, 'Thank you for a lovely evening. I hope we can repeat it soon. I'll give you a ring.'

*   *   *

Agnes slanted a sideways glance at Dan as she trotted along trying to keep up with his long strides down Springfield Road. He was so engrossed in thought he seemed unaware of her presence or her efforts to keep pace with him. She confirmed in her mind that he did indeed resemble Cary Grant. The same straight nose, dark brown eyes and cleft chin. Not much older than Cary, he was a very handsome man. Strange that Jack didn't in the least bit resemble him. He must take after his mother.

Suddenly aware of her covert scrutiny, he turned a rueful smile on her and slowed down. 'Sorry, Agnes. I was away in a world of my own there.'

'Don't worry about me, Mr Thompson. I need the exercise,' she joked. 'I'm sure you have a lot on your mind,' she added daringly, with a wise nod of the head.

A grin split his face and his eyes twinkled. 'Now I wonder what you think I have on my mind? Mm? Pray tell me.'

They had arrived at the corner of Violet Street, and, glad to be reprieved, Agnes said, 'Thanks for walking me home. Good night, Mr Thompson.' With a wave of her hand she scurried off down the street.

As he continued on down the road, Dan let his mind return to his immediate problem. Tess had been annoyed when she saw him in her home tonight. Very annoyed, in fact! But he and Alice weren't youngsters. They couldn't be expected to say good night at the corner when they both had homes to go to. Not that he wanted to invite Alice into his house – in the warmth and comfort of her home he realised how primitive his own house really was – but he had no intention of standing at a corner as if they were a pair of teenagers.

He was also very much aware that he wanted Alice, and not just as a friend. She would be the ideal partner to spend the rest of his days with. If he sought a divorce from Anne would Alice agree to marry him in a register office? Anything but marriage would be out of the question, but he couldn't see her consenting to marry him outside the Catholic church. Perhaps given time, and with a bit of friendly persuasion, he could wear her down. The biggest stumbling block would be Tess.

As he approached his house he could see light showing through the blind and expected to see Jack and Colette when he opened the vestibule door. To his surprise, it was his wife who sat facing Jack by the fireside. Before he could recover from the shock, Colette's voice called from the scullery.

'Would you like a cup of tea, Mr Thompson?'

'No. No, thank you, Colette, I've just had one.' His eyes were still fastened on Anne's face. 'What are you doing here?' he snapped.

Jack sprang to his feet and said warningly, 'Now, Dad, I invited Mam in.'

Anne smiled sweetly at Dan. 'We met in the Clock Bar and they told me they plan to marry in August, so I came down with them to discuss the wedding arrangements.'

He wondered if her toy boy had been with her in the pub, but refrained from asking. 'What's them getting married got to do with you?'

Anne collapsed back in the chair in a show of mock surprise. 'Don't act silly, Dan. I'm Jack's *mother*, after all is said and done.'

'You forgot that for a long time, didn't you?'

'Well I'm here now and I'm not going away again.'

'Dad . . .' Jack sounded nervous and Dan dragged his attention from Anne and turned to hear what his son had to say. 'Dad, Colette needs someone to talk things over with and Mam's the ideal person.'

'What about her own mother? Or her grannie for that matter?'

'Remember, Dad, her family live in Omagh.'

'That's not the other side of the world, son. I'm sure her parents would be willing to travel up now and again to make plans. They might even want the wedding to be held in their own parish church in Omagh, for all you know.'

'That's where you're wrong, Dan,' Anne piped in. 'Colette was telling me tonight that her parents don't want her to marry our Jack.'

Colette let out a wail of dismay; she had told Anne this in confidence and now here she was, blabbering her big mouth off already. She cringed as both son and father turned looks of amazement on her.

'Is this true?' Jack managed to gasp.

'No!' The consternation in her voice was acute as she threw Anne a withering glare of pure hatred. 'It's not true! They just want me to wait a year or two in case I change my mind. They think I'm too young and don't know what I'm doing.'

Dan could see how upset she was and turned his wrath on Anne. 'Get out! Go on. Get out of here before I throw you out.'

Anne slowly shrugged into her coat and with an airy wave in the direction of her son and Colette left the house. Dan followed her out on to the pavement, not wanting the others to hear what he had to say.

'If you cause any more mischief I swear I won't rest until I make you pay. That wee girl in there is devastated, so she is. You're nothing but a bloody troublemaker.'

'And whose fault is that?'

His jaw dropped and he asked, 'What do you mean by that? No doubt you're about to lay the blame at my door.'

'It's all your fault! If he had a trade he would be more acceptable to her parents. She has a future in banking ahead of her. What has Jack got? A dead end job. That's what!'

'If she loves him it won't make any difference what he works at.'

'Oh, no? Well that's where you're wrong! Didn't you see the effect it had on him? He was gutted, so he was. And another thing, in case you've forgotten . . . love doesn't pay the bills.'

'And that pleases you, does it? Why did you blurt it out like that? Obviously she hasn't told him how her parents feel.'

'He's better knowing where he stands,' she said stubbornly.

'That's only your opinion, and that doesn't count for much. You had two wages coming in and you still weren't satisfied.'

'Oh, give my head peace. You never did think much of my opinion anyway. Perhaps if you'd paid more attention to how I felt we would still be together today.'

'Perish the thought,' he snarled. 'I know now what a narrow escape I had *and* I'd like a divorce.'

She drew back, eyes widening with surprise. 'Isn't that a bit drastic? Are you going to let me telling Jack the truth separate us for good?'

'No, actually, I had already made up my mind to divorce you before this happened. I can, you know. It was you who walked out on me and ran off with another man leaving a young son behind.'

'It'll not be as easy as you think! I'll fight you every inch of the way. And what about the church? How are you going to reconcile your conscience with that?'

'Don't you worry about me. I'll manage. I just want you out of my life for good.' He turned on his heel, leaving her glaring after him.

Inside, there was no sign of Jack. Colette sat huddled on the edge of the settee, arms clasped around her as if for comfort. Big tear-washed eyes looked at him in bewilderment.

'How could she be so cruel? I spoke to her in confidence. There was no need for Jack to know.'

He sat down beside her, and put an arm across her shoulders. 'So it's true then? They don't want you to marry him?'

She shrugged. 'It doesn't make any difference to me what they want, so I can't see why Jack should be so upset.'

'It's his pride that's hurt. He'll get over it. I think you should give him a chance to cool down, love. So wipe those tears up and get yourself off home. Everything will pan out in due course. Just wait and see.'

Inwardly he wasn't so optimistic. She was very young; would her parents be able to put a stop to her wedding plans? He didn't know how these things worked. Hell roast Anne and her interference. He wished she would go and fall under a bus and give them all some peace of mind. God forbid.

Tess washed the crockery and her mother dried them and put them carefully away. It was she who broke the long, tense silence between them.

'Did you have to bring Agnes home with you, tonight

of all nights?' she asked reproachfully. 'Giving her something to gossip about.'

Angrily Tess rounded on her. 'Why should you care who knows about your *platonic* relationship – as you so nicely put it – with him?'

'Because, although it is innocent, people always think the worst in these situations and we intended to be as discreet as possible.'

'So you intend slinking about as if you're ashamed of being seen together. Is that what you're saying?'

'Actually, I was thinking of you. You seem so concerned about us.'

'I take it he's talked you into seeing him again then?'

'And why not? We both enjoyed this evening very much.'

'That's not the point, Mam. You're forgetting he's a married man!'

'Listen, girl! My conscience is clear and I'm not going to let you or anyone else for that matter dictate terms to me. So there! Now, if you'll excuse me, I don't want to discuss this any further . . . I'm off to bed.'

Tess banked the fire and checked the windows and doors automatically. Easter was fast approaching; perhaps her mother's trip to see Malachy and Rose would give her time to think and maybe see the folly of her ways. But then, that holiday break hadn't been mentioned for some time now. Did her mother not intend going after all?

She wished her Uncle Malachy's phone was sorted out. It had been out of order for some time now, and you'd think with the farm being so isolated the PO would give him some priority. Instead, it seemed it was well down the pecking order for repairs. Tomorrow she would write to him and ask him to somehow get to a phone and ring her mother and persuade her to keep her promise.

Two days after Tess posted the letter the phone rang. It was her uncle calling to tell her that at long last the line had been repaired. 'Rose was sick of running up the lane every time she wanted a word with me, so I gave in and put some pressure on the PO. I didn't think it would do any good, but it must have worked. It was connected again last week. I intended phoning earlier to let you know, but one of the ewes died and we are having to bottle-feed her two lambs. I've been so busy, what with one thing and another, I never got round to it.'

'I'm sorry to hear about the ewe, Uncle Malachy.'

'Oh, well, these things do happen and I'm not complaining. Far from it. Things could be a lot worse. I'm just explaining why I didn't phone sooner.' He lowered his voice and said softly, 'Can I speak freely?'

'Yes. Mam's out at the shops.'

'Your letter has me awfully worried. What on earth's the matter with Alice?'

'She's seeing a married man.' What she considered words of doom produced a great roar of laughter down the line that almost deafened her.

Stifling his mirth, Malachy said, 'Ah now, Tess, what do you think I can do about that?'

'It's wrong, Uncle Malachy! It's a mortal sin, so it is. You'll have to talk some sense into her.'

'Tess . . . love, I must remind you it's the nineteen sixties and things are changing dramatically.'

'I know that! But that doesn't make it right. You know what Mam is like. I don't want her to get hurt.'

'Don't distress yourself so much, Tess. When Alice

[131]

comes to visit us at Easter I'll try to broach the subject. I take it you'll not want her to know you've been discussing her affairs with me?'

'Oh, God, no! And thank you for being so understanding. But you see, the problem is, I don't think she intends visiting you at Easter.'

'Oh, but she must!' He sounded aghast. 'Rose will be so disappointed if she doesn't. She has been doing all sorts in preparation for her visit.'

'Tell Rose to phone Mam and insist that she comes to Carlingford. Tell her to put pressure on her and in no circumstances to let her off the hook. Look, I hear Mam at the door now. I'll put her on and you can tell her all the latest country gossip. That'll please her no end,' she informed him, tongue in cheek. 'Don't forget to get Rose to phone!'

Alice paused at the door to shake the rain off her umbrella. Tess hurried forward and took it from her.

'Mam, it's Uncle Malachy on the phone. The lines have been repaired at long last. He wants a word with you.'

Alice walked slowly to the phone. Tess could see her mother was reluctant to speak to her brother. She closed the umbrella and passed along the hall to put it in the kitchen sink to drip dry.

'But now, Malachy, I mightn't be able to come at Easter after all. I've a lot on my plate, you know.'

At these words Tess crossed her fingers and said a quiet prayer. Please, God, let Mam be persuaded to go to Carlingford out of temptation's way.

She reached for the kettle and half filled it with water for a cup of tea. When Alice entered the kitchen she looked at her inquiringly.

'I've told him I can't go, Tess.'

'Why? You were all for it at Christmas, so you were.'

'I know, but talk's cheap. And after all, it was just talk. You know how I hate the countryside.'

'You sounded very sincere about wanting to go, Mam. Besides, it will do you a world of good to get away for a while.'

'You're just saying that hoping that I'll split up with Dan. Isn't that it?'

'That's not true! I was delighted when you told Uncle Malachy and Rose that you'd visit them at Easter. You know that for a fact, and that was long before Dan Thompson arrived on the scene.'

Alice's voice took on a coaxing note. 'Tess . . . I'd much rather stay at home with you.'

'Me? Hah, don't make me laugh.'

'All right. You and Dan.'

'And nothing I can say will make you change your mind?'

'No . . . nothing. My mind's made up,' Alice replied defiantly.

It was Rose who was the deciding factor. She phoned and put the thumbscrews on, lamenting how hard she had worked to get her cottage ready, hoping Alice might stay for a day or two with her before going home. Telling her how she planned to take her new friend round all the local farming community.

'You just have to come, Alice. I would never dream of letting you down if the positions were reversed. Please say you'll come . . . please. I won't be able to show my face round here again if you don't come, not after all I've told them about you and Tess.'

In the face of all this determination how could Alice possibly refuse? She told Dan when she saw him that

Thursday night and was pleased when he agreed with her that it would indeed be very selfish of her not to go, but added that she must spend some extra time with him before she left. Two extra outings were arranged and Alice was inclined to think that everything had worked out for the best.

Chapter Seven

Spy Wednesday dawned wet and miserable. Alice stood at the work room window gazing up at the heavy, dark clouds hanging low over the rooftops. 'You said the weather was going to improve,' she cried plaintively. 'That sky doesn't look very promising to me.'

'Give it a chance, Mam. It's early yet, and the weather forecast did say that it would brighten up later on.'

'I don't know why I let Rose talk me into going to Carlingford,' Alice grumbled. 'I must need my head examining.'

'Because she has obviously gone to a lot of trouble getting everything in order for you coming, that's why! It would have been very unkind to let her down. Besides, a couple of weeks will soon fly in.'

Alice reared back in alarm. 'A couple of weeks? Ah, no. I've told Malachy I'd only be able to stay one week and one week it'll be.'

'We'll see. You might change your mind when you've been there a few days. You might even meet a rich, eligible farmer,' Tess teased, and was rewarded by a dirty look from her mother.

'You make it sound as if I'm on the lookout for the first presentable thing in trousers to come along,' she hissed.

'Well, aren't you?' Tess dared to joke.

'Indeed I am not,' Alice cried indignantly. 'Dan and I are just good friends. As you well know.'

Having used her absence in Carlingford for a week as an excuse for extra outings with Alice, Dan had persuaded her to accompany him to the cinema the previous Saturday night. Not wanting to play gooseberry, Tess had made herself scarce before they returned home. Now, remembering the long silences and low-pitched voices, she was sceptical about their *friendship*. Of course they could have been keeping quiet so as not to awaken her. Chance would be a fine thing, she thought derisively.

'Then two weeks won't do you any harm,' she assured her mother.

'*One* week,' Alice insisted stubbornly.

'All right! One week then. Here's the taxi.'

Tess grabbed her mother's suitcase, leaving her to carry the holdall. This was one of the times she wished she could drive. It was so costly to take taxis everywhere.

'Where to, miss?' the driver inquired.

'The bus station, please,' Tess informed him.

Ten minutes later they were unloading Alice's luggage from the boot. After paying the taxi fare Tess looked round to see where they would have to wait for the bus, but could see no sign with Newry on it. Alice had to get the bus to Newry and then a connection to Carlingford. Leaving her disgruntled mother standing with the luggage at her feet, Tess approached the reception booth. The assistant pointed to a bay where a single-decker bus was parked and Tess hastened back to Alice. 'The bus is here already. It must be early. Come on, hurry up, before it takes off without you.'

'If only,' Alice muttered bad-temperedly.

'What did you say?'

'Nothing.'

'I heard,' Tess ground out between clenched teeth, her own temper flaring. 'How can you be so ungrateful? Everybody is falling over themselves trying to help you.'

'Calm down, Tess. I never asked or wanted anyone to help me. Besides, the driver isn't even in the bus yet. It won't go off on its own, you know. It will probably sit there for another half hour. And mind you, I'm not boarding until it's ready to go.' Alice, trailing behind with the holdall, was irritated at her daughter for rushing her off her feet. In her opinion there was no need for all this haste.

They joined the small queue and, seeing the resentful scowl on her mother's face suddenly change into a wide grin, Tess turned to find out the cause of the sudden transformation. Striding across the depot was Dan Thompson.

'He said he'd come to see me off, but I told him there was no need,' her mother spluttered, pink-cheeked but obviously delighted to see him. And neither was there any need, Tess thought resentfully. As far as she could see, he could only complicate things.

Dan towered smilingly over them. Dressed in his work clothes and cement-splattered boots, he still managed to receive admiring glances from a few of the women in the queue, as they openly appraised him and mentally approved what they saw.

It never ceased to amaze Tess the way he managed to attract women's attention. Oh, he was attractive, as Agnes had rightly pointed out to her. A Cary Grant lookalike. He was a middle-aged man, yet even younger women openly admired him. She herself wouldn't dream of staring at men old enough to be her father. Still, she was inclined to think that he was totally unaware of his magnetism to the opposite sex; couldn't care less what they thought of him.

Except Alice. All of his attention was hers. He locked eyes with her and said softly, 'I couldn't let you go without saying goodbye, Alice.'

'It's very kind of you,' Alice simpered, 'but I told you not to bother.' She was looking at Dan with cow's eyes. That was the only way Tess could describe her mother's demeanour at that moment, and she felt like grabbing her and giving her a good shaking. It disgusted her to see a grown woman like her mother behaving like a young girl. It was totally unbecoming of her!

Now she muttered ungraciously, 'You shouldn't have come, Dan.'

'Why not? I won't see your mother for a whole week.'

'Two weeks, as a matter of fact.'

Dan shot her a startled glance, then turned an inquiring look on Alice. 'Two weeks?'

'She's having you on. I'm only staying one week.' Alice glared at her daughter resentfully and assured him, 'You can count on it, Dan.'

The doors of the bus opened and the queue shuffled forward. Alice hung back, reluctance in her every step. Annoyed, Tess urged her. 'Come on, Mam, if you want to get a decent seat.'

'Leave me alone, Tess. I don't care where I sit,' Alice snapped.

Dan reached for the luggage. 'Look, before you two come to blows, I'll see her on to the bus, Tess. Maybe you'd like to go on home?'

He laughed aloud when she retorted, 'No, thank you. I'll wait and make sure she gets on that bus.'

He shook his head and teased, 'Oh, ye of little faith.'

Aware that the other travellers on the bus were being entertained by the spectacle the trio was creating, Tess muttered in exasperation, 'Never mind! Just get on with it.' Giving her mother a quick hug, she said, 'Don't forget to phone and let me know you've arrived safely.'

It was with a sigh of relief that she at last waved the bus out of sight. 'Thanks for your help, Dan. For a moment there, I thought she was going to renege.'

He silently agreed with her and smiled, knowing full well that it wouldn't have taken much to persuade Alice to change her mind. 'Can I buy you a coffee?'

Tess thought about it. Why not? She wasn't in any hurry to get back home; only cleaning and tidying up awaited her. 'That would be nice, thank you, Dan. But have you not to get back to work?'

'I'm making a late start this morning. In case the bus went out late or something. You know what I mean.'

They debated where to go, but when she suggested the Ulster Milk Bar he demurred and said it was too popular and would be crowded. 'Besides, I couldn't go in there dressed like this.' He gestured to his work clothes. 'I was thinking more along the lines of a working man's café. That is, if you don't mind?'

'The Ulster Milk Bar won't be too busy this early,' she objected. 'And it's really only your boots that look dirty. Please? I love their frothy coffee. My mouth is watering just thinking about it.'

He laughed and gave in gracefully. 'All right, if that's how much it means to you.'

They turned and headed in the direction of Castle Junction, and a short time later they were seated in the Ulster Milk Bar. 'Would you like a cake or a scone, or anything else to eat, Tess?'

'No, thank you, coffee will be fine.'

She watched as he went to the counter and gave their order. The girl behind the bar greeted him with a wide grin, obviously smitten. The girl, or young woman, whom Tess judged to be about thirty, was actually fawning over him. She was attractive in her own right, so why did she get on like that over a middle-aged stranger? Or was he a stranger to her? Was she the reason he didn't want to come here in the first place? Even if she was, what business was it of Tess's whom he chatted up? What a suspicious mind I'm developing, Tess thought, disgusted with herself.

Catching Tess's watchful eye the girl gave her a bright friendly smile and winked at her before turning to serve another customer. Tess looked away in embarrassment. The girl probably thought Dan was her sugar daddy. How did he manage it? It seemed to require no effort at all on his part. And how come Anne had left him and no other woman had managed to hook him since, if he was as wonderful as he seemed? Did he play the field? Was her mother just another conquest for him? All sorts of unsavoury thoughts raced through her troubled mind as she sat watching him.

He set her coffee down in front of her and took a chair facing her. 'Tess, I want to have a chat with you about me and your mother.'

She lifted the cup and tilted it in his direction. 'Thank you.' She eyed him over the rim. 'Fire away.'

He grimaced. 'Imagine, now I have your undivided attention I don't know where to start.'

'Mam always told me the beginning is the best place to start.' She smiled. 'Especially if it is something unpleasant you have to say.'

'Your mother is, of course, quite right. But you see,

I don't really know where it began.' He eyed her intently as he confessed, 'I don't know just when I fell in love with Alice and knew I had to have her for my wife.'

She managed to place the cup carefully back on the saucer without spilling a drop. Straightening her back in the chair, she reminded him, 'You're a married man, remember?'

'That's what I want to talk to you about. If I get a divorce, do you think Alice would consent to marry me in a register office?'

'Never!' The word spat from her mouth with such venom that it startled him. 'She's of the opinion that if Catholics marry outside the church, they aren't married in the eyes of God.'

Regaining his composure he leaned across the table. 'And you, Tess. Is that what you think?' he asked earnestly.

'It's not me you're wanting to marry,' she retaliated softly.

'Ah, I know . . . but if your mother asked for your opinion, what would you say?'

'Look, Dan, I know my mother inside out. If, in a moment of sheer madness, she actually married you in a register office, she would never forgive herself and would regret it till her dying day. I'm sure you'll agree that's no recipe for a happy marriage, but that's the type of woman she is, I'm afraid.'

'So, that means you wouldn't back me, then?'

She shook her head. 'No, I'm afraid not. I wouldn't encourage my mother to do anything that I knew to be against her better principles. It would bring her too much heartache in the long run.' Suddenly suspicious, she asked, 'Have you already discussed this with my mother? Has she said something to give you hope and now you're testing my reaction?'

He shook his head sadly. 'No. I wouldn't dare suggest anything at the moment. I'm afraid she might send me packing.'

'I did warn Mam that there was no future for you two together.'

'Tess, talk's cheap and you can go into something with the best of intentions and still get your fingers burnt. One can't foresee how things will turn out. I'm hoping for a small miracle. I do admit I want your mother for my wife. I wish now I'd given Anne a divorce years ago when she asked for it. At least I'd be a free man today.'

Reaching for her handbag, Tess rose abruptly to her feet. 'Look, Dan, I can't discuss anything like this with you. It's just not right. I don't want to be involved in your private affairs.'

He was on his feet in a flash. 'I'm sorry, Tess. I shouldn't have said that. Please sit down and finish your coffee. We'll talk about something else. All right?'

Slowly she sank down on her chair, still clasping the bag on her lap as if ready for flight at the slightest provocation. She eyed him warily. 'Fair enough.'

He was quiet for some moments, his mind still on Alice. Then, making a great effort, he asked, 'Did you know our Jack will be twenty-one next Thursday?'

She smiled faintly. 'How could I? I've seen very little of him since Colette came along.'

He grimaced. 'I can't seem to say anything to you without putting my big foot in it.'

'Oh, I'm not offended,' she quickly assured him. 'Far from it. That episode in my life is over and done with long ago, I'm happy to say.'

He eyed her intently and saw she meant it. 'I'm glad to hear that, Tess. One of these days you'll meet some nice young lad who'll make you happy.'

'So it is you who's spouting off to Mam about me needing to meet suitable young men?' she accused with a twinkle in her eye.

He had the grace to look ashamed. 'I'll use any argument to win Alice over. So you've been warned, Tess.'

'Dan, I've nothing against you personally. I only want what's best for Mam.'

'I know that, love. And in my heart I don't blame you. But I've promised not to discuss that with you, so to get back to Jack . . . he has always wanted a motorbike so I've bought him one for his birthday. A second-hand one, a 250cc Triumph. It's a couple of years old but in very good nick. The guy who owns the repair shed at the corner of our street has polished and cleaned it and it looks like new. A friend of mine who works in that yard at the bottom of the street – you know, on the bend a couple of doors from us – well, he's keeping it in the yard, out of sight, until the big day. So you see, Jack's in for a big surprise. He knows nothing whatsoever about it.'

Tess had to smile at the enthusiasm in his voice. 'He'll be dead chuffed, so he will,' she said softly.

'I suggested having a bit of a do for him but he wasn't interested, so I'm taking Colette and him out for a meal and he thinks that's his present. I can't wait to see his face next Thursday morning when he sees it sitting outside our front door.'

Tess looked at this kind, thoughtful man and wished he was free to marry her mother. He would make a nice stepdad. But even if he got a divorce from Anne it could never be.

She drained her cup and he said quickly, 'Have another one.'

'I can't, Dan. I have some shopping to do before I go home,' she excused herself.

He rose and accompanied her outside. Taking her hand between his he bent down and gazed earnestly into her face, saying solemnly, 'I've enjoyed your company, Tess. I always do. I think you and Alice and I could all live very happily together. Think about it, love . . . goodbye for now.'

Tess spent the next hour shopping in High Street and Ann Street before crossing Castle Junction and catching the bus at the bottom of Castle Street. She thought of her mother on her way to Carlingford, resentful and bitter. Had she done the right thing persuading her to go? She knew that Malachy and Rose would see that she enjoyed herself while she was there, and fervently hoped they would be able to persuade her to stay for two weeks. But would it do any good in the long run? Dan was obviously a man on a mission, and by the sound of him would not be deterred. Not by Tess or anyone else for that matter.

She sighed and her mind turned to Jack. So he'd be twenty-one next week! And he would be a married man by the end of the summer. A lot had happened since she had first met him that night at the Rolling Stones concert, but her elusive Mr Right had yet to put in an appearance.

Leaving the bus at the junction of Springfield Road, and crossing over, Tess spotted Agnes coming out of the post office, accompanied by a man Tess did not recognise.

'Hi, Agnes,' she called.

'Tess! Where have you been?' Agnes cried, hurrying to meet her, the stranger following her with long loping strides. 'I've been ringing you all morning.'

'I've been down at the bus station seeing Mam off to

Carlingford. Remember? Why, what's all the fuss?'

'I forgot about your mam going away over Easter. That's great! It means you're free.' She indicated her companion. 'I want you to meet Dominic Sullivan. Remember I told you he was coming home from America to be Dennis's best man?'

'Of course. Pleased to meet you, Dominic.'

Thrusting a hand towards her, he exclaimed in a slow American drawl, 'The pleasure is all mine. Agnes has been telling me all about you, but she didn't say how attractive you are.'

Tess had just been thinking that he was quite handsome in a rugged sort of way and could feel the colour creeping up her neck at the compliment.

Agnes laughed at her embarrassment. 'He's a terrible flirt, Tess. He can't stop the compliments dripping off his tongue. He's even got Mam eating out of his hand. So don't pay any attention to him. The reason I've been trying to get in touch with you is, Dennis and Marie, Joan and her husband and Tony and I are going out for a meal and then round to the Orpheus afterwards on Saturday night. We've booked a table for seven o'clock, and we would like you to join us.'

'Oh, I don't think I'll . . .' Tess flailed about in her mind for the right words.

Softly, in that lovely drawl of his, Dominic interrupted. 'Agnes neglected to say I'm also going and I need a partner, Tess. Please take pity on me. I'd sure be honoured to have you along.' Dominic held her eye and she found herself unable to look away. Her head nodded as if of its own volition and he said, 'Thank you. I look forward to seeing you again.' He turned to Agnes. 'If you'll excuse me, Agnes, I'll leave you two ladies to get on with your business now and push off down town.'

'Dominic, there is no need for you to rush off. Tess doesn't bite, you know.'

He laughed. 'She can nibble my ear any time she likes. But really, I want to walk into town and have a look round. I've some bits and pieces I need. I'll see you later.' The tousled blond head inclined in their direction and then he headed off down the Falls Road.

They watched him for some moments – tight blue hip-hugging jeans, leather jacket and tan-coloured suede boots – then Agnes turned to her friend. 'Isn't he something else, then?'

'He sure is. He stands out like a sore thumb in those clothes. You'd think he'd just got off the stagecoach.' Tess laughed and hoped Agnes wasn't aware just how much he had affected her. 'Anyway, madam, shouldn't you be at work?'

'I've asked for some time off. I don't go back until Monday week.'

'How did the rehearsal go?'

'Great! Dominic arrived on Sunday and we had the rehearsal on Monday night and everything went smoothly. I bet he'll look great in high hat and tails. I wish you were coming to the reception, Tess. You would be great company for him.'

'I don't think he'll be stuck for company. The girls will be round him like wasps round a jam jar. And don't worry about me not coming to the reception. I'll come down to the church and have a look at all the finery. I hope the weather picks up for you all.'

'So do I.'

'Meanwhile, I must dash. I took down all the heavy curtains to get them dry cleaned and they came back yesterday. I want to hang them all today if possible.'

'I'll come up and give you a hand.'

'Are you sure? Won't you be needed at home?'

'I'm glad to get out for a while, Tess. Roll on Monday! I'll be happy when this wedding is over and done with.'

'If that's the case, I'll certainly be glad of your help. So let's go.'

Tess had shaken out the curtains and spread them over the banister and beds to remove any wrinkles. Four pairs in all to be hung, but undaunted the two girls got stuck in. The curtains were off the biggest windows and very heavy and awkward to control. The matching pelmets were a right pain to work with. Tess was glad that Agnes had offered her assistance. She would never have managed on her own.

Some time later they stepped back, hands on hips, and examined their handiwork. Tess said, 'I think you deserve more than a cup of tea after all that hard work. Will you let me treat you to a fish supper later on?'

'That sounds great. I'll nip home now and meet you on the corner about seven. Will that be all right?'

'Smashing. I'll see you there.'

They decided to go to Johnny Long's, down behind the Ritz cinema, for a change and it was while they were waiting for their order that Tess questioned Agnes. 'Did you know that Jack will be twenty-one next Thursday?'

'Yes, Tony mentioned it. He's surprised Dan isn't having a bit of a do for him.'

'Oh, Dan told me he wanted to throw a party but Jack turned down the idea, so he's bought him a smashing present instead.'

'Oh, what did he buy him?'

'I'm afraid I can't say in case you let it slip to Tony and he tells Jack. You see, it's a surprise. Jack knows nothing about it.'

'I see. I thought perhaps the reason was that Dan was a bit short of cash now he has a woman to spend his money on,' Agnes said slyly.

'If you mean my mam, I wouldn't say he's spending a fortune on her.'

'Ah, but he might be making plans for the future, Tess. He knows your mam would never consider living in Spinner Street.'

'You seem to forget, he's a married man, Agnes.'

'Do you think that really matters in this day and age?'

'Yes. As a matter of fact I do.'

'Ah well, everybody is not as strait-laced as you, Tess. Your mother deserves some happiness. She's been a widow far too long.'

'Do you think I don't know that? I'm sure she could have had many a man while I was growing up, but she didn't seem interested. Her and my dad were very close from what I hear, and I honestly think she wasn't interested in any other men . . . until now, that is! Sometimes I wish I'd never met Jack Thompson, then Mam wouldn't have met Dan. In fact *most* times I wish I'd never met him. He's brought me nothing but misery since day one.'

'Ever heard tell of fate, Tess? If it is meant to be, it was just waiting in the wings to happen, whether or not you had made Jack's acquaintance.'

Their fish suppers arrived and all else was forgotten as they tucked in.

A shadow falling across the table brought raised eyes to rest on Dominic Sullivan. Weighed down with parcels, he stood at their table.

'I was over in the Crown bar to sample their Guinness and then dandered round here to see if this chip shop was still open for business. I couldn't believe my eyes when I popped in and saw you two ladies sitting here.' He gave Agnes a reproachful look. 'You didn't mention you were coming here this evening.'

Agnes shrugged and pointed her fork towards Tess. 'Blame her. She's treating me.' Her voice was abrupt and his eyebrows rose fractionally.

'Mind if I join you?' He kept his gaze on Agnes, waiting for her response, and only when she said 'Be our guest' did he look questioningly at Tess.

She nodded her consent. Dominic tucked his parcels under the table and went to the counter to place his order. Tess looked suspiciously at her friend. 'Do I detect some sort of tension between you two?'

'Don't be silly,' Agnes muttered bad-temperedly.

During the meal, Tess watched them closely, but everything seemed normal. There was lots of banter and laughter and Tess found Dominic very easy to get on with. She put all ideas of animosity between Agnes and him from her mind. Her imagination had been working overtime lately. She would be delighted to accompany this man to the Orpheus on Saturday night.

Still not very happy with her lot, Alice descended from the bus at Carlingford in bad humour to find Malachy and Rose waiting for her. They were so pleased to see her and welcomed her with such warmth that she felt ashamed of her reluctance to visit them.

'I'm preparing lunch in my house. Is that all right with you, Alice?'

'That will be lovely, Rose. Thank you very much.'

A huge grin split Rose's face and she cried merrily, 'Right, Malachy, you see to the baggage and we'll be on our way.'

By the time they climbed into the Land-Rover Alice

was in a happier frame of mind. After all, she consoled herself, a week was no time at all and didn't they say absence made the heart grow fonder?

Rose's home was a whitewashed, two-storey detached house not too far back from the main road. She explained to Alice that her farm was about half a mile further up the lane that ran past the side of the house and that she had very little to do with the running of it these days. Her son and his wife were living there now and although, when necessary, Rose helped out, she now left the actual day to day running of the farm to them, as they would inherit it one day.

'Don't you get lonely living here on your own?' Alice asked tentatively, following her friend through the gate and down the garden path to the front door, while Malachy parked the Land-Rover at the rear of the house.

'Not a bit of it! I enjoy my own company and my two daughters bring their friends to visit the odd week-end when they've nothing better to do. And Malachy, when he's not too busy, comes round for a bit of a chin-wag. There always seems to be something for me to do, so you see I'm never too lonely.'

She led Alice into a big, sprawling, tastefully furnished room that ran the full length of the house. A turf fire burned brightly, throwing out welcome heat, and an open staircase ran up against the opposite wall.

'Oh, this is lovely,' Alice exclaimed.

Rose smiled in appreciation at her genuine praise. 'Thank you. I must confess I *am* proud of it. It wasn't like this when my husband was alive, mind you. More like a hovel, to tell you the truth. I was for ever on to him to get something done to it, so the girls could stay here when they came home from college. The farm-house is a bit on the small side, now they have grown up. However, he wouldn't hear tell of it. Said it would be a waste of good money. Oh dear, here's me rambling on and forgetting all about my guest. You'll be thinking I've no manners whatsoever, Alice. Here, give me your coat and make yourself at home, while I finish off the lunch.'

Alice chose one of the armchairs near the blazing fire, and sinking back into its comfortable depths she had a good old look around the room. The wood block floor was highly polished and good quality rugs were strategically positioned in front of the large sofa and easy chairs. The walls were adorned with watercolour prints, presumably of local sceneries. She recognised one of Carlingford Lough. A Welsh dresser graced the wall to the right of the fireplace and was home to a willow patterned dinner service. Under the staircase stood a large china cabinet. Two shelves displayed a number of beautiful porcelain figurines while the bottom shelf was cluttered with a variety of sporting trophies.

Malachy's voice broke into her musing. 'Rose has this room lovely, hasn't she? She's a real home-maker.'

Alice turned her head to where he stood at the door watching her. 'I didn't know you were there. She certainly has it beautiful. I take it this was once two rooms?' She nodded upwards to where an encased beam ran across the ceiling.

'Correct! Shortly after her husband's death, she got Seamus Corrigan, the local handyman, in. She had the partition wall pulled down, as you can see, and an extension built on at the back for a kitchen and dining room, through there.' He pointed to the door through which Rose had disappeared. 'The new bathroom is above the kitchen. She has been working hard putting the finishing touches to the house for your arrival.'

'It's all very nice. I had pictured you and Rose on adjoining farms.' Alice grimaced slightly, remembering how she was dreading muddy farmyards and yapping dogs.

As if reading her mind, Malachy said, 'Muddy yards and the like, eh, Alice? You'll be surprised when you see my farm. It's been modernised a lot since you last were here. I have only one dog now, Meg, and she's a bit long in the tooth. The worst you'll get from old Meg is a good sniffing.'

Alice grinned. 'We'll see. I'll reserve my opinion till I've run my beady eye over the place.'

Rose popped her head round the kitchen door. 'Lunch is almost ready. Perhaps you would like to freshen up first, Alice?' When Alice nodded, Rose said, 'The bathroom is upstairs at the end of the landing. You can't miss it.'

Alice returned from the very modern bathroom, full of praise. 'You really have a natural talent, Rose. Everything up there is just beautiful.'

'You're very kind, thank you, Alice. Sit here, please.'

Alice seated herself at the big pine table, which was laden with an assortment of dishes. 'There's enough here to feed an army!' She lifted up the lids of a few dishes for a quick peek while Rose's back was turned. 'And don't forget . . . it's a day of fast and abstinence today.'

'Why do you think there's no meat on the table, Alice? Rose is like you and abides strictly by the rules,' Malachy said drily.

The meal consisted of poached salmon, trout with a fine, crispy, golden coating dusted with salt and pepper, green salad and crusty bread, with different sauces and pickles. It was delicious and Alice was sincere when she said, 'That was absolutely mouth-watering, Rose. I really enjoyed it.'

'Those trout were caught early this morning,' her brother informed her.

'I could tell,' Alice assured him. 'I could taste the peaty freshness.'

After lunch they retired to the big room. 'You must have a drink before you go.' Rose sent Malachy an inquiring look. 'I'm afraid I don't have much of a selection. Just white wine and Bristol Cream.'

'White wine will be fine, thank you.'

'Will you pour, Malachy?'

Handing Alice a glass, Malachy laughed softly. 'You must be wondering why Rose is throwing me all sorts of queer looks, Alice. So let me put you in the picture. It's like this . . . she's hoping you'll stay here in the cottage with her for a few days. How do you feel about that?'

Taken unawares, Alice was tongue-tied. She had expected to go to her brother's farm first and after Easter stay with Rose for a couple of days before going home. 'Well now . . .'

Rose quickly came to her rescue. 'It was just a thought, Alice. Don't worry about it. I won't be offended if you don't want to stay.'

'Oh, but I'd love to.' She turned to her brother. 'That's if Malachy doesn't mind.'

'Actually I think it's a great idea. Rose will be able to take you out and about in her car while I'm busy during the day.'

Rose was grinning from ear to ear. 'Good! That's settled then. Would you fetch Alice's luggage and put it in the back bedroom, Malachy? You'll get a better view from there, Alice. Thanks for agreeing to stay. I'll take you in and around the town and show you some of our beauty spots.'

'I have been here before, Rose,' Alice reminded her softly, remembering that in her opinion there hadn't been much to Carlingford.

'Ah, but I know places you've never heard tell of.' Rose hugged her new-found friend close. 'I'm so glad you came.'

Before going into the house that night after work, Dan called in at the yard to have another look at the motorbike. His friend, Bob Crosby, smiled and patiently closed the big double wooden doors so that there would be no spectators. Then he went to the far end of the yard and flipped the canvas cover from the bike.

The two men stood side by side gazing at the gleaming machine in silent admiration. 'She's a beaut, isn't she, Bob?'

'She certainly is.'

'Old Geordie did a grand job of cleaning it up. It looks almost new. Do you think Jack will like it?'

'He'll be very hard to please if he doesn't. I take it he'll be able to handle it all right?'

'I've no sweat about that. His cousin had an old wreck of a motorbike and they rode about everywhere on it. My heart used to be in my mouth watching them set off. He'll be able to manage this one all right.' Dan helped Bob cover it again and said, 'I'll get away on in now, Bob. Thanks for looking after it for me.'

'Any time, mate. It's no trouble at all.'

Jack was on the early shift and was in the scullery preparing the evening meal when his dad came in.

'Hi, son. How did your day go?'

'Ach, so-so. You know what it's like.'

He sounded so despondent Dan's heart went out to him. 'Hey! Why all the doom and gloom?'

With feet that dragged Jack entered the kitchen. 'Dad, there's something I have to tell you and you're not going to be one bit pleased.'

Dan's brows gathered in a frown. 'It must have something to do with your mother then, if you think I'm not going to like it.'

Jack nodded. 'She wanted to have a bit of a party for my birthday and I knew you wouldn't take kindly to it, so I said no.'

'I see.'

'I explained that you had suggested having a few friends round here for a party but I'd said I'd rather just go out for a meal.'

'And what had she to say about that?'

'It's not what she said . . . it's what she did. She's gone and bought me an expensive present.'

'How do you know?'

'She's given it to me already.'

A ball of anger gathered in Dan's chest. 'Has she forgotten your birthday is not till next Thursday?'

'She wanted me to be able to wear it over Easter, Dad. Please say you don't mind.'

Dan wanted to rant and rave at the way Anne was sticking her oar in and spoiling everything. She must have had a right old laugh at his expense, at the thought of him taking Jack and Colette out for a meal as a twenty-first birthday present. For two pins he'd take his son down to the yard after dinner and show him the motor-bike; let him know he had also bought his son something worth talking about. He thought better of it. It was for his twenty-first birthday and that was the day he would first set eyes on it.

Curbing his temper he asked, 'And what is this expensive present she has bought you?'

'A lovely wristwatch, Dad. Would you like to see it?'

'Why not? It's obviously what she had in mind.'

'You're wrong there, Dad. Mam was afraid you might buy me a watch too. That's one of the reasons she gave it to me early. She was relieved when I told her you were just taking Colette and me out for a meal.'

'I'll bet she was,' Dan said sarcastically. 'Well now, where's this watch you're all excited over?'

Going to a drawer in the dresser, Jack removed a small dark blue box and handed it to his father. 'It's a beauty, Dad.'

'It is that, son,' Dan agreed when he opened the box and saw the slim, gold-faced watch with the black leather strap. 'An Avia calendar watch. It must have cost a pretty penny by the looks of it.'

'You won't be offended if I wear it, will you?'

'Not at all, son. I just wish I had thought of buying you something like that.' A smile tugged at Dan's lips when he thought of the treat Jack had in store.

'What are you smiling at?'

Jack's voice was suspicious and Dan hastened to reassure him. 'Nothing, honestly. I was just thinking how pleased your mother must have been when she handed it to you. I hope you and Colette will still come out for a meal with me?'

'Of course we will.' Jack looked embarrassed and muttered, 'That's another thing, Dad. Mam wants to know if she can come along too.'

'I can't believe her cheek,' Dan gasped, shaking his head in bewilderment. 'No! I'm sorry, son, but I must put my foot down. If she wants to take you out another time that's fine by me. I've booked a table for three at the International Hotel and I don't want your mother there. That's final! Now what's that lovely aroma I smell? Can we eat now and forget all about your mother?'

Jack stood gnawing at his bottom lip, at a loss as to how to change his father's mind regarding an invitation for his mother.

'Dad . . .' His voice trailed off. He was aware himself that it would be a disaster if his mother joined them. But what could he tell her? How would he be able to make her understand that he had no say in the matter; that it was his father's treat?

As he passed him in the scullery to wash his hands, Dan noted the strained expression on his son's face. He gave a short laugh. 'Don't worry about it, son. Your mother will understand that I don't want her to come with us. So sit down and enjoy your dinner.'

The meal was eaten in silence. Dan, angry that his wife was managing to take all the pleasure out of his plans, shovelled the food into his mouth. The smoked haddock tasted like cardboard. Jack was pushing his food around the plate and very little of it was reaching his mouth.

Unable to stand it any longer, Dan put down his knife and fork and gave his son a hard look. 'See here, Jack, if you would like your mother to take my place at the International Hotel with you and Colette, I'll understand. I will still pay for the treat, of course.'

Jack looked scandalised. 'You'll do no such thing! Colette would be mad. She still hasn't forgiven Mam for revealing how her parents feel about me.' He nodded his head determinedly. 'I'll just tell Mam she can't come.'

Relieved that his son hadn't jumped at the chance to decide in favour of his mother, Dan said, 'That's settled then. Eat your dinner, son.'

Appetite somewhat recovered, Jack smiled at his father and got stuck in. His mother must be made to understand that she couldn't invite herself along when it suited *her*; that she wasn't always welcome. He was beginning to realise that his father no longer had any future plans that included his wife, so the sooner he got used to the idea the better.

As if to prove him right, Dan said, 'Jack . . . Mrs Maguire is in Carlingford at the moment, but . . . she is expected to return next Wednesday. Would you be upset if I invited her to dine out with us on your birthday?' Jack kept his head down, staring at his plate. Dan hurried on. 'Forget it, son. It's unrealistic of me to expect you to accept Alice. Especially after me rejecting your mother.'

Raising his head, Jack looked him in the eye. 'No, Dad, you're quite right. I've finally accepted that the past is over and done with. By all means invite Mrs Maguire along. I only hope she doesn't hold it against me, after my fling with her daughter.'

Alice had thought that time would drag in Carlingford. Not one bit of it. The first day, taking a packed lunch, they set off early and headed for Omeath and then Newry. When Rose had suggested that they visit these two towns, Alice smothered a grimace of distaste. Hadn't she passed through both many a time and found them boring? How would they get a day in there?

However, under Rose's supervision they visited places Alice had never heard of. As they drove along with the lough shimmering on the right Rose explained that Carlingford was actually at the foot of Slieve Foye, the highest of the Cooley Mountains, and that these mountains were more jagged than the smooth lines of the

Mournes distinctively visible across the lough, the contrast being due to the different rock types that made up the mountains, formed as molten magma cooled down after volcanic eruptions millions of years ago. Alice began to view her surroundings through different eyes. Everywhere it seemed was steeped in history and Rose soon had her asking questions and wanting to learn more about the neighbouring countryside.

Near Newry, situated at the head of Carlingford Lough, they had a picnic close to the historic Gap of the North and as they sat in the warm sun Rose told Alice that in the twelfth century St Malachy had founded an abbey in Newry.

'How come you know so much history?'

'Don't forget I was born and reared here. It's only natural that I should know all about it.'

'You make me feel so ignorant,' Alice complained.

'Ah, now, don't talk like that. I'm sure you know more about Belfast and surrounding areas than I could ever imagine.'

'Well, I suppose you're right. I know this much . . . in future I'll find out all I can about the places I visit.'

Next Rose headed the car in the direction of Warrenpoint. Just before entering the town she turned into a car park so that Alice could visit Narrow Water Castle, built in 1570. Their next port of call was Warrenpoint itself, where they spent some time, and Alice learned a lot more history before they headed home.

They arrived back quite late and after a quick meal relaxed in front of the fire happy and contented, gabbling away as if they had known each other for years. On Friday Rose was surprised when Alice was a bit subdued when she suggested they should go to Dundalk.

'We don't have to go anywhere today if you'd rather stay at home,' she stressed.

'It's not that I don't want to go, Rose. It's just . . . well, it's Good Friday, and I feel I should be going to church to do the Way of the Cross.'

Relieved, Rose quickly reassured her. 'But sure, we can make our own pilgrimage by way of reparation. Believe me, on Good Friday there will be plenty of places to stop and pray.'

So on Friday they headed in the opposite direction, going along the coast and spending some time on a few quiet beaches between Carlingford and Dundalk.

Malachy was right. Alice was surprised and impressed when Rose finally drove her to his farm on Holy Saturday morning. The old ramshackle building nestling at the foot of the hills had been transformed into a pleasant homestead. The yard in front of the whitewashed building had been flagged.

'It is not always as clean as this,' Malachy informed her. 'I've given it a good hosing down so you wouldn't get those pretty boots of yours dirty.'

Just as he had foretold, the old collie, Meg, waddled over to Alice, had a good sniff and returned to her place by the door.

The Cooley Hills rose steep and jagged behind the farm and Alice couldn't believe that she hadn't really noticed them before, they were so majestically overpowering. I must have gone about with my eyes shut in my younger days, she thought, not to have noticed all this beauty.

Saturday had dawned dull and misty and a haze still obscured the Mourne Mountains, but Malachy assured her that this was not unusual and the mist would probably lift later on in the morning. He was right again. After lunch they visited the local market and Alice was amazed at all the wonderful produce on sale. By the end of the afternoon Malachy and Rose were weighed down with all sorts for their respective larders. Alice also bought some jars of pickles and preserves, all made by the farmers' wives, to take home to Belfast.

On Easter Sunday friends of Malachy's were invited to lunch to meet his sister. Everybody was so friendly and they got on so well together that an impromptu musical get-together was arranged for that evening. A buffet was laid on, the farmers brought their fiddles and flutes and they danced until the early hours of the morning. Alice was much in demand as a partner. She really was enjoying herself.

Monday was spent likewise meeting Rose's family and friends in her farmhouse. After all this sociability and activity, Alice had no difficulty in agreeing to extend her visit until Saturday to attend the wedding of a friend's son, which Rose assured her would be worth staying on for. Without hesitation she agreed to tell Dan of her decision when he phoned, as planned, on Tuesday evening.

Tess was delighted when she phoned her mother on Monday evening and discovered her change of plans. Perhaps she was having second thoughts about Dan Thompson after all and she wouldn't have to worry about them living in sin. 'Good God, I'm beginning to sound like my mother,' she thought in shocked dismay.

Chapter Eight

As the weather forecast had predicted the weather in Belfast did get better as Wednesday in Holy Week progressed and it was a dry, cool evening, the stars above sparkling bright against a dark sky, when Agnes, Tess and Dominic at last left Johnny Long's. Drawing in deep breaths of the crisp air, Dominic suggested they walk home.

'Are you not tired?' Tess asked. 'You've been on the go all day. We sat in there yarning so long I was sure Johnny would throw us out.'

'I don't usually like shopping but I enjoyed myself immensely today, trailing round the shops in Belfast, recognising some, unable to find others. It was strange. A lot of the stores have changed hands and a lot of places are missing altogether since I left.' He hoisted the bags up. 'Back home I'm a bit of a miser. All my money goes back into the business. But today I spent a fortune. I came back to Belfast determined to enjoy myself and that's what I'm going to do.'

'I can believe that, looking at all those parcels. You've every right to spoil yourself. But . . . are they heavy? Don't you think we should get a taxi home?'

'Not a bit of it! It's too good an evening to spend cooped up in a car. We'll be home in no time.'

Tess laughed and saluted him. 'If you say so, sir. Anything you say, sir.'

'I say.' He returned the salute with a smile.

One on either side of him, they stepped out smartly up Grosvenor Road. He was a great conversationalist and had them in stitches as he related episodes from the time when he was training to be a chef.

'And now you own your own catering business.' Agnes's voice was full of awe. 'That's some feat.'

'I've been lucky. And mind you, it is only a small establishment mostly catering for the Irish in our community, but I intend branching out. I have met this girl and she is a superb cook.'

'Girl friend, as in courting?' Agnes asked brightly.

He slanted a glance at her. 'Not quite, yet. But who knows what the future has in store.'

'What kind of food does she specialise in?'

'I can truthfully say that she can successfully turn her hand to most dishes. That's why I was able to come home with an easy conscience. She can be depended upon. As for her pastries and desserts, they're mouth-watering.'

'She sounds the ideal partner for you.'

He shrugged. 'Who knows? I always thought when I met the right woman I'd be bowled over. To be truthful, the people I know to have been bowled over by love are few and far between and, sad to say, a couple of the marriages have ended in divorce. So perhaps there is more to marriage than love alone. I suppose I'm just an old romantic fool at heart. Anyhow, who knows, maybe this wedding will put me in the notion and I'll go racing back to the States and fall on my knees and propose to Stella.'

Behind his back Agnes caught Tess's eye and mimed *Stella*.

*   *   *

A short time later they reached and passed Violet Street, and walked Tess to her front door. Refusing an invitation to come in for a cup of tea, Agnes and Dominic retraced their steps back down to Violet Street, both locked in their own thoughts.

Feeling cheerful, Tess made herself a mug of hot cocoa and, sipping it, slowly climbed the stairs to examine her wardrobe. She was happy to know that Dominic had a woman friend back in America whom he cared enough about to maybe ask to marry him. It put all the silly ideas out of her head. Knowing he was practically spoken for, she could now enjoy herself in his company without any romantic nonsense and take anything that happened with a pinch of salt. There was no way she would ever make a fool of herself over a man again; once bitten, twice shy. But this way, knowing he was practically engaged, she wasn't likely to be tempted. It was nice to be aware from the beginning that he wasn't available. At least she knew where she stood, and wouldn't get any silly ideas as she had where Jack was concerned.

Running her hand along the row of clothes in the wardrobe, she was dismayed. Plenty of suits, skirts and blouses hung there, but precious little else. Well, her social life didn't include dancing, so why should she have any dresses? There was certainly nothing in her wardrobe that would be suitable for a dance at the Orpheus. How on earth could she possibly accompany Dominic Sullivan to the Orpheus in a skirt and blouse? It would be unheard of. Her only two dresses, hanging forlornly on the rail, were well out of fashion. She had made them herself some years ago when Agnes persuaded her to go to a class in Sammy Leckie's to learn ballroom dancing. Her enthusiasm had waned after a time, so no more dresses were made.

Quickly descending the stairs she dialled Agnes's number. She had to let her friend know that she was unavailable, give her a chance to ask someone else. It was a pity but it couldn't be helped. It was Agnes herself who answered the phone.

Without any greeting, Tess blurted out, 'Look, Agnes, I'm sorry, but I'm afraid I can't go to the dance on Saturday night.'

'Why ever not?'

'I haven't anything to wear.'

'Don't be silly, Tess. You have some lovely clothes. Your taste is impeccable.'

'You're wrong. I haven't anything to go dancing in. I have two dresses and they are as old as the hills. Not at all suitable for somewhere like the Orpheus, I can assure you. I'm afraid you'll have to find someone else to round off your numbers.'

'You can go down town tomorrow and treat yourself to a new dress. And don't pretend you can't afford it, Tess. I know you're not short of a bob or two, so I won't take no for an answer.'

'Pay a fortune for a dress I may never wear again? You've got to be joking. I'm sorry, but you'll have to find someone else, Agnes.'

'And just who can I ask at this late stage?'

'I really don't see your problem. Dominic doesn't really need a partner. All the unattached girls will be falling over themselves to get a dance with him and, as we both know, he's not shy. Far from it. For goodness' sake, he'll be in his glory! All that talent to pick from. As for the meal . . . you can say one of your party has taken ill. It happens all the time. Restaurants must surely make allowance for things like that.'

'Look here, Tess Maguire, you promised to come and you can't let me down. You just *can't*! Do you hear me? I'm depending on you, and I'm not taking any of your old excuses. So there!'

Tess heard the dialling tone and taking the receiver away from her ear gazed at it in amazement. Agnes had hung up on her. What cheek! What on earth had got into her? Annoyed, she started to dial again, then thought better of it. She had made her position quite clear and it was now up to Agnes to find someone else to partner Dominic. Perhaps it was all for the best, Tess consoled herself. Dominic was probably a terrific dancer, whereas she had only ever learned the basic steps and would probably trample all over him.

Deciding to have an early night, she checked the doors and windows and climbed the stairs. Her mother had phoned to let her know she had arrived safely and was spending a few days with Rose before moving on to stay at her brother's farm. She had seemed quite contented and Dan Thompson's name had not entered into the conversation.

The house was quiet as a crypt and for the very first time Tess regretted not having a television. Her mother had broached the subject a few times but neither of them was keen enough to rush out and buy one. They were quite expensive, and so they kept putting it off. Perhaps when her mother came back from Carlingford they would go down town and look at some sets.

It seemed strange being alone in the house. This was the first time her mother and she had ever been separated. It was something she was going to have to get used to in the future, if Dan Thompson had anything to do with it.

Now was the opportunity to finish the book she was

reading, she thought. However, the family saga she usually had difficulty putting down tonight failed to grip her attention. After reading the same page three times, she marked her place and rose from the bed. Thrusting her feet into her slippers, she picked up her dressing gown and descended the stairs.

Something was niggling at the back of her mind. The year before, a customer had chosen velvet for her brides-maid dress and a piece of the material had been surplus to requirements. The girl had insisted it was of no use to her and that Tess must keep it. If she recalled correctly the material wouldn't be big enough for a dress for herself but a long velvet skirt matched to her best blouse might be dressy enough for the occasion.

She was beginning to think she had thrown the ma-terial out when at last she discovered it at the bottom of a drawer full of remnants. A rich dark green, it was good quality and not a wrinkle marred its softness. It would be ideal, but holding it against her she confirmed that there would not be enough for a ball dress. A long skirt it would have to be. Spreading it out on the work table, she measured it carefully.

Now if she had wanted one of those skimpy dresses that were all the style at the moment there would be no problem whatsoever. With a bit of care she would certainly be able to make one. But her mother would take a turn in her eye if she dared to wear something revealing. However, her mother wouldn't be here to see her, and what the eye doesn't see the heart doesn't grieve over. So why not? Why not be daring for a change, just for the hell of it? A dress would be so much more suit-able than a skirt and blouse!

Tomorrow morning she would go down to Anderson & McAuley's and get a pattern. She would be sure to get one of the very latest designs there. She would also let Agnes know that she had changed her mind . . . again.

Dominic and Agnes walked the short distance to her home in silence. He kept throwing sideways glances at her, aware that she was in an unhappy frame of mind but at a loss to understand why.

'Have you not enjoyed yourself tonight, Agnes?'

'Of course I have! The crack was great.'

They lapsed into silence again but when they arrived at the house and she made to open the door, with a hand on her arm he stopped her. 'Agnes, have I done something to offend you?'

She reared back like a startled deer, and gazed at him apprehensively. 'No! What gives you that idea?'

'When I first met you last Monday you were like a breath of spring, laughing and happy. The loveliest girl I've ever clapped eyes on. But since then, whenever we happen to be alone you go all quiet and moody. I feel I must have done or said something that has offended you. If I have . . . I can honestly say it was unintentional. I know I do sometimes say things without thinking how they might sound to others, but I certainly never meant you any offence.'

She clutched at his arm and shook it roughly. 'Don't you dare think like that, Dominic Sullivan. You're one of the nicest people I have ever met and I like you very much.' She shrugged and made futile gestures with her hands as if trying to shoo off a fly. 'It's this wedding. It's all we seem to talk about these days, morning, noon and night, wedding, wedding, wedding! I'll be glad when it's all over and the household can get back to some state of normality.'

'Then you'll have your own wedding to prepare for,' he reminded her gently.

She waved this idea aside. 'That's away in the future. I'll have plenty of time to get used to the idea.'

Her smile was tremulous and he felt sad. Surely a wedding was something to plan for joyously? Not an idea to get used to, he thought.

'Are you very much in love with Tony?' he asked softly.

She blinked in confusion at the question. 'Of course I am. Look, we'd better go in now. I'm sure Dennis will be anxious to get home. He has to get up early in the morning for work. So has Tony for that matter. I didn't think we'd be this late or I'd have told him to go on home straight from work.'

Slowly he released her arm and she opened the door, bewildered and confused by the emotion his touch had awakened in her. Thank God he had a girl waiting for him in America!

Tony came into the hall to meet her. He stopped abruptly when he saw Dominic. 'I was worried about you. I didn't realise you two were together.'

She smiled brightly. 'Tess and I went down to Johnny Long's for a supper and would you believe it?' She nodded behind her. 'We bumped into this fellow.'

May came into the hall. 'Would you like a sandwich, or perhaps something else to eat, Dominic?'

'No thank you, Mrs Quinn, I've already eaten.'

'A cup of tea then?'

Dennis's voice reached them from the living room. 'Dominic can have a cup of tea at home, Mrs Quinn. I've waited long enough for him.'

'I'm sorry if I'm annoying you, Dennis,' Dominic shouted back. 'But it was you who suggested that I call in here and walk home with you.'

Dennis came into the hall. 'I'm not disputing it. I just didn't realise you'd be this late. So let's get a move on. I'm whacked.' He lovingly took Marie into his arms. 'It's getting a bit crowded in here. Let's say good night outside, love. Give us a couple of minutes, Dominic. I haven't had a good kiss with Marie for a couple of days. She'll be leaving me standing at the altar if I'm not careful.' With these words he grabbed his coat off the hall-stand and ushered Marie out the door, pulling it shut after them.

As she made to enter the living room Tony drew Agnes aside. 'Let's go into the sitting room, love.'

'Why?'

He lowered his voice, a frown gathering on his brow. 'Surely it's obvious . . . just to be alone for a while with you. Is that asking too much?'

'We've got company, Tony. It would be bad manners to take ourselves off.'

'Your mam and dad are in there. I'm sure Dominic won't mind. He, apparently, has had your company all evening by the sound of things.'

In spite of Tony's low tone, Dominic heard every word. 'Don't worry about me. I'll be going home in a minute or two.'

Disgruntled, Agnes let Tony urge her into the sitting room and, when the door closed on them, rounded on him angrily. 'Don't you ever speak to me in company like that again. You're acting as if you own me.'

He drew her into his arms. 'Hold on, Agnes. I just wanted some time alone with you.'

She shrugged herself free from his embrace. 'I'm tired, Tony. There will be plenty of time for this kind of thing later on.'

Tight lipped he faced her, eyes filled with distaste.

'Will there, Agnes? Sometimes I doubt that.'

'And just what do you mean by that?'

'I'm worried about you. You seem to have ice in your veins.'

He turned on his heel and left the room. She heard him call out 'Good night, everyone' and the outer door close after him. Immediately contrite, she rushed to stop him. How could she treat him like that? She was behaving like a spoiled child.

In the hall she stopped abruptly. Dominic was coming out of the living room and said with a smile, 'I think Dennis has had enough time to say good night to Marie, don't you?' He peered intently at her. 'Are you all right? You look a bit pale.'

She started retreating into the shadows of the sitting room again, to escape his penetrating look. 'I'm fine. Good night, Dominic.'

He followed her, pausing in the doorway. 'If you don't mind me saying so, you don't look fine to me.'

Tears threatened. With a wave of the hand she motioned him out of the room but instead he came further in, closing the door. 'Have you and Tony quarrelled?'

The tears spilled over and ran down her cheeks. 'Just a silly little lover's tiff, that's all.'

He produced a handkerchief and moved closer. Gratefully she grabbed it and dabbed at her eyes. 'Thank you. It was all my fault. I'm treating Tony terrible of late. He must have the patience of a saint to put up with me the way he does.'

'He loves you, that's why.'

'I know he does and I'm not worthy of him. Everything he does is for our future and all I do is find fault.' A sob caught in her throat.

Dominic drew her into his arms and patted her on the back, just as he would comfort a child. 'There now, don't get all upset. All courting couples quarrel now and again. It will all work out all right in the long run.'

A sigh escaped her lips and putting a finger under her chin he tilted her face up towards his. 'It will be all right,' he stressed. 'You'll see.'

She smiled and looked so forlorn that without further ado he kissed her. He caught himself on immediately and quickly released her. 'I'm sorry. I'd no right to do that.' For the life of him he couldn't understand what had possessed him, kissing his brother's future sister-in-law like that and her engaged to another man. One thing he did know, he hadn't wanted to stop. She had felt comfortable in his arms and her lips had been soft and responsive.

'It's all right, Dominic. I know you only meant to be kind. I'm fine now. Thank you.'

Resisting the urge to gather her close again, he said, 'Then I'll be off. Good night, Agnes.'

The phone rang as she passed through the hall and she lifted the receiver. 'Hello.'

It was Tess saying she couldn't go out with them on Saturday night. After a brief, bitter discussion, Agnes hung up on her friend. She was at the end of her tether. What else could go wrong? Weren't troubles supposed to come in threes? Tears blinding her, she called out good night to her parents and once in the privacy of her own room threw herself on the bed and gave way to her emotions.

The dress was beautiful! Daring but beautiful. It looked so small lying on the bed she found it hard to believe it would actually fit her. But it did. She had been careful to try it on step by step as she went along, and it fitted her . . . just!

She stood by the bed in her black satin waist slip and sheer black nylon stockings and gazed in awe at her creation. Then, gently lifting the dress, she stepped into it and eased it up over her hips, wiggling it into position and securing it at the waist where it fitted snugly. Then lifting the two front panels up over her bare breasts she secured them at the back of her neck.

It fitted like a glove. The front dipped low and for the first time in her life she realised just what a cleavage meant. Her firm breasts pushed at the material and looked larger than they actually were, and a mole high on the left one tantalisingly caught the eye when she moved. Her skin gleamed translucently above the rich colour of the dress and her eyes looked enormous and glowed like emeralds. She twisted to see the back of the dress and was glad her skin was free of blemishes as it was exposed to the waist.

She stood open mouthed at the creature reflected in the mirror. Surely this couldn't be prim and proper Tess Maguire. Could it?

It was indeed! She looked and felt wonderful. But there was no way she could possibly go out in this creation! What would people think? Distractedly her mind roved over all alternatives in her wardrobe and nothing else would do. She must wear this dress or stay at home. The door bell startled her into action. A glance at the clock showed her that Dominic, Brian and Joan, whom she was travelling down with, were early. She couldn't back out now. Not with the car at the door. With one last look at her reflection she shrugged into her coat and grabbing the small suede black bag that matched her court shoes she headed for the stairs.

Agnes would soon let her know if she looked out of place.

A table was booked at the Steak House on Wellington Place and the others were already waiting outside. Tess tumbled out of the car with Joan and Dominic and Brian went to find a parking spot while the rest of them entered the building.

Tess was dismayed when the women all removed their coats. She had thought she could remain covered up until they went to the Orpheus, but Dominic was gesturing for her coat to hang on the stand and reluctantly she slipped it off and handed it to him. Her transformation was not wasted on Dominic. He hesitated so long to examine her that the others caught on that something was afoot, and all eyes turned in her direction.

Becoming aware of her embarrassment, Dominic apologised and pulled her chair away from the table for her. Thankfully she sat down. Taking his place beside her he murmured, 'You look fantastic.'

'Thank you. The dress isn't a bit over the top, then?'

He laughed. 'Just the opposite! It's way below it.' Her colour deepened and he said, reassuringly, 'It's perfect.'.

Dennis caught her eye across the table and winked and Agnes gave her the thumbs up sign. Tess relaxed and determined to enjoy herself.

In the Orpheus cloakroom Agnes delayed after Marie and Joan had left them. Those two hadn't even noticed the change in Tess, so wrapped up were they in plans for the wedding. This evening was supposed to be a break away from anything to do with the wedding, but no, that pair couldn't relax for even a couple of hours. Eyeing her friend from head to toe, Agnes said sincerely,

'You look lovely.' She had managed to stamp down the jealous pangs that reared their ugly head as she watched Dominic practically drool over Tess in the Steak House, reminding herself she was engaged to Tony.

With her friend's approval, Tess was content. She must look all right. However, Agnes couldn't resist teasing her. 'I don't know whether or not your mother would approve, mind.'

Tess grimaced. 'I can imagine her reaction, but if I have my way Mam will never set eyes on this dress.'

'If you are ever giving it away, remember we wear the same size,' Agnes remarked casually.

'I'll certainly bear that in mind,' Tess assured her. 'Though I can't see your mam being any more tolerant than mine. But thanks for your vote of confidence. I was feeling a bit overdressed.'

Agnes laughed aloud. 'In that skimpy outfit?'

Nudging her with her elbow, Tess retorted, 'You know what I mean. Shall we join the others?'

'Yes, let's.'

The evening proved to be the most memorable of Tess's young life. The dance floor was so crowded it wasn't important whether or not you knew the proper dance steps. Held clasped to Dominic's chest she relaxed and gave herself up to the rhythm of the music, swaying in perfect unison with his body.

At one point she became aware of her partner's close scrutiny and following the direction of his gaze realised he was examining the mole on her breast. Defensively her hand moved to try to cover the offending spot with some of the dress material. He caught her hand and, holding it tight in his, apologised.

'I'm sorry. But it is very eye catching, you know. Is it real?'

Her eyes widened and she gazed at him, uncomprehending.

He laughed and whispered in her ear, 'I can see that it must be. I should have known you wouldn't seek to attract attention by false means.'

Totally bewildered, she said, 'I don't know what you're talking about, Dominic.'

He sighed. 'I can see that. Don't ever let anyone take advantage of your honesty and charm, Tess. Would you like to sit this one out while I fetch you a drink?'

'That would be nice, thank you.'

Leading her back to the table, he excused himself and headed for the bar where soft drinks were served. She watched heads turn as he made his way round the edge of the dance floor and was not surprised at the attention he received. He would stand out in any crowd. He was also the nicest man she had ever met. This girl back in Florida was very lucky. Very lucky indeed.

A breathless Agnes joined her at that moment and with a nod in Tess's direction Tony followed Dominic to the bar. 'I've been watching you,' Agnes said accusingly. 'You're having the time of your life.'

Confused, Tess asked, 'Are you not enjoying yourself?'

'It's run of the mill for me now with Tony. I've danced so often with him it doesn't excite me any more.'

Tess wanted to question her friend, ask if it had ever excited her, but bit back the words. This was neither the time nor the place to probe. 'I think anyone would enjoy dancing with Dominic.'

Agnes grinned but Tess thought it looked contrived. 'He's not just dancing with you. He's drooling all over you.'

'Don't be silly!'

'Are you saying he doesn't excite you?'

Tess gave this some consideration and smiled. 'I must admit I find him very attractive. In fact, I have to keep reminding myself he has a girl back in Florida.'

'You like him that much?' Agnes gasped.

Tess smiled and reassured her. 'Don't worry. Once bitten twice shy. Believe me, I'll keep control of my emotions.'

After a cool drink and a lot of enjoyable conversation Dominic asked Agnes to dance with him. As they moved on to the floor Tony gave a slight bow and invited Tess to follow them.

He smiled down at her. 'You look very attractive in that dress, Tess.'

'Thank you, kind sir.'

'Dominic is obviously smitten with you.'

'Well now, since he has a girlfriend back home and I think him a gentleman, I'll ignore that remark.'

'Oh . . . is he engaged, then?'

'I don't think he's actually engaged, as far as a ring is concerned, but he has a close friend.'

'Agnes never mentioned it.'

'Why should she? She probably thinks you wouldn't be interested.'

For some moments Dominic and Agnes danced in silence. He was marvelling at the blonde halo of hair around a pert, exquisite face. He loved the feel of her in his arms; the closeness of her body. The tantalising memory of her lips under his. He was determined to hold her as far away as possible so she wouldn't realise the effect she was having on him. He didn't think she would take kindly to it, her being engaged to another man. Tony Burke was a very lucky fellow.

Agnes felt affronted, remembering how he had talked and laughed and drooled all over Tess. Why wasn't he talking to her? Did he dislike dancing with her that much? With Tess he had seemed so relaxed, whilst now he was stiff and unbending. Deciding to try to find out why, she broke the silence.

Looking up at him through long silky lashes, she asked softly, 'Am I boring you, Dominic?'

'No. Not in the slightest.'

Hmm! That bit of conversation didn't lead to anything, she thought. Changing tack, she said, 'Perhaps I should warn you that Tess has had a nasty experience with a boy. It took her a while getting over it. You'll be careful of her feelings, won't you?'

He looked down at her through narrowed lids. 'Tess doesn't appear to be nursing a broken heart as far as I can see.'

'No, not any more she's not. But do be careful, won't you? Remember, you're not a free agent.'

'Are you warning me off?' he muttered incredulously. 'Surely Tess can look after herself?'

'Of course she can!'

'Then why the concern?'

'Because I don't want her to be hurt again.'

He swung her round in a reverse turn to face the opposite direction. 'Can you see Tony and Tess from here?'

'Yes, I can. Do you think I'm blind?'

'And you can see that Tess is laughing and talking to Tony, just like she behaves with me?'

Agnes nodded, at a loss to understand what he was implying.

'Does that not tell you anything, Agnes?'

'No. Should it?'

'That's the first time tonight I've seen Tony look happy and relaxed. You and he dance round the floor as if you have been married about twenty years.'

Tight lipped, she glared at him. 'Remember, I was brought up never to be a temptation to the opposite sex. No long kisses or close embracing. Surely you were taught the same, Dominic? Surely the Christian brothers were as strict as the nuns where morality is concerned? Tony was reared the same as me, and we are saving ourselves for after our marriage.' She was so angry she almost stamped her foot. He might have lived in America for a long time but he grew up on the Springfield Road just as she had.

'Oh, yes. The brothers were very strict but us lads were not as easily influenced as you girls. Are you saying Tony has agreed to all this waiting?'

Now she was really angry. 'Yes, he has!' she hissed.

'Then he is a bigger fool than I thought he was.'

'He respects me.'

He changed course. 'All right. What about Tess? Does she not agree with what the nuns preached?'

'Huh! Even more so than me.'

'You wouldn't think it, to look at her. She's so relaxed and normal.'

'Are you insinuating that there is something wrong with me?'

'No . . .'

'You sound dubious.'

He shrugged. 'I just don't understand you.'

'Fortunately you don't have to.'

'No.' He sounded sad and her eyes questioned him. 'So long as Tony does. Does it not worry you that he dances so close with Tess?'

'Why should it? I trust him.'

'Are you not afraid that all kinds of thoughts may be going on in that head of his while he gazes down at that neckline?'

'The way they do when you dance with her, you mean?' she asked sarcastically.

He smiled. 'Mm. Maybe.'

She gave a very definite shake of the head. 'Tony isn't anything like you! He wouldn't ever think like that about Tess, or any woman, for that matter.'

'Hah! So it's a saint you're engaged to? Or are you implying that Tess Maguire isn't attractive enough to interest the opposite sex?'

'No! I'm not implying anything of the sort. She's lovely! Especially in that dress.'

'But you don't think Tony may be tempted by her closeness? Remember, he's holding her much closer than he holds you.'

Agnes twisted round to have another look at the other couple. She could see nothing untoward. Dominic watched her with laughing eyes. He was enjoying teasing Agnes; she was so uptight about everything. Then she flashed him a look of complete bewilderment and he caught a glimpse of the misery shadowed in her eyes, and shame smote him. 'I'm sorry, Agnes. I'm only teasing. I always seem to rub you up the wrong way.'

'No,' she said sadly. 'No, it's me. I don't seem to have a sense of humour where you're concerned.'

Annoyed at himself for having upset her, he apologised. 'I'm sorry. Really sorry. I don't know what gets into me when I'm with you.' The dance was drawing to an end and she twisted from his hold and headed for the table. He followed her and once she was seated he excused himself and left the room.

He was disgusted with himself. Why did he let her

get to him like this? Tormenting her like that on the dance floor. Ridiculing her choice of husband. Laughing at her morals. It was cruel! He ought to be horse-whipped. What did it matter to him that she was an ice queen? It was Tony she was going to marry. It was some time before he felt enough in control to return to the ballroom and face her. He had decided to ask her to dance with him again and try to put things right between them. But he warned himself not to be surprised if she refused.

Disgruntled, Agnes watched him go. What did Dominic have against her? She just wanted him to be her friend. Treat her like he treated Tess. As if she had summoned her, a breathless Tess sank down on to the chair next to hers. 'Where's Dominic? Surely you can't have lost him already.'

Agnes looked at her glowing features and said sourly, 'How do I know where he is? I'm not his keeper. And I wish you would try to look intelligent for a change, Tess. You've been acting like the laughing cavalier all evening.'

'Agnes!' Tony cried, aghast. 'What's got into you?'

Tess looked stunned. 'What on earth do you mean?'

Throwing an apologetic glance in her friend's direction, Agnes muttered, 'I'm sorry. Please forgive me, Tess. And will you both excuse me?' Grabbing hold of her handbag she literally ran from the table.

Tony rose to his feet but Tess motioned him to sit down again. She nodded reassuringly at him. 'Don't worry. I'll see what ails her.' She followed Agnes to the cloakroom, where she discovered Marie and Joan, whom they had seen little of all evening as they had spent most of the time in a corner with their partners going over wedding details, hovering around Agnes trying to find out what had upset her.

'I was just overcome with the heat! That's all. Nothing to worry about.'

Tess stood to one side for some moments and silently watched the trio. She could understand why the others were anxious, Agnes was as white as a sheet and trembling slightly. What on earth had affected her so?

Stepping forward she said, 'You girls go back to the lads. They'll be wondering what's happening. I'll look after Agnes.'

'Are you sure, Tess?' Marie turned gratefully to her and then back to her sister. 'If you want to go home, Agnes, let me know and I'll get Dennis to fetch the car,' she volunteered.

'I feel fine now. Just leave me be. Go on, leave me alone.'

The others reluctantly withdrew and Tess hovered solicitously over her friend. 'What on earth happened?'

'Nothing!'

'Come off it, Agnes, you're not in this state over nothing. Did Dominic say something to offend you?'

'No. He didn't say anything.' Heading for a cubicle, Agnes said, 'Look, Tess, do you mind? I'd really like to be alone for a few minutes. I'll come back to the table presently.'

'All right, but don't be too long or I'll come looking for you.'

'I won't. I promise.' Agnes smiled but the misery reflected in her eyes tore at her friend's heart. What could have happened, to affect her so?

Back at the table there was still no sign of Dominic. When he saw her, Tony bounded to his feet and came hurriedly to meet her. 'Where's Agnes? Is she all right?'

Tess nodded. 'She'll be here in a few minutes. I think the heat got to her.'

Dominic arrived on Tess's heels and was relieved to find that he had been reprieved and didn't have to face Agnes just yet. 'Would anyone like a drink?' he asked. He looked pale and worried and Tess decided to find out just what was going on.

'You wait here for Agnes, Tony. I'll go to the bar with Dominic.' She was determined to get to the bottom of this; Dominic had yet to look her straight in the eye and as they waited to be served she asked directly, 'What happened back there?'

'Nothing. No matter what I say, I seem to rub Agnes up the wrong way. She's a very prickly person. Has no sense of humour whatsoever.'

'On the contrary, her sense of humour is above reproach. I think it's all this talk about weddings that's getting her down.'

'I don't buy that. She's not even excited about her own wedding.'

'I know that. But then, it might never happen.'

Suddenly she had all his attention. 'Why do you say that?'

'She only got engaged to Tony because he produced the ring and asked her to marry him in front of a lot of people. Otherwise I'm sure she would have put him off.'

He sounded bemused. 'No wonder she seems indifferent to him.' Sensing Tess's surprise, he added, 'And here I am teasing her. Still, she should loosen up a bit. She takes life far too seriously.'

Determined to defend her friend, Tess said, 'It was the heat! She was too hot and that's why she left the dance floor.'

'No, I was teasing the life out of her and she couldn't take it. I wish now I'd minded my own business. I deliberately pointed out to her how relaxed Tony was with you. When they dance together they're like an old married couple.'

Whilst silently agreeing with him that all was not well with her friend's relationship, Tess nevertheless did not want to discuss Agnes's engagement with him. She shrugged. 'We're all different. Have different ways of showing affection.' Didn't she know how different? Suddenly startled, she cried, 'Look! Agnes and Tony have just left the room and she has her coat on. They must be going home.'

She started to cross the room but with a hand on her arm Dominic stopped her. 'Let her go.'

'She might need me.'

'For heaven's sake catch yourself on! She's with Tony. Why would she want you?'

His voice was so sharp she drew back and gaped at him. 'She's my best friend, so she is! I worry about her.'

He released his hold on her. 'I'm sorry. By all means go after her. I don't know when to keep my big mouth shut.'

Tess dithered. Dominic was right. Agnes was with Tony; the man she was betrothed to. She hadn't even bothered to say good night to them. 'You're right. I don't know why I feel so protective of her.'

There were still a few people ahead of them waiting to be served and he turned to her. 'Are you very thirsty? Shall we forget about these drinks and dance the night away?'

She nodded and willingly entered his arms. This was her night and nothing and nobody must be allowed to spoil it.

* * *

The rest of the evening passed in a whirl. Dominic was a wonderful companion, teasing and flirting with her. She thought him delightful. How come Agnes couldn't get on with him?

It was with reluctance that she sought out Joan at the end of the evening to go to the cloakroom to collect their coats.

She found Joan very subdued. 'Why so quiet? Did you and Brian not enjoy yourselves?'

'To be truthful, Marie and I are worried about Agnes. Marie was surprised when Tony came and asked if they could go home early. It's not like Agnes to want to leave anywhere early. Do you think she's sickening for something?'

Tess was immediately concerned. She had not considered a physical cause for her friend's apparent illness. Not wanting to involve Dominic, she said apprehensively, 'I hope not, with the wedding so near. No, I think it was just the heat getting to her.'

'I hope you're right.' Joan didn't sound in the least confident.

Collecting their coats they made their way outside to where the others were waiting to walk them to the car park.

Outside her home Dominic insisted on leaving the car and escorting her to the door. She smiled up at him. 'Thank you for a marvellous evening. I've never enjoyed myself so much.'

'The pleasure was all mine. Listen, I've persuaded Dennis to let me have the loan of the car tomorrow. Will you come out for a run along the coast with me?'

'That sounds wonderful. I'll get in touch with Agnes in the morning and see if she is well enough to come.'

'No. Let Agnes and Tony have some time together. I've been thinking that maybe I've been crowding her and Tony doesn't like it. I don't want to be a bone of contention between them. I want you to come out alone with me. I promise not to tease or do anything to annoy you. Cross my heart and hope to die.' He made a big cross on his chest and she laughed.

'Hah! Tease all you like. I think I'll be able to handle you.'

Cupping her face in his hands he whispered, 'You're so sweet . . . I wish . . .'

What he wished she wasn't to hear. With a light kiss on the lips, he said, 'Good night. I'll ring you in the morning,' and joined the others in the car. She stayed at the door and waved as it drew away from the kerb and headed up the road, before she entered the house.

Hugging herself with happiness, she waltzed down the hall and around the kitchen. She could become very fond of Dominic Sullivan if she wasn't careful. Was he really serious about this girl, Stella? Behave yourself, Tess warned. Remember you vowed you would enjoy whatever came, no strings attached. Roll on tomorrow.

Early on Sunday morning Tess rang Agnes to inquire how she felt. It was Mrs Quinn who answered the phone.

'She's still in bed, Tess. Do you want me to give her a shout?'

'No, it is quite early. I'll ring later on. How is she?'

'She went straight to bed when she came home from the dance last night, saying she had a headache. Other than that she seemed all right to me.' Worry crept into her voice. 'Is there anything I should know?'

'No. No, she left the dance early and I just wanted to make sure she was all right.'

'I'll get her to give you a ring when she gets up, Tess. Okay?'

'That will be great, Mrs Quinn. A happy Easter to you and the family.'

'Thank you. And the same to you, Tess. Goodbye, love.'

A couple of hours later Agnes still hadn't rung. Not wishing to interfere, Tess resisted the impulse to call her again. She didn't want Mrs Quinn to start questioning her daughter.

She would have to be patient and wait until Agnes got in touch with her.

Chapter Nine

There was a great big bubble of anticipation in Tess's heart as she prepared for twelve o'clock Mass in Clonard Monastery. It was another sunny day with bright blue skies and just a hint of a breeze and she knew a lot of the outfits and children's clothes that she had made would be on parade this Easter day. She always got the satisfied feeling of a job well done on these occasions, as she watched her handiwork pass up and down the aisles. Afterwards, Dominic was picking her up to go for a drive along the Antrim coast and she had prepared a picnic lunch to take along. She couldn't contain her excitement; at this moment in time life couldn't be any better.

As she mingled with the congregation leaving the church after Mass, exchanging greetings, a familiar face caught her eye. Theresa Cunningham, the young woman who had trained her in the Belart factory, was coming towards her. Tess had heard that Theresa had bought a house further up the Springfield Road a couple of years ago but this was the first time she had run into her. Theresa met her gaze and a pleasant smile relaxed her rather stern features.

They greeted each other and fell into step along Dunmore Street. 'It's a long time since I last saw you,

Tess Maguire, but I've been hearing all sorts of good reports about your factory.'

'Ah, dear God, surely they're not calling my work room a factory?' Tess laughed. 'I work from home, Theresa.'

'I know you do, but people do tend to exaggerate. Especially if they like you and you're doing well. Mind you, any reports I hear about your work are all good.'

'Thank God for that at least. Mam and I aren't doing too badly at the moment. In fact we were thinking of taking on a trainee stitcher,' Tess couldn't help boasting proudly. 'What about you? Are you still in the Belart?'

'No. I had to leave work some months ago. After me breaking out and investing in a more upmarket house. You see my mother fell ill and can't be left on her own for long periods. I don't want to put her into a nursing home. Not unless it becomes absolutely necessary. But it was either that or leave the Belart.' She sighed. 'I chose the latter.'

In times past Tess had met Mrs Cunningham in town when she was out with her daughter and had thought her a nice person. 'I'm sorry to hear that, Theresa. Give her my regards, won't you? Do you like living on the Springfield Road?'

'I must confess I do. In spite of everything, I'm glad I moved when I had the opportunity.'

They had reached the corner of Dunmore Street, from where Tess would go down Springfield Road and Theresa in the opposite direction.

'Goodbye, then. It was nice seeing you again.' Tess made to leave, but Theresa hesitated and Tess paused to hear what she had to say.

'You say you are taking on a trainee stitcher?'

Mystified at her interest, Tess said, 'Well . . . I've been

threatening to do so for some time now, but it's getting the right person. I will eventually get round to it. Why? Do you know anyone suitable?'

'Would you not be better taking on a qualified stitcher? Someone who knows all the ropes?'

'I wish I could. But unfortunately I can't afford anyone like that. We wouldn't have enough work in at any one time to justify taking on a trained stitcher.'

'Would you consider taking me on . . . on a part-time basis, that is, say a couple of afternoons a week? I wouldn't expect top wages, but a small steady income would augment the money me and Mam have coming in weekly. It would also protect the savings I have salted away for a rainy day. And, as you know, I'm more than capable of doing any job you'd give me.'

Tess studied her for a moment. 'But what about your mother?'

'I'd be all right as far as that's concerned. A friend comes to visit her two or three afternoons a week so there would be no problem me getting away. In fact they'd be glad to get rid of me for a while. And I'd only be down the road if I was needed in a hurry. You are on the phone, aren't you, Tess?'

Caught on the hop, Tess was looking at her, tongue-tied. Embarrassment brought extra colour to Theresa's face. 'Look, Tess, I'm sorry for putting you on the spot like this.' She hastened to add, 'What if I give you my telephone number and if you think it would work out, you could give me a ring. If I don't hear from you, I'll understand. Okay? There will be no hard feelings.'

Tess was in a quandary. Theresa had trained her in her first two years in the Belart factory. How would she cope with being on the other side of the fence; taking orders from Tess? 'Tell you what . . . I'll talk it over with

Mam. She's in Carlingford at the moment, but I'll let you know next week what we decide, one way or the other.'

Theresa rummaged in her bag and produced a pen and an old envelope. 'Thanks, Tess. And remember, I'll understand no matter how you decide.' Quickly jotting down her telephone number she handed it to Tess and with a final farewell hurried away.

Dominic was so easy to talk to that Tess found herself confiding in him about her conversation with Theresa.

'You know this lady?' he asked gravely.

'Yes. She taught me everything I know about the rag trade.'

He sat in thought for some moments. 'If I were going to start someone new in my kitchen, I'd prefer a mature person who knows all the ropes, and would be willing to work part time say two, maybe three days a week, to having the bother of training a greenhorn. That's just my opinion, of course. You see, while you're training a new hand to your procedures you're not doing any real constructive work yourself, and as there's only your mother and yourself in the business you could soon find yourself falling behind in your work programme. I am assuming of course that you do work to a planned schedule. You see what I'm getting at? You'll find yourself spending too much valuable time with the trainee or watching every move she makes. In no time at all you'll let some customer down and that could cost you dearly in the long run. You might make the excuse that it's only one customer. So what? But that could be a very big mistake to make; the turning point in a successful business. That disgruntled customer will tell another of your customers, there's no doubt whatsoever about that, and it will soon snowball. If you're not very careful, you could soon find yourself facing bankruptcy. I'm not telling you any old cock and bull story, Tess. I've seen it happen before in the States and it will happen again, so be very careful and give it a lot of thought before coming to a decision.'

Tess sat through this lecture in silence taking in every single word, occasionally nodding in agreement. 'Phew! That was certainly laying it on the line. I was thinking along those lines myself, actually. Not in such depth, though. Nevertheless you have made me aware of the pitfalls I could face if I took on a trainee. I'll see what Mam has to say when she returns. Thanks for lending me your ear – I'll give it back to you tomorrow – and thanks for your valued advice.'

'Any time, Tess . . . What are you going to give me back tomorrow?'

'It was a joke.'

The outing along the Antrim coast was a great success. They had their picnic on Fair Head at Ballycastle overlooking the sea towards Rathlin Island. They sat in a sheltered spot and as he viewed the lush green grass and gently swaying bushes around them, and the choppy blue-green waters below, Dominic confided wistfully, 'I really miss Ireland, you know, Tess.'

'Why did you leave?'

'Oh, me and Dad had a big row. He had all these grand ideas for his eldest son but I didn't want my life laid out for me by someone else. He thought he knew best and wouldn't listen to reason, so I made my own plans on the QT and when I had everything arranged I announced I was going to America to work. You can imagine the reception that got. I was called all sorts of unrepeatable names and warned never to come back. That's why I've never been home before. I was surprised when our Dennis wrote and asked me to be best man. He said my dad had no objections, so here I am.'

'But now you're here, why not stay? Have your parents forgiven you?'

'I think so. I know Mam is happy enough and would be glad if I stayed, but Dad is another matter. I think he's having me stay on sufferance to please Mam and Dennis, who is now his blue-eyed boy.'

'If you stayed here, I'm sure he'd come round in time to your way of thinking, and surely with all your experience you could open your own restaurant here?'

'Yes, that would be no problem. And I know I'd have no trouble selling my business in America, but . . .'

'You're thinking of Stella,' Tess guessed. 'Would she not agree to coming over here to live?'

'No. I'm afraid she wouldn't.' He turned a mischievous smile on her. 'I've a confession to make as far as Stella is concerned. You see, I failed to mention that she is happily married to a friend of mine.'

Tess blinked in confusion. 'But . . . but why didn't you say?' Comprehension dawned and she gasped, 'I know why! You don't want any romantic complications here in Belfast. Isn't that it?'

'No. You're wrong. You and Agnes assumed I was committed to Stella so I let you believe it. After all, what difference does it make?' Tess sat silent and he said, 'You're not annoyed at me, surely?'

'No. I just can't understand your reasoning. Were you afraid someone might make a pass at you? Try to get you to stay?'

He gazed across the water. 'On the contrary, I was big-headed enough to think perhaps I'd fall in love with an Irish colleen, sweep my heart's desire off her feet, and take her back to Florida with me. However, it's not to be. It would cause a terrible upheaval. Remember, I told you I was an old romantic at heart? Well, I really am. And I don't want to cause any bother to anybody. So far everyone I've met is very committed to their families and careers and that's the way it should be. I doubt if anyone would consider leaving this beautiful country, and to be truthful I don't blame them.'

Tess wished he would make himself a bit clearer. Had he a particular girl in mind? He sounded as if he had met someone he could care for. Could it possibly be her? Hadn't he told her just last night how sweet he thought her? Did he think she wouldn't leave her mother and her wee business? Well, he was right on that count. That was something she would be very reluctant to do. But hadn't he just implied that he missed his homeland and would like to come back?

He saw her bewilderment and reached for her hand. 'Tess, don't worry your head about me, I'm a survivor. I have however decided not to prolong the agony. I intend cutting short my holiday. I'll only be staying one month instead of two, as I had intended.'

She turned her head away so that he wouldn't see her disappointment. 'I'm sorry to hear that, Dominic. I'll miss you.'

Hand under her chin, he turned her face towards him. 'Let's not spoil our day out.' His lips met hers and she responded to them willingly. It was a tender kiss but when she would have moved closer he gently released her and rising to his feet assisted her up. 'Well, where do we go from here?'

She knew he wasn't alluding to the kiss but to the next stage of their journey and said, 'Let's have a look at that map.' After all, she still had over two weeks to get him to change his mind.

Tess opened her eyes to bright sunlight streaming in through her bedroom window and thanked God for another lovely day.

It was Easter Monday and she dressed with care to go down to St Paul's Church to the Nuptial Mass and to see all the wedding finery. From now on she would be out to make a big impression on Dominic every chance she got. To this end her make-up took much longer than usual to apply, and she fussed over her hair before settling the small close-fitting hat on the bright curls until everything was to her complete satisfaction. After a final look in the full length mirror and a pleased smile at her reflection, she made a final unnecessary adjustment to her skirt and left the house.

She was glad her mother was away from home or she would have smelt a rat long ago and known a man must be involved. How she now wished she was going to the reception. She was convinced that all the single girls would be attracted to Dominic. How could they help it? As far as she was concerned he was the bee's knees.

Arriving at the church early, Tess chose a pew at the front of the left hand aisle where she would have a clear view of the centre altar where the ceremony would be performed. Dennis, looking nervous, was already seated. Dominic in the role of best man was whispering in Dennis's ear, obviously reassuring his brother. Tess wanted to feast her eyes on Dominic without his being aware that she was there and this was the ideal spot for doing so.

Marie seemed to float up the aisle, hand resting lightly on her father's arm. She looked like a fairy tale princess, her face shining luminously through the fine veil, and Tess thought how beautiful she looked. Her shimmering white silk, figure-hugging dress had a long train that swept out in her wake. She carried a bouquet of roses and lilies of the valley, and young Amy walked in front looking like a small replica of the bride, scattering flower petals as she went. Behind the bride came Agnes and Joan, their dresses a warm shade of primrose.

Agnes had failed to get in touch with Tess the day before and she, taking umbrage, had made no further attempt to break the silence between them. She sorely regretted this when she saw her friend. Agnes looked so pale and fragile Tess's heart went out to her. Perhaps Joan was right and she really was sickening for something. Turning to enter the front centre pew Agnes caught Tess's eye and gave her a nervous smile. Anxious to make amends, Tess mouthed the words *See you outside* and received a nod in reply.

Throughout the service Tess found her eyes returning again and again to Dominic. He stood a head above everyone nearby, and was a commanding figure in his grey morning suit, snowy white shirt and silver cravat. The ceremony was conducted with great sincerity and the mothers of both bride and groom were in tears. Tess had a lump in her own throat as she watched them and was glad when the bridal group finally disappeared into the vestry to sign the register.

Wishing to catch Agnes before she got caught up in the taking of photographs, Tess hurried outside to wait at the church doors for the wedding group to come out. She also wanted to convey her best wishes to the bride and groom. As her eyes ranged over the crowd milling about she noted that quite a few of the wedding guests were young, attractive women and her heart sank. She could only hope that most of them were married.

Dominic spotted her immediately and, ignoring those who were seeking his attention, came to her side. She glowed with pride, glad she had worn her pale green tailored suit and close-fitting hat as his eyes swept over her from head to toes.

'You look lovely,' he greeted her. Leaning closer he whispered, 'I can't understand why you weren't invited to the reception. I'll miss you.'

'It, as you well know, is being held in Belfast Castle and will cost a fortune, and' – she nodded to the crowd milling about – 'you'll soon find consolation.'

'One more guest wouldn't have broken them, I'm sure.'

She shrugged. 'One has to draw the line somewhere, Dominic.'

They were calling for him to come over for the photographs. He sighed. 'I hate getting my photo taken. I feel such a fool in this gear.'

She wanted to tell him that he looked just wonderful but thought he was already well aware of the fact. 'You're keeping everybody waiting. You'd better get yourself over and into that group,' she said, giving him a slight push in the right direction.

St Paul's Church, being situated on the junction of the Falls Road and Cavendish Street, had no suitable background for photographs so only a few were snapped at the church doors before the group broke up and piled into the waiting limousines to go to Belfast Castle and its beautiful grounds to continue the photography session in more picturesque surroundings.

Before leaving, Agnes hurried over to Tess. 'I'm sorry about the way I've been behaving. I would have phoned Sunday afternoon but Joan told me you were away for a run in the car with Dominic. Where did you go? Did you have a nice time?'

'Along the Antrim coast, and we had a marvellous day. Dominic certainly knows how to treat a woman.' A frown puckered her brow. 'I can't understand why you've gone off him, Agnes. It's not like you. What on earth did he say to offend you?'

'I haven't gone off him,' Agnes hastened to assure her. 'I think he's great. It was all a silly misunderstanding. I'll ring you tomorrow. Okay?'

With that Tess had to be content but she was still worried about her friend, she looked so pale and tense.

Dan found the time dragging without his dates with Alice. He had been a loner before but all that had changed since Alice had come into his life. If only he were free. He wished Anne would conveniently fall under a bus or something. He immediately asked God's forgiveness for such dark thoughts. It was because he was afraid of losing Alice. She was a very attractive woman, after all, and he was inclined to think that some of the locals in Carlingford would indeed be paying her attention. And why not? How could they help it? Had she already met someone else? Perhaps some guy who wasn't short of a bob or two. A man who would be able to give her the kind of life she deserved. He thought he'd go crazy thinking about it.

But no matter, he decided. First things first. All his attention must be given to making his son's twenty-first birthday a time to remember. Nothing must be allowed to spoil Jack's great day. Dan would concentrate on that; push all else to the back of his mind. He had the motorbike, a table booked for a meal, in the International Hotel no less, so that much was settled. Now he must buy a helmet and gauntlets. He intended letting Jack pick his own leathers but a helmet was essential because it was only to be expected that Jack would want to go for a run on the bike right away. Colette would probably accompany him so he would have to splash out on two helmets.

His shopping didn't take up too much time and Easter passed quietly as far as he was concerned. Colette and Jack had packed haversacks and a tent and gone to Bray Head for the long weekend. Dan spent most of his time alone, thinking about and longing for Alice.

On Tuesday on his way home from work he went to the public phone in the Clock Bar and, as promised, rang Alice. He was all keyed up, had been thinking all day about seeing her tomorrow; planning how he would ask her to accompany them to the International Hotel. Would she agree to come, after all the hurt Jack had caused her daughter?

He was gobsmacked when Alice informed him that she intended staying on an extra few days. It was like a betrayal, after the fuss she had made about going in the first place. She explained that she was staying to please her friend Rose as she had asked her to accompany her to a wedding.

Dan's heart sank. He couldn't believe that Alice was putting Rose in front of him. Were his fears to be realised? Was there some old fellow lurking in the background plying her with compliments and gifts?

'I see,' he said, at a loss for words.

'I'll come home Saturday,' Alice promised, and paused, expecting him to say he would be at the station to meet her. To her surprise he made no such offer. 'Are you still there, Dan?'

'Yes, I'm still here. Forgive me, but I never dreamt

you'd stay on.' He wanted to add that he missed her sorely but refrained. Obviously she wasn't missing him. 'I'll see you sometime on Saturday, Alice. That is if you're not too tired. Goodbye for now, dear.'

Crushed with disappointment, he went to the bar and ordered a double Black Bush. Downing it in two gulps, he was about to order the same again but, realising the futility of it, left the bar and headed back to his empty house.

To his surprise Anne waylaid him on the way down Spinner Street. He was so deep in thought that he didn't see her until it was too late to avoid contact. She was hovering in the doorway of Lily Brady's house and as he passed by a hand shot out and grabbed his arm. 'A word, please, Dan.'

He glanced at his watch. 'It had better be a quick one. It's my turn to make the tea and I'm running late as it is.'

'Right. I'll make it as short as possible. Unless . . . would you be agreeable to my making the tea for you and Jack tonight? We could talk as I cook.'

'No, thank you. I'm not that desperate.'

'You're a hard man, Dan Thompson.'

'Not really. Not with everyone. Just those I don't have any time for.'

She bit nervously on her lip. He certainly didn't pull his punches. She forced herself not to retaliate. This was important to her. 'Dan, I think you're being very mean not allowing me to come to my own son's birthday dinner. After all, he only comes of age once and it should be a family affair.'

He looked down his nose and examined her through narrowed lids. 'Should it, now?'

'Yes, it should. You know quite well he wants me to

be there. Why, he was so embarrassed when he explained you didn't want me to come, I felt heartsore for him.'

'Did he also tell you that I offered to let you take my place? Still my treat, mind you, but he refused to consider it?'

'No. No, he didn't say.'

'It's true. You see, Anne, you offended Colette when you broke her confidence. That's not something she'll willingly forgive.'

'What do you mean? Colette and I have spoken since that episode. She has forgiven me.'

'Forgiven? Oh, yes, I can imagine her pretending to forgive you for the sake of peace. But somehow or other I don't think she'll go out of her way to seek your company ever again.'

'So that's a definite no, then?'

'Very much so, I'm afraid.'

'Tell me, Dan. Have you met someone who is really special to you? I've been told that you haven't bothered with another woman all these years.'

'Now I wonder who told you that? Lily Brady, I suppose. And how would she know? Eh? Just because I don't bring women home with me doesn't mean I'm not seeing them. As for whether or not I've met someone special, well, that's none of your business. Anyway, why the sudden interest?'

She leaned closer. 'Because if you have met someone and she doesn't come up to scratch, remember I still think we could make a go of it. I made you happy once and I can do it again.'

His head swayed from side to side and he smiled mockingly. 'Do you know something, Anne? I wish you had never come back into our lives. No one wants you about here.'

'Jack does! Only he doesn't want to offend you. But I'll continue to work on him and see what happens. I might not be at his twenty-first birthday dinner, but you mark my words, Dan Thompson! I'll certainly be at his wedding. And there is damned little you can do about it.'

'Over my dead body,' he muttered as he turned away.

'Stranger things have happened,' she hissed after him.

Bob Crosby had been decent enough in his offer to come in to work early Thursday morning so that Dan could get into the yard for the bike before Jack awoke for his breakfast. Between them they decorated the bike with balloons and a huge birthday card saying 'Happy 21st Birthday' and wheeled it along the pavement to set it outside Dan's door.

'Thanks, Bob. I owe you a pint . . . or two. I can't wait to see Jack's face when he sees it.'

'To be truthful, neither can I.'

'I'll give you a shout.'

'No need to do that. I'll be watching out for him,' Bob laughed.

Jack awoke, stretched, looked at his bedside clock and snuggled back down under the blankets again with a contented sigh. It was his birthday, he had two days off work, and he could have a lie in. At least that was his intention. The noise coming from downstairs was enough to waken the dead. What on earth was his dad up to so early in the morning?

Pulling on an old pair of jeans and a pullover, Jack descended the stairs, hair tousled and still half asleep. He was surprised to see his father sitting at the table eating his breakfast.

'What on earth are you doing? I thought you were

taking a day off work and we'd have a lie in. And what was all that noise about?'

'I couldn't sleep, son. It was those ones out there that were kicking up a racket.' Dan stabbed his fork in the direction of the front window and managed to hide a smile as Jack went to investigate.

Dan heard his gasp of surprise and joined him at the window. 'Well, say something! Do you like it or not?'

'You mean it's really mine?' The words came out on a shrill, high-pitched note and Dan put an arm round his son's shoulders.

'It's really yours, son. Happy birthday.'

Jack headed for the door but Dan stopped him. 'You don't want to go out looking like that. I've boiled a kettle of water. Away and clean yourself up and put on some decent clothes.'

After a hurried wash and shave and a change of clothes, Jack went outside and walked round and round the bike, giving it a good examination. Tears pricked his eyes when he at last turned to his father.

'Thanks, Dad. It's beautiful. If you'd asked me what I wanted for my twenty-first, and money no object, I'd have chosen a Triumph motorbike.'

'You're welcome, son. I'm glad you like it. Hold on a minute.' Dan entered the house and came out holding the biker's helmet and gauntlets. 'I'll buy you the leathers at the weekend. I want you to pick your own.'

Carefully, Jack secured the helmet on his head. 'It's a perfect fit. You've thought of everything. Thanks, Dad.'

'Well then, let's see what you look like on it.'

Dan removed the decorations and Jack swung his leg over the bike and kicked the engine into life. It fired at the first attempt. When he twisted the throttle the engine responded with a healthy roar. As if summoned, Bob immediately came from the yard followed by his two workers, and Colette and her grannie appeared at their door in their dressing gowns and just stood there gawking.

Slowly Colette approached the bike and Jack cried, 'Get your clothes on, girl, and we'll go for a spin.'

Still she stood as if mesmerised. 'Is it yours?'

'Yes.' Jack grinned at his father. 'Dad's been spending all his savings on me.'

He sounded so pleased, Dan flushed with pleasure. 'You only come of age once, son,' he said gruffly.

Bob Crosby said, 'She's a good 'un, son. You should be proud to own her.'

'Oh, I am. I am. Believe me, Bob, I'll treasure it and look after it. I can't thank you enough, Dad.'

'Any time the yard is open you can keep it there at night, but I've a feeling we'll close too early to suit you.'

'Thanks for the offer, Bob, but I've already had a word with wee Mrs McAnulty.' Dan nodded to the end house on the other side of the street whose yard was covered in and had a large wooden gate for access. 'She has agreed to let him have a key to her yard.'

Bob saluted him. 'That's good thinking, Dan. Meanwhile, if you ever need me you know where I am. Come on, lads, no more skiving. Back to work.'

During this discourse Colette had disappeared indoors. Now she came out in warm clothes with a scarf around her head to protect it from the wind.

'Climb on, love, and let's see how fast we can go.' Jack couldn't keep the happy grin off his face. Seeing his mother slowly approaching, he waved excitedly. 'Mam, see what Dad bought me for my birthday.'

Anne came to a halt beside the machine, unable to hide the resentment on her face. 'It's just as well I bought

[204]

you that watch, otherwise you'd never have received such a wonderful present from your dad,' she replied sarcastically.

Dan heard these words as he came from the house with the other safety helmet for Colette. 'If he has any doubts, Jack has just to ask Bob Crosby how long the motorbike has been in his yard. Long before you had any notion of buying him anything.'

'Please, you two. Can we call a truce for today at least? Look, Mam, I'll pick you up at Lily Brady's at eleven tomorrow morning and take you for a run, okay? Let's go, Colette.'

Climbing on to the pillion seat, Colette put her arms round Jack's waist. 'Thanks a million for the helmet, Mr Thompson.' Without so much as a glance in Anne's direction she added, 'I'm ready, Jack.'

'Take care now, Jack. Don't go mad,' Dan warned.

'Don't worry, Dad. I'll just be feeling my way at first, until I get used to the feel of her. See you later.'

They shot off up the street as Dan yelled, 'Don't forget we're going out tonight.' Ignoring Anne completely he entered the house and closed the door before his wife had a chance to open her big trap again and take all the pleasure out of the occasion. And she was the one who could do just that.

Chapter Ten

On that Thursday night of Easter week a lot of wine was supped at the International Hotel with the appetising four-course gourmet dinner. They dallied over the meal, delighting in every delicious morsel, before retiring to the lounge for coffee and brandies. The evening that stretched before them proved to be a terrific success and Dan admitted to himself that he had been wrong in thinking that Tess would have been a more suitable partner for his son. Jack and Colette were obviously made for each other. He remembered his mother saying in the old days about apparently suited couples, 'When God made them, He matched them.'

It was a very merry trio that eventually arrived back at Spinner Street. As they stood giggling on the pavement outside Dan's door while he tried, unsuccessfully, with an unsteady hand, to find the keyhole, Mrs Burns opened her door and beckoned them in. A widow in her early seventies, she rarely left the house because of arthritis but liked dabbling about in the kitchen. She delighted in providing delicious dishes for her granddaughter and her friends. Now she pointed to the table on which stood a beautifully decorated birthday cake complete with twenty-one candles.

'Happy birthday, Jack.' She smiled happily at him.

Jack, who had adopted her as his grannie, carefully, so as not to cause her swollen joints any pain, lifted the small figure gently in his arms and kissed her tenderly on the cheek. 'Thanks, Grannie. It's beautiful. It was very thoughtful of you to bake it.'

An embarrassed smile crossed her face and she said gruffly, 'Put me down, you big fool, and I'll put the teapot on.'

'You'll do no such thing, Grannie!' Releasing her, Jack led her to the sofa. 'You sit yourself down there and I'll look after the tea.'

Colette had already beaten him to it. He followed her into the scullery and they grinned happily at each other as they waited for the kettle to boil.

Standing on tiptoe, Colette kissed him. 'Gran has been working on that cake all week. It's lovely, isn't it?'

'It's a work of art. Seems a shame to cut it. All those decorations must have taken hours. And I'm sure it will taste lovely too.'

Looking pleased at his praise, Colette agreed. 'You can be sure of that.'

'Your grannie is a wonderful wee woman.'

'Yes, she is. It's been a great night altogether, hasn't it?'

'It has,' Jack agreed. Gathering her close he wheedled, 'I don't suppose you'd agree to make it even better if I stayed behind when your gran retires to bed and Dad goes home?'

'Now you know my views on that, Jack Thompson! You'll have to hold yourself in check for another few months.'

'Oh, I suppose so. You're the boss. It's just I have this terrible fear that you'll meet someone else. Someone with a bit of money. You meet so many men through your work at the bank.'

Placing her hands against his chest, she gazed earnestly up at him. 'I love you, Jack Thompson. You're in my heart and in my mind. No one or nothing is going to change that. Money or no money. Now get that into your big thick skull.'

He still looked unconvinced. 'I love you so much. I can't believe you could possibly love me in return. I don't know what you see in someone like me.' They kissed again and not wanting to overstep the mark he fought down his rising passion and changed the subject. He hadn't given up hope, though. Perhaps she would change her mind later when they were alone. 'I hope this tea sobers me up a bit. I feel quite tipsy,' he confessed.

'So do I and I didn't drink half as much as you.'

Jack wagged a finger at her. 'Ah, but then, it's *my* birthday, and . . . I haven't to go to work in the morning,' he finished smugly.

She gave him a push. 'You lucky devil! Get out of my way and let me get the cups down. Away in and talk to your dad and my grannie.'

Dan had always found Mrs Burns a good conversationalist and Jack discovered them deep into current affairs. The escalation of American involvement in Vietnam was the topic of conversation so he sat down and listened.

The tea was poured and the cake cut and as they gathered around the table the troubles in south-east Asia were quickly forgotten.

Jack raised his cup. 'A toast to the three people who have made this such a wonderful day for me.' They all drank to that and then Dan went next door to fetch the beer and whiskey he had left in to finish off the celebrations.

*   *   *

Both father and son consumed too much that night, and as a result were nursing throbbing heads the following morning.

'I wish I hadn't told Mam I'd take her for a ride on my motorbike this morning.'

'I'd forgotten all about that. You'd be as well putting her off, son. Make another date. She'll understand.' Under his breath Dan muttered, 'Maybe.'

'Ah, Dad, I can't do that. She'll be ready and waiting. I can't let her down. You know what she's like.'

Dan rose to his feet, screwing his eyes closed and wincing as the sudden movement sent pain shooting through his head. 'I'll go up to Lily Brady's and explain to your mother . . .'

'No, Dad, please don't. She has missed out on so much, I feel sorry for her. I want to take her for a ride. I won't go far, I promise. Besides, I can't wait to get back on that bike. It's brilliant, so it is.'

'Do you feel well enough to go out on it? My head's throbbing. I certainly wouldn't fancy riding on a motorbike this morning, in my condition.'

'I don't think I'm quite as bad as you, Dad. My head's clearing already. But then, I didn't touch the whiskey and I have a cooked breakfast inside me. That's two things in my favour. Shall I phone work and explain you're feeling under the weather?'

'And have them all laughing up their sleeves at me? You'll do no such thing! A couple of aspirins and a mug of strong tea and I'll be as right as rain.'

'You really should eat that fry I've ready for you.'

'I couldn't face it, son. I believe aspirin and strong tea are the cure for a hangover. They've always worked for me in the past.'

With concern, Jack watched his father down some

aspirin tablets and drink a mug of strong tea before leaving the house, declaring himself fit and raring to go. In Jack's opinion he still looked a bit drunk.

Jack found that dunking his head under the cold water tap worked wonders at clearing the remaining cobwebs of his hangover. Once washed and shaved he was in fine fettle and ready for the road. Crossing the street, he opened the high wooden gate to Mrs McAnulty's yard and wheeled the bike outside, thrilled to the core to be the owner of such a fine machine.

Anne was ready and waiting and he was glad he hadn't put her off. 'How did your birthday treat go?'

'It was great, Mam. I'm sorry you couldn't be there.'

'Are you? I very much doubt that. I think with a little persuasion you could have gotten me invited,' she grunted sarcastically.

'That's not true, Mam! You know I wanted you there, but it was awkward. I wish things could be different, but I can't do anything about it.'

'You can.'

He looked bewildered. 'How?'

'Let's you and me find a flat where we can live together until your wedding. I know more about weddings than your dad ever could and with Colette's parents not wanting to be involved my experience could prove very helpful.'

'Colette's parents will be involved. They have agreed to accept me.'

'Is that good enough for you, son? To be accepted? To be tolerated!'

'Mam . . . as long as Colette loves me, that's all that matters. And anyway we don't see much of her family these days.' He was beginning to get a bit annoyed at her attitude. 'Are you coming for a ride or do you just want to stand there arguing?' She shrugged her shoulders and he handed her Colette's helmet.

She waved it away. 'I'm not going to wear that thing. It will ruin my new hair-do.'

He shrugged. 'Suit yourself. But we're not going anywhere unless you put it on.'

Reluctantly she donned the helmet and climbed on to the bike behind him.

'Hold on tight. Anywhere in particular you want to go?'

'No. I'm just happy to be with you, son,' she said, wishing to make amends for her bad behaviour.

'Okay, let's head up the Glen Road then. It's a long time since I've been up there. An old pal lives there near St Teresa's and I want to show off my new bike, if he's about. Right. Hang on, Mam. Here we go.'

Working automatically, Dan managed somehow to get through the morning, glad that he could almost do his job with his eyes shut. By lunch time his headache had subsided and, having skipped breakfast, he began to feel the pangs of hunger. Having neglected to bring any sandwiches with him, he went to the mobile cafe that parked outside the building site every work day and purchased a couple of bacon rolls and a mug of tea.

Choosing to sit a short distance from his noisy mates, who had been ribbing him all morning about his hangover, he was just finishing the last of his rolls and feeling much better for the nourishment when he saw Billy Robson, the foreman, leave the site office and walk towards the workers. Only then did he notice the police car parked in front of the office and a terrible premonition descended on him. A cold tremor went through his whole body. He knew it was bad news; just knew it!

Silence fell as Billy passed the rest of the gang. Followed by questioning stares and concerned looks, he continued to where Dan sat alone. When the foreman stopped in front of him and said, 'I'm sorry, Dan . . .' the howl that escaped Dan's lips and rent the air was almost inhuman.

The men were all on their feet, staring over, embarrassed, not knowing what was going on, not knowing what to say or do; how to be of help.

Billy patted his arm in futile comfort. 'The police want a word with you, Dan.'

'Is he . . . dead, Billy?'

'I don't know. They wouldn't tell me anything. Just said that your son's motorbike had been involved in an accident and they needed to speak to you.'

'Oh, my God. Oh, my God,' Dan whimpered, his mind spinning uncontrollably. He was afraid to rise, sure that his legs wouldn't support his large frame.

Holding out a helping hand, Billy said, 'Come on, Dan. They're waiting for you. You'll have to speak to them.'

Gripping the proffered hand, Dan allowed himself to be hauled up. He was glad to find that once upright he was steady enough on his feet, though somewhat shaky. 'Thanks, Billy.'

The police were very sympathetic and polite, explaining that no other vehicle was involved in the accident. Apparently, on the journey up the Glen Road, a dog had run out in front of the bike and Jack had swerved to avoid it. He lost control of the motorcycle and crashed head on into a stone wall. When the ambulance arrived he was declared dead at the scene but Dan's wife had survived, although she was in a critical condition in hospital.

'Have you any transport, Mr Thompson?' At his shake of the head the police offered to take him to the hospital where he would be required to formally identify his son's body.

He sat with his head buried in his large hands in the back of the police car beside the younger of the two constables, feeling as if he had fallen into a great chasm and couldn't get out. Surely he would wake up soon and discover it was all a bad dream. Suddenly Colette entered his head. 'Has Jack's girlfriend been notified?'

'I'm afraid we wouldn't know of any girlfriend, Mr Thompson. We were only told to contact you, being the next of kin,' was the polite reply.

'I understand.' Dan glanced at his watch. 'She will still be at work at the Northern Bank in the town centre. We can't have her finding out by herself. Will it be on the radio, do you think?'

'Most certainly, but your son's name will not be released until all the relatives have been informed.'

'But she will guess. You see, he only got the bike yesterday for his twenty-first birthday. She knows he's taking his mother for a spin on it today.'

The young constable looked aghast. What a tragedy! 'I'll radio in to the station and see if they can get someone to pick her up from the bank. Will we have them bring her to the hospital?'

'Yes, please.' Where else could she go? If she landed in on her grannie with this terrible news, the poor old dear might have a heart attack. She was so fond of Jack.

Dan was taken to the City Hospital. He had always hated the disinfectant smell that seemed to permeate all hospitals, but today it really turned his stomach and he had to fight down the bile that rose in his throat as the constable led him down some stairs and along a corridor until they were standing outside the mortuary door.

'Are you ready, sir?'

Drawing a deep breath, Dan nodded. 'As ready as I'll ever be.'

Inside there were banks of what looked like large stainless steel filing cabinets. An attendant stood by one of the cabinets, his hand poised over the handle, and waited for the constable to give the go-ahead nod before slowly pulling on the drawer. It slid out effortlessly and almost silently, befitting the atmosphere in the room, to its full extent. A sheet covered the body that rested within.

The sheet was solemnly drawn back and Dan, gripping the drawer tightly with both hands as if to support himself, gazed in sorrow on his only son. There wasn't a mark or cut to be seen on his face. Dan had been worried in case Jack was so badly damaged he would be unable to recognise him. His shoulders slumped as he relaxed a little. 'That's him. That's my Jack,' he managed to mumble.

He swayed slightly and the constable quickly stepped forward and gripped his arm to steady him. Dan's other hand locked in a vice-like grip on the young man's arm, 'He doesn't look dead!' he cried shrilly. 'Are you sure? How did he die?'

It was the mortuary attendant who answered him. 'We're quite sure, sir. It was probably a broken neck, but the post-mortem will show the cause. If it's any consolation, sir, death would have been instantaneous. He wouldn't have suffered.'

The police had been quick picking Colette up and she was sitting in the corridor, hands on her lap, twisting nervously at her handkerchief. She gazed with dread at Dan as he approached. 'It's true then? It really is Jack? I kept hoping that it was some terrible mistake.' She started to sob uncontrollably.

Dan nodded speechlessly. He knew what she meant. Hadn't he felt the same?

'Can I see him?'

Dan looked askance at the constable. He answered the mute question. 'If you think it's wise, sir.'

Dan turned to Colette. 'He's not marked. Not even a single bruise. You'd think he was just lying there sleeping. I think you'd be as well seeing him, love, or you won't be able to believe he's dead. I'll wait here for you.'

Fifteen minutes later Colette returned to the corridor as white as a sheet, tears pouring down her face, her mascara, usually so attractive, now a complete mess of black smudges and streaks as she dabbed at her eyes with her already tear-soaked hankie. Dan gathered her close, comforting her as best he could.

A hand on his shoulder brought him back to attention. 'Would you like to see your wife now, sir?'

Colette pulled away from Dan, gaping at him in horror. 'Is *she* still alive?'

He nodded. 'Would you like to come with me?'

'No! No, I wouldn't. It's not fair! How come *she* survived?'

'Hush now, love. The constable will think you don't like Anne. Will you wait for me?'

The policeman interrupted. 'We'll see her home, if you like, Mr Thompson.'

Colette would like! 'That will be great, thank you.' Colette quickly accepted the offer before Dan could intervene. How could she pretend she was glad that *that* woman was still alive, when her beloved Jack was dead?

[215]

She just couldn't do it. 'I'll see you later, Mr Thompson.' She wanted to be alone in the privacy of her own home, to try to come to terms with this nightmare, but she dreaded breaking the news to her grannie.

Anne lay in the high hospital bed looking small and vulnerable. Behind the oxygen mask that covered the lower part of her face, Dan could see that she was badly marked. Her hair was scraped back from her forehead and stitches ran from the corner of one eye and down the side of her left cheek. She had two black eyes and looked battered, as if she had just gone fifteen rounds with Cassius Clay.

'She's sedated,' the nurse explained.

'How bad are her injuries?'

'A broken wrist, two broken ribs and a badly bruised sternum, which is making breathing difficult for her at the minute. She has to go back to the operating theatre for exploratory surgery, to see if there is any internal damage to the chest cavity. She did get the worst of the impact.'

Dan rounded on her in a fury. 'Are you daft, woman? She's *alive*! My son is *dead*, for God's sake.'

The nurse drew back alarmed in the face of such venom. 'I was only explaining her condition, Mr Thompson, like you asked. I think you'd as well going home for a rest and coming back later. It's been a harrowing morning for you. If we need you, you'll be notified.'

Dan had every intention of going home. Anne was not his problem. He had a son to bury. He never stopped to wonder just whose problem Anne would be. The nurse looked after him in bewilderment. He had hardly looked at his wife! Hadn't even touched her hand as any normal husband would surely do. But then, he was probably in a state of shock, poor man. After all wasn't his son lying down in the morgue?

When Colette broke the news to Mrs Burns the small woman collapsed in a heap, sending her granddaughter into a state of sheer panic. She made to dash next door to get Dan's assistance but remembered in time that he wasn't there. She knew a doctor must be called out immediately, but how? She couldn't leave her grannie alone for any length of time. She saw Mrs McAnulty leave her house, and hailed her.

Once put in the picture wee Molly took control. 'Who's her doctor?'

'Dr Giles.'

'Same as myself. Look, love, Mrs Madden up the street has a phone. I'll get her to send for him.'

Dan arrived home in time to see Mrs Burns being stretchered into an ambulance and Colette clambering in after her.

He hurried forward. 'What's happened? Is Mrs Burns all right? Do you want me to come along, Colette?' The questions poured from his mouth.

'No, Mr Thompson, you have things to see to. I'll call in and see you when I get back. I'll tell you all about it then.'

Inside the house Dan sought the remains of the whiskey and poured himself a stiff drink before climbing the stairs. Colette was right, he had things to do. People to see. From the top of the wardrobe he removed an old battered shoe box and placed it on the bed. One by one he removed documents from it. When he came to his marriage certificate he paused, fighting the urge to rip it to shreds, but these were things you were supposed to keep safe so he set it down. Finding what he was looking for he put it to one side and, replacing the other documents, closed the box and put it back on top of the wardrobe.

Downstairs he smoothed out the Britannic insurance policy on the kitchen table. Would there be enough to bury Jack? He doubted it. No matter. Jack would go out in style, he'd make sure of that, should he have to beg, borrow or steal any extra money that may be required. Having settled that in his mind he cradled his head on his hands and gave way to his grief, great sobs ripping him apart and a sea of tears streaming from his eyes. How would he be able to bear this terrible tragedy? What had he done to deserve it?

He was awakened by a loud knocking on the door and the arrival of Bob Crosby and his workers to offer their condolences. He beckoned them in; offered them a drink which they declined, and thanked them for their trouble.

'If there's anything at all we can do, you know you only have to say the word. You know that, don't you, Dan?'

'I'll remember that, Bob.'

'Well then, we'll get back to work and leave you in peace. You look absolutely shattered, Dan, if you don't mind me saying so.'

'I am a bit tired. Thanks . . . lads, for coming over.'

They had no sooner gone than there was another knock on the door. This time it was Lily Brady.

'Dan, I've just heard the bad news. I'm so sorry.' She stood on the doorstep wringing her hands in despair. He reached for them and drew her into the house.

'Thanks, Lily. I don't how I'm going to manage, but I will . . . somehow.'

She waited, gazing speechlessly at him, obviously

expecting something more. He dithered, not knowing what she expected of him.

After a pause she blurted out, 'What about Anne? Wasn't she with him?'

He thumped his head with his fist. 'Good God! I'd completely forgotten about Anne. She's badly wounded, but I think they expect her to recover.'

Lily couldn't believe her ears. He sounded so indifferent. Didn't he care at all about the fate of his wife? 'Will they let me in to see her, do you think?'

'I don't see why not. And I'd be grateful if you would go. She's in the City Hospital. Awkward to get to from here. Will that be a problem, Lily?'

'No. My brother has a car; I'll get him to run me over after tea.' Lily continued to stare at him as if he had two heads. This man had been married to Anne and had lived with her here in this very house for twelve years and they had appeared happy enough at the time. Then to everybody's surprise Anne ran off with that guy from work. Now Dan didn't seem to care whether she lived or died. He was one hard-hearted bastard. 'Goodbye, Dan. I'll see myself out.' Poor Anne. Poor lonely Anne. What would become of her?

After Lily, a long string of friends, both Jack's and his, came to the door. The continual flow of people, the talk and reminiscing, lifted Dan's mind, helping him blank out his grief for the time being.

Colette returned from the hospital with the bad news that her grannie had had a slight heart attack and they were keeping her in for a couple of days for observation.

She looked at the stacks of dirty cups and glasses scattered about and cried in amazement, 'Did no one offer to wash these?'

'They did. But I wouldn't let them.'

She sighed. 'Right. First let's get these dishes cleared up and then I'll make us something to eat.'

Dan looked at her as if she had just uttered a string of obscenities. 'Are you mad? I couldn't eat a thing. Food would only choke me.'

'Mr Thompson, you're not the only one grieving,' she retorted sharply. 'I loved Jack too. I was going to marry him, remember. And I thought I was going to lose my grannie as well. In fact I might still lose her. But life goes on and we have a funeral to arrange. We must eat to keep up our strength.'

Seeing her point of view, he backed down. 'You're right. Of course you're right. But don't make too much, eh? Just scramble a couple of eggs.'

'If that's what you want. I take it you've been in touch with the undertaker?'

He shook his head. 'Not yet.'

She glanced at the clock. 'It's too late now. But first thing in the morning you must start to make arrangements, and don't forget the parish priest while you're at it. Right. I'll scramble some eggs and toast a bit of bread, then we'll clear up this mess.' She had no intention of letting him wallow in self-pity. He must be kept alert.

In the privacy of the scullery Colette buried her face in her hands and fought for control. She must be strong! Mr Thompson obviously didn't know whether he was coming or going. She had him and her grannie to think about. She would grieve later.

Friends and neighbours continued to call during the evening and Colette acted as hostess, making tea and trying to make things easier for Dan. About midnight they closed the door on the last visitor and Colette, who had managed to keep Dan away from the bottle most of the evening, relented and poured him a large Jameson's, courtesy of one of the callers. She poured one for herself as well and sat down. She intended staying to see he retired to bed, didn't sit boozing all night.

He sat on the settee and she sat near the fire watching him. Great tears rolled down his face. Unable to contain her own sorrow, she joined him on the settee and they cried together, united in grief.

Easter week was a time of joy for Tess. Dennis let Dominic have the loan of his car while he was on honeymoon and on Tuesday morning when Dominic phoned and asked Tess out for the day she at first demurred, saying that Tony would be returning to work that day and she had half promised Agnes that they would go out somewhere together. She confided in him that she was worried about her friend and didn't want to leave her to brood on her own.

Reluctantly he agreed that she could ask Agnes to come along but warned her that if Agnes refused, Tess must still come out with him.

Agnes was only too happy to agree. She wanted to make amends to Dominic for her bad manners towards him.

They all met in Tess's house and Dominic confided, 'I've been thinking. Why don't we go down south this time. Say maybe as far as Galway? What do you think?'

The girls looked at each other. It was Agnes who spoke. 'It's a long way to travel. We'd be no sooner there than we'd have to turn back.'

'Oh, how stupid of me. I didn't think of that,' Dominic lamented.

He looked so disappointed that Tess suggested, 'We

could of course take our night things and toothbrushes and stay overnight – or even two nights, for that matter. It would be a nice wee break. There's plenty of bed and breakfast places down south and they all have a good name.'

'That sounds like a smashing idea to me,' he agreed happily.

Realising that Agnes hadn't commented, they both looked at her for her reaction. She grimaced. 'I'm afraid you will have to go without me. Tony wouldn't be too pleased if I tagged along.'

'Sorry, Agnes,' Tess exclaimed. 'I wasn't thinking straight. Can we go somewhere else, Dominic? Somewhere closer to home?'

He paid her little attention. His eyes held Agnes's, intent and probing. Suddenly, as if they had discussed it telepathically, she said, 'I'll come. I'll leave a note for Tony.'

'Good girl! That's settled then. Tess, while you pack your bits and pieces, I'll run Agnes down to pack hers and come back for you. May as well pack your little green number, in case we go somewhere special while we're down there.'

Tess hesitated. She didn't want to cause any trouble between Agnes and Tony.

As if guessing her thoughts Dominic said, 'Come on, Tess, get a move on. It wasn't your decision, after all.'

Without another word she rushed upstairs. Dominic eyed Agnes. 'Are you sure this is what you want to do?'

Without removing her gaze from his, she whispered, 'More than anything else in the world.' Without giving it any thought she knew that she just wanted to please him.

He reached for her, but what might have happened

she would never know, because at that moment Tess suddenly reappeared to inquire if one dress would be enough, and the spell was broken. However, in the car going back home Agnes was aware of a lovely warm feeling around her heart. Surely not just because she was going to Galway? Feeling Dominic's gaze on her she turned and met his eyes. No! Definitely not because she was going to Galway.

They returned to pick up Tess and then went to collect some toiletries and extra clothes for Dominic. The girls waited outside the Sullivans' house on Mackie's Height and Tess, still worried about Tony's reaction when he discovered Agnes had gone on holiday without him, asked tentatively, 'Do you think Tony will be very upset?'

'At the moment I couldn't care one way or the other. I'm fed up bending over backwards to please everybody. I need this break to sort myself out.'

'Just so long as you know what you're doing.'

'I don't really, but for the first time in my life I'm willing to take the chance.'

The journey down through the towns, big and small, was a pleasure. Even when they passed through heavy showers and the rain beat mercilessly down on the car and Dominic had to stop because it was obscuring their vision, they were at peace with the world. After all, it was April, one had to expect showers of some sort, and they were on their way to Galway.

For part of the journey Tess sat in the front of the car with Dominic. They stopped in Cavan for lunch and afterwards Tess changed seats with Agnes. Glad that she and Dominic were friends again, Agnes covertly watched him as she sat up front, admiring his strong hands on the wheel. She began to fantasise about him, something she had never done about anyone in her life before, imagining him touching her. Wondering what it would be like to be kissed properly by him; not the friendly peck he had given her before, but a full-blooded kiss filled with passion! She laughed secretly, deriding herself. What did she know about passion? This thought caused her to brood on the word, analyse it. How come there was no passion in her relationship with Tony? That was her own fault. She never gave Tony a chance to get started; but then, she never had the desire to.

Dominic caught her eye in his peripheral vision and she blushed with shame. Could he possibly guess what she was thinking? For the rest of the journey she kept her eyes on the road and engaged Tess in small talk about the passing scenery to keep her mind from running amok again.

Dominic smiled, a secret smile. He was getting through to her. At last she was coming round to his way of thinking; he was in with a chance.

After a while the girls' chatter lapsed into silence. He brought her attention back to him.

'Are you all right, Agnes?'

Startled, she swung towards him. 'Of course. Why shouldn't I be?'

'You're not worrying about Tony, are you?'

Truthfully she answered him, 'No. But I do feel mean, taking off like this. I'm sure he will understand when I explain that I just had to get away for a while.'

Dominic looked sceptical but she had to have a show-down with Tony, clear the air once and for all.

'What about you, Tess? Are you all right back there?'

No answer. A quick glance in the driving mirror confirmed that Tess was asleep. Without further ado, Dominic caught hold of Agnes's hand and kissing the palm he closed her fingers round it. 'Keep that for me. I'll get it back when you're ready.'

Agnes nodded slowly, her brow puckered. When she was ready? What did he mean?

Dominic insisted that they do it in style, his treat. He booked them into the Warwick Hotel, in Salthill on the outskirts of Galway, for bed and breakfast and inquired about entertainment. He was informed that there was no entertainment in the hotel on a Tuesday night but that dances were held regularly in a hall further up the road.

They decided that they would have a short rest and freshen up before going out for a meal and later to the dance. The girls were sharing a room and when they had each had a bath and were preparing for their evening out, Tess confided in Agnes. 'I'm glad you and Dominic are friends again. He really is a nice person.'

Suddenly apprehensive, Agnes asked, 'You haven't gone and fallen for him, have you?'

Remembering the hurt caused by Jack Thompson, Tess was cautious. 'Not really. I'm very fond of him, mind, and he has hinted that he would like to remain in Ireland, so who knows how things might turn out?'

Agnes concentrated on her eye make-up. She should have known that Tess was likely to fall for Dominic. What difference did it make, anyway? She was engaged to Tony. However, she discovered that it certainly did make one hell of a difference. The idea of Dominic maybe one day marrying her best friend devastated her. Why? She hadn't been in the least annoyed when Tess was falling for Jack Thompson.

It was raining when they joined Dominic in the lounge. A perusal of the dinner menu made them decide to remain in the hotel for their meal and avoid getting wet before going to the dance. The dance hall was packed and Tess caused a stir in her green dress. Once the local men became aware that she was unattached, she wasn't short of partners and Dominic was free to dance a lot of the time with Agnes.

Agnes dared to tease him. 'You'll be sorry you asked me along.'

'Why?'

'I'm keeping you from dancing with Tess.'

'If I wanted to dance more with Tess I'd ask her before anyone else had the chance. Am I monopolising you? Perhaps you'd rather dance with some of the local talent?'

'No,' she whispered, her voice husky. 'I'd rather be with you.'

He held her closer and was content when she didn't draw away. He was making headway.

Tess was having the time of her life as she twirled around the floor in the arms of numerous men. She could see it was giving her friend and Dominic a chance to get over their differences and was pleased. They danced until the early hours of the morning and returned exhausted but happy to the hotel.

They spent Wednesday exploring Galway and the surrounding countryside and returned to the hotel for dinner. Afterwards, in the lounge Tess slipped off her shoes and rubbed her hot, weary feet. 'I think I'll retire early. You two look quite fresh, but I feel completely whacked. Do you mind if I leave you?'

'Not at all. Will you have another drink before you go up?'

'No, thank you, Dominic. I think I'll have a hot bath

and go straight to bed. Good night, Agnes, Dominic. See you both in the morning.'

'I'll be very quiet when I come up and try not to disturb you.'

'Be as noisy as you want, Agnes. As long as I'm in bed you won't annoy me.'

At the door of the lounge she waved and they returned her salute. Slowly Dominic turned his gaze on Agnes. 'Have you ever watched the sun go down on Galway Bay?'

She laughed. 'No. I'm afraid that is something I've never managed to do.'

'I can't go back to Florida and say I was in Galway and didn't see the sun go down on the bay. I'd never hear the end of it.' He raised a brow at her.

'No. That is something you'll have to do,' she agreed solemnly.

'Will you join me?'

'I'd love to.'

'Then you will have to wrap up warmly. It gets chilly late on.'

Tess was surprised to see her friend so soon. 'I didn't expect you to be up for another hour or so.'

Agnes explained Dominic's desire to see the sun go down on the bay.

'I wish he had said sooner. I've a bath running or I'd come with you.'

Agnes hesitated, undecided. Without understanding why, she found herself praying that Tess wouldn't decide to join them. She breathed a sigh of relief when Tess said, 'I think I'll just stay here in our room. I really am very tired.'

'See you later, then.' Grabbing her coat and scarf, Agnes was out of the door before her friend could change her mind, leaving Tess staring at it, a perplexed frown on her brow.

They left the hotel and Dominic drew her arm through his and pressed it close to his side. This was an unexpected chance to make her aware of him as a man; not just Dennis's brother. She was completely unawakened. She thought that she and Tony were on the right track for marriage. Who knows, perhaps she was right. He only knew that from the moment he first set eyes on her he had wanted her for his wife.

They watched in awe as the sun slowly appeared to sink into the bay, lighting up the sky in a blazing, golden backdrop. It was an experience that Dominic would never forget.

Cuddling even closer to him, Agnes whispered, 'Wasn't that beautiful?'

He held her against his body. 'It still is.'

She lifted her face to his and nodded. With a finger he tilted her face until he had a clear route to her mouth, and then he fastened his lips on hers. She returned kiss for kiss, caress for caress. They stayed locked together for some time until he sighed and put her gently from him.

'It's time we were getting back to the hotel.' An arm across her shoulders, he led her away from the darkening horizon. 'What did you think of that, then?'

'It was wonderful.'

'It wasn't the sunset I was talking about.'

'I know,' she whispered, as if afraid to admit the effect he had had on her. 'You are wonderful.'

He sighed contentedly. 'You know now you're engaged to the wrong man, don't you?'

'Yes. But it's much too late for us. I couldn't do anything to hurt Tony. He has been so patient and kind to me.'

Dominic couldn't believe his ears. He gripped her by the shoulders. 'What about me? Don't I come into this anywhere?' She looked so bewildered, he released her. He had no intention of trying to coerce her. She must come off her own bat or not at all. 'I've shown you how I feel about you. I'm returning to Florida sooner than planned. If you care about me you must break off with Tony and come to Florida with me. The choice is yours.'

Agnes was in a state of confusion. When she dwelt on thoughts of Dominic, the happiness she felt was new to her. She had never known anything like it. However, Tony was the stumbling block. How could she do anything that would hurt him? It was on the journey home, when they had stopped once again in Cavan and got out to stretch their legs with a short stroll down the main street and then back to the same restaurant for lunch, that Agnes had a rude awakening.

She and Tess were in the cloakroom of the restaurant, refreshing themselves before continuing the journey, when Tess smiled happily at her and said, 'I'm delighted you and Dominic are friends again. Now if he decides to stay in Ireland, which I hope he does, I can pursue him with a happy frame of mind.'

Agnes turned a startled look on her. 'You mean you really do fancy him?'

'Yes. I wasn't going to tell you after all those shenanigans with Jack Thompson but I feel quite confident that Dominic likes me too.'

'Why, has he said anything?'

'Not outright, but I do know he has met someone he can care for . . . and if not me, who else? He hasn't bothered with anyone else that I know of.'

'Would you be willing to go to Florida with him?'

'Oh, no. I couldn't leave Mam, but he has implied that he would like to stay here in Ireland.'

Agnes was confused. Had she picked Dominic up wrong? Probably. After all, he had been talking in riddles as far as she was concerned. He had kissed her, and that had knocked all sensible reasoning out of her head. What kind of mind games was he playing at?

Dominic noticed the difference in Agnes's attitude towards him during the rest of the journey and could not account for it. When he dropped her off at her door a grim-faced Tony came out to meet her. A cup of tea was politely declined. Dominic tried to catch Agnes's eye but she avoided contact, so wishing them both good night he drove off.

'I wouldn't have minded a nice cup of tea,' Tess said plaintively. She was annoyed at not being given the chance to accept.

'Oh, Tess, I do apologise. That look on Tony's face put me right off,' he lied blithely. If Agnes had been more forthcoming he would have ignored Tony's attitude.

'You're right. I do hope Agnes doesn't grovel to him. Just because they are engaged to be married doesn't mean he owns her. She's too soft where he's concerned.'

Dominic agreed wholeheartedly. Had he shown his hand too soon? Would Agnes be strong enough to break off with Tony? Would she realise that they were soulmates? Or was it all only in his head? Only time would tell.

Chapter Eleven

They were home so late on Thursday that Tess was glad her mother had decided to stay on in Carlingford until Saturday. It would give her a chance to tidy up the house on Friday, get in the groceries and hide the little green dress somewhere her mother wouldn't come across it. These last few days had been so happy she was still floating on cloud nine. As far as she was concerned, life had never been so exciting.

On Friday evening she was in the work room getting everything ready for her return to the grindstone the following week when she saw Tony and Agnes approach the house. They saw her, waved, and waited to be admitted.

'This is a nice surprise,' she greeted them. 'I was just about to make a cup of tea. Will you join me?' They both looked pale and strained and this worried Tess. She wondered if Tony was still annoyed at Agnes for going to Galway without him. She supposed he had cause to be disgruntled, but surely he wouldn't continue to hold a grudge if he really loved Agnes.

To Tess's bewilderment, without as much as a hello or anything, Agnes took her by the arm, and, leading her into the living room, pushed her gently down on to a chair. 'We have some bad news, I'm afraid.'

Tess's thoughts immediately flew to Alice. 'Is it my mam? Has something happened to her?' It would be just like Malachy to try to soften the blow by phoning Agnes and asking her to break any bad news in person.

'No. Relax. Your mam is okay. At least, we haven't heard anything to the contrary.' Agnes paused and bit hard on her lip before blurting out, 'I'm afraid it's Jack. He was killed today on his new motorbike.'

Tess sat stunned, remembering Dan's excitement at buying the motorcycle. He had been absolutely over the moon about it.

Her silence worried Agnes and she asked anxiously, 'Are you all right, Tess? Can I get you a drink or something?'

'No. No, I'm fine. I just can't take it in. Mr Thompson must be in an awful state. He bought Jack that bike for his twenty-first birthday. He will be blaming himself. And poor Colette. She must be absolutely devastated.'

Glad that her friend's thoughts were all for others with no obvious signs of distress for herself, Agnes's shoulders rose and fell in a sigh of relief and she slipped off her coat. 'You stay there and I'll put the kettle on for that cup of tea.'

While Agnes was in the kitchen, Tess questioned Tony. 'When did you say it happened?'

'Early today.'

'How did you find out about it?'

'It was on the radio at lunch time but I didn't twig. You see, no names were mentioned. They just said that a man and woman were involved in a fatal motorcycle accident but names were being withheld until the relatives had been notified. I didn't know anything about the bike so I didn't give it a second thought. Then one of the lads went out for cigarettes and said he had heard

Jack Thompson's name mentioned in the newsagent's. That's when I learned who it was.'

'A man and woman?' Tess latched on to this piece of information. 'Was Colette with him?'

Tony shook his head. 'Apparently he had been taking his mother for a ride.'

'Is Anne dead too?'

'No, but I hear she is badly injured. They took her to the City Hospital.'

'Wait until my mam hears about this. She'll be gutted.'

'When is she due home?'

'Tomorrow morning. Have you been down to see Dan?'

'Yes, but I just stayed a few minutes. The house was packed and I didn't like to ask any questions about what happened. Dan's in an awful state. And to crown it all, Colette's grannie collapsed when she heard about it and she was rushed to the Royal. Agnes and I will call down in the morning and see if we can be of any help.'

'Poor Colette. Poor Mrs Burns! God, it never rains but it pours. I'd come with you but I've to meet Mam at the station. I'll see what she wants to do.' Tess shook her head. 'It's so hard to take in, that Jack is dead. I can't believe it. I'll go and give Agnes a hand with the tea, Tony.'

Agnes was pouring water into the teapot and eyed Tess keenly when she entered the kitchen. 'I was very worried when I heard about Jack. About how the news would affect you, that is. I didn't know how you'd take it.'

'No need to worry about me. I got over Jack some time ago. It's poor Colette I'm worried about. She must be heartbroken.'

'And Dan! How must he feel, having bought Jack the

bike? Eh? I must admit I'm not looking forward to seeing him tomorrow.'

Tess lifted the now laden tray. 'Let's take this into the living room.' She paused and lowered her voice. 'Is Tony all right about you going to Galway without any warning?'

Agnes shrugged. 'There's nothing he can do about it. I'm my own boss.'

'But . . . is the engagement still on?'

Agnes nodded despondently. If only it wasn't, she lamented inwardly. 'Oh, yes. It will take more than that to separate us.'

Dominic phoned later that night to invite Tess out for a meal and on to the cinema the following day. Tess explained the circumstances and reminded him that her mother was returning home tomorrow morning. 'She's bound to be upset and I don't know whether I'll be able to leave her on her own and come out with you.'

'Tell you what, I'll drive you to the bus station in the morning and we'll take it from there, okay?'

'That would be wonderful. Thank you very much, Dominic.' A time was arranged for him to pick her up, and when she placed the receiver back in the cradle she felt a sudden surge of guilt. She was happy that she would be seeing Dominic, when poor Jack was lying in the mortuary, dead.

Tess was apprehensive as she waited at the station next morning, with Dominic, for her mother's return from Carlingford. 'Do you think I should tell her straight away or wait until we get home?'

'Does it make any difference? I mean, will she be very upset? Was your mother very fond of this lad?'

'No, I wouldn't go so far as to say that. Quite the

opposite in fact. You see, Jack dated me a few times and I was upset when he dropped me and started going out with another girl. Mam foolishly held it against him. Although it didn't stop her becoming friendly with his father,' she added drily.

'Ah, now I understand. So this Jack Thompson is the lad Agnes was telling me about? The one who broke your heart?'

Tess's mouth gaped slightly at these revelations. 'Why did she tell you that? She had no right to discuss my affairs with you.'

'She was warning me off. Said you were still fragile and I must be careful not to give you any wrong ideas.'

'And were you careful not to give me any wrong ideas?'

'I hope I made my intentions quite clear to you. I certainly didn't want to cause any concern.'

He was saved from further questions as the bus pulled into the bay where they waited and Tess caught sight of her mother and waved.

Alice left the bus and stood waiting for an introduction to the handsome young man accompanying her daughter.

'Mam, this is Dennis Sullivan's brother. He came home from Florida to be best man at the wedding. He was kind enough to offer me a lift down to meet you.'

'That was very kind of him.'

Dominic gripped her hand and, flirtatious as usual, said, 'I'm very pleased to meet you, Mrs Maguire. Tess neglected to mention how lovely you are. And, by the way, my name is Dominic.'

Tess suppressed a smile as her mother preened herself and said graciously, 'I'm pleased to meet you too, Dominic.'

Introductions over, Alice let her gaze scan the bus

station. 'I thought Dan might have been with you.'

'Mam, I've some bad news.'

'About Dan?' She was alert at once. 'Has he gone back to his wife?'

Tess never ceased to wonder how everyone first jumped to the conclusion that might affect *them*. 'No, it's Jack. Did you know he was twenty-one last Thursday?'

Alice shook her head. 'No. Dan never mentioned it.'

'Well, Dan bought Jack a motorbike for his birthday and he crashed on it yesterday morning and was killed.'

'Oh, my God.' Alice's hand covered her mouth and she whispered behind it. 'Sweet Jesus have mercy on his soul. Dan must be in an awful state. I must go to him immediately.'

'Would you not be better going home first and freshening up?'

'No. Dan might need me.'

Tess glanced at Dominic and he responded immediately. Reaching for Alice's luggage he said, 'Give me directions and I'll take you both there.'

'Thank you.'

They found Dan's house locked up and the window blind down. Colette came from next door and beckoned them in. 'Mr Thompson has gone to the undertakers to make arrangements for the funeral.' She was pale and red-eyed from lack of sleep and crying.

Tess immediately put her arms round Colette and held her close, rocking her gently to and fro. 'I'm so sorry for you. So very, very sorry.'

The women were in tears and, embarrassed, Dominic moved restlessly, shuffling from one foot to the other.

Wiping her eyes, Tess said, 'Forgive me. My manners

are terrible. Colette, this is Dominic Sullivan, Dennis's brother.'

Dominic gripped her small hand. 'Sorry we couldn't meet in happier circumstances. If there's anything at all I can do, please let me know. Now I know you don't know me, but I really mean that.'

'Thanks.'

'Has Dan been gone long?'

'Here he is now,' Colette said, as she recognised Dan's step in the hall. With a light tap on the door he entered the room.

He stopped abruptly when he saw Alice. She went to him and slowly – almost reluctantly, it seemed – he opened his arms to embrace her. He released her at once, and nodded a greeting to Tess. A bit put out, Alice said, 'I'm sorry I wasn't here, Dan.'

'Don't be. After all, you had better things to do, Alice.'

Alice couldn't hide her hurt surprise at his words and curt tone of voice. To cover her mother's confusion, Tess introduced Dominic and offered her condolences.

'Mam is just off the bus from Carlingford. I'm sure she's tired, so we will leave you for now, Dan, and come back later on today or tomorrow morning. Okay?'

'Yes, Alice will be tired after her extended holiday,' Dan agreed. 'Don't worry about coming back. There will be plenty of people here over the next few days. Excuse me, please.' With these words he passed through the scullery and out into the yard, leaving a stunned silence behind.

At a loss for words and close to tears, Alice looked beseechingly at Tess. 'I think we'd better go.'

'Of course, Mam. Sorry to rush away like this, Colette, but whether Dan likes it or not we will be back.'

'I'd wait until tomorrow if I were you, Tess,' Colette

advised. 'The mood he's in at the moment, he's not very sociable.'

'That's probably good advice. We'll see you tomorrow, then.'

Dan stood in the yard and berated himself. What on earth had gotten into him? Imagine speaking to Alice like that. And in front of a stranger too. Still, if she had returned on Wednesday as planned she would have been here when he most needed her and perhaps he wouldn't now feel so steeped in guilt. He'd had no one to turn to. Well, that wasn't unusual, he reminded himself. After all, he had managed on his own all these years, so why should he need a woman now?

His guilt had stemmed from his evil thoughts. He had wished Anne would fall under a bus, God forgive him. But it had backfired. Instead he had lost his only son.

He delayed for a while outside and when he eventually returned indoors, the others had gone and Lily Brady was sitting there talking to Colette. He nodded to Lily in acknowledgement and would have passed outside to go home, but she rose to her feet. 'Dan, I must speak to you.'

Realising that he had forgotten to inquire after his wife's health, he said, 'Did you see Anne last night?' She nodded and he continued, 'How is she?'

'That's what I want to talk to you about.'

He felt apprehensive. 'Anne is no concern of mine any more, Lily. Hasn't been for the last nine years.'

'I'm afraid you're going to have to take some kind of responsibility for her, Dan. You're all she has, you know.'

Dan frowned, and Lily rushed on. 'They will let her out in a few days, so long as she has somewhere to go and someone to keep an eye on her.'

'Isn't she living with you?'

'Dan, as you well know, I've two sons. They share the second bedroom. Bill is away on a course and decided to stay with friends over Easter. Tom offered to sleep on the settee and let Anne have the bedroom for the holiday period. But in a few days' time Bill will be home and I'll have no room for Anne. She understands that. I made it crystal clear when she first came to me that it would be for a short time only.' Her hands spread in a futile gesture. 'But then this happened.'

'And what did Anne intend doing when Bill came home? She must have had some plans.'

Lily looked shame-faced. 'She had hoped that she would have persuaded Jack to set up house with her by then.'

Dan was dazed. Had he not enough on his plate without worrying about Anne? 'I've nowhere to put her,' he said curtly.

'Ah, come on now, Dan. There's two bedrooms in all these houses.' Annoyed at his callousness, Lily cried bitterly, 'Jack won't need his any more, after all.'

White with fury, Dan pointed to the door. 'How dare you. Get out! Go on, get out. Anne is not going to have Jack's room.'

Lily stepped towards the door but stopped. 'I've a message from Anne. She says to tell you that Jimmy settled a generous allowance on her when they split up and she wants to contribute to the funeral costs.'

'You tell her to stick it! I don't need or want her money.'

'And will you take her in?'

'I will not! And you can tell her that too. If she hadn't been trying to come between me and my son she'd have had a place of her own by now. And, God knows, this might never have happened. So, tough, if she has nowhere to go!'

Lily slammed the door on her way out and Dan turned to where Colette sat, wide eyed, listening to his ranting. 'Sorry about that, love.'

'I hope you don't mind my saying so, Dan, but it looks as if you will have no other option than to take Anne in for a while. She is still your wife, after all, even if in name only. You can't just abandon her.'

'She abandoned me, and Jack! I feel nothing for her. Nothing! I applied for a divorce just last week and if we live under the same roof it will only slow up the proceedings.'

Colette shrugged. She had nothing to be grateful to Anne for. She was just trying to be charitable. 'If you happen to be looking for me later on, Dan, I'll be out for a while. I'm going to the hospital to see Grannie.'

Dan's expression softened. 'Give her my regards, won't you? But hold on a minute. Will you take a look at these first, and tell me what you think?'

He took some sheets of paper from his pocket and spread them on the table. They were pictures of coffins and accessories. 'I chose this one and these handles and a crucifix for the lid. What do you think?'

Colette noted that he had chosen the most expensive items. She said, tentatively, 'Can you afford these? Everything doesn't have to be the dearest, you know. No one is going to be examining them. I think you should pick something a little less expensive, Mr Thompson.'

'Only the best will do for my son. As well as the hearse there will be two limousines. Will that be enough, do you think?'

Colette nodded silently; tears, already so close to the surface, were ready to fall again.

Dan took her gently in his arms but she pushed him roughly away. 'Leave me alone. I'll be all right! I forgot to tell you, Mam is coming tomorrow and staying for the funeral. When is Jack being buried?'

'I haven't seen the priest yet.' At her look of amazement he hurriedly gathered up the papers and turned to the door. 'I'm on my way down to St Peter's right now.'

Once he'd gone Colette closed and locked the outer door and curled up on the settee. She was exhausted; needed a good rest, needed some time to herself. If Grannie's health permitted, she would go back to Omagh with her parents. Not something she wanted to do, but there was nothing left for her here, now that Jack was gone. She dozed on and off for an hour and then, still dopey from lack of sleep, prepared to visit her grannie.

Tess invited Dominic in for a bite to eat when he dropped them off, but he had had enough of weeping women for one day and gracefully declined. 'I'll give you a ring tomorrow and perhaps we will be able to arrange something for during the week,' he suggested, placing Alice's luggage in the hallway.

'That would be nice. Thanks for everything, Dominic.'

Alice was sitting on the edge of a chair hugging herself as if for comfort. 'Did you hear the way Dan spoke to me back there?'

'Now, Mam, he's not himself. He has a lot on his plate with Jack dead and Anne in hospital and all the arrangements to make. He must be out of his mind with worry.'

Wild eyed, Alice's fear came to the surface again. 'Do you think he will have her back?'

At her wits' end as to how to reason with her mother, Tess said, 'Even if he doesn't, Mam, it will make no difference. They're still married.'

'Oh, I wish she had died instead of Jack. That would have solved all our problems.'

'Mam! Listen to yourself. How can you even think such a thing?'

'Because these past ten days away have shown me how much I love Dan Thompson, that's how! I can't picture life without him any more. We were getting on so well together and now there seems to be a great rift between us and I can't get through to him. I wish I hadn't let myself be persuaded to go to Carlingford.'

Although unspoken, the words 'It's all your fault' hung in the air. Tess was annoyed and it showed in the look she bestowed on her mother. She retaliated quickly. 'Then why didn't you come home on Wednesday as planned? Eh? To be truthful I thought someone else had caught your fancy. Perhaps Dan thought so too.'

'No one I met could hold a candle to Dan Thompson. When Rose asked me to stay over for a few extra days, I suppose I agreed because I was trying to make Dan jealous; make him realise that he really cared for me. Instead I seem to have given him the wrong impression. I've implied that I don't care for him enough. It will be all my fault if he takes Anne back.' Her body was racked by harsh sobs.

Tess knelt beside her mother and held her close. 'Forget about Anne Thompson for the time being. It might never happen. We must wait and see what *does* happen. We'll wait until tomorrow and after Mass in the morning we'll both go down and offer our assistance. Dan will have had a chance to collect his thoughts and I'm sure he will be glad of our help around the house, looking after his visitors.'

* * *

She was wrong. Next morning when once again they arrived at his house on their errand of mercy, Dan showed no inclination to accept their help, insisting that everything was being taken care of. Worried, Tess took Colette to one side. 'Is Dan managing okay?'

Colette shrugged. 'He's locking all his grief up inside himself. He doesn't say much to me.'

'When's the funeral?'

'Tomorrow, after Requiem Mass in St Peter's. The Mass is at eleven o'clock. That much I do know.'

'Won't some of the mourners be invited back to the house afterwards? Who's going to make the tea and sandwiches and all that? You can't possibly manage all on your own, Colette.'

'I've questioned him till I'm blue in the face, but he says I'm not to worry my head about anything. Just look after my mother and father when they arrive.'

'They're coming for the funeral?'

'Yes. They arrive today and go back Tuesday.'

'What will you do, Colette?'

'I'll stay until my grannie is well enough to look after herself, and then I suppose I'll go back home. There's nothing for me here any more.'

Although Tess and Alice were the only visitors, after a curt greeting in their direction Dan kept his distance, leaving Colette to entertain them.

While Tess and Colette were talking, Alice waited her chance to have a quiet word alone with Dan. Determined to get to the bottom of his obvious animosity towards her, she followed him when he muttered something and restlessly went into the scullery. Pausing on the threshold, she pleaded, 'Don't do this to me, Dan.'

She moved closer and to her relief he didn't back

away and seek refuge in the yard. 'I don't know what you mean,' he blustered.

'I think you do. You're blaming me. You're acting as if I were the cause of the accident because I stayed over an extra three days. That's the only reason I can think of for your present behaviour.'

Suddenly he gripped her by the shoulders. 'Look, Alice, I admit that at first I was annoyed at you for staying away longer than planned. Annoyed? I was consumed with jealousy, thinking you had met someone else. But perhaps it was all for the best. I treated Jack and Colette to a slap-up meal in the International Hotel on Thursday night as part of his birthday present and I wanted you to be there. I wanted you to get to know him better. See what a fine lad he is . . . was.'

'You should have said before I went away. I would certainly have come.'

He shrugged. 'I never thought for one minute you'd stay longer than planned. I couldn't have stayed away from you if the circumstances had been reversed.'

'I know. I was foolishly trying to make you jealous.'

'Ah, Alice. Well, you certainly succeeded. But that's all water under the bridge. Now I'm just keeping my distance because I know there's no hope for us. I don't want you to get caught up in anything that you might later regret.'

'Don't be silly. As far as I'm concerned, nothing has changed. We can still be friends, can't we?'

He shook his head in sorrow. 'That's not good enough for me any more. I love you, Alice. And because I love you, I did a terrible thing! I wished Anne would fall under a bus. Imagine wishing that on your own wife, just so you could be free to marry someone else. I didn't really mean it, of course. But the thought was there.

Well, I certainly received an answer to my wish. Jack was taken from me.'

Appalled at his revelations, Alice whispered furiously, 'Now you're talking rubbish and you know it.'

'Listen to me, Alice! Anne has nowhere to go. I might be forced to bring her here to stay until she recovers.'

These words floored Alice. Was her worst fear to be realised? 'Can't she go to one of her friends?'

'She hasn't any, I'm afraid. She severed all her connections round here when she left me and Jack.'

'Where was she living?'

'With a woman up the street, but she was only staying there over the Easter holidays. Lily Brady has been to see me and says she needs Anne's room back as her sons will be back in the house next week. So Anne has nowhere else to go. Now do you understand?'

He gazed at the sadness in her eyes and, drawing her further into the scullery, against his better judgement he roughly gathered her close and kissed her trembling lips. Alice hungrily responded. Slowly, he released her. 'Why did this have to happen, Alice? I had such high hopes for us. I had applied for a divorce, hoping to persuade you to marry me in a register office, but that's all hit on the head now.'

These words salved Alice's wounded pride. Register office? What did it matter. He had admitted that he loved her and wanted to marry her.

From her seat near the fireside, Tess could not see Dan, just her mother near the entrance to the scullery. When Dan's hands came into view and gripped her mother's shoulders, Tess moved to the edge of her chair, ready to intervene if anything started in there. She had to fight hard to control her impulse to interfere. Alice wouldn't thank her for it, but neither had she any intention of letting Dan hurt her mother.

At the same time, if Alice was making a fool of herself, Tess was the one who would have to be around to pick up the pieces and live with the results. She dragged her mind back to what Colette was saying.

'He assures me the catering has been arranged and a wreath ordered. This is my first funeral, Tess. Is there anything else I should be reminding him of?'

'I don't know. I was too young when my father died to pay much attention to what was going on. I'm more into weddings than anything else. I'll ask Mam . . . that is, if she can manage to tear herself out of that scullery.'

As if she had heard her, Alice entered the kitchen. She was pale and had obviously been crying, but looked more relaxed than she had previously. Dan followed her to the settee and they sat close together.

'Mam, have you and Dan been discussing the funeral arrangements?' It was obvious from their guilty expressions that they hadn't. Tess turned her attention to Dan. 'Look, I'm not being nosy, Dan, I just want to make sure everything is under control and you haven't forgotten anything.'

Dan spread one hand out and ticked off the items on his fingers. 'First, I've been to the undertaker and arranged for a new grave to be opened in Milltown Cemetery. Second, I've ordered the cars and picked a coffin. And last but not least I've seen the priest. Jack's body will be received into the church tonight at seven o'clock and he will be buried tomorrow after eleven o'clock Mass.' His eyes passed from one to the other of them questioningly. 'Have I forgotten anything?'

It was Alice who spoke next. 'Are you not bringing him home, then?'

'No, it would break my heart to have him lying here

for all and sundry to gawk at. It's much better this way.'

'Have you put a notice in the newspapers to let people know when the funeral is taking place?' Tess asked. It was a bit late thinking of that now, but better late than never. At least it could be in tomorrow's *Irish News*.

'To be truthful, I'd forgotten all about that.' He caught and held Colette's eye. 'I can't remember whether or not I mentioned to you about the newspapers on Friday night, Colette. Everything was such a blur then.' Tight lipped, she shook her head as if in anger. He apologised quickly. 'Sorry about that, but if I recall correctly, I was quite drunk at the time?' A brow was raised in Colette's direction. He received another curt angry nod. 'Anyhow, I called into the Silk & Rayon on Friday afternoon to let Jack's boss know what had happened, but he already knew about the accident. It was him who mentioned the newspapers. When I admitted I hadn't given it a thought, he kindly offered to see to it for me. We wrote out all the details between us and it was in yesterday's *Irish News* and last night's *Telegraph*. Luckily, Father McAleese later fell in with all my wishes regarding the time of admittance to church on Sunday night and the Requiem Mass at eleven on Monday.'

'Thank God for that!' Tess exclaimed. 'That only leaves the catering. Agnes has offered to help us three with that, if you will allow us.'

'There's no need. That is also taken care of. Mrs McAnulty and a few other neighbours are looking after that for me, so you see' – he spread his hands wide – 'like I said, it's all under control.'

They were all looking at him, flabbergasted. He wearily washed his hands over his face. 'I've surprised you, haven't I? Seeing to all these arrangements is what has kept me sane this past couple of days,' he admitted.

Reaching for his hand Alice clasped it and moved closer to him. He returned her grip like a dying man grasping at a straw. With one accord Tess and Colette rose to their feet.

'Mam, I'll go in next door with Colette for a while. I'll be back for you in half an hour or so, okay?'

An absentminded nod was all the reply she received and the girls left the house, closing the outer door behind them.

'I don't know what is to become of those two,' Tess confided in Colette. 'Is it all right if I come in with you for a while?'

'Of course it is. I'll be only too glad of your company. You can talk to me, take my mind off things, while I prepare something for Mam coming. I envy Dan having your mother to turn to. They can at least comfort each other. I feel so alone and empty. It would be different if Grannie were here; she's great company.'

'I'm glad your parents are coming for the funeral. They'll be there to support you.'

'Yes. I suppose I shouldn't say this, but I bet Mam's relieved that the wedding will not now take place.' Colette choked back a sob at this confession.

At a loss for words of comfort, Tess cried, 'Oh, I'm sure you're wrong.'

'You don't know my mother.'

'Colette, I know we never got the chance to become friends the way things happened, but I do like you and, if you ever need someone to talk to, I'll be here for you.'

'Thanks, Tess. I'll remember that.' Colette raised her head and peered through the net curtains. 'Here's Mam now.'

Tess rose hurriedly to her feet. 'I'm sure you'll have

a lot to talk about so I'll go now and let you get on with it.'

'You'll do nothing of the kind. You'll stay and have a cup of tea with us. You told your mam you'd come for her in half an hour or so. That was only ten minutes ago.'

Colette listened for the car door to slam and then went out to greet her parents. Colette's mother was tall and elegant. The man who followed her through the doorway was grey-haired and distinguished looking.

'Tess . . . this is my mother and stepfather. Betty and Stan. Tess is a friend of mine.'

'This is a terrible situation, isn't it?' Betty lamented. 'Such a loss of a young life.'

'At least the wedding will not now take place.'

'Now, now, Colette . . . no need to speak to your mother like that. Obviously these things are laid out for us. It wasn't meant to be.'

'Do you really believe that, Stan?'

'Yes. As a matter of fact I do. I've seen it happen time and time again. It is known as fate.'

'You mean . . . in your opinion, if I hadn't met Jack and planned to marry him, he'd still be alive today. You're talking through your hat.'

With a quick glance in Tess's direction, Stan said warningly, 'Now, Colette, let's not start any of that old nonsense.'

She looked at her mother's face, taut with anger, and relented. 'All right. I'm sorry, Mam. Everyone to their own way of thinking. I've prepared some sandwiches. I'll just go and put the teapot on.'

Dominic had obviously been kept up to date with events and phoned to ask if the Maguires needed a lift down to St Peter's that evening. Gratefully, they accepted his offer and at five minutes to seven they joined the other mourners at the back of the church to await the arrival of the coffin.

The service was brief, the eloquent words of the priest about the loss of such a young man bringing tears to all present. As the congregation shuffled out of the church afterwards, Dan remained behind, by the side of the coffin that reposed before the high altar, shoulders slumped and head bowed in grief.

Alice waited at the back of the church with her daughter, undecided what to do. It was Tess who made up her mind for her. 'Go to him, Mam. He'll be there all night if you don't.'

It was as Tess left the church that she caught sight of Anne, supported by a man and a woman. She was in great distress and beckoned Tess over. 'Is Dan avoiding me?'

'I don't think so. I don't think he knows you're here.' Pity wrung Tess's heart at the change in the woman's appearance. Black eyes, bruised face and stitched brow made her a sorry-looking sight indeed. 'How are you faring, Anne?'

'I'm not so bad. At least they've discovered there is nothing seriously wrong with my chest, which is a relief. I couldn't bear it if I had to stay in that hospital for any length of time.'

'I'm glad to hear that. All the same, I'm surprised they let you out so soon.'

'I signed myself out.' She nodded towards the woman. 'Lily is putting me up until her son comes back.' Her head inclined towards the man. 'Her brother very kindly gave us a lift down tonight. Dan never thought to let me know anything at all about the funeral arrangements.

It's as if I didn't exist. But I do! And I must speak with him. Is he still in there?'

'Yes. I'll let him know you're here. I won't be a minute.'

Dan and her mother were sitting in a pew near the coffin. Tess approached quietly and addressed them. 'Dan, your wife is in the porch. She wishes to speak with you.'

Alice visibly paled. Dan gasped aloud. 'Anne's here?'

'It's only to be expected,' Tess said reprovingly. 'Someone called Lily has brought her along. She says she needs to speak with you. Come on, Mam, let's get you home.'

Blindly Alice grasped at her daughter's arm. Dan's voice stayed her. 'I'll see you later, Alice.'

'In the morning, Dan. We'll see you then,' Tess informed him and gently led her mother down the aisle.

Tess was apprehensive as they entered the church porch, wondering how her mother would react when she saw Anne. She needn't have worried. Pity and compassion immediately wiped out any ill feelings Alice might be harbouring, when she saw the state Anne was in. Going to her she gathered her close. 'You poor, poor dear, how you must be suffering.'

Tears fell afresh at this unexpected show of sympathy. 'Oh, I am! But nobody cares. I'm just Jack's mother, after all. I've lost my only child and my husband won't even speak to me. Let me know what's going on.'

'He will. He's coming now. I'll see you at the funeral tomorrow, Anne.'

'Thanks, Alice. It's nice to know someone understands how I feel.'

When Dan appeared, Lily's brother gave him a look of utter contempt and followed Tess and her mother outside. Lily slowly relaxed the hold she had on Anne's waist and said, 'You'd better support her or she'll fall.'

'There's no need for you to leave, Lily. This won't take long.' Dan was startled at the state of his wife but he had no intention of being influenced. Nine years was a long time and this woman was like a stranger to him now.

Lily gave him a look that was positively venomous. 'Anne wants to speak alone with you. I'll be waiting outside.'

Anne put a hand against the wall for support and Dan slipped his arm round her waist. 'Let's get you inside. We may as well sit down. Why didn't you stay inside and wait for me?'

'I was afraid of you giving me the slip,' she said simply.

'Surely you don't really think I'd do a thing like that?'

'Why not?' Her voice rose shrilly and with an apprehensive glance towards the coffin he hushed her. She wanted to mock him, ask if he thought Jack could hear them . . . fighting, as usual. However, she was well aware that, if provoked, Dan could very easily storm off leaving her on her own; then what would she do? She lowered her voice and continued, 'Why wouldn't you avoid me? You're a cruel bugger, Dan Thompson. You've kept me in the dark about everything, but you're still my husband in the eyes of the law, remember, and that's my son lying up there. I intend being at his funeral, in spite of you! And afterwards, well, I've nowhere to go. What are you going to do about that?'

Dan held a tight rein on his temper. This woman always brought out the worst in him. 'You seem to forget, Anne, that you're not my responsibility any more. What about this Jimmy fellow? Are you out of touch with him completely? Won't he take you in?'

'Look, Dan.' She made a sweeping gesture with her

hands, palms down, dismissing Jimmy. 'That's all in the past. I've left all that behind me.'

'Huh! Like you left me and Jack?' Dan scoffed.

Ignoring him, Anne continued. 'Meanwhile, Bill Brady is due home on Wednesday. Lily has been kindness itself to me but she needs time to get the room ready for his return. If I stay there a couple of nights, will you put me up from Tuesday onwards? Just until I'm well enough to look for a flat.'

He wanted to argue with her; tell her to go to hell. Tell her that what she was asking was out of the question, but decided it would be useless. The cards were stacked against him. She was, after all, Jack's mother and in dire need of help. And he was the only one who could help her.

'All right. I'll see what I can do. But don't take too long finding somewhere else to live. I won't put you up indefinitely. Is Lily waiting to take you home?'

'Yes.'

'Then let's get you out of here.'

It was raining early Monday morning, dark clouds hanging low over the rooftops. By mid-morning the rain had petered out and a weak watery sun showed signs of breaking through the grey clouds. Dan didn't know whether to be glad or sad. To him it seemed fitting that his son's body should be put into the earth in bad weather. He had always felt this way about funerals. He thought it better to leave the world behind in drabness, but if Jack had been attending a funeral he had always liked the sun to shine; said it made him feel hopeful that there really was life after death.

The funeral service was, as usual, a solemn affair. Dan broke down when he did one of the readings and

Colette's stepfather, after some hesitation and a nod from the priest, took over. By the time the Requiem Mass had finished and the coffin was carried from the church, the sun was shining brightly. Dan, after conferring with the undertakers, had asked that the coffin be carried up the Falls Road, past Spinner Street and Waterford Street, before being put into the hearse. A large crowd of mourners had turned out so the lifting would be no problem. There were plenty of friends and sympathisers to lend a shoulder when required.

Dan, Tony, Bob Crosby and Colette's father took the first lift. After that friends and neighbours and workmates of both Jack and Dan took turns until Leeson Street was reached. Here the coffin was placed on Dan's shoulder again and the burden was shared by Tony and two of Jack's workmates from Silk & Rayon. They continued slowly along the road and paused at the top of Spinner Street where a crowd of neighbours had gathered as a sign of respect, and also at the bottom of Waterford Street where it seemed as if the rest of the Silk & Rayon employees had assembled. At the Springfield Road junction the coffin was put in the hearse and mourners got into the limousines and other cars that had joined the funeral cortège and rolled slowly towards Milltown Cemetery.

Chapter Twelve

As the funeral procession paused at Spinner Street, Anne, who stood, supported by Colette and Tess, at the corner, collapsed and hung heavily in their arms. Distressed, they looked frantically around for assistance. Fearing it would prove too much for her, they had tried to persuade Anne to remain indoors, but she had insisted that, since Dan had forbidden her to go to the cemetery, she must at least see her son's remains pass by his street. It would be the last she would ever see of him in this world. Compassion overcame common sense and they had agreed to accompany her to the top of the street. And this was the outcome.

The two men who worked for Bob Crosby were standing, caps in hand, close by as the cortège passed and became aware of their plight. They immediately went to the girls' rescue. The younger man swept Anne's limp figure up in his strong arms and at a nod from Tess followed her down the street to Dan's house.

Inside the house Tess asked him to lay Anne on the settee and, thanking them for their trouble, offered them a drink.

'Better not, miss. We've got work to do.' It was the older man who answered with a wistful look.

It was Colette who twigged. 'Perhaps later?' she suggested.

'That would be lovely, miss. See you after work?'

'Any time at all. You just come along when you're free, and thanks for all your help.'

He touched his forelock. 'No problem, miss.'

When the door closed on them, Colette turned to Tess in despair. 'What are we going to do with her? She can't lie there all day. The mourners will be coming back soon.'

Tess bent low and examined Anne closely. 'Do you think she needs a doctor?'

'No. I doubt it. I think she just went into a cold faint.'

'Let's get her upstairs to bed then.'

'I wouldn't dare,' Colette retorted. 'You weren't here when Lily Brady suggested that Anne could have Jack's room. Dan was furious and ordered her out of the house. He vowed Anne would never sleep in Jack's bed. He was livid, so he was. So in no circumstances would I dare risk putting her in Jack's bed. And to put her in Dan's? That would be unthinkable.'

An angry twitch warned them that Anne wasn't as unconscious as she was leading them to believe. With a wink at Colette, Tess said, 'Well then, we'll just have to get her awake and settled in that chair over there, out of everybody's way. There's nothing else for it.'

Anne's eyes shot open and she let out an exaggerated groan as she swung her feet to the floor. 'Don't talk about me as if I'm not here. And thanks for all your sympathy.'

'Oh, a fox's doze, was it?' Colette asked in an inno-cent voice. 'Let me tell you something, Mrs Thompson. You're not the only one who needs a bit of sympathy round here. You lost a son you walked out on nine years ago . . . I lost my future husband.'

Colette received a look of pure venom, but Anne was saved by the bell, as it were. There was a light knock on the door and Mrs McAnulty stepped into the room. 'Just popped over to make sure you were satisfied with the spread.' She nodded to the long, narrow tables borrowed from neighbours and covered in white sheets, along one wall. They were laden with sandwiches, savoury pies and plates of cooked ham and chicken.

'Everything is marvellous, Mrs McAnulty. You and your friends have done a great job there. Can I coax you to stay and help with the making of the tea and serving it?'

'I'd be delighted.' Without further ado the small woman removed her coat and disappeared into the scullery.

Colette turned her attention to Anne. 'If you will kindly move into that chair over there I'll fetch you a cup of tea when it's ready. Tess, here's the crowd that was at the corner. Will you let them in and I'll give Mrs McAnulty a hand?'

Tess went to this brave girl who was putting on such a show of courage. 'You have my deepest admiration, Colette. I couldn't have done it if I were in your shoes.'

Tears came to Colette's eyes at this unexpected praise. 'Everyone seems to forget about me. I'm grieving too.' Her eyes strayed to the door as the mourners began filing in. 'Here's Mam and Stan. At least I've now got someone of my own to support me.'

That was the start of the visitors. There was a constant flow of people: relatives, neighbours, workmates and just about anybody who happened to be passing by, it seemed. 'Just dropping in to offer my condolences, can't stay too long. Oh all right then, if you insist. I'll just have the one thank you and then I'll be on my way' appeared to be more or less the formula on most visitors' lips. And so it continued till the early hours of the morning.

The women left around midnight. Dominic, after paying his respects, had left in the afternoon but had promised to return about twelve for Tess, Alice, Tony and Agnes to taxi them home. This he did, dropping Agnes and Tony at her house before continuing up Springfield Road with Alice and Tess.

Weary and exhausted, Alice thanked him, and climbed the stairs to go to bed straight away, for once not worrying her head about what her daughter might get up to with the handsome American, as Alice called him.

'Can I offer you a drink, Dominic?'

'I've already had a couple of beers, Tess, and I'm driving. Any chance of a nice cup of tea?'

'Ah, a man after my own heart. Make yourself comfortable. I won't be long.'

Delighted at the prospect of having him all to herself for a while, Tess made some sandwiches and a pot of tea. Dominic relieved her of the tray and put it on a small table which he had placed ready in front of the settee. 'You look all in. Sit down here and I'll pour.'

Tess thankfully curled up on one end of the settee and watched him. He handed her a plate with some sandwiches and a cup of tea. After helping himself, he sat down beside her.

She feasted her eyes on him. He really was very handsome. 'Thanks very much. You're spoiling me.'

His eyes were affectionate and warm. 'I couldn't spoil a nicer person, Tess,' he assured her.

She laughed and wagged a finger at him. 'Now you're

flirting again,' she warned. Becoming subdued, she said, 'It hasn't been much of a holiday for you, Dominic. Running us about to the church and the funeral. Not to mention collecting Mam from the bus station. You should start up a wee taxi service while you're here. You'd make a bomb at it.'

He shrugged. 'To be truthful, I'd nothing better to do.'

'You must be bored stiff. Do you still intend return-ing to Florida at the end of next week?'

A nod was her answer as he bit into a sandwich.

'There's no chance of you staying on here, is there?'

'No.'

'Then you haven't met that lovely Irish colleen you were hoping to sweep off her feet and take back with you?'

'Well now . . . I have and I haven't.'

Tess had been moodily contemplating her cup, as if expecting some foreign object to float to the surface. Now her head jerked up. 'You have?'

He frowned. 'I thought you understood that?'

'No, but then there is a lot I don't understand about you, Dominic Sullivan. You're an enigma. You talk in riddles most of the time. For instance, I thought if you met someone special you intended staying in Ireland.'

'No. That was just a foolish dream of mine. My home is in America. I can see that now. And it would cause too much of an upheaval for anyone to return there with me. So it looks like I shall be going back alone, more's the pity.'

Tess turned these words over in her mind and said tentatively, 'But surely if a woman cared enough . . . could she not follow you out at a later date?'

'Perhaps. The question is, *does* she care enough?'

Exasperated, she cried, 'Why don't you ask her, then?'

'I intend to, but not until the last minute. I would like her to be prepared to drop everything and return with me. Cut all her ties completely.'

'That's expecting a lot, Dominic. What if she hasn't got a valid passport?'

'She has. I know that for a fact.'

Tess recalled how, last week, before Jack was killed, Dominic had suggested that perhaps she and he could make up a foursome with Tony and Agnes and go over to Paris for a few days. That is, if they all had passports, which they all assured him they had.

With Jack's death, the idea had been shelved. But had that been Dominic's way of finding out if she had a passport? Could she just up and go as he seemed to be suggesting? No, of course she couldn't. And surely even he wouldn't expect her to. What about her mother? Their dressmaking business? Maybe he thought if a woman really loved a man, that was the way she could prove it to him.

Perhaps she could show him in her own way how much she cared. She swung her legs off the settee and, placing her plate and cup on the table, moved closer. They were thigh to thigh and knee to knee. She thought the pressure of his leg against hers would make her swoon. Never had she felt such strong vibrations because of another person's nearness. It was like an electric current coursing through her entire being. She willed him to put an arm round her and pressed closer still, trying to encourage him.

Dominic sat still, watching all these manoeuvres as though mesmerised. What on earth was she playing at? Suddenly it dawned on him. Good Lord! Tess thought he was propositioning her. Wanted her to throw caution to the wind and go to Florida with him. How on earth had he managed to put that notion into her head? He thought he had made it quite plain that someone else was involved. How had he got himself into this pickle? He had always thought he was being above board with Tess but somehow he had managed to get it all wrong. Now he saw little chance of getting out of this mess without hurting this sweet, kind girl.

Tess was an attractive girl and he was no saint. The closeness, warmth, and pressure of her body; the faint fragrance of her perfume – her very willingness was arousing him. He squirmed, not wanting his body to betray him. In no circumstances must he lose control. Tess was too nice a person to be taken advantage of. He was fighting a losing battle and knew he must get away, and pronto.

Placing a hand on his thigh, she whispered reassuringly, 'It's all right, Dominic. I understand. I feel the same way too.'

He was on his feet in a flash, gazing down at her in dismay. 'Tess, this is all wrong. I'll have to go now before we do something we'll both later regret. I'll give you a ring tomorrow.'

She sat in stunned silence until she heard the outer door close and the car pull away from the footpath. Bewildered, she went back over in her mind everything that had been said. Could she possibly have picked him up wrong? Surely not. There was no other woman that she could think of in the reckoning. All she could do was wait and see what developed, now she had admitted she cared deeply for him. Tired though she was, she tossed and turned all night long, and dawn was pushing weak skeletal fingers of light across her bed before she at long last fell into a restless doze.

*　　*　　*

The rest of the week passed slowly. Alice was in constant tears wondering how Dan was coping with Anne. He had promised to phone and let her know how things went. The call never materialised and she was too proud to troop down to Spinner Street to find out how he was getting on. Tess, in a similar position to her mother, also waited in vain for the phone to ring. Surely never before was a phone so stubbornly silent!

Alice seemed disinclined to start back to work. Tess, finishing the alterations to two skirts, decided it was time to broach the subject of Theresa Cunningham. 'Mam, look, we will have to get to work on the first Communion dresses and boys' suits as soon as possible. You know we never have enough time and always finish up rushed off our feet at the last minute, so I have a suggestion to make. Remember Theresa Cunningham?'

A blank face was turned to her and a slow shake of the head denied all knowledge of anyone called Theresa Cunningham. 'Of course you remember her,' Tess insisted. 'You met her a couple of times. She trained me in the Belart.'

At last the penny dropped and she had her mother's attention. 'Ah, yes. Theresa was a nice girl, so she was.'

'Come on, Mam. Snap out of it. She still is! I was talking to her outside the monastery on Easter Sunday. Her mother is poorly and Theresa has had to give up her job in the Belart to look after her.'

'Oh, I'm sorry to hear that.'

'She congratulated me, saying she had heard how well we are doing, and we got talking about work. I'm afraid I got carried away with my own importance and bragged a bit. I said we were thinking of taking on a trainee stitcher. She thought I was looking for someone right away and suggested we take her on for a couple of after-noons a week instead.'

'Can we afford her?'

'She wouldn't expect top wages and she certainly knows all about children's fashions. She'd be an asset to us, so she would. I think we should give her a try.'

Alice sat in thought for some moments. 'As you say, we could certainly sell more first Communion clothes if we had them. No matter how early we start we never manage to make enough. Would she come for a trial period, say for a month?'

'I think she would be willing to do that. I'll give her a ring and ask her to call in and see us. What day would be most suitable for you?'

'Any day,' Alice said despondently. 'No one seems to want to be bothered with us. What's happened to that friend of yours? You know, the American.'

'Mam, Dominic is on holiday. He knows it's back to porridge for me this week, so he'll want to get out and about during the day.' Why was she making excuses for Dominic's absence? His neglecting to phone and his continued absence was bothering her. Surely he wasn't ashamed to face her? Wanting to get away from her mother's penetrating stare, she said brightly, 'I'll give Theresa a ring now.'

Theresa was relieved and delighted to hear from her. She agreed to come and see them the following day. Tess replaced the receiver and stood with one hand still resting on it, gazing at it for some moments as if will-ing it to ring. It remained mute, however, as if mock-ing her with its continued silence.

It was seven o'clock that evening when Dan arrived at the door. Alice answered his knock and he asked her if she would go to the Broadway picture house with him.

He looked so haggard that she drew him into the hall and hugged him. 'Would you not rather stay here for a few hours and rest?'

He shook his head. 'I need to get out for a while before I go mad or something. Could we go for a walk, Alice?'

'What's it like outside?'

'Not too bad, but better put on a warm coat in case it gets cold later on.'

Grabbing her coat from the hall stand, Alice shrugged her arms into it and belted it round her waist. Wrapping a head scarf round her head and knotting it under her chin, she glanced to where Tess stood watching. 'I've my key with me, love, so don't be afraid to go out if you feel like it.'

'Chance would be a fine thing. Good night, Dan. On the other hand . . . perhaps it's not good night. Maybe I'll see you later. Feel free to come back for a bit of supper.'

'Thanks, Tess. I might just take you up on that.'

Tess stood at the door and gazed after them in amazement. It was the only time she could ever remember her mother leaving the house without first checking her appearance in the hall mirror. It must really be love. Wonders would never cease.

Dan strode purposefully along and Alice had difficulty keeping up with him.

'Hold your horses there, Dan,' she chided gently. 'You're running me off my poor old feet.'

He slowed down immediately and gave her all his attention. 'I'm sorry, love. I don't know what I'm doing half the time.'

Slipping her hand under his elbow, Alice said, 'It must

have been difficult for you these past few days, with Anne living under the same roof.'

'That's what I want to talk to you about.'

Fear clutched at Alice's heart. Had Anne wormed her way back into his affections? Was he about to tell her they were going to try for a reconciliation? She held back her fears and asked gently, 'What is it you want to tell me?'

'I want to ask your advice. As you already know, Lily Brady needed the bedroom Anne was using, for her sons, so she moved in with me on Tuesday.'

'And how's it going?' Alice asked with trepidation; perhaps she would be better off not knowing.

'Bloody awful. She never shuts up about the past and how happy we used to be. She must be looking back through rose-tinted glasses. She insists we can make a go of it again.'

'And has she managed to convince you?'

'No! She hasn't swayed me one wee bit. Maybe if I hadn't met and fallen in love with you, I might have been persuaded to give it another try, just to get some peace of mind.'

Alice was in turmoil. What could she say? If Dan's marriage could be saved she should be urging him to try to save it. It was the decent thing to do. After all, while Anne was alive he would never be free to marry anyone else in the eyes of God, so why try to keep them apart?

But she couldn't bring herself to nudge him in that direction, and didn't want to sever all connections with him. She compromised. 'What do you want to do?'

'I thought that was obvious. I want to marry you.'

'But you know that can never be, Dan.'

'It could! If only you would put your scruples to one

side. I've applied for a divorce, you know, and I only hope that Anne and I being under the same roof won't jeopardise my case. If it does come through would you be willing to marry me in a register office?'

'I . . . I don't know about that, Dan. It's against everything I believe in.'

'I know that, Alice. But would you at least consider it?'

'Well . . . now . . .'

'Please, Alice. Give me some hope. Just say you'll consider it.'

Unwilling to commit herself to such a promise, Alice remained silent. It was a lonely stretch of road and Dan stopped suddenly. Gripping Alice by the shoulders he gazed deeply into her eyes.

'Alice, I'm at my wits' end. I can't live under the same roof as that woman and I can't put her out. So what am I to do? Can you give me any advice?'

Tentatively, Alice asked, 'Has she managed to get into your bed?' A blush suffused her cheeks at the very idea of it. She had no right to question him like this. After all, Anne was still his wife and, by the sound of it, would be more than willing to oblige him in that department, given half a chance.

Dan glowered at her. 'How can you even think like that?'

Relieved, Alice relaxed against him. 'I'm sorry. I should know better. Well then, you'll have to move out of the house for a time until Anne finds somewhere else to live. To be truthful I can't bear the thought of you two being under the same roof.'

'Ah, Alice, my love.' He kissed her gently on the eyes, the cheeks, the lips, longing in every touch, before replying. 'And where do you suggest I go?'

Mesmerised by his kisses she replied without stopping to think of the consequences. 'There's plenty of room in our house. You could stay with us.'

The minute the words were out of her mouth she regretted them. What on earth would Tess say? She would never agree to a man's living with them.

'Is there any chance of that?'

'Of course I'd have to talk it over with Tess first. See what she has to say about it.'

He smiled wryly. 'I can't see her agreeing. Can you?'

'It is my house, you know, Dan.'

'I know that. But I would never forgive myself if I was to cause any friction between you and your daughter.'

Suddenly in command, Alice broke away from him and turned back down the road. 'Right! Let's go back for some supper and if I get a chance I'll put it to Tess. The decision will be hers. Okay?'

On their return, leaving Dan seated in the living room where a fire burned brightly in the modern grate, Alice manoeuvred Tess into the sitting room. 'I've a big favour to ask of you, my dear.'

She knew she was about to put her daughter on a sticky spot and had difficulty framing the right words to soften the impact of her proposal. She dithered so long that Tess cried out in exasperation. 'Well, get on with it. What has you in such a quandary? You're never usually at a loss for words where I'm concerned.'

The words came out in a gush. 'Can Dan stay here till Anne finds a place of her own?'

Tess staggered back, eyes almost popping out of their sockets at her mother's gumption. 'You mean . . . you and he share a room?'

Alice's jaw dropped slightly. 'Catch yourself on, Tess.

Of course not! I'm surprised at you, so I am. I thought he might have the attic bedroom. That is, if you have no objections.'

'Why all the embarrassment then? You mean can he stay as a *paying* lodger?'

Alice smiled. 'To be truthful, money wasn't mentioned. I just suggested that he might be able to stay until Anne finds a place of her own. If you were willing, of course,' she added hastily.

'Mam, you saw the state of Anne. She won't want to show her face outside for some time to come. She is sitting there rent free with an estranged husband who supposedly hates her guts, and probably thinks she can eventually win him over. I think Dan will be here for some time to come, so he'll have to pay his way. We're not running a charity shop, you know, and the sooner he learns that the better.'

'Thanks, Tess. I'm sure he will agree to anything you say.' Alice was so relieved to think she was going to prise Dan away from his wife's clutches that she impulsively hugged her daughter.

The following day, Friday, Dominic rang and asked Tess if she would like to go to the pictures with him on Saturday night, adding that they could make up a foursome with Agnes and Tony if she wanted.

Tess bit down on her bottom lip for some moments before answering sweetly, 'You don't have to bring your chaperons along, Dominic. I can assure you that I've no intention of jumping on you at the first opportunity.'

Obviously in the dark as to what she meant he said hesitantly, 'Does that mean you'll come?'

'Only if you feel safe enough with me sitting beside you in a darkened cinema.'

He laughed, but was clearly still somewhat perplexed. 'I'll pick you up at half six then. Bye for now.'

The doorbell rang as she was about to leave the hall, heralding the arrival of Theresa Cunningham.

'Come in, Theresa. Mam has just popped out for a minute or two. She won't be too long.'

They were passing the work room and Tess said, 'Would you like to take a look around? This is where we work. It's not very big for three people to work in comfort, I'm afraid, but I think Mam would be more than willing to do her work in the sitting room when necessary.'

Theresa's eyes ranged over the room. 'It's smashing, Tess. The layout's great and you have a good stock of material by the looks of things. And *two* sewing machines! I was wondering about that.'

'Yes, that one was going at a bargain price when that factory on Donegal Road was closing down last year. It was practically new, so I jumped at the chance to buy it, hoping that we might eventually expand.'

'You're obviously a good businesswoman as well as everything else. And it takes you to have your head screwed on these days. Plan ahead, that's what I say.'

'We don't do too badly, and in a way it's all due to you. You taught me all I know about this trade, Theresa.'

'I only did what I was paid to do. The talent has to be there in the first instance for you to be able to succeed. And you have, Tess. I'm very proud to be associated with you.'

She sounded so sincere that Tess was grinning from ear to ear and red with embarrassment. 'Here's Mam now,' she said with relief when the outer door slammed shut.

Alice was accompanied by Dan carrying a couple of large suitcases.

'Hello, Theresa. It's lovely to see you again.' Alice proffered her cheek for a kiss and then introduced Dan. 'This is a friend of mine, Dan Thompson. He'll be staying with us for a while. I'll show you where to put your cases, Dan. Excuse me, Theresa. I won't be a minute; then we can sit down and have that talk.'

While they waited, Theresa confided in Tess that she would be delighted to work on these premises and sincerely hoped they could come to an amicable arrangement. She need not have worried. After a short interview, throughout which Tess let her mother do most of the talking, terms were offered and accepted.

Theresa refused a drink or a cup of tea on the grounds that her mother would be waiting impatiently to hear the good news, and left, saying she looked forward to seeing them on Monday afternoon.

The outing to the cinema wasn't much of a success. The film, advertised as an exciting spy thriller, turned out to be a mediocre affair, and so it was a glum foursome that headed up Grosvenor Road to where the car was parked in a side street. Tess had to admit to herself that if Dominic had acted a bit more friendly towards her, her attitude would have probably been very different and she wouldn't have cared one way or the other about the film.

But it annoyed her that Dominic seemed to be distancing himself from her; hadn't even held her hand during the show as he had done during their previous visit to the pictures. Did he really think she was out to get him at any cost? He should know her better than that. Shrugging off her misery, Tess tried to lift the gloom that was hanging over them like a black cloud. 'All right then, let's brighten up a bit, lads! Even a visit to the graveyard would be a lot more cheerful than this. So where do we go from here?'

Agnes looked daggers at her friend. 'That's not a very nice thing to say. After all, *they* didn't choose which picture house we should go to. In fact, if I remember correctly it was you who suggested going to the Ritz.'

'Go on now! Put the blame on me! It was supposed to be a good thriller, according to the write-up in the papers.'

'Well you're the one complaining.'

'Hey, hold on a minute, girls,' Dominic interrupted. 'Let's not start a slanging match in public. So it wasn't a great film, so what? It's not the end of the world, after all. Can I suggest that, since Johnny Long's is nearby, we go round there for a fish supper or something. I don't know about you lot, but I'm a little bit peckish.'

'Sounds good to me,' Tess agreed, turning in that direction.

As usual the succulent, crispy cod and golden chips were delicious and lifted them out of their doldrums. 'Dennis is due home tomorrow so let's make the most of having the use of his car tonight,' Dominic declared. 'Any suggestions, folks?'

'Let's take a run down to Bangor. That would be a pleasant change, and it's a nice run and not too far away.' Tony surprised them all by making a decision.

Agnes flashed him a pleasant look of surprise. He usually asked her opinion first and then fell in with her wishes. Perhaps he wasn't such a dull person after all, she thought. Maybe they *could* make a go of it once Dominic's overpowering influence was removed from the scene. Another week to go. She had been dismayed when she learned that he was shortening his holiday;

had experienced a great sense of loss which she couldn't understand. However, after some consideration she decided it was all for the best. Once she and Tony were married she would soon forget all about Dominic. Tony was a quiet, reliable man. She would be safe with him.

Dominic had never again referred to her going to Florida with him and she had mixed feelings about that. She had actually given consideration to his proposal; had in her mind's eye pictured herself running off with him, and the idea of living in a warm climate had appealed to her. Since he hadn't mentioned it again he obviously had changed his mind about her. He had been making a fool of her and she was glad she hadn't rushed in head over heels and made a fool of herself into the bargain. Mind you, at the time, after viewing that magical sunset and the wonderful joy of his kisses, the idea had been very tempting indeed; then Tess began to talk as if she had some claim on him. Was he making a pass at both of them as a bit of warped humour on his part? Something to boast about when he got back to the States?

To be truthful, she would be glad to see the back of him, then everything could get back to normal. His constant presence filled her with urges she couldn't control; she was afraid to catch his eye unexpectedly, when in his company, in case any of the others noticed the effect he had on her. It wasn't natural to feel the way she did about someone she hardly knew and it disturbed her immensely.

Without the desires she felt when in his presence, he wouldn't be haunting her dreams. Tony was the man for her. Married life with him should prove rewarding. Wasn't he willing to wait until after marriage? In truth, she couldn't see what all the fuss was about; why couples risked pregnancy by behaving immorally before taking their marriage vows and ended up getting married too young and before they were ready. More times than she cared to remember these shotgun marriages didn't last. It was a source of wonder to her.

When they left the car park at Bangor, Agnes slipped her arm through Tony's and hugged it tightly; a possessive gesture that caught Dominic's attention.

Dominic gave her a long searching look and received a defiant tilt of the chin in return. He turned his attention to Tess. 'Which direction do you want to go, Tess?'

'What about a stroll along the promenade?'

Without another word he placed an arm across her shoulders and led her away. With an apprehensive glance in the direction of their companions, Tess asked, 'What's wrong, Dominic? Did I miss something there?'

'I think they deserve some time alone. In fact I'm beginning to think they deserve each other,' he added grimly.

Shrugging his arm off her shoulders, Tess said drily, 'How thoughtful of you. I wish you were just as considerate towards *me*.'

'Ah, Tess. Don't be like that. I never meant to offend you.'

'Who's offended? I'm just the stupid eejit who went along with everything you said. You didn't even phone me when you promised you would. Why didn't you?'

'I didn't know what to say. I didn't even think you cared. You could easily have hung up on me and then what would I have done? Can't we remain friends, Tess? I value your friendship a lot.'

Friendship! He was offering her bloody *friendship*. Still, it was so uncharacteristic of arrogant, confident Dominic to be so humble, she felt her bad humour evaporate.

At least he hadn't let her make a fool of herself that night on the settee. She could still face him without feeling ashamed. Now she admitted, 'I'm afraid I over-reacted a bit. Sorry.'

'You have nothing to apologise for. This is all my fault. I should have made my intentions crystal clear.'

'No! You made no promises. It was my fault. I got the wrong end of the stick . . . as usual. For a while there I actually thought you fancied me,' she confessed in a small voice.

'You're a wonderful person, Tess. I wish things could be different.'

'There's nothing you can do about it, Dominic. Always the bridesmaid, never the bride. Good old Tess. That's me!'

'Oh, you'll marry one day, Tess. You're too nice a girl to be passed over. I only hope you get someone worthy of you. Don't you ever settle for anything less.'

She looked up at him. 'I wish you'd confide in me who this mysterious girl is. I've racked my brains and can't, for the life of me, think who it could be. Unless you've been seeing someone on the sly.'

He hesitated, undecided, and she urged him, 'Go on! Tell me.'

'If I tell you, will you promise not to say a word to anyone? Especially not to Agnes?'

She nodded her head excitedly, and vowed, 'I prom-ise. Scout's honour.'

'It's Agnes.'

If he'd smacked her full on the nose with his fist, she wouldn't have been any more shocked. She stood stock still as if pinned to the spot, and gasped, 'What? You're having me on. Aren't you?'

'Don't sound so surprised. I fell for her the moment

I clapped eyes on her. She's beautiful and sweet and Tony doesn't deserve her.'

'That's as may be, but she did choose to get engaged to Tony. Does she know you fancy her?'

'Well . . . I did tell her in a roundabout way that she was the one for me, but obviously she didn't believe me. Maybe she thought I was pulling her leg.'

'Huh! You told her in a roundabout way? I'm sure it was as clear as mud to her. Even when you think you're being straightforward, you're very vague. You talk in riddles at the best of times. Did you know that?'

'I'll try and put it into words you'll understand, Tess, and maybe you'll be able to advise me. Remember the night in Galway when Agnes and I went to watch the sun set on the bay?' Tess nodded and he continued. 'It was a wonderful experience, watching that great ball of fire slowly sink out of sight. It seemed the natural thing to do, that we kiss. And she enjoyed it, mind you. I know she did. I got the impression that Tony didn't kiss her like that. But when I suggested she was engaged to the wrong man, and she must break off with him and return to Florida with me, she said Tony was very good to her and she could never do anything that would hurt him.'

Tess wagged her head. 'That's Agnes for you. And what did you say to that?'

'Well, I had no intention of trying to force her. If love isn't spontaneous it's not the real thing as far as I'm concerned. So I told her the decision was hers. I know she's very reserved, but she has to care enough to throw caution to the winds and come away with me. Make a complete break of it.'

'And?'

'And nothing. She hasn't given me any signs that she's

even thinking about it. In fact she was so cool on the journey home from Galway, I thought she had already made up her mind to stay with Tony. I haven't had the chance to talk to her since.'

Tess recalled the conversation she had had with Agnes in the restaurant in Cavan. She groaned aloud.

'What?' he asked urgently. 'You've thought of something, haven't you?'

'Yes, I have, and it might have some bearing on your predicament. On our way home from Galway I implied that you were interested in me and wanted to stay in Ireland.'

'Ah, I see.'

'Well, you can't blame me for thinking like that! It's your talking in riddles again.'

'Probably. What did she say?'

'She asked me if I had fallen for you . . . and I admitted that I had. So there you are! I bet it's me she won't risk hurting. Not after Jack Thompson dropping me for another girl.' They strolled along in silence for some moments, gazing unseeingly at the numerous yachts bobbing on the swell. 'We'll have to do something about it, Dominic.'

'You think I might still stand a chance with her?'

'Not if you keep on the way you're going. Do what you vowed you'd do. Sweep her off her feet! Take her back to Florida with you. Above all else, speak in a language she can understand, not your usual double Dutch. Make it as simple as possible. That way there can be no misunderstandings.'

Tony and Agnes were already back at the car when they eventually returned. Tess looked at her friend with new eyes. She'd always known that Agnes was a stunner. Short, natural blonde hair, sparkling blue eyes and good figure. With looks like that, how could she be otherwise? Tony was the obstacle. If only Agnes hadn't allowed him to coerce her into an engagement. If she were free, everything would be hunky-dory. She caught Agnes's eye and before her friend could look away Tess detected a hint of what could possibly be jealousy in its depths.

Annoyed at herself for worrying what Dominic and Tess might have been getting up to, Agnes sat trying to come to terms with her misery. She sat apart from Tony, incurring anxious glances from him. An uneasy silence encompassed them on the drive back to Belfast. After dropping Agnes and Tony off, Dominic stopped the car outside Tess's house.

'It's too late to ask you in, Dominic. I forgot to mention that Dan Thompson is lodging with us at the minute. Mam and him will be in bed by now – separate beds that is. But then, how do I know what they get up to when I'm out? Good heavens, would you listen to me. I'm beginning to sound like Mam when she is worrying about me. Still, I don't want to disturb them. I want to have a private chat with you.'

Dominic turned sideways in the driving seat and eyed her. 'What about?'

'You and Agnes. Now that I've gotten over the shock, I think you two would make ideal partners.'

'You're such a good person, Tess, and fun to be with. You never cease to amaze me. I'm so sorry I'm not the one for you, but I know you *will* find your Mr Right one day.'

'That's okay, Dominic.' She smiled wryly. 'Mind you, you are going to have one hell of a job persuading her to break off with Tony. You see, she's the old-fashioned type. She'll worry about leaving him to face the music on his lonesome. Nevertheless, let's see if I can be of some assistance. Let's put our heads together and see what we come up with.'

'Right!'

'When do you leave for America?'

'I leave Aldergrove for Shannon on Sunday night, and my connection to Florida leaves Monday evening.'

'That doesn't give us much time, so let's put some plans together. And the sooner the better.'

'I think I had better mention that my parents are throwing a party for me. Just at home, like, with relatives and close friends.'

'When will that be?'

'Friday night.'

'Oh, dear, we'd better get a move on. What if we . . .'

A plan was concocted. Whether or not it would succeed was another matter.

Chapter Thirteen

Agnes was concerned to find that Dominic and Tess seemed to be closer than ever. What if he changed his mind and remained in Belfast; could she live with that? Tony was also aware of the covert looks exchanged by the pair when they were together, and thought that, with a bit of luck, they might get engaged. He would certainly be glad to get Dominic out of his hair once and for all, one way or the other. It worried him that Agnes got all uptight when the guy was around.

They had decided to cram as much action into Dominic's last few days as possible and were constantly on the go. Dennis had obligingly let his brother have the loan of the car for the remainder of his stay and on Sunday they spent the day at Newcastle. On Monday they took a drive to Portrush.

Tess cried off going anywhere on Tuesday, her excuse being that she needed to work and put in some overtime to justify taking on Theresa Cunningham who had started work on Monday afternoon. Dominic also pleaded a prior engagement and they made plans for the four of them to meet up again on Thursday for a final fling, Dominic saying he wasn't sure what was happening on Wednesday.

As the car pulled away from her doorway on Monday

night, Agnes muttered, 'I feel sure those two have made their own plans for tomorrow night. They just don't want us with them.'

Putting his arms round her, Tony said gently, 'Dominic hasn't much time left. Perhaps they want to be alone for a change.'

'Why? Do you think they've fallen in love?' She managed to keep the horror of this idea from her voice.

Unaware of her misery, Tony shrugged. 'It's not impossible. After all, they're both free to do as they please. So why not?'

'I can't see Tess leaving her mother to go and live in Florida, can you? They're as thick as thieves, those two. No, I can't see it.'

'Maybe Dominic will go back to America and settle his affairs and come back here to live. I don't think he would expect Tess to give up her business and all. If he sold up, he would have plenty of cash to start up a restaurant over here.'

Appalled at the very idea, Agnes wriggled herself free of Tony's arms. 'It's getting late, Tony, and I'm very tired. Do you mind if I don't ask you in?'

Tony did mind. He minded very much, in fact, but knew from past experience it would be useless to argue with her. Agnes always got her own way. Why did he put up with it? Because he loved her and it would be all so different once they were married. Or would it? He was beginning to have his doubts. Would he always be henpecked?

Agnes was surprised when her mother shouted upstairs at tea time the following night and said Tess wanted to speak to her on the phone. Skipping lightly down the stairs, she lifted the receiver to her ear. 'I thought you and Dominic were going it alone tonight?'

'What gave you that idea? I told you I was working late. We need a couple of Communion dresses and a boy's suit for display purposes. That way potential customers can see what they're getting for their money before placing their orders. Theresa made the boy's suit yesterday afternoon and it's beautiful. She's a great seamstress. I have a long and a short Communion dress almost ready and I want to finish them off tonight.'

'Huh! If I were to believe that I'd believe anything.'

'Do I detect a note of jealousy in your voice, Agnes Quinn?'

'You've got to be joking. What have I got to be jealous about?'

'Perhaps because you like Dominic more than you're letting on, and you're picturing me and him off somewhere on our own, having a cosy wee cuddle. Could that be the reason for your jealousy?'

Glad that her friend couldn't see her blazing face – for hadn't she been harbouring just such thoughts about Tess and Dominic? – Agnes muttered, 'Catch yourself on! Anyway, to get back to business, why did you phone?'

'I was wondering if you were seeing Tony tonight?'

'No . . . like you, he feels the need to work some overtime.'

'The reason I phoned is because I need some advice, Agnes. Will you come up here and listen to my tale of woe?'

'Now? Can't it wait till tomorrow?'

'I need your opinion as soon as possible.'

'Does it concern Dominic?'

'In a way, yes, it does. I'll explain when I see you. Bye for now.' Tess hung up before her friend could ask any more questions. Replacing the receiver in its cradle, she turned and faced Dominic. 'Well, she's coming, so be ready to get her into the car and take off.'

'What if she won't come with me?'

'Dominic! For heaven's sake think positive. If you can't persuade her into the car to go for a drive with you, you may as well forget all about whisking her off to America in a plane.'

He headed for the door. 'Wish me luck, Tess. I hope she doesn't take too long getting here or I might get cold feet and do a runner.'

'Good luck, Dominic. I've a gut feeling that this is going to work out okay.'

When the door closed on him she stood for some moments gazing blindly at it. Why was she being so helpful? Because Dominic would be of no use to her while he was in love with Agnes. It was as simple as that. Going into the work room she pulled a chair up close to the window. It could be some time before Agnes arrived, but Tess intended keeping a lookout to make sure her friend didn't run off when Dominic invited her to go for a drive. The way things stood at the moment, Agnes would probably imagine it was like being invited to go on a drive with the devil.

It was a half hour later that Agnes dandered up the road at her leisure. A frown plucked at her brow when she saw Dennis's car parked in front of Tess's house. Tess hadn't mentioned that Dominic was going to be there. Had he come unexpectedly? Would she be interrupting anything? Should she go back home? In a dither she squinted closely at the car through narrowed eyelids. Surely there was someone sitting in it.

A bundle of nerves after sitting in the car so long,

Dominic watched her approach in the mirror. When she hesitated, he quickly got out of the car and stood waiting for her.

'What's going on? Tess said she wanted to talk to me about something.'

'No, I want to talk to you.' His hands rested lightly on her shoulders, in case she turned tail and ran back down the road. 'I want you to come for a drive with me, without Tony waiting patiently in the background. I want to have a good long chat with you without any interference.'

Head high, she looked disdainfully down her nose at him. 'You make patience sound like a curse instead of a blessing.'

'No, you're wrong. Patience is a great virtue, but mine is stretched to the limit at the minute. There isn't much time left and I need to talk to you before I go back to Florida. Will you come for a drive with me? Please?'

Her eyes scanned the bay window. There wasn't a light in the room but she had a feeling that Tess was there, watching them, although everything was obscured by the street light reflecting on the glass.

'All right. Let's go.' If Tess had anything to do with this, God knows what Dominic was about to confide to her. She had better prepare herself for the worst. Her heart was thumping like a trip-hammer as she got into the car.

Tess watched the meeting take place. She saw Agnes glance towards the window and willed herself to remain motionless. After what seemed like ages, Dominic led Agnes round to the passenger side of the car. She climbed in and off they went. Where would he take her, Tess wondered. They needed to be completely alone, without any interruptions. Probably up past Whiterock Road into the countryside. Oh, to be alone in a car with Dominic and him intent on making her feel loved. Tears pricked at her eyes. For a while there she had thought Dominic was her Mr Right. Would she ever meet someone she really cared for and have those feelings reciprocated?

Stretching her cramped limbs, she squared her shoulders and entered the living room. She found her mother and Dan seated either side of the hearth like an old married couple. Dan had certainly made himself at home in their house. If at times Tess was annoyed at the intrusion into her organised life she managed to hide her feelings. After all, he had only been here a short time and it wouldn't be for ever, she consoled herself. Or would it? Her mother was waiting on him hand and foot, so why should he be in a hurry to get back to that drab house in Spinner Street, where he had to cook for himself and do the washing up and all the other housework that required doing. He knew when he was well off. 'Have you seen any sign of Anne since you moved in here?'

Dan hesitated. A quick glance in Alice's direction and a brief nod was Tess's answer. Her mother's chin rose a fraction and there was a slight tightening of her lips. Obviously he hadn't mentioned to her that he had visited his estranged wife.

Determined to get a positive answer, Tess said, 'How is she managing on her own with a broken wrist?'

'She seems to be coping okay. You'll never believe it, but remember Lily Brady's brother Pat? The one who brought her down to the church that night in the car? Well, I've since found out that he's a bachelor and a bit sweet on Anne. With a bit of luck the two of them might just hit it off together. So who knows . . . perhaps he'll take her off my hands, once and for all.'

Vexation oozing from her every movement, Alice rose and left the room in a huff. They heard her climb the stairs and a bedroom door close none too gently.

'In future, if I were you, Dan, I'd keep Mam up to date on your meetings with Anne. She has every right to know what's going on. If you've nothing to hide there shouldn't be a problem.'

'Tess, believe me . . . there's nothing going on. As I've just said, maybe this Pat fellow will talk Anne into going to live with him. I certainly hope so.'

'And what good will that do, pray tell me? You will still be a married man. I'm warning you, Dan Thompson, don't trifle with my mother's affections, or you'll have me to answer to. She's too good to be hurt by the likes of you.'

With these words, Tess rose abruptly and left the room. He followed her into the kitchen. The dinner dishes were still soaking and as she angrily thumped them about with unnecessary vigour, he lifted a glass cloth and started drying the plates.

'That is something else you could do more often,' Tess said, thumping another plate on to the stainless steel drainer. If they were chipped she would have no one to blame but herself. She was angry and intended getting all the aggression off her chest while she had the chance. 'I'm sure you had to share the chores with Jack while he was alive. So you'd better pull your weight while you're staying in our house. I for one will not become a skivvy just because a man has come to stay. *And* I certainly won't stand by any longer while you sit in there on that big fat arse of yours, and watch Mam wait on you hand and foot. So you'd better pay heed if you know what's good for you.'

Putting the last dish on the draining board she

flounced from the kitchen, throwing over her shoulder, 'And you can do the worktops while you're at it.'

His voice stayed her. 'Tess . . . I *have* offered, you know. Honestly! But your mother won't let me do any housework.'

Tess knew this to be true and it rankled. 'Ignore her! Or so help me, if you don't get your finger out, you'll be looking for somewhere else to live.'

'I'll do my best,' he promised. 'And listen, Tess, if you're not too busy could you nip down and see Colette some time? It was her I called to see, when Anne collared me. Colette's grannie is still in hospital and the poor wee dear hasn't a minute to herself. No sooner is she home from work than she's off again to the hospital. That girl's run off her feet. She can't even find the time to cook a proper meal. She deserves a medal, so she does. Anne says she's tried to help, but Colette won't have anything to do with her. Won't even come in for a cuppa or a drink or even a wee chat. For that matter, she won't have anything to do with me either. You'd think I'd offended her in some way. When I ask how she's coping she just says she's managing very well thank you, and that I'm to leave her alone and not annoy her.'

Tess was overcome with remorse. She had meant to keep in touch with Colette and encourage her to get out and about, and not to dwell on the past. But all that fuss with Dominic and Agnes had driven the girl completely from her thoughts. 'I'll go down now, Dan. It was very inconsiderate of me. I should have gone down sooner.'

'Thanks, Tess. You're an angel. And by the way . . . have I really got a big fat backside? Are you suggesting that I'm putting on weight?'

He grinned at her and she laughed at the very idea of her rude remarks as she headed for the stairs. 'Yes!'

Tess found Colette looking wan and miserable when she answered her knock. She followed the girl into the kitchen and, full of compassion, gathered her close and rocked her gently in her arms.

'Colette, I'm so sorry for neglecting you. I should have come down sooner.'

Colette sniffed loudly, tears brimming. But she remained in the comfort of Tess's embrace, glad of human contact. 'Don't be silly, I'm not your problem. But thanks all the same for thinking of me.'

Sobs began to shudder through the girl's frail body and Tess wondered what to do. 'Don't, love, don't upset yourself so. Can I get you anything?'

Easing herself from Tess's arms, Colette sat down on the settee and wiped her eyes with the back of her hand. 'You'll have to forgive me, Tess. I'm just back from the Royal. Grannie's getting home tomorrow.'

'Why, that's wonderful news,' Tess cried, at a loss as to why Colette appeared so despondent. 'I suppose it's the relief of knowing she's better that has you in this state,' she chided her. 'You'll be soon back to normal, once she's home. You'll see.'

But Colette's head was slowly shaking from side to side in sorrow, as more tears fell. 'She's not going to get better. They've given her a month at the most.'

'Oh, my God.' Tess, always the practical one, let her thoughts race ahead of her. 'Will you be able to get the time off work to look after her?'

'I don't know, but if the bank won't give me compassionate leave I'll have to give up my job. It's as simple as that. The hospital offered to put Grannie in a nursing home, but I wouldn't hear tell of it. I won't have her looked after by strangers when I'm capable of doing it myself. A nurse will call in twice daily, morning and evening, to help me bathe her and move her about to prevent her getting bedsores.'

'You've my admiration, Colette. You're a very brave girl. But if there's anything – anything at all – my mam or I can do to help, you have only to ask.'

'Thanks.'

Tess smiled wryly. 'I suppose you're taking that with a pinch of salt considering how I've been neglecting you lately. You'll be thinking, as soon as I'm out of that door it's the last you'll see of me. But I do sincerely mean it. Honest!'

To divert Colette's troubled mind away from thoughts of her grannie, Tess confided her reason for not keeping in touch with her. After all, she could trust Colette to keep her own counsel, and giving her thoughts a new direction was more important than keeping a secret that would be resolved one way or the other in a few days' time in any case. She told Colette how for a second time she had thought that perhaps fate was smiling on her at last and she had met her Mr Right, only to discover she had got it all wrong . . . again. Colette sat enthralled as Tess related how she had misread all the signs. She had thought that Dominic was wooing her, only to find out that all the while he was in love with her best friend, Agnes, and hoped to take her back to Florida with him. 'How could I have been so blind, I ask you?' she finished.

Now the consoler, Colette patted Tess's knee in a comforting gesture. 'I'm sorry to hear that. You must be so disappointed.'

'Oh, I'll get over it. I'm only too glad I didn't make

a fool of myself. This is my second disappointment, remember. Maybe third time lucky.'

'What about Tony?' Colette asked quietly.

'He'll just have to be like me. Grin and bear it. Agnes should never have gotten engaged to him in the first place.'

'Still, she did agree to marry him.'

'Under duress.'

'Poor Tony. He'll be heartbroken. There is more to him than meets the eye, you know. I got to know him quite well when I was going out with Jack. He's very obliging and wouldn't hurt a fly.'

For the first time Tess considered Tony's position in all this. So far, in her estimation he had just been one pain in the neck; hadn't deserved any sympathy. But she admitted that he did, in his own quiet way, love Agnes. Of that there could be no doubt, so of course he'd be devastated. She silently seconded Colette's words. Poor Tony. Well, I'm losing Dominic, she reminded herself. Only, to be truthful, it wasn't the same thing, now was it? Dominic had not committed himself to her. It was all a big misunderstanding on her part. Tony's case was a different kettle of fish altogether.

She rose to her feet. 'Now I've told you all my little secrets, I'll have to be getting back home.'

'Thanks for calling down, Tess. Realising other people besides myself have their own troubles has lifted my spirits a lot.'

'Your troubles are more horrendous. Nevertheless, I'll be back to keep you up to date on the saga of the yank and Agnes. Will she or won't she? Watch out for next week's episode.' She laughed, heading for the door.

Slowly, Colette followed her, a look of consternation on her face. 'I hope Agnes opts to stay with Tony.'

Tess was amazed that Colette could think along those lines. 'Do you?' she gasped. 'Why?'

'Well, it seems to me that Dominic has a lot going for him in America. He'll have so many things to occupy his mind and will soon get over his disappointment. Whereas if Agnes leaves Tony . . . he may never get over the loss of her.'

'You know, I never thought of that. You're a very wise person, Colette.'

'No, I'm not!'

'Oh, but yes you are! You've set me thinking. Look, I must run. If it's all right with you, I'll nip down tomorrow for a short time and meet your grannie.'

'Make it the afternoon. She won't be home until about three.'

'Right, afternoon it is. Bye for now.'

Agnes sat silent as the car sped up Springfield Road. She had convinced herself that Dominic was going to apologise for pretending he cared for her. She wanted to be able to assure him that it didn't matter in the slightest. That she would be only too glad to see him and Tess hitting it off and, maybe, him settling down in Belfast.

She clasped her hands so tightly in her lap that her knuckles were white, as she tried to compose herself. Would she be able to carry it off? As usual, when in his company, she was restless. Hurry up, she willed him silently. Hurry up and get it over with.

Dominic watched her from the corner of his eye. He could almost feel the tension that surrounded her; could see the different emotions flicker across her face. This was all one big mistake. He had been wrong to lure her to meet him. She would never agree to anything he proposed; never relax enough for him to talk her round to his way of thinking.

Up in the countryside, on a lonely stretch of road, he drew the car to a stop in the entrance to a field and sat gathering his thoughts. Should he turn round and take her home?

'Would you mind getting on with it? I haven't all night, you know.'

Startled by her tone of voice, he turned in his seat and faced her. She was staring straight ahead, ignoring him completely. 'Excuse me? Did you speak?'

'Yes! I said get on with it. What do you want to talk about?'

'I'm not sure that it's such a good idea now.'

'If it was important enough for you to practically kidnap me and drive me away up here, it must be important enough to talk about. Shall I make it easier for you?'

Grim faced, he nodded. 'Yes, you do that.'

'You want to apologise for making a pass at me in Galway. Right? I understand perfectly, Dominic. It was the romantic atmosphere. The setting of the sun on the bay was enough to bring out the romance in anyone.' How she wished she could forget that night. She had tried, but it haunted her dreams, filling her with longings she had no control over. In an unsteady voice she continued. 'There's no need for you to explain anything, or apologise. No need whatsoever. I felt the magic of it too. And it takes two consenting people to enjoy it. So don't go blaming yourself.'

'But I asked you a question that night, and you didn't give me an answer, Agnes.'

'Why should I? It was all make believe on your part, after all. Wasn't it? Tess made it quite clear the next day in Cavan that you were interested in her. You'd have got one heck of a shock had I pretended to have fancied you.'

'That's a laugh! You wouldn't have fooled me for one minute. The only one you're fooling is yourself. It never ceases to amaze me the way you stick to Tony like a bloody sticking plaster every time we all go out together. It must be damned uncomfortable at times, trying to drag yourself away from him.'

The air in the car was so charged with electricity that Dominic felt a flick of a switch would spark off an explosion, blowing them both to smithereens. He could see she was crying, but hardened his heart. He had come to the conclusion that he was flogging a dead horse. She wasn't in the least bit interested in him at all. Her only interest was in good old boring Tony. What an exciting life lay ahead of her.

He turned the key in the ignition. 'I apologise for wasting your precious time. I'll take you back.'

He was reversing out on to the road when he brought the car to an abrupt halt and drove forward again. 'I imagine I'll get a cursory peck on the cheek as my farewell kiss at the weekend, before I leave. So if you don't mind I'll say goodbye now.'

Aware of her blotched face and swollen eyes she made to get out of the car, away from his penetrating gaze. 'Leave me alone.'

Gently he pulled her into his arms and sank his face in her hair. 'I'm sorry, love. I really am sorry. Please forgive me. I wouldn't hurt you for the world. Can I have one kiss? Just one.'

Lifting her head she nodded and his mouth closed over hers. He seemed to draw all the breath from her body. Limp as a rag she clung to him and the kiss went on, and on, and on. His hand hovered over her breast but having got this far he had no intention of taking any chances that might go frightening her off. He drew back and gazed into her eyes, silently seeking permission. Eyes swimming in love gazed back at him, bringing a surge of tenderness to his heart. With a nod she gave her permission.

This was frustrating. There wasn't enough room; steering wheel, gear stick, hand brake and just about everything else that could get in the way was getting in the way. He didn't dare suggest they move to the back seat. That would only break the magic spell. To his astonishment, as if she had read his mind, the next time they came up for air she said, 'Wouldn't we be more comfortable in the back?'

With a sigh of relief, he assured her, 'We certainly would.'

Much, much later they became aware that dusk was falling around them. The long grass in the field in front of them had turned from forty shades of green to a dark mass swaying gently in the light breeze.

Dominic laughed. 'You know something? I didn't even notice how lush that grass was, when we first arrived.'

'Neither did I,' Agnes confessed. 'I was so worried that you were about to confess your love for Tess. I was such a bundle of nerves about how I'd hide my feelings for you that everything else was just a blank.'

Her honesty touched his heart. 'You do realise now that I was never interested in Tess?'

'I do now . . . but does she? I thought she really cared for you.'

'It was her who convinced me that I might stand a chance with you. To be truthful, I was going to return to Florida nursing a broken heart.'

'Would you just listen to yourself,' she chided gently. 'You'd have found someone else over there and I'd soon become a passing memory.'

'It's you I want.'

She laughed. 'Prove it.'

He reached for her again and there was no shyness in her response; no holding back. She returned kiss for kiss, caress for caress.

It was dark when he eventually stopped the car at her door. 'Do you want me to come in with you?'

'No. Tony will probably be in there waiting for me. He'll be wondering where I am. I think it would be better if I faced him alone. I won't break the news to anyone else until tomorrow.'

'Promise me you won't renege?'

She lightly trailed the contours of his face with her fingers. 'Do you think I could live without you now?'

Standing on the pavement she watched him drive away, a great well of love engulfing her heart. The hall door opened and Tony was there waiting for her. Good, kind, dependable Tony. How could she ever justify what she was about to do? Head up, shoulders squared, like a soldier going to war she went in to drop her bomb-shell.

Alice accompanied Tess when she went to visit Mrs Burns next day. She had an ulterior motive for visiting Spinner Street. She hoped to see Anne and have a chat with her; find out all she could about this new man Dan had mentioned. It bothered her that Anne might still win Dan over. Nevertheless, she was sincere in her offer to be of any help to Colette.

Dan had made his peace with Alice the previous night, explaining it was Colette he was worried about and that he had called in to see how she was faring, and how Anne had collared him as he was leaving Colette's house and asked him to open a can for her.

Bearing in mind that she had a broken wrist, he had felt obliged to enter the house and give her some assistance. He assured Alice he had not dallied and a few minutes later had seen him on his way. Anne had told him she also was worried about Colette, hence his asking Tess to visit her. It was all above board, he assured her.

Mrs Burns, looking very frail, was propped up on white pillows, her transparent skin rivalling them in colour.

Colette introduced them. 'Grannie, this is Tess; you've heard me speak of her?' A nod from her grannie confirmed it. 'And this is Mrs Maguire, Tess's mother.'

Mrs Burns greeted them in a husky whisper. 'It's good of you to come and see me. Now that I'm home, away from that hospital, I'll be back to porridge in no time.'

Alice bent low over the bed and gently lifted the skeletal hand, the skin stretched like parchment over the old bones, the joints swollen with rheumatism. 'Of course you will. I bet you have more work left in you than the rest of us put together. I've brought you some grapes. Not everybody likes them, I know, but it seems the expected thing to do.'

The little woman smiled and whispered, 'Actually, I love grapes. Thank you.'

Tess came forward holding out a spray of roses. 'I hope you like flowers too.'

'I do. Very much, and roses are my favourite. They're beautiful. Thank you.'

'I'll put them in some water for you.' Colette relieved Tess of the flowers and said gently, 'We'll leave you to rest for a while, Grannie. I think you've talked long enough.'

In the scullery, Tess watched Colette arrange the flowers. 'She's very frail, isn't she?'

Tears ran down Colette's face and dripped unheeded on to the roses. 'She's so weak. I can't see her lasting a month.'

Tess silently agreed with her. 'Now you listen to me, Colette. We're only a stone's throw away. Any time you need us, get a neighbour to phone. Day or night. Okay?' She wrote down her number on an old envelope and gave it to Colette.

'Thank you. Mind you, I may have to hold you to that. I've no one else to turn to in an emergency.'

'We'll be glad to help. But what about your mother? Would she not come and stay? Be here with you, keep you company during the night and be with you at the end?'

'We aren't on speaking terms at the moment. You see, after Jack died Mam wanted me to go back to Omagh with her and she's very annoyed that I didn't fall in with her wishes. It didn't matter to her that Grannie was lying in the Royal and needed someone to visit her. She'd condemn Grannie to a nursing home tomorrow without giving it a second thought.'

'What about your father? Surely he will want to come when he finds out how little time his mother has left?'

'I've tried to get in touch with him, but it's hopeless. He's been gone so long, moved about so often, no one knows where he is now.'

Alice said, 'Why don't you get Dan to try and find him? I know he'd be delighted to be able to help. After all, he was almost your father-in-law. He might know someone who knows about tracking down missing persons.'

To Tess's surprise, Colette's lip curled with scorn. 'Let's leave him out of this. I don't want any help from *him*.

Will you both excuse me, please? The nurse will be here soon and I've things to get ready for her arrival.'

Tess and her mother exchanged an inquiring glance. They knew when they were being dismissed. Tess said, 'I'll call down again tomorrow, Colette. In the meantime, if you need us, you know what to do.'

'Thank you. I'll be pleased to see you.'

'Outside, Alice turned to her daughter. 'I wonder what Dan did to offend her?'

'I was thinking the same thing myself. Whatever it is he appears to be totally unaware of it. Surely she's not blaming him for Jack's death, just because he bought the motorbike?'

'If she is, she can't blame him any more than he blames himself. Sometimes he is so engulfed in guilt that I can't get through to him no matter what I do.'

'Poor Dan. Poor Colette, for that matter.'

'Let's not go all maudlin. Since we're down here, I think it would be neighbourly to call on Anne and see how she is faring. Don't you?'

'Not really, but it's obviously what you intend doing.'

Anne answered their knock, but did not invite them in. She raised an inquiring brow at them.

'We were in visiting Mrs Burns and thought we'd call and see how you are,' Alice explained.

'Oh, never felt better,' was her sarky reply. 'Sorry I can't invite you in but I've got company.' Careful application of make-up covered her bruises and the pucker of stitches was stretching and fading.

Glad that she seemed on the mend, Alice retorted, 'Oh, excuse me for interrupting.' She was not to be deterred. If Anne wanted to discuss her affairs on the doorstep that suited her fine. 'Have you found alternative accommodation yet?' she asked sweetly.

'I beg your pardon? I can't see how that is any business of yours.'

'Oh, but it is very much my business. You see, when the divorce comes through, Dan and I will be getting married and we intend living here. I know there's a lot of work to be done to the interior, so the sooner Dan and I get started on it the better.'

Anne looked stunned. 'So you're the *other woman*?' she gasped, her surprise transparent. 'Well, well, well, what do you know! I would never have dreamt it. I'm sorry, but no, I haven't found anywhere else yet. Tell Dan he'll be the first to know as soon as I do.' The door closed on them with a decisive click.

Turning away, Alice clucked her tongue. 'Don't look at me like that, Tess.'

'What way am I looking at you? As if you've lost your marbles, Mam? Well, have you? Has Dan convinced you it is all right to live in sin after all?'

'No, of course not! He knows nothing about this. I wanted to shake her up a bit, that's all. Remind her that it's not her home any more. Do you think the boyfriend is in there with her?'

'Mam, it's none of our business who her visitor is.'

'It is, if she's carrying on under Dan's roof.'

Tess stopped and gazed in horror at her mother. She was carrying things just a little too far.

Alice threw back her head and laughed aloud. 'I wish I had my camera with me. You should see your face, Tess. I'm only pulling your leg, love. And I've no intention of marrying Dan. At least not at the moment. I think I'll just be his live-in lover. After all, it's the done thing now.' She went into another kink of laughter at her own wit, making Tess shake her head in frustration.

'Come on, Mam. Let's get you home before they cart you off to the laughing house.'

Tess received a phone call from Dominic early Wednesday morning. He sounded jubilant and thanked her for all her help in bringing him and Agnes together.

'Am I to take it that she has agreed to go to Florida with you?'

'You can. We are going down today to try and get her on the same flight as myself. She doesn't fancy travelling alone. I don't think there will be any problem. I can't believe she's coming with me. And I can't thank you enough for all your help, Tess.'

'Does Tony know yet?'

'Well, he should by now. She was to break the bad news to him last night. She wouldn't let me go in with her. Said she wanted to do it on her own. I never thought I'd say this but I actually feel sorry for the guy.'

'Never you worry about him. Agnes must really love you or she wouldn't be willing to take off with you, just like that. Tony and her wouldn't have been happy together. It's obvious, now, they weren't meant for each other.'

'That's true, but I still feel guilty. I only hope he doesn't take a swing at me. I wouldn't have the heart to retaliate.'

'And Mr and Mrs Quinn, how do they feel about it?'

'We have decided not to tell them or anyone else for that matter – yourself excluded of course – until the flight and all is arranged. Is it all right if Agnes and I call up to see you tonight? She's worried about how all this will affect you. You know what I mean.'

'Tell her not to worry, that I'll be only too happy to see you both.'

* * *

They arrived around seven o'clock brandishing a bottle of wine. One look at them and Tess sighed inwardly. Oh to be in love. They simply oozed happiness.

She fetched three glasses and a corkscrew and Dominic opened the bottle. He nodded at the glasses. 'Won't your mother and Dan join us?'

'They're away out to the pictures. Mam's favourite actor, Glenn Ford, is on in the Broadway.' She raised her glass. 'To both of you. May your happiness last for ever.'

'Thank you, Tess. Your help was invaluable.'

'You *will* be my bridesmaid, won't you, Tess?'

Flustered, Tess said, 'Well now, I don't know about that. America is a long way off.'

'Oh, but you must, Tess!' Dominic looked fondly at Agnes. 'She could easily back out, you know, if you refuse.'

'I don't think there's any sweat about that,' Tess replied wryly.

'I'll send you the air tickets.'

Tess laughed. 'Well that certainly simplify matters, but it would depend on when you intended getting married.' She shot an inquiring glance from one to the other.

Agnes answered. 'Dominic wants to get married as soon as possible.'

'And why not?' Dominic retorted.

'I see.' Tess thought for a moment. 'Let me know as soon as you set the date, and I'll see how things go. Meanwhile, tell me, Agnes. Did you manage to get booked on the same flight?'

'I did, yes, and for that I'm grateful. I can't picture myself travelling all the way to America on my own.'

'Have you told your mam and dad yet?'

'No. When we leave here we're going to tell them and then go up and break the news to the Sullivans.'

'It will be one hell of a shock for them all.'

'I know.' Agnes's voice trembled.

Dominic interrupted. 'They will still give us their blessing. I'm sure of it.'

'I don't know about that. Mam has grown very fond of Tony. We'll just have to wait and see.' Agnes looked at Tess and sighed. 'I'm afraid we've blown it as far as a final fling goes. We can't very well go out without Tony. It would be the final insult. As if I was thumbing my nose at him.'

'Ah, well! That's the way the cookie crumbles.' Tess raised her glass once again. 'To both of you.'

There was a strange atmosphere at the party on Friday night. A feeling of disbelief permeated the air as everyone gazed in wonderment at the happy couple. It had come as a terrific shock to both families, but they agreed the pair were well matched and obviously in love, which was all that really mattered.

Tony was noticeable by his absence. Tess didn't blame him. If the crowd had been aware of her designs on Dominic, she wouldn't have had the gall to show her face either. Everybody avoided mentioning his name. It was as if he had never been. Agnes had confided in her the night before how badly he had taken it.

'Do you know something, Tess? I can't see Dominic and me being happy ever after – as the saying goes – when we have inflicted so much misery on another person.'

'I know this sounds trite, Agnes, but he'll get over it, so he will. So don't you go worrying yourself over him. Didn't I get over Jack Thompson?'

'And what about Dominic? Did you really care for him?'

'No. I must admit that for a time I did have high hopes about him, but deep down I didn't really think they would come to anything. So you can rest assured, I'm not nursing a broken heart . . . and I have no intention of jumping off the Queen's Bridge when he leaves.'

Agnes laughed outright. 'You would never be that foolish, no matter what the circumstances.'

'Oh, I don't know about that now, but you're probably right. I'm too big a coward.'

'I'm going to miss you, Tess.'

'Catch yourself on. Dominic will make sure you haven't any time to mope about thinking of me or anyone else for that matter.' They were in each other's arms, tears mingling. 'You're a very lucky girl, Agnes.'

'I know! I can't believe that I almost lost him.'

They separated as the kitchen door opened and Dominic breezed in carrying some empty glasses. 'You two have been in here long enough,' he admonished. 'You're supposed to be bringing in those trays of sandwiches, in case you didn't know.' He looked more closely at them now. 'Is that tears I see?'

Putting down the glasses, he took Agnes in his arms. She melted against him and they didn't even notice Tess slip from the kitchen. How come she hadn't made the connection before, she mused. Surely there must have been some outward indication of how they felt towards each other.

Chapter Fourteen

Mrs Burns didn't last the month. Two weeks from the day she left hospital, she died peacefully in her sleep, in the early hours of the morning. The doctor had warned Colette earlier that day that death was imminent and afterwards Father McAleese had given her the last rites of the church. Tess and Alice kept a vigil with Colette during the night until her grannie slipped quietly from this world.

As she breathed her last few breaths and the death rattle was in her throat, Colette fell to her knees beside the bed, and reaching for her hand grasped it tightly.

Alice placed a warning hand on the young girl's shoulder. 'Don't call her back, love. She's on her way to heaven, I'm sure.'

'I know! I know one shouldn't call a soul back. It's just that . . . I don't want to let her go. I love her! She's all I really have.'

'And what would you be condemning her to? Eh? To lie there unable to help herself. Ah, love, she would be praying that God would release her from her agony.' Alice leaned closer to the little figure on the bed, then gently lowered the eyelids. She made the sign of the cross and said, 'She's away, love. God rest her soul.'

A mournful wail left Colette's lips. 'I wish I had done more for her when she was alive. She hasn't had much happiness since Grandfather died. I'll never forgive my father for not keeping in touch with her.'

'She had you, love. And I'm sure you were a great source of joy and comfort to her. Let's all say a wee prayer for her, then Tess can go and catch a few hours' sleep before getting back to work. Later on she'll notify the doctor of your grannie's death. No need to call him out in the middle of the night, but he'll have to come later on and sign the death certificate.'

Alice helped Colette wash her grannie's body to get it ready for the undertaker. It was as they gently moved her about that they discovered an envelope under the pillows. Colette's name was scrawled across it in her grannie's spidery handwriting. When she opened it Colette found it contained her grannie's last will and testament. The typed will was signed by a member of a firm of solicitors in the city centre, Frank Hanna and Co., and witnessed by two hospital orderlies. It confirmed that Mrs Burns had left all her worldly possessions to her granddaughter, Colette. There was also a second letter enclosed, stating that Miss Colette Burns should make an appointment at their office, at her earliest convenience, to learn exactly what she had inherited. It was signed Matthew McIlroy. In the same envelope there was a Liverpool Victoria insurance policy covering the funeral expenses.

Colette wept when she read it. 'Grannie was always so good to me. And now even in death she hasn't left me any debts to pay off.'

Alice examined the expensive looking letterhead from the solicitors and said, 'There just might be something worthwhile here. On the other hand don't build your hopes too high, Colette. The chances of your grannie having much to leave are slim.'

Colette rounded on her in anger, which quickly evaporated when Alice drew back in dismay. Quickly Colette apologised. 'I'm sorry, Mrs Maguire. But you see I don't expect her to have much to leave. It's the fact that even at the end she was thinking of me, and went to all this trouble.'

Colette decided to keep the funeral a quiet affair and three days later, with just a handful of friends present, Mrs Burns was laid to rest in her husband's grave in Milltown Cemetery. It was in a sheltered corner of the cemetery, and the sun shone high above as her coffin was lowered into the ground.

Her only son knew nothing of her demise and, in private, Colette used some choice words to describe just what she thought of this man who had walked away from all his responsibilities years ago. But then, she reminded herself, she must bear in mind that her mother had put him out of the house. She had been too young at the time to understand the ins and outs of it; could barely remember him; had no real feelings towards him, the way a daughter should have for her father. But still, no matter the differences between him and his wife, he should have kept in touch with his own mother. Then again, who knows? Perhaps the poor bugger was dead.

Her mother and Stan came to the funeral but departed shortly afterwards, explaining that they were too busy to stay any longer. They tried again to persuade Colette to return to Omagh with them but she refused. She intended to remain in her grannie's house as long as the landlord would let her, and until she decided what to do with her life. It would also give her a chance to save some money. Her grannie had some fine pieces of furniture which looked quite valuable. What would become of them, she wondered.

Tess suggested that Colette should try to get her name put on the rent book and then she would be free to stay there as long as she cared to. Taking her advice Colette called into the rent office. She was informed that her name had been on the rent book for the last four months. Mrs Burns had insisted that she needed her granddaughter to remain with her and her name should be in the book. If money had changed hands no one mentioned it.

A week later Colette presented herself at the offices of Frank Hanna and was shown into an elegant wood-panelled office.

A small elderly man with stooped shoulders, a thatch of snow white hair and bright blue eyes behind rimless glasses rose from behind a highly polished desk and came to greet her. He gripped her hand tightly in his own smooth, well manicured one and spoke in a modu-lated voice. 'My name is Matthew McIlroy and I am pleased to meet you, Miss Burns. May I offer my condo-lences on the death of your grandmother? She was a grand lady and it was my great pleasure to make her acquaintance. She was admired by all who got to know her here in the office, before it became too difficult for her to travel. But then, that was all while you were still a young schoolgirl.'

Tess was bemused. Her grandmother had been in the habit of dealing with these people, in these very offices? She had certainly kept that quiet.

He gestured to a leather chair in front of the desk. 'Please take a seat.' When she was seated, he asked, 'Would you like a cup of coffee or tea?' A shake of the head rejected his offer. Colette couldn't imagine herself drinking tea or coffee comfortably in these plush surroundings; she would be sure to spill it. But somehow or other she had no difficulty picturing her grannie sitting here, at ease in this chair, sipping coffee and conversing with Mr McIlroy. The solicitor was continuing and she brought her mind back to attention. 'Now let me acquaint you of your inheritance, my dear.'

Colette sat primly on the edge of the chair, knees close together and hands clasped tightly in her lap. She felt intimidated by all this grandeur and was anxious to get the meeting over and done with as quickly as possible. A file sitting precisely in front of the man was opened by long slender fingers and Matthew McIlroy smiled at Colette before beginning to read. 'It is short and to the point,' he said, patting the file with the flat of his hand. 'First let me inform you that you are the sole beneficiary of this will.'

His gaze returned to the papers in front of him. 'I the undersigned, Margaret Emily Burns, being of sound mind, do hereby bequeath all my worldly goods solely to my granddaughter Colette Mary Burns.' The small man raised his eyes and she thought she detected a mischievous twinkle in their depths. 'I think you are in for a nice surprise, Miss Burns. Your grandmother has left you, after all expenses have been settled, just over ten thousand pounds. She also bequeaths a few pieces of jewellery which are in safe keeping at her bank, and the contents of the house in which she resided.' Once more he glanced in her direction, preparing to deliver another bombshell. 'If I remember correctly the pieces of jewellery are very valuable. Your grandfather, not wanting all his eggs in one basket, invested in gold.' He sat back in his chair with his fingers steepled in his lap, a satisfied smile on his face.

However, one glance across the desk and he was·on his feet immediately and scurrying round it, bending in concern over Colette. 'Are you all right, my dear?'

Colette willed herself not to pass out. This man would think her such a fool. Ten thousand pounds would probably seem nothing to him but to her it was a fortune; a fantastic amount of money. She couldn't take it in. Perhaps she had picked him up wrong. He pressed a bell on the desk and a girl immediately answered its summons. 'Doris, please fetch Miss Burns a glass of water.' When Doris returned with the water, he said, tersely, 'Bring some coffee too, will you, please? I think this young lady is in shock. It's all been too much for her.'

A few sips of the cold water revived Colette to some extent and she smiled weakly at the solicitor. 'Did I hear you right, Mr McIlroy? Did you say *ten thousand pounds*?'

'Yes. You heard me right.' The coffee arrived and, more at ease now, Colette sat back in her chair. She had to; she was afraid of tumbling off it. She was trembling all over and felt light headed, her mind racing in all directions. Matthew poured the coffee into fine china cups. 'Sugar and milk, my dear?'

'Yes, please. One spoonful.'

Handing her the cup, he said, 'Drink that up. Let's get some colour back into those cheeks of yours.'

Colette sipped at the coffee. It was delicious. Not any old coffee here. 'I'm all right now, thank you, Mr McIlroy. I've gotten over the initial shock. I just can't understand how my grannie came by all that money.' Struck by a thought, she cried in alarm, 'There's no mistake, is there? You are reading the right will?'

He smiled benevolently at her. 'I can assure you, my dear, there is no mistake.'

Bewildered, she repeated, 'How on earth did Grannie come by all that money?'

'We have handled your grandparents' affairs for a number of years and I can tell you that your grandfather was a very shrewd man where the stock market was concerned. He left your grandmother comfortably off when he died. However, without his expertise, she wasn't willing to risk what she had and the money has been lying in the building society gathering interest over the years. I think she had your future welfare in mind even then. She always mentioned your name in the course of any conversation with us. She was very proud of you.'

'She was a wonderful woman. I still can't take it in.' Her eyes widened in wonder. 'I'm rich.'

'It's a lot of money, yes, but I'm sure you'll handle it sensibly. If you ever need advice or decide to invest it, or indeed part of it, I would be only too delighted to be of service to you.'

Colette walked about the town in a daze. If only Jack were still alive! The plans they would be making now. They wouldn't have to count the pennies. They would be able to buy a house, have a big wedding and an expensive honeymoon. Restless, she felt the need to share her news with someone. Talk about her good fortune. Tess was the closest she had to a friend and catching a bus up Grosvenor Road she travelled on up the Springfield Road to the stop nearest Tess's house.

Tess and Theresa were sewing away in the work room and were surprised to see Colette. As a rule, friends knew better than to visit during working hours. 'Is anything wrong?' Tess asked anxiously.

'No. Far from it. The very opposite in fact. I'm sorry

for interrupting you at your work. I never thought. I just had to talk to someone.'

Sensing that whatever Colette wanted to talk about was meant for Tess's ears only, Theresa suggested, 'It's time for a break anyway, Tess. Why don't you make the tea?'

'Good idea, Theresa. I'll bring you in a cuppa.'

In the kitchen Colette revealed her good news. 'You're having me on!' Tess gasped. 'Aren't you?'

Delighted at her friend's response, Colette assured her, 'It's true. I can't take it in myself.'

'I'm very happy for you, Colette. You deserve it. You were devoted to your grannie. She knew you loved her dearly.'

'I don't want everyone to know. That's why I didn't say anything in front of Theresa. I want to have a good think about it. Decide what I want to do. But meanwhile, let's celebrate, eh? Let's go out on Saturday night and paint the town red.'

'I'm all for that!' Tess hesitated, wondering if what she was about to suggest was the right thing. 'I wonder . . .'

'Come on, out with it,' Colette prompted.

'Would you mind inviting Tony along? He's not exactly the best of company since Agnes left, but if we can persuade him to join us it might cheer him up.'

Colette agreed willingly. 'Will you ask him or shall I?'

'I'll probably see him before you do, so leave it to me.'

Tess was already regretting her impulsive suggestion. Tony was making a nuisance of himself hanging about the road outside the house, waylaying her whenever possible. He might put a damper on their night out. He seemed to imagine that he and she should be crying on each other's shoulder, whereas Tess was just happy that things were apparently working out so well for Agnes and Dominic. The letters she received from her friend simply glowed with happiness. Dominic had bought a house and they were in the process of decorating it. Stella who managed the restaurant in Dominic's absence and Agnes got on together like a house on fire. Last but not least they hoped to marry in August. Tess was glad for her friend but wanted to get on with her own life. Meanwhile Tony was still wallowing in self-pity.

'I'd better take this cup in to Theresa, or she'll think we've forgotten all about her. Mam is at the shops and she'll be back soon. I take it you won't want her to know either?'

'Not at the moment, Tess, if you don't mind. It's too much to take in all at once. As I said, I need some time to think it over. Let it sink in.'

Tony said he would be delighted to join the girls on Saturday night, which left Tess feeling somewhat guilty. Perhaps she should have encouraged him more. He had asked her out a few times but she was afraid of giving him the wrong impression. She had no interest what-soever in Tony Burke.

Struck by a sudden thought, she recalled how Colette had championed Tony when she learned that Agnes might return his ring. Was there a chance that these two could help each other recover from their respective losses? Maybe even find romance together? Tess thought it was indeed a possibility and vowed to do all in her power to help it along.

Saturday evening was a great success. Tony deter-minedly shrugged off his gloom and was, on the whole, quite good company. With Colette not wanting anyone else to know about her inheritance they had difficulty persuading him to let her foot the bill. He said it was only fair that he paid his own way. In fact, he had a bit saved and would be only too happy to treat them. At this Colette relented a bit and said her grannie had left her a few hundred pounds and she wanted to treat him and Tess. He eventually agreed on condition that he treated them the following Saturday night.

Thus it became a habit, the three of them going out together once a week, but although Tess left them in each other's company whenever possible, romance didn't blossom between Colette and Tony. They remained just good friends.

The orders were rolling in for first Communion outfits and Tess and Theresa got on famously, working happily together while Alice made the headdresses in the back room.

The only cloud on Tess's horizon was Dan Thompson. It looked as if he was going to become a permanent feature about the house. Anne had really settled into his house and showed no signs of budging in the foreseeable future. They eventually heard that her friend Pat had moved in with her.

Waiting until her mother was out of the room, Tess confronted Dan. 'Look here, Dan, I don't mind you staying here, but don't you think you should be making a bigger effort to get Anne and her boyfriend out of your house?'

'I didn't say anything to your mother, Tess, but I have tried. Anne is claiming squatter's rights. Whether or not she can get away with it I don't know. As for her friend . . . he's proving to be one awkward customer, so he is.'

'Well, you can't live here for ever! So what are you going to do about it?'

He shrugged his shoulders and just sat staring at her. Tess turned away in disgust. In her eyes he was proving to be an unsavoury customer too, living here for next to nothing. Her mother could find no fault in him, so Tess's hands, and indeed her tongue, were tied. When she had tried to talk to her mother about the situation, Alice had implied that her daughter would find any man difficult to live with and that she had all the makings of a spinster. This had rankled within Tess, and made her question her own lifestyle. Working five, sometimes six days a week with hardly any social life, what chance had she of meeting a suitable man? But, she vowed, if married life meant buckling down to the demands of some lazy bugger like Dan Thompson, she would be better off single.

As first Communion time approached the outfits were selling like hot cakes. Theresa surprised her one day as they sewed away. 'Tess, there's a shop down the road, you know the one near the corner that sells children's clothes? Well, it's up for sale. Would you not be interested in branching out?'

Tess had indeed noticed the For Sale sign above the shop and the idea had crossed her mind only to be pushed aside. Now she voiced her thoughts. 'Where on earth would I get that kind of money?'

'Actually, I was thinking of us entering into a partnership. I've a bit salted away and I imagine you've some savings too?'

Tess sat thinking for some time. 'It's a big step to take, Theresa.'

'Not really. It's already well established as a children's clothier and we've got the ability to make a go of it. The two spinster ladies who own it are retiring to Carrickfergus. It's still a going concern so of course we would also have to buy the goodwill.'

Her description of the owners cut Tess to the bone. Is that how she and Theresa would be known in years to come? Spinster ladies? 'Have you any idea how much they are looking for?'

'No, but if you're interested we can find out. And the sooner the better. It won't be on the market much longer. It's sure to be snapped up.'

'I'll talk it over with Mam and let you know. Okay?'

'Fine. But I must warn you, I've given this a lot of thought. I'm really interested in it. If you find you can't see your way to taking a risk, I won't hold it against you, but I'll be looking for a partner elsewhere. I think it's the chance of a lifetime. Maybe the only one I'll ever get, and it's too good an opportunity to miss.'

They had become good friends; got on so well together at work that the thought of losing Theresa spurred Tess on. Knowing she would have difficulty holding a private conversation with her mother once Dan came home from work, she broached the subject as soon as Theresa had left for the day.

'Mam, did you notice that shop at the bottom of the road is up for sale?'

'Which shop's that?'

'The one that sells all those lovely children's clothes.'

'No I didn't. I'm surprised to hear it's in trouble. It seems to do a roaring trade.'

'As far as I know it isn't in trouble and is being sold as a going concern. The two ladies who run it are retiring.'

'Mm, I suppose they are getting on a bit.' Her glance sharpened. 'Where's all this leading, Tess?'

'Theresa has suggested we join resources and put in an offer for it.'

'Has she indeed! It could be quite costly.'

'Theresa has some money saved; whether or not I can match it is another matter. But it won't cost anything to find out just how much is involved. The question is, how do you feel about it?'

'Huh! For a minute there I thought I didn't count.'

'Ah, Mam! You know you and I are partners. And always will be.'

'I'm glad to hear that. Let me mull it over in my mind for a while, will you?'

'I need to let Theresa know as soon as possible. She'll be looking elsewhere for a partner if I'm not interested.'

'Is she threatening to leave?'

'It's not a threat, Mam. Just good business sense. Like myself, she's a single girl, and has to look to the future.'

'She is quite a bit older than you, Tess. But no matter, I'll let you know tomorrow morning. Is that soon enough?'

A bit peeved, Tess nodded. For the life of her she couldn't understand what her mother had to think over. All she had to do was agree or disagree. Unless of course she wanted to talk it over with Dan.

Tess didn't have to wait until the next morning for her mother's reply. Dan retired early that night, much to Tess's surprise, and obviously at her mother's instigation, strengthening the feeling that indeed her business had been discussed with him. Usually he sat her out these nights and she had little time alone with her mother. She didn't like the idea that their business had been mulled over, as her mother put it, with Dan, but what could she do about it?

Alice broached the subject directly. 'I've been thinking over what you said about that shop, Tess, and I think it would be a good investment.'

Pleased, Tess replied, 'You think we should go for it then?'

'Why not? As you are well aware, you'll be twenty-one in July . . .'

'You won't believe me, Mam, but I'd forgotten all about that.'

'Well, when you were born your father and I took out a small endowment policy on you. Nothing big, mind you. Just a few shillings a month. We had planned to bump it up, but somehow or other it was pushed into the background. Then when your dad died I never got round to it. Careless of me,' she admitted sadly. 'Just last week I received a letter from the Prudential reminding me that the policy would mature at the beginning of August.'

Tess watched her mother wide eyed, hanging on her every word, not knowing what was coming next.

'And what do you know?' Alice continued. 'With final bonuses they reckon it will be worth somewhere in the region of twelve hundred pounds.'

Tess sat in stunned silence, trying to take in what her mother was saying. 'You mean . . .' Her voice trailed off; she was afraid to put her thoughts into words in case she was wrong.

'I intended using some of the money to throw a surprise birthday party in your honour, but I think the money itself would be more beneficial to you, if you're interested in purchasing this shop. So as soon as the cheque comes I'll give it to you.'

'Ah, Mam, what can I say?'

'Don't say anything. Just be sure you're not throwing good money away.'

'Never you fear! Theresa and I will go into it very thoroughly. She has a very shrewd business mind and is also quite competent at ordering goods and the like. She looked after the books and all at Belart for a time, so I have every confidence in her. She certainly won't let anyone pull the wool over her eyes, that's for sure.' Going to her mother, Tess fell to her knees beside the chair and gripped her hands tightly. 'You're a wonderful woman, Mam. I'll never be able to thank you enough.'

Alice cupped her daughter's face in her hands. 'I don't want any thanks. You've been a good daughter to me. I'm just glad the money is coming at the right time and will be there when you need it.'

The excitement proved too much for Tess. She didn't sleep a wink that night. She was downstairs twice during the night making cups of tea and wandering about the house, cup in hand, her mind in turmoil with the possibility of being part owner of the shop. In her mind's eye she could envisage the name over the shop: *Maguire & Cunningham – Children's Outfitter*. It was during her second rambling that she first learned that Dan was sharing her mother's room. She was shocked to the very core. Her mother was such a puritan, had questioned everybody else's morals, and here she was, cavorting with a married man. How long had it been going on? Sleep was completely out of the question after that discovery. Tess's mind swung between the excitement of buying the shop and her mother's fall from grace. She kept telling herself it was none of her business; nevertheless she had difficulty hiding her feelings at breakfast next morning. No wonder they acted like an old married couple. There would be no rush to get married now, and *he* would certainly be in no rush to get back to his own home.

Why should he leave a nice comfortable house where he was lifted and laid to return to a cold, dingy house in Spinner Street?

She phoned Theresa and told her the deal was on. Where did they go from here?

'Our first call will be to the estate agents. Once I get Mam settled I'll ask a neighbour to sit with her and I'll pick you up at . . . say eleven?'

'I'll be ready and waiting,' Tess promised.

Theresa parked her car outside the estate agents in Lower Donegall Street. She warned Tess not to appear too enthusiastic. They would pretend it was a casual inquiry and that they had other property to view.

The young man in charge of the agency introduced himself as Barry McGuinness and was full of praise for the premises on Springfield Road. Sadly, he informed them that an offer had already been made for it.

Disappointed, Tess remained silent, having been told to follow Theresa's lead. Theresa had done her home-work well. She knew there was an empty shop on the Falls Road with a different agency. Now she said sweetly, 'Thank you for your attention, Mr McGuinness.' She headed for the door. 'I guess we will just have to have another look at that shop near Waterford Street, Tess. It should prove to be cheaper, as it's been empty quite a while.'

'Just a minute, Mrs . . . Oh dear, I'm afraid I've forgotten your names already.'

'It's *Miss* Cunningham, and you never asked for our names, which was very remiss of you. This is Miss Maguire. I think perhaps we should speak to your superior. When would that be possible?'

Thoroughly flustered now, the young man apologised profusely and pulling two chairs away from a desk said, 'If you will take a seat, please, I'll show you what we have on our books.'

'We're only interested in the clothes shop near the corner of Springfield Road,' Theresa warned. 'So don't think you can dump anything else on us. You'd be wasting your time.'

Barry opened a cabinet, took a file from it, and spread it out on the desk. 'I was telling the truth when I said an offer has been made for it . . . but well below the asking price.'

Theresa leaned forward, elbows on the table. 'Someone you know? Is that why you were reluctant to tell us about it?' Barry's face blazed with colour but she let him off the hook. 'Okay, let's hear about this offer you've received.'

They discussed all the details. At last Theresa seemed satisfied and rose to her feet. 'We'll be in touch with you, Mr McGuinness. Thank you for all your help.'

Outside, Tess looked in bewilderment at Theresa. 'Even at more than they were offered it still sounded good to me. Less than we expected it to be. Wasn't it?'

'Trust me, Tess. Whoever put that offer in was chancing their arm. They will be willing to go higher. Much higher, if I'm not mistaken.'

'Does that mean we're out of the running?'

'No. We're going to visit the two ladies who run the shop. Find out how much they want for the goodwill.'

'Goodwill?'

'Names, addresses, contact numbers for their clients.'

'Does that matter?'

'Oh, yes. It matters very much. They might also have

some stock on their hands we could get at a bargain price.'

Tess was beginning to realise there was more to buying a property than she had ever imagined. She was glad Theresa was in control.

It turned out that the two elderly ladies, one thin as a whippet and the other plump and jolly, were sisters. When the bell above the door tinkled, the thin one bustled out from a room at the back of the shop and came to the counter.

'Can I be of any assistance, ladies?'

'Yes. We are interested in buying these premises and would like to speak to the owner.'

After giving them a considering look and obviously deeming them trustworthy, the woman lifted the flap at the end of the counter that gave access to the rest of the shop, shouting over her shoulder, 'Mary, there are two young ladies inquiring about the shop. Just go on through there,' she instructed. 'I'll close up for a short while.'

A small plump woman came forward to meet them at the entrance to the back room. Thrusting her hand towards Theresa, she introduced herself. 'My name is Mary Donnelly, and' – she nodded to the thin woman – 'that's my sister Cissie. Just what is it you'd like to know?'

'Well, first of all, what do you think of the offer that has already been submitted to the estate agent?'

Mary's chin lifted in the air and her nostrils flared in anger. 'Insulting! That's what we think.'

'Is the goodwill included in your asking price?'

Sensing that this was a genuine inquiry and not just someone being nosy, Mary led them through to yet another room, comfortably furnished, and nodded to a small settee. 'Let's sit in here and discuss this in comfort. Would you like a wee cup of tea, my dears?'

An hour later they all stood on the threshold of the shop and exchanged handshakes.

'We will need to arrange a loan from the bank,' Theresa said. 'But there will be no problems there, we can assure you. Meanwhile, you say you will turn down the offer already made?'

'You can count on that,' the sisters chorused.

'What if they come up with a better one?' Tess voiced her worry.

'We are more than happy with your offer,' Cissie assured her. 'And we are so glad that you will continue to sell children's clothes. We spent years building up this wee business and are glad to know it won't become an electrical goods shop, which is what the other client intended.'

'We shall submit a written offer first thing tomorrow morning and make an appointment to see about a loan from the bank. I'm glad we called to see you person-ally. It was a pleasure meeting you. You've been a wealth of information.'

'We'll keep in touch. Anything you want to know about suppliers and buyers, you only have to ask.'

Goodbyes were said all round and Theresa and Tess headed to where the car was parked in McQuillan Street. At the corner of the Falls Road they stopped and faced each other.

'Well? What do you think?' a breathless Theresa asked.

'I think, if it all goes through without a hitch, we're getting a smashing bargain,' Tess enthused.

'So do I. We will have to go to the bank first thing tomorrow morning and see about a loan.'

'I'll phone Colette. I'm almost sure she works in the department that deals with business loans. Do you think we'll have any trouble getting one?'

'Of course not. We only need a small loan to let us retain some of our savings as security against the unexpected.'

As soon as she got home Tess phoned the bank and asked to speak to Colette. As she had hoped, her friend did indeed work in the business loans department and immediately made an appointment with her superior.

That evening she called in on Tess and surprised her by offering to lend her the money personally, interest free.

'Oh, but I couldn't take your money,' Tess exclaimed, profoundly touched by her generosity.

'Of course you can. I trust you. How much do you need?'

'It's not just for me, Colette. Sit down and I'll tell you all about it.'

Colette listened as Tess related how Theresa had suggested they go into partnership and put in an offer on the shop, and how they had gone down to see the estate agent and then up to the shop in question and the agreement they had struck with the two sisters.

'Wow! You certainly hit it lucky there, getting Theresa as a partner. It sounds as if she knows her onions all right. You will definitely make a go of it. Both of you are such hard workers, it's bound to be a success.'

'Thanks, Colette. We can only give it our best shot.'

'I've been a bit busy myself lately,' Colette confided. 'I wrote to my friend in Canada and I got a reply from her yesterday. She's going to try and get me fixed up with a job out there. She said that with my banking experience I'm more or less guaranteed a job. It will be a complete change for me and I'm looking forward to it. I'm all excited.'

'I'm sure you are. It's a great opportunity for you. Too good to miss.' Tess felt a twinge of sadness; she had become very attached to this young girl. 'I'll miss you, so I will.'

'Not a bit of it! You'll be too busy making your fortune to notice my absence. I'd better run. I let Tony talk me into going for a walk up the mountain loney.'

Tess's eyes widened and she said, 'Why, that's wonderful news.'

'It's not, you know. All he'll do is talk about *you*. But it will get me out of the house for a couple of hours. Here, did I tell you I've been to the Ulster Bank and had a look at the jewellery Grannie left me?' At Tess's shake of the head she continued with a huge smile on her face. 'Six pieces in all and worth, I've been assured, at least another five thousand pounds. They are absolutely gorgeous. I don't know what to do about them.'

'Oh, you lucky devil! You're set for life.'

'And all because of my grannie, God bless her. Look, I'd better run on or Tony will think I've stood him up. Don't forget my offer of the loan. I'm dead serious about it, Tess. I mightn't see you at the bank in the morning – you'll be interviewed in one of the private rooms – but if not, I'll see you Saturday night as usual.'

On Saturday night the trio went to the Carlton steak house and then on to the Hippodrome. Although everything appeared all right on the surface, Tess sensed that Colette was worried about something. Knowing that she didn't like her affairs discussed in front of anyone else, not even Tony, she held her tongue but had every intention of finding out what was worrying her friend.

With this in mind Tess called down to see Colette on Sunday afternoon. As she awaited an answer to her knock, she let her eyes roam over Dan's house, noting that the door had been freshly painted and crisp white net curtains hung at the windows. Anne was certainly making herself at home.

She was turning to leave, thinking that Colette must be out, when the door opened just a fraction and Colette peered out. 'I'm not very good company at the moment, Tess. Could you come back later?'

Tess dithered. Had Colette someone with her and didn't want Tess to know? She looked closer and was concerned to note that her friend had been crying. 'Are you sure you wouldn't like someone to talk to? It was obvious to me last night that you were unhappy. That's why I'm here now. To see if I can be of any use.'

Slowly the gap in the doorway widened enough for Tess to enter and Colette confessed, 'I'm in a quandary. Don't know where to turn. You see, once I speak about it, there'll be no turning back.'

They sat together on the settee. 'Let me guess. Your friend in Canada has changed her mind and doesn't want you to go out there now. Am I right? Is that why you're so down in the mouth?'

'Far from it. That might set me back a bit but it would be the least of my worries right now.'

Intrigued, Tess insisted, 'Trust me, Colette. You know I can keep my big trap shut when I have to.'

Colette covered her face with her hands. 'I'm so ashamed. But it won't go away, so I suppose I may as well tell you. You'll know soon enough anyhow. Everyone will. *I'm pregnant!*'

You could have knocked Tess down with a feather. This was the last thing in the world she would have expected to hear. At last she got her breath back. 'Has Tony . . .'

A bewildered frown gathered on Colette's brow. 'Tony? Of course not! You've got it all wrong. When I missed my first period I thought it was the upheaval of Jack's death, but when I missed the second one I realised I was expecting a baby. Oh, Tess, what am I going to do?'

Tess could only guess at her friend's predicament. Wasn't she herself gobsmacked at the news? Colette had been so happy, looking forward to a new life in Canada . . . and now this. 'As you say . . . this is something that can't be kept a secret very long. Your mother will have to be told—'

'*Never!* Do you hear me? I'm trusting you to keep your mouth shut like you promised. I'll think of something. I just haven't got my mind round it yet. But I won't give my mother the satisfaction of saying, "Didn't I tell you so?"'

Remembering Colette's intention of going down the aisle a virgin, Tess was sad. If only she had persevered. But these things do happen in the heat of the moment. 'Whatever you decide to do, I'll back you all the way,' she promised.

'I don't want this baby.' At Tess's startled look, Colette cried, 'Oh, I'm not thinking of an abortion! But I won't keep it! I will get it adopted.'

'It's early days, Colette. Let's get used to the idea first and then we'll put our heads together and see what we can come up with. Remember, I'll help you all I can.'

'I feel a great deal better already. Just having some-one to talk to makes all the difference. I thought I'd go away in the head this past few days. Thanks, Tess. Thanks for being so understanding.'

'That's what friends are for. But never you fear. Between us we'll sort something out.' Tess sounded confident but for the life of her she couldn't see any way out of this dilemma without involving Colette's mother.

Chapter Fifteen

After a few minor hiccups, everything went smoothly regarding the purchase of the shop. They had been invited to examine the premises, so on the advice of their bank had hired an assessor to do it on a professional basis. When they got his favourable report they put down a deposit as a token gesture of good faith to show their intentions as genuine buyers. The sisters had kept the shop in a good state of repair and would be vacating it at the beginning of August. The girls would be able to move in straight away. Tess and Theresa proudly had cards printed and sent out to their regular customers informing them of their new business address. The future was beginning to look rosy indeed.

They had sold far more first Communion outfits than they normally did. They had also worked hard finishing off two wedding outfits at the end of June. On the whole, a good few months' hard graft had reaped substantial dividends. Theresa was overjoyed with the bonus she received for all her hard work, happy in the knowledge that her trial period was over. She was now part owner in a small but going concern.

Alice advised them to take a break during the Twelfth fortnight as she would be around to collect the weekly payments from their regular tick customers. The girls readily agreed that this was a good idea indeed as, with most firms closing down for two weeks in July, a lot of families chose this time to take their annual holidays and there would be few orders coming in. August and September would see them working on the wedding outfits already in their order books for the autumn, and then there would be Christmas dresses and children's party dresses, so now was certainly the time for a well earned holiday. Theresa happily began making plans to take her mother away to visit a cousin in Bundoran for a week; she had a lot of boasting to do about her new status in life.

Tess's thoughts flew to Carlingford. Her Uncle Malachy had phoned a few times reminding her of her promise to visit him, but she had thought it unlikely that she would be able to get away due to pressure of work. However, the employment of Theresa had changed all that and now she decided she would give him a ring and make arrangements to visit the farm for a week or two.

As yet unaware that Tess knew she was sharing her bed with Dan, her mother was in her element, looking forward to having the house all to herself and the love of her life. Tess could not deny that her mother looked fulfilled and happy, wandering about the place with a perpetual smile on her face, but for the life of her Tess couldn't get it out of her head that Dan wasn't a free agent. Would it all end in tears? Still, as she kept reminding herself, it was none of her business. Since her confrontation with him, Dan was contributing more money for his keep and generally pulling his weight about the house. Nevertheless, Tess missed her own privacy. Things were a lot different with a man, practically a stranger, around the house.

Before getting in touch with Malachy, she decided she would endeavour to persuade Colette to accompany her to Carlingford. Tess had kept in close contact with Colette over the past weeks, ever ready with an attentive ear or a sympathetic shoulder to cry on. As yet her friend had not come up with any concrete plans for the immediate future, saying there was plenty of time as she wasn't even showing yet. Perhaps if Tess could get her away from Belfast for a while to the peace and tranquillity of Malachy's farm she would be able to talk her round to her own way of thinking. At the moment Colette was adamant that she would not keep the child and that her mother must never know about the pickle she had landed herself in. Betty seemed to worry Colette more than anything else and Tess thought it tragic that one couldn't turn to one's own mother in such circumstances. It seemed such a pity that the baby would go to complete strangers and might never know its natural grandparents, one at least of whom would lavish it with love.

Now, when the proposition of a holiday was put to her, Colette shook her head determinedly and said, 'I can't go to Carlingford with you, Tess. I'd be a wet blanket, always moaning and groaning about one thing or another. I'd only spoil your holiday and you'd end up wishing you'd never invited me along in the first place. Thanks anyway for asking, but . . . no thanks.'

'Look, Colette, you need to get away for a while. Give yourself a break, a chance to think things through more rationally in the quiet of the countryside.'

'I've already thought it through. I've turned it over in my mind time after time after time and always come up with the same answer. I'll work as long as I can and then I'll go away somewhere and have the baby.'

'Huh! Just like that?'

'And why not? Other girls have done it. I'll get in touch with one of those homes for unmarried mothers where I'll stay until the baby is born. Afterwards, the authorities will find a good home for it, someone who'll love it more than I ever could. No one need be any the wiser. Thanks to Grannie, money won't be a problem.'

All this sounded so cold and calculated and not one bit like the Colette Tess had grown to like and respect. A perplexed frown on her brow, Tess asked tentatively, 'I know you must feel very bitter about Jack leaving you in this predicament, but after the birth you might feel different. They say that once you hold your baby in your arms, you don't want to let go. Don't you think you should at least tell Dan you are expecting his grandchild? It seems only fair that he should know about it. In fact, he would be the ideal person to rear the child and Mam would be only too delighted to help him. I mean, they're still quite young and I'd also be there to give a hand when needed. You wouldn't have to go away to have it, and I'm sure your friend in Canada wouldn't mind waiting a bit longer for your company. Everybody would understand the circumstances and the child would be here if you should ever change your mind. Think about it, Colette. It's the sensible thing to do.'

'Look, Tess, I know you mean well, and I wish things could be different, but they can't. Meanwhile, I don't want anybody to know I'm pregnant. No one. Do you understand? So don't you dare break your promise . . . please.'

Feeling as if she had come in in the middle of a play and had missed the beginning of the plot, Tess vowed, 'Colette, unless you give me permission, I will never utter a single word about it to anyone. But you can't blame me for speaking my thoughts to you; giving you my opinion. Don't deny the child its family connections.'

'Look, Tess, this is getting us nowhere fast. Could we change the subject, please?'

Noting the stress lines on her friend's face, Tess quietly agreed. 'All right. But you do need a holiday, you know. Can you get two weeks off in July?'

'Yes, but—'

'No buts about it! You look as if you could do with a good rest. And you know what they say . . . a change is as good as a tonic.'

Colette could see the logic in her friend's words and admitted, 'You're right. I'm not getting much sleep these nights. I'd love to come to Carlingford with you. That is, if your Uncle Malachy doesn't object.'

Malachy was delighted to receive Tess's phone call. He had given up all hope of seeing her this side of Christmas. 'Of course you must bring Colette along. Wait until I tell Rose,' he cried. 'She'll be over the moon. And Tess, since you're coming down here I'll be able to give you your birthday present in person.'

'That sounds intriguing. Can I ask what it is?'

'You certainly can, but that's as far as it goes. It's my big secret and will remain so until you get here. But I know you'll be delighted with it.'

'Well, if you're not going to tell me, I'll just have to wait then, won't I?'

'I'm afraid so. I'm glad you're bringing a friend along. Rose and I will do all we can to see you enjoy your stay. I'll call her when you hang up and tell her the good news. Bye for now. See you soon.'

*　　*　　*

Alice couldn't contain her excitement at the idea of having Dan all to herself for two whole, uninterrupted weeks. No having to slip out of each other's bedrooms in the wee small hours, in case Tess guessed what was going on. No keeping their hands to themselves when they were alone. Although she admitted to herself that the need for secrecy added spice to their affair.

She often pondered on how she had managed to end up in this glorified lust; how she, above all people, had managed to suppress her conscience enough to cohabit with Dan. He on the other hand wanted her to look out for a place of their own where they could live together openly. She had soon put that idea out of his head. *Openly in sin?* How could he even contemplate it? What would people think of the high and mighty Alice Maguire's fall from grace? She was totally mortified at the very thought of it. Why, she would never be able to hold her head up in public again.

Dan was also off work for two weeks and she couldn't get Tess out of the way quickly enough. It would be marvellous being in the house all alone with him. Just like being on her honeymoon. The first night she intended making a special meal and a bottle of champagne was hidden at the back of the fridge.

The Twelfth of July fell on a Monday this year and Saturday morning the tenth saw Tess packed and rarin' to go. As Alice hovered about impatiently waiting to say her goodbyes the taxi arrived, and Tess couldn't help taking the opportunity to tease her mother.

'Mam, I think perhaps we should wait and travel down tomorrow morning. The roads won't be so busy then. What do you think?'

'But . . . what about your taxi? It's sitting outside waiting for you.'

'I can always send it away.'

Seeing all her plans evaporating into thin air Alice cried, 'And what about Colette? Won't she be expecting you to pick her up soon? She'll be sitting there all packed and ready to go. You can't let her down.' Tess's eyes twinkled and Alice realised she was pulling her leg. 'You're having me on, aren't you?'

'Do you think I don't know about all your shenanigans with Dan?' She watched the blood creep up her mother's neck. 'Ah, Mam! I've got eyes in my head. I've known for some time how it is between you two.' She wanted to add, 'How could you?' but didn't. Why spoil things for her mother with snide remarks? It certainly wouldn't stop her carry-ons.

To her surprise Alice said sadly, 'I know what you must be thinking and I don't blame you, love. I don't know where it all started. I've always been so bloody sanctimonious. But it's too late now. I just can't help myself.'

'Mam, I understand. I'm a big girl, you know. He *is* handsome . . . in fact Agnes Quinn thinks he's the spittin' image of Cary Grant.'

'Does she?' Alice's face brightened as she gave it some thought, and with a wag of the head she conceded, 'She does have a point.'

'And we must remember you're a very attractive woman. If he was free, there would be no problem whatsoever.'

Dan, descending the stairs, put an end to their little *tête-à-tête*. 'So you'll be off soon then, Tess? See and enjoy yourself. I'm glad Colette is going with you. She needs a break too.'

Tess allowed him to peck at her cheek. 'My taxi's sitting outside.'

Dan lifted the two suitcases. 'I'll carry these out.'

Tess wrapped her arms around her mother in a bear hug. 'No use telling you to be good, but at least be careful. If he ever hurts you, I swear I'll swing for him. And you tell him that. Goodbye, Mam.'

'Goodbye, love. And I know *you* will be good. See you when you get back.'

Tess laughed at the very idea. 'I don't think there will be any chance to be otherwise. From what I hear all the farmers' sons and daughters are spoken for practically from birth.'

'Well then, don't you go upsetting the apple-cart by catching some lad's eye,' Alice warned, with a twinkle in her own. 'Enjoy yourself, love.'

When Tess arrived in the taxi to pick her up, Colette greeted her friend eagerly. 'You know, I didn't think I could get excited over this holiday . . . but I am!'

'Oh, I'm so pleased to hear you say that. Just forget all your troubles and woes and let's enjoy ourselves for the next two weeks, eh?'

'I'm all for it!'

The warmth of their welcome at Carlingford nearly brought tears to Colette's eyes. Once introductions were made, she was hugged and kissed as if she were the prodigal daughter. Old Meg had died and Malachy had acquired a new Border collie to take her place. He had named her Florrie and she frisked around them, running back and forth between the girls and a shed close to the house.

'She wants you to go and look at her litter,' Malachy explained.

'A litter already? Impossible!' Tess exclaimed.

'I took her off a friend's hands when he realised she

had been playing around. Luckily, as it turned out, it was another Border collie she was having fun with. I shouldn't have any bother getting homes for her six pups.'

Colette was enthralled with the wiggling bundles of fur. 'I've always wanted a dog,' she said, cradling one of the pups against her cheek.

'No problem. I'll be only too glad to let you take one home with you. Take your pick. Mind you, they need plenty of exercise,' Malachy warned.

Colette flashed a startled glance at Tess. 'Well now . . . I . . . I don't know about that,' she spluttered. 'I might be going away in the near future.'

Before Tess could intervene on her behalf, Malachy said, 'No sweat, Colette. I'll not force you to take one. Think it over. The decision's all yours.'

While Malachy worked in the fields by day, Rose took them for drives to the outlying villages and Colette was enchanted. In the evenings, weather permitting, Malachy took them further afield.

'I could stay here for ever.' Colette confided. 'You never told me how beautiful it was, Tess.'

'And spoil your first impression of it?'

'There is still so much to see.'

'Well, we have another week and by the sound of things it's going to be a hectic one. For instance, Malachy is throwing a small party to celebrate my twenty-first birthday on Saturday night.'

'He's very fond of you, Tess. You're very lucky to have relatives who truly care for you.'

'I know. Everybody needs someone close that they can discuss their troubles with. And remember, I'm here for you, Colette.' Always ready to press a point home, she asked tentatively, 'Have you changed your mind at all about the baby?'

'Now Tess . . . behave yourself. Please?'

'All right! All right, I'll not say another word.'

Saturday started off damp and miserable. 'I hope it's not going to rain today of all days. It will spoil all my carefully laid plans,' Malachy moaned. The two girls were spending a few days at Rose's home, and today Malachy had been invited to join them. As they ate breakfast at the big table in Rose's kitchen he gazed dolefully out over the wet hedges and fields at the blanket of mist hanging over the mountain tops.

'The forecast for today is good, actually,' Rose informed him.

'Ach! They're not always right. Far from it,' he said pessimistically.

'What's so important that a little rain will spoil it?' Tess queried.

'Tonight I want everything to be just perfect. First we are going for a meal in that new restaurant near Dundalk and then we're coming back here to meet a small gathering of friends. All in honour of your twenty-first. I know your big day isn't till the end of the month, but I do want to be there when you see your present. It's a bit large to send in the post.' He caught Rose's eye and they shared a secret smile.

Looking from one to the other, Tess said, 'Ah! The plot thickens! I can't wait to see this mysterious present, whatever it is.'

Rose nodded her head sagely. 'You won't be disappointed. I can understand Malachy not wanting it to be raining.' She too peered out at the mist and drizzle. 'But with those dark clouds scudding overhead, I can understand his misgivings.'

'I'm looking forward to this evening, Uncle Malachy.

We'll enjoy ourselves no matter what the weather is like,' Tess assured him.

'Of course we will,' Rose agreed. 'Meanwhile, I want to take you girls to the market today. So while the bathroom is free, you two get cleaned up and I'll clear up in the kitchen, all right?'

'No it's not all right. We'll help you in the kitchen before we get ready to go out,' Tess declared.

'She sounds determined, Rose. Better let them help out.' With a wide grin on his face, Malachy headed for the stairs. 'Besides, the bathroom won't be empty much longer.'

By mid-morning the sun had broken through the now thinning clouds, and the girls left for the market in a happy frame of mind. It was going to be a fine day after all. As they drove along the road they saw Malachy in the distance and pointing to the sky he gave them the thumbs up.

'You know, I can't help wondering about this mysterious present Uncle Malachy has bought for me.' Tess slanted her eyes at Rose. 'I don't suppose you'd give me a clue, would you?'

Rose gazed at her in amazement. 'I wouldn't dare! Malachy would murder me if I said a single word about it. So I'm afraid you'll just have to contain your curiosity a little longer, my dear.' Her smile was full of mischief. 'But I can assure you, it's worth waiting for. You won't be disappointed.'

They spent hours wandering about the open-air market. There were stalls offering all sorts of wares — 'You can get anything here from a needle to an anchor,' as Rose had so aptly put it. Tess was pleased to find beautiful hand-painted vases for her mother and Theresa, a leather belt with his name etched into it for Dan, and a pale blue mohair wrap for Theresa's mother to match her still sapphire eyes. Colette bought some small ornaments for workmates and they ended the afternoon having tea and cream scones in the big marquee erected for that purpose, before returning to Rose's house to prepare for their night out.

The restaurant near Dundalk stood in its own grounds; acres of lawns and gardens, and a small lake that was home to a pair of majestic swans. Before entering the magnificent building, they took a leisurely walk in the gardens admiring the colourful display of flowers and shrubs.

Indoors they were led by the head waiter to a table reserved in a spacious booth. The booths were in an alcove to one side of the room and each was overlooked by a high window. 'I'll send the wine waiter over, shall I, sir?'

'Please do.'

When he came over Malachy ordered two bottles of medium dry white wine.

As Tess sank down on to a plush velvet-covered seat she muttered to Colette, 'This must be costing Uncle Malachy a bomb.'

Rose heard her and whispered, 'It is! But you only come of age once and he regards you as the daughter he never had.' She hesitated before adding, 'Malachy did invite your mother and Dan, you know, but Alice said they were busy making their own plans for your birthday. She wished us all the best.'

Not wanting Alice to appear uncaring, Tess assured her, 'Mam has been very generous too.' She went on to explain about the endowment policy and how she would be able to buy her share in the shop with it. 'Besides, I know why they didn't want to come,' she added with a twinkle in her eye.

As the waiter poured the drinks they perused the menu and chose their starters, of which there was a long intriguing list. Each ordered something different, something they had never heard of before, so that they could find out just what some of the mysterious names actually were.

While they waited for the starters, Rose looked inquiringly at Malachy. He gave a little nod and delving into her handbag she retrieved a small parcel. Reaching across, she placed it in front of Tess, who smothered a secret smile. Too big to send through the post, eh?

'Happy birthday, Tess.'

'Thank you.' Tess carefully removed the silver wrapping paper to display a jeweller's box. Inside nestled a watch with a fine mesh gold strap, obviously expensive, and a card bearing the greeting, 'To my friend Tess. From Rose, Happy Birthday.'

'Oh, Rose . . . this is far too expensive! I can't possibly accept it.'

'Tess, Malachy talks so much about you I feel as if you are already family. And since—'

She stopped abruptly and shot Malachy a guilty look. He spread his hands wide and shrugged. 'Trust a woman not to be able to keep a secret. Go on, you may as well tell them.' Although he pretended to be annoyed, the girls could see he was pleased and rather chuffed.

'Malachy has, in fact, persuaded me to become part of the family. We are getting married next spring. He's right, it's a bit early to be talking about it, but I'm hoping you'll make my wedding suit for me, Tess.'

Tess left her chair and going to Rose kissed and

hugged her. 'Oh, I'm so pleased for you, and thank you for this beautiful watch. It's gorgeous! And of course I'll make your suit.'

Before returning to her chair she hugged Malachy. 'Rose is a lovely person and I'm so happy for you. I hope you will have many years together. Can I tell Mam? She'll be delighted.'

Colette offered her congratulations, then she too produced a small parcel and gave it to Tess, saying shyly, 'Happy birthday, Tess. I know it's a week early, but I hope you like it.'

Colette's present was a small gold crucifix on a chain. Tears in her eyes, Tess said, 'Oh, Colette. It's beautiful. Thank you very much.' Reaching for her friend's hand she squeezed it tightly. 'I don't deserve such expensive presents.'

'You've been a good, loyal friend to me, Tess, when I really needed one. I couldn't have coped without you since Jack died.'

The three women were almost in tears and an embarrassed Malachy was glad when the waiter arrived with their starters.

The meal was delicious, from the unusual starters and main courses to the mouth-watering desserts. A sated, happy party retired to the lounge for coffee and mints prior to returning to Rose's house to have a bit of a do with the neighbours. Just as they were finishing a waiter approached Malachy and whispered in his ear. A grin split his face and he rose quickly to his feet, offering his arm to Tess. 'Please accompany me, madam. Your transport has arrived.'

A puzzled frown puckering her brow, Tess looked to Rose for support. Rose gave her a confident nod and, gathering her and Tess's belongings, signalled for Colette to accompany them outside.

Striding forth in a grand manner Malachy led his bemused niece out of the lounge, across the foyer and through the revolving doors. He came to a halt outside and turned to watch Tess's reaction.

She couldn't believe her eyes. Parked outside the main entrance was a gleaming, bright red Austin Mini, sporting a large placard saying 'Happy Birthday Tess. From Uncle Malachy.' It sat in full glory, the chrome trimmings glistening in the late sunshine.

Her reaction was more than Malachy could have hoped for. She took a startled step backwards and her enormous green eyes looked as if they were about to pop out of her head. Her mouth hung open in astonishment. Closing it with a gulp, she turned a stupefied gaze on her uncle and managed to splutter, 'Is it really mine?'

'It's really yours,' he assured her solemnly.

Throwing herself into his arms she hugged him tightly, tears pouring down her face. 'Oh, it's wonderful! I'll never be able to thank you enough, Uncle Mal.'

'I've been keeping in touch with Theresa Cunningham and she assures me you drive her car like an old hand.'

'And she never said a word,' Tess exclaimed. 'Although, mind you, I did wonder why she insisted that I learn to drive her car. It seemed such a waste of time since I thought it would be years before I could afford one of my own. And now this! My very own car. I can't believe it. I just can't believe it.'

'Mind you, it's not brand new, but it had just one careful owner.' Malachy handed Tess the keys with a flourish. 'In you go. Let's see you drive it to the car park at the rear while I settle the bill. That wee waiter is watching us like a hawk. I imagine he thinks we're about to do a runner.'

Nervously, Tess glanced at Rose and Colette, who were standing silently in the background. They each gave her a nod of approval and timidly she turned the key in the lock and for the first time got into her very own car. She felt at home almost immediately. Adjusting the seat and driving mirror, she started the engine, and confidently drove the car round and round the building before expertly reversing into a parking space at the rear.

'Well . . . what do you think of it?' Rose asked, peering in at her.

'It's absolutely out of this world, so it is.' Tess got out of the car and walked slowly round it, her hand trailing admiringly along its smooth bodywork as she went.

'I told you it was worth waiting for, didn't I?' Rose said coyly.

'And it certainly was, Rose. I would never have guessed Uncle Mal would have bought me a car. It's breathtaking, so it is! I'm not surprised that he couldn't post it to me,' she joked.

Returning from the restaurant Malachy waved her back into the car. 'In you go, girl! You're driving home.'

'But . . . I'm not insured.'

'Oh, yes, you are. This car comes with six months' insurance and road tax.' Seeing tears about to fall, he added sternly, 'And no more tears. Do you hear me? Good God, girl, you're supposed to be happy.'

'Oh, I am. I am!' Tess sniffled and clambered back into the driving seat.

With Rose and Colette leading the way in the Land-Rover, and Malachy in the passenger seat of the Mini, Tess drove all the way back to Carlingford. Her uncle nodded approvingly as she turned into the driveway and smoothly pulled up outside the house. 'Theresa was right. You're a natural driver, Tess.'

'Ah, Uncle Malachy, thank you! Thank you very much. This has been the happiest day of my life.'

'Just one of many, Tess, I hope. And it's not over yet,' he added, as with a fanfare of sound and a blaze of light the front door burst open and friends and neighbours came pouring out to congratulate her.

After another hectic week, the girls decided to have a quiet night in before returning to Belfast on Saturday morning. Tess elected to take an early bath and disappeared upstairs. Saying she wouldn't be long, Rose nipped over to Malachy's with some freshly baked soda farls.

It was a beautiful evening with just a nip in the air and, left to her own devices, Colette took a stroll down towards the lough. Choosing a spot close to the shore she sat on a bench and watched the stars reflecting on the smooth water. It was lovely and peaceful here. If only they could stay a little while longer, but duty called and it was back to porridge in the morning.

She was surprised at how smoothly her pregnancy was progressing. No morning sickness and just a slight thickening of the waist. No one would ever dream that she was carrying a child. Of course she was aware that this state of affairs could not last much longer. She would soon be obliged to see a doctor and then what? The idea of applying to one of those homes for unmarried mothers was abhorrent to her. She pretended to Tess that she was tough, but deep down she was scared stiff. What was going to become of her? She suddenly felt very frightened and alone.

Rose studied Colette's still figure from a distance. In repose the young girl looked so sad. She left the road and slipped down on to the bench beside her before Colette was aware of her presence.

'Are you saying your goodbyes to Carlingford?' she asked gently.

Sadness dispelled, a smile transformed Colette's features. 'Something like that. It's a beautiful spot you live in here, so close to the Cooley Mountains. You don't realise how lucky you are. All this peace and tranquillity. Thank you for having me here this past two weeks.'

'It's been our pleasure having you.' Silence reigned for some moments and Rose broke it by asking tentatively, 'Have you made any plans for the future?'

'Well, a friend in Canada has been asking me to join her for some time now. She says I'd have no trouble at all getting a job there. There was a time when I wouldn't have been able to afford to go, but my grannie made that all possible by leaving me a large sum of money. So now I hope to eventually emigrate to Canada.'

A bewildered frown appeared on Rose's brow. 'But what about the baby? Do you intend taking it with you?'

Colette cringed away from her. 'Tess promised never to mention that to anyone,' she wailed.

Gripping her hand, Rose gave it a slight tug. 'Listen to me, Colette. Tess never said a word about you being pregnant.'

Slowly Colette relaxed and looked in confusion at Rose. 'Then how did you know? I never told anyone else.'

'I'm a country woman, remember, Colette. The signs are obvious to me. I'm sorry if I startled you, but . . . it isn't something you can hide for ever.'

'I know,' she replied sadly.

'Why are you keeping it such a big secret then? Don't you want Jack's child?'

'It's a long story, Rose. When Jack died I was devastated. I was so low that I even contemplated suicide. If Tess hadn't come into my life then, I'd probably not be here today. Tess doesn't know about this, so I'd appreciate you not mentioning it to her. Well, after a while I got my mind straightened out and began planning a new life for myself. Unfortunately the planning stage was as far as I got, due to an acute shortage of finances. Then when Grannie left me the money my dream of getting away from it all became a real possibility. I was in a position to go to Canada to start a new life. And then . . . I discovered I was pregnant. It was a terrible shock, I can tell you.'

'And now you've gotten over the shock what do you intend to do?'

'I don't know. I honestly don't know. I feel I must be some kind of monster not to want my own baby.' She turned towards Rose and gripped her arm. 'But I don't want it! I honestly don't!'

Putting an arm round her shoulders, Rose soothed her as best she could. 'Let's get you indoors and we can discuss it further, over a nice wee cup of tea.'

Walking back to the house, Rose said, 'What about your mother? She's the obvious one to help you. Won't she be annoyed when she finds out you've kept her in the dark all this time?'

'She's the last one I'd turn to. A child born out of wedlock? She would run a mile. She'd disown me.'

Rose smiled slightly. 'I think you're wrong there. Most mothers threaten dire penalties to try to protect their offspring, but if something happens they rally to the cause. It's only natural.'

'Believe you me, my mother is not in that category.'

At the finality in her voice Rose did not pursue the subject any further.

It was chilly, and when they entered the house Rose went straight to the grate and put a light to the fire that was already laid. They sat either side of the hearth and suddenly Colette leaned across and gripped this kind woman's hands. 'Rose, I'm not really a monster, you know.' Her voice pleaded for understanding.

'I know you're not. I find you a very kind and caring person, Colette.'

'If you only knew how much I regretted that night. I'm so ashamed every time I think of it. One night when I wasn't in full control of my senses and my life is ruined for ever.'

'I think you're being a little harsh on yourself. When you're in love these things happen quite naturally, no matter how good your intentions are.'

'But you don't understand! It should never have happened. I'll regret it till my dying day, so I will.'

Rose roughly shook her hands. 'Now you listen to me, Colette Burns. Regrets are futile. Many a time I've said If only . . . What if? But it does no good. You just have to put whatever it is behind you and get on with your life.' Colette opened her mouth to dispute this. How could you put the imminent birth of a child behind you? Rose forestalled her. 'I know your problem seems insurmountable, but it's a case of finding the right solution. Trust me. Things will work out somehow. They always do.'

Tess descended the stairs in her dressing gown, towelling her wet hair. 'My, but you two look solemn,' she said, joining them by the fire.

Wanting to leave the friends alone so that Tess could

be brought up to date on affairs, Rose volunteered, 'I'll put the teapot on, shall I?'

'That would be lovely,' Colette readily agreed, glad of the respite.

At the huskiness in her voice Tess peered closer and saw the signs of recent tears. Concerned, she sat close to her friend. 'What's wrong?'

'Rose knows I'm pregnant.'

Immediately, Tess straightened her back. 'I swear I never said a word. Honest!'

'I know you didn't. She read all the signs.'

'Of course, I should have known. She's a country woman, isn't she? But I do know this much. You can trust her. If you ask her to keep her mouth shut she will.'

'I've been waiting for you to come down, so we can discuss it. See what options I have, before it drives me round the bend with worry.'

Tess breathed a sigh of relief; her prayers had been answered. Now there were two of them to persuade Colette to keep the baby.

Rose returned with a tray laden with teapot, milk, sugar and a plate of still hot soda farls dripping with butter. Setting it down on a coffee table she went back to the kitchen for the cups and saucers. They ate in silence, each buried in her own thoughts. It was Rose who finally spoke.

'When is the baby due?'

'January.'

'You must have some idea what you intend doing?'

'I was thinking that I'd write to one of these homes for unmarried mothers and when the baby is born have it adopted.'

Rose gnawed at her bottom lip for some seconds,

while Tess willed her to come up with some pearls of wisdom. But Rose's argument was the same as hers. 'Do you not think Dan would be happy to take responsibility for the baby? After all, it's his grandchild.'

'No. No, I don't think that would be a good idea.'

'Why not?'

'Because then everybody would have to know.'

'Has the doctor given you an approximate date?'

'I haven't been to the doctor yet.'

Rose nodded her head. 'I thought as much. Perhaps that's a good thing. While I was making the tea I was trying out ideas in my head. Shall I tell you what I came up with?'

They both nodded eagerly and Rose continued. 'You'll be able to work for another couple of months. Right?' A nod from Colette confirmed it. 'What if I arrange for my doctor to look after you?'

'I don't see how that could help, Rose. Remember I live in Belfast.'

'I don't want you to rush into anything, Colette, but I'm going to make a suggestion and I want you to give it some careful consideration before you answer, okay?'

'Okay.'

'When you feel the need to leave work, why not come here and live with me? After all, you did say what a lovely spot this is. I'd be glad of your company and my doctor is a very understanding man. He would look after your welfare while you were staying here. I would tell him you're a young friend in trouble. He would understand and wouldn't ask any awkward questions.'

Tess couldn't believe her ears. Here was her future aunt offering her friend a solution to her immediate troubles. Her prayers had indeed been answered. She looked expectantly at Colette and was dismayed to see her sadly shake her head.

'Thank you, Rose. You're very kind. But you see I want to go away so no one in Belfast need ever know the truth. What you're suggesting wouldn't remain a secret for very long.' She glanced towards Tess. 'For instance, Mrs Maguire would know and through her Mr Thompson. And then he would start pestering me regarding the baby's future.' The head shake became more definite. 'No, this way it wouldn't work out.'

Tess had been taking all this in and turning it over in her mind, quickly coming to a decision. Now she interrupted. 'Mam wouldn't necessarily have to know. When the time comes that you have to leave work you could suddenly get the chance to go to Canada to see how you feel about working over there on a permanent basis, and not have time to say goodbye. No one else connected with the family, except Uncle Malachy of course, need ever know you're here. I think it's a great idea. It could work out for the best, Colette.'

'Do you think it possible? It would be lovely to come here instead of being away among a lot of strangers. I really do love Carlingford. Everyone I've met has been so nice and friendly towards me.'

'With a bit of careful planning it can be managed,' Tess assured her. 'I'll keep your secret no matter what. Trust me!'

'Mind you, I'd still want the baby adopted.'

Tess and Rose stared at each other and a silent pact was made. They had plenty of time to persuade Colette to change her mind.

Chapter Sixteen

Next day Tess drove proudly home in her new Austin Mini. She left Colette, much relieved now that a decision had been made about her immediate future, on Spinner Street and proceeded up the Falls Road to Springfield Road. She had phoned her mother and told her about all her presents, especially the car, and now she sat outside her home expecting Alice and Dan to come rushing out and fawn all over it. Not a bit of it!

No sign of life at all. Such a difference from Carlingford. And to crown it all, today – the 24th – was her actual birthday. Feeling desolate, Tess got out of the car and unlocking the boot proceeded to unload her suitcases and parcels. Just what had she expected? Was her mother going to be awkward about the car? Did she resent Uncle Malachy's buying it for Tess, as she had with the Christmas present he had given her? Surely not. She had sounded so pleased on the phone when Tess told her all about it. Had insisted on talking to her brother and thanking him for his generosity. But the reception here in Belfast was one big disappointment.

Her reverie was broken by the sound of the front door opening and her mother, followed closely by Dan, Theresa and a few other friends, clattered down the steps to greet her. Alice hugged her as she wished her a happy birthday. 'Sorry it took us so long coming out,' she apologised. 'We've been on the lookout for you all day and then, wouldn't you know, as soon as we turned our backs you arrived at the door. Something came up at the last minute to distract us. But you'll hear all about that soon enough.' She turned her attention to the car. 'Oh, my, but isn't that car one wee beaut. I love that colour.'

Pleased at her reaction, Tess watched closely, but her mother seemed genuinely sincere in her admiration. Dan was also giving the Mini the once over. 'It certainly is. It's a grand wee car. Happy birthday, Tess. Here, give us a hug.'

Theresa was tugging at her sleeve. 'Let them drool over your lovely car all they want, but you must come inside, Tess. There's a load of presents to be opened.'

'If I could just give you mine now, Tess. I have to rush off.' Tony Burke thrust a parcel into her arms and pecked her on the cheek. 'Happy birthday. I'll see you tomorrow.'

Theresa grabbed his arm. 'What about dinner tonight?'

Gently he released her hold. 'I don't think so. Bye for now, Tess. Have a nice time tonight.'

'Bye, Tony, and thanks for the present.' She looked in bewilderment at Theresa. 'What on earth's up with him? And what's all this dinner business?' she asked.

'If you'll just come inside I'll explain.'

'Dan, can I leave you to look after my cases?'

'No sweat, Tess. Away you go.'

When she entered the hall a whiff of remembered perfume hung in the air. Alerted, she quickly entered the sitting room only to come to an abrupt halt and stand gaping speechlessly. There, looking like a million dollars in a suit that fitted like a glove, stood a smiling Agnes Quinn, her arms held out wide to embrace her best friend.

'When did *you* get here?' Tess managed to splutter.

'Just before you. That's why they were so slow at going to the door.'

'Where's Dominic?'

'He couldn't afford to leave the business again so soon, so he arranged all this behind my back. I didn't know I was coming until yesterday. It was a last minute rush. So you can guess I've hardly any clothes with me.'

'I don't believe that for one second. Anyway, how long are you home for?'

'Just a week. It was a cancellation so Dominic got it cheap.'

They were wrapped in each other's arms, hugging and kissing, tears mingling as if they hadn't seen each other for years. 'Oh, I'm so glad to see you again, Agnes. This is the best birthday I've ever had.'

Agnes pointed to a large box on the table. 'That's my present. It arrived long before me, since I didn't know I was coming. I'm afraid it's a winter jacket. But then I didn't know you'd be the proud owner of a car. It's lovely, by the way. I had a wee peek at it from behind the curtains. Imagine you being able to drive, eh, Tess? Wonders will never cease!'

Tearing off the wrapping paper and opening the box, Tess exclaimed with pleasure when she saw the dark green ski-type jacket. She slipped it on and examined herself in the mirror. 'Oh, it's lovely! And as you well know, a winter coat will never go to waste over here, Agnes.'

'I suppose not. It goes with your eyes. I'm glad you like it.' Agnes nodded to where Theresa stood beaming at them. 'I believe you are also part owner in a shop now?'

'Yes. Isn't it wonderful? I take it you've already met Theresa? Me and her get on like a house on fire.'

'I'm pleased to hear that, Tess. I hope I meet someone like her out in America. At the moment it's a bit lonely over there as I hardly know anybody, but Dominic takes me round introducing me to his friends every chance he gets.'

'Here's your mam and Dan coming in now,' Theresa exclaimed. 'Let's move into the living room. There's a bottle of champagne waiting to be opened. My mam is in there too, patiently waiting to give you your present.'

Linking her arm through Agnes's as she always did, Tess happily led the way. What a lovely homecoming it had turned out to be, and there's her thinking that everyone had forgotten her big day. She gave an involuntary sniffle at the thought. The twenty-fourth of July was going to be a great day. Apparently a table had been booked at the Royal Avenue Hotel for eight o'clock that night. Her best friend was home for a week. Life couldn't be better. The only fly in the ointment was Tony. She would phone later that afternoon and thank him for the perfume he had bought her, and perhaps she would be able to persuade him to join them for dinner. Did he still care so much for Agnes that he couldn't bear to be in the same room as her? He would have to get her out of his system, or he would end up a grumpy old bachelor.

The weekend was an exciting time for Tess, the dinner and subsequent birthday party going with a swing. The cheque from her mother was gratefully received and was now deposited in the business account of Maguire & Cunningham.

Agnes willingly spent some of her holiday helping the girls clean and polish the shop fittings, in preparation for the big opening day. Theresa listened raptly in the background while the two friends babbled away, exchanging bits of gossip as Tess brought Agnes up to date on all the latest news and scandals. It was during one of these conversations that she discovered that Tony and Agnes had been engaged. She surmised this to be the reason why Tony had refused to come out with them on Saturday night. It surprised her, as she had been inclined to think he was very interested in Tess.

Soon Tess was saying a tearful goodbye once more to Agnes, amidst promises of going out to Florida to be her bridesmaid when a definite date had been set. When Agnes had departed it was no holds barred as, with final papers signed, she and Theresa began moving into their new work premises and shop. They had all agreed that it would be best if Alice were to continue working at home.

A lot of thought was put into the window display. The public were used to seeing children's clothes in this shop window. Tess and Theresa didn't want to appear as if they would be dealing only in children's wear, so a bridal ensemble took up the centre of the display, complemented by a variety of outfits for children. Having bought all the previous owners' stock they had plenty of autumn wear for sale and were free to start working on bridal wear and Christmas dresses.

Tess, Tony and Colette still had their Saturday night outings together and Tess was surprised at how well her friend managed to hide her pregnancy with loose clothes as autumn approached. After Theresa left for the day, Colette spent a lot of evenings in the shop, sewing on buttons or pressing or assisting with anything else that didn't require too much expertise.

On these occasions she could relax and discuss any problems she might have with Tess. It was late September when she handed in her notice at the bank and Tess began to drop hints to her mother and Dan about Colette's wanting to go to Canada for a trial period.

Dan was the first to voice his objections. 'What does she want to go to Canada for?'

'To get away from all the memories around here, that's what. There are good opportunities out there for someone with Colette's experience. Besides, if she doesn't like what she sees, she can always come home.'

'What has her mother got to say about that?' Alice queried.

'I couldn't say. She never discusses her family with me.'

'Talk her out of it, Tess.' Dan sounded disturbed. 'She was almost my daughter-in-law. I feel I should be keeping an eye on her for Jack's sake.'

Tess flashed him a look of derision. 'Hah! That's the best gag I ever heard! Just what have you done for her since Jack died? Go on . . . tell me!'

Dan held up his hands in defence. 'All right! All right! So I haven't done very much. I admit that. However, it wasn't for the sake of trying. She just kept giving me the brush-off. But I always listen whenever you talk about her. I know she's doing all right. If there was ever a hint of trouble I'd be the first one in there fighting the good cause. You've got to believe that, Tess. I feel a good deal of responsibility where she is concerned.'

Tess could see he really was perturbed. Amazed at

how smoothly the lies rolled off her lips, she said, 'Perhaps nothing will come of it. It's all talk at the moment. But, Dan . . . if she does decide to go . . . if I were you I wouldn't interfere. She won't thank you for it.'

'Oh, won't she? Well, I can't see me just standing around holding my tongue.'

'Let's just wait and see what happens and not go flying off the handle, eh? As I said, she might change her mind.'

Two weeks later Tess drove Colette to Great Victoria Street station and put her on the train to Newry. Malachy would be there to pick her up. That night Tess broke the news to her mother and Dan that Colette had left for Canada.

'She's away and all?' Dan exclaimed. 'And you never said a word about it?'

'Here, hold on a minute. I didn't know.' Tess lied through her teeth. 'It was all arranged from Canada. Her friend persuaded Colette to go and see what it was like out there. She arranged it all.'

Dan shook his head in disbelief. 'And she hadn't even time to say goodbye?'

'She didn't want a lot of goodbyes. She said goodbyes always made her weepy.'

'Did you drive her to the airport?'

This was the snag as far as Tess was concerned. She was the obvious one to have driven Colette to the airport, but she hadn't been away from home long enough for that.

More lies came to her lips. 'No. One of the managers from the bank was going to a conference down south and gave her a lift to Shannon.'

Both Alice and Dan still looked unconvinced and, flustered, Tess cried, 'I don't know what all the fuss is about. You hardly ever see her anyhow, so what difference will it make? Even if she decides to make her home in Canada she'll be back to settle her affairs and say her farewells. Anyway, it's none of our business what she does.'

'Still, I wish I'd known. I could have perhaps talked her out of it.'

Dan left the room and they heard him climb the stairs. With a reproving glance at her daughter, Alice followed him.

Dismayed, Tess wondered just what she had got herself into. Letters would be expected from Canada over the next couple of months. What excuse would she give when they failed to arrive? She would have to play it by ear. At least Colette was in safe hands, not away somewhere surrounded by strangers, and that was Tess's primary consideration at the moment. Dan's hurt feelings didn't enter into it as far as she was concerned.

To Tess's surprise, Tony showed no great interest in Colette's departure. When Theresa heard about it she smiled and said, 'I bet Tony is delighted. I think he thought her a bit of a gooseberry.'

'What do you mean?'

'It's obvious he fancies you, and now with Colette out of the picture he will feel free to show his interest. You mark my words, Tess.'

'Tony . . . fancy me? Don't be silly. We're just good friends.'

Theresa laughed outright. 'Just you wait and see.'

'I hope you're wrong. Because believe you me, I am not in the least bit interested in Tony Burke.'

*　　*　　*

As expected, questions *were* asked about the absence of letters from Canada, or any other communication for that matter. It was a Sunday afternoon and Tess and Alice – Dan having gone for a walk – were having a cup of tea and catching up on each other's news when, taking Tess unawares, Alice wondered aloud about Colette's welfare. Absentmindedly Tess almost assured her that she was doing well and everything was under control. The words were on the tip of her tongue and just in time she swallowed them and muttered, 'It would be nice to know.' She was very annoyed with herself, realising how close she had come to letting the cat out of the bag. So easily done! Exasperated, she cried, 'Mam, if Colette wants us to know her business she'll write in her own good time! Okay? Meanwhile, I wish you and Dan would stop pestering me about her. What makes you think I know any more than you do?'

At her daughter's tone of voice, Alice drew back affronted. 'You can't blame Dan for being worried, Tess.'

'Actually, Mam, I can and I do blame him. He should have been more attentive when she was here and maybe she wouldn't have gone off in the first place.'

'He tried. You heard him. But she wouldn't let him help her.'

'We've only his word for that, Mam. Colette certainly never spoke to me of him offering any help. And anyway, it's none of Dan's business what Colette does or doesn't do.'

Alice rounded on her in anger. 'Are you saying he lied?' she cried indignantly.

'No, Mam, I'm not. What I am saying is that if she didn't want his help before, she won't want it now, so let's forget about Colette for a while. I've more important things on my plate at the moment. If I do get any news you'll be the first to know. Okay? After all, Colette and I weren't exactly bosom pals.'

With a look of disdain, Alice lifted her cup and left the room. Tess buried her face in her hands; so much for a quiet chat over a cup of tea! She prayed she would be able to keep up this deception. At least it was near the end of November; not all that much longer to go now. According to Rose, Colette was still talking about adoption and wanted Rose to get in touch with the proper authorities on her behalf. A distracted Rose informed Tess that if they couldn't change her mind she really would put the baby up for adoption and go off to Canada.

Every Wednesday after closing the shop for the day Tess would settle down and have a good old chin-wag with Rose and Colette before going home, to find out how things were going. They assured her that so far everything was fine and Colette always reminded Tess not to drop her guard and let anyone know where she was.

Christmas day fell on a Saturday this year and the girls were closing shop from Wednesday night for the Christmas break. On Tuesday night Rose rang Tess at home, something she had never done before. It was Alice who answered the phone, and after a short conversation with Rose she called Tess into the hall. 'It's Rose. Something about a pattern for her wedding suit,' she explained.

It was so unlike Rose, to phone out of the blue to discuss her suit, that Tess had a premonition that something awful had happened. Gingerly picking up the receiver, she delayed as long as she could before saying softly, 'Hello, Rose.'

Quick on the uptake, Rose whispered, 'I take it it's not safe to talk at the moment?'

'Not really.'

'I'm sorry. But I couldn't wait any longer. I just had to let you know. Colette has had a baby boy, and I'm afraid of her doing something rash. She wants to see you as soon as possible. Is there any chance of you getting down here tomorrow?' She sounded really worried.

'Why, that's wonderful! Yes, I think I could get down some time tomorrow to have a look at it. It would be a pity to let such a piece of material pass you by as you seem to have your heart set on it. I'll ask Mam if she will help out in the shop.'

Alice was sitting with her ears pricked when Tess put her head round the living room door. 'Mam, Rose has the chance of a beautiful piece of worsted material for her wedding suit,' she lied glibly. 'Is it all right if I go down tomorrow after the shop closes and stay overnight? Or better still, could you possibly help Theresa in the shop tomorrow and let me get away early? We shouldn't be too busy. Just a couple of customers are working and can't pick up their orders until the last minute, so it means keeping the shop open. It's not fair to leave Theresa on her own.'

Alice pulled a wry face. 'Can Rose not hang on to the material until after Christmas? I've to go down to the market tomorrow for my turkey and fresh vegetables. I daren't leave it till Christmas Eve. It'll be murder then.'

'Tell you what, Mam. You get your veg down the road and I'll ask Uncle Malachy to get us a turkey. He should be able to get us a nice one down there.'

Alice pondered for a moment. 'All right. I suppose that's fair enough.'

Tess ran back to the phone. 'Hello? Are you still there, Rose?'

'Of course I am.'

'I can be in Carlingford early tomorrow. Mam will help Theresa in the shop and we're closed on Thursday so I'll be able to stay overnight if that's all right with you? And, Rose . . . would you ask Uncle Malachy to get me a turkey, please?'

'Of course you can stay as long as you like. The turkey will be no problem. I'll see you tomorrow then, Tess. Bye for now.'

On the journey down to Carlingford. Tess said over and over to herself, 'A boy. A little boy.' She wished she knew more about it but her mam would have been suspicious if she and Rose had started whispering on the phone the night before. Not that Alice would ever have guessed the truth, but she would have known that something was going on and would have tried to find out what. That was something they could do without while the baby's fate hung in the balance.

When she got out of the car, Rose quickly left the house, closing the door behind her.

'Oh, I'm so glad to see you, Tess. Colette's in an awful state. She will hardly look at the child and he's absolutely gorgeous. I hope you can talk some sense into her.'

'So do I! What weight was he?'

'Just over seven pounds. It's obvious she wants to hold him but is afraid of getting too attached to him. She's still determined to go to Canada. I don't think we'll be able to put her off that idea.'

'The baby's early, isn't it?'

'Early *and* quick! She went into labour at about seven o'clock yesterday evening. I thought it would take hours and I delayed sending for the doctor. He came in as I was delivering it myself around nine o'clock. I thought I'd wait until you closed for Christmas before letting you know but Colette wouldn't wait. That's why I rang you last night. I'm sorry I put you on the spot, but I couldn't do anything else. She wants to talk to you on your own. So up you go.'

Still Tess dithered. 'I don't mean to sound suspicious . . . but did the doctor say anything about it arriving early?'

Rose stared intently at her. 'No, but then he wouldn't. If Colette told him anything in confidence he wouldn't break that confidence. Just what are you implying, Tess? Do you think maybe it isn't Jack's child?'

A bewildered shake of the head was her answer. 'I honestly don't know. I'll go up now and see her. We'll have a chat later.'

Colette was in despair as she awaited the arrival of Tess, torn by thoughts of her son and how he had come to be conceived. Would Tess understand and lend a sympathetic ear, or would she be disgusted with her friend's despicable behaviour? Heaven knows, she couldn't be any more disgusted than she herself was right now. How she regretted that night. She had thought of little else since it had happened. Jack just a few hours dead and she had betrayed him! If only she could turn back the clock.

In all honesty she hadn't realised Dan was so drunk. As for herself . . . unused to strong alcohol, it had not only deadened the pain of the loss of her beloved Jack, it had lulled her into a sense of false security. When Dan's comforting pats had become sensual caresses she had swayed with the wind as it were, willingly gratifying her desires, urging him on, wanting to blank out reality. It had seemed so right at the time! And she was honest enough to admit to herself that, in her drunken state, she had even enjoyed it. However, it was all over in a very short space of time and she was horrified when the enormity of what she had done hit her. Her great worry was having to face Dan again.

She had tried to waken him but he was dead to the world. Throwing a blanket over his prone form she skulked from the house, engulfed in shame.

The next morning she had waited in trepidation for Dan to come and apologise. She waited in vain. When he did eventually arrive to discuss the funeral arrangements with her, she was dismayed that he did not mention what had taken place between them. Not a word. In fact he appeared to be unaware that anything *had* happened.

At first she couldn't believe that Dan didn't remember what had taken place between them the previous night; had thought he was being evasive about the whole matter. However, it soon became clear to her that he had no recollection whatsoever of their encounter. He had either erased it from his mind or perhaps convinced himself it was all a dream. Either way he had shown no outward sign that anything had occurred between them. How she wished that she could do likewise, but she would never forget that night and the deep shame she felt would stay with her till her dying day.

As time passed she was glad that he did not remember. It meant that she could put it behind her and no one need be any the wiser. By the time she discovered that she was pregnant it was too late to confront Dan about it. Even if she had picked up the courage to do so, would Dan have believed her? She very much doubted it. It was obvious by then that he had eyes only for Alice Maguire. The only solution she could see open to her was to have the baby adopted, but now that she had seen her beautiful son there was no way she could ever give him up. Hearing footsteps on the stairs she closed her eyes and tried to arrange her thoughts. The time of reckoning had arrived and she must confess her guilty secret to Tess.

Tess quietly entered the bedroom and at a glance saw that Colette was sleeping. Her thoughts were in turmoil. Did she really think that Colette had been stringing them along pretending the baby was Jack's? Tiptoeing over to the cot in the corner, she gazed down in wonder on the sleeping child. He was indeed beautiful, with a mane of jet black hair and small perfect features. Whether it was because she wanted it to be so, she didn't know, but she thought he resembled the Thompsons. Not Jack, no, but to her he was the spitting image of his grandfather.

Colette's voice brought her back to reality. 'He's lovely, isn't he?'

Tess glanced towards the bed and big dark haunted eyes gazed back at her. 'He certainly is.'

'Thanks for coming so quickly.' Pushing herself painfully into a sitting position, Colette patted the bedclothes and said, 'Come and sit here. I want to talk to you.'

Hesitantly Tess approached the bed and stood gazing at Colette in concern. 'Are you all right? Do you feel up to talking? I'm staying overnight. We can talk later if you like, after you've had a good rest. I'm sure you're exhausted.'

'I'm fine. Just the stitches are a bit sore when I move.

Please sit down. We mightn't get another opportunity to speak in private.'

Reluctantly Tess sank down on to the bed. She didn't want to know if Colette had been playing around whilst engaged to Jack. She felt betrayed that her friend had used Rose and her to cover up her deceit.

Determinedly, Colette held Tess's eye. 'I've a confession to make, and it isn't pleasant listening. Jack is not the baby's father.'

Even although she was already thinking along these very same lines, Tess couldn't hide the shock and distaste that coursed through her.

'Don't look like that, Tess! Why do you think I was so ashamed when I discovered I was pregnant? If it had been Jack's I'd have been over the moon. But it isn't! And that's why I wanted to get it adopted. The only snag is that now I've seen him I've changed my mind. I certainly don't want him to go to some strangers.'

Tess's thoughts had gone into overdrive. If Jack wasn't the culprit, then who was? Only one other person came to mind.

She voiced her shocked thoughts. 'Is it Tony Burke's?'

Colette smiled sadly. 'I wish it was. But do you think if it had been Tony's I'd have been afraid to tell him? Even if he was engaged to Agnes at that time, Tony is a very responsible person. He would have taken care of me, no matter what.'

'Then *who*?' Tess cried in exasperation. 'Who were you afraid to tell? What bad bastard left you in the lurch? Was it someone at work?'

'No. No, nothing like that. Look, I don't know how to put this into words, so I suppose I'll just have to tell you as simply as I can.' Hands clasped tightly in front of her, Colette continued in a monotone. 'Do you remember when Jack died and Grannie was taken into hospital?'

At a nod from Tess she went on. 'I was distracted. Completely at my wits' end. I didn't know you very well then, and had no one to turn to. That night, after everyone else had gone, dreading going into an empty house, I stayed behind to comfort Dan . . . and, I suppose, to get comfort in return. He holds his drink so well I didn't realise he was already drunk and I poured us both a large whiskey. I hate the stuff, but I made myself drink it hoping it would deaden the awful pain inside me. And it did!' Tears trickled down Colette's cheeks and dripped unheeded on to her nightie.

Having an inkling where all this was leading, Tess reached for Colette's hands and gripped them tightly. 'Don't upset yourself so.'

'I have to tell you, Tess. You see, you're the only one I can really trust. You're my best friend. And . . . you'll know what to do.'

'Me?' Tess squeaked in dismay.

'Yes, you. The whiskey, and I suppose the grief, had taken its toll on me. At first I didn't realise Dan's comforting pats had become sexual pawing.' Her eyes begged Tess to understand. 'It was such a comfort to be wanted.' Tears fell faster at the recollection of it. 'I didn't even try to prevent it happening. You've got to believe me, Tess, when I tell you it seemed the most natural thing in the world. It's the God's honest truth, so it is.'

Tightening her grip on Colette's trembling hands, Tess gasped, 'Are you telling me that Dan Thompson took advantage of you?'

Colette looked blankly at her. 'I suppose he did. I never thought of it like that. I was so confused by my actions, especially as I had refused Jack the night before.'

'What did Dan have to say about it?'

'That's just it! I was afraid to look at him the next day, but he seemed unaware that anything had happened. I thought he was putting on an act and inwardly called him all the bad names I could think of, and some more. However, as time went by he seemed so caring I believed he really had completely blanked it from his mind. So, although I wanted nothing at all to do with him, I was at least glad to be able to put the episode behind me.'

'And when you discovered you were pregnant?'

'I'll never forget it! I nearly went out of my mind. It's awful, you know, to be in my position and have no one to turn to.'

'Why not me? We were friends by then.'

'Come on now, Tess. Be honest about it. Could I have told you? Dan and your mother were becoming so close I didn't know what kind of reception I would get, and I didn't want to lose your friendship. You were the only person I could talk to about being pregnant. Of course I couldn't tell you it was Dan's. I was too afraid of losing you.'

'Oh, God. This is awful. Imagine you having to rely on the likes of me. It's not right! Dan mustn't be allowed to get away with it! He must be made to face up to his responsibilities.'

'That's why I want to talk to you. What happens next will depend entirely on you.'

'Me? I don't understand. What have I got to do with it?'

Leaning closer, Colette said urgently, 'Think of the scandal if I speak out now, Tess. The whispers and the gossip. The people that would get hurt. Your mother for one. And the finger of shame would always be pointed at that poor innocent baby. Think about it!'

'But . . . you've got to agree, Colette, Dan Thompson must be made to pay for his part in this. Why, you could have had him up for rape if you had spoken out sooner. He took advantage of you, the dirty bastard!'

'No! No, Tess, you're wrong. I was a willing partner. But if it became common knowledge, it could be miscon-strued. Is that what you want? The man your mother appears to love, being branded a rapist? If it got out of hand it would probably be spread across the front of the local papers, you know. He might even go to jail. Is that really what you want?'

'It doesn't matter about that. Mam would never condone anything like this. She would want to see him pay the penalty for his sin.'

Colette looked sceptical. 'Maybe . . . but would she be grateful to us for opening her eyes? Let's face it, Tess. It was a one off! It's not something that is likely to happen again. And think of Anne! She'd have a field day. Do you want to put your mother through all that humiliation?'

Before Tess could answer, the baby whimpered and she made to go to him. With a hand on her arm, Colette stopped her. 'Don't get too fond of him until we get this sorted out between us.'

'Surely you can't consider letting him go to strangers now. He's beautiful.'

'No. Rose has offered to look after him for me and she says Malachy is more than willing. But it's not the ideal situation. Her son's wife is expecting a baby in March and I don't want his nose put out of joint.' Tess still looked stunned and Colette added sadly, 'I know how you feel. I've been awake all night thinking about it. One thing I do know, I will not have him adopted. Not now.'

'Thank God for that at least! You're not going away then?'

'Oh yes, I'm still going to Canada. Do you think I could look at that wee child's face every day and not remember that I had betrayed my beloved Jack? And with his father of all people? I just couldn't do it, Tess.'

Tess gazed at her in confusion. 'But you didn't really betray Jack. You were drunk and vulnerable, remember. Oh, I wish I could get my mind round this. Just what do you intend doing?'

'I have a suggestion to make, Tess. It all depends on you. You could take the child home with you tomorrow and introduce him as either Dan's son or his grandson. The choice is yours. As Dan's son . . . he will cause a lot of unhappiness and misery, although I don't doubt for one minute that Dan will take on the responsibility of rearing him, even if it means losing your mother's friendship. As Dan's grandson, he will be greeted with delight by all concerned.'

'And what about Rose? How much does she know?'

'She knows nothing. She still thinks it's Jack's. Everyone else will think so too, unless you say otherwise.'

'But why tell me?'

'Because you're my friend and you have been good to me. Your mother's happiness is at stake here. To be truthful, it's not just your mother I'm thinking of. I myself don't relish the scandal that will erupt if the truth is told. They will say terrible things about me as well, you know, but I'll be going far away where it won't hurt me. Where no one will be any the wiser.'

The baby cried out, louder this time, and there was

a tap on the door. Rose's head appeared round it. Her eyes took in the two tense figures on the bed, and she made to withdraw then paused to say, 'Sorry for interrupting. I was just going to take him downstairs and change his nappy. If that's all right?'

'Thanks, Rose. You do that, please.'

When the door closed on Rose, Colette advised, 'Sleep on it, Tess. The decision is yours. And please don't think me awful for wanting to get away. I'll go nuts if I stay in Belfast and live a lie for the rest of my life.'

Reaching for her, Tess gathered her close. 'You poor, poor dear. What you've come through is nobody's business. You must have felt so isolated. I think you're a very brave girl, so I do. I'll go downstairs now. I can't wait to hold that wee fellow. Have you thought of a name for him yet?'

Colette smiled. 'No matter which way it goes, I think Jack will be the most appropriate name. Don't you?'

'You're right there! Jack it will be.'

Downstairs, as she crooned over the baby, Tess could feel Rose watching her covertly, but as yet there was nothing she could tell her.

'Colette is going to name him Jack,' she volunteered.

'And do you still think it might not be Jack's baby?'

'Oh, he's a Thompson all right. The minute I set eyes on him I could see that,' she said convincingly.

'I don't want to appear nosy, but has she said what she intends doing?'

'Rose . . . after all you've done? You could never appear nosy in my book. She wants me to take him back with me tomorrow and introduce him to Dan.' But in what capacity? What a decision to have to make.

'And are you going to do that?'

'Yes, I think he has the right to know about the baby. And I'm sure when he hears that Colette still intends going to Canada he will want to make himself responsible for his upbringing.' She glanced sadly at Rose. 'You must feel let down. Colette says you offered to take him.'

'Don't worry about me! My son's wife is expecting a baby in March. I can spoil that rotten. I just wanted to ease Colette's mind; to let her know that I'd be here if she needed me.'

'You're such a good person, Rose. I hope Uncle Malachy appreciates what he is getting.'

'Don't you worry about that. I'll make sure he does!'

The journey back to Belfast the next day was a different kettle of fish from the one to the farm. Then she had thought that Colette had played the dirty on her and Rose. Had used them. Now she knew the whole sordid story and the part she was required to play in it. From time to time she glanced at the baby's carrycot strapped securely on the passenger seat beside her. Her mother would delight in helping to rear him. And it would also be a blessing in disguise. With Dan out at work every day Tess felt her mother resented working in the house alone while she and Theresa worked in the shop. With a baby to look after she would be happy and contented with her lot.

But could she deceive her mother on such a serious issue? After all, as Colette had pointed out before she left, one way or the other the child would be Dan's responsibility. She would have to play it by ear. See if Dan showed any signs of guilt. If he did, it would mean that he remembered the part he had played in the baby's conception. Even though he had been unaware of the consequences, in that case Tess could not see herself being able to hold her tongue.

One thing was certain. Whatever decision she made today, she would have to stick by it. There could be no turning back.

Drawing the car up to the front of the house she quickly got out and, checking the baby was all right, closed the door.

Dan came out as she opened the boot. 'Your mother asked me to make sure you have a turkey back with you.' He stood gazing in amazement at the variety of baby stuff packed in the boot. 'In the name of God, what's all this? I know it's Christmas, but this is ridiculous.'

'The turkey's in that box.' She indicated a cardboard carton. 'Would you take it in along with my case, Dan? I'll explain everything inside.'

Alice came out in a rush. 'Dan says you've a lot of baby stuff home with you. Who's it for?' Her eyes searched Tess's face. 'You're not . . . Are you?'

Tess smiled at the very idea that she might be pregnant. 'No, Mam, I'm not.'

'Theresa then?'

'Wrong again, Mam. Come and see.'

Tess opened the car door just as Dan returned. Alice gaped in wonder at the sleeping child. Her head swivelled towards Tess. 'It can't be Rose's, surely.'

'Mam, will you stop making these stupid guesses. Dan, will you carry the cot inside, please. Mam, you help me empty the boot.'

Dan had placed the cot on the settee and was gazing intently at it. When Tess came into the room she watched him very closely. He looked totally relaxed. No sign of tension.

Still keeping a close eye on him, she announced, 'Colette gave birth to that child two days ago in Carlingford.'

Dan swung round and his eyes were blazing. 'You mean to tell me that Colette was in Carlingford expecting my grandchild and all along I was led to believe she was in Canada? And no one thought fit to tell me?' He turned on Alice. 'Did you know anything about this?'

'No, I honestly didn't know a thing. I thought she was in Canada too.' She looked accusingly at her daughter. 'Why all the secrecy, Tess?'

'She still intends going to Canada, and actually she was going to have him adopted and not say a word about it.'

'She was going to have my grandchild adopted without my permission?'

'She didn't need your permission, Dan . . . Or did she?' she added slyly, still very attentive to his reactions.

'As a grandfather I must have some rights. Why did she do this, Tess? How could she be so cruel?'

She could see he was completely bewildered. No sign of guilt or evasion. If he was putting on an act, he deserved an Oscar. She stood in thought for some moments before moving to the next scene in the saga. 'When some women are pregnant they get all mixed up. She thought you'd object to her still wanting to start a new life in Canada. Thank God she changed her mind about the adoption. She wants you to take care of him. What about it, Mam? Would you be willing to help Dan? It's a big step to take at your age.'

Alice had lifted the child into her arms and was crooning softly to him. 'Don't be silly! I'm not over the hill yet, girl. It would be the nicest thing that could possibly happen to me. He's the picture of his grandfather. But what about baby food? Shouldn't Colette be breast-feeding him?'

Tess held her breath, but there was still no reaction

from Dan at this allusion to whom the baby resembled. 'Dan? What about it? Are you willing to take on the responsibility? Colette doesn't want to become too attached to her son, so the doctor advised Rose what milk to start him off on. The baby clinic will advise you later on.'

'Willing? To bring up my own grandson? My own flesh and blood? Why, it would be as if Alice and I were rearing our very own son.'

Tess's eyes examined his face once more. Was he being sarky? No, there were no innuendos there. She took the final plunge. 'Well then, meet your grandson. Colette has named him Jack. She'll be coming up to say good-bye to him and the rest of us before going off to Canada. And please be kind to her when she gets here. She's been through the mill these last lot of months.'

Gently, Dan took the tiny infant in his arms, his face wreathed in smiles. 'Of course I will. And I'll love this wee lad as if he was my own son. What a lovely Christmas present, eh, Alice?'

'The nicest ever.'

Such a happy picture they make, Tess thought. But . . . only time would tell if she had made the right decision.

Sworn to Secrecy

To all my friends and readers

Acknowledgements

I would like to thank the staff at Belfast Public Library for their assistance with my research.

And special thanks to Peter and Louie – they know who I mean. Their help was invaluable.

Author's Note

The geographical areas portrayed in *Sworn to Secrecy* actually exist and historical events referred to in the course of the story are, to the best of my knowledge, authentic.

However, I would like to emphasise that the story is fictional, all characters fictitious and any resemblance to real persons, living or dead, purely coincidental.

1

Belfast 1971

'There . . . I think that's just about right.' Tess Maguire smiled brightly from where she knelt at the feet of May Ross, pinning the skirt up to the required length for alteration. Drawing back she squinted at her handiwork. 'Take a look in the mirror,' she advised, 'and tell me what you think.'

May surveyed herself in the full-length mirror. 'Well now . . .' She turned round one way and then the other before saying haltingly, 'Do you not think it's just a wee bit too short? I know the mini is still popular at the minute but my legs are too fat for it.'

Tess's heart sank. She was due to collect Dan Thompson's grandson from school soon and the big hand on the clock was relentlessly heading towards that time. Her business partner had promised to be back early enough to let Tess nip over to St Paul's School for young Jackie, but there was no sign of her yet. Theresa could at least have phoned and let me know that she couldn't make it back on time, so that I could make other arrangements, she thought resentfully.

If only the school in Cavendish Square was still open, it would be so handy! The new one, which had opened a couple of years ago, was on Mica Drive off Beechmount Avenue, and although not a great distance away it still took a little longer to reach.

Still smiling in as friendly a manner as she could muster, under the circumstances, Tess said, 'I noticed the length of your coat and assumed that all your outdoor coats would be the same length. If this skirt's any longer it will hang below them. You wouldn't want that, now, would you?'

May laughed aloud. 'Would you just listen to yourself? Coats indeed,' she scoffed, emphasising the plural. 'I should be so lucky! This is the best . . . in fact, the only decent full-length coat I possess. Still, I think you're wrong. I think it is too short. Tell you what . . .' She reached to where the coat lay draped over the back of a chair. 'I'll try it on and see what it's like over the skirt.'

To Tess's relief the coat and skirt swung level with May's knees in perfect unison. 'There you are then, not as short as you had imagined.'

Obviously taken aback, May said, 'Now that is surprising! I would have thought it much shorter than this coat. But you're right! Any longer and it would look ridiculous. This is the length most suited to me.' As Tess rose to her feet, May looked enviously at her long slim legs, encased in black plastic knee-length boots with a skirt hem some inches above them. 'I wish I'd legs like yours.'

'Don't be silly. You look fine. I'm too skinny, so I am. But I'm glad you agree with me about the length of your skirt,' Tess said with a silent sigh of relief. She wanted to urge May on her way, but knew it would be unwise to do so. May was a relatively new customer and the

2

way business was going at the moment Tess didn't want to risk offending her. Where the hell is Theresa? she fumed inwardly.

As if she had conjured her up, the door opened and Theresa Cunningham breezed in, apologies sprouting from her mouth. 'Sorry I'm late, Tess.' A glance showed her that Tess was fully occupied, and by the look her friend threw her it was obvious that she was in a foul mood. 'Shall I take over there?' she asked apprehensively. 'Or shall I go on over and pick young Jackie up from school?'

Not in the least bit appeased by her partner's airy attitude, and even less so by the sight of the man who followed her through the door, Tess turned to May. 'Would you mind if I hand you over to my partner? I have to rush out for a short while.'

'Not in the slightest! I know what it's like. I'll be going to pick my girls up from St Dominic's soon. It was great when they were able to come home under their own steam, but now I collect them every day, just to be on the safe side. It doesn't do to take any chances. Those couple of years of comparative peace and plenty of work have spoilt us. Then all that trouble flared up in '69. Now the work is drying up and unemployment is a scourge again, you never know what's going to happen next. That's the cause of all this unrest. Ah, listen to me rambling on. Away you go. Don't let me hold you back. I'm sure this young woman will be quite capable of looking after me.'

'Thank you, Mrs Ross.' To let her know that she was still displeased with her, Tess avoided her partner's eyes, as she addressed her. 'Theresa, you have just to jot down the details of the alteration and how much it will cost. I really must run now or I'll be late.' She smiled gratefully at the pleasant young woman. 'Thanks for your custom, Mrs Ross.'

'You're welcome. When will the skirt be ready?'

'Any time from Tuesday onwards.'

Mrs Ross hesitated and then said tentatively, 'I don't suppose you could have it ready for Saturday?'

A refusal was on the tip of Tess's tongue; two days was short notice, and they didn't normally do alterations at all, but in the present climate they had decided not to turn away any orders, no matter how small. However, in the background, a slight nod of the head informed her that Theresa would be willing to do the alteration. That meant she would have to work late tonight or come in early tomorrow morning. Well it served her right! She wasn't pulling her weight lately, not since Bob Dempsey had arrived on the scene.

With Easter so near they'd had a bit of an upsurge in their business and they still had a bridal gown to finish off and some children's dresses and Easter bonnets to make. And although Theresa wasn't aware of it yet, Alice Maguire had informed her daughter the night before that she and Dan had decided to tie the knot at Easter and Tess was sure her mother would want a new outfit for the big occasion. And why not? One didn't get married every day of the week.

'I'm sure we can manage that, Mrs Ross. Theresa will check and make sure. See you soon.' With these words Tess pulled on a black plastic coat that just reached her skirt line, earning another admiring look from May, and quickly left the shop.

Tess's reliable Mini – a twenty-first birthday present from her Uncle Malachy – had been pinched from outside the house on Springfield Road and was later found, a burnt-out shell, at the top of the Whiterock Road. Another sad statistic of these troubled times they were presently living in. She had received compensation from her insurance company but decided to wait until things improved before investing in another car. She sorely missed that Mini, her very first car; it had been the joy of her life. Meanwhile, they were using Theresa's old and not too dependable banger, a Ford Prefect, for business purposes. Hurrying up the Springfield Road and along Crocus Street, Tess tried to control her temper. Since Theresa's mother had died last year, her friend was proving to be so unreliable. It was all Bob Dempsey's fault. Theresa had met him about six months ago and had fallen hopelessly in love. He was attractive, had the gift of the gab and Theresa could see no fault in him.

Whereas, try as she might, Tess found it difficult to find any saving graces at all. He was by far too smug for her liking and she was sure that only heartache would come out of the relationship, especially him being ten years younger than her friend. During a couple of verbal altercations, Theresa had had the audacity to suggest that perhaps Tess was jealous. Huh! Jealous over a layabout like him – indeed.

Arriving at Mica Drive, Tess joined the other young women outside the school waiting to collect their children and nodded in acknowledgement at their greetings. She didn't often collect Jackie, that was her mother's job, but today was an exception. She knew most of the women by sight. Some were old schoolfriends and a few were regular customers in her shop.

Her mother had often complained that Jackie was nearly always the last pupil out and today was no different. At last he appeared, dark hair standing on end, socks sagging down around his ankles, shirt-tail hanging

5

out over his trousers and coat slung over a shoulder. He looked a proper little Just William.

'How did you do today, love?' Tess greeted him as she put his coat on and buttoned it up before pulling his socks up to his knees.

Ignoring her question he gazed anxiously up at her. 'Where's Grannie?'

'She had to go into town today, Jackie, to do some shopping, and she asked me to collect you.'

'Are we going to your shop?'

'Just for a short while, until Grannie comes back.'

'I want to go home and watch TV,' he whined plaintively.

'All in good time.'

'Ah, Auntie Tess, please take me home now. I don't want to miss *Thunderbirds*. It's my bestest programme, so it is.'

'My *favourite* programme,' she corrected him.

Surprise widened his eyes. 'Yours too? I didn't know that, Auntie Tess.'

'Oh, never mind.' She couldn't suppress a smile at the very thought of it. 'I've work to do, Jackie. Now let's get back to the shop.'

'But . . .'

'Quiet now, and no buts about it.'

Deciding she deserved a break away from the shop and the unwanted company of Bob Dempsey, Tess took the other, longer route home along Beechmount Avenue and down the Falls Road. They trudged along in silence until they reached the Springfield Road junction. Jackie, usually a talkative child, was in a sullen mood and Tess tried to cajole him into better humour. 'Grannie won't be much longer, so cheer up, Jackie. Here, hold tight to my hand and let's get across this busy road.'

Reluctantly he took hold of her hand and stood in glum silence at the kerb as she went through the Green Cross Code with him. 'Look right, look left . . .'

At last there was a break in the traffic and together they crossed over. Tess was sore at heart every time she crossed this section of the road and got the full impact of the steel grille that protected her shop window. It spoiled the beautiful display. You couldn't get a clear view of anything through the heavy wire mesh. Although removable, it was too heavy for her and Theresa to take down and put up every day. Theresa had suggested that they ask Bob to do it but Tess refused. He loitered about the shop enough as it was, disturbing their work routine, without needing a legitimate excuse to hang about even more. Her eyes roved along the row of shops. They were all in the same boat, grilles covering the windows or, in some isolated cases, the windows boarded up because their owners could no longer afford the ever-increasing insurance premiums, which kept rising at an alarming rate. This was still a busy shopping thoroughfare but people had less money to spend now.

Back at the shop Theresa was attending another customer, and recognising her as an old and valued client, Tess greeted her warmly. 'Hello, Margaret. I hope you're keeping well?'

'Ach, not too bad, Tess.'

'I'm glad to hear that. There's a lot of flu going around at the minute.'

'Don't I know it! Most of my family have caught it, but so far I've managed to escape the bug.'

'Me too, thank God.'

Passing through a door to the workrooms at the rear of the shop, Tess was annoyed to find Bob Dempsey still there and very much at home, brewing tea on the small stove in a corner of the room. Tight-lipped, and without a word of greeting, she bent and helped Jackie out of his coat.

'And a good day to you too,' Bob said drily.

Tess threw him a look of disdain. 'Can't you get any kind of job, and leave Theresa free to get on with hers? Instead of always hanging on to her skirt tails.'

Bob's lips tightened and he warned himself to stay calm. He was very fond of Theresa and didn't intend letting this spiteful bitch come between them. 'Ah now, Tess, you know jobs are hard to come by these days. Why, it's like looking for gold in the street.'

'Hmm. It must be especially hard if you don't even make the effort to get yourself out and look for work. Even so, if you were half a man you would let Theresa get on with hers.'

Bob set a steaming mug of tea on the work bench close beside her and silently hoped it would choke her. She was becoming a real pain in the arse as far as he was concerned, a constant bone of contention between him and Theresa. He turned his attention to Jackie. 'There's some orange juice here, Jackie. Would you like a drink?'

'No.'

'Mind your manners, Jackie. Say no thank you,' Tess reprimanded him.

Bob laughed and said with a sneer, 'He's just following your example, Tess. I didn't hear you say the magic word.'

Put on the spot, Tess blushed bright red. 'Forgive me, Bob. Thank you for the tea,' she said sweetly. What she would have liked to say to him was unfit for the child's ears.

'I hope there's one in that pot for me, Bob,' Alice Maguire said as she entered the room, slipping her coat off. Draping it over the back of a chair, she threw her daughter a warm glance. 'Thanks for collecting Jackie, Tess.'

Alice gathered up the young lad, who had thrown himself into her arms, and hugged him close. She loved this child as if he were her and Dan's very own, instead of the offspring of Dan's dead son. He had been just two days old when Tess had brought him to them from Carlingford where his mother, Colette, had given birth to him.

'There's plenty for everybody, Mrs Maguire,' Bob assured her.

Arms wound tightly round his grandmother's neck, Jackie whispered, 'Grannie, can we go home now?'

Gently disentangling herself from his hold, Alice held him from her and gazed fondly into his young face. 'Can I have a cup of tea first, Jackie? I've been on my feet all day, love.'

'Ah, Grannie, I want to see *Thunderbirds*. You can make the tea when we get home.'

'I'm afraid Lady Penelope will have to wait, Jackie. I'm very thirsty. I promise not to be too long,' Alice insisted. She smiled at the fair-haired young man who carefully turned the handle of the mug towards her before handing it over. 'Thanks, Bob. Any sign of a job yet?'

Bob had his back turned to them pouring himself a cup of tea, and a grimace twisted his lips. Why couldn't they mind their own bloody business? The sooner he persuaded Theresa to break all connections with the Maguires the better. They were far too nosy for his liking. He wanted to tell them that he was indeed chasing jobs, even if he didn't boast about it. He bit back the words hovering on his tongue. He didn't have to explain to them that he was trying to get work. It was none of their

9

bloody business. However, his bitterness and resentment were well masked as he turned the full charm of his smile on Alice.

'Unfortunately no, Mrs Maguire.' Unable to resist his appeal, Alice gave him a wide grin of pleasure in return. Pleased that his charm had worked as usual, Bob kept the smile fixed on his face. It seemed to work on everyone but Tess, the ice queen. But then, he thought wryly, Tess was typical old maid material; couldn't hold on to a man if she were glued to him. From what he'd gleaned from Theresa, Tess had been let down by two men in the past few years and had sent another one packing. A pity really. With that hair and those big green eyes she wasn't all that bad looking. He let his eyes travel over her body. Nice figure too.

Alice eyed him over the rim of her mug. 'I hear they're looking for a caretaker at St Comgall's School. Would you not apply for that?'

It wasn't a job he would be interested in, but aware that the position would be snapped up in no time, Bob lied, 'I've already put in for it, but I'm not holding my breath waiting for a reply. There was dozens after it. And I'm sure a lot of them will have more experience of that kind of work than me.'

'Well, you never know your luck.' Alice sipped at her tea before adding thoughtfully, 'Dan knows a teacher there. I could get him to put a good word in for you, if you like.'

Bob managed to hide his dismay and tried to appear grateful. 'That would be great, if it's not too much trouble, Mrs Maguire.'

'I'll have a word with him tonight.' Alice was already regretting her rash offer. Dan Thompson would not be too pleased about it. He shared her daughter's dislike for

Bob Dempsey. Alice couldn't understand what they had against him. As far as she could see he was a very likeable young man, and always trying to please.

She finished her tea and rinsing her cup under the tap placed it on the small stainless steel draining board. 'That was lovely, thank you, Bob. Now, Jackie . . .' She reached for his coat and held it for him to put his arms in. 'Let's get this coat on. And try and look a bit more pleasant, young man, or there'll be no TV for you today. You'll go straight to bed, so you will. Goodbye, Bob.' She grabbed her own coat. 'See you at teatime, Tess.' She longed to give her daughter a good ticking-off, and tell her to wipe that scowl off her face and all, but knowing it would be of no avail, she held her tongue.

The customer was paying for her purchase, and Alice delayed until she had left the shop to have a quiet word with Theresa. 'How are things between you and Tess these days?'

Theresa pulled a face. 'Not so good, I'm afraid. There's no pleasing her at the moment.'

'Go easy on her. She's worried about the business.' Alice waved her hands vaguely about the shop, at the empty shelves that at one time had been weighed down with stock, as if to emphasise her point.

'And you think I'm not?' Theresa exclaimed. 'I've invested all my savings in this business as well, you know. So it's not only Tess who's worried. Everything was so wonderful when we first started. The orders were flooding in, we could hardly keep up with them, and then the troubles had to begin again. We used to have a lot of good custom from the Shankill Road and the Donegall Road. Our wedding gowns were quite famous. And affordable! Now it's all dried up.'

'Yes, I know all that, but if you keep at it surely things

11

will pick up again. Once the army goes home everything should hopefully get back to normal.'

Theresa smiled sadly. 'I can't see that happening in the foreseeable future. To tell you the truth, I think we should cut our losses – get out while the going's good.'

A horrified look spread across Alice's face. 'You can't possibly mean that.'

'I'm afraid I do, Mrs Maguire. Although, to be truthful, I think we've left it a bit late for that. Who in their right mind would want to buy a shop practically in front of a police station, with all that shooting and bombing going on?'

Inwardly, Alice agreed. Who indeed? At a loss what to say, she changed the subject. 'I'm sorry now I'm getting married at Easter. Tess can't see why we want to tie the knot since Dan and I have lived happily together all these years. I suppose if we'd married when his divorce first came through, it would have been different. To be honest, I don't know why Dan is so set on the idea. It's not as if we'll be able to do it in church, and a register office doesn't exactly appeal to me. I'd rather go on as we are.'

Theresa hurried around the counter, a grin on her face. 'Congratulations! This is a surprise.' She hugged the woman who had been a second mother to her since her own mother had died. 'I didn't know anything about it.' She continued in a consolatory tone, 'I suppose Mr Thompson is thinking of Jackie. He'll want to make sure everything is legal. The way things are nowadays, when you go out you never know whether or not you'll come home. But once you're married to Mr Thompson, you'll be Jackie's legal guardian and his mother won't be able to claim him if anything should happen to your husband.'

'I don't know about that. She'll still be his natural mother. I'll only be his step-grandma. But you're right.

That's probably why Dan's so keen on getting married. I never thought of it that way, but I don't think it will make any difference in any case. Colette will always have the law on her side. Didn't Tess tell you about our decision, then?'

'No. No, she didn't. I wonder why?'

'Perhaps she hasn't had time yet. We only broke the news to her last night and she wasn't exactly over the moon about it.'

'That explains it then. I was in late today and we haven't had a chance for a natter.'

'Grannie . . .'

'All right, Jackie! I'm coming. I'd better go, Theresa, before this wee rascal has kittens. See you tomorrow.'

Troubled thoughts plagued Alice as she walked up the road past the shops. She waved in acknowledgement at the barber as he worked at the window of his shop, clipping away at a young lad's hair, mentally reminding herself that Jackie needed his hair trimmed. Perhaps she'd take him in after school tomorrow, if the barber's shop wasn't too packed. The greengrocer was busy too, as was the butcher. The hardware shop also had quite a few people browsing around. Such a busy stretch of road. If only it wasn't facing the police station.

This thought brought her gaze to dwell on the Springfield Road barracks at the corner of Violet Street. It was heavily fortified with high metal mesh fencing and security lights but still a potential target for the bombers. She could just about make out a head watching from behind the darkened bullet-proof glass of the look-out tower. Alice continued the short distance up the road to her home with a heavy heart. She knew only too well how worried her daughter was about the way business

13

was dropping off. In 1966 when Tess and Theresa had sunk all their savings into the purchase of the shop, things had looked very promising indeed.

There was comparative peace at that time and the Springfield Road was a pleasant place to live and work, with a constant stream of people in and out of the shops. At first the troubles didn't amount to very much and the business continued to flourish. Their fame had spread, and girls came from far afield to have their wedding outfits made by Tess and Theresa. 'The Two Ts', as they had become affectionately known.

Then in '69 the troubles had intensified in Derry, and Belfast got really caught up in the riots. Civil rights marches took place. Rioting broke out in the city and gun battles raged on the Falls and Shankill Roads. Houses were petrol-bombed on both sides of the community and hundreds were made homeless. It was always the innocent who suffered most. Families with nowhere to go, doubling up with relatives in safer areas of the city or in church halls, losing their dignity and self-respect.

Barricades were built across the tops of streets and manned by the residents to keep out undesirables and protect their homes from petrol-bombers and looters. As the rioting escalated out of control the British government sent the troops in to restore law and order to the province. Peace walls were erected to keep warring factions apart.

Although not a welcome sight to some, the army did at first make a great difference and for a time things quietened down. The following year, 1970, had started off quietly enough and business had improved a little, bringing hope to all. But it was not to last. Explosion followed explosion until it was almost a daily occurrence. Everyone was living on their nerves, and in neighbourhoods with

14

mixed denominations, families who had existed in harmony for years began eyeing each other with suspicion. The more sensible people avoided the city centre. This should have helped local businesses like Tess's, but so many were thrown out of work that money was scarce and new clothes were the last thing on people's minds.

Alice jerked her mind back to the present. This year, 1971, didn't look very promising either. A few weeks back, on 20 March, the prime minister, Chichester-Clark, had resigned with the intention of calling Westminster's attention to the worsening state of affairs in the province. A few days after his resignation Brian Faulkner took over the reins and everybody waited with bated breath to see if he could make any worthwhile change. Nothing was different. Atrocity continued to follow atrocity. So what was the use of trying to sell the shop the way things stood? Better to hang on and hope for the best. Still, Alice knew how worried Tess was. Her daughter had great difficulty in coping with her disappointment at the downturn in business. Unless things picked up soon, the money they kept in reserve for emergencies would disappear, and then what would happen?

She was dismayed that Theresa was talking about pulling out of the partnership. Had she mentioned it to Tess? Alice didn't think so, as Tess hadn't said anything to her mother about it. If it should come about and Theresa wanted to bail out, would Tess have enough money of her own to buy Theresa's half of the business? And would she be able to continue running it on her own? Alice very much doubted it.

Settling Jackie in front of the TV, she went out to the kitchen to prepare his meal. Like so many children of his age Jackie was no great lover of vegetables, and to avoid a confrontation with his grandfather every evening, when he would have had the child gagging on cabbage or whatever vegetable was on the menu, Alice always made Jackie his tea before Dan got in from work. Beans or peas were his favourite veg.

Jackie was normally a happy wee fellow and Dan doted on him. So did Alice for that matter. Theresa's words came back to trouble her. Did Dan really think that Colette might one day turn up on their doorstep and demand her son back? After all, she had apparently left him behind without too many misgivings when, shortly after his birth, she had packed her bags and taken herself off to a new life in Canada. Still, things had been quiet then, and how was Colette to know that soon her son would be living in a war zone? With money left to her by her grandmother which she had invested wisely – thanks to good advice from her bank colleagues – Colette had apparently done very well for herself in Canada, and besides sending money home on a regular basis for Jackie's upkeep had set some aside in a building society account for a college education when he left school.

She had recently become engaged to a manager at the bank where she worked and intended marrying him over there in Canada some time next year. It was Tess she corresponded with, and in her last letter she had confessed how worried she was at the state of affairs in Northern Ireland, sending warning bells ringing regarding Jackie's future here.

Alice was inclined to think that if anything should happen to Dan, Colette would have the excuse, and rightly so, to claim her son and take him back to Canada, away from all the shooting and bombing and constant rioting. After all, their house was deep in the heart of the troubles. Dan had tried to persuade Alice to sell up and seek accommodation elsewhere as the army posts and RUC barracks continued to be the target of the bombers and gunmen, and living so close to the Springfield Road barracks put them in a very vulnerable position indeed. However, Alice refused to be driven from her home. In this instance she was staunchly supported by Tess.

Financially, Alice wasn't in any way dependent on Dan, except of course that he was expected to hand over money each week towards the housekeeping. The house had been paid for with her late husband's compensation, awarded when he'd had a fatal accident at work. It was also Tess's inheritance. Dan was just Alice's live-in lover. Lord, but that sounded so exciting, and at the beginning it had seemed very daring. Now they were just like any other old married couple rubbing along together. Besides . . . what was she thinking of? Nothing was going to happen to Dan.

Long after Bob Dempsey had left the shop the two girls worked in a strained silence. Theresa was fed up with trying to persuade her partner to give Bob a chance to prove his worth and waited for Tess to break the awkward lull, but in vain.

At last, unable to bear it any longer, she said plaintively, 'Why didn't you tell me your mother is getting married at Easter?'

Tess gave a slight start of surprise. 'Oh! I'd forgotten all about it,' she confessed. 'That will probably mean another suit to make.' She gave Theresa a rueful smile.

Glad now that she had broken the ice, Theresa returned the smile. 'Two! What about yourself? You'll probably be bridesmaid, won't you?'

'You know, with it being in a register office I never thought of anyone else being involved. Stupid of me, of

17

course. You're right. I'll probably be bridesmaid. But I'm sure I'll find something suitable to wear in my wardrobe. I only found out about their decision to marry last night, you know, and I haven't had time to give it any thought.'

'You have a lot on your mind at the moment.' Theresa wondered if now was the opportunity she'd been waiting for to mention leaving the business. Bob was continually on her back to give her partner notice. But before she could broach the subject, Tess agreed with her.

'I know. Everyone's in the same boat at the minute. I'm lucky to have you for a partner, Theresa. Thanks for putting up with my sulks.'

Tentatively, Theresa tried to make use of this opening. 'Sometimes I wonder if it's worth all the worry, the way things are at the moment.'

'Of course it is.'

'Do you not think we'd be better off cutting our losses and calling it a day?'

Tess was flabbergasted. 'After all the hard work we've put into building up the business? Not a chance.' She became intense. 'Surely you don't really think we should sell up?'

Put on the spot like that, Theresa found she couldn't add to Tess's worries. She did an about-turn. 'No. Well . . . at least not at the moment.'

'Thank God for that! For a moment there you had me worried. We've got to hang in, Theresa. We've too much to lose. You'll have to be more patient. Things are sure to pick up, you'll see.' But even to her own ears the assurance sounded very hollow.

Theresa nodded. She hoped Tess was right but thought her partner was living in her own little dream world. Wait till Tess heard that she was putting her house on the market. She could just picture her reaction. She would blame Bob, and the worst of it was, she would be right. Theresa wasn't at all sure she was doing the right thing, but she was afraid of losing Bob. What if he set his sights on some other girl? One younger and prettier than her. She had noticed that when they went dancing he quite often made covert eye contact with young women and she was aware of the encouragement he received in return. Now she would have to placate him regarding giving Tess notice. It wouldn't be easy. Far from it. He could be very awkward with her when he didn't get his own way.

'I've put my house on the market. What do you think of that?' The words were out of her mouth before she could stop them. Now why had she said that? Did she really want Tess's opinion?

Tess's head shot up. 'You've got to be joking.'

'No. That's where I was today. At the estate agent's. Someone will be out on Saturday afternoon to value it.'

'Don't be daft! Where will you go?'

'Bob has asked me to move in with him.'

'But you told me he lives in a bedsit over on University Avenue.'

'He does.'

'Is it big enough for two?'

Picturing the one room with a curtained-off area containing a stove and sink glorifying in the grand name of a kitchen, Theresa confessed, 'Well . . . just about.'

'And after all the improvements you've done to that big house of yours, you're going to leave it and move into a crummy wee bedsit?'

'Why not? It'll be worth it. I do love him, Tess.'

'And your furniture. What'll you do with it? Store it?'

An indifferent shrug was her answer, before Theresa ventured to say, 'I suppose I'll have to sell it.'

19

'You're mad, so you are. You have some lovely pieces. You'll only get a fraction of what you paid for them. It's Bob Dempsey who's put you up to all this, isn't it?'

'No. I've been thinking of it for some time now,' Theresa lied. 'I'm lonely in that big house on my own.'

'You never said.'

'No. What good would it have done?'

'Wouldn't it be better if Bob moved in with you? That way you would have him living with you – which is what you want – and still keep your independence.' And your lovely home, Tess added silently.

'Bob doesn't want people to get the wrong idea and think he's living off me. You know, like a kept man.'

'Why not? Isn't that what he's doing anyway? Aren't you keeping him in cigarettes and beer money? I'm sorry, Theresa, but as far as I can see, he's nothing more than a scrounger.'

Startled, Theresa cried, 'That's very unfair, Tess. Is that what people are saying about him?'

Tess spread her arms in frustration. 'How do I know? I don't listen to tittle-tattle. I can only vouch for myself and that's how it comes across to me. Loud and clear. He neither works nor wants. Please think very carefully before you give up your home, Theresa. You'll thank me in the long run, so you will. You've too much to lose. At the moment things might be a bit tight where the shop is concerned, but at least we're not on our uppers yet. Business is bound to pick up some time. Stick in there with me and we'll ride out this bad patch together. Wait and see what the future holds.'

'You sound as if you think Bob is after my money.'

'I'm sorry, but yes, I do.'

'What money? If you mean the little bit of insurance that was left after I buried my mother, that's almost gone.

20

As for the house . . . I'll probably sell that at a loss.'

'I don't understand you. If that's what you think, why are you even talking about selling it?'

'I don't know.' Theresa rummaged in her overall pocket for a handkerchief and dabbed at her eyes, warning Tess that she wasn't too happy with the way the conversation was going.

Immediately she left her machine and putting an arm across her friend's shoulders said gently, 'Come on, let's go into the wee room and I'll make us a nice pot of tea. And I'll tell you what. While the kettle's on I'll nip up to the bakery and get us a couple of fresh cream cakes. It's a long time since we had a good old talk.' They were both feeling much better already.

Sitting close together on the small sofa, the girls sipped at their tea.

'Theresa . . . I know you think I'm jealous of your relationship with Bob, but I'm not, honest.'

Quickly Theresa interrupted her. 'Look, I know you're not! I'm sorry. I should never have said that. Tony Burke was a good catch, and attractive into the bargain, yet you turned him down, so why should you resent me hitting it off with Bob?'

'Tony and I were just good friends.'

'I don't think he saw it quite like that.'

'Well, forget about Tony. That's water under the bridge.' Tess took some moments to choose her next words carefully. She didn't want Theresa to get the hump up and do something rash. 'Now, Theresa . . . I don't want you being offended at what I'm about to say, but please take your time about selling your house. Don't rush blindly into anything. If I were you I'd insist on Bob moving in with you, and if he loves you he'll do

21

it. Whereas if you do manage to sell the house, any profit will be squandered in no time at all and you know that. To be truthful, I don't think you'll have any bother selling it. So many people were burnt out of their homes and are looking for somewhere to live. Your house is situated in a good spot, and if all else fails, this new Housing Executive they've set up will buy it for displaced families.'

'Huh! They'll not give me much for it.'

'From what I've been reading, I think they have to at least give you the market value, and I remember you telling me that you got it at a bargain price, so you're bound to make a fair profit on it. That's all the more reason why you should wait a few years and get as much as you can. It's an investment for your future. And if you're really lonely or nervous living on your own, and Bob won't listen to reason, I'd be more than willing to move in with you for a while.'

'You'd do that for me? Honest?'

'Of course I would. We're best friends. You should have said before.'

'Do you want the truth, Tess?'

'Go on.'

'I'm afraid of losing Bob. He's the first lad that has ever been serious about me. I'd just die if he left me.'

'Theresa, you're not giving yourself a chance to find out if other men would be interested in you. You're an attractive woman. Remember, you've always looked after your mother. You hadn't the time or the inclination to get out and about to meet men when you were younger.'

Theresa was silently nodding in agreement with all Tess said. 'I know! I know all that, Tess,' she interrupted. 'That's why I'm so desperate. I'm forty years old, for God's sake, and I don't want to finish up an old maid.

If Bob and I get together now, I might possibly conceive. I know he wants children so I can't afford to hang about much longer. Can't you see my predicament?'

'And a bedsit is the ideal place to bring up a family?' Tess said sarcastically. 'Do you not think you'd be better off on your own? If you fall in with Bob's plans you'll be making the biggest mistake of your life. Something you'll live to regret.'

'You really do think I'm making a big mistake, don't you?'

'Yes, I do. Well, not necessarily. But you could have your cake and eat it, you know. Play the waiting game, and if Bob loves you he'll go along with whatever you say. If he doesn't . . . you're better off without him.'

'I wish I was as strong-willed and as sure of myself as you, Tess.'

'I'm not strong. I'm in the same boat as yourself, Theresa, hoping to meet a nice fellow I can depend on.'

'Why did you ever send Tony Burke away? He was daft about you. You could have been married by now and had a couple of kids.'

'Tony was all right, but he wasn't the one for me. I'm still looking for my Mr Right. Now don't try changing the subject, girl. Have you decided what you're going to do?'

'I'll wait and see what the estate agent says on Saturday and then I'll make up my mind.'

'I'm glad to hear that. And for God's sake, whatever you do don't rush into anything. Take your time. If they try and push you for a quick decision, just you tell them that you want some time to think it over. Don't commit yourself. Remember, I'm always here for you if you want to talk about it.'

Although Theresa wouldn't admit to the wisdom of

her friend's advice, Tess could see the relief etched on her face.

Dan Thompson got off the bus and trudged across the Springfield Road to the house he had shared with Alice Maguire for the past five years or more. He was in despair. He had been paid off. He had seen it coming for some time but Alice thought he was indispensable. How was he going to explain it to her? Could he now afford to marry her at Easter? Then again, could he afford not to? The way things were, Colette would be justified in coming home and demanding that Jackie return to Canada with her, away from all this trouble and strife. Dan was the boy's grandfather and had cared for him from birth, but no papers had been signed; there was nothing legally binding them except their blood line. To be fair, Colette had right from the beginning regularly sent money for her son's welfare, so she couldn't really be accused of neglect. It should help if he and Alice were married, then if anything happened to Dan she would at least be Jackie's guardian and could, if necessary, fight for custody of the boy.

At one time Dan had been very fond of Colette, had thought her an excellent match for his son. What had turned him against the girl Jack had intended to marry before his fatal motorbike accident was the knowledge that she had been so secretive, going to stay with a friend of Alice's brother Malachy in Carlingford to have the baby. Had she really thought Dan would care that his grandson was to be born out of wedlock? As if that wasn't bad enough, she had intended to have the child adopted without telling Dan anything about it. His grandson sent away to be reared by strangers? All this was planned on the sly, and to make matters worse . . .

she had been aided and abetted by Tess Maguire. Imagine that! It didn't bear thinking about. To this day he didn't know all the ins and outs of it.

If only Jack hadn't been killed, he and Colette would have married and they would have all lived happily together, or as happily as other families managed to do in spite of the troubles. He would never understand just why Tess had helped Colette during her pregnancy, but because she had managed to persuade Colette to let him rear the child, Dan had forgiven her.

Squaring his shoulders, he put his key in the lock and turned it. As was usual, Alice came into the hall to greet him. He wished he could do more for this woman he loved so dearly. Taking her in his arms he burrowed his face in her hair.

Aware that something was amiss, Alice gripped him tight. 'What is it, love?' she whispered fearfully. 'What's wrong?'

'I've been laid off, Alice.'

'What? How can they do that? You've worked for Martin's since you were a fourteen-year-old apprentice.'

'That doesn't make any difference. They've given me the boot.'

Thoughts were tripping over each other in Alice's mind. How would Dan live with it? He who had always had a job to go to; always had a pay packet to take home each week. He who was never short of a bob or two. What must he be going through now? Alice herself had given up her position as milliner in Tess's business – except for the odd tricky bridal head-dress which would take up too much of the girls' time – in order to look after Dan's young grandson, Jackie. Something she had never regretted. Pushing her worries to the back of her mind, she concentrated on consoling Dan.

'You must be devastated, love. It's so unexpected.'

He laughed ruefully. 'No it's not! I've been expecting it for some time. I'm just surprised I lasted so long.'

'You never said. I thought your job was safe.'

'I didn't want to worry you. Nothing's safe nowadays, Alice. Where's Jackie?'

'He's in the bath. Away up and see to him while I lift your dinner.'

Tess arrived home while Dan was still upstairs and Alice filled her in on the bad news.

'Poor Dan, he must feel so let down. He's worked there for such a long time, hasn't he?'

'That's what I said too. Actually it's the only firm he has worked for since leaving school.'

'It's sad that it has come to this. There seems to be no end to these miserable times.'

They set the table in silence, each buried in their own private thoughts. When Dan came downstairs with a pyjama-clad Jackie in his arms, he greeted Tess and went into the living room to see if there was anything suitable on TV for Jackie to watch. Once they were seated at the table Tess expressed her sorrow at him losing his job.

He nodded glumly and addressed Alice. 'I think we'll have to forget all about getting married at Easter, love.'

'I don't mind in the slightest, Dan. I'm happy the way things are,' Alice assured him.

Tess fixed a stern gaze on him. 'Why have you decided to postpone the wedding, Dan? You'll get redundancy money, won't you?'

'Yes, but I'll have to be careful with it. It will be all right if I get a job right away, otherwise the money will soon disappear. I won't get any dole, you know, not for a while.'

'I know what you mean, but would it not be in your

best interests to marry Mam now? I don't understand how these things work, but could Anne, for instance, being your ex-wife, claim half your redundancy and any money you have in the bank if you and Mam aren't married and something happened to you? Knowing Anne, I imagine she would certainly try to get her hands on it.'

Alice had been listening to her daughter mouth agape. 'You never cease to amaze me, Tess. Last night you couldn't understand why we wanted to get married. You seemed quite annoyed at the very idea of it. Now you're suddenly all for it.'

'Things were different last night, Mam. Dan had a job then and you were secure enough. But now that redundancy is involved I would like to see you safely married, at least in the eyes of the law if not the Church. You know what Anne Thompson's like, she'll know all the ins and outs of these things. Look how she squatted in Dan's house in Spinner Street until she eventually got the key. No one else would have had the gall to do that. And look how she keeps in touch with Dan because of Jackie.'

'Ah, but Dan didn't really want to go back there or she wouldn't have found it so easy to get the key to the house. As for keeping in touch . . . why shouldn't she? She's the child's grandmother, for goodness' sake.'

'Do you think she would bother about Jackie if his mother hadn't a bit of money behind her? Remember, Colette's grandmother left her a lot and she seems to have invested it wisely. Anne Thompson's no dozer. She'll be aware of all this. Hence the doting grannie act. Didn't she run off and leave Dan when her own son was at a vulnerable age? Do you really think she would bother her arse if there was no money involved? I don't think so. She's a right gold-digger that one.'

27

Dan had listened to all this in silence, weighing up Tess's words. Now he joined in the conversation. 'Tess is right, Alice. I never thought of that. We'll go ahead and get married as planned. I really do sincerely want to make an honest woman of you, and this way, if I kick the bucket, then all my finances will be legally yours.'

Alice smiled fondly at this big kind man who held her heart. 'I know you do, Dan, but I'll not feel any better than I do now if we marry in a register office. It's the Church's blessing I want.'

'That's not the point, Alice. We will be better off tying the knot. I'd hate for Anne to get her claws into anything that's meant for you. We'll spend some of the lump sum on a wedding and invest the rest in your name. How does that sound to you, Tess?'

'Sounds fine, Dan.' Contented that he was in agreement with her, Tess tucked into her dinner.

In the weeks that followed, Tess had nothing but the utmost admiration for Dan. Every morning saw him up early tramping round building sites looking for work. So different from Bob Dempsey. Dan also got into the habit of removing the security grilles from the shop window before setting out on his daily quest and replacing them in the late afternoon. This pleased the girls no end and their Easter display encouraged passing shoppers to stop and admire, and often come in to buy something. They also had two wedding dresses plus all the accessories on their order books for May.

Another thing that gave Tess heart was the fact that Theresa hadn't put her house on the market. She had stuck to her guns and eventually Bob had moved in with her. And why wouldn't he? Tess thought wryly. He knew when he was on to a good thing. On the whole, things were beginning to look up.

The Easter weekend passed quietly enough, at least as far as they were concerned, and Alice was married on the Tuesday of Easter week. She looked radiant in a pale blue suit and white blouse made by the girls. A small close-fitting hat, its feathers curling about her face, set the outfit off. At short notice Tess had to make do with the suit made for Uncle Malachy and Rose's wedding almost five years ago, though it was still quite fashionable. Alice had insisted that Dan buy a new suit for the occasion and he looked very handsome in dark grey serge, and Jackie was proud as Punch in a black velvet page-boy outfit complete with white ruffled blouse and satin cummerbund.

It was a quiet affair with just a few close friends invited. Tess was bridesmaid and Malachy was best man, or witnesses as they were called in register office nuptials. After the brief ceremony there was a slight hiccup when Jackie got the idea into his little head that the lucky horseshoe was a plaything for himself. Tess had a bit of trouble coaxing him to present it to his grannie and grandad, explaining that it had magic powers and would bring lots of good luck to them. He eventually succumbed and handed it over with a broad grin.

After the photograph shoot they all returned to the house, where Malachy's wife Rose had stayed behind to help Theresa and Bob prepare a buffet lunch.

Pouring them all a glass of wine, Malachy toasted the happy couple and then raised his glass to Tess. 'It will be your turn next, I hope.'

'Don't count on it, Uncle Mal. I don't think I'll ever get married. I can't imagine why, but I seem to scare men off.'

'What happened to that nice young lad we met the last time we were up here? Tony something or other. He certainly seemed keen enough on you.'

'Tony Burke. Oh, that never came to anything. As a matter of fact, Mam invited him and his girlfriend to the wedding but he was going away for the Easter break and didn't expect to be back in time.'

'He was a nice lad. I liked him.'

'We all like him,' Alice interrupted, with a wry smile at her daughter.

'Mam, it wasn't meant to be!'

'If you say so, dear.'

Embarrassed that all eyes were on her, Tess was glad to be rescued by the chimes of the doorbell.

'I'll get that,' she said before anyone else could make a move. Escaping into the hall, she threw open the front door, a wide grin on her face. The smile slipped a little when she saw Tony Burke accompanied by a pretty fair-haired girl standing on the top step.

Immediately aware of her manners, she stood aside. 'Come in. Glad you could make it after all, Tony.'

The couple passed her and paused in the hall. 'Tess, this is Geraldine Harris. Geraldine, meet Tess Maguire.'

The girl thrust out her hand and Tess gripped it. 'Pleased to meet you, Geraldine.'

'I feel I already know you, Tess, Tony talks such a lot about you.'

Tess gave the conventional answer to this. 'Not all bad, I hope. Come on in and meet the others, Geraldine.'

After introductions were over, silence reigned for some time as they all did justice to the tasty buffet.

It was Malachy who broke it. 'How are things faring at the moment, Tony?'

'Not too bad, Malachy. Has Tess told you that me

30

and a friend, Pat McVeigh, have branched out on our own? We've rented a yard and we're doing all right at the moment. I think there'll always be work for plumbers.'

'You're right there. I hope it works out for you. No word of you getting married yet?'

'Not in the foreseeable future.'

Malachy noted that Geraldine bestowed a long, questioning look on Tony but he avoided eye contact with her and she did not contradict him. In Malachy's opinion it was a pity that Tess wasn't fond enough of Tony to consider marriage. As far as he could see, the lad had all the makings of a good husband and father. But then, there was no accounting for taste.

2

Alice and Dan left for the station to catch the Dublin train. They were spending a few days there and would return early Saturday. Having lived together for some years, they were calling it a long-awaited honeymoon, albeit with an excited Jackie for company. Tess had offered to look after the child but they would not hear of leaving him behind. Malachy said he and Rose would run them to the station and they were waved off by the others in a shower of confetti. Theresa and Bob made their excuses and left shortly afterwards.

Alone with Tony and Geraldine, Tess felt uncomfortable in their company. Inwardly she derided herself. The arrival of Geraldine on the scene had made her all too aware that she still regarded Tony as her own property. Did she really want him to hang around until she was sure that she had no other option? Certainly not intentionally, but she had to admit that she had received a shock when he arrived at her front door with this attractive girl in tow. She had known that he dated other girls but he had never been known to go public like this with anyone. Had he decided that Geraldine was the one for him?

Tess examined Geraldine. Pale gold hair cut close to the skull, small elfin face and big dark blue eyes. A definite resemblance to Agnes Quinn, she noted. Was that the attraction? Becoming aware that Geraldine was looking enquiringly at her she smiled. 'I was admiring your hairstyle,' she said in explanation of her blatant scrutiny, and went out of her way to make them feel welcome.

In spite of their clashes of opinion Tony had been a very good friend to her, when her best friend Agnes Quinn – who had been engaged to Tony at the time – and Dominic, the man Tess had become attracted to and had dared to think cared for her, had announced out of the blue that they had fallen in love. Agnes had apologised for all the upset this caused but would not be swayed from her decision to go to America with Dominic, vowing that they would soon marry. It had been such a bolt out of the blue and both Tess and Tony had been devastated. They had sought solace in each other.

With hindsight Tess had soon realised that Dominic and Agnes were meant for each other. They had married the following spring and Tess had flown out to Florida at their expense to be bridesmaid. It was a day she would never forget. How she had envied Agnes her new-found happiness in the Sunshine State.

Tess had tried to pair Tony off with Colette, the mother of young Jackie, but by this time he was professing to be in love with Tess herself. She had managed eventually to make him see sense and convinced him that nothing would ever persuade her to marry him, and that was the last she had seen of him for some time.

Surprised at how much she had missed him, Tess was delighted when he once more appeared on the scene. However, by this time Tony was a changed man. No more did he cajole her to go out with him; he was still a good friend but a distant one. He assured her that he was there for her should she ever need him, and Tess convinced herself that it was better that way. After all, it was her decision that they should just be good friends; no strings attached. She couldn't expect him to hang around indefinitely in spite of what she had said. And, true to his word, he was always there when she needed him. Although her mother had invited him to the wedding and told him to bring a friend, Tess had nevertheless expected him to come alone, if he was to turn up at all. Now here he was sitting in her own home flaunting a very pretty girlfriend.

Wanting to learn more about this attractive young woman, she enquired, 'Do you live about here, Geraldine?'

It was Tony who answered. 'She lives in Beechmount Parade. Imagine that, almost the girl next door. I don't know how I didn't notice someone as pretty as her before.' He smiled and confessed, 'Of course she's some years younger than me. I suppose that's why I didn't see her around.'

Geraldine smiled back at him and their eyes clung for some moments, making Tess aware that Tony was apparently in love. 'When you first came to my attention, Tony, I was in my last year at school and I had a crush on you. However, you were engaged to another girl at the time and had eyes for no one else. As far as I was concerned, you were out of bounds. It was only recently that I heard you were a free man again.' Her eyes now met Tess's. 'That's when I set out to try and catch his eye. Did you know this girl who did the dirty on him?'

Tess looked at Tony and saw colour rise in his face. Just how much had he confided in Geraldine about his

34

engagement? she wondered. Not wanting to put her big foot in it, she took time to consider her answer. 'Well now, I don't know what exactly Tony has told you about Agnes Quinn, but she was my best friend and a thoroughly good person. A girl of great integrity; someone whom I have absolute trust in. When her sister and Dennis Sullivan decided to get married, his brother Dominic, who had emigrated to America some years earlier, was asked to be best man. He agreed and came over from Florida and swept Agnes off her feet during his short stay here. She certainly didn't set out to hurt Tony or even fall for Dominic. It just happened! Agnes is a very kind-hearted person. And she did fight the attraction she felt for Dominic. This I know for a fact. However, love will not be denied. In the long run Tony and I didn't stand a chance.'

Tony sat tight-lipped. 'In my eyes she made a complete mug of me,' he growled bitterly, showing that his pride was still hurt. 'You have to agree with me, Tess. You know she must have been playing around behind my back, and I never twigged. She gave no warning of her intentions until the very last minute. Showed no consideration whatsoever for my feelings. I felt a proper Charlie, I can tell you. I was so ashamed to show my face outside for weeks because I thought that everybody would be laughing up their sleeves at me. If it hadn't been for the kindness of you and Colette, I'd probably be living like a hermit now.'

'No you wouldn't! You're too sensible for that, Tony. But remember this, people can't help falling in love. I was besotted with Dominic, I was hurt as well. It was just one of those things you have to accept, then get on with your life. They were meant for each other. Agnes knew that once she was sure Dominic was the one for her, it would have been a disaster to marry you. Surely you realise that? Especially now you've met Geraldine.' Tess was testing the waters now. For some unknown reason she needed to know if Tony considered himself in love with this girl.

Tony shrugged. 'It took a long time. You got over Dominic quickly enough. You can't have been all that involved with him.'

'I was, very involved. But it's no use crying over spilt milk. That's my motto.'

He eyed Tess intently and said, 'That's one thing I did come to realise in time, thank God. It's certainly no good fretting over something you can't have. It took me a long time to come to terms with that, but now I've decided to put the past behind me and make a fresh start.' He turned and smiled at Geraldine. 'I think we should be making a move now, Geraldine. Your mam will be expecting us.'

Well now, that certainly answered Tess's unspoken question. He had as good as admitted that he'd got over her and Geraldine was now the one for him. Tess smiled to show she understood, but as she waved them off, a sadness settled on her heart. She sat for some time trying to figure out why she felt so confused and sad. Much as she liked Tony Burke, she didn't love him. They had never even shared a proper kiss. At least not in the passionate way a man should kiss the woman he hoped to marry. She had shared passionate moments with Dan's son Jack before he met Colette, and she had been passionately aroused by Dominic Sullivan, so why wasn't she indifferent to Tony's affection for another girl?

She was selfish, that was why! It had been handy having him around if she wanted to go somewhere in particular and needed a male escort. Good old Tony! He could always be relied on to step into the breach at short notice. Was that all about to change? Probably. Geraldine wasn't likely to let Tess have any influence over her man. The sooner she realised that she couldn't have her cake and eat it, the better.

With a resigned sigh she started to clear away the dirty dishes, wanting them washed and out of the way before Malachy and Rose returned. The couple got so little time away from the farm that Malachy was taking advantage of the break and had made some plans for the next few days. He had bought tickets for the Opera House for that night to see a show that was getting rave reviews. The shop being closed for the week, they had bought Tess a ticket, and insisted that she must enjoy her break from work and accompany them on all their outings.

On Wednesday they spent the day at the Botanic Gardens and the museum and then drove across town to Bellevue Zoo. Afterwards Malachy treated them to a meal at the Steak House. This brought back happy memories for Tess, of the time, all those years ago, when she had first accompanied Dominic Sullivan on a date. That had also been to the Steak House at Easter and after the meal they had gone on to the Orpheus ballroom. They had been having a night out with Dennis and Marie, the prospective bride and groom, and some friends. Agnes was partnered by Tony, to whom she had become engaged the previous Christmas, and Tess had been invited along to partner Dominic.

Tess remembered vividly the emerald-green dress she had made for the occasion. Unconsciously, colour rose in her cheeks as she remembered how sexy she had looked in it. Not something she would normally wear, it was very much a current trend at that time. Being short of material the skirt had been very brief indeed. It, and a plunging neckline, had left little to the imagination. She had felt quite daring in it, and if her mother hadn't been on a visit to Malachy's farm at the time, Tess would never have dared make that dress, let alone wear it. She had thought it wise to hide it away from the critical eye of her mother, who, before her affair with Dan Thompson, had been so strait-laced. Still was for that matter, as far as other people were concerned. To this very day Alice had yet to set eyes on that cute little number.

Dominic had told Tess that she looked ravishing and his eyes had said a lot more as they wandered over her body. Sure that he fancied her, she revelled in the emotions he was arousing while twirling her round the dance floor. It had been a wonderful evening as far as she was concerned. But even then, unknown to anyone else, he had already fallen in love with Agnes. He had certainly hidden his feelings well, forever picking on Agnes and even reducing her to tears on some occasions. Tess discovered later that his treatment of Agnes was because he was in despair that she wouldn't admit her feelings towards him.

And to be fair, once he realised there was a chance that Tess might fancy him, he had tried to warn her off; let her know that he cared for someone else. Desperately trying not to hurt her feelings, but not wanting to reveal his love for Agnes, he had neglected to make it crystal clear and she, fool that she was, had got her wires crossed and thought he was insinuating that he cared for her. In due course, she and Dominic had a confrontation. She had ended up actually helping to bring Agnes and him together. Sadness lengthened her face as she recalled Dominic's fine physique and handsome face and the way he could make her laugh and so easily arouse her emotions. If only things had worked out differently, she mused forlornly, how wonderful life would be now.

Malachy watched his niece intently from under lowered brows. It troubled him to see her look so sad. 'Tess . . . Tess? Come back to us, you're miles away.'

She came to with a start. 'Sorry, Uncle Mal. I was indeed miles away. I was remembering the last time I was in here. It seems so very long ago now. What were you saying?'

'I was asking what you thought of Geraldine Harris.'

'Mmm. She seems nice enough.'

'Oh . . . and you don't feel in the least bit jealous?'

Rose interrupted her husband. 'Malachy! Give over. Don't be so nosy.'

'I'm not being nosy. I just wonder what happened. Tony seems a nice bloke. It was obvious that he cared for Tess, so what went wrong?'

'Oh, he is a nice guy. One of the best in fact,' Tess quickly assured him. 'Geraldine is a very lucky girl.'

'Then why . . .' With raised brows Malachy let his query trail off, waiting in expectant silence for her answer.

Tess laughed aloud. 'I know what you're thinking, and I agree. Tony is a good catch. But, I ask you . . .' She spread her hands wide. 'Is that enough? Am I wrong to expect some excitement and a bit of humour during courtship? That's what was lacking between Agnes and Tony, and look what happened there. For heaven's sake, they were more like brother and sister than a courting couple. And that's how it is between Tony and me. No wonder Dominic swept Agnes off her feet. She was vulnerable and fell head over heels in love.'

'Is that what you're waiting for? Someone to sweep you off your feet?'

39

'Well . . . something like that.'

'And Tony doesn't excite you at all?'

'I'm afraid not. Certainly not the way Dominic did, and as it turned out, even he wasn't the right one for me. How's one to know? Tony's a wonderful friend but I can't see him in the role of husband and lover.'

Hesitantly, Rose offered her opinion. 'You know, Tess, my first marriage had exciting moments but I was very unhappy most of the time. You can have a very happy marriage without a lot of excitement, you know. For instance . . .' She threw an apologetic glance at her husband. 'Malachy and I were just friends at first, but now we have a wonderful relationship that a lot of our friends envy. We are very happy together.'

Embarrassed at these revelations Tess said seriously, 'I know you are. But you two are a different kettle of fish altogether. You're . . .' Not wanting to give offence, she was at a loss as to what to say.

'Two old fogies, is that what you're trying to say? Don't know the meaning of excitement?' Malachy teased solemnly.

Horrified that he could put into words such an exact interpretation of her thoughts, Tess opened her mouth to protest, but in time caught the twinkle in her uncle's eye. 'Of course not. I only hope that one day I'll meet someone like you. So kind and caring.'

'There's only one Malachy,' Rose said fondly. 'When they made him they threw away the mould.'

Tess beamed at her uncle. 'There you are then. That must be why I'm not having much luck meeting the right man.'

'Your day will come. When you're least expecting it someone will walk into your life and love will blossom. You mark my words.'

'Hmm. I'll not hold my breath waiting. After all, it's not everyone who is destined for marriage. For all we know I might even end up in a convent.'

Malachy raised his hands in defeat. 'I give up. Let's change the subject, eh?'

'About time too,' Rose agreed. 'I warned you to mind your own business.' She turned her attention to Tess. 'Remember, we have only one day left, so let's make plans for tomorrow. Have you any suggestions?'

They eventually agreed that should the weather be good tomorrow they would go for a run to the Glens of Antrim.

They awoke to a warm but cloudy day and tucked into an Ulster fry prepared by Malachy, who was used to being up at the crack of dawn. The weather continued to hold and they set off, stopping at each village they passed through to have a look in the souvenir shops until they were about ready to drop. Rose was obsessed with hunting for special presents for her two granddaughters.

Tess had insisted that they allow her to return their hospitality and had booked a table at the Chimney Corner Inn for seven o'clock that evening. They returned in the early afternoon and rested. Refreshed, they had a quick look around the shops in Glengormley before heading for the Chimney Corner. Both Malachy and Rose were impressed with the inn and the quality of the food. They had a delicious meal and, fully sated, decided to call it a day.

Back at the house, tired but happy, Malachy and Tess relaxed in front of the TV with a drink while Rose reluctantly retired upstairs to pack.

Tess smiled fondly at her uncle. 'Thank you, Uncle Mal, for taking me out with you. I've enjoyed myself immensely. It's done me the world of good.'

41

'It was our pleasure, Tess. You need a break now and again. Tell me, how's Theresa coping with the loss of her mother?'

'She misses her something terrible, of course, but for the first time in her life she is free to do as she pleases. You know, with her mother ailing all those years Theresa hadn't much of a life. She hardly ever got over the door except to go to work. Now she's besotted with Bob Dempsey.'

'You sound as if you don't think that a good thing. Surely she deserves some happiness?'

'Bob's ten years younger than Theresa. To tell you the truth, I'm worried in case she gets hurt. I can't see it lasting.'

'Age doesn't come into it where love is concerned, Tess. *You* have your own very definite ideas about love and what you expect in a man. But everybody has different needs. One man's meat and all that . . . Mm?'

She smiled wryly. 'I know that! Perhaps that's why I can't hold on to a man. I expect too much of him.'

'As I've said before . . . your turn will come. You're the nearest I have to a child of my own, and as I'm sure you're aware, I care very deeply for you. I long to see you happily married.' Sensing her embarrassment, with a slight smile he changed the subject. 'Alice has been telling me that Colette is questioning the logic of young Jackie staying here with her and Dan.'

Tess sighed. 'I suppose we can't really blame her, but it will break Dan's heart, and me mam's for that matter, if Colette takes that child away to Canada. I'll miss him and all. He's so much a part of our family, I can't imagine life without him.'

'It wouldn't be fair for Colette to take him away. She was glad enough to leave him behind when she took

42

herself off to Canada. She was even considering adoption at one time, if I remember correctly.'

'There were extenuating circumstances that no one knew about back then, Uncle Mal. She just had to get away and she was in no position to take a baby with her. And you have to admit that with all the bombings and killing, things have changed dramatically here in the past few years, and there's no sign of a let-up. Colette has every right to be worried about Jackie's welfare.'

'Well, remember . . . any time you're worried for his safety, Rose and I will be glad to have him. We're very fond of him as you well know, and he'll be safe enough with us in Carlingford.'

'Look, Uncle Mal, I know it's dangerous here living so close to a police station the way things are at present, especially since the army is also using it as a barracks, but I have no say whatsoever in the matter and I don't think Dan and Mam would take very kindly to your offer. They love that child so much they can barely let him out of their sight for any length of time. Besides, what about school?'

'I understand all that, Tess. I'm just suggesting a way out that could alleviate Colette's worries. Jackie would be safe with us over the border. If necessary I'm sure I could get him into the local school. Still, I can see Alice and Dan's point of view. There are lots of families living in high-risk areas of the city, and they just make the best of it and get on with their lives.'

'I know that. But Colette's argument will be that Jackie doesn't have to live in Belfast. And who can argue with that?'

'You're right, of course,' he said resignedly. 'Ah, there you are, Rose. Come and sit down, love. I've a drink poured for you.'

43

Rose sank gratefully on to the settee beside her husband and cupped the brandy glass in her hands. Raising it in Tess's direction she said, 'Thanks for everything, Tess.'

Tess raised her glass in return. 'Thank *you*, for letting me tag along. I've really enjoyed myself these last few days.'

'The pleasure's all ours, love.'

'It's a pity you can't stay over and see Mam and Dan before you go back home. Is there no chance?'

'It wouldn't be possible, Tess. I've got to get back to the farm. We've been away too long as it is. But we've had a lovely time, thanks to you. Remember we hope to see you later on in the year.'

'I can't make any promises. I do hope to get away this year, but we have to take any orders as they come. There's no picking and choosing now. It's practically impossible to plan ahead.'

'You're welcome any time, Tess. Any chance you get. No need for advance warning, remember that. Just pack your bags and come down. You might even have a young man by then.'

Tess laughed. 'He never gives up, sure he doesn't, Rose.'

'He's a hopeless case. But do try and visit us in the summer, Tess. And feel free to bring a friend. Not necessarily of the opposite sex.'

'I will. And thanks again for all your kindness.'

Carefully draping the white satin and pearl wedding gown on to the hanger, Tess hung it on a rail beside a pale pink brocade bridesmaid dress and stepped back to admire the effect. A few more stitches and the white flower-girl dress was ready to join them. Theresa carried it over and hung it beside the others. This was the second of the May wedding ensembles completed and they were happy with another job well done.

Theresa joined Tess in her admiration. 'They're beautiful, aren't they?'

'Just perfect. Or as near perfect as we can make them,' Tess agreed.

'Jean Peters will look fantastic in that dress. She'll make a lovely bride. She has the figure for it. I can just picture her walking down the aisle like someone in a Hollywood movie.'

'She certainly has the figure, and she's so attractive as well. This will be great publicity for us.' Tess's answer was heartfelt. Sometimes girls chose patterns that were all wrong for their figures and would not be persuaded otherwise. However, this should be a stunning wedding. Tess and Theresa would certainly be at the church to see the result of their labours.

It was Tuesday but custom was slack, and the girls had spent all their time putting the finishing touches to the dresses. They had taken longer than expected and were looking forward to their evening meal. Between them they carefully covered the dresses with a dustsheet.

Tess glanced at her watch. It was after five o'clock. 'If you don't mind, I'll head on home now, Theresa, and see how Mam's getting on with the head-dress. It's a really complicated one but the result should be spectacular. She told me she will need some more of those pearls.' Tess nodded towards a box of beads. 'If I bring them up now she'll probably finish the tiara tonight. It should be beautiful, Mam has such a delicate touch for detail.'

'You do that, Tess. I'll just hem this dress and then I'll be off myself. What about the shutters?'

'Dan had an interview for a job this afternoon. He said he would come down after tea and put them up.'

'Away you go then. See you tomorrow.'

Tess dandered slowly up the road. The shops all stayed open late in the summertime and she paused to look in the windows, stopping to buy some fruit at the green-grocer. She was delighted to find that the home bakery had some scones left and bought half a dozen for supper before continuing on, at peace with the world. Business was looking up again. Easter had proven to be a prof-itable time for them, and so had May. June would bring plenty of trade in the form of First Holy Communion outfits. They also had another young girl coming at the weekend to choose the material and patterns for her wedding and bridesmaid dresses for early July. All in all they had a lot to be grateful for.

A set of wine glasses caught her eye as she passed the hardware shop. After examining them in the window she decided they were worth further scrutiny and turned into the doorway. They were running short of glasses at home.

It took just a few minutes for Theresa to finish the dress. She folded it carefully and put it away in a drawer. A knock at the door brought her through into the shop, a frown creasing her brow. Had Tess forgotten something? Her eye lit on the box of beads on the counter. She certainly had. Cautiously opening the door, which she kept on the safety chain whenever she was alone in the shop after closing time, Theresa was surprised to see Bob standing in the hallway.

'What brings you here?' She greeted him with a smile as she released the safety chain. 'I thought you were going to see your mother.'

'I am, but I wanted you to be the first to hear the good news. I've got a job. At my own trade too. Isn't that great?'

'Oh, that's wonderful, Bob.' Her arms reached for him and hugged him close. She knew just how much this meant to him and there was a hint of a tear in her eyes. 'Just wonderful. Tell me all about it. Who will you be working for?'

'My mam will be waiting for me. So let's go out tonight and celebrate and I'll tell you all about it then. Okay?'

'I'm all for that. Where will we go?' Her eye once again fell on the box of beads and she said impulsively, 'Look, Bob, will you do me a favour?'

'Sure.'

'Tess is not long gone, and knowing her, she'll be in and out of the shops up the road. Will you catch up with her and give her this box? Mrs Maguire will need it tonight. If you can't find Tess, will you go on up and hand it into the house?'

'I'm on my way.'

Bob strode quickly up the road. He would be delighted to tell Tess Maguire that he had got a job; wipe that derisory smirk off her face every time work was mentioned. He was aware that Tess regarded him as a layabout and thought he wasn't trying very hard to get work. Why could she not take him at face value? Lord knows he had always tried to be pleasant enough to her, and up until a year ago he had worked as hard as any other man lucky enough to be employed.

He had served his apprenticeship as a joiner and once he was fully trained he had worked on building sites all over the province, doing the woodwork on houses. He was a first-class joiner, even if he did say so himself. But he had a big mouth and a short temper. On one site the foreman had shown favouritism in the allocation of jobs and he couldn't hold his tongue. It had resulted in him walking off the site. He had been on the dole ever since.

He saw Tess come out of the bakery. Saw her pause and look into another shop window. A flurry of activity across the road outside the RUC station caught his attention. For some seconds Bob stood and stared. Soldiers were urgently ushering people off the premises. Bob had a premonition of trouble and the hair stood on the back of his neck. There was something drastically wrong over there. He could sense it. The tension was so electric he could almost touch it. Quickening his step he was abreast of the shop, and as Tess turned into the doorway he was right behind her. A deafening explosion erupted and the front of the barracks was blown out. People were lifted off their feet by the blast and chunks of masonry and a car were thrown across the road. A cloud of choking black dust filled the air.

Bob was thrown against Tess. Covering her head with his arms he pressed her body against the door and protected it with his own, burying his face in her hair to save her from flying debris as windows crashed in and shards of glass flew dangerously everywhere.

Pressed against the door of the shop, Tess thought she was going to suffocate. She felt the ground beneath her feet heave and then the door was blown off its hinges. Lying winded on top of the door in a daze, she panicked when she was unable to move the weight that kept her pinned down. A scream rose in her throat but she choked it back. She had difficulty breathing with all the thick dust and the weight on top of her. Obviously a bomb had gone off. Was she buried alive? To her relief the weight shifted and she found herself gazing into Bob Dempsey's eyes.

Bob rolled to one side and, propping himself up on an elbow, looked down at her. 'It's all right, Tess. It's all right. You're safe.'

Fear-filled green eyes searched his before taking in the area about her. Voice shrill, she gasped, 'It's a bomb, isn't it?' He nodded. 'How did you get here?' she asked in bewilderment.

His eyes scanned her face intently as if seeing her for the very first time. Confused at the effect that being crushed against her body – even in these dire circumstances – was having on him, his voice was unsteady, 'They've bombed the police station.'

'Oh my God. I knew it! I just knew it. It was waiting to happen. I just *knew* this was bound to happen sooner or later,' she gabbled, then slumped in despair. Bob gathered her close to comfort her, marvelling at the feel of her in his arms. What was he thinking of? This was Tess Maguire. The girl who never had a good word to say about him. Who always picked on him at every opportunity.

Soldiers loomed in the rubble-laden hole that only a couple of minutes ago had been a doorway. They picked their way cautiously through the debris and thick dust, calling out, 'Is anyone in there?'

'Over here, mate.'

Bob gently helped Tess to her feet. She was shaking like a leaf and he kept a supportive arm round her waist.

A young soldier peered into her face. 'Are you all right, miss?'

Bob answered for her. 'We're fine, but I heard someone cry out in there.' He nodded towards the back of the shop. 'They might be injured.'

The soldiers went further into the shop and Tess turned to Bob. 'Bob . . . the shop. Theresa's still down there. Will you see if she's all right? I'll go on up to our house and see how they are.'

Loath to leave her alone, he eyed her anxiously. 'You

don't look too good to me.' Inwardly he disagreed. She had never looked better in his eyes. 'Are you all right? Are you sure it's safe to leave you on your own?'

Surprised at his concern, she smiled, a wobbly smile. 'I think so.' Gingerly moving her arms and legs, she said, 'See? Just a few small cuts and bruises. Nothing serious I hope. At least I've no broken bones.' Their eyes locked and at the expression in his she looked away in confusion. 'What about you? You seem to have taken the full impact of the blast.'

Her glance caught sight of his bloodied hands and she gasped. 'You're injured.' The backs of his hands were slashed as if with a razor, small slivers of glass glistening in some of the cuts. Turning them over she was dismayed to see the palms also had angry-looking gashes. She gently touched them with her fingertips then reached up to touch another gash down his cheek. 'These look bad. They need seeing to. You'll have to go over to the Royal, so you will.'

Embarrassed at her show of concern, he shrugged. 'They're only superficial cuts. They look worse than they really are. Look . . .' He flexed his fist and blood flowed freely. 'See . . . nothing broken. I'll be all right once the splinters are removed. You know what they say, it's hard to get rid of a bad thing. Theresa sent me after you to give you this box.' He glanced at his hands and motioned towards his jacket. 'Can you get it out of my pocket?'

Delving into his pocket she pulled out the box of beads, and found herself saying stupidly, 'Oh, I forgot these.' As if he didn't already know. She must be more shocked than he'd imagined, the way she was getting on.

The ceiling above them gave a resounding creak and lumps of plaster rained down on to their heads. Taking hold of her arm, he said, 'What am I thinking of, keeping

50

you here? Let's get you outside before the building crashes in round our ears.'

The devastation that faced them was horrendous and Tess was unable to stop the whimpers that came uncontrollably from her throat, pressing her hand tightly over her lips to try and suppress them. The front of the barracks had been blown out and was now a huge gaping hole. People were lying about the road awaiting medical attention, some obviously in a bad way. Others like herself – the walking wounded – were shocked and trembling with fright. There was dust and rubble everywhere. A soldier passed by cradling a small boy in his arms. The child seemed to be badly hurt. She recognised Father Lowry from St Paul's tending to the injured.

Army lorries and a bulldozer were quickly on the scene and were soon clearing the debris along the Springfield Road. The immediate area was cordoned off, and while some police took names and statements, others organised a sweep of the district in an attempt to find the bomber. Father Lowry, police and soldiers were trying to comfort the more seriously injured as they waited for the arrival of the ambulances. Men and women were wandering about in a daze, crying out names, looking for companions or loved ones.

Tess shivered and immediately Bob put an arm round her shoulders. 'I can't leave you like this, Tess. You're in shock. I'll take you up to your house and then come back and see about Theresa and the shop. I don't think there'll be much damage down there.' He caught sight of Dan Thompson pushing his way towards them. 'Ah, help is at hand, here's Dan.'

Dan's arms embraced Tess. 'Thank God you're all right. What's your shop like?'

Bob answered him. 'We don't know. I'll go down now

51

and find out. I didn't want to leave Tess. You take her on up to the house, she's a bit shaky on her feet, and I'll find out how Theresa and the shop fared.'

'No!' Tess cried. 'I'm all right now. I want to see how Theresa is. You two see if you can be of any use here.'

'If you're sure . . .'

'I'm sure. And Dan . . . see he gets those hands seen to.'

Dan looked at Bob's bloodied hands. 'Don't worry, I'll make sure he's looked after. Will you give your mother a ring, Tess? She'll be worried stiff about you.'

'I'll do that.'

Still Tess dithered and Bob gave her a gentle nudge in the direction of the shop. 'Perhaps I could be of more use here, I've done a first-aid course,' she whimpered.

'Tess . . . you're in shock, love. You'd be no use to anybody the state you're in. Get away down to the shop and see how things are there.'

Without another word, Tess, confused and miserable, picked her way gingerly through the rubble and headed down the road. For a few seconds Bob gazed after her, amazed at himself. He had just called Tess Maguire *love*. He must be suffering from brain damage. With a shake of the head he turned his attention to an elderly lady sitting on the pavement, her back to a wall, moaning and holding her head in her hands.

Theresa was hovering about on the pavement in front of the shop to deter any would-be looters. The window was like a giant spider web, shattered but still held together by some unseen agent. When she saw Tess she ran to meet her and gripped her close. Tears running down her face she gasped, 'Thank God you're safe. I was afraid to go up in case some eejit finished off the damage to our window and destroyed the stock.'

Theresa pulled her partner the rest of the way until she was in front of the window. 'Just look at that mess.'

'I'm glad you stayed put.' Tess surveyed the window listlessly. 'It's not all that bad, Theresa. You should see the state of the shops up there. And a lot of people are injured. Some might even be dead for all I know. It seems so selfish to be worrying over a stupid old pane of glass.'

Always the practical one, Theresa said, 'That may well be, Tess. But life must go on and we have to look after our own interests. What will we do? Can we afford to replace this window?'

'We'll just have to. When I see a shop window boarded up I think it looks like the beginning of the end for the owners. We'll have to get the glazier out and get this lot sorted.'

'What about the insurance premiums? They'll jump sky high.'

Tess glanced upward and was relieved to see that the upper windows were intact. 'It's only *one* pane of glass, for heaven's sake. We'll pay for it out of our own pocket and not bother with the insurance company, otherwise we could wait for weeks before they even think about sending someone out to assess the damage.'

The ambulances had arrived and TV crews were setting up cameras. The police and army had cordoned off the area down to the Falls Road and pedestrians and traffic were diverted away from the scene. Crowds of people had by now gathered and stood huddled in small groups watching the rescuers. They stood gaping in horrified silence, unable to believe their eyes. The girls understood just how they felt. The bombing had intensified and hardly a day passed now without an explosion going off somewhere in the city, but the full impact of the devastation was only brought home when one was caught up in the midst of it.

Theresa eyed some youths standing near the shop. They were probably innocent onlookers, but remembering how looting always seemed to follow a bombing, she decided to take no chances. 'I'll bring out a chair and you can sit in the hallway and keep an eye on that lot, while I make you a nice cup of sweet tea. They say it's good for shock.'

'Who says that?' Tess asked gravely.

'I'm not sure, I think it was Biddy Smith.' Theresa smiled. 'Anyway, it's the done thing in times of emergency. You take my word for it.'

'Oh well then. Away in and make it. But . . . Theresa, don't put any sugar in mine.'

'But then it won't be sweet, so what's the point?'

'I know, but I can't stand sweet tea.'

Theresa gave in gracefully. 'All right. No sugar. No point in giving it to you if you won't drink it.'

They realised the stupidity of the conversation and shared a silly smile before Theresa went indoors to put the kettle on.

Dan and Bob arrived as they sat outside drinking their tea.

'Was anybody killed? What about that wee child I saw?' Tess asked fearfully.

'Not that we know of, but there's still some unaccounted for. One poor army sergeant's in a bad way. According to the rumours flying about he was shielding some children when the bomb went off and took the full brunt of the blast.'

These words brought Tess's attention to Bob. She turned to Theresa. 'This man of yours is a true hero. He saved my life, so he did.'

54

Embarrassed colour flooded Bob's face. 'Don't be at it. I don't think you would have been badly hurt, even if I hadn't been there,' he protested.

'You didn't know that, so stop being so modest,' Tess insisted gently. 'Thank you very much.'

Theresa went to Bob and kissed him full on the lips, then looked at Tess. 'I told you he wasn't all that bad.'

'I didn't say he was.'

'Oh no?'

'Not really,' Tess insisted as she remembered past conversations with Theresa. 'I never used the word *bad* . . . did I?'

Help came from unexpected quarters as Bob snapped, 'Will you two stop yacking as if I weren't here. I only did what anyone would have done in the circumstances, so give over.'

Dan butted in. 'Leave the poor lad alone, for heaven's sake. Can't you see he's mortified the way you two are getting on? I got a wee nurse to clean his wounds and bandage them. She says he doesn't need any stitches.'

Bob held up his hands for them to see.

Theresa's gaze became intense. 'Will you still be able to start work on Monday?' Her look swung to include the others and she said proudly, 'Bob's got a job.'

A bit annoyed that he hadn't managed to take Tess unawares with his news, Bob eyed her closely. He could see she was somewhat taken aback. So it looked as if she really did think him a layabout. Ah well, what the hell, you can't win them all. 'I imagine I'll be all right, Theresa. If not, given the circumstances I think they'll allow me some time to recuperate.'

'I sincerely hope so. And thanks again, Bob.' Tess was persistent with her thanks.

Unable to bear all this gratitude, Bob wagged a

bandaged hand in her direction. 'Ah, give my head peace, Tess.'

He disappeared into the shop, and with a wink at Dan and Tess, Theresa followed him. 'I'll give him a wee bit of comfort.'

'Did you phone your mother, Tess?'

'I couldn't get through, Dan. I suppose everyone is trying at the same time, or that bloody bomb has damaged the lines.'

'I'll get these grilles up, and then we'll go on home. Your mother will be beside herself with worry.' He lifted the steel grille from along the wall and carried it outside. Pausing beside Tess he said with a slight smile, 'By the way, Tess, I got a job too.'

'Oh, that's great, Dan. Congratulations! I never did ask you where the interview was.'

'Actually it wasn't the job I went after. I'll not know about that one until next week, but I'm not very hopeful. I called into the Clock Bar on the way home and the owner and I got talking and he offered me a job as bar-and cellar-man.'

Tess's mouth dropped open. 'What did Mam say about that?'

'She doesn't know yet. I was just over the doorstep when the bomb went off and I came straight down to see if I could be of any help.'

'I don't envy you having to tell her.'

'It's a job, Tess. And until something better turns up, I'm taking it. No matter what your mother says.'

He lifted the grille up against the window frame and started to lock it into position. Tess sat in a daze. Her mother would indeed have something to say about that. Dan Thompson working in his ex-wife's local? Which Anne definitely frequented. Hadn't Tess first met her there? Tess couldn't see Alice allowing that to happen. Not if she had any say in the matter.

The smell of soot stung their nostrils as Dan and Tess entered the house. It hung in the air and a fine black film covered everything. Alice was making a valiant attempt to clear up the mess caused by the bomb blast.

'The damned stuff's everywhere,' she moaned, 'and two of the front upstairs windows are cracked.'

Jackie came running into the hall, his teeth a white gash in his black face. Dan swooped him up in his arms. 'I bet you're enjoying this, you wee rascal.'

'I'm helping Grannie to clean up,' Jackie said proudly.

This brought a smile to Alice's wan face. 'You can guess how helpful that is,' she retorted.

'We'll give you a hand.' Dan removed his jacket and hung it in a cupboard away from the soot.

Tess headed for the stairs. 'I'll get into some old clothes. I'll be back in a minute.'

After an hour or so of hard graft things were comparatively clean again. Tess put the kettle on and got the cups and plates out while Alice made some sandwiches, then they all settled in front of the TV and avidly watched the news. It was even worse than Tess had first imagined. They were appalled at the youths who jeered when the young sergeant who had risked his life to save some children was stretchered to an ambulance. It was hard to believe that people could behave like that towards their fellow man. What a sad world they lived in.

Alice wiped the tears from her eyes. 'God forgive them. How can anyone sink so low?'

'How would they have felt if it had been one of their own? A brother or friend? They're brainwashed with all the propaganda that's flying about at the moment. That's what it is.' Tess sniffed and furtively dabbed at her own eyes.

Alice rose to her feet. 'I'm going up to Clonard to light some candles for those who were injured.'

'I'll come with you, Mam.'

As the women put on their coats, Dan gave Tess a beseeching look. Tess knew what he was asking of her. During the clean-up operation her mother had indeed put her foot down right away at Dan's proposal to work in the Clock Bar. When Dan insisted that he must take whatever job he could lay his hands on, Alice had left the room and hadn't spoken to him since. Tess didn't think she would be able to change her mother's mind, but she gave a slight nod in Dan's direction to let him know that she would do her best.

Clonard Monastery was almost full. Word had quickly spread that the Redemptorist fathers would be leading prayers for the injured. The rosary was just starting as they sidled into a pew near the back and sank to their knees to join in the prayers. Afterwards they lit some candles and sat in silent prayer for some time.

An hour later they were on their way home. 'Mam, why are you so against Dan taking that job in the Clock Bar?'

Alice snorted. 'Surely you know the answer to that as well as I do.'

'Because it's Anne Thompson's local? Have a titter of wit, Mam. You know he can't stand the sight of that woman.'

'She's still a very attractive woman. And we both know she'd jump at the chance to have him back.'

'If he wasn't interested in her before, he'll be even less interested now that he's married to you. And he'd be happier and safer working on the Falls Road than travelling every day. You should be glad for him, Mam. He says the money's not near as good, but he's not a young man any more—'

Alice interrupted her. 'The money's not all that important. We don't need very much to get by on.'

Bewildered, Tess said, 'Then why? Eh? Why object to him working there? After all, it's only a stopgap while he looks around for something better.'

Alice shrugged. 'Oh, I don't know. I suppose I'd be worried every time he comes home late.'

'Mam, I don't think Dan would ever do anything stupid enough to give you reason to doubt his love for you.'

Alice turned a confused look on her daughter. 'Do you really think so?'

'I know so. You needn't worry about Anne. That marriage was over a long time before you met him. I know.'

Alice was quiet and withdrawn the rest of the journey home and Tess knew she had given her mother food for thought.

Next morning they heard on the radio that the army sergeant who had gallantly saved the children from the explosion had died. Such a waste of a young life. He left behind a wife and two young children of his own. It was estimated that almost thirty people had been injured, and it was just by sheer luck that more hadn't been killed.

Theresa phoned the glazier first thing that morning but was told it would be a week at least before the glass could be replaced.

'We'll have to keep the shutters up meantime,' Tess said as they cleared the window display. 'Thank God we got that wedding dress finished. I don't feel like doing any stitching at the moment. My nerves are shot to ribbons the way things are going. By the way, what kind of job did Bob get? If it's glazing, he's landed on his feet,' she joked.

'On a building site. You know, fitting the window frames and stairs and rafters on houses and things like that.'

'You never said he was a joiner.'

'You were never interested one way or the other what he was. There's one snag, however. It's over the border. Too far to travel every day, so he'll be away during the week. I'll only see him at weekends.'

'You'll miss him, so you will.'

'You can say that again. Look, Tess, I've a cheek asking, but I was wondering if you'd mind sleeping in my house during the week? If it's not convenient just say so. I'll understand.'

'If that's what you want. No problem.'

'Thanks. I don't fancy being on my own in that house now I've got used to having company.'

The horror and misery continued as one explosion followed another. Families on both sides of the community were burnt out of their homes. Some were forced to seek refuge down south.

Dan started work in the Clock Bar and Bob went to work on a building site in Sligo. As Tess had predicted, Communion outfits for the month of June kept the wolf from the door, and people still wanted to tie the knot in spite of the troubles. During the week Tess slept at Theresa's house and she spent the weekends at home.

Theresa missed Bob and never stopped talking about him. Thus Tess learned a lot about him and it became evident that she had badly misjudged him. According to her friend he was kind and considerate and caring. But

60

. . . wasn't it said that love was blind? However, after his care and attention during her bombing ordeal Tess was willing to give him the benefit of the doubt.

She allowed herself to be coaxed into accompanying the pair of them out a few times to dances at Romano's and to an old haunt of hers, the Club Orchid. Unfortunately Tony was no longer available to partner her, and feeling a bit of a gooseberry most times she politely declined their offer.

One night when they were in the Club Orchid there was a bomb scare and everyone was ordered to vacate the building as quickly as possible. There was a rush for the exit and Bob ushered them down the stairs and out on to King Street to join the crowds pouring from the Glenshesk pub below the ballroom. They were directed along Castle Street towards Castle Junction with the rest of the crowd until the police decided they were a safe distance away should the suspect object explode before the army bomb disposal unit arrived.

The girls had not been allowed to collect their coats and now they sheltered in the hallway of the London Mantle Warehouse away from the cold night air. A friend of Theresa's from the Belart factory was there and struck up a conversation with her. Not wanting to appear inquisitive, Tess moved slowly along the long hallway looking at the fashions displayed in the windows.

Bob followed her, and as they neared the door at the entrance to the shop itself, he said softly, 'What does this remind you of?' Tess turned to face him, a perplexed frown on her brow, and he continued quietly, 'Not so long ago, Tess, we were crushed up against a door like this one. Remember?'

Her face cleared and she smiled slightly. 'I'll never forget it. I was terrified.'

'Neither will I forget it, Tess. For a lot of reasons I'll not forget it.' Bob was having difficulty coming to terms with the feelings Tess had aroused in him at the scene of the explosion. Even at this moment he wanted to hold her; touch her. Was it all one-sided? He couldn't live in limbo, not knowing. Had she felt anything at all for him? He just had to find out.

The look in his eyes caused Tess to blush. What on earth was he getting at? He was embarrassing her.

'Tess . . . listen.' Her eyes glanced over his shoulder and she relaxed. Sensing that Theresa was behind him he turned with a resigned sigh as she joined them. 'I was just saying to Tess that this reminds me of the bombing of Springfield Road Barracks.'

Before Theresa could answer him raised voices called out telling everyone it was a false alarm and they could return to the building.

The crowd started to troop back up Castle Street. 'What were you saying, Bob?'

'It wasn't important, Theresa.' They were climbing the stairs to the dance hall, and he added, 'Do you girls want to stay for the last few dances or collect your coats and go on home now?'

'I want to have another word with that girl from the Belart. She's just gone up to the cloakroom so you two have a dance. Give me your ticket, Tess, and I'll fetch the coats while I'm up there.'

Theresa continued on up the second flight of stairs and Bob led the way into the ballroom. Bowing slightly he said, 'Shall we?'

Diffidently, Tess preceded him on to the dance floor. She had danced with him quite often but there was something different about him tonight and it disturbed her. She remembered the tension in the hallway of the London

Mantle Warehouse and part of her wanted to cry off. Deciding she was being silly, she entered his arms.

Bob drew her close; closer than he usually dared. Tess drew back and looked at him in amazement. That look was back in his eyes. She couldn't put a name to it, but was aware of an answering warmth within her. Her breath caught in her throat and, flustered, she mumbled, 'I need to powder my nose, Bob.' Pushing free of his arms she quickly left the dance floor and climbed the stairs to the cloakroom.

Bob stared after her, a pleased smile on his face. She did sense that there was some kind of attraction between them. But would she ever admit it?

3

Dan settled happily into his new job at the Clock Bar. He knew most of the patrons and joined in the good-natured banter, and not having to travel outside his own environment was a bonus. All in all he was contented with his lot. However, Alice wasn't so happy about the state of affairs. She fretted that he was out most evenings, but he insisted that until something better turned up he would continue working there.

They fell into an uneasy routine and everything went smoothly enough until the night Anne made a right fool of herself in the pub. Surprised and pleased at being able to see him most nights if she had a mind to, she got into the habit of flirting with Dan. He managed to keep her at arm's length by treating it as a bit of fun, and teasingly accused her of cradle-snatching as her escorts were always men who appeared young enough to be her sons.

This particular night, however, she had drunk more than her usual quota and Dan quietly advised her companion to take her home before she made a spectacle of herself. Low though his voice was, Anne heard and immediately got on her high horse.

'Are you insinuating that I'm drunk, Dan Thompson? I'll tell you something . . . I could drink you under the table any day of the week.'

'Ha ha! You don't have to tell me that. I don't for one minute doubt it. If I remember correctly, you always could hold your liquor. There were times when I even thought you must have hollow legs.'

Her expression softened and she looked appealingly at him. 'So you do remember the good old times, then?'

He grimaced. 'You being drunk? How could I ever forget? Though I wouldn't go so far as to call them the good old times.' She swayed on the edge of the seat and he turned to her companion again. 'If I were you, son, I'd take her home now, before she passes out.'

Having said his piece, Dan was leaving the serving hatch that divided the small lounge from the bar when Anne's voice stopped him. 'I'll go home right now, Dan, if you'll walk down with me.'

'Sorry, I can't. Remember, I don't own the pub, I only work here. I can't just take off when I feel like it.'

She became maudlin and weepy. 'Please, Dan.'

Her young friend gave a resigned snort and lifting his coat said, 'Right! That's it. I've had enough. She's all yours, mate. I'm outta here.'

'Hi! Hold on a minute. I bet she's been forking out for your drinks all night. At least have the decency to see her home.'

Angry colour flooded the lad's face and he became belligerent. 'Actually, no! You're wrong. I've paid my share and I've better things to do than pander to a drunk who's making passes at her old man.'

'Why you little twerp . . .'

'So long, mate. She can be quite entertaining when she's sober. But then, being her ex, I suppose you already know that. Give her a couple of cups of strong coffee and maybe she'll sober up. You'll be all right then. Know what I mean?' He gave Dan a sly wink and headed for the door. Dan's hands curled into fists and he wished there wasn't a wall between them. Then he could have smashed one of them into the cheeky bastard's face.

Glad that the lounge had emptied by this time and no one else was aware of the spectacle that had been going on, Dan eyed his ex-wife warily. She was still swaying unsteadily, and looked on the verge of passing out. It was near time for knocking off, and sure that his boss wouldn't object to him getting a drunk woman off the premises, he went to have a word in his ear.

Having got permission to leave early, Dan shrugged into his jacket and with a good night to his boss, and the lingering bar regulars, left the pub and went round the corner to the entrance to the lounge. To his dismay Anne was slumped over a table. With great difficulty he managed to struggle her into her coat and with an arm around her waist hauled her upright and supported her out into the damp night.

The cold air appeared to revive her somewhat and lifting her head she looked around her in confusion. 'What's happening, Dan?' Surprise entered her voice. 'Are you seeing me home?'

'I had no choice in the matter. Your toyboy took himself off.'

To his amazement she actually chuckled. 'Why, the young rascal. Wait till I get my hands on him. Still, his loss is your gain. Eh?' she added slyly.

It was beginning to dawn on him that Anne had been putting on a bit of an act. She was drunk all right but not as bad as she was pretending to be. He released his hold on her. 'I think you're sober enough to see yourself home now, Anne, so I'll be on my way. Good night.'

Immediately her hand gripped his arm. 'You're wrong, Dan. I couldn't make it on my own.' When he hesitated her fingers dug harder into his flesh. 'For goodness' sake, it will only take a few minutes.'

With a resigned shrug he started to walk down the street. She clung to his arm like a limpet, pressing her body suggestively against his. He ignored her actions and quickened his pace, surprised to find that he was becoming aware of the softness of her breast against his arm, the pressure of her thigh against his. Wanting to be away from her he lengthened his stride until they were practically racing down the street.

This brought cries of dismay from Anne. 'Hey, hold on. You're running me off my feet.'

He ignored her, and soon they were standing outside her door. Inwardly relieved, he prised her fingers from his arm.

'Good night, Anne. Sweet dreams.'

'They'd be a lot sweeter if you'd join me,' she said wistfully.

'No thanks. I've been down that road before, remember.'

'At least come in for a cup of tea, Dan. What harm will that do?' she wheedled, adding coyly, 'I promise I won't try to seduce you.'

'No thanks. Alice will be wondering what's keeping me.'

'I must say, I have to hand it to Alice. She certainly has you under her thumb, something I was never able to do.'

'Alice is an entirely different species altogether. Something you wouldn't understand.'

'A real lady, eh? You must have changed. If my memory

serves me correctly you used to like a bit of rough. Anywhere, any time.'

'That's all in the past, when I was young and a bit headstrong. I didn't know any better. Since I met Alice I couldn't be happier.'

'I wish I could have made you happy, Dan.' Her voice was sad. 'As a matter of fact, I thought you were quite contented with our marriage.'

'We were far too young for a start!' He leaned towards her. 'We hadn't even discussed marriage. We weren't ready to settle down, Anne, and you know it.'

'Then you should have been more careful, shouldn't you?'

'I thought I was being careful. I got the shock of my life when you told me you were pregnant.' He sighed, his mind recalling that night. 'Look, it's no good raking over dead ashes, I'm away home.'

'This used to be your home, remember?' She moved closer. 'It could be again.'

A frown furrowed his brow. 'You haven't heard then?'

'Heard what?'

'Alice and I got married at Easter.'

The muscles of Anne's face slackened and she gaped at him. 'How come I didn't hear about it?'

'It was a quiet affair. We've been living together so long we didn't exactly advertise it. Still, I'm surprised you didn't hear. You don't seem to miss much, especially where I'm concerned.' She seemed dumbstruck, and he took the opportunity to bid her good night again and started off back up the street.

On the way home Dan pondered on his reaction to Anne's closeness. He had better steer clear of her in future, that was for sure. She could be a real turn-on when it suited her. And she was right. In those early days he had always been ready, willing and able, any time, any place. She had been a sexy wee minx in her younger days. One of the many things that had gone wrong in their marriage was that she had lost interest, and he had got bored. Had it just been sex that had held them together all those years? Sex and their son Jack. If she hadn't become pregnant he would never have married her. He knew that now.

He debated whether or not to tell Alice about seeing Anne home. His mind twisted this way and that and in the end he decided it would be more diplomatic not to say a word. After all, none of Alice's friends frequented the Clock Bar, so she was unlikely to hear anything about it, and there was nothing underhand going on. His conscience was clear, so why disturb his wife's peace of mind?

He was soon to regret his decision. The following afternoon, after checking that the cellar had all the necessary stock and that the pumps were flushed out and working, he went home for his dinner break before returning for the evening shift.

Alice didn't meet him in the hall as usual, and he assumed she had something heating on the stove that she couldn't leave. He shouted a greeting to her and joined Jackie in the living room.

'How did you do at school today, son?'

Without taking his eyes off the TV screen his grandson muttered, 'Fine!'

With a sigh Dan opened the *Daily Mirror* and was soon lost in current affairs. Youngsters nowadays were spoilt; you couldn't prise them away from the telly for love or money.

'Your dinner's on the table.'

Alice's voice brought Dan back from the troubles of the world. 'Oh . . . thanks.' Setting the newspaper to one side he entered the dining room and stopped dead in his tracks. The table was bare.

'I've set the small table in the kitchen for you. I had mine with Jackie earlier,' Alice said drily.

Suddenly becoming aware of the frosty atmosphere, Dan eyed his wife closely. 'Is anything wrong, Alice?'

'You tell me!'

The episode with Anne immediately leapt to mind, but he pushed it aside. Who on earth would want to make trouble by telling Alice about that? Then he knew. Of course! It had to be Anne herself, the scheming bitch. He had played right into her hands. She must be behind this. But how?

'I've no idea what you're on about.'

'Really? Well let me refresh your memory. I had a phone call earlier on, from your ex-wife no less.'

He felt the colour drain from his face and dread entered his heart. Had Anne embroidered what had really happened? Most likely. Dear Lord, he could do without this hassle. Apprehensive now, he went into the kitchen and sat down at the table. 'What did she have to say?' he asked and lifted his knife and fork.

'Actually, it was you she asked for. Was disappointed to have missed you. She was under the impression you didn't work in the afternoons. I got the notion she was annoyed that you hadn't told her.'

'Why should I? It's none of her business what hours I work.'

'I don't think she would agree with you there. She wanted to thank you for seeing her home last night.' Alice was watching him closely and he knew she must surely see the guilty colour that flooded his face.

70

He set the cutlery down, having yet to touch his food. 'Now, Alice, don't you go letting your imagination run away with you,' he warned. 'Anne was drunk and the guy she was with left her to fend for herself. She could hardly stand, let alone walk. She needed someone to support her. What else could I do? I just walked down the street with her and left her at her front door. That's all there was to it. Was I home late, eh?'

Picturing him with his arm around his ex-wife, Alice's lip curled in scorn. 'And why *you*? Could no one else look after her? She told me you managed to get away early.'

Dan was determined to contain his temper and remain calm. Trust Anne to make a meal of it. 'Did she now? And did she say it was only a few minutes early, Alice? Just a few. As I've already said, she could hardly stand and the boss let me away to see her home. And that's all I did. Played the Good Samaritan, left her at her door and came straight here.'

'She implied that you asked to go in for a drink but she was too tired and sent you on your way. She hopes you're not too offended. Perhaps another time, she told me to tell you.'

Damn that bitch to hell! Dan lost the battle to keep his temper in check and now it erupted with a vengeance. Pushing roughly away from the table, he rose to his feet and towered over Alice. 'I can't believe that you stood and listened to all that garbage,' he bawled. 'She was winding you up, for God's sake, and you swallowed it, hook, line and sinker. Why didn't you just hang up on her?'

Alice's chin rose in the air. 'And give her the satisfaction of knowing she'd hit a raw nerve? No thanks. If it was all so innocent, why didn't you tell me about it when you got home last night?'

71

'Because I know you don't like me working in the Clock Bar, but I do, Alice, and I'm not going to leave because you choose to listen to a pack of lies about me. Tell me something. Have I ever, in all the years we've been together, given you any cause for concern?'

'No. Well, not so far.'

'Not so far?' He was astounded. 'Tell me this. After all this time, am I still on probation?'

'Don't be silly. Sit down and eat your dinner before it gets cold.'

'Do you know something, Alice? I've completely lost my appetite.' He brushed past her into the hall and grabbed his jacket from the stand.

Alarmed she cried, 'Where are you going, Dan? It's too early for your shift.'

'I don't know, and I don't care.' He was starving and the appetising aroma in the kitchen made him want to back down, but he knew if he didn't make a stand now his life could become a living hell. Opening the door he threw over his shoulder, 'Maybe if I ask her nicely, Anne will make me a bite to eat. Now that's an idea,' he added as if the thought appealed to him.

The big heavy door shuddered on its hinges. Alice gazed at it for some moments then burst into tears. He must be hiding something or he wouldn't be acting like this. Did he regret marrying her? Had Anne got her claws into him again? Had Alice driven him into his ex-wife's arms? How could she bear him to continue working in that pub after this?

Their raised voices had brought Jackie from the TV to investigate. He stood in the living-room doorway gazing wide-eyed at her. Not understanding what was going on, he was nevertheless whimpering in sympathy. 'Grannie . . . what's wrong? Where's Grandad gone?'

72

Wiping her eyes with the corner of her apron, Alice forced a feeble smile. 'Your grandad will be back in a minute, love,' she said, gathering the young boy close. But would he? her mind asked. How could she have been so foolish, ranting on at him like that? She'd tried him, judged him and found him guilty without listening to his side of the story. He was such a handsome man that she never had been able to control her jealousy where he was concerned.

'Come on, love, let's run your bath.'

Tears forgotten, Jackie played happily in a mass of bubbles. Desolate, Alice sat on the toilet seat and watched him with unseeing eyes. Ten minutes passed before the sound of the outer door opening brought her rushing to the top of the stairs. Dan came along the hall and stood looking up at her.

'I'm sorry, love. I shouldn't have lost my temper like that. It's just so frustrating that you can't trust me.'

Relief flooded through her. 'I'm the one who's sorry. I behaved like a wee child.'

Dan slowly climbed the stairs and she eagerly filled his arms. 'Is Jackie in the bath?' he whispered against her lips.

She nodded. 'We've about ten minutes before he gets bored and wants out.'

'Well then, let's not waste any more time.'

'What about your dinner? It's in the oven keeping warm.'

'Ah, so you knew I'd be back. You didn't dump it in the bin, then?'

'I *hoped* you'd be back,' she corrected him gently.

'Come on then, let's get on with it. Dinner can wait another ten minutes,' he whispered and urged her into the bedroom.

Although aroused, she questioned the logic of their intentions. 'Should we do this now? What about Jackie? Will he be all right in the bath?'

'Alice . . . he's only next door, and he's making enough noise to waken the dead. No harm will come to him.'

Won over, she gladly surrendered herself to his gentle lovemaking, returning kiss for kiss, touch for touch; suddenly writhing in alarm when he became too rough. Lifting his head he apologised. 'I'm sorry, love. I don't know what came over me.'

He knew quite well what had come over him. Anne had brought back memories of what it used to be like with her: the wild, mind-blowing, passionate frenzy. He would have to be very careful in future, Alice was not that kind of woman. And he had done without that kind of excitement for a long time before he met Alice, so why think of it now? Because of Anne's recent behaviour, of course!

The summer dragged on, filled with unrelenting violence and unrest, and no sign whatsoever of peace. Those who could afford it were going away for the Twelfth fortnight, and Tess and Theresa decided that with business at such a low ebb in July they would finish off any commitments they had and also close down for the two weeks. Bob's firm was on a rush job and he could only manage to get one week off in July, the second week of their holiday, so Tess invited Theresa to accompany her to Carlingford for the first week.

Jackie, who loved being on the farm, where he played happily with Rose's two granddaughters, had been packed off to Carlingford when his school closed for the summer break. Rose told Tess he was very excited at the idea of seeing her and Theresa and was expecting her to bring him a wee present. Tess assured her that that had already been taken care of.

They packed their suitcases, plus bits and pieces they had bought for Jackie and the two wee girls, and set off on Saturday the tenth, although not as light-heartedly as they would have liked. They couldn't keep their minds off the shop. It was depressing leaving it vacant, even though it was locked and shuttered.

Suddenly Tess laughed aloud. 'Would you just look at the two of us! The picture of misery. No one would ever guess we were going on holiday. You'd think we were going to a funeral instead. Let's forget all about the shop for a while. Remember Murphy's law? "Anything that can go wrong will go wrong." So why bother our heads worrying about it? We'll have to cheer up, put a big smile on our faces. We can't turn up on the farm tripping over our bottom lips. Uncle Mal might just send us straight back home if we arrive all doom and gloom.'

Theresa agreed wholeheartedly. 'We certainly can't. Tell you what. Let's stop at some wee pub on the way down and have a drink to fortify us, eh?'

'That sounds like a very good idea.'

They stopped at Banbridge for the promised drink. It was a lovely sunny afternoon and they sat at a table outside the pub and watched the world go by. One drink led to another and, about to start her third half, Theresa suddenly gasped in alarm. 'What am I thinking of? I'd better not drink that! Do you think two halves of Tennant's will put me over the limit, Tess?'

'I've no idea,' Tess confessed. 'It never entered my head about drink-driving.'

'I wish I'd stuck to the one half. This warm weather makes me so thirsty, I just never thought of the conse-quences if we should get stopped.'

Knowing that an old car like Theresa's could very likely get stopped going over the border, Tess's reply was heartfelt. 'It doesn't bear thinking about.' She rose to her feet. 'I'll ask the barman to make us some coffee. That should help. Meanwhile, there's some Trebor mints in my handbag. Help yourself to them.'

The coffee when it came was far too strong and Theresa, not a great lover of the brew at the best of times, screwed up her face with distaste. 'There's no need for you to drink this revolting stuff, Tess. It's like tar,' she whispered, with a furtive glance in the direction of the barman, who didn't usually serve coffee but was doing them a favour. 'Only the fear of losing my licence is forcing me to drink this muck.'

'I feel duty bound to keep you company, sip for sip,' Tess said gallantly and reached for her cup.

'Don't be daft. If the positions were reversed I wouldn't dream of drinking it.' Draining her cup with a grimace, Theresa reached for Tess's. 'I'll drink yours too, just to be on the safe side. You may as well have my lager,' she said, looking longingly at the cool drink. 'Silly to let it go to waste.'

'I daren't. I don't want to arrive at the farm tipsy. What would Uncle Mal think? Me drunk in the middle of the day, I ask you?'

'That would never do.' Theresa did, however, insist that Tess also suck some of the mints. 'If we're stopped, any smell of alcohol inside the car could mean me being breathalysed. Oh, how I wish we were already at the farm.'

Thinking that a strong smell of peppermint might just be suspicious enough to cause concern, Tess felt like laughing at their antics, but to keep her friend pacified she did as she was bid. Just outside Newry they ran into a tailback of traffic at a checkpoint and the girls looked at each other in dismay. 'Shall I turn and go back?' Theresa asked fearfully.

'No. That's the worst thing you could possibly do. We'll just have to sit it out. If we turn back now we'll certainly look guilty. They'll think we have a bomb or guns or something suspicious in the boot and they'll come after us, and things could really get out of hand if that happens. It doesn't bear thinking about.'

They sat in nervous silence eyeing the armed soldiers in full camouflage gear lying on the wide grass verges by the roadside, rifles trained on the vehicles, ready for action if called upon. At last it was their turn. A young soldier motioned them forward and then with a raised hand stopped them and approached the car.

'Good afternoon, ladies.'

Theresa's voice came out in a squeak. 'Good afternoon.'

'Can I see your driving licence, please?'

'Sure.' Theresa had the licence ready and handed it over, trying not to breathe any fumes in his direction.

After a close examination of the licence he handed it back and ducked down to take a look at her travelling companion, grinning back at the big smile directed at him. 'Are you ladies going south on business or pleasure?'

'Pleasure. We're going to Carlingford on holiday.'

'Have a nice time.' With a sweep of his hand he waved them on and went to meet the next vehicle.

Theresa sighed. 'What a relief. He was a nice lad, wasn't he?'

'He was, God love him. I suppose his mother is worried stiff about him being over here in the midst of all our troubles.'

Tess gave her friend a sideways glance. 'There must be something up, you know. They don't usually bother stopping *all* vehicles. Most times they have a list of registration numbers and photographs to check against. They know who and what they're looking for and wave you on through. That's the first time I've been stopped in all the years I've been coming down here. There must have been another bombing or somebody has been shot or something.'

As they pulled slowly away from the checkpoint they noticed a couple of cars and a van with the contents strewn on the grass verge. The occupants were standing with their hands on the roofs of the vehicles and soldiers were covering them with their weapons while officers questioned them.

'There's no bloody end to it,' Theresa lamented. 'I'll be glad to stay on the farm for the week. It'll be quiet there, won't it?'

'Quiet, but very pleasant. That is something I can promise you. You'll enjoy your stay in Carlingford.'

When Malachy and Rose had got married some four years back, Rose moved into Malachy's house and hers was kept for occasions like this, when family or friends visited. Theresa was expecting a small country cottage with no running water and an outside toilet. Tess hadn't enlightened her and was pleased at her friend's gasp of delight when she directed her to pull up in front of an impressive-looking two-storey building.

'Is this it?'

'Yes. You've to go up the lane to park at the back. Let's take the cases out of the boot first and I'll get the front-door key from its hiding place.'

Inside, Theresa was enchanted with the layout of the house. 'It's beautiful. Rose must have been very reluctant to leave here.'

'Oh, Uncle Mal has his farm all modernised, and now Rose has the best of both worlds. She can spend weekends here when her two daughters visit from Dublin for the odd weekend. She handed over the running of her farm to her only son after the death of her first husband. All in all she's a very contented and happy woman. Malachy and her dote on each other.'

'I could see that the few times I've met them. Lucky her.'

'Your turn will come.'

'Huh!'

'Oh ye of little faith. Let's get unpacked. Rose will be here soon.'

Carlingford always lived up to Tess's expectations and she was glad to see that Theresa was as taken with the beauty of the countryside as she was. They had a wonderful week, and although she confessed to missing Bob, it was with reluctance that Theresa bade them goodbye and headed across country to Sligo to pick him up at his digs, as arranged. The pair of them were going to Bray for the week, and Theresa promised to collect Tess on the way back, saving Malachy a journey to Belfast. In turn Malachy persuaded Theresa to return on the Friday and stay overnight, promising he would take them all out to dinner. Theresa was delighted with the idea and set off to meet the love of her life in a happy frame of mind. Tess watched her go and was slightly perturbed, but for the life of her she couldn't understand why.

The second week flew by. The weather remained warm and bright, and Tess was content to join Rose in keeping the children entertained and to help Malachy do odd jobs about the farm. Her favourite chore was collecting eggs.

Malachy had warned the women that he had a treat in store for them and wanted them looking their very best for a special night out. Early Friday afternoon Tess retired upstairs for a leisurely soak in the bath while Rose took the three children over to her son, saying she would get ready up at his place and leave the bathroom free for Theresa and Bob.

Freshly bathed and hair shampooed, Tess stood in front of the cheval glass and examined her reflection. Far from beautiful, she mused, but not altogether unattractive. The sun had heightened the highlights in her hair and it shone like burnished copper. Her pale skin was now a warm apricot and freckles dusted the bridge of her small, straight nose. The pale green dress made from a silky material clung to the curves of her body and deepened the colour of her eyes. She had darkened the thick lashes that framed them and they sparkled back at her from the mirror like emeralds.

Today was her twenty-sixth birthday. She had not mentioned it, not wanting anyone to make a fuss or go to the expense of buying her presents, although it saddened her that she had not received a card from her mother and Dan. They had apparently forgotten all about her birthday.

A commotion outside brought her to the window to gaze down into the front garden. Theresa and Bob had arrived and Malachy was helping Theresa carry their overnight cases into the house, leaving Bob free to park the car. Tess found herself examining Bob. Working on the building site had darkened his skin to a rich golden tan and his fair hair was bleached the colour of ripe corn. As if aware of her presence he looked up and caught her eye. They remained locked in each other's gaze for some seconds, caught in a magnetic trance, before he lifted a hand in greeting. Theresa followed his glance and with a brief word to Bob grabbed her case and entered the house.

Tess found she couldn't take her eyes off Bob. There was a stirring in her blood and she licked lips that had gone dry. He glanced up at the window once more and a satisfied smile spread across his face before he got into the car. Annoyed at herself, Tess was glad of the short respite before her friend arrived in the bedroom. She was relieved that she was able to regain her composure, to a certain degree. Theresa apparently didn't notice anything different about her.

'You look great, so you do, Tess. Is that a new dress?'

'Yes. It's only a cheap one. Rose and I took the kids to Dundalk the other day and I saw it on a stall in the market and fell for the colour.'

'You suit it.'

'Thank you. You're looking well yourself. You've certainly caught the sun. Did you enjoy yourself in Bray?'

'It was great. We had a wonderful time. You should see the tan Bob has. He's like a Viking god. Of course I'm prejudiced.'

A sad note had crept into her voice and Tess eyed her closely. 'Is everything all right?'

Theresa sighed. 'To be truthful, I don't know. Nothing I can put my finger on, but somehow or other Bob seems different. He's still attentive enough and kind, but . . .' She shrugged her shoulders. 'Oh, I don't know! Perhaps he's met someone over in Sligo. I wouldn't be a bit surprised. A fine figure of a man like him? I'm sure he gets plenty of attention from the local girls.'

'Didn't you ask him? Set your mind at rest. It's probably your imagination, you know, playing tricks on you.'

'I was afraid of what he might say.'

'Don't be daft! He loves you.'

'You've changed your tune!'

'I know I used to doubt him but I was wrong. He's obviously a nice person and he seems to care a lot for you.'

With a bewildered shrug, Theresa agreed. 'Oh, I suppose you're right.' She changed the subject. 'Where's Malachy taking us tonight?'

'I haven't a clue. He hasn't even mentioned it today.'

'That doesn't sound like Malachy. You say he's always full of any plans he's making and likes to discuss them to make sure he hasn't forgotten anything.'

'Yes, it is unusual, but he's been very busy. I've hardly seen him these past couple of days. Besides, he likes wee surprises. Look, I got ready early to leave the bathroom free for you and Bob, so away you go.'

'Look after Bob for me.'

Tess hesitated. 'I've a few things to do, but I'll be down shortly.'

When Tess at last reluctantly descended the stairs, Malachy rose from his chair. 'Ah! There you are. I need to nip over to the farm to get ready before we go out, so I'll leave you to entertain Bob.'

'Sorry, Uncle Mal, I didn't know you were still here. You should have given me a shout. Away you go, I'm sure I can entertain Bob for a short while.'

Tess sat on the wide windowsill. She couldn't have chosen a better background had she planned it. The slight breeze from the open window fanned her hair and the sun's rays emphasised the coppery highlights as she unconsciously moved her head to one side. Her face in shadow was quite beautiful; her eyes dark and mysterious. To Bob she was a vision of beauty.

He openly admired her and raised the glass he was holding. 'Join me in a drink?'

'I'll have a Coke, please.'

He filled a glass and handed it to her. Clinking his own against it he said, 'Cheers.'

'Cheers.' Tess sipped some of the cold liquid. 'So, how was Bray?'

'Great. We enjoyed the break.' His eyes were closely examining her face and hair. 'You look a million dollars, if I may say so.'

Tess felt the colour rise in her cheeks. 'Thank you. You can tell me that any time you feel like it.'

'Is that an invitation? Why, I do believe you're blushing, Tess Maguire.' He sat down on the windowsill beside her and give her a sideways glance.

There was ample room for two but he deliberately sat close to her and the pressure of his thigh against hers was electrifying. Nerves on edge, she flailed about in her mind for something sensible to say in case he became aware of the effect he was having on her.

'Would you like another drink, Bob?'

He gave her a quizzical look and indicated the almost full glass in his hand.

Really agitated now Tess started to rise but with a hand on her thigh he stopped her. 'Don't run away from me, Tess.' His breath fanned her face and she felt weak and vulnerable. The hand on her leg felt hot through the thin material of her dress and moved caressingly up and down. 'We'll have to face up to this sooner or later, you know,' he said softly.

Not wanting him to remove his hand she nevertheless whispered furiously, 'I have no idea what you're talking about, Bob Dempsey. And please take your hand off my leg.'

'If you weren't enjoying it, you'd have pushed it away long ago.'

'I don't understand you.'

'I think you do.'

'What if Theresa were to see us, eh? What on earth would she think?'

'She'll have to find out sooner or later.'

Eyes wide with alarm, Tess hissed, 'Find out what?'

Bob leaned closer, but before he could state his case the front door opened and Rose hurried into the room. 'Bob! I didn't realise you were back.' She gazed vaguely around the room. 'Where's Malachy?'

'We arrived just a few minutes ago. Malachy said he was going to the farm to get ready.'

'He asked me to remind him about something, I wonder if he remembered himself. Did you have a nice time in Bray?'

'Quiet, but nice.'

Tess rose abruptly to her feet. 'I'll go up and see if Theresa needs anything.'

Rose looked after her, an enquiring frown on her brow. 'Did I interrupt anything?'

'Nothing that can't be resolved later,' Bob assured her. At least he certainly hoped so.

'If you don't mind me leaving you, Bob, I'll nip over and see if Malachy has organised everything. I'll be in hot water if he has forgotten anything since he asked me to remind him.'

'I'm quite content to sit here and have a rest, Rose.'

'See you later, then.'

On the drive out to dinner Tess was so wrapped up in her own thoughts she failed to realise where they were heading until they passed through the entrance gates. It was the same posh restaurant her uncle had taken them to on her twenty-first birthday. Even the mallard ducks preening themselves on the lake looked as if they had barely moved.

'Oh, how lovely,' she exclaimed. 'What a pleasant surprise.' She was seated beside Malachy in the front seat of the Land-Rover and now she turned to him. 'You certainly kept this quiet!'

His eyes slanted in her direction. 'I wondered when you'd twig. You were away in a world of your own there. Are you worried about anything?'

'No. No, I was just wool-gathering. I never expected you to bring us here again. It's so expensive.'

'On a special occasion like my only niece's birthday? How could you expect anything less of me?'

'To be truthful, Uncle Mal, I thought you had forgotten all about it,' she confessed ruefully.

'Have I ever forgotten your birthday, Tess? Even when I was struggling to make ends meet on the farm, I always managed to get you a present. Albeit it sometimes only a small one.'

Her hand rested on his forearm for some moments. 'Sorry. With Mam and Dan not mentioning it, I thought everyone else had forgotten as well.'

'As if I would. Shame on you for even thinking such a thing.'

They left the Land-Rover and waited while Rose drew her car into the parking lot beside them. Malachy assisted Rose from the car and Bob and Theresa clambered out of the back.

Theresa eyed the impressive building. 'Wow. This is going to cost you something, Malachy.'

'Nothing's too grand for my niece on her birthday.'

Theresa rolled her eyes at Bob. 'I'm glad now we brought our wee present with us, Bob. I would have been mortified, so I would.' She made a wry face in Malachy's direction. 'We thought you'd all forgotten.'

'What kind of an uncle do you take me for, eh?' Offering one of his arms to Rose and the other to Tess, Malachy led the way up the steps and through the revolving doors into the foyer.

The head waiter hurried forward, snapping fingers to bring another waiter springing to attention. 'Your other guests have arrived, sir. May Declan take the ladies' coats?'

Other guests? Who else had been invited? Tess wondered as they trooped behind the waiter into the restaurant. Maybe some of his farming friends. A couple seated at a table in the spacious lounge rose to greet them and Tess knew why they hadn't all piled into Malachy's Land-Rover. They would need two vehicles for the journey back to the farm.

'Mam! Dan! What a lovely surprise. I'm so glad to see you.'

Alice hugged her daughter. 'Isn't your uncle just wonderful, arranging all this? I hope you didn't think we'd forgotten your birthday, love. Surely you know what that Malachy fella's like by now. He wanted to surprise you. He loves arranging the unexpected.'

'And I can't think of a better surprise, Mam. It's lovely to see you. You too, Dan.' She tilted her cheek for Dan's kiss and Bob looked on enviously.

The restaurant lived up to its reputation for good food and service and everybody noisily enjoyed their chosen dishes. They retired to the lounge for coffee and it was here that a beautiful birthday cake was carried in and placed on their table, bringing tears of delight to Tess's eyes. The wine waiter arrived with a magnum of champagne and filled their glasses before crunching the bottle into the ice bucket beside them.

Malachy raised his glass. 'May I propose a toast?

Happy birthday, Tess, and all the very best for the future, love.'

They all raised their glasses and chorused, 'Happy birthday, Tess.'

'Thank you. Thank you all so very much. I'm absolutely speechless. I don't know what to say.'

'It's not over yet, Tess. We can't manage a car at the moment, but I think this will come in handy.'

Malachy handed her an envelope. It contained a birthday card and Tess caught her breath at the sizeable cheque inside from her uncle and Rose.

'Oh! Thank you very, very much indeed!' She dabbed at her eyes as the tears started again.

Another card containing a cheque was forthcoming from her mother and Dan.

'Have you lot gone and won the pools or something? Thanks, Mam, Dan. Can you really afford this?'

'Oh, the wolf's not sniffing at the door yet,' Alice assured her.

'Do you know something, Tess Maguire? I'm so embarrassed because we haven't a cheque for you,' Theresa teased, and thrust a small flat package into Tess's hands. 'I hope you like it. It was Bob who picked it.'

With fingers that shook Tess carefully removed the gold-coloured wrapping to reveal a flat box. Inside a necklace of fine smooth green stones lay on a white velvet lining.

'Oh, it's beautiful!' she whispered in awe. 'Thank you both very much.'

Bob moved to stand beside her. 'Let's try it on.'

Tess watched as his long, sensitive fingers removed the necklace from the box, then, standing behind her, his body brushing hers, Bob placed it around her neck. He secured the clasp with cool hands that lingered on her nape, sending a tremor coursing through her body. Was it her imagination or was it a caress? It certainly felt like it. Agitated, and hoping no one would notice how distracted she was, she quickly put space between herself and Bob and, fingering the necklace, repeated, 'It's gorgeous, so it is. Thanks again.'

There seemed to be no end to the festivities. Back at Malachy's farmhouse, a finger buffet was laid on and neighbours whom Tess had come to know during her many visits had been invited along. Each couple had a small birthday token for her and she was overwhelmed with gratitude at their generosity.

The visitors tucked into the buffet and when they all had eaten their fill the tables and chairs were pushed to one side and the entertainment began. Two of the guests had, as was usual on these occasions, brought their fiddles along and the strains of Irish jigs soon filled the air. The heat became stifling and the windows and doors were opened wide, and couples drifted outside to dance in the cool night air.

All the male guests made a point of dancing with the birthday girl and Tess was inebriated on wine and happiness. It was while the fiddlers were having a rest and records were put on that Bob asked her to dance with him. Determined to show him how indifferent she was to his charms, Tess willingly entered his arms and they circled the farmyard in a slow waltz.

They danced in silence for some moments and, relaxed and happy, Tess allowed herself to be drawn close. Becoming aroused at the nearness of her and not wanting to frighten her off, or for that matter make a spectacle of himself, Bob pushed her away from his body. Taken unawares, she stepped back abruptly and caught the heel of her court shoe on an uneven flagstone. The next thing she knew she was sprawled on her bottom. Clasping her ankle she grimaced and looked up at him in bewilderment. 'What did you do that for?'

Before he had a chance to apologise, all attention was directed at her. Theresa, who had been dancing with a young farmer, rushed to her side, quickly followed by Alice. 'What on earth happened? Are you hurt?'

Gently, Bob helped her to her feet. 'Let's get you inside and have a look at that ankle.' His arm circled her waist and she hobbled beside him across the yard.

Tess assured everyone as she went, 'I'm all right. Carry on dancing. Please don't let me spoil the evening. It's probably just a sprain.'

Bob shooed them away. 'She's right. There's no need to stop the entertainment. I'll look after her.'

Seeing she was in safe hands, Alice and Dan led off the dancing again and others followed suit.

Tess sat on a kitchen chair and, kneeling in front of her, Bob gently eased the shoe off her already swollen foot.

'I'll get the first-aid kit. I noticed one in the bathroom,' volunteered Theresa, who had followed them into the kitchen.

Alone with Tess at last, Bob gazed into her eyes and apologised profusely. 'I'm so sorry, Tess. Really, really sorry. I don't know what happened. One minute we were dancing and the next you were on your backside.'

Convinced that he had deliberately pushed her away, Tess nevertheless shouldered the blame. 'It wasn't your fault, it was my own clumsiness. My heel caught on a flagstone and the next thing I remember is being helped to my feet.'

Cool fingers gently examined her ankle. 'I think it's just a sprain. A cold compress will soon get the swelling down.'

Finding that his touch was sending all kind of thrills coursing through her, making her slightly breathless, Tess inwardly chastised herself. It was the wine that was affecting her like this, she wasn't used to drinking so much. Not really convinced, she was relieved when Theresa returned with the first-aid kit.

Hearing Bob's words Theresa peered over his shoulder. 'I think you're right.' She went to the freezer. 'Will a packet of frozen peas be any good?'

'That should do the trick. Would you get me that pouffe in from the big room, Theresa?'

Bob placed Tess's foot on the pouffe and taking the bag of peas crunched the frozen mass between his hands to loosen the contents before laying it gently against the injured ankle, causing Tess to inhale sharply at the sudden coldness.

'Thanks, Theresa. I feel so stupid. Please don't let me spoil the evening. Keep the ball rolling out there, will you?' Tess glanced out of the window. 'That young farmer is waiting for you. Away out and dance with him.' She winked at her friend. 'Give him something to dream about.'

Theresa dithered. 'Are you sure?' She looked askance at Bob. 'Do you need any help, love?'

He jerked his hand in her direction. 'Away you go. We'll be fine. I'll soon have Tess back on her feet again.'

'Give me a shout if you need me.'

Bob was concentrating on applying the frozen compress to the swelling, and as Tess gazed down on his blond head the urge to touch it was overwhelming. Confused by the emotions that were coursing through her body, she clasped her hands tightly together on her lap and fought for self-control. Unable to bear it any longer and needing to put some distance between them, she said in a shaky voice, 'I would love a cold drink, please.'

He rose resignedly to his feet and gazed down at her. 'Don't you think for one minute that you're fooling me, Tess Maguire.'

Aghast that he might guess what was going on in her troubled mind, she gasped, 'I don't know what you're talking about.'

'Oh yes you do! And I know you do, so stop kidding yourself, because sooner or later Theresa will have to be told. And the sooner the better as far as I'm concerned.'

'You listen to me, Bob Dempsey! Theresa is my dearest friend and I will never do anything that will hurt her, so leave me alone.'

Going to the kitchen door Bob closed it, then returned and leaned over Tess. 'First I must do something, then if you still want me to leave you alone, I will.'

Tess gazed at him apprehensively. Before she became aware of his intentions, he tenderly cupped her face in his hands and touched her lips with his. As the kiss deepened she reacted violently. Where she got the willpower from Tess would never know, because she was crying out for his kisses, for the touch of his hands, release for the passion that had engulfed her. Somehow she managed to push him roughly away and rising to her feet hobbled a few steps from him.

'Don't you ever do that again or so much as lay a finger on me. Do you hear? I don't trust you, I never have, but Theresa does and I'm not going to let you use me as a lever to hurt her. She loves you and I hope and pray you will never let her down.'

He gripped her shoulders to stop her frantic endeavours to get away from him and forced her back down on to the chair. 'What about me? Eh? Am I supposed to keep my trap shut and go on as if nothing has happened?' She struggled to rise again and he snapped at her, 'Sit down until I bandage that ankle before you do more damage to it.' He reached for the first-aid kit. 'And don't worry. I'll never bother you again. That you can count on. You're not worth the effort.'

Grim-faced, he deftly wound the elastic bandage round her ankle, and secured it with a safety-pin, then ordered her, 'Wait here.'

When he returned he handed her a couple of aspirin and a glass of water. 'If you're sure you're all right, I'll leave you now. *Are* you all right?'

'I'm fine. Just go away.'

'I'll send someone in to keep you company.'

'That won't be necessary, I'm going to bed.'

'I'll help you up the stairs.'

'I can manage on my own, thank you.'

'Not on that foot you won't. Come on.'

She looked so woebegone he said kindly, 'Don't worry, I won't bite.'

She clung to his arm and he helped her from the kitchen and up the stairs.

On the landing he hesitated. 'Which is your room?'

'That one.' She indicated it with a nod.

He pushed the door open and helped her to the bed. 'Stretch out there and take the weight off that foot. I'll send someone up to sit with you.'

Tears she had managed to hold at bay toppled down her face. Keeping her face turned away from him she said, 'I want to be alone.' Good Lord, I'm beginning to sound like Greta Garbo, she thought.

Gently he turned her face towards him. 'What's all this? Why the tears?'

'I don't know,' she wailed.

Throwing caution to the wind he wiped her cheeks with his thumbs, trying to stem the flow. Then the expression in her eyes made him gasp and with a muttered exclamation he claimed her lips. This time she didn't draw away and the kiss deepened. Gathering her into his arms he covered her face and neck with feverish kisses, all the while declaring how much he loved her.

At first she was reluctant, but then the passion within her spilled over and she returned his embraces with a fervour that left him gasping for breath. He released her and, gazing down on her flushed face, said gravely, 'You're a wonderful girl and I've fallen hopelessly in love with you. We'll have to bring this all out into the open. Theresa must be told. Surely you can see that?'

She pushed him away. 'All what? It was only a kiss, for heaven's sake. It should never have happened in the first place and it must never happen again.'

'You know it was no ordinary kiss. Tess—'

'Wasn't it?' she interrupted angrily. 'What was so special about it, then?'

Before he had a chance to reply, footsteps on the stairs and Rose's voice calling out brought Tess upright in alarm.

Gripping his arm, she begged, 'I can't face her now. Put her off, please, Bob.'

With a resigned sigh, he quickly left the room, pulling the door closed behind him. Tess heard their muffled voices and then receding footsteps. Burying her face in the pillow she punched it repeatedly and cried as if her heart would burst. Why did she have to go and fall for Bob Dempsey, of all people? How had it come about? Why, she hadn't even liked him to begin with; far from it! She would go so far as to say that she had probably hated the man; thought he wasn't good enough for

Theresa. But what he said was true. It *was* no ordinary kiss. It was more like a commitment. The most wonderful thing that had ever happened to her. But now it was up to her to convince Bob otherwise. There was Theresa to consider. She could say goodbye to the partnership and Theresa's friendship if she encouraged Bob any further. She wouldn't be able to run the business on her own, that was for sure! Oh, why the hell did Bob Dempsey have to go and confuse things?

4

Tess felt as if she were wallowing in deep clinging mud. Panic-stricken, she struggled through a thick fog towards wakefulness, writhing in desperation to escape invisible hands that were pulling her back into a frightening nightmare. She was half aware that she was caught up in a very bad dream but couldn't break the spell. She was sweating profusely. Something was terribly wrong. Someone or something was trying to get her attention, but for all her efforts she found she couldn't move any faster. At last she managed to throw off the restraining cloak of sleep and, forcing her eyes open, gazed fearfully about her bedroom. Emerging from the ugly blackness of nightmare, she had expected the bedroom to be shrouded in darkness, but was surprised to find it bathed in a pale dawn light.

A quick glance at the luminous dial on the bedside clock told her it was just after half four. What on earth was going on? she wondered through the tangled cobwebs of her mind as she struggled to sit up. Then she realised what had wakened her. There was a terrible commotion coming from outside.

Apprehensive, she threw back the bedclothes and crossed cautiously to the window, inching aside the curtains. The sight that met her eyes caused her to step back involuntarily and brought a strangled gasp of fear from her throat. Armoured personnel carriers, jeeps and army lorries were crawling along the road and the foot-paths were crowded with police and soldiers who were banging on doors. When they were not answered quickly enough, they forced their way into the houses. Not every house was targeted, but from those that were, men, some of them still half asleep, were pulled out bare-footed and in various stages of undress and bundled into Saracen personnel carriers or canvas-topped lorries. Through the open back of one of the army lorries she could just make out some men sitting handcuffed on wooden bench seats running the length of the lorry. A soldier sat between each of the men, keeping a watchful eye to prevent any communication between them.

The officers seemed to have specific addresses on their lists. They were going about their task methodically, but then surprise would be on their side. Tess realised that the racket that had wakened her was not coming from the police or troops. From her high vantage point she could see crowds of women and youths gathered at the corner of Crocus Street. They were banging bin lids and saucepans on the pavement, blowing whistles, and shouting abuse at the troops, kicking up such a racket that it could easily have wakened the dead, let alone alerted neighbouring streets to what was going on; warning them what was in store for them.

Tess stood rooted to the spot. She knew that the Faulkner Government had been pressing the British authorities for a long time now for internment for those suspected of being involved in terrorist activities. Had the weekend of horrific killing and rioting resulted in them getting their wish? Was this the start of the internment operation? Were the Protestants on the Shankill Road being subjected to the same indignities as these poor men?

Why was she so surprised? It had been a terrible weekend. The shooting dead of a civilian outside the Springfield Road RUC barracks had triggered off rioting that had continued over the weekend, spreading across the city like a cancer. Tess was alone in the house at the moment, her mother and Dan having gone to Carlingford on Friday to collect Jackie; a fact for which she was thankful. They intended to stay the week. It was Monday the ninth of August.

As she watched, an army officer looked towards her house then scanned the clipboard he was holding before ordering his troops on past her door. She surmised that Dan wasn't on their wanted list. Her thoughts flew to Bob Dempsey. Had he been lifted? A great dread flooded through her. Pulling on her dressing gown, she raced down the stairs to the phone. It rang just as she reached it. Theresa Cunningham was on the line. A very distraught Theresa.

'Tess? Oh Tess, do you know what they're doing?' She almost screamed down the line, not giving Tess time to answer. 'They're arresting all the men!'

'Calm down, Theresa. I know all about it. I've been watching them from my bedroom window for the last ten minutes. They're lifting them down here as well. What about Bob?'

A sob caught in Theresa's throat and Tess heard her gulp deeply before saying, 'They've taken him away. Oh Tess, what will become of us if all our men are interned? What will become of the families of the married ones?'

Tess's heart sank at the news of Bob's arrest but she endeavoured to comfort her friend. 'Shush, Theresa, they're not lifting *all* the men and they can't hold them without just cause.'

'Oh, can't they? You don't really believe that, do you?' Theresa retorted scornfully. 'Can I come down to your house, Tess? I'll go away in the head if I stay here another minute longer, so I will.'

'Of course you can. But take care. Wait until things have quietened down and the army has moved on. Or they might just lift you as well.'

'I will. I'll be very careful. I've to get washed and dressed yet anyway. Oh Tess, I'm so worried.'

'Take care, love. We'll talk about it when you get here.'

Slowly Tess replaced the receiver and sank down on to the bottom stair. She gazed about her with unseeing eyes for some minutes, striving to get her thoughts in order. Bob had been arrested! God knows what was happening to him, but she must not, under any circumstances, give any outward sign to Theresa of how terribly concerned she was. She felt absolutely gutted. How would she be able to hide her true feelings from her friend?

She had stuck to her word that nothing could come of the emotions that had flared with the slightest provocation between Bob Dempsey and herself. How on earth no one else seemed to notice she would never know. She was nevertheless aware of anything and everything to do with him. Since that night she had sprained her ankle she had never given Bob an opening to try and influence her to his way of thinking. God knows he had tried often enough to contact her, to persuade her to see him on her own, but she had blocked his every move and was always careful never to be alone with him. She didn't dare! He was constantly on her mind and she didn't trust herself.

Now strong emotions engulfed her as she considered his plight. Bob was a very headstrong person. He would not have gone quietly. What if something awful happened to him? He'd resist every inch of the way. Burying her face in her hands, Tess wept long and hard, harsh sobs erupting from deep within her.

Theresa arrived at the house dishevelled and distressed. She and Tess clung to each other for some moments in silent anguish, patting each other on the back as if it would lessen the pain. Then, glad that Theresa was too preoccupied to notice her swollen eyes, Tess asked, 'How did Bob react at being arrested?'

'What do you think? He lashed out, of course, and received a couple of baton thumps for his trouble. I don't suppose any of them went quietly. Imagine youngsters waking up in the middle of the night and seeing their dads or big brothers being frogmarched from their homes by soldiers with faces covered in camouflage paint and carrying rifles and machine-guns? It must have been terrifying. What on earth will become of those families? It will affect the kids' minds for the rest of their lives.'

Tears flowed again, and putting an arm across her shoulders Tess led her friend along the hall. 'Come into the kitchen, I've the kettle on for tea. The cure for all ills.'

'If only it were. If only it were,' was the sad, muttered reply.

Theresa sat dejectedly at the kitchen table, hands wrapped round the hot mug, finding comfort in its warmth. Tess put the pan on the stove and threw some rashers of bacon into it.

A bewildered look on her face, Theresa asked, 'What on earth are you doing?'

'What does it look like? I'm making us some breakfast.'

'I'm ashamed of you. How can you even think of food at a time like this?'.

'What good will it do Bob and all those other poor souls if we starve, eh? Tell me that!'

Theresa threw her a baleful glare. 'Do you know something, Tess Maguire? There are times when I can't comprehend your way of thinking.' Putting the mug to one side, she rose from the table, adding disdainfully, 'I don't want anything, thank you. I couldn't eat a thing. I'm too upset.'

A rough push sent her sprawling back down on to the chair. 'You'll eat something! Do you hear me? Or I'll ram it down your bloody throat. Do you think everybody will be like you, just sitting at home whingeing and moaning and feeling sorry for themselves? No! They'll be out there trying to find out what's going on and how they can get their men back. If we go down to the shop we'll be kept up to date on what's happening. Who knows? We might even be able to help out in some little way.'

'You're opening the shop today?' Theresa sounded scandalised. Was there no end to her friend's treachery?

'Of course I am!' Tess found herself shouting. She was so frustrated she longed to give Theresa a good shake. 'And what's more, whether you like it or not, you're coming with me,' she warned. They had heard on the early-morning news on Radio Ulster that over three hundred men had been arrested. 'We'll find out more about our own community if we're in the shop. How many men from the district were arrested and where they're being held. Things like that. You do want to know what's going on, don't you? Where they've taken Bob, for instance?'

100

Theresa brushed a weary hand across her face. 'You're right, of course. I'm sorry.'

Putting the bacon on a warm plate, Tess cracked a couple of eggs into the pan. Her face was a grim mask of contemplation. Where on earth were they going to put all those men? Crumlin Road jail was big, but not big enough to accommodate another three hundred prisoners. Or anywhere near that number, for that matter. And, as Theresa had pointed out earlier, what would become of the married men's families, particularly the innocent ones? God only knows.

For all her brave talk Tess found that she couldn't force the food down her throat. She pushed the plate away. Shamefaced, Theresa looked from Tess's full plate to her own, which was almost empty, and pushed it to one side also.

'I've a cheek to talk,' she whimpered, gesturing towards her plate.

'You were hungrier than me,' Tess consoled her.

While they were washing the breakfast dishes, Alice phoned from Carlingford. They had been following the news of the rioting all weekend and phoning regularly. Now they had just heard about the internment raids on RTE Radio and were anxious to know just what was going on. Tess relayed all the news about the early-morning raids on Springfield Road and explained about Bob being lifted. She promised that as soon as she heard anything more about the state of affairs in the district she would let them know.

'Did the army come to our house?'

'No. It appears they had specific addresses in mind, and believe you me, they knew exactly where to go.'

'We've decided to come home today, Tess.'

'Don't be silly, Mam. Keep Jackie away from here as

long as possible. There will be repercussions, you mark my words! Our ones won't take this lying down, you know.'

'I'm aware of that. I just don't like the idea of you being there on your own.'

'I won't be on my own. Theresa's with me at the minute, and with Bob being lifted, she'll stay as long as she wants. You know she doesn't like being alone in her own house. Meanwhile, you and Dan stay put. We're going down to the shop shortly. We'll find out more on the grapevine down there and I'll ring later and let you know how things stand.'

'That's a good idea. Watch yourself, love. I'll be praying for you.'

'Goodbye, Mam.'

Tess was right. The shops along the road were all putting on a brave front and opening for business as usual. People had to get on with their lives. After all, not everyone's husband or son or friend had been arrested. But still, so many homes had been disrupted that customers were few and far between. It was as if everyone was in mourning. The road was pretty well deserted and the shop-owners gathered in small groups discussing the happenings of the early-morning raids and whether it was worthwhile staying open.

As Tess had foretold, she and Theresa learned a lot of things via the local grapevine, news that would never be heard on TV or radio. It seemed that men from all walks of life had been arrested. Business and professional men, tradesmen and labourers and those on the dole. It was even said that a blind man had been lifted. A very mixed bag indeed. They were given a list of the local men arrested and discovered that Tony Burke's name was included. It was also alleged that the men had not been treated with kid gloves, to say the least, and tempers were high at this revelation. It was thought that those arrested were being held at Girdwood Park Barracks on the Antrim Road, and on the *Maidstone*, a converted troopship moored at Belfast docks. It was also believed that all those arrested were Catholics. Tess didn't for one minute believe this. Even the Government wouldn't be so stupid as to condone something like that. They knew there were terrorists on both sides.

Monday was a day of ferocious rioting and shooting. Two soldiers and nine civilians were killed, including a priest at Ballymurphy who was shot whilst administering the last rites to an injured man. All this was relayed on the grapevine and the shopkeepers decided to put the shutters up early and call it a day. Tess and Theresa spent the rest of the day glued to the TV. They felt so helpless, having been unable to find out just where Bob or Tony were being held. They had tried ringing round different RUC stations in the district. When they eventually got through to someone they were asked what their relationship was to the two men, and when they explained that they were just friends they were politely but quickly cut off. The sound of constant gunfire and explosions could be heard outside; there was no sign of any let-up.

Tess phoned her mother and again advised her to stay in Carlingford, but Alice was reluctant to do so.

'I'd rather come home, Tess,' she insisted.

'Mam, you'd be much safer staying where you are. It will be too dangerous travelling on the roads the way things are at the moment, and it would be unfair to expect Uncle Mal to drive across the border when it's not necessary.'

'We could get the train! I'm worried about you. All that rioting going on, anything could happen.'

In exasperation, Tess ridiculed her. 'And you'd be able to stop it, eh? Is that what you're trying to tell me? Wise up, Mam!'

Her hump up at her daughter's scorn, Alice retorted, 'At least I'd know what's going on. I wouldn't be sitting here biting my nails to the quick, wondering how you are. Not everything is reported on the news or in the newspapers, as you well know, and I'm worrying myself sick.'

Tess's tone softened. She knew this was all too true. 'Mam, please stay put. I promise I'll keep you up to date on anything that happens around here, and in case you think I'm holding things back, you may as well know now, we heard that Tony Burke was also lifted.'

Alice was scandalised. 'Why? Sure everybody knows that Tony Burke wouldn't harm a fly.'

'Neither would any of the men we know that have been arrested. They're all honest, hard-working men with families. And wouldn't you know! It's said that in spite of lifting so many, the army still didn't manage to net the ones they were really after. So surely all these men should be home soon. Wouldn't you think so?'

'I wouldn't count on it. The Government won't admit that they've dropped one almighty clanger this time.' There was a pregnant pause, then Alice said, 'So you think I should stay here?'

'Yes, Mam, I do.'

A short silence as her mother gave this advice some thought. 'Tell you what. I'll stay until Friday as planned, and see how things go from there. Okay?'

'Yes, I'll give you a ring at teatime tomorrow. Give my regards to everyone there. Good night, Mam.'

The shooting and bombing continued throughout the province. It was alleged that Tuesday was the worst day of violence in Belfast since the troubles had started in 1969. Ten people were reported to have been killed in the city. In the more dangerous areas terrified families fled their homes in fear of their lives – some, it was alleged, even torching their own houses to prevent 'the other side' moving in. Hundreds of homes were destroyed by fire; all the precious possessions gathered over the years gone in a matter of hours. All those poor people, homeless through no fault of their own. Where would it all end?

The phone rang in the early hours of Wednesday morning, awakening Tess from a fitful sleep. As she made her way downstairs to answer it, she had a fairly good idea who would be on the other end of the line. She was right. Colette Burns had been phoning regularly since the explosion at Springfield Road Barracks. Her voice was fraught with worry. 'Tess, I've just seen the latest news on TV. Are you lot okay over there?'

'We're all fine, Colette. Jackie's in Carlingford with me mam and Dan at the moment.'

'Thank God for that. Look, Tess, I've come to a decision. I can't bear all this worry any longer, dreading getting bad news about my son every time the .phone rings. We'll have to have a serious talk about Jackie's future.'

'It's Dan you'll have to talk to, Colette, not me.'

'*He* won't want to give him up.'

'Huh! Can you blame him?'

'Still, you will help me persuade him that it will be in Jackie's best interests if he comes over here to live with me, won't you, Tess?'

'Colette, I'm not going to get involved in any more wrangling between Dan and you. We've been down that road before, in case you've forgotten. Dan and my mother love that child. They'll fight you tooth and nail to keep him. And remember, Jackie hardly knows you. You'd be uprooting him from everything he's familiar with and taking him away to live among strangers in a foreign country. Dan and Mam have reared him since he was two days old. I think they stand a good chance of keeping custody of him, troubles or no troubles. Don't you?'

'You're forgetting I'm his mother. That will count for a lot.'

'I'm not forgetting anything. However, not knowing the legal implications, I imagine the court would be inclined to think that you abandoned him. I think if you push it, the courts will be sympathetic towards Dan.' Tess had no great faith in the courts, she just hoped to put Colette off, but without any success.

'Well, if conditions don't improve over there, I'll have no option but to fight Dan for custody. If anything should happen to Jackie, I'd never forgive myself. And Tess . . . remember you swore never to tell the truth about his birth.'

'I won't break my word, Colette, but I beg you to think hard before you do anything rash. You might be opening a big can of worms.'

'If that's how it goes, so be it. I'll keep in touch. Good night.'

'Good morning.'

Wide awake now, Tess decided to have a drink. There was some brandy left over from the wedding and she poured herself a little. Curled up on the settee she sipped at the fiery liquid and let her mind wander back over the last few years. Her mother and Dan deserved the happiness they shared. She couldn't let all that be ruined. She would just have to persuade Colette to leave well alone. Tess shuddered to think of the effect the truth would have on her mother, should it ever come out. Would Alice be able to live with the fact that Jackie was Dan's son? *Not* his grandson, as Tess had led them to believe all those years ago. If her mother had learned the truth then, would she have agreed to let Dan stay in their home, knowing he had betrayed her with Colette, his dead son's fiancée? Would she ever be able to forgive his treachery? Forgive Tess for deceiving her? Tess thought not. Both Dan and herself would get the full brunt of her mother's wrath. But then again, Colette would never admit that she had betrayed the man she had been betrothed to, with, of all people, his own father. Therefore, the truth would never be known unless Tess herself broke her solemn promise, and that she would never do.

So if Colette chose to fight for custody of her son through the courts, she could very well win her case. She was his biological mother after all! And no one else, bar Tess, knew that Dan was the biological father of the boy he had loved and reared as his own grandson since birth. Not even Dan himself, to her knowledge, was aware of this.

His son Jack had died in a motorcycle accident on his twenty-first birthday. Dan had bought him the bike for the special occasion, and therefore was devastated by grief and guilt. According to Colette – who was at the time engaged to Jack – she and Dan had sought comfort in each other that fateful night and things had got out of hand, leaving Colette pregnant. Apparently Dan, who had been quite intoxicated, had blanked the episode from his mind. Tess derided Colette when she heard this. She didn't think it possible that a man could do what he had done and be incognisant of the fact, no matter how drunk or grief-stricken he was. However, Colette convinced her that she believed Dan had no recollection of the act, and after some consideration Tess thought it feasible that in the circumstances this could actually have been the case.

The door opened and Theresa peered fearfully round it, rousing Tess from her depressing reverie. 'I thought I heard sounds down here. Couldn't you sleep?'

'Didn't you hear the phone ringing?'

A shake of the head. 'Who on earth would be calling at this unearthly hour?' Hope brightened her face. 'Was it anything to do with Bob?'

'No, it was Colette Burns.'

'What did she want?'

'She's worried about Jackie. She's talking about taking him to live in Vancouver with her.'

'Surely she can't do that.'

Tess sighed. 'I'm very much afraid she can.'

'I remember you bringing Jackie home from Carlingford, but I never did hear the ins and outs of it, Tess. It was none of my business anyhow. But I got the distinct impression that she had washed her hands of the child at birth, so surely she can't just waltz back into his life again and claim him. She hasn't been back all that often. Jackie hardly knows her.'

'Look, Theresa, I don't know the legal implications of it, but I do know the mother usually gets custody of the child, should it come to a legal wrangle. Especially in these circumstances, with Colette being comfortably off and able to take him away from all the misery and danger that surrounds us here.'

'It all seems so unfair,' Theresa lamented.

Tess sat up and straightened her shoulders. 'Right,

enough of that for now. We'll cross that bridge when we come to it.' She nodded towards the brandy bottle. 'I think you could just about manage to squeeze another one out of that, so sit down and join me and we'll forget all about our troubles for a while.'

They drank in companionable silence and eventually climbed the stairs to the sound of distant gunshots shattering the stillness outside. The gunfire continued throughout the rest of the night and they were both aware that a lot of the shots were now close at hand. God alone knew what awful news the morning would bring.

Wednesday dawned and they heard on the radio that all kinds of atrocities were reported to have taken place. There was, however, one bright aspect to the day. Some of the men arrested in the early hours of Monday were to be released, and the two girls waited impatiently for news of those who were to be freed. With no let-up in the shooting, they decided to stay at home for the day. When Bob appeared on their doorstep that morning he was a sight for sore eyes. He was unwashed and unshaved, his clothes crumpled and dirty, but he was greeted as if he were Richard Burton himself. Theresa hugged him close, while over her shoulder Tess anxiously examined his face and her heart went out to him. He looked drawn and haggard, and dark shadows under his eyes told of a lack of sleep.

'Are you all right, Bob?' Tess asked softly, and although she didn't know it, her eyes spoke volumes to him.

He nodded, then sniffed and confessed, 'I'm certainly not smelling of roses at the minute, that's for sure! Can I use your bathroom, please?'

'Of course you can. I'll run a bath for you.'

He gently released himself from Theresa's embrace. 'I'll need some fresh clothes, Theresa. Perhaps I should go up to your house and have a bath there?'

'No, no. As you've obviously guessed, I've been staying here with Tess. There'll be no hot water or fresh milk up in our house at the moment, so I'll nip back and get the clothes for you.' She hugged him again. 'It's great to have you back, love. I won't be too long.' Before he could raise an objection she had grabbed her coat and was out the door in a flash.

Bob's eyes locked with Tess's. She stood spellbound, longing to go to him, to offer him solace. At last she reluctantly broke free from his gaze. 'I'll get that bath running for you,' she mumbled.

'I know you're a hard girl, Tess, but I didn't realise just how hard. Were you not just a wee bit worried about me? Aren't you glad to see me?'

'You know I am!'

His arms stretched towards her and his eyes held a plea. Slowly she moved towards him, all the while cautioning herself not to let this happen, until his arms closed round her. It was heavenly to be held against him; to know he wanted her, even though he did smell a bit rancid. All her good resolutions evaporated and she raised her lips to his. He claimed them eagerly, clinging to her like a limpet and sucking all the will-power from her being, reducing her to a limp rag. In panic she tried to push him away.

He refused to release her. 'I need you, Tess. It was only the thought of you that kept me going these last two days. Please say you care . . . just a little.'

'You know I care. But we have been over all this before, Bob. Nothing has changed. There's no future for us. I wish there was but you're committed to Theresa and that's that. She loves you.'

'She'll meet someone else.'

'She doesn't want anyone else.' Tess at last managed to push herself free from his embrace. 'I'll run that bath now.'

She almost flew up the stairs to escape from her own desires. If Bob knew just how near she had come to giving in to his demands he would never stop pestering her until she eventually succumbed. She had to be strong. Theresa would be back shortly. It wouldn't do to be caught in a compromising situation. She was dismayed at these thoughts. Would she have allowed his advances to develop if her friend's return wasn't imminent? She would have to be very careful in future; she wanted him so much.

Bob followed her slowly. Both taps were running and she was leaving the bathroom as he reached the landing.

'I can't go on like this, Tess. I can't lead Theresa on a wild-goose chase any longer. I'll have to tell her that I've met someone else. If you won't have me, I'm going down south to live.'

She felt as if her heart would explode. 'And what about Theresa? You'll break her heart.'

'I can't possibly marry her feeling as I do about you. That would still break her heart. It wouldn't be fair on any of us.'

'But why move away?'

'There'd be no point in staying round here if you won't have me. Will you? If I break with Theresa will you be my girl?'

'You know I can't do that, Bob.'

'Then I'll settle down in Sligo. It's lovely down there and the people are very friendly and easy to get on with.'

'You've already got someone down there, haven't you?' she accused him, and was annoyed at the jealousy that was evident in her voice.

'No I haven't. But this might surprise you, Tess. Some women do find me attractive. Mind you, I've had a few offers, but when I was tempted to go out with them I thought of you. There was no point dating any of them if I stood a chance of having you. I've never felt this way about anyone else. I know we're meant for each other, but if you're so determined to block me out, I might as well date some other girl; get to know them. Who knows, in time I might even manage to get you out of my mind. If I stay here I'll never be able to do that. I'd always be looking out for you.'

It didn't surprise her in the slightest that women found him attractive. What did surprise her was how she had failed to notice this attraction sooner. She made no effort to hide her misery. 'If that's what you want, Bob.'

He gripped her roughly by the upper arms and shook her, such was his frustration. 'It's *not* what I want! But if you won't listen to reason, what else can I do? I'll have to get out of Belfast for good.'

Tess was saved from answering by the sound of the front door opening. 'I'm back.'

Theresa removed her coat and hung it on the hall-stand, then eagerly climbed the stairs. Tess met her at the top. 'Bob's in the bathroom. I'll go down and get the pan on for him. I'm sure he must be starving.'

'I'll scrub his back.' It was obvious that Theresa was over the moon at his return, her face one big beam and her voice light and airy. 'Oh, I'm so happy! I can't believe he's back so soon.'

'I'll phone around and see if I can find out anything about Tony.'

Theresa watched thoughtfully as her friend descended the stairs. So that was why Tess had been so uptight this past couple of days: she was worried about Tony Burke.

112

Did she really care for him in spite of all her denials?

Mrs Burke's quiet voice answered the phone. 'Hello.'

'It's Tess Maguire here, Mrs Burke. Is there any news of Tony?'

'Not yet, love, but I'm praying for him. The other two men lifted from this street are back home now.'

'Will you ask Tony to give me a ring when he comes home?'

'*If* he comes home. I'm at my wits' end, Tess. He's done nothing wrong, you know. Surely they can't hold him . . .' Her voice broke and Tess hastened to comfort her.

'He'll be home soon. Our friend Bob Dempsey has just arrived back.'

'Oh, I do hope so. I'll get him to ring you.'

Tess found that she couldn't stay in the house and cook breakfast for Bob as she had promised. She couldn't bear to think what he and Theresa might be getting up to upstairs, so she decided to go and open the shop. She would make a start on the wedding ensemble that had to be ready for the final fitting at the end of the month. Shouting up the stairs to let them know she was leaving, Tess, without waiting for a reply, slipped on her coat and left the house.

She and Theresa had made futile attempts to get going on the ensemble, but with the trauma of the past few days they had grabbed at any excuse for delaying the work. Now Tess set to with unnecessary vigour. It would keep her mind off Bob Dempsey and his threats to settle in Sligo. How would she be able to bear it?

It was approaching lunchtime when Theresa eventually walked into the shop. Tess finished serving a customer and followed her into the back room. Her friend seemed a bit subdued. Had Bob told her about his plans?

113

'I thought we weren't opening today?'

'I wanted to give you and Bob some time to your-selves,' Tess lied convincingly.

'I see you've cut out the flower-girl dress.'

'Yes. We need to get a start on these without any further delays. We're behind with them as it is. Perhaps, since you're here, you'll do the sewing while I'm cutting the others?'

'Good idea.' Theresa noisily sorted out the thread and lace she would need and without further ado settled down at her machine. Tess eyed her covertly. She definitely wasn't herself. Something must have happened between her and Bob. Had he carried out his threat?

'You seem very quiet. Is anything wrong?'

'I'm just so angry at the things people get away with.'

Tess relaxed. It wasn't Bob she was talking about. 'What do you mean?'

'You should see Bob's body.'

If only I were so lucky, Tess thought, bringing a fleeting smile to her face. It was soon wiped off as Theresa continued.

'You wouldn't believe the state he's in. He's a mass of black and blue bruises, so he is. You'd think he'd been run over by a trolley-bus he's so badly marked. Not his face, mind you! Oh no, they were crafty enough there. Just his body. God knows what permanent damage they've done to him.'

Tess stopped cutting and set down the large scissors; she didn't feel they were safe in her hands at the moment the way she was shaking. 'What do you mean?'

'I think he's been given a good hiding by those vicious bastards, but he won't talk about it. He just says he's all right. Says he's been very lucky, and I should see some of the other poor guys.'

Horrified at the thoughts invading her already troubled mind, Tess urged her friend, 'Go home and look after him, Theresa. Go on! I'll be all right here on my own.'

'It's okay. I gave him some aspirin. He's asleep now. I'm better down here working. It'll keep my mind occupied for a while. He wasn't even capable of . . .' She hesitated, colour flooding her face, then gestured feebly. 'And he's so embarrassed about it. You know what I mean.'

Tess was pleased at this revelation. In spite of immersing herself in her work, she had been tortured by vivid images of Theresa and Bob together in bed. At least if he moved to Sligo she wouldn't be bumping into him every weekend. Wouldn't have to watch him and Theresa cavorting about together. But what about Theresa? She would be heartbroken if Bob left and it would all be Tess's fault.

If only Bob hadn't kissed her she could have gone on pretending that she didn't care for him. But he had and she did! And could she blame him? Wasn't I crying out for it? she thought distractedly. Perhaps it was fate and she and Bob were meant for each other. But Theresa would always be there – the stumbling block. There was no way Tess could hurt her friend. She knew what it felt like to be betrayed. Hadn't Jack Thompson ditched her when Colette Burns appeared on the scene?

The shooting and bombings continued throughout the week. The Taoiseach, Jack Lynch, had instructed the army authorities to make ready for an influx of refugees across the border, and it was estimated that thousands of people were seeking refuge there and in other safe enclaves within the city itself.

In spite of Tess's pleas, Alice refused to delay any longer in Carlingford. She and Dan returned to Belfast on Friday afternoon as planned, bringing young Jackie with them.

Tess waited until after they'd had their tea and Jackie was settled in bed before telling them about Colette's phone call. To say Dan was incensed when he heard about Colette's plans to come for Jackie would be putting it mildly. He paced the living room ranting and roaring like a wounded lion. 'Who the hell does she think she is? Eh? Does she take me for a bloody eejit or something?'

Seeking to ease the tension, Tess reminded him gently, 'She *is* Jackie's mother.' All in vain.

'How can you sit there and say that? She's never been a mother to him,' he snarled. 'And you know that for a damned fact!'

'She did give birth to him, and that counts for a lot in the eyes of the law.'

'Don't make me laugh. If she had wanted the child at all, she would have taken him to Vancouver with her in the first place. Wouldn't she? Other women have reared kids on their own.' He swung round to face Alice. 'What do you think of all this?'

Taken by surprise, Alice was flustered. She didn't want to upset Dan more than he was already. His face was blood red and his eyes bulged as if about to pop out of their sockets. She had never seen him so angry. Fearing a heart attack she dithered. Her diffidence only made matters worse.

'Surely you don't think I should give our wee Jackie up. Do you?'

After a pause, during which time Dan stood hands on hips glaring at her, Alice decided she must tell the truth as she saw it. 'I think she has every right to want her

116

child to be safe. I'd feel exactly the same in her position.'

'Huh! You wouldn't leave your child in the first place.'

'No. But then everybody's different.'

'That's no excuse. I'd never forgive a woman for abandoning her child. No half-decent mother would do it.' He continued prowling restlessly about the room clenching and unclenching his large hands. 'No matter what it costs, I'll fight her for custody. I will, you know! If it takes every penny I've got, I'll fight her to the bitter end.'

'If things die down she probably won't carry out her threat,' Tess intervened optimistically. 'Let's just wait and see what happens.'

'If you really think things are going to quieten down here after all those shootings and bombings, you've another think coming, girl. I never imagined you could be so daft.'

'Thanks! Thanks a bunch. I didn't realise you thought so highly of me.'

Dan threw his hands in the air. 'Ah, Tess. No offence meant. You know what I mean, don't you? Why, if that wee girl was standing in front of me at this very minute, I think I'd strangle her with these bare hands.'

With a sigh, Tess confessed, 'Yes. I know what you mean, Dan.'

Still seething with rage, he left the room. Tess eyed her mother. 'What do you really think about all this?'

A frown puckering her brow, Alice said, 'You've lost me, Tess. What do you mean?'

'I don't know how to put this . . . but would it not be better all round if Colette took Jackie to Canada, where he'd be safe? It would be for the child's own good.'

Alice looked bewildered. 'I still don't understand. Are

117

you insinuating that I don't love Jackie enough? That I'd be glad if he went to live in Canada?'

'No, Mam, no! What I'm trying to say is . . . Jackie would be safer and have a brighter future if Colette got her way. He's young enough to settle over there, and in time forget about life here, and you and Dan would have some years to yourselves. You're not getting any younger, you know. You deserve some time together.'

'Are you implying that Jackie would be happier with Colette and that Dan and I are too old to look after him?'

Tess shook her head in frustration. 'To be truthful, I don't know what I'm trying to say. I'm as confused as you. I just think it's a good opportunity if you wanted some time alone with Dan. You've done your bit. Given the child a good start in life. He'll know he's loved by you.'

'No he won't! He'll think we've abandoned him, poor wee soul. He's too young to understand what's going on. Better to wait until he's older and can choose for himself. That's what I say!'

'What if anything happens to him meanwhile? What if he's killed or maimed? Will you be able to live with that? There are a lot of people out there who'd give their eyeteeth to send their children somewhere safe.'

'You're wrong there! This isn't like during the war, Tess, when city children were evacuated to the country for a while. If Jackie goes to Canada we might never see him again, and he'd soon forget us. That, Tess, would be the death of me and Dan.'

'Ah, now, Mam, Colette's not that heartless. You'd have access to Jackie.'

'How do you know that? Eh? She gave her child up at birth. If that's not heartless, I don't know what is.

Besides, it's not just across the Channel you're talking about, Tess. It's halfway round the world as far as we're concerned. Where would we get the money to fly back and forth to Canada?'

Tess sighed dejectedly. 'It was just a thought, Mam.'

'Well for goodness' sake don't say anything like that in front of Dan. There's no way he'd give up that child without a fight. And I must say I agree with him. We'd be lost without Jackie. Our whole world revolves round him.'

Tess shrugged. 'It was only a suggestion. Both of you have done a great job bringing him up. He's a lovely, well-mannered wee boy and you can be very proud of him.'

'Oh, so you admit we've done a good job, eh?'

'Of course, Mam. Did I ever say otherwise?'

'Then why do you want us to hand him over to Colette?'

'I don't! I just think you mightn't have any other choice. I suppose I'm just trying to prepare you for the worst scenario. Colette's his natural mother! That will count for a lot if it comes to the crunch. But then, who knows? Perhaps Dan will talk her into changing her mind.'

Families refused to pay rent and rates in protest against internment, and the revenue lost to the council ran into tens of thousands of pounds. The shootings continued and by the end of August a total of thirty-five people had been killed.

Towards the beginning of September Colette phoned without any warning and announced that she had booked a flight to Belfast and would be accompanied by her fiancé. When Tess offered to put them up she said that they had already booked into a hotel and would be in touch when they arrived in the city. She obviously meant to keep all this businesslike and above board.

Tess relayed this message to Dan and her mother. Tight-lipped, Dan said, 'Right! Tomorrow I'll go see a solicitor and find out where I stand.'

Having made an appointment, and sure that they would receive advice in their favour, Dan and Alice set off in good spirits the following morning, saying that they would call into the shop on their way back to let Tess know the outcome of the meeting.

It was lunchtime when they trooped despondently into the shop. One look at Dan's face and Tess guessed that the news was bad. Tentatively she asked, 'Well, how did it go?'

'Not too good, I'm afraid. Mr Morrison thinks we'll have one hell of a fight on our hands. His advice is to come to some arrangement with Colette.'

'Well, that sounds like good advice.'

'Good advice my ass. How often do you think we'd see the child? Once in a blue moon, if we're lucky.'

'What do you intend doing then?'

'I'll get a second opinion. That's what I'll do!'

Behind Dan's back, Alice rolled her eyes at Tess and confessed, 'Mr Morrison says that with the way things are here at the moment, the court will no doubt give priority to the child's mother since she can take him away from the troubles. He said he would feel guilty taking our money to fight a losing battle in court.'

'We'll soon see about that. Come on, Alice. Let's go back to the house. I want to phone around and see if I can find another solicitor. See you later, Tess.'

Theresa had been listening to their conversation and when Tess entered the workroom she said gently, 'Mr

120

Morrison must be a decent man. Some of those solicitors would string Dan along and take him for all he's got.'

'That's exactly what I was thinking.' Tess shrugged in despair. 'Obviously Dan doesn't see it that way.'

'Poor Dan. He's determined to lose a lot of money as well as Jackie.'

'It's not fair on my poor old mam, so it's not – piggy in the middle – but she'll back Dan to the hilt.'

'Perhaps Colette will see reason.'

Tess laughed aloud. 'You sound as dubious as I feel.'

Tess had been thinking that Theresa looked happier than she had for some time. Bob had cried off coming home the previous weekend. Now Tess questioned her. 'You look quite pleased with yourself, girl. Can I take it Bob will be home this weekend?'

'Yes. Yes, he is. I can't wait. It seems so long since I last saw him. I hope he doesn't make a habit of staying in Sligo at weekends.'

A warm glow flared up in Tess's heart. She was going to see Bob! Albeit it not as much as Theresa would. Still, one had to be thankful for small mercies. Her heart thumped and her pulse raced. Roll on Saturday.

5

Dan made an appointment to see another solicitor, Mr Mortimer Jr. from the law firm Mortimer, Ratcliffe and Mortimer. Mr Mortimer agreed to accompany Dan to meet Colette and her lawyer when she came over from Canada. He emphasised that the mother usually had priority in custodial cases, unless it could be proven that she was unfit, through one reason or another, to look after a child. He didn't think this would be the case here. The powers that be would agree that the boy would be better off in Canada with his mother than remaining any longer in riot-torn Belfast. Nevertheless, he jotted down all the details and said he would look into Colette's background and be prepared to take on Dan's case if he thought it worthwhile. Satisfied that wheels were in motion, Dan was quietly confident as he prepared to await the summons from Colette's lawyer.

Colette, however, took them totally unawares. Without further ado she arrived on their doorstep. It was Saturday afternoon, and having closed the shop early, Tess had the house to herself. She answered the knock and was somewhat surprised and very impressed by what she saw.

Colette looked stunning in a figure-hugging cream suit. Her dark hair, sculpted to her head, gleamed ebony in the sunlight and her Mona Lisa face was perfectly made up. She was a couple of years younger than Tess but looked far more mature and self-assured.

'Colette! Why, you look wonderful!' Tess cried, genuine in her praise. She put out a hand and drew her friend inside. 'You should have let us know you were arriving today. I'd have baked a cake,' she joked.

'Actually, we got here yesterday.'

'Oh . . . I see.' This sounded ominous. Tess eyed the gentleman who entered on Colette's heels. He was immaculately dressed in a dark serge suit, crisp white shirt with a pale yellow tie, and a pair of black shoes so shiny you could probably see your reflection in them. This handsome middle-aged man must surely be her solicitor, Tess mused. Where then was the boyfriend?

They paused in the hallway and with a flick of the hand towards her companion Colette made the introductions. 'This is Lesley O'Malley, my fiancé. Les, meet my dear friend Tess Maguire.'

Tess was so surprised she gasped aloud, 'Your *fiancé*?'

The man smiled slightly and extended his hand to clasp hers. 'I'm very pleased to meet you, Tess. You look surprised and I don't blame you. I'll never be able to fathom what Colette sees in me. I'm a very lucky man.'

Colour flooded Tess's face and she hastened to make amends. 'I'm so sorry. I didn't mean any disrespect. Come into the sitting room.' She led the way, saying over her shoulder, 'Mam and Dan have taken Jackie to the Botanic Gardens and museum. They've been gone quite a while now so they shouldn't be much longer. Take a seat, please. Can I offer you a cup of tea? Or perhaps you'd prefer coffee?'

'Tea would be nice.' Colette smiled at Les. 'Les loves the tea over here.'

'That's nice to hear. Would you like a sandwich, or some biscuits?'

'No thank you. We've already had lunch. A cup of tea will be fine.'

'If you'll excuse me, I'll put the kettle on.' Tess gratefully escaped to the kitchen, an amused Colette close on her heels.

'That man must think me awful, Colette. I honestly didn't mean to be rude,' Tess apologised. 'I naturally expected your fiancé to be much younger.' Her hands spread palm up in frustration. 'There I go again. That's another thing I shouldn't have said. I just don't know when to keep my big trap shut.'

Colette laughed at her embarrassment. 'You're only speaking the truth. He *is* older than me, but the silver hair makes him look older than he really is. It does make him very handsome and distinguished-looking, though . . . don't you agree?' she parried.

Tess nodded and grinned. 'Yes, I'll grant you that, he is very attractive. And O'Malley? He must surely have Irish connections.'

'Irish grandfather, French grandmother.'

'Why wasn't he snapped up before you met him?'

'He was when he was younger,' Colette assured her. 'Now he's a widower.' She changed the subject. 'Tell me something, Tess, does Dan have a lawyer, or solicitor as they are called over here?'

'As far as I know he has.'

'I saw Mr McIlroy yesterday. Remember him? The elderly solicitor who looked after my grannie's affairs?' Tess nodded, and Colette continued. 'He invested some of my money as well and has done very well for me these past few years. I have the utmost confidence in him.'

Tess nodded. 'Yes, I remember, you thought a lot of him.'

'Well, he has advised me that it would be better for all concerned to settle this amicably between ourselves, out of court.'

'That's exactly what I've been telling Dan. But he won't listen to reason.'

'I'll just have to try and change his mind then, won't I? Meanwhile, what do you think of Les? As well as being handsome, that is.'

'Ah come on now, Colette. I've only just met the man. I know nothing whatsoever about him.'

'He's forty-two, but you see, I'll be safe with him, Tess. Young men make me feel uncomfortable and insecure.'

Safe? Tess could hardly believe her ears. Not one word about love. Completely mystified, she asked, 'Do you love him?'

'Of course I do! There are different kinds of love, Tess. I don't think I'll ever get over Jack Thompson. He was my first love. My only true love.'

Tess shrugged. She was remembering that Colette's father had walked out on her and her mother when she was still a child. Was her friend looking for a father figure? Someone who could be both husband and father? Was that why, in her grief, she had succumbed to Dan's drunken passion? She pushed these unsavoury thoughts from her mind. 'You're right, of course, Colette. Besides, it's none of my business. Everybody to their own taste.'

'As I said, Les is a widower. He and his wife were very kind to me when I first arrived in Vancouver. Carol, his wife, took me under her wing and introduced me into their circle of friends. Sadly, she died in a car crash two years ago. Les was driving at the time and blamed himself for her death. It was a winter's night with a lot of ice on the road and he lost control of the car. He was inconsolable. The shock turned his hair silver overnight. He turned to me for comfort and we became very close. I was happy to say yes when he asked me to marry him. His wife couldn't have children, you see, so he'll be only too delighted to adopt a lovely little boy like Jackie.'

'Obviously that bit of comforting didn't lead to a pregnancy, more's the pity, or you wouldn't be over here now looking for Jackie, upsetting my mother's and Dan's peace of mind,' Tess said bitterly. She was immediately ashamed of her outburst but she couldn't help reminding Colette of how Jackie had been conceived and who his real father was.

Colette drew back in dismay. 'That was below the belt, Tess. You know how it was back then.'

'I'm sorry.' Tess flapped her hands in regret. 'I suppose it's just my way of reminding you who Jackie's father is. Does Les know?'

'No. You're the only one who knows my guilty secret. If everything goes according to plan and we marry, I shall tell Les the truth before he adopts Jackie.'

'How can you be sure he'll be sympathetic towards you?'

'He loves me.' The words came out simply but with conviction.

'Lucky you. Does he not deserve some love in return?'

Colette smiled. 'You're the only one I've ever let close to me, Tess. You alone know all about me, so I forgive this intrusion into my private life. As I've already said, there are different kinds of love. I care deeply for Les. I'll be a good wife to him. What about you? Have you let Tony wear you down yet?'

Tess shook her head and laughed at her friend's change of subject. 'No. No chance of that. He was one of those lifted during the internment raids and then released, you know?' At Colette's shake of the head she continued, 'He was one of the lucky ones. So many are still locked up. I've seen very little of him lately. He seemed to be serious about another girl for a while there, but internment changed him. As you already know, he's always been very quiet. Internment made him even more withdrawn. As far as I know it's all over between him and this girl. But he is not the one for me, you know. We're just good friends.' Tess lifted the tea tray and hesitated. 'It must be nearly eighteen months since you were last here, so just remember that Jackie may not recognise you,' she warned Colette. 'Well then, let's go keep Les company or he'll think we've deserted him.'

Tess was surprised when a few minutes later Theresa and Bob called in. She had expected Theresa to keep Bob to herself over the weekend. If the positions were reversed, she certainly would not have shared him. After introductions had been made, Tess excused herself. 'I'd better put the kettle on again. My friends will entertain you.'

Glad to get away from the unsettling effect Bob's presence was, as usual, having on her, Tess retired to the kitchen, her thoughts focusing on him and how well he looked in his light grey suit. Gone was the tension that had hung over him like a dark cloud in the early days after detention. It was good to see him looking more relaxed; more like his old self. She missed him keenly and had begun to despair of ever seeing anything of him over the weekend, so was delighted that they had unexpectedly dropped in. Just the sight of him was enough to set her nerve-ends tingling. To her delight, he joined her in the kitchen. Standing close behind her at the table as she cut some of his favourite Dundee cake he said softly, 'Have you missed me at all?'

'Please, Bob. Not now. Don't get me all agitated,' she warned. 'I've people out there to entertain.'

'Ah, so I can agitate you? I'm glad to hear that.'

'You know you can.' The longing she felt for him was all too evident in her voice and eyes.

He wasn't even touching her but she felt as if he was caressing her; his breath fanning her hair was sending a thrill down her spine. A strangled moan of pleasure and longing escaped her lips and she willed him to move away before she lost all self-control.

Instead he shortened the slight distance between them until he was actually brushing against her. Turning, she pushed him roughly away. 'Stop it! Do you hear me? Stop it at once!'

'Stop what?' he enquired innocently, a teasing smile on his face. 'I haven't done anything.'

'You know very well what I mean.'

Footsteps in the hall hastened her to find sanctuary in front of the stove, her back towards the door. Pulling a chair away from the table Bob sat down. It was Colette who entered the kitchen.

'Can I use your bathroom, Tess?'

Tess answered without looking round, giving her complete attention to spooning tea into the pot. 'Of course you can. You know where it is.'

'Theresa and Les are getting on like a house on fire in there. I've never known him to relax with a stranger so quickly. He's inclined to be a bit on the reserved side. I won't pee long,' Colette quipped and laughing at her own wit, left the room.

Bob was on his feet the second Colette left. His arms

circled Tess and she was lost. Twisting in his embrace she pressed close and let him savage her lips. But just for a minute. Only a minute. Common sense quickly intervened and she angrily pushed him away. 'Don't do this. Do you hear me? It's not fair.'

'We can't go on like this, Tess.'

'Do you think I don't know that? Somebody is bound to catch on.'

Pleased at this admission, Bob reached for her again. 'To hear you, anyone would think we were having an illicit affair.'

She eluded him just in time. The door opened and Colette said, 'Can I be of any help?' One look at them and she backed out of the kitchen in embarrassment. 'Oh! I beg your pardon. Please forgive me. I'm sorry for the intrusion.' She retreated, hurriedly closing the door behind her.

Tess gaped at Bob in dismay. 'Now look what you've done!' Her voice was shrill with alarm.

'We weren't doing anything!'

'Obviously Colette seemed to think otherwise,' Tess lamented. 'Oh, why can't you behave yourself?'

'She won't say anything.'

'How do you know? You've only just met the girl and I'll have you know, she's Jackie's mother.'

'I guessed as much.' He sighed. 'Theresa was saying something about her wanting to take him back to Canada. I still can't see why you're so worried. After all, she's hardly likely to let the cat out of the bag. Why should she?'

'Maybe I'm just over-reacting,' Tess admitted. 'Bring that tray in,' she ordered. 'And behave yourself! Or I'm warning you, there'll be wigs on the green.'

*   *   *

Dan and Alice arrived home as they were finishing tea. As was his custom, Jackie rushed ahead of them into the sitting room to tell Tess all about his adventures. He came to an abrupt halt when he saw the strangers and started backing away. Dan stood in the sitting-room doorway and eyed Colette sternly and Alice peered round him to see what was wrong. Without a word, Jackie slowly retreated and squeezed past his grandfather until he was cowering behind him, tugging at his coat-tail.

Pushing past her husband Alice broke the awkward silence. 'Hello, Colette. This is a pleasant surprise. How are you?' Going to Colette she kissed her on the cheek in welcome, making up for Dan's lack of hospitality.

'I'm fine, Mrs Maguire.' Her face broke into a broad smile. 'Oh, excuse me, it's Mrs Thompson now, isn't it? Congratulations.' Her glance included them both. 'What about yourself, how are you keeping?'

'Not too bad, except this business regarding Jackie is very disturbing to us all.' Alice looked at Les and raised an enquiring brow.

Quickly, Colette made the introductions and, to her credit, although she had – like her daughter – jumped to the wrong conclusion and surmised that he must be her solicitor, Alice welcomed Les without batting an eyelid. She then took Jackie by the hand and drew him gently forward. 'Don't you remember your mummy, love? She's come all the way from Canada to see you.' The child just snatched his hand away and cowered against his grandfather.

Dan, who had remained tight-lipped and inflexible, with just a nod in Les's direction, gathered the boy to him and said, 'I see you've had tea, so let's get down to business, shall we? Is this gentleman also your solicitor?'

So far they had kept all knowledge of Colette's visit

and the reason for it from Jackie, and now Tess interrupted. 'I have to go down to the shops. Will you come with me, Jackie, and you can tell me all about what you saw at the museum while I get something for your tea?' To her relief he agreed without the usual griping. He disliked going to the shops but Tess wasn't really surprised. She knew he wanted to get away from his mother. Surely Colette could see the effect she was having on the child.

As they left the house, Tess hoped that the presence of Theresa and Bob would keep a civil tongue in Dan's head.

She by-passed the shops. There was always something in the house for the child's tea. That had just been her excuse to get Jackie out. She didn't like being anywhere near the police barracks, especially when Jackie was with her. This area of the road looked like a blitzed site with windows in some of the shops and houses still boarded up, the residents loath to get them glazed until things quietened somewhat. Who could blame Colette for wanting to take Jackie away from all this?

They crossed the road at the Falls junction and headed for Dunville Park. It was a warm day and sitting on a bench they watched children skipping and playing in the now defunct fountain.

Wrapped in her own troubled thoughts, Tess hadn't realised just how quiet Jackie had become, until a small hand thrust into hers gained her attention.

'What's wrong, love?'

Eyes brimming with tears he said, 'Sure you won't let my mam take me away, Auntie Tess?'

Tess gathered him close. Poor wee soul. In spite of all their good endeavours to keep him in the dark, he had figured out in his own little mind what was going on and was worrying himself sick.

'What do you mean, love?'

'She wants to take me far away to live with her, doesn't she? I heard Grandad and Grannie talking.'

'She *is* your mother, Jackie, and she worries about you living here with all this shooting and bombing going on.'

'I don't care! I don't want to go with her. I want to stay with you and Grandad and Grannie. I love you. I don't like her!'

'Ah, now, she loves you, Jackie, and Canada is a wonderful place. You'd soon settle down and get to like it over there. You'd even get to see real Mounties.'

He pulled away from her. 'No! I won't go with her. Do you hear me? I won't go.'

'Your grandad is going to try and arrange for you to stay here, Jackie, but he mightn't be able to get permission.'

Big tears spilled over and ran down his face. Tess found herself crying in sympathy with him. 'There, love, please don't cry. We'll just have to wait and see what happens. Besides, if you do have to go, we'll visit each other. Won't that be great fun? You will be able to show me all the sights of Vancouver, won't you?'

'No!' he howled. 'I won't go! I don't want to go.' And he charged off across the park with a distracted Tess in hot pursuit.

Back at the house there was no sign of Alice or Dan. It was Colette who quietly put Tess in the picture.

'I'm afraid we couldn't come to any sort of agreement, but I didn't want to leave without seeing Jackie. Dan wants us to discuss the situation with our solicitors present, get their advice. We've arranged a meeting with them for Tuesday morning.'

'I'm very sad to hear that.'

'Can you blame me, Tess? I nearly died when I saw the state of that road out there. It was bad enough seeing it on TV over in Vancouver, but to actually witness it with my very own eyes was terrifying. Les felt the same. I'm even more determined than ever to take Jackie away.'

Jackie had a tight grip on Tess's skirt. Colette knelt in front of him but refrained from touching him, afraid of outright rejection. 'Any chance of a big hug for your mammy, Jackie?'

Jackie pressed closer still to Tess. Bending down, Tess said softly, 'Give your mother a hug, Jackie. She has to go now.'

At the realisation that he wasn't expected to go with Colette, Jackie inched cautiously forward. Colette put her arms round him and whispered. 'I love you, son.' Kissing the top of his head she released her hold on him and rose to face Tess. 'We'll have to go now. Perhaps I'll see you on Tuesday, Tess?'

'More than likely.'

Theresa and Bob, who had obviously sought refuge in the kitchen during the debate, had come into the room and stood talking quietly in the background. Now Theresa came forward. 'Tess, Colette is meeting the girls she used to work with tonight for a drink. Les doesn't want to go out with a crowd of strange women and I thought that you and he could come out with me and Bob. We could take him to Romano's. That is . . .' She turned apologetically to Les. 'Forgive me for being so presumptuous. Would you like to join us?'

'I'd be delighted, if that's all right with you, Colette?'

Colette's strained face relaxed slightly. 'Thank you, Theresa. You've just taken a load off my mind. I was feeling a bit guilty about leaving Les on his own in a strange city.'

'That's settled then. Where shall we meet?' Bob asked quickly, before Tess could think up some excuse not to go.

Colette answered him. 'Would you three like to come over to our hotel and have a meal with us first? I'm not meeting the girls until nine o'clock.'

'That would be great!' Theresa cried. 'Let's get a move on, Bob. I've a lot to do.'

Tess prepared for her night out with trepidation. She knew that if they went to Romano's, Bob would be sure to dance with her. Much as she longed to be close to him, she knew there would be no great pleasure in this; she would be a bundle of nerves all evening, afraid someone would twig how she felt about him. She was aware that they were now under Colette's scrutiny, having noticed her covert glances since the episode in the kitchen. Her friend must think that she was carrying on with Bob behind Theresa's back.

Tess held her hands out straight in front of her; they trembled so much that she gave them a vigorous shake. This would have to stop! Her mind latched on to her recent thoughts regarding Tony Burke. His romance with Geraldine Harris had obviously petered out, and he had intimated that he was available again should she ever need him as a stand-in partner. Perhaps if she tried hard enough she would be able to cultivate some emotion towards him.

She decided it was time she developed that relationship. She had felt great passion with Jack Thompson, to no avail; just abject misery when he had met and fallen for Colette Burns. Then the passion she had felt for and had thought was returned from Dominic Sullivan had been all in her imagination; he had fallen in love with her best friend, Agnes Quinn. Wasn't it on the cards that the same thing could happen where Bob Dempsey was concerned? How could it be otherwise with Theresa to consider? She remembered Colette's words about Les: 'I'll be safe with him.' Perhaps Colette had the right idea after all. Maybe it would be better to feel *safe*. She would be secure with Tony. No great explosions of passion there, but then again, no great depths of despair either, just a warm, cosy companionship.

Yes! It was time she woke up to the fact that passion and excitement were not meant for her. Her mother was right, she read too many romantic magazines. Tony Burke would be the ideal partner. Everybody thought so, so why not give it her best shot? The next time she saw Tony she would ask him to take her out somewhere or other; get the relationship moving. With this decision she felt at peace within herself.

The serenity lasted until Bob and Theresa called to collect her, and then everything flew out the window. Just looking at Bob made her all agitated and nervous. Did she want to go through life like this? A nervous wreck; not in control of her own life? No! This would definitely have to stop, she silently vowed. Tony Burke was the man for her. Unwittingly, she gave Bob a look of such venom he actually stepped back in alarm. Startled, Tess glanced at Theresa, afraid to see her reaction. As usual, her friend didn't notice anything amiss. Was she just thick or something? There were times when she thought Theresa didn't deserve Bob.

This was the first real outing since Bob's release from internment and Theresa was bubbling with happiness and excitement. 'I'm really looking forward to this evening. We deserve a night out, so we do. What do you think, Tess?'

'Well, I agree, but I can't help thinking we're going out to enjoy ourselves whilst those poor men are still stuck behind bars.'

Theresa's face dropped, her happiness diminished like a deflated balloon. 'I thought you'd be the first to say that us sitting at home wouldn't be of any benefit to them, Tess Maguire. There's no pleasing you, so there isn't.'

Immediately, Tess apologised. 'I'm sorry, I don't mean to be a wet blanket. It's all this worry about Jackie. Perhaps I should just stay at home in case I spoil the evening,' she ventured.

Dan and Alice were supposed to be watching TV in the living room, but were obviously eavesdropping on their conversation. Her mother's voice reached her. 'You'll do no such thing, girl! You'll go out and enjoy yourself. Do you hear me? Sitting here won't change anything.' Her voice rose still higher. 'Bob?'

'Yes, Mrs Thompson?'

'Please make sure Tess enjoys herself.'

'I will indeed. Here's our taxi now. Good night all. See you next weekend.'

Les and Colette had booked into the Stormont Hotel on the Upper Newtownards Road. They were waiting to welcome their guests in the cocktail bar and soon they were all drinking and chatting away while awaiting a summons to the restaurant. The better she came to know him, the more Tess agreed with Colette that Les was a lovely man, polite and unpretentious. Colette was a very lucky girl, she mused. And, she reminded herself determinedly, Tony was also a fine upstanding gentleman.

The meal was delicious; everyone voiced their satisfaction. Afterwards they had coffee in the lounge. Colette sat sipping hers, one eye on the clock.

'Look, I'll have to be going soon. I'd better ring for a cab now or I'll be late.' She got to her feet, but with a raised hand Bob stayed her.

'Why don't we share a taxi?' he suggested. 'We can drop you off on the way to Romano's.'

'I don't want to rush you, Bob. You see, I really ought to be leaving now.'

'No problem.' Bob drained his cup and looked expectantly at the others. They followed suit. Rising to his feet, he headed for the reception desk to ask them to phone for a taxi.

'Tell them we'll need a six-seater,' Tess reminded him.

They all piled out of the taxi at Castle Junction. Colette's friends were already there waiting for her. The others had decided to continue the short distance to Romano's on foot. Colette reached up and kissed Les and with a wave of farewell hurried across the road. They watched her until she joined her friends and with a final wave towards them headed down in the direction of High Street. They were going to a bar they used to frequent on Cornmarket.

Les watched her go with a fond look on his face. 'She's a wonderful person, you know.'

He dropped behind Bob and Theresa walking up Castle Street. Tess fell into step with him and was quick to agree. 'I know she is.'

'I think she has every chance of getting custody of the boy.'

'So do I,' Tess agreed. 'The mother always seems to win in these cases unless she's unfit to look after the child, and Colette has everything going for her in that department.'

'It's all such a shame. Can't you persuade Dan to come to some agreement and save himself a lot of money and grief?'

A sad shake of the head. 'He won't listen to reason. And remember, Jackie doesn't want to go. That will be in Dan's favour.'

'He's a bit young for his opinion to hold any sway. It's a pity that Dan won't see reason.'

They turned the corner at Queen Street and Theresa greeted them gaily. 'Come on, you two slow-coaches. I was beginning to think you'd run off together.'

The girls handed their coats to the cloakroom attendant, got their tickets and joined the men in the dance hall. Les eyed the moving mass of bodies in surprise. 'It's a bit packed, isn't it? Are they always this keen over here?'

'It's like this most weekends. And yes, they're always this keen. Do you dance, Les?'

'A little, if there's enough room. Let's find out, shall we?' He made a gesture towards the dance floor with his hand and smiled. 'After you.' Tess preceded him on to the dance floor. It was a quickstep, and taking her in his arms he swung her expertly in and out of the couples, some dancing and some slouching across the floor. Not a great ballroom dancer herself, Tess was pleasurably surprised and forgetting everything else surrendered herself to the beat of the music and the guidance of his steps. He didn't put one foot wrong, and she sighed with disappointment when the music ended. He drew her to a halt near Bob and Theresa, who had been watching them in amazement.

Les bowed slightly. 'Thank you very much, Tess. I really enjoyed that.'

She beamed at him. 'Me too.'

138

A waltz was announced and Les turned his attention to Theresa. 'May I have the pleasure?'

With a nod she entered his arms and was whisked away. Bob looked at Tess and scratched his head. 'Les will be a hard act to follow, mind you. Do you think you could bear to moody round the floor with me?'

Eyes glued to his, she warned, 'We would be better not, you know.'

'Well then, let's find some dark corner where we can sit and talk.'

'Tut! Bob, what am I going to do with you?'

'I could suggest a few things, but we would need to be somewhere a lot more private than here, and I don't think for one moment you'd agree to that.'

She grabbed his tie and pulled him on to the dance floor. 'Come on. At the moment this is the better of two evils.'

Clasping her close to his chest, Bob was so quiet that after some moments she glanced up at him. Head bent, he was gazing down at her, eyes almost closed.

'What are you looking at?'

'I'm just thinking how beautiful you are, Tess Maguire,' he said sincerely.

She blushed fiercely and laughed aloud. 'Now I know you're having me on.'

'Beauty is in the eye of the beholder and I think you're beautiful. And . . . I know you're a kind and generous woman. I can't believe there was a time when I actually hated the very sight of you. I must have been off my rocker.' He pulled her closer still and brushed the top of her head with his lips. 'I love you.'

She looked up at him, eyes aglow. 'Oh, Bob . . .' Words trembled on the edge of her tongue but she bit them back.

'Say it. Go on! Admit you love me.'

She shook her head. 'Don't be silly. You're imagining things.'

'If you say so.'

They danced the remainder of the waltz in silence and it was with some reluctance that she withdrew from the comfort of his arms.

They were all determined that Les should enjoy himself, and in spite of the sound of a bomb exploding not too far away, bringing anxious looks all round, the moment passed, and the evening was a success. After the last dance they left the hall and lingered outside chatting. Les thanked them profusely and left in a taxi to return to his hotel.

'Do you girls want to wait for another taxi, or walk home?'

'It's a lovely evening. I'd prefer to walk if you're up to it, Bob. Remember you've an early start in the morning.' Theresa confided in Tess, 'Bob has to get back to Sligo tomorrow morning. There's a big rush on to get the job finished on time and ensure the men get their bonuses.'

'Oh, I'm a healthy young man! I'll still be up with the lark. Is that all right with you then, Tess?' Bob asked anxiously.

Tess nodded her willingness, and she and Theresa linked their arms through Bob's and started off up Castle Street. 'All that dancing has given me an appetite. Does anyone fancy a fish supper?' he asked.

'I could never say no to a nice bit of fish,' Tess admitted. 'But will anywhere be open this late?'

'I imagine so. This is when they make their money, when all the entertainment places are closing. We'll soon find out.'

They hadn't gone far when they found a chippie open. The sit-down area was packed, so Bob bought three fish suppers to eat on the way home. All her good resolutions regarding Tony forgotten, Tess was bursting with happiness, pretending in her mind that Bob was her date and Theresa the gooseberry. They dallied at her doorstep and she invited them in for a cup of tea; Bob graciously accepted, but Theresa declined. Grabbing Bob's hand, she reminded Tess that he had to be up early in the morning, and that they had a lot of catching up to do and needed some precious time alone together.

Tears filled Tess's eyes as reality trespassed into her fantasy world and her happiness crumbled. She turned blindly away to hide them. Bob gently released himself from Theresa's clasp and mounted the steps to Tess's side. 'It looks like everyone is asleep. Let me see you safely indoors.' He took the key from her shaking hands and opened the door, ushering her inside. A glance over his shoulder showed that Theresa had elected to walk slowly on up the road, unaware of what was going on. Pushing the door to with his foot, Bob gathered Tess close. She clung to him, the tears streaming down her face. Oblivious to the fact that Alice or Dan might at any moment appear on the scene, he devoured her mouth and neck, drawing the breath from her body. There in the warm darkness of the hall, tears pouring down her cheeks, she mutely offered him her all.

Reluctantly putting her gently from him, he said, 'One of these days I'll make you mine. That's a promise, Tess Maguire. You remember that!' With one last bruising kiss he left her breathless and gasping for more. If things continued the way they were she had no doubt that one day he would indeed make her his. And for once thoughts of Theresa didn't trouble her mind one iota. She had come to the conclusion that Theresa was either blind or just hadn't a clue what was going on around her!

Sleep eluded Tess for some time as she tossed and turned, torturing herself with thoughts of Bob and Theresa together. At last, as dawn was pushing skeletal fingers of light through the slight gap in the thick curtains, she drifted off into an uneasy slumber. The shrill tones of the phone woke her. A quick glance showed her it was eight o'clock. She had forgotten to set the alarm.

Grabbing her dressing gown she hurriedly descended the stairs. 'Hello.'

'Tess? It's Les here. I'm so sorry to disturb you this early. Colette didn't come home last night and I'm worried stiff. I don't know what to do.'

All kind of ideas raced through Tess's mind. 'Does the hotel lock the front door at any particular time? Could she have been too late and gone home with one of her friends?'

'I don't know, but she does have a key. I'm really worried, Tess. Do you think I should call the police?'

Remembering the explosion they had heard the night before while they had been in Romano's, Tess felt icy fingers grab at her heart. Alice had followed her downstairs, and covering the mouthpiece, Tess turned to her. 'Did you hear where that bomb went off last night?'

'Somewhere near Ann Street, I think. There were three people killed and a lot more injured.'

'Oh, sweet Jesus.' Tess returned to the phone. 'Could you stay there for a short while, Les? I'll be with you as soon as I can.' Without waiting for his answer, she hung up. She couldn't start sharing her worries with him over the phone. It might be a bit premature. There could be a dozen reasons why Colette hadn't returned to the hotel. Nevertheless Tess was filled with a dreadful premonition.

She turned to Alice in anguish. 'Mam! Oh, Mam, Colette didn't get back to the hotel last night. She was somewhere round Cornmarket celebrating with those friends of hers and that's at the top end of Ann Street. I'll have to go over to Les, he'll need some company, poor man, just in case anything has happened to Colette. Will you order a taxi to come in twenty minutes, while I go up and get washed and dressed?'

Les rang just before Tess's taxi arrived. He sounded distraught. 'Glad I caught you, Tess. The police are here. Someone answering Colette's description and carrying a Stormont Hotel key is in the City Hospital. They say she was caught up in an explosion last night and is in a critical condition.'

'Oh, dear God, I was afraid of something like that. Look, Les, my taxi has just arrived. The police will take you to the hospital and I'll meet you there. Okay?' Silence reigned and she thought they had been disconnected. 'Les? Are you still there?'

She heard a deep, shuddering sob. 'Yes, I'm still here.'

'I'll see you at the hospital, then. Okay?'

'Yes. I'll meet you there.'

Dan and Alice were hovering about, not knowing what to say or do. Her face drained of the last vestige of colour, Tess said, 'It appears that Colette may have been caught up in that bomb explosion last night. I'm meeting Les at the City Hospital to find out if it's really her.'

'Would you like me to come with you, Tess?' Dan was quick to offer.

'No, I'll be all right. Mam, will you let Theresa know? I'd better run. These taxi drivers get nervous sitting about here. See you later.'

* * *

Tess arrived at the hospital first. She saw the police car pull up and Les jump out. She hurried towards him and gripped his arm in sympathy. He looked old and haggard, and at his first sight of the old building that in bygone days had been the workhouse he was unable to hide his dismay.

'Don't worry, Les,' Tess quickly assured him. 'The doctors here have a good reputation, and remember, they're used to saving the lives of bomb-blast victims. God knows, they've had plenty of practice.'

The reception area was packed. Some people were standing in tears, hugging each other or being comforted by family or friends; others milled about looking bewildered. Tess headed straight for the reception desk and Les followed as if in a daze. As they waited for attention a girl approached them.

'Are you looking for Colette Burns?'

'Yes.' It was Les who answered her. 'Do you know anything about her?'

'I thought I recognised you. I was with her last night. It was awful. As far as I know, Colette is in intensive care. One of our friends, Anne Marie Kerr, was killed outright. I was one of the lucky ones. Just a few scratches and bruises was all I got. I'll never forget it till God takes me. One minute we were all laughing and reminiscing . . . the next there was this almighty bang and we were thrown all over the place like rag dolls. I knew nothing until I woke up here. I've just been released. Oh, here's my dad to collect me now. I hope Colette's all right.'

They waited impatiently at reception for their turn. After a lot of questions, a harassed nurse was dispatched to take them to where Colette lay. They followed her in frustrated silence.

At the door to a ward the nurse stopped. 'I'm afraid you will have to wait here. I'll see if I can find a doctor.

144

I may be a while. Everybody's rushed off their feet at the minute.'

As the nurse disappeared through swing doors further along the corridor, Tess pressed her face against the small window in the ward door where they were standing. There were only two beds but it didn't look like any intensive care unit that she had ever seen. There were no monitors, nor did there appear to be anyone in attendance. A curtain pulled around the bed nearest the door obscured both beds and she couldn't see the patients.

Tess suddenly realised that Les had barely spoken a word since they had met outside the hospital. A glance showed her that he was deathly white, his expression glazed. Probably in shock, she surmised. There was a bench along the wall and she motioned him to it.

'Let's take the weight off our feet.' Gratefully he sank down on to the bench and buried his head in his hands. Sitting beside him she placed a sympathetic hand on his arm. 'Let's not think the worst, Les. Be optimistic.'

'Why won't someone see us, explain what's going on? This waiting is killing me. It's awful not knowing how Colette is.'

'They will get round to us eventually. The medical staff will have their hands full at the minute.' Tess sought for words of reassurance but could find none. 'I'm sure a lot of victims from last night's bombing were brought here, judging by that crowd out in reception.'

The nurse returned with a small elderly man in tow. He introduced himself. 'I'm Dr Madden. You are enquiring after Miss Burns?'

'Yes,' they chorused.

'Are you relatives?'

'I'm her fiancé. We're over here on holiday from Canada.'

A look of sorrow darkened the doctor's face. 'I'm afraid she didn't pull through. Miss Burns passed away an hour ago. There was nothing we could do to save her.'

Les's legs buckled, and gripping his shoulders Dr Madden pressed him back down on to the bench and pushed his head between his knees. 'Take a deep breath,' he ordered.

He eyed Tess. 'Are you a relative?'

'Just a close family friend.'

Les straightened up, brushed his hands over an ashen face, and taking a deep breath squared his shoulders. 'I'm all right now, thank you. Can I see her?'

Dr Madden pursed his lips and said doubtfully, 'I don't think that would be advisable at the moment.'

'I want to see her.' Les hesitated and asked, 'Is she badly marked?'

'No, hardly at all. It's you I'm thinking of. If you're sure you're up to it?' Les nodded and the doctor said, 'Follow me.'

He led them into the ward and only then did Tess realise that it was Colette behind the drawn curtains. The other bed was empty.

She looked as if she were sleeping; hands clasped on her chest. 'You say she's dead?' Les queried.

'I'm afraid so. It appears she was thrown with terrific force by the blast and hit the back of her head. She never regained consciousness. We did all we could but we were always fighting a losing battle.'

Tears poured down Les's face. The doctor squeezed his arm in sympathy and murmured to Tess, 'I'm so sorry. I must leave you now, but don't let him stay too long. The police will want to interview you before you leave the hospital. They've set up an incident room in one of the offices close to reception.'

* * *

146

The next few hours passed in a blur. After a short interview with the police, Tess insisted that Les check out of his hotel and spend the remainder of his stay at her home. There was much to be done and he would need companionship: someone to discuss things with; someone to help him through his trauma. She accompanied him to the hotel and packed his and Colette's belongings while he settled the account. Tears streamed down her face as she packed the clothes. Colette was so young, should have had her whole life ahead of her. Hatred for the perpetrators of the bombing filled Tess's heart. They were nothing but cold-blooded murderers.

Tess had phoned ahead and Alice had a room ready for Les. He asked if he could be alone for a time and Alice showed him to his room and left him.

Dan sat hunched over the fire, elbows resting on his knees and wringing his hands. Tess could only look at him in bewilderment, unable to account for the state he was in. There was certainly no love lost between him and Colette. Alice beckoned her into the kitchen and explained, 'Dan's blaming himself for Colette's death.'

'*What?*'

'I know! It's absurd, but he's distraught, so he is. You see, some time before the accident Dan had wished his wife would fall under a bus, and so when Jack had taken her for a spin on his new motorbike that tragic day and was killed in the crash, Dan thought Jack had been taken from him because he had wished Anne dead.'

'Silly man. But . . . I still don't understand, what has that got to do with Colette dying?'

Looking furtively over her shoulder towards the door, Alice continued, 'When she and Dan couldn't come to an agreement regarding wee Jackie, Dan told me he had wished in his heart that she were dead so that he wouldn't be in this pickle. He truly thinks he's the cause of her being killed in that explosion.'

'What a load of rubbish! Tell him to pull himself together. Les will need all the help he can get. The poor man's devastated, so he is.'

No one felt like eating so Tess made some sandwiches and tea for the evening meal. Les asked permission to phone home and let their friends know what had happened. Alice told him he didn't need to ask and to feel free to phone any time for as long as he needed and they left him to do his talking in private.

Theresa, when she heard the news, had come down and collected Jackie and taken him out for a walk, away from all the grief, promising to take him to her own home afterwards and keep him there until things had quietened down. Early evening Tess phoned Malachy to let him know of Colette's tragic death. He was shocked and saddened by the news and said he would come up the following morning and see if he could be of any assistance, and if they liked, he would take Jackie back to the farm with him. That settled, Tess left the house and walked up the road to call on Theresa.

Her friend opened the door, a finger to her lips. 'Jackie's asleep at long last. I thought he'd never go over, but he seems to be in his night's sleep now.' She eyed Tess closely. 'You look shattered, love. Come in and I'll make us a cup of tea.'

Tea poured, they sat in silence, each buried in their own thoughts, for some moments. What did one talk about at times like this?

Tentatively, Theresa asked the inevitable. 'How's Les taking it?'

'He's in an awful state, but bearing up as well as can

be expected under the circumstances. He's been in touch with Colette's lawyer back in Canada, a friend of his, I believe, and he's flying over on the first available flight. It will be good for Les that he has a friend with him for company. We're all strangers to him over here. He has also been in touch with Mr McIlroy, Colette's solicitor over here, and he wants to see us all tomorrow morning in his office.'

'All of you?'

'Well, he wants Dan and me to accompany Les, and no doubt Mam will tag along. She'll not want to miss out on anything,' Tess said wryly.

'But why does he want to see *all* of you?'

'I imagine it will concern Jackie's welfare. Dan will probably now get custody of the child.'

'It's an ill wind . . .' Theresa's voice trailed off and she sat in thought for some seconds. 'I still don't understand . . . Why *you*?'

'I've no idea.'

'Do you think . . .'

Tess shifted uncomfortably in her seat. She could guess what her friend was thinking. To her shame the same idea had entered her own mind only to be pushed aside. Now she was adamant that it couldn't possibly be. 'No, Theresa! I can guess what you're about to suggest and the answer is . . . no!'

'Oh . . .'

'Theresa! We know Colette was well off, but she wasn't a millionaire. Why should she leave me anything?'

'I didn't say that.'

'No, but it's what you're thinking, isn't it? Besides, I'm sure her estate will be in the hands of her Canadian lawyer. I can only suppose that Mr McIlroy wants to see me in connection with Jackie in some way.' Theresa still looked sceptical and Tess changed the subject. 'Does Bob know about Colette?'

'Not yet. I'll tell him when he phones later on.'

'Can you keep Jackie here till we see how things go?'

'Sure. Mind you, he knows something's wrong and wants to go home.'

'Malachy is coming up tomorrow morning with Rose and they will probably take Jackie back with them until things get back to some sort of normality. God, I can't believe all this is happening. I expect to wake up any minute and find it's all a bad dream.'

'That's exactly how I feel. But at least you saw her body. You saw for yourself that she's dead. Was she badly injured?'

'No, Theresa, looking at her you wouldn't think she was dead at all. You'd have sworn she was just lying there sleeping. I could hardly believe my own eyes. I suppose we've that to be thankful for. Look, I'd better get back home. It's awfully awkward at the moment, everyone just sitting around like dummies; we don't know what to say to Les.' She shrugged. 'What can you say?'

Early next morning they took a taxi to the solicitor's office. In the reception area Mr McIlroy himself came out to greet them and ushered them into his office.

Once coffee was served and introductions had been dispensed with, Mr McIlroy clasped his hands on the desk in front of him, cleared his throat and began to speak. 'You'll be wondering why I asked you all to come here today.' It was a statement, not a question, and they all silently returned his look. He met and held Les's. 'I'm sure you have informed Miss Burns's own lawyer of this tragic accident?'

'Yes, Colette's lawyer, Mark Benson, is a personal

friend of mine. He is on his way over even as we speak.'

'Good! Good! The reason I asked you here today is regarding Miss Burns's will. When she inherited her grandmother's wealth, she asked me to manage her affairs.' He smiled, a sad twist of the lips. 'Investing in the right commodities at the right time, my colleagues and I did quite well for her. On this side of the Atlantic she was a fairly wealthy young lady. Such a shame she will not be here to enjoy the fruits of our efforts.'

He reached for some papers and shuffled through them. 'When Miss Burns became pregnant she came to see me and made a will, should anything happen to her.' Once again he held Les's eyes. 'When she came to see me last Friday we had no time to discuss her affairs so I don't know whether the will I hold here for her was ever revoked by a later will or codicil. Can you enlighten us to that end, Mr O'Malley?'

Les shook his head. 'I don't think so. She did mention making a will here but not in Canada. We intended making joint wills when we got married.'

'If that's the case, the will we hold in this office will be deemed legal and binding, but I think perhaps I should meet with . . .' he had a quick glance at his notepad, 'Mr Benson before divulging its contents, just in case another will does exist. Is everyone agreeable?'

Les nodded and Mr McIlroy asked Dan, 'Is that all right with you, Mr Thompson?'

'Yes! That's fine by me, sir.'

'Then when Mr Benson arrives I shall meet with him and compare notes, so to speak. Then we shall all meet back here again. I'll keep you informed.' He rose to his feet to indicate that the meeting was at an end, at the same time apologising for bringing them out on a wild-goose chase. Then he paused, as if struck by an afterthought.

'Another thing I would like to mention: Miss Burns also intimated to me that should anything happen to her she would like to be interred in her grandparents' grave. It was just a remark in passing and I don't know if things have changed. Perhaps she may have indicated somewhere else since. I just thought I'd mention it. Thank you for coming. If Miss Maguire would remain behind for a minute, I'd like a quiet word with her.'

When the others had left, Tess nervously inched to the edge of her chair and fixed her eyes intently on the solicitor.

He smiled kindly at her. 'Miss Burns held you in high esteem, Miss Maguire. She told me you were a very good friend to her.' Opening a drawer he took out an envelope and passed it across to her. 'She tried to cover all eventualities and asked me to give this to you should anything unforeseen happen to her. Remember, this was some years ago, before she left for Canada.'

Tess gazed down at the envelope. Her name was written across it in Colette's neat handwriting. 'Thank you.'

'I was in Miss Burns's confidence and privy to the contents of the letter. If you ever feel the need to talk to someone, just give me a ring.'

Pushing herself upright, Tess carefully put the letter in her handbag. 'I'll remember that, Mr McIlroy. Thank you once again.'

'If I may say so . . . I think it would be most prudent to open the letter when you are alone. Good day to you, Miss Maguire.'

6

Tess was pleased that her mother hadn't accompanied them to the solicitors. She would have pounced on her daughter the minute they left the building, pressing to know why Mr McIlroy had asked her to stay behind. She would have demanded that Tess open the letter there and then; let her see the contents. Alice would not have been in the least deterred by the fact that the solicitor had advised Tess not to open the letter in anyone's company. Her mother considered anything to do with Tess was also her business. In a way Tess agreed. Normally she would have gone along with her mother's wishes. But Mr McIlroy had her intrigued. Why the big mystery? She sighed. Until she had a chance to read the contents of the envelope she would be none the wiser. Only then would she decide whether or not to confide in her mother.

The letter was burning a hole in her handbag as she hastened to the entrance. To her dismay she found Dan and Les waiting in the reception foyer, deep in conversation. Although their eyes questioned her, neither man had the gumption to enquire as to why she was asked to stay behind, and she didn't enlighten them. She had already told the men that she had some shopping to do and now she chastised them for waiting for her.

'You should have gone on home. I won't be too long. Tell Mam I'll be home as quick as I can.'

'Are you sure you don't want us to tag along? We'd be only too happy to keep you company; carry your shopping,' Dan added gallantly.

'Mm . . . I bet you'll be all disappointed not to be trekking round the market after me,' she said and added drily, 'But sorry, I wouldn't be able to concentrate on what I was after with you two hovering at my elbow. So get yourselves away on home! I'd rather be on my own, thank you.'

'Well, if you insist,' said a relieved Dan.

'I insist. Goodbye, Dan, goodbye, Les.'

'See you later then.'

Glad of the respite, Tess made her way round to Donegall Place and her favourite café. Seated at a corner table in the Ulster Milk Bar, she ordered a coffee and a gravy-ring. While she waited to be served she opened her handbag and took out the envelope, fingering it gingerly. It was light and flat. She guessed that it held only a single sheet of paper.

She tut-tutted, impatient with herself. What was she thinking of, sitting here in a dream? There was only one way to find out what was inside. Still apprehensive, she took her time, carefully easing the flap open and slowly removing a single sheet of pale blue paper. Her coffee and gravy-ring were brought to her and she paid for them before spreading the sheet of notepaper carefully on the table with the flat of her hand.

The letter was short and to the point.

Dear Tess,

Thank you for all the kindness you've shown me over the years. You'll never know how much I appreciate all your help since Jack's death. I couldn't have got through the pregnancy and all the trauma without you being there for me. I hope one day to be able to show just how much your friendship means to me. Meanwhile, in the event of my premature death (God forbid) I have written this letter to release you from your promise to me regarding the identity of my son Jackie's father. Should, for instance, my parents learn that they have a grandson and try to lay claim on him (although I don't think it likely). If it ever becomes necessary and you decide it advisable to disclose his father's identity you have my full permission to do so. Of course I hope to live to a ripe old age and you'll never know this letter ever existed. But accidents do happen and I want to be sure that you know that I leave everything regarding Jackie's welfare in your more than capable hands. If you do receive this letter from my solicitor it will mean that I'll no longer be in this world. Please look after my son's interests on my behalf. I trust you to do what is best for him. Again my sincere thanks.

Your ever grateful friend,
Colette

For a brief moment Tess had forgotten where she was, she was so wrapped up in Colette's letter. It was as if Colette were speaking to her from beyond the grave. She blinked furiously to hold back the tears that threatened, in case she made a fool of herself in public. It had completely slipped her mind that Colette's parents had no knowledge of Jackie's birth. Her mother was so strait-laced, Colette had been adamant from the moment she discovered she was pregnant that she must never know of the child's existence. Had they been notified of their daughter's death? Did Les know of their whereabouts? They were in for one hell of a shock. Not only would they learn of Colette's death, they would also discover they had a grandson. How would they react to that?

Tess had met Colette's mother and stepfather twice; both sad occasions. The first time was when they had come to Belfast for Jack's funeral. She had met them briefly; didn't even know their surname. Colette had introduced them merely as Betty and Stan, nothing more. They had thought Jack wasn't good enough for their daughter and Colette had accused them of being snobs and glad that he was dead and that there would now be no wedding. Tess imagined that their stay had been an uncomfortable occasion.

The second time she had just seen them from a distance, at the funeral of Colette's grandmother some weeks later. She remembered how enraged Colette had been when Betty and Stan had left immediately after the funeral, saying they had things to do and couldn't stay any length of time. Colette had thought them very disres-pectful, but perhaps they had urgent business elsewhere. Colette had been left to wind up her grandmother's affairs. She had earlier confided in Tess that she intended returning to Omagh, saying that with both her grannie and her fiancé gone there would be nothing to keep her in Belfast. However, after witnessing her parents' selfish attitude she had decided to remain in the city. In due course, and to her great surprise and delight, she had found out that her grandmother had left her quite a substantial sum of money, plus some items of expensive jewellery.

Tess recalled Mr McIlroy's warning; did this mean Colette had confided in him? It looked very much like she had! Somehow or other this made Tess feel better. If she ever needed to talk to someone, he would be the perfect choice, although it seemed Colette's secret was safe. If Dan, as Jackie's grandfather, were to be trustee to Jackie's inheritance there would be no need for anyone to know that he was also the child's natural father. Alice's happiness would be secure and that was what mattered most to Tess.

Slowly folding the sheet of paper, she returned it to the envelope and put it back in her handbag, grateful that Mr McIlroy had advised her to read it when she was alone. Her mother would have been practically sitting on her shoulder as Tess read the letter. She wouldn't have rested until she knew exactly what Colette meant regarding Jackie's father and then there would have been all hell to pay. Tess fervently hoped that Dan wouldn't mention to her mother that she had been asked to stay behind after the meeting closed.

Quickly drinking the cooling coffee, Tess left the café and headed for the bus stop. Her shopping would have to wait. She must remind Les to contact Colette's parents if he hadn't already done so. And the sooner the better; too much time had already elapsed.

Malachy and Rose had arrived while they were out and Tess found the family gathered round the kitchen table discussing the tragic events. Tess greeted her uncle and Rose, and then asked, 'Did you take Jackie to school today, Mam?'

'No, but Theresa took him down to the shop shortly after you left in the taxi. I decided he's better off there.

157

He's too young to understand, and the less he knows about this awful business the better,' Alice replied.

'I just wanted to be sure he wasn't here before I spoke.' Tess turned to Les. 'Les, has anyone notified Colette's parents of her death?'

He blinked and looked blankly at her. 'Not that I'm aware of,' he confessed.

'Dan?'

'No, Tess. I must admit, I never gave it a second thought. I only met them a couple of times at the funerals, remember, and didn't even have a proper conversation with them.'

'Do any of you have an address or a phone number for them?'

Everyone shook their heads and Tess cried, 'I feel so awful about this. I'm the one who should have remembered. I don't even know their surname. They'll have to be told, but how do we go about finding them?'

Bored with all the sitting around twiddling his thumbs, and glad at last to have something to do, Les volunteered. 'I'll find out. First I'll ring Mr McIlroy. He might know,' he said, heading for the phone.

He came back waving a slip of paper. 'Success. Elizabeth and Stanley McCormack, and an address in Omagh. Now, do we phone them or ask the police to notify them . . . or go in person to break the bad news?'

'I think it would be only proper for someone to go and see them in person.' Tess paused a moment before dropping her bombshell. 'They're in for a double shock. You see, they know nothing about Jackie.'

Dan's jaw dropped. 'You never said!'

'Colette didn't want you to have any dealings with them, if she could help it. She said her parents would disown her if they found out she had a child born out

158

of wedlock and she didn't intend giving them that pleasure. She said it would be easier to sever all connections with them. So she didn't give them the opportunity to reject their grandchild. It's a sad state of affairs I know, but Colette and her mother never did see eye to eye.'

'So that explains why they never visited or sent Jackie any birthday cards or presents at Christmas. I thought it strange many a time, but decided that they resented Colette leaving him in my care, and I didn't want to do anything that might upset the apple-cart. But I never dreamed for one minute that they didn't know of Jackie's existence.'

Les stood sadly shaking his head. 'It's tragic. When Colette first came out to Canada, my wife and I persuaded her to keep in touch with her parents. And for a time she did, she wrote dozens of letters to them, but their replies were always the same. They kept insisting that she come home and this always upset her. Eventually the correspondence petered out. It was obvious that they didn't really understand or care what she wanted out of life; didn't even consider her wishes. It was a very selfish attitude they took. They just wanted her to return to Omagh. We did intend visiting them when we were over this time, and inviting them to our wedding,' he confessed. 'But now . . .' His voice broke and he hurriedly left the room.

Tears brimmed in Rose's eyes, she was so overcome with emotion. She found it hard to believe that any mother would be so indifferent to her own flesh and blood. 'Poor man. How sad for him. How very, very sad,' she murmured.

'Sorry about that,' Les apologised as he made a dignified return. 'If I remember correctly, I believe Omagh is a fair distance away. About seventy miles or so . . . is that correct?' Dan nodded, and Les continued, 'I can't go there today, I want to be here when Mark Benson arrives. If I hire a car, will you accompany me tomorrow, Tess? Will Theresa be able to cope on her own?'

'Of course she will, and I will be glad to accompany you, Les.'

'Look, Les, you've never met them, so if it's all right with Dan I'd be more than happy to run him and Tess to Omagh after lunch,' Malachy volunteered. 'But I really do think it would be better if we got young Jackie away from here as soon as possible.'

'You're right, Malachy. There's no need for him to know what's happened. Not yet, anyhow,' Alice said.

Malachy smiled ruefully at his sister. 'Meanwhile, talking about lunch . . . I'm starving, Alice.'

Alice was on her feet in a flash. 'Sorry, Malachy. I've been so preoccupied, the thought of food never entered my thick head. If you'll all get out of my kitchen I'll make us a bite to eat. Go on, shoo. And will someone please go down and ask Theresa to close the shop for an hour and bring young Jackie up and join us for lunch.'

'I'll go,' Les offered. 'I'll be glad to get out and stretch my legs for a while. I can't bear all this hanging about doing nothing.'

Theresa came from the back of the shop when she heard the door open and her heart went out to Les as he entered. His shoulders drooped and his face was drawn. Such a change from the vibrant man she had first met on Saturday.

'Les . . . please come through.' She held a warning finger to her lips. 'Jackie's asleep.' Lifting the counter flap she motioned towards the back of the shop. 'Any news?'

160

'Would you believe that no one thought to inform Colette's parents? We've all been so remiss.'

She smiled slightly. 'Well, they haven't been in the picture much all these years, so I suppose it wasn't hard to overlook them.'

'I've been sitting up there twiddling my thumbs, wishing I had something constructive to do while waiting for Mark Benson to arrive. I could have had all this business sorted. I feel so stupid!'

Detecting a tremble in his voice Theresa went to him and put her arms around him. 'My heart goes out to you, it must be very hard for you, Les. Stuck here in this godforsaken town among a lot of strangers.'

He gripped her close, glad for the comfort of her embrace. 'You've all been very kind and supportive, but I must confess I do sometimes feel so alone. I can't believe Colette's dead. Everything will be different once Mark gets here. We're close friends, he's like a brother to me.'

'If you ever feel the need to talk to someone, don't hesitate to come to me. I'll be here for you.'

'Thank you, Theresa. You're most kind. I'll remember that.' He gently put her from him and, taking a handkerchief from his pocket, blew his nose. 'See? A few kind words and I'm almost reduced to tears.'

She was about to tell him to go ahead and have a good old cry, it would do him the world of good, when the tinkle of the shop door opening again caused her to grimace.

'Sorry, Les. I won't be a minute.'

It was Tony Burke who stood at the other side of the counter. 'Theresa . . . I've just heard!' he exclaimed. 'I'm devastated. To come all that way and to die like that. I just can't take it in. Tess left a message for me but I was working away for a few days and I've just got back. Is she here?'

'No, she's not in today, but Colette's fiancé is here. Come through and I'll introduce you.'

After introductions the two men shook hands and Tony offered his condolences.

In the awkward silence that followed Les suddenly remembered why he was there in the first place. 'Good Lord, I forgot! Alice sent me down to invite you and Jackie back to the house for some lunch, Theresa. Her brother and his wife have arrived from Carlingford.'

Tony nodded to the sleeping boy. 'I'll carry Jackie out to the car. It's parked outside.'

Without further ado, Theresa immediately reached for her coat. She ushered them out of the shop and turning the sign to Closed followed them out and locked the door. 'You come too, Tony. Tess will be glad to see you.'

Tess *was* pleased to see Tony. The now wide-awake Jackie was seated in front of the TV. During lunch Tony was brought up to date on all the happenings of the past few days. He would not hear of Les hiring a car and offered to take Tess to see Colette's parents, that afternoon if necessary.

Tess was quick to accept his offer. 'That would be great, Tony. The sooner the better. Can Pat manage without you for the rest of the day?'

'He'll be all right on his own.'

'We'll go directly we've finished lunch, if that's okay with you.'

Tony rose to his feet. 'Fine! I'll nip home and freshen up first. And call in and explain to Pat what's going on.'

'Finish your lunch,' she admonished him.

Tony laughed and nodded towards his empty plate. 'Do you want me to scrape the pattern off?'

* * *

162

Half an hour later Tony returned and waited at the kerb, engine idling, until Tess joined him. The journey to Omagh took almost two hours. Twice they were stopped by army patrols and their car searched. Tony put this down to his Belfast licence plates. Once they reached Omagh they spent some time looking for Betty and Stan's road, but eventually they found it. It was a quiet, secluded cul-de-sac in the more opulent part of the town. The house was a stone-walled bungalow with a manicured lawn and neat, well-tended borders. A gleaming Vauxhall car was parked outside an open-doored garage inside which could be seen an array of gardening tools.

'They're obviously keen gardeners,' Tony observed and lifted the brass knocker.

It was Betty who answered their knock. She gazed blankly at Tess, a slight frown on her brow. 'Yes, can I help you?'

Taken aback, Tess began in a hesitant manner. 'Mrs McCormack? We met some years ago . . .' A flicker of recognition dawned on the woman's face.

Someone came up behind her in the hall. 'Who is it, Betty?' Stan McCormack peered over his wife's shoulder. 'Why, it's young Tess Maguire! What are you thinking of, Betty, keeping the girl standing on the doorstep? Come in, Tess. Come inside. What are you doing in this part of the world?'

Betty moved to one side and as they passed, apologised. 'Of course. I remember now. Sorry about that, Tess, I just couldn't place your face for a moment. Is our Colette coming home on a visit? Do you know something . . . it's a disgrace, but we've only seen her twice since she went off to live in Canada. Two quick visits during which we couldn't agree on a single thing.'

Stan was eyeing the visitors closely, sensing that this

wasn't any social visit. 'Sit down. I've a feeling that Tess is the harbinger of not too good news. Is that right?'

Tess turned to him gratefully. 'Yes. I'm afraid I am.' She gestured towards Tony. 'Do you remember Tony Burke? He was Jack Thompson's best friend.'

Betty just gave him the briefest of nods but Stan thrust out a hand and Tony gripped it and they exchanged greetings. 'Betty, put the kettle on, love. I'm sure these young people could do with a cup of tea if they've travelled through from Belfast.'

Tess couldn't bear to wait while tea was made. She was a bundle of nerves, wanting to get this over with and get away as quickly as possible. Having a biased opinion of Betty, she hadn't given much thought as to how the woman would react to the news of her daughter's death. Now she was regretting coming here. She hadn't prepared herself as to what to say or even how to say it. With hindsight she realised they should have let the police break the bad news. But then what about Jackie? She would still have had to let them know about their grandson. Tess knew it was bound to be a terrible shock and needed to get it over with quickly. Full of trepidation, she said, 'We can't stay for tea, thank you . . .' Her voice trailed off and her eyes sought Tony's, pleading for his help.

He quickly came to her assistance. 'I'm afraid we've brought some very bad news.'

Betty looked very apprehensive but she managed a derisive snort. 'Colette has married someone totally unsuitable and can't bear to tell us herself. Is that it? Has she sent you to break the ice?' As if struck by a certain thought she headed for the hall. 'Why isn't she here? Is she sitting in the car out there? I don't understand . . . she was never afraid to face us before. Was always defiant, so she was! We didn't think that Jack Thompson was good enough for her, but if he hadn't died in that crash Colette would have insisted on marrying him, regardless of our objections.'

As she passed him, Stan reached out and gripped his wife's arm, drawing her back into the room. 'I think you had better sit down, love.' He pushed her gently down on to an armchair, and perching beside her put a comforting arm across her shoulders. 'Somehow or other, I don't think Colette's out there.'

Tess and Tony had remained standing. Stan nodded to the settee. 'Please sit down and tell us why you're here before my wife has one of her turns.'

At a loss, and still flailing about in her mind for the right words to soften the blow, Tess bit hard on her lip and said in a choked voice, 'I don't know where to start.'

With a perplexed glance, and to give her time to gain control of her emotions, Tony interrupted. 'On second thoughts, perhaps we should have that cup of tea after all.'

Without another word Betty rose to her feet and left the room. Stan sat down on the chair facing them, leaning forward, arms resting on thighs, fingers laced. 'The news isn't too good, is it?' he said quietly.

'No, it isn't. I'm sure you heard about the bomb in Belfast at the weekend that claimed three lives?' Stan nodded and Tess continued, 'I'm afraid Colette was one of those killed.'

The last vestige of colour drained from the man's face. 'Oh my God!' He slumped back in the chair, hand pressed to his forehead, and repeated, 'Oh my God. This is terrible. It'll kill Betty. She always clung to the hope that Colette would somehow see sense and come home and make a fresh start here in Omagh. Marry some suitable young man and give us grandchildren. It's what she's been praying for all along. That's why she didn't want her to go to Canada in the first place. We didn't think it was too much to hope for.' He shook his head in despair. 'If you don't mind, I'd like to be the one to break it to her.'

He looked enquiringly at Tess, and much relieved that the onus had been taken from her she nodded. He rose, squaring his shoulders, excused himself and followed his wife to the kitchen.

Tess turned to Tony and said in a low voice, 'I'm glad now you came with me. I didn't think it would be so hard to tell them. With Colette and her mother apparently always at loggerheads I thought it would be easy. I should have been more prepared. With hindsight I could at least have discussed it with you on the way here; had some idea what I was going to say. I don't know what I was thinking of. The police would have handled it more diplomatically. They're trained in these matters. Whether she and Colette were close or not, that poor woman is bound to be devastated when she hears. Thanks for helping me out, Tony.'

'I wondered what on earth had happened to you. It's not like you to be stuck for something to say.'

'It suddenly struck me that Colette was Betty's only child. Did you hear what Stan said about grandchildren? This could get very awkward, Tony. What if they want to claim Jackie and bring him up as the grandchild they've been praying for? They'll think their prayers have been answered.'

'Hush . . . lighten up, Tess. I don't think they would stand a chance.'

'I don't know about that. They could claim that they had been deceived all along. Not given the chance to get to know their only grandson.'

166

'That doesn't change the fact that they're complete strangers to the boy. Dan and your mother have had him since birth. I can't see there being any hitches as to who gets custody.'

A scream of anguish, like that of a wounded animal, came from the kitchen. Tess jumped quickly to her feet but Tony restrained her. 'Leave them to their grief, Tess. They won't welcome your intrusion.'

Some minutes passed and then the door opened and Stan put his head round it. 'I'll just bring the tray in.'

He disappeared for a few moments, then returned carrying a laden tray and placed it on an occasional table. 'Betty will be back shortly. She has just nipped into the bathroom.'

Tess again rose anxiously to her feet. 'Is she all right, Stan? Shall I go to her?'

'No, you sit down, love. She's best left alone for a few minutes. She's a very strong character is our Betty. When her first husband ran off with another woman, Colette was only four at the time. There were faults on both sides, of course, but Betty never once said a bad word to Colette about her father, never even mentioned the other woman. She wanted Colette to have good memories of him. So of course Colette though he was a saint and her mother had driven him away and was to blame for the broken marriage and subsequent divorce.'

'I'm sorry to hear that. I'm afraid I only ever heard Colette's side of the story.'

'I'll bet she hadn't a good word to say about her mother.' Betty entered the room and took the seat across from Tess. Her eyes were puffy and red-rimmed but she sat composed, wringing a small lace handkerchief in her hands. 'Mind you, it wasn't easy bringing her up on my own, before I met Stan. I worked hard to give her a good education; had no kind of a social life at all. I was really peeved when she went to visit her Grannie Burns. You see, she too blamed me for the break-up of our marriage. She doted on her worthless son. He could do no wrong in her eyes. She thought I must have done something terrible for him to run off with another woman. I don't know how long he'd been carrying on behind my back but it certainly didn't happen overnight. I must have been blind! But then he always did fancy himself as a bit of a ladies' man. Not once did Mrs Burns give me credit for rearing Colette on my own! Not once!' Now the floodgates were open there was no stopping her. All the bottled-up resentment came pouring out. 'When Colette got a job in Belfast and decided to live with her grannie to be near Jack Thompson, I was hurt; dreadfully hurt. I'm afraid I handled it all wrong; told her to get on with it and ruin her life if that was what she wanted. Can you blame me? After all I'd done for her. All the sacrifices I'd made to give her the best of everything. I was very annoyed that Jack didn't even have a trade! A lovely girl like Colette could have done so much better.'

'Jack was a nice lad,' Tess defended her friend. 'And his was a similar story to yours. His mother left Dan to run off with a work colleague. Jack was twelve at the time and it broke his heart. I suppose that's what brought the two of them together in the first place. A common denominator. But they were well suited and grew to love each other very much. I think they would have been very happy together. It was tragic that he died so young.'

'I knew nothing about his background. Colette and I never really had a good long talk. She never discussed anything with me. However, I soon realised that they were in love, and I had become resigned to the idea of them marrying.' Her eyes flew to Stan. 'Isn't that right,

Stan, didn't I say so?' He nodded in confirmation, and Betty continued, 'But I didn't get a chance to explain this before Jack died in that awful accident. Afterwards I took the brunt of Colette's anger. She accused me of being glad Jack was dead. Imagine! As if anyone could be so callous. She refused to come home with us. We parted with the usual animosity between us. I thought if I left her to dwell on it, she'd eventually come round to my way of thinking. After all, with Jack dead, there was nothing to keep her in Belfast.'

'Your mother-in-law was very fond of Jack. She had a heart attack when she heard of his death. Colette didn't want her put into a nursing home so she stayed in Belfast to nurse her.'

'I realised that afterwards, but at the time I thought she was being her usual stubborn self. When Mrs Burns died I thought Colette would surely come home. But no, for months not one word from her. Then the next thing I heard she was flying off to Canada.'

'Did you know that her grannie left her a tidy sum of money?'

A bewildered shake of the head. 'No, I didn't! She certainly kept that quiet, which wasn't surprising. How much did she get?'

'I'm not quite sure,' Tess lied. 'But I believe it was enough to make her sufficiently confident to try and start a new life in Canada.' Tess licked her dry lips and confessed, 'I've something else to tell you.'

Sensing from her tone of voice that it was more bad news, two pairs of eyes full of dread fixed on her face as she paused. With trepidation Tess dropped yet another bombshell. 'You have a grandson.'

The silence was deafening. It was Betty who eventually spoke. 'Are you sitting there telling me that my

Colette married out in Canada and hadn't the decency to let us know?'

'No. She didn't marry. That's why she never told you about young Jackie. She told me you wouldn't understand. That you would disown her and her son.'

Betty shook her head in frustration. 'God, but that girl had a very low opinion of me. As if I would be that cruel! How old is this child?'

'Five. He's a lovely wee boy. Full of life and mischief.'

'You know him, then? She brought him home to meet you and never came to visit us? God, how she must have really hated me.'

'No. No, you've got it all wrong. Jackie was born here in Ireland, before she went to off Canada.'

Tess could practically hear Betty's mind ticking over. 'Jack Thompson's child?' she queried. 'Why didn't she come to me when she discovered she was pregnant? You'd think with her grannie dead I'd be the obvious one to turn to.'

'She was afraid to come to you for help. Said you always threatened to disown her if she fell pregnant outside marriage. That the shame it would bring on the household would finish you off.'

Betty looked flabbergasted. 'What a mixed-up girl she was, and I never once guessed. Every mother says things like that but never really means a word of it. Did your mother never threaten you to try and keep you on the straight and narrow? I'll bet she did!'

Tess had to nod her head in agreement. Alice had indeed warned her many a time of the dire consequences if she did anything wrong and brought shame to the door. Why hadn't Colette realised that her mother's warnings, like any good mother's, were only empty threats? Why for that matter had Tess not realised and pointed it out to her friend?

'See what I mean? I can't believe I'm hearing all this. Where is the boy now?'

'Dan Thompson and my mother have reared him from birth.'

Betty was more astounded still. 'You mean to say she didn't take him to Canada with her?'

'No.'

'And your parents never thought to inform me of his existence? How could they be so cruel?'

Her voice caught in a sob, and Stan, seeing that his wife was stretched to breaking point, interrupted. 'Tell us, what's happening now, Tess?'

'Well, actually, Colette was engaged to a very nice Canadian businessman, Les O'Malley. He came over to Belfast with her last Friday.'

Betty interrupted her. 'Was he caught up in the blast too?'

'No, he wasn't with her. She was out having a drink with some girls she used to work with when the bomb went off. Les has phoned her Canadian lawyer, who should be arriving today and will meet with Colette's solicitor in Belfast. Between them we hope everything will be sorted out.'

'Will we be able to see Colette? Is she badly . . .' Betty's voice trailed off.

Tess hastened to assure her. 'No, I've already identified the body. There's hardly a mark on her. I don't know how these things go, but I can't see any reason why you shouldn't see her.'

'Have you any idea when we will be able to bury her?'

Tess sat in stunned silence and again it was Tony who intervened. 'We really don't know what will happen, Mrs McCormack. I imagine that there will have to be a post-mortem. Perhaps you could phone tonight and speak to her lawyer? That way you can find out what they intend doing. I'll give you the number.'

Betty was staring vacantly into space, twisting her hanky into a knot, great tears rolling down her cheeks. Stan rose abruptly to his feet. 'Yes, we will most certainly do that.' He held out his hand in farewell and Tony gripped it. Kissing Tess on the cheek, he said, 'I'll see you out.' At the door he added quietly, 'Please forgive Betty. She's absolutely devastated.'

They said their goodbyes and, climbing into the car, drove off.

Only when he returned indoors and clasped his wife close did Stan notice the laden tray and realise that their visitors had gone without touching a thing.

On the way back they soon picked up the road to Dungannon. In the countryside outside Omagh, Tony pulled into the first lay-by they came upon. Stopping the car, he drew Tess into his arms and cuddled her close. 'You're freezing. We could have done with that cup of tea.'

'I know. That was my fault. I made such a mess of everything, didn't I? Everything I said seemed to come out different to what I meant.'

'No you didn't.'

'What made me think that a mother could be indifferent to her daughter's death no matter about their differences of opinion? How could I have been so stupid? The poor woman was wrecked with grief.'

'Colette and her mother obviously had a very mixed-up relationship. The problem was they didn't seem to talk to each other. Mrs McCormack let her daughter live in fairyland as far as her father was concerned, thus Colette surmised that he was the good guy and her

172

mother the evil witch. I remember thinking it strange that her da hadn't even kept in touch with his own mother. He must have been a right nasty piece of home-work! Old Mrs Burns was a lovely wee woman. Do you think she realised at the end that he was no good and that's why she left Colette all her money?'

'I don't know. Colette did her best to find him when she knew her grannie was dying, but without success.' Tess sighed. 'I must admit, listening to Colette's side of the story, I had put all the blame on her mother.'

'It will certainly teach us not to be so presumptuous in future. Relationships can be so complicated. Only the people involved know what really goes on and you only hear their biased version of things, you know, the things they want you to hear. If we've learned anything today, it's to listen to both sides of a story before passing judge-ment.'

'Do you think they'll respect Colette's wishes and let her be buried in Milltown Cemetery with her grand-parents?' Tess asked.

'God only knows. They might want to open a new grave of their own in Omagh so that they can tend to it and later be buried with her. You can't blame them if they do.'

'I wish everything was settled.' Seeking comfort, Tess cuddled close. Tony trailed her neck and face with gentle kisses.

Tess nestled against him and lapped up all this tender-ness. She had been wrong about Tony, and her mother and Uncle Malachy right. Tony would make an ideal husband. He was such a good man; could be depended on. Wasn't he always there when she needed him? He respected her and as a good Christian was saving his passion for when they were married. That was how it should be. She gazed blindly over his shoulder. Her feelings for Bob were purely lustful. It was a sin to even think of him the way she did. Theresa would get hurt if they carried on the way they were. She'd have to put a stop to it, once and for all, before it got completely out of hand. She snuggled closer still and with a contented sigh Tony gave her a lingering kiss before putting her gently from him.

'Let's get you home, love, before we get carried away, eh?'

Relieved that she had been right about him respecting her and not trying anything on, with a sigh she agreed. 'Yes, let's.'

Mark Benson was in his mid-forties; tall, handsome, with well-groomed black hair, he had an air of authority about him. He certainly looked the part of a lawyer. At least the part portrayed in American films.

Regretfully declining their offer to put him up, he explained that he and Les would be very busy and he had booked them both into the International Hotel. Les was upstairs packing when Tess and Tony got back.

In his absence Dan introduced Mark and then asked, 'How did it go, Tess?'

'Awful! That poor woman is devastated. She had great hopes that Colette would eventually tire of Canada and come home and marry a local lad and give her and Stan a few grandchildren.'

Dan gave a start of surprise at these words and Tess quickly explained, 'Communications between Colette and her mother were obviously strained to say the least and that makes it even harder for her to bear. She's in an awful state, so she is.'

Dan looked stunned. Remembering how distraught he

had been when he learned that Colette had kept her pregnancy a secret, that she had actually, at one stage, considered putting his grandson up for adoption without his knowledge, he could imagine how Betty felt. She had his deepest sympathy. He, at least, had ended up rearing his grandson.

'Did you tell her about Jackie?' Tess nodded and Dan prompted, 'Well . . . what did she say?'

'She accused us of being cruel for keeping her in the dark about him.'

'Didn't you explain that Colette didn't want her to know?'

'Of course I did! But I imagine that she thinks we should have used our influence to get her to change her mind. That's what we should have done. Hindsight is a wonderful thing.'

'I suppose you're right,' Dan reluctantly agreed. 'But then, it wasn't up to us. We couldn't go against Colette's wishes. Do you think Betty will want custody of the boy?'

'I imagine so. He's the only grandchild she'll ever have, Colette being her only child.'

'Huh!' Dan thumped himself on the chest. 'Remember, Jack was my only child too.'

'Nobody is arguing about that, Dan. We will just have to leave it in the capable hands of Mr Benson and Mr McIlroy.' Tess looked across at Mark.

He quickly responded. 'I've already been in touch with Mr McIlroy and we are all invited to his office tomorrow morning.'

'Everybody?'

'Well . . . Les, Dan, and you, Tess, are to meet him. Colette's parents will also be there.'

'Why would he want me to attend?' enquired Tess.

'Patience, Tess. All in good time. Your Uncle Malachy

and his wife were asked to come along but they can't make it as they don't want to leave young Jackie behind in Carlingford, so we shall be writing to them in due course.'

The meeting was scheduled for eleven o'clock, and when they arrived with five minutes to spare, they found Stan and Betty already sitting in the foyer. Greetings were exchanged and they were all shepherded into Matthew McIlroy's office. Space there was limited and an embarrassed silence reigned as they waited in close proximity. The two solicitors entered from an adjoining room, where they had obviously gone to confer.

'Good morning, ladies and gentlemen. Sorry for keeping you waiting, but Mr Benson and I had notes to compare and matters to discuss,' Mr McIlroy apologised as he bustled into his office.

He sat at his desk and remained silent until Mark had seated himself beside Les. Then, clearing his throat, he addressed Stan and Betty. 'Please accept my sincere condolences. It must have been a shock for you finding out about your daughter's death as you did. She was a wonderful young lady. She and I had become friends over the years.' They both nodded mutely and Betty dabbed furtively at her eyes.

'Now to get down to business. Mr Benson has informed me that he has carried out a search, and to the best of his knowledge Miss Burns never made another will or codicil since arriving in Canada.' His bright blue eyes rested on each of them in turn. 'So the will she made shortly before leaving Belfast and which is in my possession is legal and binding.'

He once again looked around at each of his audience to ensure that he was being understood, before drawing some legal documents across the desk towards him. Pausing dramatically, he cleared his throat again to give an air of gravity to the proceedings. 'At that time, having inherited a substantial sum of money from her grandmother, another lovely lady whom I had the honour of serving for a number of years, Miss Burns was quite well off. She died a fairly wealthy young lady.'

Tess was seated next to Betty and heard her slight intake of breath.

'Just how wealthy, Mr Benson and I have yet to determine. She had some property and had invested wisely in stocks and shares both here and in Canada. Yes, she was a fairly wealthy young lady.' Once again he cast his gaze over his captive audience, pausing for effect. 'However, the beneficiaries will remain unchanged as she never drew up another will. She has left the bulk of her estate in trust to her only child, Jackie Burns. The trustees, nominated by Miss Burns, are myself, Mr Daniel Thompson and Miss Teresa Maguire. Mr Daniel Thompson, being the child's grandfather and guardian, will, each month, receive a sum of money – the amount to be agreed – for his upkeep, as well as further payments as and when required and agreed by the trustees in the interim, until the child reaches the age of twenty-one years. I will now read the will of Miss Colette Mary Burns.'

Tess, tense with anticipation, leaned forward in her chair. What surprises had Colette in store for them? Would she disclose Jackie's real father's name?

It was very brief and simple, written in her own words.

I, Colette Mary Burns, leave to my dear friend Tess Maguire the sum of £1,000 and to my mother and stepfather the sum of £2,000. I also leave £500 to Mr Malachy Lynch and his friend Rose Donaghy

*for looking after me during my pregnancy. The
balance of my estate will be held in trust until my
son reaches the age of 21 years.*

Another glance round the beneficiaries and Matthew
McIlroy said, 'Although Miss Burns died a wealthy lady,
thanks to Mr Benson . . .' he nodded in Mark's direction, 'diligently looking after her affairs in Canada, and
to the staff here in this firm, these legacies will still
remain as bequested. The bulk of the estate, which is
quite substantial, will go into trust for the child. You
will all be notified formally when probate has been
granted, which should be in about three or four weeks'
time.'

There was silence for some moments and then Stan
said hesitantly, 'Does this mean that Betty and myself
won't have a say in young Jackie's upbringing?'

'Not unless you are invited to do so by the boy's grandfather, Mr Thompson.'

'I don't understand.' Betty's voice was low and
Matthew leaned over the desk to catch her words. 'I'm
Colette's mother. She was my only child. Stan is her step-
father. Surely that counts for something?'

'I'm afraid not. Mr McCormack is only a grandfather
by marriage. There is no blood connection.'

'What if we disagree with you? What if we insist that
we have some rights?' Betty went on. 'Say we want to
challenge your decision?'

'That is your prerogative, Mrs McCormack, but I
would advise that you and Mr Thompson try to come
to some arrangement. If that fails, you would have to
take legal advice on the matter.'

'Thank you, sir.'

'You are welcome. Has anyone any further questions?'

Stan raised a hand. 'When will we be able to bury our daughter?'

The two solicitors exchanged looks. It was Mr McIlroy who spoke. 'When Miss Burns made her will she told me that if anything should happen to her she would like to be buried in the same grave as her grandparents, in Milltown Cemetery. Nothing was ever put in writing to this effect but perhaps she has mentioned somewhere different to Mr Benson.' His eyes questioned the Canadian lawyer.

'Nothing was said to me, but one must not forget that Colette was a young lady, planning to get married to my good friend Mr O'Malley.' He tilted his head towards Les. 'Death and funerals were the last things on her mind. Did she ever express any preference to you, Les?'

'No, never. As you've just said, Mark, death and funerals were the last things on our minds. We were planning for a future together, preparing plans for our wedding in the spring. We had discussed making joint wills, but places of burial were never mentioned.'

'Then the choice will be ours,' Betty insisted hopefully.

'I'm afraid you will have to decide that among yourselves. We have no say in the matter. Any further questions?'

Heads were shaken all round. 'Well then, that's all the preliminaries taken care of. The beneficiaries of the will shall receive their cheques in due course. All funeral expenses will of course be deducted from the deceased's estate.'

Chairs scraped the carpet as they all rose to their feet and hands were shaken and farewells made. In the reception foyer Alice conferred with Dan and then approached Betty and Stan. 'Would you like to come home with us for a chat and a cup of tea?'

'No thank—' Betty automatically started to refuse but with a hand on her arm Stan stopped her.

'That would be lovely, thank you, Alice.'

Les and Mr Benson had other business to attend to, and after making arrangements to pick up Tess and her mother and Dan to take them out for a meal, they left the building. Dan asked the receptionist to call for a taxi, but Stan quickly insisted that there was no need as they could all travel in his car.

Tess was in despair as Dan directed Stan from the city centre to Springfield Road. From her position diagonally behind Betty she observed the look of horror on the woman's face when she spotted the graffiti on the gables of houses and hoardings along the way. She looked as if she were about to pass out when she saw the state of the RUC barracks. What on earth had possessed Alice to invite these people back to the house? Did she not realise the impression Stan and Betty would get? What must they be thinking? They would surely now be more determined to fight for custody of their grandson, if only on the grounds that they lived in a safer environment; to get him away from the heart of the troubles.

Inside the house, Betty was sincere in her compliments as she looked around. 'What lovely big rooms. I've always loved high ceilings, they give off such a feeling of grandeur. And you have it very tastefully decorated and furnished.'

'Thank you,' Alice said, and making her excuses headed for the kitchen.

'Would you like a drink?' Dan asked politely. He was now having his doubts and wished he hadn't agreed with his wife to invite the McCormacks back. 'We have sherry and whiskey.'

180

Stan said, 'A whiskey would be nice, thank you. Just a small one with a dash of water. Remember I'm driving.'

'Will you have a whiskey as well, Betty?'

'No thank you, I'll wait for the tea.'

Dan busied himself at the drinks cabinet and Betty turned to Tess. 'Will we be able to meet young Jackie?'

'I'm afraid not. You see, he's staying with my Uncle Malachy in Carlingford until everything is settled up here.'

'Is that the same uncle who looked after Colette during her pregnancy?'

'Yes. He and Rose married shortly after Colette left for Canada.' Tess was polite but abrupt. She didn't want to get into a conversation about that particular time in their lives.

'Oh, I see. When would it be possible to meet our grandson, then?'

It was Dan who answered. 'You are free to come and see him any time you like, Betty, once this whole business is over and done with and things get back to normal. But . . . let's get the poor girl buried first, eh?'

'That's another thing we want to discuss. Stan and I would like to bury our daughter from our church in Omagh and on to the family cemetery there. We don't want to be travelling to Belfast every time we want to visit her grave. Omagh is where she belongs.'

'Well, the way I see it, she would be better buried in Milltown Cemetery with her grandparents. Or with my son, who is after all the child's father. That way we can take Jackie to visit them.'

'That remains to be seen. I must warn you that I will fight for custody of the boy . . .' Betty's voice was high with a mixture of excitement and determination.

'Here, hold on a minute,' Dan interrupted her. 'You

haven't even met the lad yet. Suppose he takes a dislike to you? What happens then, eh? Believe me, it's been known to happen.'

'He's young enough to settle anywhere. That road out there is like a war zone. I can't see any court letting a young child remain here when we can offer him a comfortable home in a lovely rural district.'

Tess, who had listened to all this in silence, rose to her feet in despair. 'If you'll excuse me, I'll give Mam a hand.'

In the kitchen she hissed in Alice's ear, 'What on earth were you thinking of, inviting them back here? You need your head examined, so you do.'

Amazed at her daughter's suppressed anger, Alice retorted, 'I don't know what you're talking about. I was only being polite.'

'I'll tell you what I'm talking about. One look at the state of that police barracks and Betty is talking about getting custody of Jackie. She wants to take him to Omagh to the lovely quiet district she lives in. And who can blame her?'

Alice sagged against the worktop. 'I don't believe you.'

'You had better believe me. Come on, let's get this tray in. They'll have Dan tied up in knots by now.' She lifted the tray and headed for the door. 'You bring the rest of the stuff.'

They found the atmosphere strained and silent, but apparently Dan had held his ground, and although Jackie wasn't mentioned again talk was politely sporadic. Stan and Betty ate a sandwich each and quickly drank up, as if in a hurry to get away from the house.

'That was lovely, thank you.' Stan sprang to his feet and motioned to Betty. 'We must go now, but we'll be in touch.'

182

Having given them directions to the motorway and waved them off, a relieved trio returned indoors. Sinking down on to the comfortable settee, Dan rubbed his chin and released a sigh. 'Thank God they've gone.' He gave his wife a rueful smile. 'We did the wrong thing inviting them back here, love.'

'Don't you start! Tess has already given me the rounds of the kitchen about that. I didn't stop to think. I was only trying to be sociable, so I was. I feel so sorry for that poor woman.'

'I know, love. I should have foreseen the pitfalls and made some excuse for not inviting them back.'

Tess moved restlessly. 'I hope they agree to Colette being buried with her grandparents. It's what she would have wanted.'

'Well they now know it's her wish to be laid to rest in Milltown, even if nothing is written down on paper. I can't see them insisting on burying her in Omagh.'

'That's another thing that's just struck me,' said Tess. 'It doesn't have to be written down in black and white. Her spoken word is as good as a written contract. I'm just surprised Mr McIlroy didn't say that.'

'I wasn't sure myself,' replied Dan, 'but that's what came to my mind when the solicitor mentioned it. Maybe he didn't want to get involved in our domestic wrangle. After all, the meeting was called for the sole purpose of reading Colette's will. Any other business would have to be dealt with at another time. Well spotted, Tess. It's ammunition to keep up our sleeves, in case Betty is adamant about burying Colette in Omagh.'

Colette's body had been released and lay in the chapel of rest while it was decided who would make the funeral arrangements. For the rest of them it was work as usual.

Friday night Dan was working in the bar and the owner was attending to the hatch that served those in the lounge. Anne Thompson couldn't believe her ears when people going to the hatch to order drinks shouted their condolences through to Dan.

'Glad to see you back, Dan. Sorry to hear about your friend,' one man commiserated.

'That was tragic news you got, Dan, for such a young girl to be killed like that. Terrible!' another sympathised.

A confused Anne took all this in and gazed around the lounge in bewilderment. In an effort to know what they were talking about, she voiced her thoughts. 'Who's dead? Will somebody please tell me what you're all on about?'

Everyone was vague. 'Don't know her name. Just heard it was a friend of Dan's who went abroad years ago,' said one man.

'Some girl Dan knows was killed in that explosion at

the weekend,' another man, a neighbour of Anne's, volunteered. 'Can't remember her name. Just the rumour that she's somehow connected to Dan.'

Anne turned this over in her mind trying to figure out who it could be. Certainly not Tess, she would have heard about that all right. For one thing Dan wouldn't be working. He'd be at home holding Alice's hand. And even if Dan hadn't seen fit to let her know, she would have seen the death notice in the *Irish News*. And it certainly wasn't Tess's business partner . . . she had spoken to Theresa in the chemist that very morning.

Seeing her confusion a woman confided in her. 'Did you not read in the paper on Monday about the young girl that was killed?' Anne still looked bewildered and the woman continued, 'There was no mention of a name, mind you, but I suppose they were waiting until all her relatives had been informed. It seems that this young girl was home on holiday from America or Canada. I've a terrible head for names and places. I forget which one it was. Anyhow, she was killed in that explosion at the weekend. It's quite possible that's who they're all talking about.'

Anne's thoughts immediately flew to Agnes Quinn, lovely blonde-haired Agnes, a close friend of Tess's. She had gone off to Florida some years ago to marry some bloke who was originally from the Springfield Road. Had they been home on holiday? Was it Agnes they were talking about? What a shame if it were; she was such a lovely girl. Waiting her chance, when business was slack she went to the hatch and catching Dan's eye beckoned him over. 'Who's this girl everybody's talking about?'

'What girl?'

'The friend of yours who was killed in that bomb blast.'

'Haven't you heard? Colette Burns died in that explosion at the weekend. I thought you knew.'

Anne was gutted; Colette had never entered her mind. 'No, I didn't know. How could I? Why didn't you tell me?'

'This is the first I've seen of you since it happened. I was sure you'd already know, seeing that you don't miss too much that goes on around here.'

Ignoring the implication that she was nosy, Anne accused him, 'And it never entered your thick head to let me know?'

'Why should I?'

'Because she was almost my daughter-in-law! Have you forgotten that?'

'In this instance, almost isn't quite good enough I'm afraid. If I remember correctly, Colette wasn't all that keen on you.'

'Whether she liked me or not doesn't come into it. You're forgetting she's the mother of my grandson, for goodness' sake! And don't forget we were next-door neighbours for months when she lived in Spinner Street. We got along all right, all things considered. I'd the right to know! Did it not dawn on you that I might want to pay my respects to the poor girl's parents?'

'You still can. She's not buried yet.'

'Whyever not?'

'Her mother wants to take her home to Omagh. I personally would like her to be buried in Milltown with Jack, but it seems she expressed the desire to be buried in her grandparents' grave. Until it can be resolved one way or the other, you can drop into the chapel of rest and say a wee prayer for her,' he said slyly, sure that she wouldn't be interested enough to do that.

She called his bluff. 'Good idea. I'll do that!'

*   *   *

Dan wasn't surprised when Anne presented herself at his door the following day. It was Alice who answered her knock and with a resigned sigh invited her in. Mark Benson had returned to Canada, leaving Les to work with Mr McIlroy in his stead. That morning Les had come in person to let Dan know that Colette's parents had won the right, being the next of kin, to bury their daughter in Omagh. He had also warned them that Betty and Stan had filed for custody of their grandson.

'I've been told that we could appeal against the ruling, but if the McCormacks dug their heels in it could take weeks,' Les explained. 'I'm aware that you would like Colette buried in Milltown Cemetery, either with your son or with her grandparents as she wished, but as I say, it could drag on for weeks . . .' His voice trailed off as he awaited Dan's reaction.

'No! It wouldn't be fair keeping you hanging about here for ages. And I'm sure everybody concerned will want the funeral to take place as quickly as possible. Let her parents make the necessary arrangements to bury her in Omagh.'

Les visibly sagged with relief. 'Thank God for that. It breaks my heart to think of her lying alone in some room, yet I'm ashamed to say that I can't bear to sit with her. I feel so useless.'

'That's understandable. I know just how you feel, Les. Let's get the poor girl laid to rest, eh?'

'Thanks, Dan. I'll go down and see Matthew and let him know.'

After a light tap, the living-room door opened and Anne preceded Alice into the room. Both men rose respectfully to their feet.

Dan made the introductions. 'Les, this is my ex-wife, Anne. Anne, meet Les O'Malley – he was engaged to Colette.'

At the sight of the tall, distinguished man with the mane of silver hair, Anne straightened to attention and it sickened Dan to see a coyness come over her. She took the hand Les thrust out and muttered the first thing that came into her head. 'You're much older than Colette, aren't you?'

Les's lips tightened. What was it with the Irish? Was it frowned upon for a girl to marry an older man? 'How do you do?' His greeting was abrupt. 'I think we've just about finished our business for the moment, Dan, so I'll leave you now. I'll let you know when the funeral will be.' He acknowledged Anne. 'Good day to you, madam.'

Alice led the way out and at the door apologised for Anne's tactlessness. 'Anne didn't mean any harm, you know, Les. It's just that her big mouth goes into over-drive before her brain gets into gear.'

He smiled wryly. 'I'm just a bit touchy at the moment. You Irish seem very aware of age differences, as if it weren't right.'

'No, Les, you're wrong. You only have to look at Theresa and Bob to know that age doesn't matter. Actually I think Anne was making you aware that *she* was more in your age group. She's a compulsive flirt, you know.' In spite of the circumstances, she couldn't resist teasing him. 'I think she fancies you.'

Les's lips pursed. 'God forbid. To be truthful, I did wonder about Theresa and Bob.' He laughed slightly at his own admission. 'So I've a cheek to talk, haven't I? Somehow it seems different when the woman is older than the man. In my eyes Theresa is a very mature woman and makes Bob appear even younger than he is.'

Alice gave him a light peck on the cheek. 'We've decided to go out for a meal tonight. No disrespect meant.

188

Just to get away from these four walls for a while. Would you care to join us?'

'I'd like that very much, thank you.'

'We'll invite Theresa and Bob along. I'll give you a ring about time and place later. See you then.'

Anne's eyes followed Les out the door. 'What a handsome man. He looks like that film star, John Forsythe. You know, the one who was in *Madame X* with Lana Turner.' Her voice was dreamy and Dan gave her a look of reproof.

'Forget it! Remember he has just lost the lovely young girl he was going to marry. He certainly won't be interested in an old boiler like you,' he said scornfully.

Anne didn't take any offence at his sarky remarks. 'Pity.' She brought her attention back to him and said with a wag of the head, 'You know me only too well, Dan Thompson. At least you think you do. Have you found out yet where Colette will be buried?' she queried, changing the subject.

He nodded. 'Yes, that's why Les was here. He called in to tell us that Colette's parents, being next of kin, have been granted the right to bury her in Omagh.'

Anne sensed his disappointment and said softly, 'I'm sorry.'

He shrugged. 'Some you win, some you lose.'

Alice had heard the tail end of their conversation as she walked back along the hall. Now she asked, 'And what about custody of Jackie? Any news on that?'

Dan shot her a warning glance but she wasn't looking in his direction. 'No word on that score at all. That's something that won't be decided in a hurry,' he said flatly, hoping his wife would twig and be quiet.

Anne, however, had noticed the warning look and

189

was intrigued. 'Surely they're not trying to get custody of the child?' she countered. 'A bit late in the day if they are. Apparently they weren't interested in him before, so why now? Why, you've had little Jackie since birth.'

'Ah, but that's because they didn't know about him,' Alice said forlornly.

Dan almost groaned aloud; he wished Alice would keep her mouth shut. You'd think she'd have enough sense not to blurt out their private business in front of Anne, of all people. The less she knew the better. To his dismay Anne was really interested now. She continued to probe. 'Are you telling me Colette never let them know that they had a grandson?'

Alice opened her mouth to speak again but Dan jumped in first. 'If you don't mind my saying so, I don't think that's any of your business, Anne.'

Anne's head shot in the air and her chin stuck out in defiance. 'Well that's a matter of opinion. In a sense it is indeed my business. Very much so in fact! After all, I'm Jackie's grandmother in case you'd forgotten. I've as much right as Colette's mother to have a say in where he should live, and I wouldn't want him to be reared in Omagh. Why, I'd never see the lad. Surely my feelings count for something?'

'I don't think it's likely to happen, Anne. After all, as you've just pointed out, Alice and I have had him since birth, so I really don't think there's much chance of him being taken from us. Now if you don't mind . . .' He gestured towards the door. 'I'm going in to work for a while. We're going out tonight and I've promised to put in a few hours this afternoon.'

Anne rose to her feet with reluctance. 'I'll walk down with you.'

Dan wasn't having any of that! He knew how persuasive she could be and he wasn't going to give her the chance to wheedle any more information out of him. 'No you won't. I've things to do first.' He kept on the move, forcing her to retreat into the hall, then, turning towards the stairs, said to his wife, 'Will you show her out, please, Alice, while I get ready? Good day, Anne.'

Anne lingered on the doorstep and Alice was too courteous to close the door on her. She waited patiently for her to leave.

Anne dallied, choosing her words carefully. 'It's awful sad, isn't it? Colette was such a lovely wee girl.' Alice nodded her agreement and Anne continued, 'Surely her parents won't have the cheek to fight for custody of Jackie?' Alice remained silent. Anne stared at her for some moments, unwilling to let the matter drop. 'What are they like, these parents of hers?'

'Don't you remember them? Surely you met them at your son's funeral.'

'No, I didn't! Not to speak to, that is. You're forgetting that I was on that motorbike too when it crashed. My face was a mess . . . remember? I stayed out of sight. But from what I did see of them from a distance, they seemed too wrapped up in each other to notice what was going on around them.'

'A close happy couple is not to be sneered at.'

'I'm not sneering! I'm just explaining how they appeared to me. I was far from well, so I was.'

'Of course, I remember now. You signed yourself out of hospital against the doctor's wishes to go to the funeral, didn't you? How could I ever forget the likes of that? You wormed your way into living in Dan's house.' Alice's voice was bitter as she now recalled all too clearly the jealous emotions aroused when she had first learned that this woman was living under the same roof as the man she herself had come to love and cherish. 'You placed Dan in an awful awkward predicament, so you did!'

Anne quickly retaliated to the implied criticism. 'At least it gave you plenty of ammunition, and my, you were quick to jump on the bandwagon,' she retorted. 'Hah! Good-living Alice Maguire, my arse! You were no better than the rest of us! Given the chance, you invited Dan to move into your house. I bet that set some tongues wagging round here. Oh, you knew what you were doing all right. You bloody hypocrite! Who knows how things would have turned out had he remained down in Spinner Street with me. Eh? You were willing enough to be talked about rather than take the chance of Dan and me living under the same roof. Away from your influence, I would easily have won him back. And you know that!'

Alice's cheeks burned bright with anger as she reared to her full height at the effrontery of this woman. 'I can assure you, he was not living with me, as you so crudely put it. At that time he rented a room from my daughter and me. It was all innocent and above board, I'll have you know. He was determined to get away from you and your malicious interference, so he was! If Tess and I hadn't taken him in, he would have found somewhere else. I did nothing whatsoever to encourage him. Nothing at all. It was he who approached me. Believe me, I had no influence over him. He just couldn't get away from you quick enough.'

'Why was he so keen to get away from me, eh? Did you ever ask yourself that, Alice? Could it be that I still held some attraction for him? Was he afraid he might give in to temptation? That's the impression I got. The short time we shared the house it was as if he was walking on eggshells. The first chance he got, he upped and ran like a scared rabbit; he was so afraid of me, pure and simple, that's what!' She brushed the air with her hands to show her disdain, then, altering her tone of voice, she continued, 'But no matter, that's all water under the bridge now. Tell me . . . is there any chance at all that this couple will try to get custody of Jackie?'

Anne had hit a raw nerve, awakening memories of past grievances, and Alice tried to regain the high ground. 'Some people, like *you* for instance, would be after all they could get. Maybe the fact that Colette died a wealthy woman might influence the McCormacks to try for custody, but they don't stand a chance. It's the child's grandfather and Tess who have been nominated trustees. They will be in charge of Jackie's fortune until he is twenty-one. Now good day to you, Anne. I've better things to do than stand here having a slanging match with you.' For once, having reached the end of her tether, Alice completely forgot her manners and took great satisfaction in closing the door in Anne's astounded face.

When her anger had evaporated, Alice was besieged with guilt. Dan must never know that she had told Anne about Colette's wealth. Anne was a blabbermouth whereas Dan was a very private person who wouldn't want people to know any of his business. Not that Anne could interfere! Alice consoled herself with the fact that Dan's ex-wife was only Jackie's grandmother, after all. She would have no say in the matter. None whatsoever.

Anne walked slowly down the road, head bowed, a perplexed frown on her brow. She was glad now that she had called up to Alice's house instead of phoning as she had originally intended doing, otherwise she would not have discovered that Colette's parents might bid for custody of their grandchild. Neither would she have learned that Dan as grandfather would be a trustee.

Imagine being in charge of lots of money. She certainly had plenty of food for thought.

Bob Dempsey was in a quandary. He sat across the table in the Chimney Corner Inn and watched the antics of Tess Maguire towards Tony Burke. What was she playing at? Was she deliberately trying to make him jealous? It was hard to believe that exactly one week ago, in the hallway of her home, she had almost eaten him alive. And it hadn't just been a mad impulse of passion, of that he was convinced. All that evening in Romano's he had been aware of her mute desire. It came across strong, in the covert glances she had shot at him and the way she had pressed against him on the walk home from the dance. Normally a very composed and self-assured lady, she had been out of control for a change; had wanted him as desperately as he'd wanted her. If Theresa had not been waiting outside the door Tess would have been his for the taking that night and there would have been no going back. Now it looked as if she was having second thoughts. She seemed to have made up her mind to keep him at arm's length again.

Disappointment was a heavy lump in his chest. Not even the tragic news he'd received about Colette's death had been able to banish excited thoughts of Tess from his mind. All week he had relived the memory of her in his arms; the feel of her lips under his. He had been planning a showdown this weekend, glad that at last their true feelings were about to be brought into the open; that they could show their love for each other. He had been prepared to break the news to Theresa that he was in love with someone else. Now this. What had got into Tess? What was she playing at?

A gentle touch on the arm brought his attention back

194

to Theresa. 'You're very quiet tonight, love. I suppose it was the shock of hearing about Colette.'

He covered her hand with his, gently squeezed it, and lied, 'You're right. It was an awful shock. To tell you the truth, I still can't take it in.'

'I suppose I shouldn't say this, but it's an ill wind and all that.' She nodded across the table. 'Tony took Tess to Omagh to break the news to Mr and Mrs McCormack, and look at them now. I think she has at last acknowledged that he's the man for her. And about time too. I must say, he's been very patient. It's funny how tragic events can bring out the best in the people we take so much for granted.'

Bob allowed a tight smile to crease his face. So he wasn't being paranoïd. Everyone was apparently aware of the change in Tess's attitude towards Tony and was giving her their silent blessing. Needing to be sure, he asked quietly, 'Has she said as much?'

'No. But sure, she doesn't have to. You've just to look at them.'

Bob wished that he could *stop* looking at them. It was breaking his heart to see all his hopes evaporate before his eyes. To his relief their starters arrived and he was able to concentrate on his prawn cocktail and for a short time force himself to ignore the shenanigans across the table.

A worried Tess tucked into her Chef's Special. It was a delicious vegetable soup, but her throat was so knotted with nerves, she was sure that it would choke her. It dismayed her that she could actually feel the anger that was directed at her every time Bob's eyes met hers. He was so full of wrath that she did her best to avoid any eye contact with him. He mustn't get the opportunity to weaken her resolve. She didn't blame him in the slightest for his attitude towards her; just hoped that no one else would notice. There was nothing she'd like more than to be in Theresa's position, seated at his side hanging on to his every word, knowing that he was hers. But it was not to be. Life wasn't as simple as that! It threw obstacles in your path, and sometimes, as was the case here, they were insurmountable. There was nothing she could do to change things. She blinked back tears. It was going to be a long, long evening.

Theresa and Bob had travelled across town with them in Tony's car and Tess had been very aware of Bob's displeasure. He had hardly spoken a word during the journey. The few words he did speak were full of innuendoes for her ears only. She prayed he wouldn't do anything stupid.

She was unconsciously pushing vegetables around in her soup when she was startled from her musing by his voice addressing her. 'Theresa's been telling me, Tess, that you and Tony went to Omagh to break the sad news to Colette's parents. It must have been a terrible ordeal for you.'

'It was awful! But Tony was a tower of strength.' Bob's lips tightened as Tess gently touched Tony's sleeve in a light caress and received a surprised, pleased look from him in return. 'It made me realise his worth.'

Bob's nostrils flared and Tess thought she had gone too far, but he controlled his temper and only remarked, 'Indeed? When will Colette be buried?'

It was Les who answered. 'Mr McIlroy said it will probably be Tuesday. He'll find out for sure tomorrow and let us know.'

'I don't think I'll be able to get back from Sligo to attend.'

'Don't worry about that, Bob, you hardly knew the girl,' Dan retorted. 'We wouldn't expect you to go.'

'Still . . . if I can, I'll be there.' Bob's eyes fixed on Tess as he added, 'I've some other unfinished business to attend to.'

The food was delicious but praise for it was sparse. Everybody seemed to have other things on their mind. They finished the evening with coffee and a drink, and soon after left for home.

Before leaving the car park Alice invited them all back to the house, but Bob quickly declined. 'Theresa and I have a lot of catching up to do,' he explained, and putting an arm around her waist drew her close, dropping a kiss on the top of her head. He noted the pain in Tess's eyes. Before she turned away, he rubbed salt in the wound. 'You know how it is, Tony. So if you don't mind, could you drop us off at Theresa's?'

'No problem, if that's what you want.'

When the car drew to a halt outside the house, Bob helped Theresa out before leaning towards the passenger window and gesturing for Tess to open it. Apprehensive, Tess wound the window down and nervously looked askance at him. Touching her on the shoulder he said, 'May I say you're looking very lovely tonight, Tess? You must be in love.' He peered across at Tony. 'Are congratulations in order, Tony?'

Tony gave an exaggerated sigh. 'I wish they were, Bob.' He looked fondly at Tess. 'Unfortunately she still hasn't said yes, but I'm working at it.' He laid a possessive hand on Tess's thigh and gently caressed it.

Seeing this, Bob's fingers bit cruelly into Tess's shoulder. 'Ah well, the signs are obvious for all to see. Keep up the pressure, Tony. I think she's about ready to tie the knot.' His reward was a tight-lipped smile from Tess and a wide grin from Tony. 'Well, good night.'

Theresa had opened the door but remained on the step

to shout a final farewell and wave them off. 'What was that all about?'

'Just wishing them good luck for the future.'

'You shouldn't have!' she admonished him. 'Did you see Tess's face, it was like thunder. She doesn't like to be pushed into things.'

Bob shrugged indifferently. 'I suppose it depends on who's doing the pushing. Let's get inside, I'm hungry.'

'Bob Dempsey! You couldn't possibly be hungry after that big meal.'

'Who's talking about food?'

A big smile of delight spread across Theresa's face. Bob had been morose all day. She hadn't dared to hope he would be in a loving mood. Taking his hand she drew him towards the stairs. 'What are we waiting for?'

She was to be disappointed. Bob laboured in vain and she was frustrated when he at last turned from her in despair.

'I'm sorry, love,' he muttered. 'I don't know what's wrong with me.'

'Don't be silly! These things happen to everybody now and again.'

He buried his head in the pillow and muttered, 'It's never happened to me before.'

This was exactly what she was thinking. It had only happened once before, after he was released from internment. So why now? Was there another woman in Sligo? Was it guilt that was upsetting his performance? There was definitely something wrong. With a swift movement she left the bed to stand staring down at him in bewilderment.

'I'm sorry,' he repeated. 'Please forgive me.'

'It's okay. Can I get you anything? A cup of tea perhaps?'

198

He turned his head and smiled at the idea that a cup of tea would solve anything. 'No thank you.'

Abruptly leaving the room she quickly descended the stairs. In the kitchen she filled the kettle and stood looking blindly down at it hissing away on the hob; what had got into him? He was a good lover, considerate and kind, always trying to satisfy her, make it pleasant for her as well. Never before had he failed. She tensed when the kitchen door opened and he came to stand close behind her.

'I'm truly sorry. I honestly don't know what happened. Can you forgive me?'

She turned and buried herself against him and mumbled, 'These things happen. We can try again, if you like.'

Knowing why he had failed and afraid of it happening again, he said, 'Better not. Maybe it's because I'm dead beat. I'll sleep on the settee. Let you get a proper night's sleep.'

'No, Bob! You don't have to do that.'

'I insist. Good night, love.'

Fetching some bedclothes, he made up a bed on the settee. He needed space to sort out his troubled thoughts. Silently he cursed Tess Maguire. She certainly brought out the worst in him. Still, the longing for her tormented him, and with the remembered feel of her in his arms he tossed and turned all night. Unable to face Theresa, he was up and away long before she awoke next morning.

Outside her house, Tess had difficulty putting Tony off. Les's car was still parked out front, and she used him as an excuse. 'I'd rather you didn't come in, Tony. Les is still here and we must respect his loss. We're all grieving over Colette, but it's easy to forget now and again for a few minutes. Les must be gutted, although he puts on a brave face. We are, after all, strangers to him. There'll be plenty of time for us to get to know each other when this is all over and done with.'

'If we don't know each other now, Tess, we never will,' Tony cried in exasperation. 'You know I love you. Won't you give me some definite sign? Agree to marry me! Let me buy you a ring . . . please.'

Dismayed at the misery that suddenly engulfed her at these words – how could she possibly accept a ring from another man, feeling as she did for Bob? – Tess pleaded, 'Not yet, Tony. What with the business and all, I'm not ready to think of marriage just now.' Even if she did decide that the right thing to do was to marry Tony, now was not the time to flaunt a ring in Bob Dempsey's face.

Pulling her into his arms, Tony smothered her face with kisses. Tess felt repulsed. He had no right, she thought wildly. Or had he? Wasn't she leading him on? He had every right to believe that she welcomed his advances. And I will, she vowed inwardly. One day I'll respond to his kisses. I'll marry him and make him a good wife. But not just yet!

Meanwhile, having been in Bob's company all evening, it was easy to picture him in her mind's eye; it was his kisses she relived as she returned Tony's caresses. He released her slowly and gazed into her eyes. 'I can't understand why you won't accept a ring from me. You seem to like me well enough.'

Tess didn't blame him for being confused. God forgive her! She was a right bitch. After all, he didn't know Bob had been the recipient of her kisses. Silently she vowed to make it up to him one day.

'All in good time. All in good time. Good night, Tony. I'll let you know when the funeral will be.'

'You'll let me drive you there, won't you?'

'Of course.'

'I'll wait for your call then. Good night, Tess.'

The funeral took place after the eleven o'clock Requiem Mass on Tuesday morning. Tess was sad but relieved when Bob sent his regrets that he would be unable to make it to the service. Closing the shop for the day, Tess, Alice and Dan travelled to Omagh in Tony's car, leaving Les to follow them, giving Theresa a lift in his hired car.

They met Malachy and Rose outside the church as planned. After a long discussion on the phone the night before, it had been decided that Jackie must be told about his mother's death and not just arrive at the church unaware that it was his own mother's funeral he was attending. Rose had broken the news to him as gently as she could. Big dark eyes held hers throughout the narrative and she was deeply worried when he showed no outward reaction whatsoever to what she was telling him. They had brought him through to Omagh with them and he cowered beside Malachy outside the church, until he spotted Dan walking through the church gates. Running to him, he threw himself into his grandfather's arms and was hugged close, before Dan gently released him and, clasping him by the hand, led them all into the church.

It was packed! Obviously the McCormacks were well known in the district and the tragic death of their only daughter had brought everyone out to pay their last respects. There wasn't a dry eye in the church at the eloquent sermon delivered by the parish priest, who was able to recall Colette's earlier days, punctuating his praise of her intellect and charm with lovable stories relayed to him by her mother and a few schoolfriends.

Tess, sitting in a pew to one side of the splendid coffin, couldn't come to terms with the fact that Colette's young body lay in it. Life was so unfair; she'd had so much to live for. But at least Dan would not now have anything to worry about. It was in black and white, written by Colette's own hand, that as a trustee he was to be in joint control of Jackie's affairs. And Tess was relieved that she would not now have to explain to her mother about Dan's betrayal. Alice need never know the awful truth.

It was a beautiful day, the air crisp and laden with the smell of freshly cut grass. Colette was laid to rest in a corner of the church cemetery and Tess couldn't control her emotions and let the tears flow freely. Tony moved closer to her side and laid an arm across her shoulders and she buried her head in his shoulder. Afterwards the mourners were invited back to the bungalow for refreshments. They eventually drifted away in twos and threes until there were only the family members left.

Tentatively Betty approached Jackie where he sat on a stool close to his grandfather. Kneeling on the carpet in front of him she reached for his hand, but he pulled it away and cowered closer still to Dan.

Undeterred, she said softly, 'I only want to have a wee chat with you, love. You don't know me yet, but I'm your Grannie McCormack, your mam's mother, and I just know we'll be best friends.'

Jackie stared at her wide-eyed and she continued, 'You and I will have to get to know each other, Jackie. Now your mammy has gone up to heaven you'll need your grandparents to look after you. You'll be able to come and stay with me here in this house. Won't that be nice, love?'

'No!' Jackie turned and buried his face in Dan's jacket and wailed, 'I want to go home with you, Grandad. Don't leave me here. Please take me home.'

'Of course I'll take you home with me, son. Don't you worry your wee head about that.' Distressed, Dan threw Tess an anxious glance and she quickly came to his aid.

Bending towards the boy she said, 'Hush, love. Don't be upset. Your Grannie McCormack only wants to get to know you better. Come with me and I'll get you a glass of lemonade before we go home.'

Keeping a wet-eyed, terrified stare fixed on Betty's face, the child sidled nervously past her and gripping Tess's hand allowed himself to be led away.

Betty slumped back on her heels with a long-drawn-out sigh, her face bathed in mixed emotions. 'I only want to get to know the poor wee soul,' she said forlornly to no one in particular. Her husband gently helped her to her feet and put an arm across her shoulders, all the while whispering words of comfort in her ear.

Dan felt heartsore for the woman, but warned himself to be wary and not be swept away by her grief. To be very careful not to make any promises he might later regret. 'You see how it is, Betty?' he remonstrated. 'The child doesn't know you.'

'That's not my fault, is it?'

'That's as may be, but you must be patient. It will take time to win him round. And remember, we were only carrying out Colette's wishes. It wouldn't be fair to change the child's routine now. He's mixed up enough as it is.'

'It's easy for you to say that now,' Betty taunted. 'I'm sure things would have been different if we had lived in Belfast. Colette would have had to acknowledge us then. Good God, I'm her mother. How can I be sure that she didn't want us involved? How do we know you just didn't want to share our grandson?'

Dan's voice hardened. He wasn't going to buckle under her accusations. If they had lived in Belfast things might very well have been different, but they hadn't, and Colette had made it plain to Tess that she didn't want her parents to know of Jackie's existence. Betty must understand right from the outset that Dan was in charge now. 'You're talking nonsense, and you know it.'

'We'll see what the law has to say about that, Dan Thompson! We've as much right as you.'

'I agree with you there! About the law, that is. It *is* best to leave any dispute in their hands; let them sort it out legally.' Dan rose to his feet. 'Now if you'll excuse us, we'll be on our way.'

Betty opened her mouth to protest further but Stan put a warning hand on her arm. 'Our solicitor will be in touch with you, Dan.'

'Not directly with me, please . . . with my solicitor,' Dan informed him.

Theresa and Les had travelled to Omagh in comparative silence. Now, on the journey back to Belfast, Theresa commiserated with him. 'I'm sure you're glad this is all over, Les. It must be a relief to know that Colette is at last laid to rest.'

'Yes, I hated the thought of her lying alone in that chapel of rest. However, I'm still worried about little Jackie.'

'Oh, you needn't worry on that score. Dan and Alice think the world of that wee boy. He'll be all right with them.'

'I know that. But what if the McCormacks fight for their rights? They must have some, you know. I don't for one minute think they stand a chance of getting complete custody . . . but I imagine they will be granted some sort of access to him.'

'By access, what exactly do you mean?'

'Maybe one weekend a month and some of the school holidays. Something like that.'

'I'm sure that Dan and Alice would agree to that. But what if the child doesn't want to go and stay in Omagh?'

Les shrugged. 'Something will be worked out.'

'Poor Jackie, he's so confused.'

'Poor Jackie indeed.' After a short silence, Les spoke again. 'As you know, I return to Canada on Friday. You have been most kind to me and I would like to take this opportunity to thank you.'

'There's no need for that. I was only too glad to be of assistance. It must have been awful for you over here in such circumstances and not knowing anyone.'

A sob caught in his throat and he swallowed before confessing, 'You know, I haven't really accepted that Colette is gone. At the back of my mind I'm deluding myself that once I get home everything will be back to normal, but of course it won't.'

His face was drawn and grey and Theresa said, 'All this has proved too much for you, Les. Would you like to take a wee break before we get back to the house? Let's stop somewhere along the way and have a nice cup of tea or coffee. It'll help you relax.'

They stopped off at Dungannon and parked the car in a side street. Making their way to the town square, Theresa spotted a café and entering, headed for a vacant table in the corner.

Deciding on tea and sandwiches they waited for someone to take their order. Les leaned across the table. 'Forgive me for remarking on it, but you seemed a bit down earlier on. Was it just because of the funeral, or . . .' He let the question hang in the air and she responded.

'Oh, you noticed then! You're right, I was depressed, but it had nothing to do with the funeral.'

'Would you like to talk about it?'

'I don't know what ails me. No, that's a lie! I just can't bring myself to talk about it.'

'Does it concern Bob?'

'Yes, very much so.'

'A lovers' tiff. All couples have them from time to time,' he said consolingly, his hand reaching across the table to touch hers briefly.

'You're a good man, Les O'Malley. It's not fair that us Irish have robbed you of your future wife. How you must hate us! I bet you can't wait to get away from here.'

'Not a bit of it! I admire your fighting spirit. I'm also a great believer that when your time's up you'll go, no matter where you are.'

She looked at him in surprise. 'Do you know something? I believe that too. If you're born to hang you certainly won't drown. My mam was forever coming up with those old pearls of wisdom.' Suddenly she looked sharply about her and laughed. 'Do you know something else, Les? I think this is a self-service café, so shall I go to the counter or will you?'

He glanced around and saw she was right. 'Allow me. It's as well you caught on or we'd have been here all day.'

'Oh, I think someone would have noticed and let us know.'

They ate their sandwiches and indulged in small talk. The break was good for Les. He was more relaxed when they left the café and they decided to take a stroll round the town square. Theresa stopped at a pawnbroker's shop to admire the antique jewellery displayed in a corner of the window.

'I think it's sad when circumstances force people to part with their family heirlooms. Look at that locket! Isn't it beautiful? I bet it broke some poor woman's heart to part with that.'

Les laughed softly. 'You're too soft. That locket was probably part of a haul some burglar passed on. I'm not saying that the pawnbroker knew it was hot. Nor am I saying the original owner wasn't heartbroken, but I bet she was well recompensed for it.'

'Only if she was insured. You'd be surprised how many people can't afford to insure their valuables.'

Les quietly agreed with her. 'You're right, of course. Look . . . please don't be offended, but will you let me buy that locket for you?'

Theresa turned a look of astonishment on him. 'You'll do no such thing! I won't hear of it. Look at that price tag, for heaven's sake! It's thirty pounds, so it is, and it isn't even new.'

Les was manoeuvring her into the shop doorway. She resisted his efforts but he was determined, and managing to get the door open he pushed her none too gently inside. They were immediately pounced on by the owner and Theresa couldn't get away without creating a scene.

'Can I be of assistance, sir?'

Before Theresa could open her mouth Les said, 'Yes, we'd like to have a look at the locket on tray fifteen, please.'

The small dark man exclaimed, 'Ah yes, a beautiful piece of jewellery. You have good taste, sir.'

He removed the tray from the window and brought it to the counter. Spreading the fine gold chain across the back of his hand he showed off the locket to advantage, displaying its beauty before handing it over to Theresa.

Carefully she took it from him and examined the intricate design on the front. 'Oh, it's beautiful, so it is, but I can't possibly accept it.' She thrust the locket back towards the man.

Seeing a sale fading before his very eyes the owner urged, 'It opens. Try it.'

Theresa's hands were shaking and she fumbled with the catch. Taking it from her, Les opened it and Theresa was relieved to see it was empty.

'May I say that a picture of you and your husband in there would complement it beautifully.'

Blushing at the assumption that they were married, Theresa asked him, 'What about the owner? Won't she be back for it?'

'When someone leaves an article with me, I retain it for six months. During that time they can redeem it for a nominal charge. This locket has been in my possession for eight months now, so I'm at liberty to dispose of it as I see fit.'

'I feel guilty. What if some poor woman is still hoping to recover it?'

'Believe you me, if it was that precious to someone, they would have come back and asked me to extend the deadline. Which is something I often do.'

Theresa opened her mouth to argue some more but Les gently forestalled her. 'I think we can purchase it with an easy conscience, Theresa.' Used to doing deals, he eyed the shop-owner and said, 'Will you take twenty pounds for it?'

The man threw his hands in the air in horrified amazement. 'That would be daylight robbery. Why, you may as well have a mask on. I'll let you have it for twenty-seven.'

'Twenty-five.'

'I can't possibly let it go for less than twenty-six.'

Les took the locket from Theresa and made to hand it back over the counter. Sensing that he would not be swayed, the owner said, 'Oh, all right then! You drive a hard bargain. Shall I put it in a presentation box for you?'

'There will be no need. My friend will wear it now.' Standing behind Theresa he dangled the locket in front of her, and when she lifted the hair from the nape of her neck he secured the clasp.

Her eyes filled as she gazed down at the gold gleaming against the red sweater she wore. 'Thank you. Thank you very much. I'll treasure it always.'

She kept gazing down and fingering the locket on the journey back. Overcome by his generosity and her emotional reaction, she did not want to face the others and told Les she would rather go straight home, where she would ring Tess and make her apologies. He drew the car to a halt in front of her house and leaned across to give her a farewell peck on the cheek. Unaware of his intention she turned her head to speak and his lips met hers.

He immediately drew back, a startled look on his face. 'Oh . . . I'm so sorry about that. It was an accident, honest. I just meant to give you a little peck on the cheek as a thank-you for sticking by me today.'

'Look, Les. There's no need to apologise. We're both adults, and anyway, I thought it was a nice little gesture. I actually enjoyed it,' she confessed with a shy smile.

'Thank you, Theresa.' After a brief, awkward silence he ventured, 'Look! I've been wondering . . . I'd like very much to keep in touch with events here. Would you answer my letters if I write to you?'

'That would be nice, and I'd be delighted to.'

'I'll write soon.'

'And once again, thank you for this lovely locket.' She reached across and deliberately touched his lips with hers; just a brief kiss, but enough to bring a blush to his cheeks.

'Thanks, Theresa.'

'Thank *you*. Would you like to come in for a drink?'

'I'd love to, but I'm so tired I'd probably fall asleep the minute I sat down. But thanks for the offer. If I wasn't heading home soon I'd ask you for a rain-check on that drink.'

'I'm shattered, myself. I think I'll make an early night of it.'

Once more her hand went unconsciously to the locket. It was the loveliest thing anyone had ever bought her. 'I'll treasure this locket for ever,' she whispered, and getting out of the car, with a final wave disappeared into the house.

8

Alice arranged drinks and a finger buffet on Thursday night to wish Les bon voyage. He had regretfully declined to make a big night of it, reminding them that he was leaving for Aldergrove very early on Friday morning to catch the shuttle flight to Shannon on the first stage of his journey home. He would be gone long before the others were awake. There was no need for Tony to take him as he would drive up to the airport in his hired car and drop it off at the rental office there.

It was just the usual small gathering of Colette's friends that Les had come to know and like, plus Anne, who had heard talk in the Clock Bar on Wednesday night that the handsome visitor was leaving on Friday. She had dropped in to wish him a safe journey home and been asked to stay. At first it was a sad affair; everyone picking their words carefully, afraid of upsetting Les by saying the wrong thing in front of him, or mentioning Colette. After some desultory conversation about death and grief, however, Anne decided enough was enough. Rising to her feet and raising her glass she said, 'I would like to propose a toast. To Colette, may she rest in peace.'

211

They all stared at her in stunned silence and then Les joined Anne in her toast. 'To my darling Colette. I'm sure she'll never be forgotten by any of us, but she would be the first to say – it's time to move on.'

He bowed his head respectfully and everyone responded to the toast. After that the atmosphere brightened up somewhat. Tess put a Dean Martin LP on the turntable as soft background music, and the conversation became more light-hearted. To the delight of Alice, who had thought she had overdone the sandwiches and savoury dishes, the buffet slowly but surely disappeared.

'They're right, you know,' Tess said quietly to Theresa. 'I'm glad Anne spoke out like that. Colette wouldn't want this wee do to be all tears and gloom.' Her eye lit on Les where Anne had him cornered near the buffet table. He was looking decidedly uneasy. 'Will you just look at that! What the hell is she playing at now? Shall I go over and rescue him or will you?'

'Leave it to me.' Theresa smiled grimly. 'She hasn't got a clue, that one! She probably thinks it's about time Les showed some interest in another woman. As if he possibly could, the poor dear.'

Crossing the floor, Theresa touched Les gently on the arm. 'Can I have a word with you, Les?'

Les turned to her gratefully. 'Of course you can, Theresa.'

'If you'll just follow me, we can talk in the kitchen, it will be more private. Will you excuse us, Anne?'

'Why? Where are you going?'

'I need to have a quiet word with Les. We won't be too long.'

A venomous look bored into their retreating backs as they left the room. In the kitchen Theresa turned to face Les and gave him a wry smile. 'I hope you don't mind me rescuing you like that, but you looked trapped by that silly woman.'

'Mind? I was glad of the interruption. I had run out of things to say to her.'

'I'm surprised she gave you a chance to talk at all. Usually you can't get a word in edgeways when she starts rabbiting on.'

'Now and again she gave me an opening, but I couldn't think of anything to talk about to keep the conversation going. We were on a completely different wavelength. So thank you very much for coming to my rescue.'

An awkward silence fell. They both spoke at once. 'I suppose . . .'

'I was wondering . . .'

Les gestured with his hand. 'Ladies first.'

'I was just going to say, I suppose we had better rejoin the company. And you were about to say?'

'I was wondering if you had heard from Bob?'

A slight grimace crossed her face. 'Just before I left the house tonight he rang to let me know he will be working overtime this weekend and it wouldn't be worth his while coming home for a few hours.'

Les pursed his lips and said tentatively, 'And you don't believe him, do you?' He stepped impulsively towards her when her face crumpled and tears threatened.

A raised hand kept him at bay. She blinked furiously and managed to stem the flow. 'I don't want to talk about it. I'll only start blubbering and then how will I be able to face everybody in there?'

He glanced at his watch. 'Look, it's getting late. Go powder your nose and fetch your coat. I'll walk you home.' He stopped, overcome with embarrassment at his own presumptuousness. 'Unless of course you'd rather stay a while longer.'

She smiled kindly at him. 'No! I'll be glad to leave now, and I'd be happy if you would escort me home. As you say, it's getting late and you have an early start in the morning. I'll pop up to the bathroom. I won't be long.'

'I'll wait in the living room.'

A few minutes later Theresa bade everyone good night and she and Les left the house, leaving their friends exchanging questioning looks. They strolled up the road in companionable silence for some minutes.

Les spoke. 'You know, it's not everyone I feel this comfortable with. Everybody I have met since I arrived here has been great, but I'm a very reserved kind of person and like to keep myself to myself. My ordeal has been made a lot more bearable by your mere presence.'

'I'm glad if I've been of some comfort to you and helped you cope with all the trauma you've been through.' They had reached her door and she paused. 'Would you like to come in for a coffee?'

'No thank you. I'd better get back and let everybody get to bed.'

'Okay, but you can be sure Anne won't leave without seeing you again. I'm sure her tongue started wagging the minute the door closed behind us.'

'Theresa . . . I hope you won't mind me saying this, but if things don't work out between you and Bob and you feel the need to get away for a while, please let me know and you can come over and visit me in Canada. I'll make all the arrangements. It will be my treat.'

'Oh, I couldn't impose on you like that. You're—'

He interrupted her. 'Don't give me an answer right now. Just bear it in mind, won't you? Canada is a beautiful country and I'll show you all around where I live in Vancouver. I'll introduce you to my friends and believe me, an attractive woman like you will be a very welcome sight indeed. You'll be bombarded with all kinds of offers.'

She laughed. 'Flattery will get you everywhere, thank you. You've made my day. I was feeling a bit jaded. I suppose it's what comes of falling in love with a younger man. Always on edge and waiting for the day he tells me that he's met someone younger. I honestly don't know what I'd do if that happens.'

'Bob's a fool if he lets you slip through his fingers.'

'You know something, Les? You're a very sweet person. I'm sorry you lost Colette in such tragic circumstances. In due course I hope you meet someone who will make you happy. It's what Colette would want for you. And if I do need to get away, I'll remember your kind offer.' She reached up and kissed him on the cheek. 'God bless, and safe journey home.'

Tess closed the door with a decisive click and descended the steps to the pavement, her temper at boiling point. The weather did nothing to improve her humour; if anything it only made it worse. Fierce winds roaring down from the Black Mountain whipped at her clothes, moulding them round her figure and almost lifting her off her feet. As she paused and struggled to open her umbrella, the wind lifted the hood of her ski jacket from her head and her long hair blew all over the place as the rain beat relentlessly down, quickly giving it the appearance of rats' tails plastered to her face and neck. The umbrella, once she had managed to get it open, was clasped firmly behind her head and shoulders as she headed down the Springfield Road, but in spite of all her efforts, when she reached the corner of Malcomson Street a cross-blast of wind caught it and blew it inside out.

With a grunt of anger she made as if to throw the broken brolly from her. In time she realised the damage it might cause to someone or something, and restraining the impulse she tucked the mangled frame firmly under her arm. Adjusting her hood she gripped both ends of it tightly under her chin and continued down the road, carried along more quickly than was safe and almost getting lifted off her feet by the sheer force of the wind.

She was daft to even think of opening the shop today, she inwardly lamented. Customers would be few and far between. Who in their right mind would come out in this foul weather? But then . . . she just had to get out of the house this morning. She was fed up listening to her mother and Dan going on and on about young Jackie. The boy had been out last weekend with his other grandparents and had come home looking far from happy. It had been Jackie this and Jackie that ever since; a continuous moan all week long. You would think the McCormacks had physically abused the boy, instead of plying him with sweets and toys. To be truthful, Tess was inclined to think that maybe little Jackie was playing the grandparents against each other. He was an intelligent child and at an age when most children craved attention and soon learned how to get their own way, so why not throw the odd tantrum now and again just to keep them on their toes?

The McCormacks were supposed to have him again tomorrow – Saturday – and now Dan regretted giving his permission for them to collect him. The week had been spent debating what to do and how best to go about it. Every mealtime, and every opening that presented itself, Dan was ranting on about it. It was a case of should he put them off or not? He couldn't make up his own mind one way or the other and had asked Alice or

216

Tess on so many occasions that Tess felt at the end of her tether. She just had to get out of the house or go stark raving mad.

Both grandparents had been advised by their solicitors that it would be better if they sorted something out between themselves, as going to court could prove very costly. So they had talked it through and agreed to come to an arrangement whereby the McCormacks could have access to Jackie.

Obviously it was going to be more difficult than they had imagined. One Saturday afternoon was enough to make Betty and Stan aware that they needed to spend more time with their only grandchild. A few hours a week was not going to be enough to get to know the boy; they had a lot of lost time to make up. They wanted him to stay overnight at their home in Omagh, get to know their neighbours and the district; they wanted a chance to show how much they loved him. The state Jackie got into when this was put to him caused Dan such concern that he immediately knocked the idea on the head. Last night he had phoned and told the McCormacks that they could collect Jackie tomorrow as promised, but after that they wouldn't see him again as it was causing the lad too much distress. The only way that they would get access to him in future would be through the courts, that is, unless Jackie agreed to see them. They couldn't continue upsetting the boy. Even having decided this, Dan was still in doubt whether it was for the best all round.

Tess was fed up to the teeth with the problems Dan had brought to their home. If it wasn't one thing it was another. She and her mother had been very happy living together on their own, and then Tess had managed for years to conquer her resentment and appear to live amicably under the same roof as Dan. At first there had been the chance that the romance would peter out and Alice and Dan would eventually go their separate ways, but it soon became obvious to Tess that her mother truly loved Dan and that he reciprocated her love. The marriage ceremony in the register office proved just how much Alice cared for him, otherwise she would never have married outside the Church. Whether Tess liked it or not, Dan was there to stay. And really, Tess knew deep down in her heart that it was no big deal. She was happy to see her mother so content. It was just that lately everything seemed to revolve around Dan and little Jackie, and at times she felt as if she were an intruder in her own home. It wasn't that she didn't love the lad. She did! But he wasn't her responsibility. She wanted space to live her own life. All this talk about the boy, the McCormacks and the courts was driving her up the wall.

Supposing, just supposing she married Tony? Would they have to buy a house of their own? Probably. The house on Springfield Road was her inheritance and she loved it, but only after the death of her mother would it become hers, and she sincerely hoped Alice would live to a ripe old age. Meanwhile, she certainly didn't intend starting married life sharing a home with her mother and Dan. But then there would be no need to. Should they marry, Tony could afford to buy a house, so why was she worrying unnecessarily?

She was willing to admit to herself that she was letting everything get on top of her at the moment. And all because of Bob Dempsey. Try as she might, Bob still intruded into her thoughts and she was no nearer to giving in to Tony and agreeing to marry him. Whoever said 'out of sight out of mind' didn't know what they were talking about. Her longing to see Bob grew more

218

acute with each passing week. She knew she would probably be even more upset if she did see him, but she
couldn't help herself. She ached for the sight of him. Was
she hoping for a miracle? Some indication as to what
was the right road to take? Surely she could never feel
justified in breaking Theresa's heart, no matter what.

And what about Tony? She had been leading him on
for weeks now and there was no way she could break
off their relationship. Agnes Quinn's treatment of him
had almost caused him to have a nervous breakdown
and Tess shuddered to think what another rejection
would do. No! There was no turning back, she had
burned her bridges, so she had better wake up to reality.

As she struggled to open the door of the shop, a car
horn hooted and a glance over her shoulder showed
Theresa's old banger passing and turning down the Falls
Road.

Putting the kettle on to boil, Tess took two cups down
from the shelf and added milk and sugar to the tray. On
a cold wet morning like this, after she had parked her
car in McQuillen Street or wherever she could find a
space, Theresa would surely call into the bakery and buy
something nice for their morning cuppa. She was right;
her friend bustled breathlessly into the shop on a great
gust of wind, bearing gifts of fresh cream cakes. Tess
eyed her covertly. Bob hadn't been home since he had
upped and left early the Sunday morning after the outing
to the Chimney Corner Inn – the weekend before Colette's
funeral. Consequently Theresa was withdrawn and
depressed. When Tess had tried to broach the subject of
Bob's abrupt departure and her obvious unhappiness, her
friend had politely but effectively told her in as few words
as possible to mind her own business. Thus Tess didn't

know whether the romance between Bob and Theresa was still on. Today was the first time she had seen Theresa look even remotely happy. She seemed more relaxed than usual and a faint smile hovered on the corners of her lips. Was that a good sign? Or a bad one, depending on how you looked at it?

They drank their tea and scoffed the cakes in comparative silence; only the weather apparently worthy of idle chatter. Unable to wait any longer, clearing away the empty cups, Tess voiced what was nearest her heart and prompted Theresa. 'You're looking quite cheerful this morning. Does that mean Bob's coming home this weekend?' She waited with bated breath for her reply.

'Huh! Chance would be a fine thing. He phoned last night with his usual string of excuses. Surprise, surprise! He's been asked to work over the weekend . . . again. He did, however, promise faithfully to come home next weekend. Isn't that just wonderful?' she said sarcastically. 'He's too good for words! I almost told him not to bother his backside, but decided I would get more satisfaction telling him to his face that it's all over between us. Not that I think for one minute he'll worry too much. He's obviously got another woman in tow somewhere.'

'Ah now, Theresa, you can't know that. Don't do anything rash. You don't really want to drive him away for good now, do you?'

Theresa shrugged and brushed the air with her hands to show her frustration. 'Can't you understand, Tess? I just don't know where I stand with him these days. I've come to the conclusion that he's working up the nerve to break it off with me. I just want to beat him to the punch. I only hope I get my word in first, that's all. He can't possibly care anything about me or he wouldn't treat me like this. He wouldn't be able to stay away if he loved me.' A sob caught in her throat. 'I'm so disappointed in him, so I am. He's treating me like dirt. In the beginning I had such hopes for us. I don't know where it all went wrong.'

Knowing fine well what had changed Bob's attitude towards Theresa, Tess asked anxiously, 'What if he decides to stay in Sligo? What will you do then?'

Theresa shrugged and a sad smile tugged at her mouth. 'Sit on the shelf and grow old gracefully, I suppose. And I'll tell you something else, Tess Maguire . . . If I were you, I'd marry Tony Burke before he gets tired of hanging around or we'll end up like the last proprietors of this shop. Two spinster ladies. Genteel ladies, but spinsters nevertheless.'

'Oh don't even joke about it, Theresa.'

Theresa laughed out loud. 'You should see the look on your face! Mind you, it could very easily happen, so let Tony put a ring on your finger before some other girl beats you to it. Come on, let's wash these cups and get stuck into the stock-taking. And Tess . . . I'm sorry if I was rude and seemed to shut you out lately. I know you meant well, but I was too hurt to talk about it. Can you forgive me?'

The girls had soon discovered that a lot of their customers who paid for their purchases on the never-never had been forced from their homes because of the rioting and arson attacks. Most of them were now living far away from the district and therefore were unable to meet their weekly payments, resulting in a severe drop in the shop's income. They were fortunate that the money from the September weddings would help keep the bank manager happy, but it wouldn't last very long.

They conducted the stock-taking in glum silence. 'Do you think business will ever pick up again, Tess?'

'Now, Theresa, every year about this time you ask that same question.'

'Ah, but it's worse this year. You know it is! Internment has already made a difference and there's no end to those bloody explosions. Hardly a day goes by without some atrocity happening. If it keeps up, Belfast will be in ruins. Folk are hanging on to their money in case they lose their jobs or have to leave town in a hurry. And I can't say I blame them. I can't see any end to it.'

'Be reasonable, Theresa. The troubles have been with us for a long time now, and we've managed to keep our heads above water.' Tess laughed harshly and pointed to where the rain was pouring down the outside of the window. 'At the moment I mean that quite literally. But you know we're always slack in October,' she remonstrated. 'Even folk who feel secure are either paying off their summer holidays or saving for Christmas. This time next month we'll probably be up to our eyes in wedding preparations and there'll still be Christmas party outfits to look forward to. Most firms are going on as usual if they can afford to. Hopefully that will bring in orders for dresses. And we usually get at least two weddings to make ensembles for between now and Christmas; troubles or not, people are still getting married, thank God. And kids keep outgrowing their clothes. Ours isn't a bad wee business to be in. Even if it's not flourishing at the moment I think we'll make out. And I've faith in the people who owe us money. I bet you they'll get in touch with us in due course and pay us what we are owed. Now, is anything else worrying you?' Tess stood, hands on hips, looking at her partner questioningly. The eternal optimist.

'After that catalogue of hopes? Not really.' The faint smile came back to hover about Theresa's lips. 'I got a letter from Les O'Malley this morning and that cheered me up no end.'

'You mean *the* Les O'Malley?'

'Yes. Before he went back to Canada he asked me if I would answer his letters if he wrote to me. I never mentioned it before because I thought it was just small talk . . . you know what it's like. But,' she patted her pocket and the smile returned to tug at her mouth, 'what do you think? I got a letter this morning.'

Tess waited some moments, but when it became apparent that she was not going to be shown the letter she asked, 'How's he managing?'

'He seems to be coming to terms with the loss of Colette now that he's home amongst his friends and relatives.'

'Perhaps in time he'll meet someone else.'

'I hope so. He's such a lovely man and deserves some happiness.' Theresa was ashamed at how chuffed she was to receive the letter. It made up for Bob's neglect of her. Not wanting Tess to probe any further she changed the subject. 'Are you doing anything exciting this weekend?'

'Not that I know of. If we're going to the pictures tomorrow night would you like to come along?'

'And play gooseberry? No thanks. You and Tony will want to be alone.'

'You're wrong! It's not like that. We don't mind company.'

Theresa fixed a quizzical gaze on her. 'Why not? Don't you want to be alone with him? You don't see him all that often.'

'Tony's very well behaved, as you know. He's very careful not to overstep the mark, so it's easier for him if someone else is there.'

'Huh! Sounds a bit strange to me.'

Tess was remembering how she had worried about Agnes Quinn when she had been engaged to Tony. Hadn't she more or less had the very same conversation with Agnes? But that had been because she had thought herself passionately in love with Jack Thompson and had been blatant in her desires when with him. She had made a right fool of herself where Jack was concerned and hadn't been able to understand why Agnes didn't feel the same about Tony. To her they appeared to act like an old married couple.

Since seriously dating Tony she had come to the conclusion that there must be different kinds of love. 'Well yes, I do agree. I used to feel differently but now I think it's better not to indulge in heavy petting that might lead to other things. Heaven knows, it brought me nothing but misery.'

'Oh, so you've felt you wanted to . . .' Theresa stopped, embarrassed. 'You know what I'm trying to say?'

'No. I can honestly say, not with Tony. He doesn't impose himself on me. He's comfortable to be with.'

'You sound like an old married woman.'

Annoyed at her friend, Tess said, 'It's not unusual for people to wait until they're married, you know. In fact, I was reading in *Woman's Own* that more couples are prepared to wait than you'd imagine. They just don't brag about it.'

'But you have wanted to . . . you know . . .'

'Yes. Actually I've felt attracted to two other men, if that's what you mean. I thought I was in love with them at the time, but nothing ever happened! That's not a crime!' Not that I didn't want it to, her mind taunted her.

'No! No, it's not. I suppose you're right. You do well to wait until Mr Right comes along.'

Feeling affronted, Tess blushed. 'For your information, Tony and I do cuddle and kiss. We just don't let ourselves get carried away. Not everybody is like you and Bob, you know, who think it's all right to live together,' she muttered.

'Oh, I'm quite aware of that! In fact some of my neighbours take pride in reminding me they're respectably married and look down their noses at me. But what's done is done! Perhaps if I had made Bob wait he'd still be hanging around, instead of chasing some other woman in Sligo. And I'd still be a virgin.'

'I'm sorry, Theresa. I didn't mean any offence. Everybody's different. And you don't know that Bob's chasing another woman.'

'I know everybody's different! It's just hard to know what to do for the best. I let Bob move in with me because I wanted a child before I was too old. You tried to talk me out of it, remember, and I think I'd have done well to listen to you. I should have waited. I'm glad now that I took your advice where selling the house was concerned. At least I've still got my independence. It's him who will have to find somewhere else to live when he's in Belfast. Now I don't know what to do for the best.'

She looked so forlorn that Tess urged, 'Well don't sit at home brooding on it. Come out with us tomorrow night. We're going to see the new James Bond film, *Diamonds Are Forever*.'

'If you're sure!' A quick nod confirmed that her friend was. 'Thanks! It beats sitting alone in the house wondering what Bob is up to. And I just love Sean Connery, I think he's gorgeous.'

'That's settled then. We'll pick you up about half six.'

'Thanks a lot, Tess.'

* * *

225

By lunchtime the rain had eased off. Anne Thompson was curled up in front of the fire trying to get interested in a crime story. Becoming aware of the brightening sky, she shook herself free from her morose thoughts and rose abruptly to her feet. A plan had been niggling at the back of her mind for some time now and the moment had come to look at it. She had been playing about with it, wondering what to do for the best. Let sleeping dogs lie or upset a hornets' nest? Perhaps now was the time for action. After all, as yet it was all in her mind. No one would be aware if she got egg on her face, if she did something foolish. Maybe a walk down to Theodore Street would help her make up her mind.

Covering her head and neck with a warm scarf, she put on her winter coat and gloves, lifted a shopping bag and ventured out to face whatever the elements had in store for her. Leaving Spinner Street behind, she cut down Lower Clonard Street into Cairns Street and made her way through to Dunville Street. As was usual after heavy rain, the park was a sorry sight. The grass was sodden and she knew from experience it would be a muddy, slippery hazard.

Having forgotten to put on boots she decided it would be more prudent to walk along Sorella Street than cut through the park to reach the Grosvenor Road, so she hurried along in that direction.

Some minutes later she paused at the top of Theodore Street and gazed pensively along the row of terraced houses. She had no idea which one Alfie Higgins lived in. Was she doing the right thing? If Alfie's wife were still alive she wouldn't be here in the first place. Rita would soon have sent her on her way with a flea in her ear. But she had heard that Rita Higgins had died some months ago back in Manchester where she and Alfie had

226

lived since their marriage many years ago. There had been no children.

After Rita's death, Alfie had come back to Belfast to live with his elderly mother here in Theodore Street. Since his return, Anne had yet to clap eyes on him. But then she hadn't been in the least bit interested in him before. As far as she had been concerned, Alfie may as well have been dead and buried.

All this talk of young Jackie's inheritance had made her sit up and take notice, however. It was a big step she was contemplating. There was Dan and Alice to consider, and she didn't think Alfie would be all that delighted either when he heard what was on her mind. He was another one who was in for the shock of his life.

The waters would be muddied, that was for sure! There would be a lot of dirt flying. And once started, there would be no turning back! Would it be worth it? She didn't even know how much money was involved or how the will was made out. She wasn't stupid! There would be other trustees besides the grandfather. To crown it all, Alice might have been spouting her mouth off about a paltry thousand or two, and Anne certainly didn't want to land herself with the rearing of her grandson unless it was worthwhile. An old adage came to mind: 'When in doubt, kick it out'. She decided not to be too rash. Her steps faltered. She would wait a while longer, she decided; try to find out more about the conditions attached to Jackie's inheritance. After all, there was no big hurry.

Slowly she retraced her steps up Grosvenor Road. There was no hurry at all; she had all the time in the world. Meanwhile, now that she was out and about she may as well do some shopping and then call up and visit her grandson. She had made a point of seeing him on regular occasions, like his birthday, Christmas, Easter and other times in between when she wanted to make a nuisance of herself and used Jackie as an excuse, so he was quite familiar with her. It would be worth her while now to get to know him even better.

Alice was returning from collecting her grandson from school and crossing Springfield Road when she saw Anne pass Malcomson Street and approach the house.

'This is an unexpected surprise,' Alice said. 'What brings you out in this foul weather? There's a lot more rain forecast, you know.'

'Oh, I don't mind a bit of rain, so long as my hair doesn't get wet. I'm just glad that the wind has died down. In fact if you ever need someone to collect him from school don't hesitate to give me a shout,' she said, nodding towards the boy.

Alice gazed at her suspiciously. 'What's brought all this on? You've never offered your services before.'

'Well I've been thinking . . . if he does go to live in Omagh, I'll see very little of him, so I thought I'd better make the most of him while I still can.'

'Hmm! Why now? Why all the sudden interest in him?'

'What do you mean? Sudden? I often visit him, as you well know. I don't want him to forget about me now these new grandparents have come on the scene. It must be confusing for the wee soul, all these grannies.'

Still sceptical, Alice eyed her closely. 'Are you coming in for a cup of tea then?'

'Thank you. I'd like that.' Plunging her hand into her shopping bag, Anne produced a paper bag and handed it to Alice. 'I bought one of those chocolate rolls Jackie loves.'

Alice became even more suspicious. Beware of Greeks

bearing gifts, she thought. It wasn't often Anne brought Jackie a present, no matter how small. What was she up to now? 'That's very kind of you,' she said, taking the bag from her. 'Thank you.' Turning the key in the lock she led the way inside.

While Alice was in the kitchen, Anne examined Jackie as he lay on the floor, elbows on the carpet and chin propped in his palms, watching *Jackanory* on TV. She was perplexed; couldn't understand it. She couldn't see any resemblance to her son, who had been long-faced and gangly. Many a time she had wondered how Dan had never twigged that Jack wasn't his. She thought back to the time she had told him she was pregnant. When he had shown doubt and questioned her about it, she had accused him of not loving her. Eventually he had accepted that he was the father and nothing more was said about it.

There was a definite resemblance to the Thompsons. Of that she was positive, although as he had grown older young Jackie had become more like Colette. And didn't they say that people who lived together grew to look like each other? Or was that just married couples? Probably an old wives' tale! Surely she couldn't have made a mistake all those years ago? Impossible!

'Penny for them.'

Anne came to with a start. 'Actually, they're not worth a penny. Looking at young Jackie lying there is bringing back memories from the past.'

Alice looked at this woman who had been foolish enough to walk out on Dan Thompson and their son when the lad was only twelve. 'Sometimes it's better to forget the past. I'm sure yours is littered with regrets.'

'True . . . but I'm sure you had your share of them as well, eh, Alice? You can't expect me to believe that you've had no regrets about living in sin with Dan these past years. And as far as most people round here are concerned . . .' she gestured at Alice's left hand, 'that ring makes no difference whatsoever. While I'm alive, they'll still regard you as a Jezebel.'

About to hand her a cup of tea, Alice had to curb the impulse to accidentally spill it on Anne's lap. 'Would you just listen to yourself!' she sneered. 'Anyone would think you were the abandoned little housewife. You're jealous because you just can't hold on to a man. That's what's wrong with you. All these young men that pass through your hands . . . they're just using you, and you haven't the brains to see it. You should be ashamed of yourself. And you've the cheek to call *me* names? If I'm a Jezebel, what the hell does that make you? Eh?'

Anne sighed and said, 'It could be the other way about. I could be using *them*, you know.'

'No chance. You're well past your sell-by date. You should try to get someone more your own age for a change, and maybe settle down before it's too late.'

'Like you did?' Anne taunted. Seeing Alice was about to retaliate, she hurried on. 'It's a good idea right enough. Take Les O'Malley, for instance. Now there's a very handsome man and obviously well-off too. If you would give me his address I could write and enquire after his welfare, you know, get a pen-pal thing going between us and you never know where it might lead. I can be very persuasive when I set my mind to it.'

'Dream on, Anne! Do you think for one minute he'd even look at you?'

'Why not, eh? But perhaps you're right. After all, he seemed to be attracted to Theresa Cunningham.'

Alice's mouth gaped in astonishment. 'Oh, but you've a nasty tongue in your head. Les is too much of a gentleman for that sort of thing. He was grieving the loss of Colette! There was no way he'd have played around.'

'Did I say he was playing around? No! That was your interpretation of my words. I said he was *attracted* to Theresa. And, mind you, I stand by that. If he hasn't a soft spot for her, I'm a Dutchman. Now for heaven's sake close your mouth and sit down, Alice, and let's forget the past. We've insulted each other enough for one day, and in front of the lad, too. Shame on us. Tell me . . .' she nodded in Jackie's direction, 'have the other grand-parents given up yet?'

Alice was only too pleased to change the subject. Anne Thompson could try the patience of a saint with her insinuations and Alice was never sure which way to take her. Aware that her daughter was fed up listening to her grievances about the McCormacks, she was only too glad to have a fresh ear to bend. A glance at Jackie showed he was wholly engrossed in the TV. Leaning forward, she confided in a conspiratorial whisper, 'Not yet! It looks like we'll be going to court after all.'

'Oh, I am sorry to hear that. Dan must be worried stiff.'

'Yes, we're all worried. I'm no expert on these kind of things, but I don't think they've any chance of getting custody.' Alice wagged her head wisely. 'Only Dan, Tess and Mr McIlroy are the named trustees,' she said import-antly. 'Betty, like you, is only a grandmother. She won't get a look-in.'

'There must be a fair amount of money involved or surely they wouldn't be bothered fighting for access? Still, I suppose with them living in a lovely house in a quiet suburb they would hope that eventually they'd get custody some day and gain access to Jackie's inheritance. Especially if it's worthwhile.' The implied question hung in the air.

Immediately on guard, Alice replied, 'I wouldn't go so far as to say it was a vast fortune. But then, I don't understand the ins and outs of it. A lot of the inheritance is invested in property and shares and the like. It seems that the solicitors here and in Vancouver have done very well for Colette with the money that Grannie Burns left her. If things go well, Jackie should be quite wealthy by the time he comes of age. We're not interested in the money. We love the child! We would keep him for nothing, so we would. We'll only touch the money for his education and the remainder will be there for him when he needs it.'

'It will take a lot of money to give a child a good education these days.'

'You're right there! But the money will be safe in Dan and Tess's hands. They're both above reproach. They'll do what's best for the child.'

To Alice's amazement Anne burst out laughing. 'You really believe that, don't you?'

'Believe what?' Alice cried in bewilderment.

Anne laughed louder. 'That Dan's above reproach.' She dabbed at her eyes with a hanky. 'You're deluding yourself, so you are. No man's that good.'

Afraid that Anne might know something she didn't, Alice wasn't so certain now. 'Dan is,' she insisted fearfully. 'And anyway he has to get Mr McIlroy and Tess's okay before they can spend a single penny. Oh, I can assure you, the money will be quite safe.'

Anne reached for her coat where she had left it over the back of the settee. 'I'm glad I came, Alice. It's a long time since I've had a good laugh.' She did the buttons up, then held out her arms to her grandson. 'Come and say bye-bye, Jackie.'

Completely wrapped up in *Jackanory*, the lad failed to hear her.

Anne grimaced. 'It's obvious he's not everybody's little ray of sunshine. Thanks for the tea. I'll see you soon, Alice.' She was still chuckling away to herself and shaking her head as Alice watched her descend the steps and set off down the road.

Away from the house the laughter was quickly stifled. That was a waste of time. She was still none the wiser. Property and shares indeed! Those assets would probably be reinvested until Jackie came of age. She wondered if there was any other way she could find out how much hard cash was involved. She would just have to sniff around a bit more. Meanwhile she would have to renew Alfie Higgins's acquaintance. He might not want to have anything to do with her and she couldn't force him. That would put paid to her plan and she would have to retire gracefully.

To Tess's astonishment when Tony called on Friday night he was annoyed when she told him that she had invited Theresa along to the pictures the following night.

She gazed at him wide-eyed. 'I honestly didn't think you'd mind.'

'I don't understand you, Tess. Of course I mind. It's only normal that I should want to be alone with you. I don't get many chances as it is. What with your mam and Dan always at home, we have very little time alone together.'

Still smarting from Theresa's comments, anger rose in her breast. 'Why? Tell me why you want to be alone with me,' she demanded. 'What do we ever do that needs some privacy? Eh?'

He drew back at her tone of voice. 'Because we're courting. That's why! Can you think of a better reason? We've things to talk about. Plans to make.'

'Are we? Are we really courting? You know . . , sometimes I wonder about that. We're more like brother and sister. As for talking, tell me, what difference will it make whether or not Theresa comes along with us? Unless, that is, you've something different planned for us tomorrow night. Are we going to expand our sexual activities?' she taunted.

His lips tightened. 'Don't be obscene,' he retorted and changed tack. 'Actually, I did hope we'd go to Romano's tomorrow night. It's a long time since we've been to a dance.'

'You're right! It is a long time, but that's all the more reason why Theresa should join us. It will give her a chance to meet other people. As I've already explained to you, Bob isn't coming home this weekend – again – and she's feeling down in the dumps. So . . . shall I tell her of our change of plan?'

'Suit yourself!'

'You had better be civil to her, mind you. Or I'll want to know the reason why!'

The outer door closed with a resounding slam as he left the house.

'My, what was that all in aid of?' Alice asked, descending the stairs. 'Who ruffled his feathers?'

'He's annoyed because I invited Theresa to come out with us tomorrow night.'

'That doesn't sound like Tony. He's usually very accommodating.'

'I know that. I don't know what's got into him. This is our first real row.'

'That sounds promising. Perhaps he's bought a ring and wants to spring it on you while you're alone.'

'He wouldn't dare do it otherwise. I'm not as understanding as Agnes Quinn. I won't be railroaded into doing

234

something I don't want to do, just to save his face.'

Alice looked at her daughter's flushed, obstinate countenance and said gently, 'Don't you think it's about time you put the poor man out of his misery? You do love him, don't you?'

'That's just it, Mam. I don't know. What exactly *is* love?'

'Look, if you're in doubt, don't marry him. On the other hand . . . there's different kinds of love, and I for one think he'd make a wonderful husband and father, and I know Dan agrees with me.'

'Does he indeed? Have you two been discussing me?'

'Not really. We just worry about you. We're afraid that Tony might get fed up hanging around and find someone else to shower his affections on. You've got to admit that he's a good catch and he has been very patient where you're concerned.'

'To tell you the truth, Mam, I don't care one way or the other. If he wants to marry me, he'll just have to wait! Otherwise he can get himself someone else. I won't be rushed into anything.'

'Hmm, I don't think there's any danger of that happening. Just be careful, or some other girl might snap him up. I can't understand why he's so patient with you. Whatever happened between him and Geraldine Harris?'

Tess sometimes wondered about that herself. She had assumed that Tony had thought himself to be still in love with her and that was the reason for the split with Geraldine. When she had tentatively questioned him he had been evasive about it, so she hadn't pressed him any further. Had he perhaps been using her to make Geraldine jealous and it had backfired on him? She knew for a fact that Geraldine was seeing someone else now. So who was Tony in love with? For all her brave words to Theresa, in her heart of hearts she thought that if he loved her he would want more than just a few kisses. It was time to set the record straight.

Theresa was delighted when Tess told her of the change of venue. 'That's great! I love Romano's. It's always got a good mixture of people. Not all young ones. Who knows? I might even click.'

When Tony arrived to pick up Tess he seemed resigned to escorting two girls to the dance and was in a genial enough frame of mind. Because he was being so nice about it, Tess felt the need to apologise. 'I'm sorry I asked Theresa along without consulting you first. I honestly didn't think you'd mind.'

'Normally I wouldn't, but I think it's time we had a serious talk, and I had hoped we'd do it tonight.' He flashed a smile at her. 'Still, we can, I hope, drop her off first and with a bit of luck your mum and Dan might be in bed when we get back. Will it be all right with you if I come in for a while?'

Apprehensive, she nodded her agreement. What else could she do? Didn't she also want to clear the air? She only hoped that he hadn't bought an engagement ring and was about to pop the question. She would not be forced into anything the way Agnes Quinn had been. Tonight all should be revealed.

9

The car drew to a halt in front of the house and Tess got out to let Theresa know they had arrived. It had rained earlier, and head down she picked her way across the uneven wet pavement. The door opened and she glanced up with a welcoming smile. Bob Dempsey was standing there, and the smile was erased from her face as she gaped at him in amazement. Her step faltered and she landed in a puddle, splashing her feet. She grimaced slightly as the water seeped over the top of her shoes, soaking her tights, but her eyes remained fastened on Bob. An electric current seemed to flow between them, making her feel light-headed. Gulping deep in her throat she dragged her eyes away from his as Theresa followed him out the door, the picture of happiness, and behind his back gave Tess a thumbs-up sign.

Avoiding further eye contact and afraid to lose her self-control again, Tess gathered her wits about her and said, 'This is a surprise. I thought you were working this weekend, Bob.' Her gaze fastened questioningly on Theresa.

'He found he just couldn't keep away.' Thrusting her

arm through Bob's, Theresa rubbed her cheek against the sleeve of his jacket and Tess could almost hear her purr with contentment. 'Isn't that right, love?'

His eyes fixed on Tess, Bob curtly agreed. 'That's right! In spite of myself I found I couldn't stay away. The attraction here was too much to resist.'

A toot of the horn brought their attention to Tony. 'Come on, you lot, or we'll be meeting them coming out of Romano's.'

In the car he greeted Bob warmly. 'Good to see you again, mate. I'm glad you're coming along. Tess said you were working overtime this weekend.'

'I managed to get away. I've things to get sorted out up here before the job comes to an end and I decide where I go next.'

'Any idea where the next job will be?'

'We'll be working in Donegal for a short spell and then the boss is looking for volunteers for a contract he's managed to win in Manchester early in the new year. He hopes it will lead to bigger things and that he'll get a foot in the door over there, as it were. Of course the married men with families are a bit wary, and you can't blame them. They won't hear of disrupting their lives for the sake of a few months' work, but me and half a dozen others said we'd think about it. I mean, when you've no family ties there's nothing to stop you going over and giving it a try, is there? And as the boss says, it could become permanent.'

Tess felt as if they had driven into a big dip in the road and she clenched her fists tight against her body as her stomach lurched at these words. Manchester! Across the water; she might never see him again. Then another part of her mind told her that perhaps it was all for the best. An omen that she was meant to marry Tony. She wished she could make up her mind what to do. Perhaps she would get some sign over the weekend, now that Bob had deigned to grace them with his presence.

Tony stopped at the junction of Castle Street and Queen Street, and turned in his seat to look at Bob. 'The money is good over there. I know a few blokes who're working in Birmingham. They're making a mint with all the overtime that's available.'

'I know, and I'm sorely tempted. I'll have to see how it goes first. If things work out all right it might be a good place to settle down.'

'You'd be foolish not to go, mate. It'll give you a chance to get away from these bloody troubles. Look, I'll drop you all off here and park the car. I shouldn't be too long. I'll follow you in.'

In the cloakroom at Romano's, Tess busied herself fussing with her hair. Her friend eyed her warily, not knowing what to expect. Just that very morning she had been ranting on about Bob, vowing that she would give him a piece of her mind; even going as far as threatening to break off their relationship. Now she was aware that she was fawning all over him; she couldn't help herself. She hoped Tess would keep her tongue in her cheek and not make any sarky remarks. Give her a chance to sort things out for herself in her own laborious way.

It was soon obvious that Tess had no intention of minding her own business. She smiled at Theresa in the mirror and asked casually, 'What made Bob change his mind, then?'

'I'm not really sure. He phoned and said he was on his way and I said that was just too bad as I had already made arrangements to come here with you and Tony. He said that was fine and could he join us.' The look of scorn on Tess's face nettled her. 'Oh stop looking at me like that, for goodness' sake! I haven't forgiven him yet for the way he's been treating me, mind you,' she added defensively.

'Huh! You could have fooled me, the way you were all over him back there.'

'I know. But I was so delighted to see him, Tess, I couldn't help myself,' Theresa admitted. 'And we haven't had time for a proper talk yet. He's not long here. I was getting ready for you coming when he arrived and then he had to freshen up, so everything was a last-minute rush.'

'Did he mention Manchester to you?'

'Yes. Yes, he did as a matter of fact. Why do you ask?'

'Would you be willing to live in Manchester if he asked you?'

'Tess! I've just told you we haven't had time to discuss anything yet. The chances are he won't even ask me to go with him.'

'But if he does?' Tess insisted.

Theresa was evasive. 'I don't know. I'll have to wait and see what he says.'

'*If* he goes to Manchester he won't want to be flying back and forth every weekend. It would be far too expensive,' Tess warned.

'No, he probably wouldn't,' Theresa agreed.

'So you'll probably go over with him?' Tess probed. She could see that Theresa was getting irritated, and hated herself for displaying so much interest in their personal affairs, but she had to have some idea of what was going on.

'What's up with you, Tess? Why the interrogation? If he marries me then I'll go anywhere with him, it's as simple as that. There now, I've gone and said it! He'll have to marry me or I'm staying put. I'm certainly not

240

going to continue the way we were, not knowing what he's up to half the time. It will be up to him whether or not I go. The ball's in his court!'

Tess had her answer. Plunged into despair, she changed the subject. 'What about the shop?'

Relieved, Theresa hastened to reassure her. 'Ahhh! So that's what this is all about. Well, I can set your mind at rest there. Don't you worry about the shop! If I do go to Manchester, I'll have to sell my share in it, of course, but I would be willing to wait. No matter how long. I wouldn't put any pressure on you, Tess.'

The shop was the furthest thing from Tess's mind at the moment. If the worst came to the worst, she had a nice little nest egg which had swelled considerably thanks to the birthday money from her mam and Uncle Malachy, and she would soon receive the thousand pounds that Colette had left her. Financially she was okay, so the shop was the least of her worries. All she wanted was to find out what Bob Dempsey was up to, and she wasn't getting much joy out of Theresa.

Frustrated in her efforts, she muttered, 'Okay then, let's join the men, you can bring me up to date later.'

Tony obviously was out to impress Tess. As each dance was introduced he ushered her quickly on to the floor until during a quickstep she cried for mercy. 'Tony, you know I enjoy dancing but you're tiring me out. I'm dead whacked, so I am.'

He twirled her to the edge of the dance floor and laughed into her flushed face. 'I know you love dancing and I want you to enjoy yourself tonight. I don't want to bore you by sitting out any of the dances.'

'Let's sit this one out, eh? Perhaps if I ask you nicely, you might even buy me a drink.'

Tony was mortified. 'Oh, Tess, forgive me! I never thought. What would you like?'

Smiling at his embarrassment she said, 'That's all right. You're forgiven. I'll go powder my nose while you get the drinks. Make mine a Coke.'

'Okay, I'll see you back here.'

Glad to find the cloakroom empty, Tess refreshed her make-up and was struggling to comb her unruly curls into some kind of order when the door opened and she saw Geraldine Harris reflected in the mirror.

'Hello, Geraldine. Haven't seen much of you lately.'

'Oh, I've been about. How are you keeping?'

'Fine. A friend of ours was killed in that explosion in Ann Street and it upset us all for a while. But we're managing to pick up the pieces and get on with our lives. There's nothing else for it.'

'I heard about that. I still visit Mrs Burke from time to time, you know. I get on well with her and she told me all about it.'

Tentatively Tess said, 'I hope I wasn't the reason you and Tony split up.'

'Did he tell you that?'

Perturbed at the inflection in the other girl's voice, Tess turned and faced her. 'No, he was very evasive about it and I didn't press him. I could see he didn't want to discuss it.'

Geraldine concentrated on colouring her lips and fluffing her pale blonde hair. 'Are you serious about Tony?'

'Geraldine, if he let you down, I swear it had nothing to do with me.'

'No, he didn't let me down. Actually, I was the one who broke it off. Do you get on all right with him?'

'I've known Tony for a long time. We get along just fine.'

'You mean you're just close friends?'

Perturbed, but not knowing why, Tess confided, 'He's asked me to marry him, if that answers your question. How would you feel about that?' she added tentatively.

An expression flitted across Geraldine's face so quickly that Tess was unable to put a meaning to it. Did this girl still burn a candle for Tony? Was she jealous of Tess? She felt somewhat uneasy standing here being grilled by Tony's ex.

'It wouldn't bother me, one way or the other,' Geraldine assured her. 'Have you said yes?'

'Not yet.'

'But you do intend marrying him, don't you?'

Tess wanted to tell her to mind her own business but something made her reply, 'To be truthful, I haven't made up my mind yet. Why are you so interested?'

Ignoring her question Geraldine eyed her intently and said, 'Do you think he would be able to make you happy, Tess?'

'I don't see why not. He's kind and thoughtful, and I think he would make a wonderful father.'

'True, he has all those qualities in his favour. But – excuse me if I'm wrong – he's not very . . . exciting . . . is he? Or perhaps you think he is. Maybe you see him in a different light from me,' Geraldine conceded. 'Tell me to shut my big mouth if I'm overstepping the mark, Tess.'

'I'm not interested in what you think, Geraldine. Everyone's entitled to their own opinion. You'll have to agree, however, that there's more to married life than excitement, as you so nicely put it. There's love and companionship and much more.' Seeing the look on

Geraldine's face, Tess drew back offended. What right had this girl to pity her? 'Besides . . . you've a cheek so you have! It's none of your business what goes on between me and Tony.'

'I know that. I'm sorry, Tess. But tell me . . .' The cloakroom door opened and a couple of noisy girls entered. Geraldine glanced at them over her shoulder and said in hushed tones, 'Do you not think he's one of *those*?' One hand at her waist, she flapped the other in the air. 'Think about it! But whatever you decide to do, Tess, good luck.'

Tess returned to the dance hall in an agitated state, going over Geraldine's accusations in her mind. She was convinced that Geraldine was still interested in Tony and that no matter what she said it had been him that had broken off with her. There was no way that Tony Burke was queer. She took the glass of Coke from him with a muttered 'Thank you,' and eyed him warily over the rim.

He peered at her face which even in the muted light looked flushed. 'Is anything wrong, Tess?'

'Not really. I was talking to Geraldine Harris in the cloakroom. She was asking after you.'

'Oh, I see.'

'Why did you tell me it was you who broke it off with her?'

'Here, hold on a minute, Tess. I never mentioned who broke it off. I would hope I was too much of a gentleman to kiss and tell.'

'I thought you did.'

'No, you assumed I did and I never contradicted you.'

'Why? Why didn't you tell me the truth?'

'We went on to talk about other things and I didn't think it important enough to bring up again. Anyway, what difference does it make? We parted amicably.' An angry scowl twisted his face. 'Why? What has she been saying about me?'

'Nothing important really.' The lie stuck in her throat. Nothing important indeed!

'Geraldine thought I was a square, as she so aptly put it. Did she tell you *that*? I think I bored her, but the parting was mutual. That's why I'm so afraid of boring you. I want us to get out and about more on our own. Learn to please each other.'

They were standing at the edge of the dance floor sipping their drinks and watching the dancers twirl past. Tess tucked that word away in her memory bank for future reference: *please*, what an unusual word to use. Geraldine had also implied that Tony would prove boring. Was that such a big deal? Couldn't she live with a bit of boredom now and again? And didn't they already please each other? At least as far as friendship went. He was always ready and willing to fall in with her every whim. So long as she was happy, he was contented. What more could she ask for? Just as long as he wasn't . . . Her mind shied away from the word. Could she have picked Geraldine up wrong? No! There was no mistaking the fruity gestures.

The music ended and Bob and Theresa came to stand beside them. Tony quickly asked what they wanted to drink then disappeared towards the bar.

'I'll have to powder my nose. Are you coming, Tess?'

'I'm just this minute back, Theresa.'

'I won't be long then.'

'There's an empty table.' Bob led the way to where a couple had just vacated their seats.

Tess followed more slowly. She was uneasy at the prospect of being alone with Bob in case she couldn't control the emotions he aroused.

'For heaven's sake, Tess, don't look so apprehensive! I'm not going to bite you.'

'I don't know what you can possibly mean. I don't feel in the least apprehensive. I was just thinking of something else,' she said defensively.

She sat down and he leaned across the table. 'You're avoiding me,' he accused.

'No I'm not!'

'This is the first time you've sat down all night.'

'That's Tony's fault, not mine.'

'Huh! You expect me to believe that?'

She shrugged. 'Suit yourself. Nevertheless, it's true. Ask him if you don't believe me.'

'Listen, Tess, we've got to talk. Have the next dance with me, okay? I have to know where I stand with you.'

Tony came back with the drinks and Tess quickly nodded at Bob to let him know that she would not object if he asked her for the next dance.

As the strains of a waltz filled the air, Bob rose to his feet and bowed slightly in Tess's direction. 'May I?'

To Tess's surprise, Tony laughingly placed a possessive hand on her shoulder. 'Sorry, mate, I've tired her out and she wants to sit this one out, Bob. Don't you, love?'

Theresa joined them in time to hear this. 'Never mind, Bob. I'll dance with you.'

Tight-lipped, Bob led the way on to the dance floor. Tess cast a glare of anger at Tony. 'What do you think you're playing at? I'll decide who I dance with.'

'But you said you were shattered. I thought you wanted to rest. I actually thought that for once I was doing the right thing. Do you know something, Tess, it seems I can't do right for doing wrong where you're concerned.' He rose abruptly to his feet. 'If you want to dance, then let's dance.'

A few heads nearby turned at his raised voice and Tess gestured at him. 'Oh, sit down! You're right. I am a bit tired. I just don't like people making decisions for me. As if I don't know my own mind.'

Mollified, he pulled his chair closer to hers and reached for her hand. 'We could make an excuse and go home early and have that talk we have promised ourselves,' he coaxed.

She couldn't quite control the grimace of distaste that crossed her face, and he straightened up in his chair and pushed roughly away from the table in disgust, afraid of saying something he might later regret. 'Do you know something, there's no pleasing you, Tess Maguire!' Face livid with anger, he muttered his excuses and strode off towards the door. She gazed after him in miserable contemplation.

Holding Theresa close, Bob Dempsey had stayed near the edge of the dance floor and watched these shenanigans with grim satisfaction. 'Tess seems a bit upset. Do you think we should join her and find out what's going on?'

Theresa swivelled her head round towards her friend and agreed with him. 'She does look a bit put out. I wonder what's wrong?'

'Tony's just stormed off in a temper. Perhaps they had words.'

'Then I think we should mind our own business. She won't thank us for our concern. In fact she's more likely to accuse us of interfering in her affairs. She's funny that way, you know.'

Bob ignored her warning and waltzed her over to the table. 'Are you all right, Tess?'

Tess glared at him; she could sense Theresa's concern and inwardly bristled. How dare they stick their noses in where they weren't wanted! Why couldn't they just leave her alone? 'I'm fine, thank you. Don't let me keep you two from dancing. Here's Tony coming back now.'

Tony nodded at them but remained standing. When the music started for the next dance, a foxtrot, he bowed slightly in Theresa's direction. 'Can I have this dance, Theresa?'

With a slightly bewildered look at Tess, and an 'Excuse me' to all, Theresa nodded and let him lead her on to the dance floor. Tess gazed sullenly down at her clenched fists resting on her lap. How dare Tony treat her like this! How dare he ignore her in front of her friends!

Very much aware of Bob's presence, she waited for him to speak. The silence stretched. Unable to bear it any longer, she shot a furtive glance across the table. Bob was watching her intently and she quickly averted her eyes.

He leaned closer. 'Can I have this dance . . . please?'

Reluctantly she rose to her feet and made her way on to the dance floor. He drew her gently into his arms, his gaze willing her to look at him. She held her body stiff and as far from his as she could. With a resigned sigh he admonished her, 'Relax, Tess. At least pretend you're enjoying yourself even if you're not. This might be the last time we'll ever dance together.'

Like a startled fawn her head jerked up and she returned his look. 'What do you mean, the last time?'

'I have to decide whether or not this job in Manchester is right for me. I've got to make up my mind pretty soon.'

'What's that got to do with me?'

'Everything! And you know it. Are you going to admit you love me?'

'What difference would that make, eh? There's still Theresa to consider. Besides, I've practically told Tony that I'll marry *him*.'

He shook her roughly. 'You're a bloody fool, Tess. You can't marry him. You love *me*.'

'Will you ask Theresa to go to Manchester with you?'

'I'll do better than that. If you won't have me, I'll ask her to marry me. She's a lovely person and I'll do everything in my power to make her happy, have no doubts about that. I *can* make her happy. I realise of course that it will be easier if we go to live in Manchester away from your influence.'

Tears welled up in her eyes, and seeing them he crushed her roughly against him. 'Do you know something, Tess? You're your own worst enemy. Why can't you think of yourself for a change?'

'Can't you understand? I could never hurt Theresa. She's my best friend!' To her dismay the tears fell fast and furious.

He drew her outside the ballroom to a small sofa in a corner of the foyer. Holding her in the crook of his arm, he sheltered her from view and thrust a handkerchief into her hand. 'I want no more tears, Tess. The last thing I want to do is make you unhappy. Just say you love me and I'll take care of everything. I'll explain to Theresa and Tony myself, and everything will pan out. You'll see! Just trust me.'

But he could see that she was not to be swayed. Her head was shaking from side to side and pushing him away she rose to her feet and hurried to the ladies'.

He followed and caught hold of her arm just as she reached the cloakroom door. 'Tess, I'm running out of time here. I mightn't get another chance to talk to you.'

'You have my answer. I could never do anything to hurt Theresa.'

With a frustrated grunt he released her arm and turning

249

on his heel headed for the ballroom without a backward glance.

The rest of the evening passed in a blur for Tess. She returned from the cloakroom to discover that Bob and Theresa had made their excuses and left the dance early to catch a bus home. Bob had obviously washed his hands of her.

'I'm surprised that Theresa left without waiting to say good night to me. It's not like her.'

'I suppose they have a lot to talk about, what with this new job in England and everything. Do you think Theresa will go over there with Bob?'

'If he marries her she will.'

Tony's face broke into a delighted grin. 'Now there's an idea, Tess . . . what about a double wedding? Would you like that?'

Aghast at the very idea, Tess said, 'Catch yourself on. When I get married I want a day of my own. After all, you only get married once.'

'Anything you say, love. You look tired. Have I over-done it with the dancing? Would you like to go home now?'

She accepted gratefully. If they went home now her mother and Dan would most likely be up and the long-promised talk would have to be put on the back burner yet again. Geraldine Harris had raised doubts in Tess's mind and she certainly didn't want to discuss their future together. At least not tonight.

At the door she invited Tony in. 'Mam and Dan will probably be in bed,' she said, while she prayed for the contrary.

Her prayers were answered; voices were coming from the living room. Tess looked apologetically at Tony. He gestured towards the sitting room and mouthed, 'Let's go in there.'

Before she could think up an excuse the living-room door opened and Alice came into the hall. 'I thought I heard you. Don't mind us, come on in. I'm just about to put the kettle on.'

Tony declined the offer on the pretext that he was tired and would head on home. Tess saw him to the door.

'I'm sorry about that, Tony. I thought they'd be in bed.'

He eyed her intently. 'Did you, Tess? Did you really?'

'Of course! Why would I lie about something like that?'

He looked sceptical. 'Why indeed? Good night, I'll call over tomorrow some time.' Giving her a peck on the cheek, he turned and left.

She sighed in relief. 'Good night, Tony.' Listening to her mother and Dan lamenting the most recent developments between them and the McCormacks would be preferable to making plans with Tony. She wasn't in the right frame of mind to start planning her future just now.

Anne Thompson was tired of loitering about the Grosvenor Road. For a week now she had been dandering down Leeson Street and along Theodore Street and gazing into shop windows along Grosvenor Road, hoping to bump into Alfie Higgins. She was beginning to think that he no longer lived in the area.

She went at different times of the day: early morning hoping to perhaps see him leave for work; noon and afternoon in case he wasn't working and would be in the bookies or doing some shopping for his mother. She had searched in vain. She didn't really believe he would be working. It would be no easy task at his age to get a job, she would have thought. He must be in his mid-fifties by now and employment was a bit hard to come by these days. Still, wonders would never cease. He just might have the right connections and have got himself a job.

Her mind drifted back to the night she had first met him. Rita had been in the same class as Anne at school. Younger than Alfie, she had been a bit of a snob and had considered Alfie a good catch. Anne knew him from seeing him with Rita, although Rita had never deigned to introduce him. He had been out on his stag night when Anne had spotted him in the Crown Bar downtown. She was with a few friends celebrating one of their birthdays.

To her amusement Alfie had had one over the eight by the looks of him. She had never seen him with as much as a hair out of place before. But tonight his mates had him tipsy and his hair was all over the place and a silly grin was plastered across his face. If prim and proper Rita could just see you now, she thought, she would be mortified. His pals led him from the pub and Anne forgot all about him until later, when she was walking home.

The girls had split up and gone off in different directions and she was alone with Marie Walker; they had enjoyed themselves and were quite tipsy, laughing and singing and dancing arm in arm up Grosvenor Road. It was after midnight, and as they neared the Falls Road junction, there was Alfie, tied to a lamp-post.

Anne had burst out laughing when she saw him. 'Ah, Marie, would you just look at the state of that. Isn't he a sight for sore eyes?'

Marie was scandalised. 'Who did that to you?' she solicitously asked an embarrassed Alfie.

'I think this must be his stag night, isn't it, Alfie? You're getting married on Saturday, aren't you?'

Hardly able to remain upright, he sagged against the post and muttered, 'Come on, girls. Please get these ropes off me.'

'But this is your big night, Alfie. Your mates will probably come back later and strip off all your clothes.'

These words sobered Alfie somewhat. 'God forbid!' he gasped in horror.

'That's what your mates usually do on a stag night, you know,' Anne teased him and continued to worry him further. 'Then they usually send word for the future bride to come and get you. They'll be very annoyed if we release you.'

'Please, girls, don't let me get into a worse state than I'm already in or I'll never live it down.'

Anne eyed Marie. 'What do you think? Shall we come to his rescue?'

'Well now, I don't know . . .' Marie teased.

'Please, girls,' he pleaded.

'Oh, all right then. We'll have you out of this mess in no time at all.'

They soon discovered this was easier said than done. The knots were so tight they had great difficulty undoing them. At last they managed to loosen them and he wriggled free, but had to grab at the post for support.

'He's drunk. We'll have to walk him home, so we will,' Anne announced in disgust.

'I'm not really drunk,' he objected. 'Just stiff and cramped from standing here tied to this damned lamp-post.'

'Do you know where he lives?' Marie asked.

'I think he lives in Theodore Street. Is that right, Alfie?'

'I'm afraid he'll have to manage on his own then,' Marie retorted. 'I haven't time to walk back down there. I'm late already. My da will be like a bear with a sore head. I was supposed to be in before twelve.'

'Okay then, but let's see if he can walk on his own.'

They each gripped an arm but he pushed them away. 'I'm all right now! Thanks for your help.' He straightened himself and walked off. Not a bad effort, but without their support he was soon staggering all over the footpath.

Anne, who lived with her grannie, knew she would have retired to bed long ago and it wouldn't matter how late she was. 'You go on home, Marie. I'll walk down with him. Make sure he gets home safely.'

Arm linked through his, she guided him back down Grosvenor Road. Fumbling a packet of Park Drive from his pocket, he asked her to light one for him.

'Have you got a lighter?'

He gestured to a pocket and she dipped her fingers in and fished out a box of Swift matches. She lit the cigarette for him at the third attempt, and he dragged the smoke hungrily into his lungs, gazing at her with heavy lids through the haze of smoke as he exhaled.

'Thanks! You're an angel. I needed that. I'm not as drunk as I appear, you know. It's just that I'm not used to drinking spirits and the lads insisted I take a couple of whiskeys and it made me very sleepy. I would probably have fallen asleep against that lamp-post if you hadn't come along. I shudder to think what might have happened if the lads had come back.' He raised a brow at her. 'Is it true what you said? Do they really strip the groom, or were you having me on?'

Anne could see that he did seem a good deal more sober. 'From what I hear, yes, that's what they do. But they leave you in your socks and Y-fronts. You do wear underpants, I hope?' She had a chuckle at the very thought of it. By now they had arrived at the corner of the street and she said, 'You'll be all right now, so I'll leave you to it. And I wish you all the very best for Saturday. I hope the sun shines for you and Rita.'

He was eyeing her quizzically. 'I know you, don't I?'

Anne laughed. 'Well, you know me to see. I went to school with Rita. Good night, Alfie.'

'I'm afraid you're one up on me there. I don't know your name.'

'Anne. Anne Gilroy.'

She was moving off when he touched her on the arm. 'Please stay and talk for a while. My mother will probably be in bed but sometimes she waits up for me, and as tonight is my stag night she'll no doubt feel duty bound to stay up till I get home. I'd like to sober up a bit more before I go in. That is, if no one's waiting up for you?'

'No, I'm staying with my grannie and she'll have gone to bed as soon as the ten o'clock news finished.'

She made to lean against the wall but he stopped her. 'You'll dirty that nice coat of yours against that wall. Here, lean against me.' He propped a shoulder against the wall and opening his jacket drew her in against the warmth of his body. 'It's getting quite cold now.'

'Yes, it is a bit chilly for August,' she agreed and snuggled close to him.

'Tell me about yourself,' he prompted.

'There's not much to tell.'

'You're not married, are you?'

'How did you guess? Have I the spinster look about me?'

'Heavens, no. You're a very attractive young girl. I noticed you're not wearing a ring.'

'You're very sharp. I'm seeing someone, but I'm not daft enough to get married just yet. I intend to enjoy myself first.'

'Do you think Rita is foolish to get married so young?'

'Well, obviously she must be more mature than me. I wouldn't dream of getting married for another couple of years. But then . . . you're a good deal older than her, aren't you?'

'Yes, quite a few years. She'll be all right with me. I've a good job waiting for me in England.'

'I thought as much. I said to Marie earlier on that Rita must think you a good catch.'

'What do you mean?

'Nothing. Forget I said that.'

Raised voices and laughter caught their attention. 'It's them! It's the lads. You were right, they have come back.' Alfie drew her further down the street, into deep shadows.

Four men stopped at the corner and peered down the street. Their words reached Anne and Alfie on the still night air. 'Well, he's not about here either. Only some courting couple. How on earth did he get out of them ropes?' one asked.

'Someone must have taken pity on him, worse luck.'

'You're probably right, Jerry. Ah well, the fun's over for the night. We may as well go on home now.'

Alfie had slouched down and buried his face in Anne's hair to hide. He remained like this until the voices faded into the distance.

Anne laughed up into his face. 'I think you had a narrow escape there.'

'Thanks to you and your friend.'

She pushed herself free of him; she was getting too comfortable in his embrace. 'I'll have to go on home now.'

'Have you far to go?'

'No. Just to Linden Street.'

'I'll walk up with you.'

She laughed at his proposal. 'In case you've forgotten, I've just walked you home. If we keep this up we'll be walking each other up and down the Grosvenor Road all night like a couple of eejits. So you see, there's no need. You get yourself on home, I'll be all right on my own.'

'I want to. It will help sober me up.'

'You seem to have sobered enough already. Your mother couldn't possibly find fault with you. That's if she's still up at this hour. You're back in control of your senses, whereas I still feel quite tipsy.'

'All the more reason why I should see you home.'

She shrugged. 'Okay, if you insist.'

They discovered as they walked along the road that they had a lot in common and Anne found herself thinking that Rita was very fortunate to be marrying this man even if he was a lot older than her. Although no oil painting, Alfie Higgins nevertheless was a very nice man, a real gentleman.

She opened her front door and stepping inside turned to offer him her hand. 'Good night, Alfie. I've enjoyed meeting you.'

He took her hand and followed her into the small hall. 'And I you. Thanks for everything.'

He bent to kiss her but she avoided his lips. 'Good night, Alfie.'

'Can't I have one little kiss?'

To get rid of him she reluctantly lifted her face to his. His mouth was warm and moist and she found herself parting her lips and returning the kiss. It went on for some time and she strained closer to him. She could tell that he was experienced where women were concerned. More so than Dan Thompson. But then, Dan was always very careful not to lose control of the situation.

Alfie edged her to one side and kicked the front door closed behind them, then gathered her closer still. She had been aware that she should send him on his way, but by this time, in the warmth and privacy of the enclosed space of the hallway, she was enjoying the bodily contact with him; wanted more. One thing led to another, and before she knew what was going on they were hard at it.

When at last he set her free he was all apologies. 'I'm sorry. I'm ashamed of myself. I got carried away.'

She was also ashamed of her lack of self-control. He must think her a right tart. She muttered, 'It's okay. After all, it takes two.'

'But I should have been more careful. I'm much older than you. I should have known better!'

She shushed him. 'Never mind! I enjoyed it.'

'Did you? Did you really?'

'Yes, really. Now get yourself away home.'

He quite literally beamed down at her. 'You think I'll be able to make Rita happy, then?' He saw a puzzled frown gather on her brow and hastened to explain. 'Me being older than Rita . . . well . . . she wanted to wait.' A blush covered his face.

'So you knew what you were doing!' she accused him. 'I thought it was spontaneous, but you were just using me. A trial run before the big day, or should I say, big night. Is that it?'

He looked appalled. 'No! No, I never intended to go that far. But you're a very sexy and attractive girl and I got carried away in the heat of the moment.'

She accepted his apology. After all, what was done was done. 'Don't worry, I'll not say a word.' She laughed ruefully. 'Consider it a wee wedding present from me to you.' If she had known then just what he had left her with she wouldn't have been so forgiving. 'Now away you go.' With a gentle push she sent him on his way.

Her thoughts had been far from charitable when she later discovered that she was pregnant. She had, in her mind, ranted and raved on about Alfie taking advantage of her vulnerability in her tipsy state. Her relief had known no bounds when she managed to convince Dan Thompson that the child was his. The ensuing shotgun wedding had certainly taken the joy out of their marriage and the scarcity of money in the rush-up to the wedding had put paid to any honeymoon she might have been dreaming of.

She came back to reality with a start at the top of Leeson Street. Perhaps it was fate that she couldn't bump into him, a warning for her to leave well alone. She was a superstitious woman; a great believer in fate. Before going home she crossed the Falls Road and headed for Gilliland's shop at the corner of Clonard Street. It was noted locally for its bacon, pork sausages and meat pies; she might as well treat herself to something tasty for her evening meal.

Inside the shop as she waited to be served she glanced casually out of the window and started in amazement. There, on the pavement, stood Alfie Higgins, the focus of her recent quest. Unable to believe her eyes she closed them for a few seconds, thinking she must have dreamed him up, so intently had she been looking for him. When she opened them again he was still there, nodding and beaming in at her.

In a daze she ordered some sausages and bacon chops, peering furtively out of the shop window again to see if he was still there. He had changed very little: a bit of extra weight maybe and a slightly receding hairline, but she would have known him anywhere. He had his back to the window now and was looking up and down the road. Suddenly she realised there was a bus stop outside the shop. What if he was waiting for a bus? She had no reason to believe that he had recognised her and was waiting to speak to her.

Mind in a spinning turmoil, she wordlessly urged the shop assistant to hurry up with her order, but in vain; the conversation was too good. Normally she would have joined in the gossip, always on the lookout for bits of scandal, but today she branded them all nosy parkers with nothing better to do. A bus drew up to the kerb and she watched breathlessly, letting out a silent sigh of relief when Alfie made no attempt to board it.

'Anything else, Mrs Thompson?' the assistant enquired as he wrapped up her purchase.

'No thanks, and I'm in a hurry if you don't mind.'

She paid him and left the shop and Alfie was immediately there beside her. 'Hello, Anne. You're looking very well, I must say.' She was so surprised at him approaching her after all her endeavours to bump into him that she must have had a blank look written all over her face, because he said hesitantly, 'Don't you remember me? Alfie Higgins?'

'Of course I remember you. I heard you were back in Belfast. I was very sorry to hear of your wife's death.'

'Thank you. I miss her like hell.'

'I'm sure you do,' she said consolingly. 'Are you back living with your mother?'

'No. I was living with her but she passed away some weeks ago. We'd sold her house and bought one up in La Salle Drive. You know, above the Broadway picture house?'

'Yes, I know where you're talking about. A bit on the posh side, aren't they?'

'Oh, I wouldn't go as far as that, but they are very nice. Mam loved living up there but she died shortly after we moved in.'

'I'm sorry to hear that. I hope she didn't suffer too much.'

'No. Thank God for that. She passed away in her sleep. She was eighty-six, you know.'

'At least she got a good long innings. You intend staying in Belfast, then?'

'Yes. When Rita passed away I took early retirement. So I'm a man of leisure now. Living the life of Riley.'

For once at a loss for words, Anne hesitated.

He was quick to notice. 'I'll walk along to Linden Street with you.'

She laughed. 'I don't live there any more. I live over in Spinner Street.'

'I should have guessed you'd moved. I heard you got married. Would your husband object if I carried your shopping home for you?'

She laughed. 'He'd better not. We're divorced.' He reached for her bag. Not wanting to appear too eager she demurred. 'It's not very heavy, Alfie. Haven't you better things to do?'

He grimaced. 'I've a confession to make. I've been hanging about this part of the road for weeks now, hoping to bump into you.'

Anne smothered a gasp. Who would believe it? While she had been haunting the Grosvenor Road, he had been doing the very same thing here on the Falls Road. It must be Fate with a capital F contriving to bring them together. She would have to tread carefully here, she thought, and let him do all the running. Let things take their own course.

261

'In that case why don't you come down and have a cup of tea and a wee chat?'

She relinquished her bag and taking it from her he said, 'I'd love to.'

In the small scullery, brewing a pot of tea, Anne marvelled at how things were panning out. Alfie had been looking for her and seemed interested in her. In her mind's eye a whole new avenue was opening out in front of her. Who knew where cultivating Alfie's interest might lead. She intended finding out. But first, she must play hard to get. The old catch-me-if-you-can game never failed.

He rose and relieved her of the tray and set it on the coffee table. She was impressed; manners as well as money. Goodness me, whatever next?

Pouring a cup of tea she offered it to him. 'Help yourself to the biscuits.'

'Thank you. You have this room lovely.'

Mentally she agreed with him. If Dan Thompson were to come to visit now he wouldn't recognise the transformation of the house. All nicely decorated now, and new furniture too. She refrained from telling Alfie how she had come by the house; squatting there until Dan had relented and arranged with the landlord to let her have the key.

'I do my best,' she said demurely

'You're obviously a natural homemaker. Can I ask if you have any children?'

'One boy. He died some years ago. He left his girl-friend pregnant and my husband ended up rearing the child. He's a lovely wee boy. His name's Jackie.'

'You're very lucky. Rita and I didn't have a family.'

'Was that from choice or . . .' Her voice trailed off. 'I'm sorry. I didn't mean to pry.'

'That's okay, Anne, I don't mind. Rita underwent a

262

number of tests and the doctors could find nothing wrong. My sperm count was normal too, so we never did find out why we were childless. It's one of those things I suppose; we just weren't meant to have children and there was nothing we could do about it. However, we both had good jobs and a good social life so we pretended it didn't matter.'

'It's obvious to me that you would have liked to have had a child. Have you any brothers or sisters you're close to?'

'Heavens, no. I've one brother whom I haven't set eyes on in twenty years. He lives in Australia. And I've a sister, a nun in the Poor Clares. She's in a convent over in England somewhere, so I don't see anything of her. I'm just a lonely old man. Perhaps you will take pity on me and come out with me now and again?'

'I'd be pleased to go out with you, Alfie. I think, given the opportunity, we could become good friends.'

'What about tonight, then?' he asked, unable to hide his delight. 'Or is that rushing things?'

Not wanting to appear too eager, Anne hesitated. 'Well now, it is a bit short notice . . . but I suppose I might be able to fit you in tonight. I'll have to consult my diary first and make sure you're not clashing with any important engagements,' she joked. She appeared to give it some thought. 'Yes. Yes, I'll see you tonight.'

'Where would you like to go?'

'Pick me up at seven and we'll decide then.'

'Thanks, Anne. You've just made my day.'

She walked him to the door and watched as he strode up the street, a spring in his step. When he was gone, she hugged herself and waltzed around the kitchen. Things were really looking up now! Who knew what the future had in store for her?

* * *

To say that Anne was surprised when Alfie drew up to the door in a brand-new Hillman Minx car would be the understatement of the year. Alfie laughed in delight at her awe.

'I may as well spend my money now. I've no one to leave it to and I can't take it with me.'

'You must have had one hell of a good job over in England.'

'I rose to the top of my profession and I got a golden handshake when I retired. All in all I did very well for myself, I suppose.'

He held the passenger door open and Anne sank into the comfortable seat with a sigh of pleasure, her nostrils filling with the newness of the car. When he joined her she fluttered her eyelashes at him. 'Just what did you work at?'

'I was in insurance. You know, a finance company.'

'Not really, but it certainly paid off. You're a very lucky man, Alfie.'

'In some ways I suppose I am. But sure I've no family to leave it to. Where would you like to go?'

'Well now . . . since we have wheels, can we go for a run along the Shore Road to Carrickfergus?'

'Your wish is my command.'

It was a beautiful night with a hint of frost in the air. At Carrickfergus they left the car in the car park and walked past the old castle and along the pier. They stood for some time watching the anglers fishing off the end of the pier. Anne noted that they were landing a fair amount of bluey-green and silver striped fish among others. This was all a new experience for her, as the nearest she had ever been to a fish was in a paper bag with chips. She was mystified as to what kind they were, and when she enquired of an elderly angler he informed her that they were mackerel, cod and pollack. If they hung around for a while, he added, they might be lucky enough to see a conger eel or two being landed from one of the little boats fishing further along close to the harbour wall. 'They're dangerous big buggers them congers. If you're not careful you could lose a couple of fingers, or worse,' he warned.

She thanked him, saying, 'You learn something new every day,' and they stood for some time watching the fishermen and gazing out over the water, which was shimmering in the fading light.

Not normally a great admirer of nature, Anne couldn't help but whisper, 'Isn't it just so beautiful and peaceful here?'

'It is that, but it's also getting a bit chilly to be hanging around here much longer. That breeze would skin a fairy. Is there anywhere we could get a meal?'

'Well, the Coast Road Hotel gets a good name for its grub. It's only a few minutes away, so we can leave the car where it is and walk over. Do you want to give it a try?'

'I'm willing to try anything once,' he replied. 'Lead on, Macduff.'

Saying a farewell to the anglers, she took Alfie's arm and pressed herself against his side in anticipation of a pleasant evening ahead of them. Then they retraced their steps and headed for the hotel.

10

The minute Tess clapped eyes on Theresa Cunningham's radiant face coming through the shop doorway on Monday morning she guessed that her fate had been sealed and mentally said goodbye to Bob Dempsey. He had obviously carried out his threat and asked Theresa to marry him. There could be little doubt of that. Her friend absolutely oozed happiness.

A great burden of depression settled like a cloud on Tess's heart and she floundered about in misery. Somehow managing to conceal her anguish behind a big smile, dredged up from some inner reserves, she exclaimed jokingly, 'Just look at you! You must have won the pools or something!'

'Oh much, much better than that. I just hope I'm not dreaming.' Hands above her head, Theresa did an Irish jig around the room. Coming to a dramatic halt in front of Tess, she grasped her by the shoulders and looked intently into her friend's eyes. 'Please tell me I'm not dreaming, Tess. Tell me this is for real. Bob has asked me to marry him. Would you believe it?'

In spite of the tight control she had on her emotions,

Tess felt tears well up and fought to keep the dismay from her face. Afraid that in spite of all her endeavours her expression might still give her away, she reached out and clasped her friend in a close embrace. 'I assure you, you're not dreaming. This is for real. It's wonderful news! I'm so pleased for you, Theresa. You deserve some happiness.'

Holding her gently at bay, Theresa gazed earnestly at her. 'You don't mind? I was afraid that you mightn't approve of us tying the knot.'

Tess managed to keep the smile in place. 'It's what you wanted, isn't it?'

'Of course. It's what I've been hoping for; praying for in fact. I just thought you mightn't see it that way.'

'And, pray tell me, why would I begrudge you such happiness?'

A slight lift of the shoulders. 'I don't know. Somehow or other Bob seems to think that you'll be against us getting married.'

Silently Tess cursed Bob Dempsey for making her out a killjoy. 'Did he indeed? Well then, that's where he's got it all wrong. There was a time when I thought he wasn't good enough for you. A bit of a layabout. But now he's got that job and appears to be sticking with it, well, I think he's all right. I wish you both all the very best.'

'Thanks, Tess. Remember what I said . . . you're not to worry about my share of the business. I've told Bob that if we move over to England I wouldn't rush you into anything, and he agrees with me. You can have all the time you need.'

'Thanks. I'll have to give it a lot of thought and decide whether or not I'll be able to keep it going on my own.'

'I'll feel so guilty if you have to sell up. Take your time! Give yourself a chance and think it through. We'll make a loss if we sell now, and I don't want you to lose out because of me.'

'I know that, but if I buy you out and then find that it's too much of a burden on my own and I have to sell eventually, I'll lose even more money.'

'Advertise for a partner. I'm sure plenty would jump at the chance to join an established business like this one.'

'To be truthful, I don't think I could start all over again with someone new.'

Now Theresa was close to tears. 'I'm so sorry, Tess, but I'll keep my word and wait as long as is necessary.'

'I know you will and I really do appreciate your offer, Theresa. And don't you worry about it. It will be my problem. Where's Bob now?'

'He was off early this morning again. We spent yesterday going through our affairs. Sorry about Saturday night, by the way, but Bob wanted to talk urgently about this job in Manchester. Or at least that was his excuse for leaving Romano's early.' She smiled dreamily and sheepishly admitted, 'We had a lovely reunion.'

Tess thought of the state Bob had left her in while he had waltzed off for a happy reunion with Theresa. She could just imagine that reunion and a great fist of misery squeezed her heart. Hell roast him! He wasn't worth all the misery he was causing her. She managed to find a level voice. 'Don't worry about it. Has he decided to apply for that job then?'

'Yes. He'll go over first and see how the land lies. If he thinks we could settle there, he'll accept the offer of the job and look around for a house. Meanwhile I'll have to see about selling my own house and start making preparations for our wedding. Would you mind if I slipped out to the estate agent's some time today?'

'Not at all. You know we're never busy on a Monday. Why not go now, before you take off your coat? Look, I hope you won't think me a pessimist, but do you not think you're being a bit hasty? What if Bob doesn't like Manchester and in the meantime you get an offer for your house? What will you do then?'

'Providing the offer is good I'll go ahead with the sale. You see ... Bob doesn't want to remain in Belfast. If Manchester falls through, he wants me to go to Sligo with him. Do away with all the travelling back and forth to work and only seeing each other at weekends.'

'I see. Well, away you go then! And remember, bring something nice back for a cup of tea.'

'Thanks, Tess, I sure will, and the treat's on me. You're a true friend.'

Still defying the tears to fall – it would never do to let Theresa come back and find her all puffy-eyed from crying – Tess sat for some time pondering what was to become of her now she had driven Bob into Theresa's arms. She had obviously pushed him to the limit and he had at last taken no for an answer. A great feeling of bereavement settled on her and she stifled a sob.

There was nothing else I could do, she lamented. Theresa deserves some happiness! But what about me? Did I not deserve some happiness too? In her heart, had she wanted Bob to take the decision out of her hands, over-ride her wishes and tell Theresa the truth? Surely not! There was no way she could have betrayed her best friend. Then why did she feel as if her heart was breaking?

The tinkle of the doorbell heralded the arrival of a customer, and glad of the temporary respite from her dark thoughts, Tess went through to the front of the shop. To her surprise Anne Thompson stood on the other side of the counter. Although they sold tights and gloves and other small articles of women's wear, Tess could never remember Anne ever shopping here before.

'Good morning, Anne. And what can I do for you?'

'Good morning to you, Tess. I'm looking for a pair of fine black tights.'

'I think I can help you there. What size?'

'Small. Medium are more comfortable around the waist but in time they wrinkle around the ankles and make me feel like an old woman. Do you have that problem?'

'Not at all.' Tess wanted to point out that she was much younger and slimmer than Anne but contented herself with, 'Medium suits my long legs fine.' Bending down, she hauled some boxes from under the counter and placed them on top.

'Let's see what we have here.' She delved into the boxes and took samples from each, spreading the various brands out for Anne's inspection. 'Anything there that catches your eye?'

Anne examined them closely and chose a pair of the finest denier. 'These will do lovely. I've a big date tonight and want to make a good impression,' she confided.

'Very nice. Anybody I know?'

'No. It's someone I knew years ago when I was courting Dan Thompson. He's lived in England for a long time but came back home after his wife died.'

'Obviously not a young lad, then.' Tess threw her a suggestive smile.

Anne grinned, accepting the sly dig. 'Far from it! I admit it will be a change for me. Alice will be thinking I'm following her advice.'

'How's that?'

'She told me to get someone my own age and settle down before it's too late.' A smile tugged at her lips. 'Perhaps she's afraid of Dan changing his mind.'

'I don't think there's much chance of that, do you?'

Anne chuckled. 'No. I'm only joking. But mind you, stranger things have happened.'

'Not much stranger!'

While Tess was busy wrapping the purchase and sorting out change, Anne broached the subject that had brought her to the shop in the first instance. 'How's things coming along regarding young Jackie's other grandparents?' she asked as casually as she could muster. 'Have they managed to get access?'

Tess was not one to be fooled easily, and a frown gathered on her brow at the question. 'I've no idea,' she said curtly.

Anne hadn't come in here to spend money just to be fobbed off like that. Concealing her resentment at Tess's attitude she smiled and continued to probe. 'There must be a lot of money involved for them to go to such lengths to try and get custody of the child. Why, they hardly know the poor wee mite, and surely they wouldn't want to be saddled with a resentful child at their time of life unless it was worth their while. Did Colette leave a lot of money, then?'

Tess drew back and looked down her nose to show her disdain. 'I beg your pardon. It's really none of your business, Anne. Even if I did know how much was involved, if any, I wouldn't dream of discussing it with you.'

'Don't you play the innocent with me, Tess Maguire. As one of the trustees you must know exactly how much money Colette Burns was worth.'

In spite of herself Tess was intrigued and showed it. 'Who told you I was a trustee?'

'Your mother! Who else?'

Tess sighed; she should have guessed. 'As I said, Anne,

it's none of your business. Now, is there anything else you wish to purchase?'

'Huh! Excuse me for breathing. I was only trying to make conversation, you know. Besides, it is my business. I'm also one of Jackie's grannies, remember. If he does go to live in Omagh I'll hardly ever see him. So surely I'm allowed to show some concern. I must have some rights. Forgive me for saying so, but the way you're getting on you'd think you had something to hide, young woman.'

At the look of chagrin on Tess's face, Anne quickly grabbed her change and flounced from the shop in a huff, letting the door slam behind her.

'And good riddance to you too,' Tess muttered. That woman had better mind her tongue before it got her in trouble. Trust Alice not to keep her big mouth shut. Tess would have to have a quiet word in her ear and warn her to be more circumspect in future, especially when she was discussing family matters with the likes of Anne Thompson.

Theresa left the car in McQuillen Street and hurried back to the shop. As she rounded the corner at Springfield Road she bumped into Anne. 'Oops, sorry,' she cried, gripping Anne's arm to steady her. 'Oh, hello.' She didn't know Anne very well but she gave her a friendly smile. 'Are you all right, love?'

'I'm fine.' Anne smiled in return. 'I can see you're in a happier mood than your partner. She could barely afford me a kind word, that one. She'll scare custom away if she isn't too careful.'

Theresa was nonplussed. 'That doesn't sound like Tess. She's always very courteous to customers. Believes that the customer must always be regarded as right, even when they're not.'

Anne looked sceptical. 'Huh! Not as far as I'm concerned.'

Sensing deep resentment and not prepared to discuss her partner with this woman, Theresa changed tack. 'Actually, I do have a lot to smile about at the moment,' she admitted. 'I've just got engaged, and I must confess I'm over the moon about it.'

Anne's eyes strayed to her bare left hand and Theresa hastened to explain. 'He only asked me at the weekend. We'll choose a ring next Saturday.'

'Who's the lucky man then?' A pleased look dawned on Anne's face. 'Tell me, is it that handsome Canadian? Oh, how romantic! Has he come back for you?'

'Canadian?' A puzzled frown marred Theresa's happy countenance.

'Colette's friend?'

'Les? Heavens above, no! What on earth made you think it might be him?'

'I'm sorry. I seem to have got the wrong end of the stick. You see, I thought Les fancied you. I even mentioned it to Alice at one time and she near ate the bake of me, so she did. Said he was still mourning Colette and there was no way he'd be thinking of another woman. But the way I see it . . . you can't help your emotions and I could see he was attracted to you.'

Taken aback, Theresa assured her, 'Ah no, you're mistaken there. We were just good friends.'

A slight shrug of the shoulders indicated Anne's disagreement. 'If you say so. Who's the lucky man then? Anyone I know?'

'Yes, I think you do, it's Bob Dempsey.'

'Ah, he's a nice lad too. Congratulations, love.'

'Thanks.'

Theresa continued on to the shop deep in thought.

Imagine Anne thinking that Les O'Malley fancied her. What on earth had given her an idea like that?

Tess was on her knees tidying the boxes of tights away. She straightened up from her task and peered over the counter when the shop door opened. 'You weren't very long, Theresa. I thought you'd be away a couple of hours at least.'

'The estate agent told me that I could have saved myself a journey and phoned. He says he can do nothing until he views the property, so he is coming out tomorrow with a surveyor. By the way, I bumped into Anne Thompson at the corner. She's giving off about you being so grumpy.'

Tess rose to her feet full of ire. 'Was she indeed? That woman annoys me no end. Has she ever come in here to buy anything while you were in charge?' At Theresa's shake of the head she continued, 'I thought as much. She bought a pair of tights . . . big deal! It was soon obvious why she'd come in. She was trying to find out how much money Colette left. Why she wants to know is beyond me. She certainly will never get her hands on any of it.'

'Don't let her get under your skin, Tess. She's not worth it.' It was on the tip of Theresa's tongue to mention Anne's remarks about Les O'Malley but she resisted the impulse. Anne must have got her wires crossed and she didn't want Tess to ridicule her for paying any attention to that woman's wild assumptions. It wasn't as if there could possibly be a grain of truth in what she'd said. 'I bought some cream cakes, so let's have a nice wee cuppa and forget all about Anne Thompson.'

The rest of the day was a terrible strain on Tess. They were busier than usual for a Monday, but between serving

274

customers and working on a wedding ensemble Theresa wanted to involve her friend in all her plans and chattered away nonstop.

When she at last got a word in edgeways Tess asked, 'When do you plan to marry?'

'We haven't decided that yet, but it will have to be soon. Maybe a Christmas wedding.'

'Will you want a white wedding with all the trimmings?'

'Definitely not! I think a suit would be more appropriate. And . . . Tess . . . will you be my bridesmaid?'

Tess managed to hide her dismay and inwardly berated herself. She should have seen this coming and been more prepared. Who else would Theresa ask? How could she possibly stand beside Theresa whilst she married the man Tess loved? She flailed about in her mind searching for an excuse. Knowing it was useless, she nevertheless grasped at straws. 'What about your cousin? Won't she expect to be asked?'

'Amy Blake? I shouldn't imagine so. I haven't seen her in years. It's a long time since I've bothered with any of my relatives.' A slight shake of the head as she gave this some thought. 'No, I've no one close enough to ask.' A definite shake of the head. 'No. It will be a quiet affair. Just you and your parents and Tony, as far as I'm concerned. Bob's mam will be there of course but I haven't any idea who else he'll invite. Please say you'll be bridesmaid, Tess. You're my best friend. In fact, you're my only friend.'

Tess found herself nodding in agreement. 'Of course I will, it will be an honour, Theresa.' Under the circumstances what else could she possibly say? But how would she be able to bear it on the day?

* * *

At dinner that evening, to break the monotonous talk about Jackie and the McCormacks, Tess mentioned that Anne had been in the shop that morning.

'That doesn't sound like her!' Alice was quick to point out the obvious. 'Has she ever bought anything from you before?'

'No . . . but this morning she bought a pair of tights. An expensive pair I might add. Our sale figures nearly went through the roof,' she joked. 'Seems she has a date on tonight and wants to make a good impression.'

'Well, what do you know. Did you hear that, Dan? Anne has a special date on tonight.'

'Whoever he is, he's welcome to her,' Dan said dismissively.

'Did she mention his name?'

'No one we know, Mam. I think she was trying to impress me. It was just an excuse to come into the shop. She was after a bit of information.'

'Information about what?'

'She was fishing to find out how much money Colette had left Jackie.'

Alice gasped aloud and Dan straightened up in his chair. 'She what?' he roared.

'You heard me.'

Dan looked stunned. 'What on earth made her think you would know that?'

A quick glance at the look of guilt on her mother's face made Tess act vague. 'Oh, somehow or other she figured out that because Colette and I were so close, I was bound to be a trustee and would be able to tell her all she wanted to know.'

'She knows you're a trustee?' Dan was flabbergasted.

'Yes, she does indeed. Anyway, I told her in no uncertain terms that it was none of her business.'

Alice shot her a look of gratitude, and before Dan could question her further Tess told them her other news.

'Bob proposed to Theresa at the weekend.' She hadn't wanted to tell them until she had got used to the idea herself and could put on a brave face, pretend she was delighted at the news, but to avoid further interrogation about Anne, her hand had been forced.

'Oh, I am pleased to hear that! He's a lovely lad,' exclaimed Alice, only too glad to change the subject. 'When's the big day?'

'Theresa says probably some time around Christmas.'

'Why the big rush? She's not . . .' Alice squirmed with embarrassment, 'you know? Is she?'

'No, Mam, she's not! Bob has the chance of a job over in Manchester starting early in the new year and they want to marry before they leave Belfast.'

Now Alice was concerned. 'They'll never get booked in anywhere for a Christmas reception this late.'

'They just want a quiet affair. Theresa has no one bar ourselves that she wishes to invite, and at the moment she doesn't know how many will be going from Bob's side, so it will probably be a very quiet affair.'

'Strange,' Alice mused aloud. 'Her not knowing how many of Bob's family will be invited.'

'There's nothing strange about it!' Tess defended her friend. 'After all, they just got engaged at the weekend. She hasn't even met all his family yet.'

'Surely she's met his mother?'

'Yes, she has, and they get on quite well together, as far as I know.'

'Has he any brothers or sisters?'

'I haven't a clue, Mam.' Strange, thought Tess inwardly. She knew very little about Bob, except that he could wrap her around his little finger; worse luck.

'I was just wondering who will be her bridesmaid.'

'Wonder no more, Mam. She's asked me.'

Alice was delighted. 'Why, that's wonderful, Tess.' She glanced across at Dan. 'Maybe if there isn't too many to cater for we could put the reception on here as a wedding present for them. Mm, Dan?'

'And have you spend the day cooking and running after everybody, worrying in case you've forgotten anything? No thank you! If there's a reception, you're going to enjoy yourself. I'll see to that!'

'No! You've got it wrong. I mean get professional caterers in to do the work.'

'Would that not be very costly?'

'I wouldn't think so. I'll wait and see how many will be invited before I say anything to Theresa. If there's not going to be a big crowd, will it be all right with you, Dan, if I suggest the idea to them?'

'Oh, I suppose so.' A grin relaxed the grim lines of his face and he turned to Tess. 'Jackie could wear that wee suit you made for our wedding and let him present the bride with a horseshoe.'

'That will be easy to arrange and he'll look a treat, so he will.'

'He will that! He will that,' Dan agreed.

Tony was delighted when he heard the news. They had been to a concert and he had whispered nonstop between acts about the engagement and coming nuptials. Tess sat silent most of the time, wanting to forget about Bob and Theresa and their impending marriage. Tony, too excited to notice how distracted she was, continued to prattle on during the drive home.

It was one of her nights for sleeping at Theresa's house and it was quite late when they arrived there. Tess was dismayed to find the house in darkness. Where was Theresa? She hadn't mentioned anything about going out.

Tony had invited himself in to congratulate Theresa on her engagement and Tess could see he was glad that they would apparently have the house to themselves for a while.

'I'll put the kettle on.'

Taking her by the arm Tony led her into the living room. 'Forget the tea. Now is our chance to have that talk we've been promising ourselves. Eh, love?'

Resigned, Tess headed for an armchair, but slinging an arm across her shoulders, Tony manoeuvred her over to the settee. With a smothered sigh she sat down, sinking back into its comfortable depths. Sitting beside her he put an arm round her and pulled her close.

'It's wonderful to have you all to myself. I get very frustrated sometimes, you know, we get so little time alone. Marry me, Tess. Make me the happiest man in the world.'

Tess wriggled uncomfortably and tried to free herself. 'Let's wait until Theresa and Bob have tied the knot, eh, Tony? We don't want to take away from their big day,' she reasoned. 'Do we?'

'To hell with that idea!' he retorted. 'We have ourselves to consider.' Seeing she was unconvinced he coaxed, 'At least let me put a ring on your finger. We don't have to set a date right away. I just want to let everyone know you're mine.'

Tess stared earnestly into his eyes. He had been so patient with her, so kind, that compassion overruled her reticence. After all, engagements could be broken and it would help keep her mind off Bob Dempsey if she too got engaged. Wouldn't it? She had a feeling that

Bob was trying to call her bluff. If she let Tony buy her a ring Bob would soon get the message that she was serious and stop pestering her. At least she hoped so, and with this in mind she made her commitment to Tony.

'All right then, have it your way. Let's get engaged.'

'You mean it?' he gasped.

'Yes, but don't you try to rush me into marriage,' she warned. 'Marry in haste, repent at leisure is my motto for the day.'

'And a well-chosen one too. I'll wait as long as you want, just so long as you have my ring on your finger. Will we go down tomorrow and choose it, or perhaps you'd prefer Saturday?'

'We'll go down to H. Samuel on Thursday afternoon. I'm not sure if they close half-day Wednesdays, and Saturday is our busiest day, and as it's the only time Theresa can go with Bob to choose her ring I'll need to be in the shop then.'

'That's even better, love. Thursday it is. I'll take the afternoon off.' He was practically buzzing with excitement. 'I can't wait to tell everyone. My mam and dad will be so pleased. They think you're such a lovely girl.'

'I'm glad to hear that. I imagine they thought we would be forever just good friends.'

'Bob and Theresa will get a surprise.'

'A shock, more like it.'

'We can all go out together and celebrate on Saturday night. Shall I book a table somewhere for dinner?'

'Best wait until I have a word with Theresa. They might have other ideas of their own.'

Tony had jumped to his feet with joy at her acceptance; now he sat down and gathered her close again. 'I love you, Tess. More than you'll ever know. You'll always come first with me and I'll never do anything to cause you any concern or hurt.'

Agnes Quinn came to Tess's mind. Hadn't he been daft about her too?

As if reading her mind he said, 'Tess, believe me when I say that I love you more than I have ever loved anyone else, and that includes Agnes. She was my first love, you're my greatest.'

'Thank you, Tony.'

Feeling compelled, she unwillingly offered him her lips. He devoured them like a hungry man. To her surprise she enjoyed the feel of his moist lips on hers and opened her mouth, returning the pressure. They became so engrossed in each other that they didn't hear Theresa come in until she spoke. Tess sat in a daze and eyed Tony. He had certainly surprised her. He had hidden depths; no doubt about that. Different entirely from Bob; more tender, more caring, not just lustful.

The passion Bob aroused in her was overwhelming but she had enjoyed Tony's advances. It had been a very nice little interlude indeed. Was her yearning for Bob because he was the forbidden fruit? Would she always want what she couldn't have?

Oh, forget about Bob, she told herself. Hadn't she enjoyed herself just now with Tony? Everyone was different and she didn't think she was going to find Tony in the least boring, no matter what Geraldine Harris might think. Not in the bedroom department anyhow. How dare that girl insinuate that he might be queer! Surely she must have picked Geraldine up wrong. There was nothing different about Tony. He was all man. But hadn't she allowed Geraldine to plant the seed of doubt in her mind? God forgive her. The next time she saw that silly girl she would soon set her right.

A wide grin on her face, Theresa paused in the doorway and teased, 'Hey, would you just have a look at these two lovebirds, Bob.'

A bright blush flooded Tess's face when Bob Dempsey followed Theresa into the room and stood staring in stunned silence, his disapproving glance taking in Tess's dishevelled clothes and flushed countenance.

Tony rose to his feet tall and proud, while Tess buttoned her blouse and smoothed her hair into place with her hands. She felt embarrassed at being taken unawares, especially by Bob. What was he doing here on a Monday night anyway?

'You may well look astonished,' Tony confided as he thrust a hand in Bob's direction. 'I didn't expect to see you so soon. I believe congratulations are in order, Bob . . . Theresa.' His arms enfolded Theresa and he gave her a bear hug. Then he glanced at Tess with a raised brow. 'May I?' A nod gave permission as Tess rose to her feet to face Bob. 'We've some news too.' Tony put an arm round Tess's waist and drew her close. 'Tess has agreed to marry me.'

With a happy cry, Theresa embraced them both. 'Oh, I'm so pleased for you, Tess. I'm glad you've put Tony out of his misery at last. Congratulations, Tony. You're a very lucky man to have won this girl.'

'You don't have to tell me that, Theresa. I still can't believe that she has accepted me.'

'Isn't this wonderful news, Bob?'

'It is indeed.' At last Bob approached Tess and, avoiding her eyes, gave her a peck on the cheek. 'I hope you'll be very happy, Tess. You too, Tony.'

Unable to stop grinning Tony said, 'Thank you. Now explain yourself, Bob! Why are you here on a Monday night and not in Sligo?'

'I got word that my mother had suddenly taken ill, so naturally, fearing the worst, I was on the next train home. Our Tommy, my cousin, thought it was a heart attack and panicked and sent for an ambulance. Thank God it was only a case of bad indigestion and she's all right now. Theresa and I have spent the last couple of hours in the Mater Hospital with her. They're allowing her home tomorrow, so it's back to Sligo for me. No rest for the wicked.'

'She's a lovely person, and delighted about us getting engaged, so she is,' Theresa chimed in.

'Shall we all go out next Saturday night and celebrate?' Tony asked excitedly.

'Why not?' Bob agreed. 'Meanwhile I'll have to get to my bed, I've to be up at six o'clock to catch the train.' His eyes fixed on Tess he added, 'Besides, I don't want to waste this opportunity to be with Theresa. You know what I mean?'

'I'll give you a lift to Sligo if you like,' Tony was quick to offer.

'I won't hear tell of it. I'll get the train. I'll see you all as usual next Saturday.'

Tony turned to Tess. 'What about you, Tess? Will you be staying here tonight now Bob is home?'

Tess got a bit of her own back on Bob. 'And play gooseberry? No thank you. Anyway, we've also got better things to do.' Reaching for her coat, she shrugged into it. She couldn't get away from Bob Dempsey's presence quickly enough. He was masking his displeasure under an affable smile but she could sense the intense anger directed at her. Just what did he expect her to do? Gratefully she turned to Tony. 'You can take me home now, Tony, and if Mam and Dan are still up we can break the news to them. I know they'll be over the moon when we tell them. Good night, Theresa, you too, Bob.'

That had been a wasted journey, Anne lamented mournfully to herself as she thumped down the Falls Road in a foul mood. She had laid herself wide open for that snobby cow Tess to deride her! And for what? Nothing! She was none the wiser for it. Maybe she should just forget the fact that Alfie Higgins was Jackie's real grandfather. After all, she was the only one who knew the truth and she had to admit that Dan was doing a fine job bringing up the lad. He and Alice doted on the boy. Whereas Alfie was a comparative stranger to her. She had no idea how he'd react if he found out that he had a grandson, especially if he learned all the ins and outs of it. She knew he thought highly of family, and if he decided to apply for and maybe win custody of the lad he could just as well take himself and Jackie off to England again, leaving her in the lurch and a lot of heartache in his wake. So why not let sleeping dogs lie? For the moment, at least, that would be the most prudent tactic, she convinced herself.

Her first date to Carrickfergus with Alfie had gone off well. The meal at the Coast Road Hotel had been delicious, and although not a great walker, she had even enjoyed the stroll along the beach afterwards. On the drive home they had discovered that they had a lot in common. At her house he had helped her to alight from the car and watched while she unlocked her front door. When she invited him in he had declined. Surprised but pleased that he wasn't rushing her, she had thanked him for a lovely evening and bade him good night. She was very pleased when he had asked to see her again. This time they were going to the Broadway cinema, where a Gary Cooper Western was showing.

That was why she had laid herself open to insults from that stuck-up bitch Tess Maguire: to try and acquire more knowledge; to understand how things stood regarding young Jackie, and find out if there was a lot of money involved. Money aside, however, Alfie had the right to know that he was the biological grandfather, and who knows, perhaps with her being the grandmother they would liaise about the boy's future, which, with a bit of luck, might even include her. Jackie would be very lucky to have such a rich grandfather. But what about everybody else? There would be ructions, no doubt about that! All hell would be let loose. Dan Thompson wouldn't just hand Jackie over to a complete stranger without one hell of a fight, even if it was proved that Alfie was his real grandfather.

Dan would argue on the grounds that he had reared the boy from birth believing him to be his very own grandson. No doubt about it. He would fight tooth and nail for that child. If it went to the courts, could he possibly win? Not knowing anything about the ramifications of custody laws, she had no idea. She shook her head in despair. But that was all in the future; meanwhile she would cultivate Alfie's friendship and play it by ear.

There was no great hurry. She might as well make the most of her chances with Alfie and get a few dates before he found out about her past shenanigans and dropped her like a hot potato. For if the truth were to become known, she was only too aware that Dan would soon let Alfie know how she had rushed him into a shotgun wedding by convincing him he was Jack's father; and had later abandoned their son, leaving Dan to rear Jack on his own when she ran off with another man. More recently, too, she had been seen cavorting about with men young enough to be her sons. What would Alfie think of her then? Not a lot, that was for sure! Alfie was from old-fashioned stock. To say the least, he would be shocked and dismayed at her behaviour.

She blinked back tears of self-pity. It was too late now for regrets. She would enjoy herself while she could. All sorts of unattached women, once they learned of his lovely home and new car, not to mention his bank balance, would soon be setting their sights on Alfie Higgins. Women younger and more attractive than her, she had no doubt. And when he learned of her past she wouldn't blame him if he sought female company elsewhere. How she now wished that she hadn't flaunted her relationships with those young men, trying to impress Dan Thompson with her conquests, and earning herself a reputation as the local trollop.

It had never bothered her before that she was the talk of the district, but it did now. Had Dan but known it, only one of the lads she drank with had taken her interest. The rest were too young for her taste and she was often left lonely and friendless. It was just the *company* of a man she craved. But who would believe her? Nobody! It was much, much too late for regrets. She had been a very foolish woman and had earned herself a bad reputation into the bargain.

They had planned to meet outside the Broadway picture house so that Alfie could leave his car in the garage at home. Anne alighted from the bus at Willowbank Park and saw his tall figure already pacing up and down in front of the cinema. Catching sight of her he strolled to meet her, with that lovely loping gait that she so much admired. To her surprise she felt her heart beating faster and she trembled slightly. Surely she wasn't falling in love with him? God forbid! That road could only end in heartache.

'You look lovely, Anne. We're both early. I thought I'd have to wait a while for you. Maybe we're both keen, eh?' he hinted hopefully.

'Maybe,' she agreed, her blue eyes shining happily at him, and she felt confident enough to slip her arm through his. He smiled down at her and pressing it close to his side escorted her into the cinema.

In spite of all this promising show of affection the film was almost over before he ventured to hold her hand, and she berated herself for being too forward. Had she frightened him off?

Outside the picture house she formally offered him her hand. 'Thank you for a lovely evening, Alfie. I really enjoyed myself. It's been a long time since I last went to the pictures on a date.'

He grasped her hand between his and clung on, gazing anxiously at her. 'Have I offended you in any way, Anne? I'm trying to be so careful not to give you reason to stop seeing me.'

Hiding her pleasure at this revelation, she managed to look somewhat bewildered. 'No . . . no, you haven't offended me at all. What makes you think that?'

He shrugged. 'Then why are you rushing off?'

'I thought it would be silly for you to see me all the way home when you just live a short distance away and I can easily hop on a bus.'

'Anne, I would like to show you my house. Will you come home with me now, and I'll make you a bite of supper?'

'I'd like that, Alfie. I'd like that very much.'

He pulled her hand under his arm and they walked the short distance up the Falls Road in silence. The house he led her to was near the top of La Salle Drive, facing the boundary wall of the Christian Brothers' home. Semi-detached, it stood back off the road with a small, neat garden fronting it. It was a hundred times superior to the house Anne rented in Spinner Street and she fell in love with it immediately. 'This *is* very posh, Alfie.'

She could see that he was pleased. He unlocked the front door and motioned her into the wide, spacious hall. 'The people I bought it from have different taste from me, but I'll soon get it decorated the way I want. But meanwhile, it's still quite nice.'

In the lounge she stopped and gazed around. 'This is a beautiful big room, but I see what you mean.' A sweep of her arm took in the lovely jade-green leather three-piece suite, and the dark oak occasional tables that graced each side of the marble fireplace housing a gas flame fire. 'You'll need some nice wallpaper and the best of curtains and carpet to show off all this beautiful furniture.'

He led the way through the dining room, as yet unfurnished, into the kitchen. Anne's breath caught in her throat as she followed him. She stood gazing around her at the gleaming work surfaces and splendid appliances. 'This is absolutely wonderful, Alfie. It would be heaven to work in a kitchen like this.'

He was beaming from ear to ear at her praise. 'I'm glad you like it. You go and sit down and I'll make us something to eat.'

'I'll give you a hand.'

Taking her by the arm he gently pushed her out of the kitchen. 'I insist you sit down. It won't be anything great, mind you. Just a few sandwiches. You can switch on the TV or put a record on if you wish. I'll be as quick as I can.'

Anne sank into one of the comfortable armchairs and

looked around the room. A nice rich green carpet and curtains would complement this furniture no end, she thought. Some watercolour prints on the walls and a couple of matching table lamps and it would be beautiful. Some lucky woman would soon make this house into a lovely comfortable home.

She awoke from her musing when Alfie came back. He pulled one of the tables over in front of the fire between the two armchairs, flashed her a smile and soon returned with a laden tray.

She gazed at the sandwiches and cakes and biscuits. 'I thought you said it wouldn't be much? There's enough there to feed a regiment.'

He laughed. 'You do exaggerate a bit. Will you be mother?'

She poured tea into fine china cups and remarked, 'This tea-set is exquisite.'

'Rita liked the best of everything, and since we had no children we could indulge ourselves in the best of material goods. A poor substitute I admit but better than nothing.'

The thought had crossed Anne's mind that perhaps material things had meant more to Rita than a family, and so she had made sure she didn't conceive. It was a terrible thing to think, that someone who had everything going for them could be that selfish . . . but how come a one-night stand had produced Jack? Surely Rita wouldn't have deliberately deprived a man like Alfie of a family? No, the poor woman must have been barren.

'Have you been divorced long, Anne?'

'Dan and I have been separated many years but we've been divorced about four. He's been living with Alice Maguire six years or so, but it was only this year that they decided to marry.' She looked at him, a twinkle in her eye. 'It was soon after he was made redundant that they tied the knot. They were married at Easter this year. Maybe she was afraid I'd be after a share of his redundancy money.'

'Surely not?'

She shrugged. 'It's only a thought . . . but many a true word is spoken in jest, they say.'

'Do you work at all, Anne?'

Her mind scurried about looking for an answer that wouldn't incriminate her. She decided to be as truthful as she could. 'Well, after me and Dan split up I went to live for a time with a man from Greeves Mill where I worked. He was in higher management and wasn't short of a bob or two, so when we parted he gave me a nice little annuity. It's paid into my bank account at the beginning of each month. Thanks to him I don't have to work, although, mind you, I wouldn't say no to a nice wee part-time job if the money was right.'

'I see. And there's no one in your life at present?'

'If you mean men friends, I've dated from time to time but haven't yet met one that has caught my eye. I prefer living on my own.' She could have bitten her tongue off. Now he would think she was giving him the cold shoulder.

To her relief he eyed her closely and said, 'You're far too attractive to be on your own. Perhaps one day you'll meet a man you're attracted to who you'd like to get to know better and maybe settle down with.'

She smiled at him sweetly and agreed. 'Perhaps. I must admit that sometimes I do feel very lonely. Especially at holiday times when everyone else seems to be out enjoying themselves.'

'Well now, since you're not working maybe I could interest you in a wee job. I'm sure a bit of extra money won't go astray.'

She settled back in her chair in surprise. 'You know someone who might actually employ me?'

He nodded.

'In what capacity? I've only ever worked in the mill, you know.'

'I think you're a true homemaker, Anne. What I've seen of that wee house of yours in Spinner Street is lovely. You seem to have a good grasp of interior design. Would you consider taking on the decorating of this house for me? You know, choose the paper and paint and soft furnishings and do the actual work yourself.'

She was struck dumb for some seconds and nibbled at a ham sandwich before putting it carefully down and giving him her full attention. 'Do you really mean that?'

'I certainly do.'

A warm glow filtered through her body. What a kind man he was. 'If you trust me to make a good job of it, I will certainly accept your offer.'

He was on his feet instantly. 'Let's shake on it.'

She took the proffered hand and he pulled her to her feet and into his arms. His lips met hers and she returned the kiss before easing her body gently away from his. 'Are there any strings attached?'

He released her immediately. 'No. No strings attached unless you decide otherwise.'

'Let's take it easy, Alfie. You know, one step at a time, eh?'

'I don't mind waiting. Remember, I know what the reward will be like if I play my cards carefully. I've been there before, and do you know something, Anne? I've never forgotten that night. Meanwhile, finish you tea and I'll take you home while I can still resist the temptation.'

She smiled at him. 'That's because it was forbidden then. It might not be so exciting now.'

'I've often thought of you over the years,' he confessed. On the verge of admitting that his marriage had not been very exciting, he bit the words back and nodded towards the plate of sandwiches. 'You haven't eaten very much. Shall I wrap up some of those and some cakes for you to take home, otherwise they'll only end up in the bin?'

'Only if you're sure you won't eat them. I'll take a couple and a cake; that'll do me for a cup of tea when I get home, if you don't mind.'

'Good. Pick what you want and I'll pack them. Now, shall we go shopping tomorrow and you can choose the wallpaper and paint for the lounge?'

'That would be lovely. I can't wait to get started.'

The house was in darkness when Tony drew the car up to the kerb. He turned in his seat and looked at Tess. 'Are you going to invite me in?'

'It's late, Tony. We don't want to spoil things by getting carried away now, do we?'

'I'm glad you agree with me where that's concerned. I want to show how much I respect you, Tess. I know what a good person you are.'

'Here . . . hang on a minute, Tony. I'm no angel.' He had been Jack Thompson's best friend when they first met. Had Jack ever confided in him how she had thrown herself at him? She was thoroughly ashamed of that episode in her life.

'I don't want an angel. I want you the way you are.'

'Tony, please don't put me on a pedestal. Then you won't be disappointed.'

'I love you, Tess. All I want is the chance to make you happy.'

'I know you do, but let's not go overboard about it, eh?' She brushed his cheek gently with the back of her hand. 'I'll wait until you come over tomorrow night before I tell Mam and Dan our news. Okay?'

He nodded. 'I can't wait to see their reaction. Good night, Tess. And thanks for at last saying yes. I'd almost given up hope that you'd ever have me.'

She smiled. 'See what patience can do? Good night, love.'

Removing her shoes, Tess silently climbed the stairs, avoiding the loose one that creaked, hoping not to awaken her mother, who was a light sleeper. She undressed slowly and crept into bed. Lying in the semi-darkness she gazed blindly at the ceiling and tried to sort out her tangled thoughts. First her surprise at Tony's lovemaking. How come he had never aroused her before? But then, she had never given him the chance before. She had always been too wrapped up in some other man. Was he just catching her on the rebound; had her response anything to do with Bob's rejection? Would it be different when they were married? Questions, questions, questions! But no answers.

When Tony had been dating Agnes Quinn, Tess had been besotted with Jack. Then Dominic Sullivan had come along, and now Bob Dempsey. She had lost the other two; was she grasping at straws because Bob was now also lost to her? Was she deluding herself? Would she be able to make Tony a good wife? If she married him she would certainly give it her best shot. Would that be good enough? More questions. Would she ever find any answers? And if she did, would they please her? On the other hand, perhaps she was meant to be a spinster. God forbid! She would dearly love a family of her own.

Bob's suppressed jealousy had given her a sense of pleasure. Although she had feared – or had she secretly hoped? – that he would blurt out the truth in front of Theresa and Tony, she was nevertheless glad he had been angry. Did that mean he would always come first in her eyes? If so, it wouldn't be fair to marry Tony. She groaned aloud. What on earth had she let herself in for?

The misery and sense of loss she had fought against all day suddenly overwhelmed her and she sobbed silently into her pillow until she fell into an uneasy sleep.

Alice and Dan were delighted when Tess and Tony told them their news. Alice actually wept. She had been worried when she had noted her daughter's pallid complexion and dark-ringed eyes at breakfast that morning. Tess had waved her concern aside, saying it was that time of the month and she'd had a restless night.

'Oh, I'm so pleased, Tess,' Alice said now. 'I've prayed that I'd see you settled before I die.'

'Thanks, Mam. Thanks a lot. I didn't think I was already on the shelf as far as you were concerned.'

'You know I didn't mean it like that, love. It's just that you're so choosy and I was afraid Tony would get fed up waiting. And you'll not get any better than him, you know.'

'Can I get a word in here edgeways, please?' Dan shouldered Alice gently out of the way and embraced Tess. 'For what it's worth, Tess, I never thought for one minute that you were on the shelf. You're too bloody attractive. Congratulations, love. I hope you're going to have a great big white wedding, because I'd be proud to walk you down the aisle.'

'Marriage is a long way off yet, Dan.'

Dan shot a glance at Tony. 'Why's that?'

Tony held up his hands defensively. 'Not my fault. I'd marry her tomorrow, but I've promised to wait until she gives the go-ahead.'

Seeing the annoyance on her daughter's face Alice quickly intervened. 'For goodness' sake, Dan, behave yourself. Let them enjoy being engaged for a while. Shall we throw a party for you?'

'No, Mam. On Thursday we're going downtown to buy the ring, and on Saturday we're going out to celebrate with Theresa and Bob. And remember, I don't want any surprises. Is that clear?'

Alice pulled a wry face. 'Crystal.'

Making sure that her mother had got the message, Tess pressed on. 'Thanks, Mam. I don't want any fuss and I know I can trust you to keep your word.'

Dan put a hand over his mouth and turned aside to hide a smile.

'What are you smirking at?' Alice asked crossly. 'I can and will keep my word.' She looked at Tess. 'Can I at least have a snack ready for the four of you when you come home on Saturday night?'

It was Tony who put paid to these plans. 'I'm sorry, Mrs Thompson, but I don't think that would be advisable. We'll probably be home very late. You see . . .' He faced Tess. 'I didn't want to say anything till I was sure I could get four tickets. There's a show band, don't ask me which one – I just thought it would be a change from Romano's – playing at the Floral Hall on Saturday night and I've made enquiries about tickets. They're getting back to me later. All right, love?'

'That's smashing, Tony, but what if Theresa and Bob want to go somewhere else?'

'I can't really see them objecting, can you?'

'No, I can't. And even if they do object, we can go on our own, can't we? We don't need any other company to enjoy ourselves.'

Tony was overjoyed at these words. 'You don't know

how pleased I am to hear you say that.' He reached for her and she willingly pressed against him and offered her lips.

Alice smiled fondly at the young lovers, and taking Dan's elbow she motioned him ahead of her out of the room. Tess and Tony were completely unaware of their departure as they clung together and kissed passionately. To Tess's joy she once again wondered how Geraldine Harris could have got it so wrong.

11

Tess dearly wished she could work up some more enthusiasm as they stood in H. Samuel's jewellery shop on Donegall Place, pondering over trays of rings. She imagined that the assistant serving them was giving her odd looks but it was probably just her own guilty conscience. Lord knows Tony showed enough excitement for both of them.

She had told him that she didn't want a conventional engagement ring but would like a cluster of stones. Nothing too big. Or too expensive, she hastened to add, but was told that money was no object. Tony assured her that he could afford a relatively expensive ring without breaking the bank.

After dithering between an emerald and a sapphire, each surrounded by a circle of diamonds, she chose the emerald.

Tony grinned at her. 'I didn't want to sway you while you made your decision, but I'm glad you chose that one. It matches your eyes,' he said softly.

The assistant who was attending to them caught these words and quickly glanced at Tess. Meeting a flash of deep green irises ringed with thick lashes, he smiled and said, 'May I be so forward as to say that I agree with your fiancé? It is the exact shade of your eyes.'

Blushing bright red Tess thanked him for the compliment and Tony grinned from ear to ear, proud as Punch.

Outside the shop she automatically turned right to return to where the car was parked. Tony stayed her with a hand on her arm. 'Let's go round to Mooney's and have a drink to celebrate before going home.'

'But you're driving,' she reminded him.

'Just one drink. One pint won't make any difference, so it won't.'

Tess didn't agree with him but compromised. 'I'll come, so long as you trust me to drive your car home. Then you can have a couple if you like.'

'But that's not fair. Then you won't get a drink.'

'This might come as a surprise to you, Tony, but I don't particularly like drinking this early in the day. A Coke will do me fine.'

Seated in Mooney's at a window table looking out on Cornmarket, Tony raised his glass and said, 'This is the happiest day of my life. To the future Mrs Burke.'

Still in a dormant state, Tess felt that she was a mere spectator, standing outside herself observing all that was going on, and sought for the right words to respond. Raising her glass she said, 'Mrs Burke . . . mm, that has a nice ring to it.' She lifted her left hand and examined the emerald. 'As for *this* ring, it's absolutely beautiful. Thank you, Tony.' She leaned over and kissed him lightly on the lips.

'We should have picked our wedding rings while we were at it,' he grumbled.

'Now, Tony . . . you promised not to rush me.'

'Sorry, love.' He looked sheepish and diplomatically

298

changed the subject. 'I wonder what kind of ring Theresa will choose?'

'She was talking about a solitaire. But then she might have changed her mind by now. We'll find out on Saturday.'

'Tess, I'm glad I was able to get those tickets for the show band in the Floral Hall. Do you think Bob and Theresa will be willing to come with us?'

'I'm sure they'll be glad to go somewhere different. After all, it's a special occasion and they'll be more than happy for a change from the old routine.'

'I think you're right. Would you like another Coke?'

'No, but don't let me stop you. Go on, have another Guinness.'

'Only if you join me.'

'Thanks all the same but I'd rather go home.' Afraid she sounded ungracious, she added, 'I can't wait to show off my ring.'

Tony drained his glass and rose to his feet. 'I'm all for that. Let's hit the road.'

'I'll just nip into the loo first. You head on back to the car and I'll follow you.'

As Tess left the ladies' room she passed Geraldine Harris on her way in. Doing a U-turn she followed her.

Geraldine laughed. 'We'll have to stop meeting like this, Tess, or people will start talking about us. What are you doing out drinking at this time of day?'

'Never mind that. I've a bone to pick with you, madam.'

Geraldine looked at her wide-eyed. 'Oh?'

Making sure the loo was still empty, Tess said, 'If I ever hear about you making besmirching remarks about Tony Burke again I'll have you up for slander.' She thrust her face close to the other girl's and prodded her gently in the chest. 'Do you hear me? Tony is all man. I just hope you get one half as good. Understand?'

Geraldine gave an indifferent shrug. 'Ah, now listen, Tess. I didn't mean any harm. Everyone is entitled to their own opinion. I can't help it if he came across like that to me. I suppose the fact is that he's just too quiet for my liking. I prefer someone who's a bit more extrovert. I'm glad you're happy with him. I really am.'

Tess held her eye. 'Just you be careful what you say in future,' she warned, then held up her left hand for the other girl's inspection. 'Tony and I have just got engaged. That's my excuse for being in a pub this early, and by the way, drinking Coke. What's yours?'

Geraldine examined the ring. 'I'm with a couple of girls from work. We sometimes come here for our lunch break. That's a beautiful ring, Tess. I wish you and Tony all the very best. And I promise I'll be more careful what I say in future.' She laughed. 'I certainly wouldn't like to tread on your toes. What more can I say but . . . sorry I upset you. Obviously he just wasn't the man for me. But then, in my heart I guessed that he wasn't fully interested in me and that he still carried a torch for you. Congratulations, Tess.'

Mollified, Tess said, 'Thank you.'

'Where is Tony? Shall I come out and offer my congratulations?'

'No! He's away on over to the car. It's parked in Rosemary Street.'

'I'll see him another time then. Meanwhile give him my best regards.'

'I'll do that. See you around.'

Saturday night at the Floral Hall was a success. It was packed and there was little room for private conversation as they gathered at the side of the dance floor between dances, and for this Tess was grateful. As she had implied to Tony, Theresa had indeed chosen a solitaire diamond and, joined by Dan and Alice, they had drooled over each other's rings before leaving the house.

Bob was on his best behaviour, not giving Tess any cause for complaint. As time passed without incident, she relaxed and started to really enjoy herself. It was towards the end of the evening before Bob eventually asked her for a dance. Immediately her emotions took over and her nerves started tingling. With great reluctance, she followed him on to the dance floor. She could do without this, she thought. Entering his arms, she braced herself against the closeness of his body. To her surprise he made no effort to draw her near.

They danced for some moments in silence. He smiled down at her. 'You'll be glad to hear that you've made me see sense, Tess. I think you and Tony will be ideal together.'

She refused to meet his eyes, bracing herself for the punch line, the snide remarks. He didn't disappoint her. 'You two deserve each other. No excitement! No passion! You'll bore each other to tears in no time.'

Her head snapped up. 'Oh, and you're such a wonderful person, eh? God's gift to women. Is that what you're implying? The world's great lover?'

'I'll show you how great a lover I am if you'll give me half a chance. But then you're too scared to let your hair down and enjoy yourself,' he taunted. 'Afraid you might like it too much. Isn't that it, Tess?'

'I don't have to prove anything to you, Bob Dempsey! I'll have you know that Tony is an exceptional man. He has qualities you couldn't possibly possess or would ever be able to understand. Most of all, he's trustworthy.'

He glowered at her. 'Are you insinuating that I'm not?'

She laughed derisively. 'Surely even you in all your arrogance can't really believe yourself trustworthy? The way you carry on behind Theresa's back? Don't make me laugh. If it were known, most people would call you an utter rogue.'

'I doubt that. Actually most people like me. Even so, isn't it a well-known fact that women love a rogue? Maybe that's why you can't get me out of your head? And I am in your head, Tess. I know that. Just like you're in mine, making everything else seem insignificant.' She arched an eyebrow at him in disdain and opened her mouth to repudiate his claims. 'Don't bother denying it! I'm right, and you know it. And now that I've managed to get your undivided attention at last . . .' He glanced around. They were close to the edge of the floor and near the open French windows that led out into the surrounding grounds. Before she was aware of his intention, he quickly waltzed her across and out the door. 'Let's go out here where we can continue this conversation in private. You can tell me how awful I am, and with a bit of luck I'll persuade you to change your mind.'

Outside, with a grunt of annoyance, she immediately pushed herself free of him and turned to go back in.

He gripped her arm. 'Just talk to me for a few minutes, Tess.'

'We have nothing to talk about.'

'Please. Just a few minutes. I want to apologise. I'm sorry for what I said back there. I didn't really mean it. I'm just so disappointed. I can't get you out of my mind. I got an awful shock when I saw you with Tony the other night. I can't bear to think of you and him together like that. It tears me apart, so it does.'

His grip on her arm tightened and he drew her round

302

the duck pond into the shadows. To her shame she made no effort to escape his clutches. She was torn in two. One half of her longed for his touch; the other despised him. Once out of view of the French windows he swung her into his arms and held her fast. It was bitterly cold away from the warmth of the dance hall and she shivered. Without releasing his hold on her he managed to open his jacket and wrapped it round her. Crushing her closer still, his lips trailed her face. 'Tess, Tess, I love you. Let me show you just how much. You'll never look at Tony again if you let me make love to you. You'll never regret it. I promise.'

Despite the tight control she had on her emotions, her passion rushed in a great surge of heat to meet the obvious need in him. She clung to him, every nerve alert as she wantonly returned his caresses. But even as she lapped up his kisses she fought desperately against her urgent desire; warning herself that this physical arousal was fruitless, a betrayal of Tony. Determinedly, she gradually won the struggle with temptation. Finding the strength to rebuke him, she cried, 'Leave me alone! You're despicable, so you are.' She struggled roughly against him, lashing out with her fists and kicking wildly at his shins in an endeavour to be free, and resentfully he released his hold on her.

Grim-faced he glared down at her. 'You're a fool, Tess Maguire. We could have something wonderful between us.'

Her temper flared out of control, but aware that there might be people within earshot she hissed, 'You're right! Perhaps we could, but for how long? Eh? Tell me that! How could I ever trust you? You're practically married to Theresa and you're still trying it on with me. Why, I'd worry every time you were out of my sight. I'm glad

303

I realised how fickle you are before I made a complete eejit of myself. I only wish I could tell Theresa the truth. You don't know how much I long to make her aware just how contemptible you are. She's such a good person, she's wasted on the likes of you, so she is.'

He closed in on her, forcing her to retreat deeper into the shadows to avoid further contact with him; afraid that if he held her again she would weaken. 'Aren't you forgetting something?' he snarled. 'You betrayed her every bit as much as I did. You deserve all the misery in store for you.' Tess shivered at the sheer fury that emanated from him. 'You've been leading me on. Pretending you were interested – that you cared. Well, you weren't thinking of Theresa then, were you? And as for you telling Theresa the truth . . . you do that. Do you think for one minute she'd believe you? Catch yourself on. You're the one who would lose out. Theresa Cunningham is worth ten of you. And while you make a mess of your life with Tony, I promise you that I'll keep Theresa fulfilled and happy.'

'Hah! Only until you set your sights on some other poor soul.'

Her eyes flashed green fire and colour defined her high cheekbones. To him she had never looked more lovely and inwardly he mourned the loss of her. As far as he was concerned she was the only one for him. Why wouldn't she give him the chance to prove it? His demeanour changed once more and he cried in frustration, 'Tess, don't do this. You're making the biggest mistake of your life. We were meant for each other. Your way nobody will be happy.'

Shaking with fear and cold, she wanted to run away from this demon side of him she had never seen before, but warned herself to take it easy and keep her cool. He stood tensed, nostrils flared, and keeping her eyes fixed warily on him, she skirted round him and past the duck pond. He reached out to stop her but she managed to elude his clutches and hurrying across the lawn made her way indoors, heading straight for the cloakroom; she needed to compose herself before facing Tony and Theresa. Bob was so two-faced she assumed that he would be able to put on a big act as if nothing had happened. She was now convinced that he was a Jekyll and Hyde character – a schizophrenic.

She wasn't disappointed in her assumptions. Back in the dance hall, Bob was talking and laughing with the others. To look at him no one would have imagined that anything untoward had occurred. He was so relaxed and unconcerned, acting as if he hadn't a care in the world. No one would have guessed the demented rage he had shown just a few minutes ago. How could Tess have been so blind?

On the other hand, Tony and Theresa both showed concern at her paleness, Tony leading her to a chair and hovering solicitously over her. 'Bob said you felt faint, love, and he had to take you outside for some fresh air. Do you feel any better now? There's only a couple more dances left, but maybe you'd rather go on home now?'

'No, let's not spoil the evening. I feel much better now, thanks. I'll just sit here for a while.'

'Are you sure, Tess? We don't mind leaving early.' Theresa touched Bob's arm. 'Sure we don't, love?'

'Not in the slightest, if that's what you want, Tess.'

'No! I'd much rather sit here a while. Get my breath back. You two go ahead and dance.' When they declined she said, 'Please. Don't let me ruin the night for you. This is supposed to be a very special occasion.' She held Bob's eye. 'It's not every day one gets engaged to be married. Please don't let me spoil it.'

Theresa moved to sit on the other side of her, patting her on the back of the hand. 'You're not spoiling anything. I want a bit of a rest myself.' They sat in silence, with just a trivial remark now and then, watching the dancers, and gradually Tess managed to calm her racing emotions.

When the last dance was announced, Bob led Theresa on to the floor. Tony put an arm round Tess's shoulders and reaching for her hand held it tightly. 'Forgive me if I'm wrong, Tess, but . . . I've a funny feeling that Bob has done something or other to offend you. Am I right? Has he?'

'No!' Realising that she sounded too emphatic she smiled in an endeavour to relieve the tension. 'Whatever made you think such a thing? I told you, I just felt a bit queasy and we went outside for a minute to get a breath of fresh air. I'm all right now.'

'He didn't try anything on when you were out, then? Did he?'

She marvelled at how Tony could be so perceptive. She would have to be on her guard in future. If Tony thought for one minute that Bob Dempsey was pestering her, he would soon sort him out in no uncertain terms, and God knows where that would lead. All the sordid details of her infatuation over Bob might be exposed, and how would she be able to face Theresa? She cringed with shame. How could she ever have imagined that she loved Bob Dempsey? She must have been out of her mind.

Now she was in a dilemma, wondering if she should tell her friend the truth. If she did, she would lose Theresa's friendship for ever, of that she was certain. Theresa was blind to Bob's faults. She didn't want to hear anything bad said against him. Tess decided that to confess would only make matters worse. Theresa must never find out how fickle Bob was. She was too much in love with him. It would break her heart.

Tony broke in on her troubled thoughts. 'Is that the truth?'

She nodded and he said, 'I will never let anyone hurt you, love. Remember that. I'll always be here for you, no matter what. And God help anyone who thinks different. Unless they have a liking for hospital food.'

Impulsively she lifted his hand to her lips. He was such a good, caring person. Her knight in shining armour. How could she have kept this dear, kind man dangling on a string for so long? She could very easily have lost him to Geraldine Harris. What a foolish girl she had been. 'I know you will always look out for me, Tony. And I'm so grateful for that.'

Her eyes were drawn like a magnet to Bob's compelling gaze across the heads of the dancers and the expression in his eyes caused an involuntary shiver to run through her. 'Someone walked over my grave just now,' she joked in case Tony noticed.

Tony was on his feet immediately. 'Right! Come on. You've obviously caught a chill out there. Let's get the coats and wait for the others in the foyer.'

The following weekend was an occasion for more rejoicing as far as Dan and Alice were concerned. Saturday afternoon Betty and Stan McCormack had arrived back from their outing with Jackie in a sombre mood. They explained that seeing the boy once a week on a Saturday wasn't working out as they would have liked. They admitted that they were used to taking weekend breaks away to the seaside and down south, but didn't think that Dan would allow Jackie to accompany them on these trips. A definite shake of the head confirmed their suspicions. They said that since it looked as if going to court could take months, perhaps years, they had decided to wait until Jackie was old enough to choose for himself if and when he wanted to come and stay with them. They asked if they could take him out during school holidays and at set times just to keep in touch. To this Dan readily agreed; he was happy so long as he was in control of the situation.

When the McCormacks finally left, Dan was so overjoyed he was all for them going out to celebrate, since it was his weekend off. But it was a cold, wet evening, and Alice said it would be wrong to take Jackie, who had a touch of the sniffles, out again into the damp night air. She suggested that they stay at home and invite Theresa and Bob to join them for a drink and she would rustle up something to eat.

Still smarting from Bob Dempsey's accusations, and unwilling to be in his company so soon after their last encounter, Tess objected. 'I'm sure Theresa would rather have Bob to herself for a change.'

'You think so? Mm . . . perhaps you're right. Still, I think you should phone and at least give them the chance to refuse, Tess. Otherwise they'll wonder why we didn't invite them.'

'For goodness' sake, Mam, they don't have to be included in all our affairs. They're not family! They don't even have to know that we have an excuse to celebrate. It's none of their business! To tell you the truth, I think we all need a break away from one another.'

Alice eyed her daughter shrewdly. There was something not quite right here, of that she was sure, and by hook or by crook she was determined to get to the bottom of what was making Tess so ratty.

In spite of feeling justified in her endeavours to rid

herself of anything to do with Bob Dempsey, Tess was nevertheless besieged with guilt as she moved restlessly from room to room waiting for Tony to arrive. Some time in the near future Theresa was bound to hear talk of the McCormacks' change of heart and would wonder why she had been left out of the celebrations. Over the years she had been treated as one of the family and invited to everything that was going on. To be suddenly excluded would be bound to hurt and bewilder her. If things had been normal, Tess would have been on the phone to her friend right away inviting her down, but as matters stood she dreaded the prospect. Unable to bear it any longer, she forced herself to lift the phone and dial Theresa's number, hoping against hope that she would have made prior arrangements.

Not so! Theresa, after a muffled conference with Bob in the background, said they would be delighted to come down and what time would they be expected? Tess advised her to come about eight and rang off with a heavy heart.

Alfie parked the car and he and Anne made their way round to North Street to look around the wallpaper shops there. They were in and out of different shops for what seemed like a lifetime to Alfie, as Anne, spoilt for choice by the huge variety of wallpaper on display, and unable to make up her mind, dithered about different patterns.

At last Alfie could bear it no longer and cried out, 'For God's sake, Anne, can't we take a break? I ate very little breakfast and my belly thinks my throat's cut. If I don't get something to eat soon, I think I'll collapse.'

Anne winked at him. She was in her element here and her happiness was all too blatant. 'Sorry, Alfie, I'm enjoying myself too much,' she admitted. A glance at her watch brought her up short. 'Heavens above, I didn't realise it was that time. You should have spoken out sooner. Let's go and find somewhere nice.'

It being the lunch hour, most of the places were crowded, and after going into a few and unable to find a vacant table Alfie suggested they go home, have something to eat there and then come back downtown.

Anne reluctantly agreed but was struck by a sudden thought. 'Hold on a minute. I'd like to try one more place before we give up.'

'Is it far? I don't think I can last out much longer and we could be home in no time at all,' Alfie reasoned.

They were by this time in Donegall Place. 'No, it's not far if we take a short cut, and by the time we get there the crowds should be thinning out. People have to get back to work, you know. Not everybody is as lucky as us.'

She led Alfie up Fountain Lane and along Fountain Street out on to Wellington Place, and soon they were standing outside the Carlton Steak House.

From the doorway her gaze scanned the interior. 'What did I tell you? There's a couple of empty tables over in yon corner.'

'Thank God for that. I'm so hungry now, I could eat a horse.'

Anne pretended to be dismayed. 'I don't think you'll get any of that in here.'

Alfie was puzzled. 'Any what?'

'They do lovely steaks but I'm certain it isn't horse meat.'

He threw back his head and laughed. 'I should hope not! Come on, get yourself inside before I pass out on this pavement.'

*   *   *

Some time later, well fortified, they were back on the prowl for wallpaper and paint. Well fed and with a pint under his belt, Alfie watched Anne with an indulgent smile as she stretched out a roll of thick embossed wallpaper for his opinion. 'What do you think of this, Alfie? Would you fancy it for the lounge?'

Alfie kindly refrained from pointing out that it was one of the first patterns she had looked at this morning. He spread his hands wide. 'I think it's lovely, but you're the boss, Anne. Pick the one you like best.'

'But I want you to like it too. You're the one who'll be living with it.'

He thought it would be imprudent to hint that he would like her to live with it too. Hadn't she told him not to rush things? 'I think it's the most suitable we've looked at all day,' he agreed and was rewarded with a huge grin.

She beckoned to the assistant who was hovering nearby. 'We will have eight rolls of this paper. There won't be much waste as the pattern is small so we might only need the seven. Will you take one back if we don't use it?'

'We will indeed, madam. Just keep your receipt and you can drop it in any time and get a refund.'

Anne opened her mouth to say that they weren't married, but with a twinkle in his eye Alfie winked at her. 'That will be great, thank you. Now I think my wife would like to choose some emulsion and gloss.'

'Will that be coloured emulsion or white?'

A warm rosy blush coloured Anne's cheeks and she tore her eyes away from Alfie's fond gaze. 'Brilliant white gloss paint, please, and brilliant white emulsion. We will also need some undercoat.'

'Come this way, please.'

Anne followed the assistant in a happy daze. If only

this could last. Why, oh why, had she been so stupid in the past? she inwardly lamented.

Alfie paid for their purchases from a thick roll of notes and asked the young assistant to carry them to a spot near the door. He slipped the man a tip for his trouble and gestured to Anne.

'You stay here and I'll bring the car round. It will save us struggling with that lot.'

On the journey home Anne confided, 'I didn't realise that wallpaper was so expensive. I didn't overdo it, did I?' she asked apprehensively.

'Don't you worry your pretty little head about money. I've already told you, I'm not short of a bob or two. Where now? My house or yours?' She hesitated and he continued, 'If we go to my house we can get stuck in after we've had another bite to eat. Will that be all right with you? I trust you will let me help with the heavy work?'

She nodded happily. 'That'll be fine. I'll be only too glad of your help, but you'll have to stop off at Spinner Street first so I can change into some old work clothes.'

The next couple of weeks passed all too quickly for Anne. Alfie kept his promise to keep his distance physically, but gave in to Anne's every whim.

They worked well together and the room slowly blossomed under Anne's careful planning and expertise. Standing back, hands on hips to admire her handiwork, she said, 'You won't really see how well it looks until you get new carpets down. Can you afford new ones?'

'Of course I can. We'll go downtown tomorrow and have a look round. See if anything catches your eye.'

She almost purred with contentment. 'Alfie, you don't know what it's like not to have to count the pennies. All my life I've had to be very careful how I spent my money.

I'd be delighted to pick some good-quality carpets. Only the best is good enough for this house.'

'Anne, can I ask you something?'

'Of course you can,' she murmured distractedly, still admiring her handiwork, and he decided not to press his luck just yet; give her a little more time before asking her to move in with him.

Turning, she gave him her full attention. 'Mm?'

Her eyes were soft and dreamy, and throwing caution to the winds, he began haltingly, 'Anne, I know you told me not to rush things, but I want you to know that I'm very attracted to you, and I was . . .'

A raised hand stopped his faltering words.

'No, please, not yet, Alfie. Give me a bit more time.'

Sensing his frustration she went to him and placing her hands on his chest, looked earnestly up at him. 'I've made a lot of mistakes in my life, and this time I want to be very, very sure that I'm doing the right thing. I need time to decide what's for the best. Can you be patient with me, just a little bit longer?'

His arms loosely circled her waist. 'You can have all the time in the world as far as I'm concerned, but remember, we're not getting any younger. Especially me! It seems a great shame to waste so much precious time that we could be sharing together.'

'We see each other most days, Alfie,' she reminded him gently.

'Don't play games with me, Anne! You know what I mean. But in case you're really in the dark, I'll spell it out for you. I want you here in this house with me, all the time.'

Her heart thudded against her ribs, sending the adrenalin surging through her blood. 'Are you asking me to move in with you?'

'More than that! I want you to marry me.'

She gulped deep in her throat, not believing her ears. Finding her tongue she muttered, 'Remember, Alfie, I'm divorced. We won't be able to marry in church.'

'Don't use that as an excuse, Anne. We can marry in a register office. So long as you're legally mine and I have someone to care for, it doesn't matter to me where we get married. Or don't you want to marry me? Is this your way of letting me down gently?'

'No! No, not at all,' she hastened to reply. 'But I'm too old to give you children,' she warned. 'You could marry a younger woman and start a family. You'd like children, wouldn't you?' She waited breathlessly for his reply. Perhaps she was wrong and he wasn't all that keen on kids running round his house.

'It's you I want, Anne. I gave up on children a long time ago. Who's to say that I'm not the one who was at fault in my marriage to Rita? Why, I could marry a younger, fertile woman and still not produce any children. Besides, what young woman in her right mind would have me, eh? I need someone mature, someone who knows what she's getting herself into, taking on a grumpy old bugger like me. You know, I've lived with the memory of that encounter with you all my life and I'd very much like to have more of it. I think we'd be good for each other.'

She turned away from him and, disconcerted, he reluctantly let go his hold on her, watching her with worried eyes. With her back to him to hide the tears that fell, she muttered, 'You don't understand, Alfie. I'm not worthy of you.'

'Ach, come on now, Anne. I'm no saint myself, you know, and I certainly don't expect you to be one either. Marry me, please. I just know we'll be good together.'

She was sorely tempted to accept his proposal. It would be heaven to put the past behind her; marry this man and live here in this lovely house with him. Given the chance she could make him happy. She knew she could. But didn't he deserve to know he had a grandson? Wasn't it his right to know he had left part of himself behind? No matter what the cost to her, he had to be told the truth. She turned to face him and he was beside her immediately, reaching for her in concern.

He gripped her shoulders and gave her a gentle shake. 'Here now, what's all this? There's no need to cry. I didn't mean to upset you, you know.' Pulling her close he pressed his cheek to her hair and patted her back comfortingly, all the while whispering endearments. 'I'm sorry. I was stupid to rush you. You warned me not to and I should have paid more heed. I'll wait until you're ready. All right, love?'

'You haven't upset me. I just need a little more time, that's all.'

He edged her back and looked down at her tear-stained face. Gently brushing her damp cheeks with his thumbs he teased, 'These tears had me fooled, you know. I thought you were going to reject me.' The words brought a slight smile to her face and he continued softly, 'However, as I've already said, I'll wait as long as you like. But no more tears! Okay?'

He sat down on the settee and drew her down beside him. 'I have to confess that I've fallen in love with you, Anne. Is there any hope at all for me?'

The sound that escaped from her lips startled him. It was like a wild animal caught in a trap. 'Ahhh, Alfie. What have I done?' She struggled from his hold and stood gazing down at him, a picture of total misery.

Bewildered, he returned her look. 'What on earth's the

matter with you? I thought I was paying you a compliment asking you to marry me.'

Her head swung from side to side in abject dismay. 'Please take me home, Alfie. I promise to give you my answer tomorrow night. I've got to think this through, give it a lot of thought and decide what to do for the best.'

At a loss to understand her reaction, he rose slowly to his feet. 'I'm sorry, Anne, I can't drive you home. I've had a few whiskeys, remember, and that Black Bush is strong stuff. I had hoped to persuade you to stay the night. In the spare room of course,' he hastened to add. 'But if that's what you want, so be it. I'll phone for a taxi.'

She passed him talking on the phone on her way to the bathroom and he turned to her and said, 'As it's Saturday night, they say it will be a while, maybe as long as an hour, before a cab comes. Is that all right?'

She nodded and continued on up the stairs. In the privacy of the bathroom she splashed cold water on her face and examined her reflection in the mirror. She looked drawn and haggard. Time had run out on her. With his proposal of marriage Alfie had made her aware that she must now make the crucial decision. But what should she do? Grab at her last chance of happiness and marry him and let him live in ignorance? Or take her chances and tell him the truth and maybe finish up on her own again?

She sat on the edge of the bath for some minutes, contemplating her options, going down each avenue open to her. Alfie didn't need to know the whole sordid tale. Hadn't he said the past didn't matter, that he just wanted to be with her? All she had to do was keep her big mouth shut. Her troubled thoughts swung back and forth like a pendulum, tearing at her conscience, driving her to distraction, until she could bear it no longer. With a strangled sob she made her decision. Quickly wiping her face dry she applied a few licks of face powder and a brave dash of lipstick and, squaring her shoulders, left the bathroom.

On legs that trembled, she tentatively descended the stairs. One look at her pale, drawn face and Alfie jumped abruptly to his feet as she entered the room. She motioned him to sit down and sat in the chair opposite his. He remained standing and gazed anxiously down at her for some moments before sinking slowly down, eyes alert to her every movement.

'I have something to tell you, Alfie. It's going to be hard for me to do this.' She grimaced. 'Believe me, I don't relish the idea of telling you what a stupid, selfish person I've been.'

'Anne . . . listen now. I don't want any confessions about your past. I've already told you that! That's all over and done with. Water under the bridge. I just want to spend the rest of my life with you. I don't care if there have been other men! I'm not in the least bit interested in that. Is that so hard to understand? Nothing else matters but that we be together.'

'If only that were possible,' she whispered, tears welling. She blinked them away and when he opened his mouth to argue raised a hand and motioned him to be silent. 'To be honest I don't want to tell you the truth. I would love to marry you and let you live in blissful ignorance, but it wouldn't be right. I've learned to care for you these past weeks. Really care. Know what I mean?'

He leaned forward and reached for her hands, gripping them tightly between his. 'Then do it! Forget the past. Marry me. I'll be only too happy to live, as you put it, in blissful ignorance.'

Her hands returned his grip and before she could renege on her good intentions she blurted out, 'You had a son!'

He gazed at her blankly. Frustrated, she shook his hands. 'Do you hear me? I gave birth to your son all those years ago.'

At last comprehension dawned and Alfie said slowly, 'Let me get this straight. Are you saying that I left you pregnant that night?'

She nodded, and releasing her hands he straightened up in the chair, his bewilderment obvious. 'Surely not . . . I don't understand . . .'

'How could you? To this day, no one except myself knows the truth.'

'And what about the man you married?'

'Oh, I convinced him the baby was his.'

A look of utter contempt, quickly subdued, flashed across Alfie's face.

'Don't look at me like that!' she wailed. 'Think about it! Put yourself in my shoes, for heaven's sake. What else could I do, eh? Chase over to England looking for you? And there was no chance, even if I had found out where you lived, that you'd want to know I was pregnant with your child. Imagine . . . you just married to Rita, a whole new future ahead of you, and me arriving on your doorstep saying, Congratulations, Alfie! You're about to become a dad. What are you going to do about it? You would soon have got shot of me! I was desperate, I didn't know which way to turn, and thankfully Dan believed the baby was his, and we got married in one hell of a hurry.'

He just sat there too stunned to speak and she waited

318

fearfully for his reaction. Shaking his head in disbelief he said, 'I can't take this in. Rita always implied that it was my fault that we had no children. She had me convinced I was infertile, so how can you be so sure I'm the father?'

'You infertile? Far from it. That one-night stand left me pregnant and ruined my whole life. Besides, Dan was always careful and took precautions.'

'Didn't you love this man?'

'I thought I did. He was my first serious boyfriend, but we hadn't even talked about marriage. We were far too young. Planned to have a good time before settling down. My condition soon changed all that. It was a bad start to married life, I can tell you. A shotgun wedding and everyone pointing the finger? Upsetting to say the least. And we were stony broke into the bargain. I have to admit that Dan was terrific. With only the slightest sign of doubt he performed his duty well and stood by me. I was the one who was unhappy and discontented.'

'Would you and he have eventually married anyway, do you think?'

Anne shrugged. 'Who knows? Probably not.'

Alfie still sat, the dazed look on his face almost tangible. At last he muttered, 'You know, I can't believe I fathered a child. I really can't take it in.'

'I know. It must be a terrible shock to discover you had a son.'

'You keep saying *had*. Was he the boy who died? The one who crashed on the motorbike?'

A sad little dip of the head confirmed this. 'Yes, I only had the one child. At first we didn't want any more. We managed to get the key to that house I'm living in now, in Spinner Street, but it needed a lot doing to it. So we decided to wait until we were in a better position to afford another baby. Later . . . well, we just kinda drifted apart, so that put paid to that idea.'

'You must have been devastated when the boy died. Him being the only child and all.'

'If I sat here talking about it till doomsday, I could never make you understand just how much. You see, by then Dan and I had been separated for a long time. I was living in Whitehouse. I returned to Belfast shortly before the accident.' She longed for him to come to her and take her in his arms, offer some comfort, but he remained in his chair, a kind of aloof wariness on his face. He was obviously gobsmacked, but surely he believed her? Why would she lie about something that could spoil her chances with him? Bravely she continued, 'I was just getting to know my son again . . .' She sniffed and groped for her handbag. He rose and handed her a handkerchief but returned to his seat with no further sign of compassion. And could she blame him? He must be completely flummoxed.

'I was on the pillion seat the day Jack crashed.'

This certainly brought him out of his trance; focused his attention back on her, away from his son. 'Good God! Were you injured?'

'Not badly. You see, I was thrown over the wall and landed on a soft patch in a field. I just received a broken wrist and some cuts and bruises.' Her hand hovered for a moment over the faint scar that ran from eye to lip. The scar he had never questioned her about; afraid she might think he found it unsightly. 'The worst part of it was, Dan ignored me, refused to give me my rightful place as Jack's mother. I didn't know at the time, but he was already courting Alice Maguire and I suppose he thought I'd upset his apple-cart. When he continued to exclude me from the funeral arrangements I had no choice but to sign myself out of hospital to attend my son's funeral. It was an awful time, I can tell you.'

'Yes, I can imagine.'

She shook her head sharply. 'No! You couldn't possibly imagine what it was like. I was absolutely devastated.'

They fell silent, and after a long pause Alfie said, 'You've mentioned a grandson . . . Is he . . .'

'Yes, he's yours. His name's Jackie. Dan of course thinks he's *his* grandson and when Colette – the child's mother – took off to Canada, she left him in Dan's care. Just two days after his birth she parted with him. I couldn't believe it! I suppose she was afraid of getting too fond of him. Dan has reared the boy ever since. And I must say he's doing a fine job with him.'

'Why did his mother leave him behind?'

'I never did get to the bottom of that. She was away off to Canada before I even heard tell of his birth. I think everybody was in the dark, except maybe Tess Maguire, Dan's stepdaughter. She and Colette were as thick as thieves, so they were. Colette and Jack weren't married. I assumed she couldn't live with a constant reminder of how much she had lost. They were very much in love. She fell to pieces when he died. That I do remember.' Anne paused, remembering that awful time. 'Colette shut herself off from everyone. Devoted herself to the only other person she really cared about, her grannie, who had a heart attack when she learned of Jack's death. Mrs Burns died shortly afterwards leaving Colette a good deal of money, from what I've heard. That's how she was able to make a new start in Canada. I suppose it was out of the question to bring a very young baby with her.'

He frowned. 'I would have thought that you and she would have been brought closer because of your common loss. Especially as she was expecting your grandchild. And why didn't she ask you to look after it? Surely it would have been more natural to ask a woman to look after a baby.'

Anne shook her head, dismayed at the turn the questions were taking. 'We had been at loggerheads for some time because Colette's parents thought Jack wasn't good enough for her,' she admitted. 'I was very annoyed but Jack was beside himself with worry when he found out what they thought of him.' What if it ever became known to Alfie that she was the instigator of all her son's pain? She had betrayed Colette's trust and told her son how the McCormacks felt about him, and that this was the reason for the rift between her and Colette. She cringed at the very idea.

'Why did they think he wasn't good enough?'

'Because he worked in the Silk and Rayon factory and hadn't a trade, whereas Colette had been given a good education and held a position as junior manager in one of the banks in the city centre. I think it was the Ulster Bank.'

Alfie shook his head as if to clear it. 'Then why didn't she leave the child with her parents?'

Vexed with herself, Anne shook her own head. 'I'm telling this all wrong. Let me explain. Colette was a strange wee girl. It seems her father walked out on her mother when she was a toddler and she blamed her mother for driving him away. Actually . . . did I mention that Colette came home for a visit recently and was killed in that bomb explosion in Ann Street?'

'No, you didn't. Good God, have you any good news to tell me?'

Anne sighed. 'I'm hopeless explaining anything, so I am. Well, Colette was killed in that explosion. It was a terrible time. When her mother and stepfather were eventually contacted it seems they were completely in the dark about their grandson. Had no idea whatsoever that he even existed. There was a right old to-do when they found out. Now they're applying to the courts for access, I suppose with a view to getting custody. As far as I can make out, Colette left young Jackie a lot of money.'

'You think these people are after his money then?'

'I've no idea. I really don't know them. You see I only met them the one time and that was very briefly at Jack's funeral. Even so, I can't see Dan giving up wee Jackie. Even if it was proved that he isn't the grandfather, he wouldn't give in without a fight. If the McCormacks should somehow win custody it would be terrible as far as I'm concerned. You see, they live in Omagh. I'd hardly ever see the child.'

Alfie sank back in his chair. 'I'd love to meet this boy. Not,' he hastened to add, 'to lay any claim on him, but just to see what my own flesh and blood looks like. That is if I really am his grandfather.'

'Oh, you're his grandad all right. Although, mind you, he doesn't look in the least like you. He doesn't resemble Jack either. Still, I'll see if I can arrange something so you can get a good look at him.'

Anne lifted her handbag from the seat beside her and opening a small compartment at the back of it withdrew a snapshot of a young boy. 'Who does that remind you of?'

Alfie gazed at the picture of a boy in short baggy trousers and wellies and laughed. 'Where did you get this? Why, that's me when I was about ten years old.'

'No, it isn't you. That's your son Jack when he was eleven.'

'I can't believe this is happening. I've missed out on

so much.' His eyes scrutinised the photograph and he came to a sudden decision. 'I'd very much like to meet my grandson. Can you arrange it?'

Anne nodded but warned again, 'He doesn't look in the least like you.'

'I'd still like to meet him.'

'I'll see what I can do.'

They were alerted by a car horn sounding outside the house.

'That'll be my taxi!' Anne reached for her coat, hoping against hope that he would insist that she spend the night here after all. But no, he helped her into her coat, handed her her handbag and accompanied her out the door. Wishing her good night, he paid the taxi driver to take her home.

'I'll see you soon, Anne. Take care.'

No goodbye peck on the cheek. No 'I'll see you tomorrow'.

'Good night, Alfie.'

Alfie felt heartsore for her as he watched her climb into the taxi and almost put out a hand to restrain her. What other surprises had she in store for him? Best to wait and see.

Anne wept all the way home in the back of the cab. She wept for the loss of her hopes and dreams. Most of all she cried for the loss of Alfie. He was the best thing that had ever happened to her. Dumbfounded by the revelation that he had fathered a son, he had appeared to have no sympathy whatsoever for her. The impression had come across that he thought her a right bitch for deceiving Dan. But what else could she have done? She had not been in a position to rear a child on her own. However, it had confirmed her belief that there was no way Alfie would ever forgive her for running off and leaving Dan to rear Jack on his own when he was only twelve. No way in this whole wide world, and she didn't blame him. She had been her own worst enemy. Why did she have to go and open her big mouth? Talk about shooting yourself in the foot. She was the expert at it.

Back at the house she sat for a long time hugging herself for comfort, trying to sort out what to do. Now that Alfie knew the truth he wouldn't stop until he saw young Jackie. It would be better if she arranged a meeting between them, than maybe him go barging in and introducing himself to Dan.

She repaired her make-up at the wall mirror and tidied her hair, then, shrugging back into her coat, headed out again. The Clock Bar would still be open, with people dawdling over their drinks, and Dan was always one of the last out; with any luck she could still catch him.

She went into the small lounge, which was empty, and approached the serving hatch. There was no sign of Dan. One of the barmen was deep in conversation with a customer and she hailed him. 'Hey, Bobby, is Dan still around?'

'It's his weekend off, Anne.'

'Oh, I see, I forgot all about that. Sorry for disturbing you. Good night.'

'No problem, Anne. Good night to you.'

Outside, Anne debated what to do. She would have preferred to speak with Dan alone but she was aware that if Alice hadn't retired for the night she was sure to want to sit in on their conversation. Perhaps if she asked Dan if she could speak with him on a personal matter Alice would take the hint and leave them alone.

She silently rebuked herself at the very idea of Alice ever leaving her and Dan alone, even for one minute.

Chance would be a fine thing. Still, she wanted to let Alfie see that she intended to do all she could to help him meet his grandson. Shaking like a leaf, she set off to face the music.

Promptly at eight o'clock Theresa and Bob arrived. Tess answered their knock and greeted them warmly. 'Come in. The others are in the living room.'

Tony came into the hall, and bidding him a good evening Theresa left Bob to bring in the bottle of wine and some cans of beer they had brought and followed her friend into the kitchen.

Closing the door with suppressed excitement, she leaned against it and whispered, 'Don't keep me in suspense any longer, Tess. Why all the mystery? What are we celebrating?'

Tess laughed aloud. 'I'm afraid I've given you the wrong impression. It's no big deal. The McCormacks have decided not to proceed any further for custody of Jackie after all. Dan is so relieved that he insisted we have a little celebration party. So we invited you and Bob down to join us.' She shrugged. 'It's as simple as that.'

Theresa sighed. 'I'm glad for Dan's sake, of course, but I have to admit I got carried away with my own imagination. For a moment I hoped that you had decided to get married on the same day as me. Now, that would be worth celebrating.'

'What on earth made you think that?'

'Wishful thinking on my part, I suppose.'

'It certainly was! I want a big day of my own with all the trappings.' Theresa's face lengthened and Tess chastised her. 'Don't look so disappointed, Theresa. You already knew that.'

'You can't blame me for hoping you might change your mind, now, can you?'

'No chance.'

'You will still help me with all the preparations for mine, won't you?'

'Of course I will. That goes without saying.'

'You see, Bob will be working all the overtime he can get so I won't see much of him and it will be up to me to keep the ball rolling.'

'Hmm, why's that? I thought he couldn't stay away.'

'That's as may be, but he has no choice. We need all the money we can get, Tess.'

At once alert, Tess asked, 'Is he putting any pressure on you to sell your share in the shop?'

'No, he isn't.' Seeing the doubt in her friend's eyes, Theresa was quick to deny this. 'Honestly! Even if he was, Tess, I wouldn't hear tell of breaking my promise to you.'

'Thanks, Theresa. I'll not keep you hanging about. I'll let you know as soon as I can.' She tilted her head. 'Listen to that!' The strains of 'Danny Boy' filtered through the walls. 'That shows just how relieved Dan is. He usually needs to be quite tipsy before we can get him to sing and I know for a fact he's only had one drink so far this evening.'

A rapt look on her face, Theresa listened intently. 'My, but doesn't he have a lovely voice?'

'He has indeed.' Tess covered plates of sandwiches and cakes with a clean cloth. 'Let's join them.'

The evening went with a swing, with everyone contributing to the sing-along. Even Tess, when she'd had a few Pernod and limes – courtesy of Tony – was persuaded to sing her mother's favourite song, 'The Old Bog Road'. In the midst of all this merriment Jackie fought sleep but at last gave up the battle and nodded off on his grandfather's knee.

Sweeping him up in his arms, Dan smothered his head with kisses. 'You're mine, love, and no one is ever going to take you from me. Not while I've a breath in my body. I'll put him to bed.'

The three women had retired to the kitchen to set out the food when there was a knock on the front door.

'I'll see who that is,' Alice volunteered and went to open it.

Anne had been willing Dan to answer her knock and she stood gazing blankly at Alice in disappointment.

'Anne! This is a surprise. What can I do for you?'

Anne now wished she hadn't come. She could hear the murmur of voices and someone laughing. A man started to sing only to be told to put a sock in it because he was tone deaf. She realised that they had company. Diffidently she said, 'I was hoping to talk to Dan in private for a few minutes, but if he's too busy I can come back another time.'

Alice, curiosity aroused, had no intention of letting Anne get away without first finding out why she wanted a private word with Dan. 'Come inside. I'll tell him you're here.'

Dan was on his way back down the stairs and his voice reached them. 'Who is it, Alice?'

'It's Anne. She wants a word with you, Dan. Come in, Anne, you're letting all the heat out.'

Anne forced her reluctant feet over the doorstep. In the hall her eyes locked with Dan's, full of entreaty. 'Can I speak with you alone, please?'

It was obvious she didn't want Alice to be present, but Dan was unmoved. 'Anything you have to say can be said in front of my wife.'

Anne turned to go. 'Look, I can hear that you have company. I'll see you another time.'

328

'Whatever you have to say must be important, to bring you out at this time of night.' Dan opened the sitting-room door. 'We can talk in here.' Alice pretended to hang back but he motioned to her. 'You too, Alice.'

With a slight shrug Anne resigned herself to telling Dan her awful secret in front of Alice.

Dan peered intently into Anne's face and had an uneasy feeling at what he saw. She looked as if she were on the verge of a breakdown. 'Alice, would you fetch Anne a drink, please. Something strong. She looks like she could be doing with it.'

Alice reluctantly left the room and Dan gestured for Anne to sit down.

Glad to take the weight off her trembling legs, Anne perched on the edge of the settee and said urgently, 'Dan, I have something very important to discuss with you. Can I please speak to you on your own. Please?'

Alice returned and handed Anne a glass containing a finger of whiskey and two lumps of ice. She thanked her and took a gulp. The strong spirit caught at her throat and she spluttered, covering her mouth with her free hand.

Dan waited patiently until she had regained her breath. 'You can speak in front of Alice, we have no secrets. Sure we haven't, love?'

A slight shake of the head was her answer. Alice's attention was fixed on Anne. Concerned, she joined her on the settee. The woman was in a right state, shaking all over. 'What is it, Anne? Something has certainly upset you. It must be serious.'

Anne turned to her in desperation. 'Alice, I need to speak with Dan alone. What I have to say can only be discussed between the two of us. Please!'

Overcome with pity, Alice decided to give up her right

to intrude into their private conversation. After all, Dan would tell her everything later. 'I'll leave you two to it, then.'

Anne shot her a look of gratitude but Dan, who had remained standing in front of the hearth, with an imperious shake of the head, said, 'You'll stay where you are, Alice. As I've already told you, Anne, we have no secrets. So please tell us what's so important that it brought you up here?'

Alice stared in astonishment as Anne thrust out her chin, squared her shoulders and rose to her feet. Good gracious, anyone would think the woman was going into battle.

That was exactly how Anne felt. Indeed, she would rather go a round with Rinty Monaghan in a boxing ring than tell Dan Thompson how she had duped him into thinking that Jack was his son. After a short pause, while she gathered her wits about her and decided where to start, she drew air into her lungs, cleared her throat and began. 'Dan, cast your mind back to the time we were going out together. Remember?'

A frown gathered on Dan's brow and he swayed uneasily on his feet. 'Do you know something, Anne? I've a feeling that this isn't going to be very pleasant.'

'You can say that again. Very *unpleasant*, in fact. I would advise you to sit down. You're not going to like what I have to say. Not one wee bit.'

He remained standing, a scowl settling on his face, and growled, 'Just get on with it, will you!'

'Remember the night I told you I was pregnant?'

Suddenly alert, Dan looked down at her. 'Where's this all leading, Anne?'

Annoyed by his condescending attitude, Anne's demeanour changed. Slap it into him, she thought. The

330

arrogant big shite. Why should she try to soften the blow for him? He was such a pompous fool, he deserved all he got. 'You were stunned, if I remember correctly,' she said sweetly.

'That's putting it mildly.'

'Why are you men always surprised? You were no saint, you know. But you doubted that the baby was yours and I had to convince you otherwise. Remember?'

'As if it were yesterday.'

'Well you were right! It *wasn't* your baby.'

Dan moved threateningly to tower over her, fists clenched. 'Are you telling me that Jack wasn't my son? That you rushed me into a shotgun wedding when it was someone else's child you were carrying?'

'That's it in a nutshell.'

Flabbergasted, his face drained of all colour, he stood speechless for some time. Then his wrath erupted, the sheer force of it causing her to stumble backwards with fear. 'I don't believe you! You wouldn't have had the gall to do that to me,' he hissed.

Voice trembling with fear she muttered, 'It's the truth, Dan. I swear.'

His arm rose menacingly in the air and Alice was quick to intervene, jumping up from the settee and grabbing at it before he could strike out, then managing to insinuate her body between him and Anne. 'Why are you telling Dan all this now?' she panted from the exertion of restraining her husband. 'You must have a very good reason for doing so.'

Anne was now glad that Alice had stayed. If she hadn't, Dan would surely have smacked her. He was absolutely beside himself with rage, and he had every right, she conceded. 'The man I'm seeing at the moment is Jack's biological father.'

'This guy you're dating? Do I know him?'

'No.'

'What kind of a man is he that he never tried to see his own son?' Struck by a thought, Dan's mouth dropped open and a scandalised look passed over his face. 'Or *did* he see him? Was our marriage a complete farce then? Were you carrying on with him behind my back? Was he a married man and wouldn't leave his wife for you?' Dan paused for breath as he ran out of questions. 'There's something fishy going on here, and I'm going to get to the bottom of it. Was our marriage a front so that you and he could carry on as lovers?'

'No! No! It was a one-night stand. He left for England a few days later and has only recently returned to Belfast. The first he knew about Jack was tonight when I told him.'

'Why? Why tell him?' a puzzled Alice intervened. 'With Jack being dead, what do you hope to gain by your confession?'

Anne kept a wary eye on Dan as she delivered her final bombshell. 'He wants to see his grandson.'

Dan's legs could support him no longer. They felt as if they had turned to jelly. Reaching blindly behind him, he groped for the chair and flopped down on it, leaning forward, his head in his hands, trying to control the panic that gripped him. That this should happen now that the threat of the McCormacks had passed filled him with a renewed dread.

Alice went to him, and kneeling by his side, with a comforting arm across his shoulders, fixed a contemptuous look on Anne. To think that she had felt sorry for her. 'What have you been up to? Have you persuaded this man to seek custody? Is that why you were trying to find out how much money Colette had left? Eh? Do you think that you and your friend can just waltz off with Jackie and his fortune? Over our dead bodies, you scheming cow.'

'You've got it all wrong! Alfie is a good man. He and his wife didn't have any children, so it's only natural that he wants to see what Jackie looks like. You'd do the same in his place, so you would.'

Dan's mind was working overtime. This man had no children. This was an even bigger threat than he had at first thought. Was this man friend of Anne's about to claim his Jackie? What chance did Dan stand if he took him to court? Dear God, what had Anne let him in for? He rose slowly to his feet. 'You can tell this Alfie . . . what's his name? Is he from around here?'

'Higgins. And yes, he's originally from Theodore Street but has lived in England these past twenty-five years or more.'

'You tell this Alfie Higgins, whoever he is, to stay well away from me and my grandson or I won't be responsible for my actions. You make sure you tell him. Show her out, Alice.' With these words Dan abruptly left the room and thumped angrily up the stairs.

12

There was so much noise from the raised voices and laughter going on between the girls that Tony popping his head round the kitchen door was the first they knew that something was amiss. 'What's all the cackling about?' he queried.

'We're just reminiscing about all the good times we had before the troubles started and caused such a division between the communities. Times when one could go anywhere and talk to anyone about anything under the sun without fear of repercussions,' Tess said, with a long-drawn-out sigh of regret for good times past. 'There's some great shops on the Shankill Road, you know. I used to do a lot of my shopping there for material and trimmings, but the troubles put paid to all that! I'd be afraid to go there these days. I suppose the Protestants feel the same way about us. More's the pity.'

'I see. Well, girls, sorry to interrupt all this merriment, but I thought you should know that that was Anne Thompson at the front door,' he informed them.

'Yes, we know.' The girls swapped mischievous smiles.

'We were eavesdropping and heard Mam invite her in. Is she still here? We wondered why Mam was taking so long. What does Anne want?'

'I've no idea, but she's been in the sitting room with your mam and Dan quite a while now, so she has. Bob and I are a bit worried. You see, we think something might be wrong because we heard raised voices and they didn't sound too friendly to us. In fact, just the opposite, if you ask me.'

Tess's interest deepened. 'Did you hear what was said?'

With a wry twist of the lips Tony confessed, 'Well, we did listen, but these walls are so thick we couldn't catch any definite words. But even through the walls we could tell that Dan was very angry. So angry in fact that me and Bob were going to barge in on them in case things were getting a bit out of hand!'

Tess hesitated. 'Strange . . . it would take a lot to anger Dan tonight. He's so relieved that the McCormacks have decided not to take him to court.' She pursed her lips in contemplation and asked, 'Do you think I should go in and see what's going on?'

'I think that might be a good idea, love. Unless you'd rather I go?' Seeing Tess's uncertainty, he assured her, 'I don't mind.'

'Oh, no! That would never do. She might be here on some private business or other. If that's the case you can't just go barging in. In fact it would be better not to interrupt at all. If it's nothing too serious Mam is sure to invite Anne to stay and have a drink with us. After all, she is Jackie's grannie and she'll be glad to hear that the McCormacks are dropping the custody proceedings. She's certainly not one bit keen on him going to live in Omagh.'

'Still, it won't do any harm to find out if everything's all right,' Tony persisted, and added laughingly, 'It's all gone too quiet for my liking. There might be a couple of dead bodies in there for all we know.'

'Don't even joke about it, Tony,' Tess chastised him, and drying her hands on the towel draped round her waist to protect her dress, she removed it and gave him a playful punch on the chest. 'I suppose since you're obviously worried, I'd better go and investigate.'

She was disconcerted as she entered the hall to see Dan blundering blindly past her, his face like thunder. She watched in alarm as he climbed the stairs two at a time. She could see that he was terribly upset. What on earth was that woman up to now to cause him such anger? Apprehensive, Tess listened at the sitting-room door for some moments but only slight sounds caught her ear, as if someone was weeping softly. Perturbed, she tapped lightly on the door and after a slight pause inched it slowly open.

Inside the room the tension was palpable, and Tess stood alert in the doorway looking uneasily from her mother to Anne. 'What on earth's going on in here? Dan just charged past me like a raging bull. He nearly flattened me in his mad rush for the stairs,' she exaggerated.

Anne remained silent, dabbing tears from her eyes with a sodden hanky, and Alice grimaced in Tess's direction. 'I'm not surprised. I'm afraid this woman here knocked all the stuffing out of him. Come in and close the door, Tess.'

Unable to comprehend what could have brought Anne Thompson here at this time of night and caused such a rumpus, Tess closed the door and gingerly approached the two women.

Eyes glued to her daughter's face, Alice said, 'What do you think, Tess? It appears that Anne tricked Dan into a shotgun wedding. According to her, it wasn't his child she was carrying all those years ago when she coerced him into marrying her. It's some other bloke's. Jack wasn't Dan's son, so as you can imagine, he's terribly upset. And you'll never guess who Jack's father is? None other than this new man she's been swanning about with. At least so she very conveniently claims.'

Anne thrust a wrathful face in Alice's direction. 'It's true! Wait and see. You just have to look at him to know that I'm telling the truth. Jack was the spitting image of him, and you know yourself that he didn't resemble Dan in the slightest. I couldn't believe my luck when Dan didn't twig years ago.'

Tess mulled all this over in her mind, recalling how, when she had first met Dan, she had thought that Jack must take after his mother, since he didn't seem to have inherited any of Dan's handsome looks. Then when Anne had returned to Belfast shortly before her son's death and Tess had met her for the first time, she had noted that he didn't resemble his mother very much either, although you could tell they were related.

However, such things did happen, Tess consoled herself, trying not to think of all the repercussions that might arise if it were proved that Dan wasn't Jack's biological father. Jack could quite possibly have taken after his grandfather or grandmother's side of the family. It wasn't unheard-of for families to have second-generation throwbacks. And Anne had shown more than her fair share of interest in Jackie's inheritance. Had she and this man concocted something between them? Were they going to try and pull the wool over Dan's eyes? One thing was for sure, Dan wouldn't be easily hoodwinked a second time, especially when his pride and joy – young Jackie – was involved.

Tess gave herself a slight shake and tried to gather her wits about her. She would think this through later. She'd have plenty of time. There was no way anyone would take Anne Thompson's word. She would need unequivocal proof, and plenty of it, before anyone would pay attention to what she had to say! Meanwhile they must all hold their tongues; not start any idle speculation. Because no matter what, now that Anne had opened her Pandora's box, it would all be so disruptive and heartrending.

'No doubt we'll see for ourselves in due course,' Alice was continuing, her voice sceptical. 'But tell me this, why did you have to tell this man about Jackie? That's what I can't comprehend. Do you honestly think this Alfie what's his name can just waltz into our lives and take control over wee Jackie and his inheritance?' She cracked her fingers in the air. 'Just like that? And on *your* say-so? Have a titter of wit! What exactly are you up to, woman?'

'I'll have you know, Alice Maguire . . .' in her distress Anne reverted to Alice's former name, 'Alfie's quite wealthy in his own right. He doesn't need Jackie's money. He has more than enough to do him the rest of his life. In fact, Jackie would be very lucky to have him for a grandfather. He'd be Alfie's only rightful heir.'

'And you'd be the grannie to help this man rear him? Help him spend the lad's inheritance. Is that your idea?'

'No! I didn't think that at all.'

'I don't understand. If what you say is true and he doesn't need the money, then why tell him about the boy? Don't you think that Dan has had enough heartache with the McCormacks, without this new worry hanging over him?'

'Look, Alice, I know you don't have a very good

opinion of me, and I don't blame you. I admit I've done a lot of things in the past that I'm ashamed of, but Alfie Higgins did me the honour tonight of asking me to marry him—'

'Congratulations,' Alice interrupted sarcastically.

'Oh, I don't think he'll want to now that he knows the truth. It has certainly lowered his opinion of me.'

'Then why on earth did you break your silence after all this time?' Tess quickly intervened. 'What do you hope to achieve? You can't get your hands on his money, you know. Not without my and two others' say-so.'

'I can put my hand on my heart and truthfully say I'm sorry now that I opened my big trap, so I am. I thought Alfie would be sympathetic towards me, but he wasn't. I thought he'd be so glad to hear he had a grandson that he'd overlook the fact that Colette hadn't considered me a good enough grandmother to leave Jackie with. I realise now that I should have let sleeping dogs lie and kept him in total ignorance. No one would ever have been any the wiser. But I've grown very fond of him and I wanted things to be straight between us. He has no one to call his own, you see, so I thought he had the right to know that he has a grandson,' she ended virtuously.

No one to call his own? A cloud of dread settled on Tess like a damp cloak. It was all too apparent to her that if Dan wasn't Jack's father, then he couldn't claim to be Jackie's grandfather. And it sounded like this man would want to get acquainted with his grandson. Even if Anne married him, she was much too old to give him children. What a predicament this silly woman had caused because she couldn't keep her big mouth shut. So much for their little celebration party. Was there no end to their troubles?

*   *   *

In spite of the best endeavours of Tess and Alice to keep the party spirit going and also to mask Dan's long silences, it went without saying that the evening was a flop. Tess had politely but firmly asked Anne to leave, saying that she was sure Dan would get in touch with her in due course. Anne had warned her to tell him not to delay too long or Alfie might take matters into his own hands, and if he brought the law into it, God knows what would happen.

God knows indeed, Tess inwardly lamented. Since it was now quite late she had offered to get Tony or Bob to walk Anne home but she refused and left the house with an angry flounce.

With Anne out of the way, Alice had cajoled Dan into coming downstairs again and trying to put on a big show of being relieved and happy. And he did try, she silently applauded how hard he tried, but Tony, Bob and Theresa, unaware of the unexpected turn of events, continued reflecting on his good fortune until he could bear it no longer and with a strangled sob excused himself and hurriedly left the room.

An uneasy silence ensued as they all sat shuffling their feet and looking everywhere and anywhere but at Alice, who sat head bowed praying for inspiration. It was broken after some moments by Tony, who, without raising his eyes, dared ask, 'It's obvious something awful has happened to change things. Have the McCormacks decided to go to court after all? Is that what this is all about?'

He looked at Tess but it was Alice who answered him. 'No, everything's fine as far as that's concerned. I'm afraid Anne Thompson has brought some very bad news tonight that has knocked the stuffing out of us. It's a bit personal and nothing we can talk about at the moment, you understand. We must wait until it can be confirmed that what she's told us is the truth.'

The two men exchanged glances and Bob suggested, 'In that case perhaps we should go on home now . . . give you a chance to discuss it among yourselves.'

'No! I won't hear tell of you leaving.' Alice smiled bravely. She desperately wanted to go and comfort her husband, but you couldn't invite people to a party and expect them to up and go just because the host was upset. 'I don't want to be left with all that food on my hands,' she joked. 'Let's eat, drink and at least try to be merry.' She headed for the kitchen. 'Help me in with the grub, girls, and you men keep the drink flowing. A bit of bad news isn't going to put a damper on my party. Not if I can help it.'

However, the spark had already gone out of the celebrations and conversation dragged. Soon Tony, Bob and Theresa said their farewells and left. Tony had stopped Tess in the hall and tentatively offered to stay behind, but Tess told him that she wanted to have a word in private with her mother before Alice retired for the night.

Between them Tess and Alice quickly got through the dirty dishes, and when they were all cleared away Tess insisted that her mother leave the kitchen while she made a pot of tea.

'I must go up to Dan. He'll be devastated.'

'Another ten minutes won't make any difference. Let's talk this through first, Mam, see if we can come up with something constructive.'

'I suppose you're right, though I can't think what difference the two of us can make. If Dan isn't Jack's father then he can't be Jackie's grandfather. It's as simple

341

as that.' Alice trailed forlornly into the living room where the dying fire still offered some comforting heat.

Tess's thoughts were running riot as she waited for the kettle to boil. Was her mother about to learn of Dan's betrayal after all these years of silence? It would break her heart. Would she believe that Dan was completely in the dark as far as fathering Jackie was concerned? Tess very much doubted it. Even knowing the true facts, hadn't she herself found it very hard to comprehend? Alice would find it a bitter pill to swallow. Pouring two mugs of tea, she joined her mother by the fireside.

Alice sat hunched over the glowing embers. She gratefully accepted the mug and wrapped her hands around it for warmth, then looked up at her daughter, her brow furrowed with worry. 'That was a turn-up for the books, wasn't it? Who on earth would believe that something like that would resurrect itself after all these years? What on earth will Dan do now? It will break his heart if he loses that wee lad.'

'First we must wait and see if there's any truth in what Anne has told us,' Tess cautioned. 'She might just be trying it on. Not for one minute do I trust that woman. Not for one single minute! It could be the money she's after. Why, as far as I remember she was making none too discreet enquiries about how much Colette had left before this man was even on the scene. She told me she had a date with him that day she came into the shop for tights. I thought at the time that the tights were only an excuse to question me about Jackie's inheritance. Now it looks like I was right. She said she wanted to make a good impression on a new boyfriend, so I imagined that he had just come into her life. Maybe they are trying to work some kind of scam.'

'But she said that he had plenty of money.'

Tess looked incredulous. 'And you believed her? I told you, Mam, don't believe a single word that comes out of that scheming bitch's mouth.' Tess was so worried that her language was running out of control.

Alice's frown deepened and she gnawed at her bottom lip. 'I don't know why, but somehow or other it rang true to me. I think for once she's telling the truth. If, as she claims, she's fond of this guy, why would she lie? I mean, he won't exactly be over the moon at her for raking out all these skeletons. There's no way she'll come out of this smelling of roses, so she had no other reason to shoot off her big mouth.'

'You're forgetting, Mam, there's money at stake. A lot of it! Just take anything Anne Thompson says with a pinch of salt. She's not to be be trusted. You mark my words.'

'No, I'm not forgetting about the money. But supposing she's telling the truth. If this man has no family, perhaps Anne really does think she's doing him a big favour by telling him he has a grandson. Especially if he already has money of his own. He'll want an heir to leave it to, and it's true, you know, that blood's thicker than water. She maybe thought that her being the child's grannie would bring them closer together. I do think that she wants to be straight with him and that's what started all this off. She hasn't thought it through properly, though, and appears to have bitten off more than she can chew.' Her shoulders lifted in a negative shrug. 'Anyway, that's what I think, for what it's worth.'

Tess turned this all over in her mind. Perhaps her mother was right. Maybe Anne was trying to be honest with Alfie. In that case couldn't her mother see what this meant? Obviously not. Tess set out to put her wise. 'Mam . . .'

She hesitated so long sorting out her words that Alice,

sensing she was about to hear something unpleasant, straightened up in her chair. 'Well? Come on, out with it, girl, for heaven's sake.'

'If what you say is true, you do realise that this means Dan is not Jackie's grandad?'

'Yes, I know that! I can work that out for myself, I'm not thick.'

'Well . . .' Tess dithered. Was now the time to tell her mother the whole sorry tale? The seconds dragged by and she was sorely tempted, but unlike Anne, she decided to keep her mouth shut. With a bit of luck all might yet be saved. 'When the McCormacks hear about this, their whole outlook might change. If it's proven that Dan isn't the rightful grandad, they and Anne might gang up on him. With Dan out of the running the McCormacks might think that they are in with a better chance of custody. After all, biological grandfather or not, Alfie is a stranger, whereas the McCormacks have managed to get to know and like Jackie. As for you and Dan, you wouldn't be in the count as far as the law is concerned.'

'Oh no, you're wrong there!' Alice was adamant. 'You're forgetting that the will states that Dan, being the grandfather, and you, Tess, will be in charge until Jackie comes of age and after that he'll be at liberty to do what he likes. No one else can interfere.'

'Mam, that's what I'm trying to point out to you. If Anne convinces Alfie Higgins that he has a grandson, he'll do all in his power to get custody.'

Alice looked stunned. 'Oh my God! I never thought of that. Then if what Anne says is true, this man has a genuine claim to Jackie. Is that what you're telling me? If he went to court he could win custody of the child?'

'I'm afraid so. That is, *if* he's the real grandad. Which would have to be proven beyond a shadow of doubt.'

'Do you think they'll be able to prove it?'

'Yes, I do. Anne is sure to have some family photographs, and I imagine they will go a long way to proving that this man fathered Jack. I never did think that Jack looked like Dan. What about you?'

'I didn't either, but that doesn't mean anything. You don't look in the least like me, you took after your father.' A puzzled look passed over her face. 'Mind you, I've always thought young Jackie strongly resembles Dan, so how do you account for that?' Tess held her breath; her mother was almost there. Would she at last twig? But Alice was shaking her head in denial. 'No, you must be wrong, Tess. Dan must be the grandfather. The boy's the spit of him. There's something fishy here and I can't put my finger on it.'

Tess didn't agree or disagree with her. Perhaps her mother would eventually figure things out for herself. The evidence was all there for her to see. 'Jack certainly didn't look like Dan. I think we can safely believe Anne when she claims that Alfie is Jack's father, but I don't for one minute think this will be sufficient proof for Dan. He'll probably insist on a blood test, and that would involve Jackie.'

'Would this prove beyond a shadow of doubt to the court that this Alfie person is the grandfather?'

'Only if his blood and Jackie's are an exact match. I'm no expert in these matters, but I think that would be sufficient evidence to grant custody.' Tess could only hope and pray that it wouldn't come to blood tests or all hell would be let loose. Didn't she know that the blood samples wouldn't match? Was she going to have to put Alice wise to the fact and break her heart into the bargain? Should she speak out and tell Dan the truth: that he was Jackie's father?

345

'Why did this have to happen to us?' Alice wailed. 'I wish Anne had kept that big mouth of hers shut. That woman will be the death of us.'

Exhaustion showed in every line of Alice's body. 'Away you go on up to Dan,' Tess said gently. 'He probably needs someone to talk to.'

Alice rose groggily to her feet. The trauma of the past few hours had taken its toll on her and she moved like a rheumaticky old woman. 'He's probably asleep by now, but I'm whacked out so I'll go on up anyhow. Good night, love.'

'Good night, Mam.' Tess watched her mother slowly leave the room and was torn with love and pity. She dreaded to think what effect the truth would have on her mother. As she had predicted a long time ago, she would be the one left to pick up the pieces if anything went wrong between Dan and Alice. And she didn't relish the thought one bit.

In the back room of the shop on Monday morning, as they toiled away at their machines, Theresa kept throwing Tess covert glances but managed to contain her curiosity. Tess could see her friend was having great difficulty holding her tongue and decided to put her in the picture as far as she dared.

'Theresa, I know you're bound to be wondering what all the commotion was about on Saturday night, but it's not my place to talk about it. Dan has asked Anne up to the house tonight to talk something over. As soon as we know how things stand and I'm free to speak, I'll tell you all about it. Okay?'

Theresa shuffled about on her chair with embarrassment. 'I'm sorry. I didn't know I was so transparent. I know it's none of my business, Tess, but I have to admit that I'm all agog with curiosity. However, I do understand your predicament and I pray everything works out for you all. So let's change the subject, shall we?' A beautiful smile wreathed her face. '*I've* got some good news, for a change. What do you think! I had a letter from Les O'Malley this morning.'

'Oh, that's marvellous! Does he know you're getting married?'

'Yes, I wrote and told him just after Bob proposed. I also happened to mention that I'd be seeing very little of Bob between now and the wedding, as he would be working all hours in Sligo to get enough money for all the essentials, and what do you think? Les wants me to pay him a visit. See his part of Canada before I settle down. He says Vancouver is beautiful at this time of year. He has even offered to pay my air fare.'

'Why, that's wonderful news!' Tess enthused. 'Just wonderful!'

'Don't be silly. I couldn't possibly go. Bob would never hear of it. But it was very kind of Les to offer, don't you think?'

'More than kind, I reckon! Don't give Bob any say in the matter. Just tell him it's the chance of a lifetime and too good to miss out on and you intend taking Les up on his offer. You'd be a fool if you don't,' Tess warned. 'You'll never get an opportunity like it again.'

'Do you think it's possible? I'm not being selfish, am I?'

'Of course not. A couple of weeks away from this place will do you a world of good. Believe me, Bob will have no reason to object to you going.'

Theresa still looked dubious. 'I'll talk it over with Bob, but I can't see him agreeing. Besides, what about you? I'd be leaving you in the lurch. And what about all my wedding preparations?' She gave her head a sad shake. 'No, I couldn't possibly go.'

Tess felt like giving her a good shake. 'Forget about Bob, forget about work, forget about wedding preparations. Stand up for yourself just for once, for God's sake. We'll work all the necessary overtime to keep abreast of the shop orders before you go and when you come back. Meanwhile Mam and I will be organising the reception. You are going to let Mam and Dan hold the reception in our house, aren't you?'

'Oh yes. It's more than generous of them.'

'Bob will just have to look after anything else that crops up to do with your wedding plans. I'm sure that won't kill him! It will only be for two weeks, after all. Tony and I will keep him up to date with all that's happening, and we'll be here to help out if need be.'

'It's awfully good of you, Tess, but I'll have to give it a lot of thought first. I don't want Bob to get the wrong end of the stick and think I don't love him any more. That wouldn't be a very good start to a marriage.'

'And do you love him? You're absolutely sure he's the right one for you?'

Theresa looked at Tess as if she had taken leave of her senses. 'Of course I love him! There has never been anyone else. See . . . that's what I mean, Tess. He'll doubt my love for him if I do go off to Canada.'

'He knows damn well how much you care for him! Besides, he'd have a cheek to object since he'll be in Sligo most of the time, and it's not as if you'll be spending a lot of money. Les will see to that. I'm sure Bob will send you off with his blessing.'

Theresa still dithered. Tess watched conflicting emotions sweep across her face. She couldn't fathom how her friend couldn't see Bob Dempsey for what he was.

348

He could stay away for weeks on end without considering her feelings yet she couldn't bring herself to leave him for two short weeks. But then hadn't Tess been the same herself for some months? Blind to Bob's faults, letting him play on her infatuation. 'Go for it,' she urged.

'You really think he won't mind?'

'I really do.' Tess had her fingers crossed when she said this. Bob Dempsey could be a contrary bugger at times, but at the first opportunity she would have a word in his ear; make him feel too ashamed to deny Theresa this treat.

Rain was pelting down like stair rods, bouncing off the pavement as the Hillman Minx slid smoothly to a halt at the kerb. Despite the heavy downpour Anne and her companion had arrived promptly at eight. Tess, who was watching from the bay window of what had once been her workroom and had now been converted back into the sitting room, warned the others, 'They're here,' and rushed into the hall to open the door for them. They crossed the pavement at a fast sprint but were still quite wet when they burst through the open doorway into the hall.

Tess gave their wet coats a good shake before hanging them on the hall-stand, then chided, 'You should have waited for a break in the weather. That rain can't last much longer, you know. At least not this heavy or we'll all be washed away.'

'We didn't want to be late. I remember how finicky Dan is about punctuality and we don't want to start off on the wrong foot, now do we?' Anne confessed. Removing her headscarf and shaking it free of raindrops, she fluffed her hair out with her fingers. The man smoothed his own hands over his wet hair and Tess was

349

quick to offer some assistance. 'Would you like a towel?'

Bright blue eyes twinkled at her from behind expensive lenses and she felt herself warming to him. 'I'll be all right, thank you. There's not that much hair left to worry about.'

With a smile she motioned them into the room where Dan and her mother waited expectantly.

Dan gave a slight start of surprise; knowing his ex-wife's taste in men, he had expected someone about her own age or younger, not this distinguished-looking mature man entering the room. He quickly recovered his composure and courteously advanced to meet them. However, further examination of the man sent his heart plummeting to his boots. It was obvious that he was looking at the father of the lad he had reared as his own son for twenty-one years. The same gangly frame, long face and crooked smile. There could be no doubt about it. Jack had been this man's double. How had he been so blind all these years not to see that he had been cuckolded?

Anne's voice had a nervous quaver as she made the introductions. 'Dan, this is my friend Alfie Higgins. Alfie, this is Dan Thompson and his wife Alice, and their daughter Tess Maguire.'

Introductions over and hands shaken all round, Alice gestured towards the settee. 'Sit down, please. I'm sure you're as anxious as we are to get this over and done with.'

'I'll leave you lot to it, then.' Tess started to back out of the room. Half of her longed to remove herself from these proceedings, have nothing to do with it, but the other half wanted to know at first hand just what would transpire from this meeting.

'Don't go, Tess. This is as much your business as the

rest of us. After all, you're one of Jackie's trustees,' Dan insisted.

When she would have still retreated he urged, 'Please stay, Tess.'

Dan cleared his throat and, eyes fixed on Alfie's face, said in an authoritative voice, 'I hear that my ex-wife has led you to believe that the boy I reared as my own son for twenty-one years was fathered by you.' He had no intention of pulling his punches or making it any easier for them by showing the slightest hint of doubt.

'Oh Dan, surely you can see that I told the truth?' Anne cried, gesturing towards Alfie. 'You can't possibly have any doubt now. Just look at him! Even you will have to admit that Jack was the picture of him.'

Dan's eyes swung and glared at her. 'You wouldn't know the truth if it jumped up and bit you on the arse!' he snarled. 'Our whole married life must have been one big lie from beginning to end.' Bringing his eyes back to Alfie, he continued, 'Pardon me for that outburst but this woman has that effect on me. What I want to know is just exactly what you intend doing about this matter.'

'All I want at the moment is to see my grandson.'

'Why? Why do you want to see him, eh? Even if you prove to be his biological grandfather, what difference will it make? You're a complete stranger to the child. Jackie has lived under this roof since he was two days old. Alice and I have devoted our lives to him, as has Tess. That will count for a lot, you know, if push comes to shove. So don't you expect to walk off with him just because *she* says you're Jack's father.'

Alfie could see that the man in front of him was getting very agitated. He resolved to tread carefully and not upset him too much. 'I only want to meet the boy. Surely you can grant me that,' he said mildly.

351

'And that will be it? You won't come back here again?'

'Ah, come on now. I can't promise you that. All I know at this moment in time is that I'd like to see the boy, perhaps determine for myself whether or not there is any truth in what Anne says.'

Anne rounded on him in anger. 'Surely *you* believe me? I showed you Jack's photograph and you thought it was an old picture of yourself.'

'I didn't think you bothered to take any photographs of Jack with you when you ran off with your fancy man and left me to rear him on my own. You appeared to have no regard whatsoever for his welfare,' Dan snarled and she cringed back in shame.

Floored by these revelations but noting how upset Anne was, Alfie reached across and gripped her hand. 'Anne, I'm *not* doubting you. If Mr Thompson will only let me see and talk to the boy, then we can go away and talk things over and decide what to do next.' He met Dan's gaze. 'I shall make my own decision regarding parentage when I see the young lad. I don't think that's asking too much.'

Dan nodded abruptly at Tess, and taking this as a hint to fetch Jackie, who was already in bed and probably asleep by now, she left the room.

The boy was still awake, sitting up in bed, smiling and talking to himself as he read the *Beano*.

'You're supposed to be asleep, young man. That must be a good story judging by that big grin all over your face. What mischief's Dennis the Menace up to now?'

Reluctantly Jackie dragged his eyes away from the comic and gave her his attention. 'I wasn't sleepy, Aunt Tess. I was sent to bed early and I didn't even do anything naughty, so I didn't. Honest! I can tell something's going on downstairs and I think that's why I'm in bed so early.'

Surprised at these words of wisdom from one so young, Tess questioned him. 'And just what do you think is going on down there, young man?'

'Ach! How would I know? Nobody tells me anything in this house. I only know everybody's acting funny.' He scrambled out of bed and stood looking entreatingly at Tess, tears hanging on the ends of long, thick lashes. 'Am I going to have to go and live with my Grannie Betty in the country? Is that what this is all about?'

Tess pulled him close and cupped his face in her hands. 'Don't you fret, my wee love. This has nothing to do with your Grannie Betty. Your Grannie Anne . . .' she paused as her mind cursed the idea of all these grannies; not a bit of wonder the lad was so confused, 'has brought someone to meet you. They're downstairs now.' She kissed him gently. 'Put your slippers on, love, and we'll go down and meet Grannie Anne's friend.'

He had to be coaxed and cajoled all the way down the stairs, Tess tugging his hand and whispering encouragement at his reluctance. At the sitting-room door he still hung back, face puckered with unshed tears of dread for the unknown.

Tess crouched over him and whispered in his ear, 'Don't be frightened, love. Your grandad is in there and he'll protect you. All you have to do is have a chat with a nice gentleman. You'll like him, honest.'

'What if I don't like him, Aunt Tess? I won't know what to talk about.'

'He'll do most of the talking. All you'll have to do is answer any questions he might ask you.'

Jackie blinked back the tears. 'What if I don't know the answers?' he wailed. The child couldn't control the tremors that took over his young body.

Alarmed at the state of anxiety he had worked himself

353

into, Tess hugged him close. 'Then just say you don't know. He's a nice man, and Grandad will be there to stop him if he asks too many questions or if he upsets you. In fact, you could sit on Grandad's knee if you like.' Tess was now debating the wisdom of bringing Jackie down here. On an impulse she decided to take him back up to bed. She could pretend that he was sound asleep and she didn't want to disturb him.

But she had left it too late. Before she had the chance to move, the door was pulled open and Alice stared at her in bewilderment. 'Why are you standing out here?' she exclaimed in surprise. 'We thought he must be asleep and I was coming to fetch you.'

'Just look at the poor wee soul, Mam. He's a bundle of nerves, so he is,' Tess warned. 'I was trying to set his mind at rest before going in.'

Anne's voice was bitter as she came towards the door. 'Telling him what to say, more likely. Is that what you were doing? Putting words in the child's mouth, eh?'

Alice glared at her and taking Jackie by the hand shouldered roughly past her and drew him gently into the room. 'Come on in, son. You mightn't think it by the sound of her, but your Grannie Anne has come to visit you.'

Alfie's first glimpse of the boy confused him. As far as he could see he didn't look in the least like anyone in his family. Fixing a firm eye on Anne he asked, 'Is this the boy you were telling me about?'

'Yes. Remember, I told you he doesn't look in the least bit like you. He doesn't resemble your son either, believe me, but he *is* your grandson.'

Putting an arm across Jackie's shoulders, Dan gave him a reassuring hug and introduced him to Alfie. 'Jackie, this gentleman has come to see you. Alfie, this is my grandson

Jackie, and a nicer wee boy you're never likely to meet.'

Crouching down on his hunkers, Alfie smiled at Jackie, and such was the magnetism of his personality that Jackie, who had been cowering against Dan, smiled shyly back. 'You look a clever little lad, how are you getting on at school?'

'Great! I got a big star yesterday for being the best writer in my class. Didn't I, Grandad?' A pleased grin on his face, he glanced up at Dan.

Dan ruffled his hair. 'You certainly did, son.'

'That's very good,' Alfie praised him. 'I bet your grandad was pleased too.'

'I was indeed,' Dan claimed.

Alfie scrutinised the boy's features closely then held out his hand. Not sure what was expected of him, Jackie held out his own small hand in response. Alfie's great fist closed around it. 'I'm very pleased to meet you, young man. Perhaps I can visit you again some time?'

Completely won over by the man's charm Jackie agreed. 'Sure you can.'

Rising to his feet Alfie caught Anne's eye. 'I think we should go now.'

To Dan's dismay, Alice, proper hostess to the end, intervened. 'Won't you stay and have a cup of tea first?' At Alfie's shake of the head Dan sighed his relief. It was a short-lived respite as his wife persisted. 'Maybe a drink then?'

'No, thank you for your kind hospitality, but the rain appears to have abated and we had best be on our way while the going's good. Anne and I have a lot to discuss.' He faced Dan. 'May I come back and talk to this young man again?'

Dan hesitated. 'So long as you don't make a habit of it. The lad is confused enough as it is.'

'Thank you.' His gaze swept the rest of them. 'And a good night to you all.'

Dan saw them out and Tess took Jackie back up to bed. She read him a story until he fell asleep, then tucked the bedclothes around him, sighing as she did so. Where would this all end? What was to become of the child? Why had Colette put the onus on her whether or not to tell Dan the truth? If only she had been honest back then, brought it all out into the open, how different would things have been today? Would her mother have forgiven Dan then, or would Dan be living somewhere else, rearing the child on his own as he had done with Jack?

That was something she would never know. If all was revealed now, Alice would be facing her daughter's betrayal as well as Dan's. Would Tess be able to make her understand that what she had done she had thought was for the best for all concerned? She very much doubted it.

The rain had stopped and stars sparkled above the rooftops in all their splendour, clinging to an inky blue background. The galaxy went unnoticed by Alfie and Anne, who were locked in their own troubled thoughts as they arrived at Spinner Street in a stony silence. Outside her house Alfie turned in his seat with an exasperated sigh and faced her. 'Anne, I have to admit that I'm very puzzled. I don't know what to think. I'd like to come in and talk things over with you, if you don't mind?'

Anne reluctantly nodded her consent, knowing that an interrogation was awaiting her inside her home and dreading what the outcome would be. Climbing out of the car, she unlocked the front door and preceded him into the house. 'Would you like a cup of tea . . . coffee?'

'Coffee would be nice, thanks.'

Removing his overcoat, he folded it neatly and draped it over the banister, then, avoiding the settee, chose one of the armchairs. He didn't want to sit too close to Anne. She had managed to keep him at arm's length so far and his mounting desire for her might tend to make him over-look some of the awful deeds she had committed in the past. He chided himself for thinking along these lines. Hadn't he told her, not once, but time and time again, that the past didn't matter? It was the future that counted.

However, the situation had now changed completely. He was pleased but somewhat uneasy to learn that he had a grandson. But was the child really his flesh and blood? It would be wonderful if he was, but as far as looks went, he had his doubts. He intended to get to the bottom of this business and wanted to see Anne's face, look her straight in the eye, when he put some pertinent questions to her.

Anne handed him a mug of coffee and sat on the chair facing him, a defiant tilt to her chin.

'Aren't you having one?' he asked quietly.

'Maybe later. I'm a bundle of nerves at the moment.' In her agitated state Anne ran her fingers distractedly through her hair, leaving it standing on end. Then, managing to compose herself a little, she asked appre-hensively, 'Now, Alfie, tell me what it is that puzzles you so much?'

He set the cup deliberately to one side and spread his hands wide as if he were some Shakespearean actor about to make a dramatic opening speech on stage. 'Everything! First, what makes you so sure that I'm Jack's father? I mean, you were having a relationship with Dan Thompson at the time you and I . . .' he flapped his hands, at a loss for the right words, 'you know, came together.'

Anne wanted to laugh at his quaint way of putting things. When she just nodded, he continued.

'How can you be so sure then that I was the father?'

'Because Dan was always careful and you weren't! You were a bit tipsy at the time as I remember. Dan did his best to avoid any accidents. That's why I was convinced it was yours. Then once the baby was born there was no doubt whatsoever in my mind who the father was. I just knew! Even then I could see he strongly resembled you. How Dan didn't guess I'll never know.'

'In spite of all these precautions you say he took, he still believed you when you told him you were pregnant?'

'Of course he did. He had some reservations at first, but as far as he was aware there was no one else in the picture. If I hadn't met you that night there wouldn't have been. I honestly don't know what possessed me. Contrary to what people might think, I wasn't that type of girl. Besides, it could so easily have been Dan's, so why should he doubt me?'

'Still . . .'

There was enough disbelief in that one little word to bring Anne jumping to her feet, nostrils flaring in temper. 'We had been going out for some months, okay? Careful or not, we both knew it could still happen. He thought it had and stuck by me, and in no time, no time at all, he had put a ring on my finger.'

'He seems a decent enough bloke.'

'He was. Still is, as a matter of fact.'

'It's a shame you had to trick him, though. How come you couldn't make a go of it with him?'

'Because I was a bloody fool, that's why!' she snapped. 'I wasn't ready for marriage. I felt trapped. I tried hard to be a good wife to him, honest I did, but I was bored. Once Jack started school I couldn't bear being stuck in the house all day long, no spare money to go anywhere or buy anything, so I got a job in the mill. For a while everything was fine. With the extra money coming in I was able to buy nice things for the house. Wee treats for Jack. Then, unfortunately, I got friendly with one of the bosses, who happened to be single and had a bit of money behind him. He was willing to take me to places I'd never been before, give me a good time, and I jumped at the chance. The rest you know.'

'You fell in love with this other man?'

'No.'

Her voice was a shamed whisper and he leaned towards her. 'I can't hear you.'

'I said *no*! If you must know, I liked the attention he was paying me. I was flattered that he sought me out and wanted to lavish money and gifts on me.'

'You mean to tell me that you left your husband and child because this guy spent money on you and bought you things?' Alfie couldn't hide his disgust.

'I suppose you could say that.' Shame blazed colour into her cheeks.

'Is that why you decided to tell me the truth? Eh? Did you think that if I could prove I'm Jackie's biological grandfather you and I could rear him together? Are you only interested in money, Anne? The child's money as well as mine?'

'No! That's not true.' Tears rushed to her eyes but she fought them back and glanced away from him in frustration. 'How can I expect you to believe anything I say?'

'Try me.'

She sank down on the chair and haunted eyes met his. 'I don't know where to start. I can't possibly justify the terrible things I've done.'

'Try!' he demanded sternly.

Her head swayed from side to side. 'I can't. I've no excuse. Dan did his best. He thought he had done well by marrying me, and for a short time, on the surface at least, everything seemed fine. But I wanted more out of life than a house in Spinner Street and I became restless.'

He drew back and eyed her thoughtfully. 'But you're still in Spinner Street.'

She grimaced. 'Yes, and glad I was to return here. Since I'm being truthful, I may as well tell you that I forced Dan to put me up when I came out of hospital after the accident. He wanted nothing to do with me but I had nowhere else to go. We were still married at the time, though living apart, so I talked my way back into his life. Mind you, he wasn't one bit happy about it. Neither was his then lady friend, Alice Maguire. Eventually he moved in with her and Tess until I could find alternative accommodation. I actually squatted in this house until he got my name put on the rent book. Oh, I was a lovely person back then!' she finished sarcastically. 'And I suppose there are those who will say that I haven't changed much.'

Alfie listened quietly, digesting her every word. He prided himself on being a good judge of character, and below all the brave admissions coming from her he sensed how lonely and unwanted she must have felt, having ostracised herself from friends and family.

'Then I began to date—'

He quickly interrupted her. 'I don't want to hear anything about other men. I just want to know anything relating to this boy you say is my grandson.'

'But he *is* your grandson!' she insisted.

'There is not a single molecule of me in that boy,' he stated flatly. 'What are you really playing at, Anne?'

'Look, Alfie, I know for a fact that you were Jack's

father, so it's only common sense to believe that you're Jackie's grandfather.'

'Is it?'

She blinked in confusion and exclaimed, 'Of course it is!'

He watched her closely as little twitches convulsed her face and urged, 'Think about it, Anne.'

She gave her head an abrupt shake as if to clear it of some hidden dark thoughts. 'Just what are you implying, Alfie?'

'Don't tell me you can't see that the boy has a lot of Dan Thompson in him. Surely you must have noticed how alike they are.'

She nodded her head. 'Yes, but . . . what are you saying? You've lost me, Alfie.'

'Come on, Anne, use your brains, for goodness' sake. Imagine you're a neutral onlooker and you've never met Dan Thompson before. Take a step back and examine the facts.' She obeyed him, giving him her full attention, eyes narrowed to slits as she concentrated. He continued slowly, 'If, as you have convinced me, I was Jack's father . . . how come the boy looks so much like Dan Thompson, eh? A blind man could see the similarities.'

She took her time dwelling on these words, then said flatly, 'What you're insinuating is not possible.' She was obviously bewildered. 'Dan didn't have any other children, so it was no son of his that fathered Jackie,' she said defiantly. Did Alfie think her that stupid?

'Exactly!'

Still Anne eyed him in a confused state, then her brow cleared as comprehension dawned. 'No! He wouldn't! Not Dan Thompson. Not with the young girl who was engaged to his son.' Again she shook her head as thoughts fought each other in contradiction. At last she expressed

361

doubt. 'Besides, why would he? He was in love with Alice Maguire.'

'I can only guess that he perhaps had an impromptu encounter, such as we had, and Jackie is the result.'

She was still unconvinced. 'There must be some other explanation. Believe me, Dan wouldn't have risked losing Alice. He was nuts about her. And Colette was very much in love with Jack. She was willing to give up everything for him.' She shook her head in disbelief. 'No, you've got it all wrong, Alfie. There has to be some other logical explanation. There just has to be.'

Alfie rose to his feet with a slight shrug of defeat and reached for his overcoat. 'Sleep on it, Anne,' he advised. 'I'll come down tomorrow night and you can tell me what you think. But for heaven's sake don't discuss it with anyone else until we've talked it over and decided what to do.' He pecked at her cheek. 'Good night.'

She struggled with her emotions. Feeling it was only a matter of time before he gave her the shove, she called out to him as he closed the door, 'Goodbye, Alfie.'

13

Tess spent a long sleepless night, tossing and turning, her tortured thoughts not allowing her mind to rest. As the blush of dawn started to push the dark wraps of night from the room, making her chances of sleep even less likely, she gave up the struggle and decided to go down and make herself a cup of tea. Wrapping herself in a warm towelling gown she pushed her feet into her slippers and descended the stairs.

Dan had beaten her to it. He sat, elbows resting on the kitchen table, chin cupped in both hands and a mug of tea cooling in front of him as he gazed blankly down at it. He was the picture of abject despair and her heart went out to him. He turned a tired, haggard face in her direction. 'Couldn't you sleep either, love? There's plenty of tea in the pot, help yourself,' he invited.

She poured a cup and sat down facing him. 'I've been up half the night. Just couldn't settle. What are you going to do now, Dan?'

'Not very much at the moment. I can only wait and see what Anne and that friend of hers come up with. What else can I do?'

'What if Alfie turns out to be Jack's father? What then, Dan?' she dared ask.

His lips tightened. 'I'll fight him tooth and nail, so I will. Even if I'm not Jackie's grandfather, surely I must have some rights. Good God, I've reared that boy since birth, Tess. Everybody knows that! It must surely have some bearing on his future. Don't you think?'

She remained silent, eyeing him closely, but could see no outward sign that he was putting on any kind of act. Deciding to put him to the test she said, 'You know, Dan, it's funny, but I've always thought that Jackie resembled you more than Anne or Jack and he certainly doesn't look in the least like Alfie. There was never any doubt in my mind but that he was a Thompson. It was a terrible shock when Anne implied he wasn't.'

He was quick to agree. 'I've got eyes in my head, Tess! I know he looks like me but I just can't figure out how.'

'Can't you?'

Confusion blotted all emotion from his features as he stared at her in bewilderment. 'No! I can't! Why, can you?'

She decided to play him along. 'Well, now that I've met Alfie Higgins, I'm beginning to think that Anne is telling the truth and Jack *was* his son. After all, Jack did look a bit like him, don't you agree?'

Dan nodded his head in despair. 'More than a bit, I'd say. It's uncanny. I can't believe that I let that bitch hoodwink me like that. I must have been blind not to twig. But I can't doubt the evidence of my own eyes. Alfie is Jack's father, I'm convinced of that. That's why I'm so worried. I can't even sleep for thinking about it. But biological father or not, I loved that boy! When Anne ran off with that guy from Greeve's mill, I devoted my whole life to rearing him.'

'I know you did, and I know how much you loved Jack and how much he loved and respected you, but that doesn't change the situation at hand. As things stand, Jackie can't be your grandson, but somehow or other I don't think he's Alfie's either. So, do you know anyone else that could fit the bill?'

'No. I can't even think straight, for God's sake.' He lifted his head, a hint of realisation dawning in his eyes, and looked at her intently. 'Are you suggesting that Colette might have been carrying on with somebody behind my son's back?' he asked fearfully.

She wanted to laugh in his face at the very idea that he could think Colette Burns capable of such deception. She had been such a good person, a paragon of virtue in fact, who was deeply in love with the man she was to marry. She had just been overwhelmed by circumstances beyond her control when she got herself pregnant by Dan. He was much older, and should have been more in control of his emotions at the time. But then his son had just been killed in a motorbike crash, so Tess supposed that there were extenuating circumstances.

She was convinced by now that Dan really didn't know he was Jackie's father. No one could put on such a plausible act. Not even the great Laurence Olivier himself. 'I'm just looking at all the possibilities, that's all,' she conceded. 'After all, someone fathered Jackie.'

Dan thrust his face towards her. 'Believe me, even in jest I'm not for one minute suggesting it was an immaculate conception. It's gone far beyond a joke! This is a very serious matter, very serious indeed,' he stressed, and she smiled grimly. Didn't she already know that? More serious than even he realised. 'Now you were closer to Colette than anyone I know.' His look dared her to disagree. When she remained silent he continued, 'If she

365

confided in anyone it's you! You knew all about the pregnancy and birth long before your mother and me. We were kept completely in the dark. I have to admit that I was astounded you could be so devious. I can remember how hurt we were to be kept in the dark all those months during her pregnancy. But at least you prevented her from putting the child up for adoption, and for that I'm very grateful. I might never have known I had a grandson if you hadn't intervened.'

Ashamed of the part she'd had to play, Tess interrupted him. 'No, Dan. You're giving me more credit than I deserve. I don't for one minute think Colette would really have gone through with her plans for adoption after seeing the baby. Once she held him in her arms.'

'Perhaps not,' he agreed reluctantly. 'But what about it, eh, Tess? Did she tell you who the father is? If you do know his name, for God's sake speak out now! I need to know the truth. I promise not to be angry if she was betraying Jack. It's all too long ago. Nothing matters but that we find out who fathered Jackie. Do you know anyone else she was interested in? Think, Tess. Anyone at all? Did she ever mention any other man in her conversations with you? Any man at all?'

For some moments Tess gazed into his troubled eyes and willed him to see what would soon be obvious to everyone. At last she sadly shook her head. 'No! I don't know anyone else who looks in the least like you, so how can you explain it?'

'I can't! I've racked my brains until I think my head will burst and still I can't explain it. To me there's no logical explanation.'

Tess sighed. It was even more apparent to her that he really hadn't an inkling that he was Jackie's father. He must have completely blanked his night of passion with Colette out of his mind. She remembered how sceptical she had been when Colette had confessed the whole sordid tale to her. She had been inclined to think how convenient it was for Dan to forget the incident. Had actually derided Colette for giving him the benefit of the doubt, stating with conviction that no man could behave like that and not remember a thing about it, no matter how drunk he was. Against her better judgement she had allowed Colette to persuade her otherwise. Now she really did believe him. It must have been all the trauma and grief of his son's sudden death that had caused such a massive mental block.

'Then we'll just have to wait and see how things pan out.' Spirits low, she rose from the table. 'I'm going back up for an hour before I get ready for work. You should do the same.'

'Maybe I will,' he said dully without looking in her direction.

Tess climbed the stairs in despair. She dreaded what was in front of them. It looked very much like the truth would have to come out. There was no alternative that she could see. How would she deal with it? How would her mother react?

The next morning in the shop, feeling the need to talk things over with an outsider, someone more or less neutral, Tess put Theresa in the picture as far as she could without breaking Colette's confidence.

Her friend sat for some moments in stunned silence. 'I can't take this in. Dan's not Jackie's grandad? My God! Then who is?' she gasped.

'Who do you think? None other than Anne Thompson's new boyfriend. That's who!'

'You mean Anne knew this man when she was dating Dan?'

Tess nodded and smiled grimly. 'Yes. You're getting there.'

Theresa battled with these words, trying to analyse them. At last she said slowly, 'So Dan forgave her and married her out of pity when he learned that she was pregnant? Is that what you're trying to tell me?'

'Far from it. Anne palmed the baby off as Dan's and rushed him into a shotgun wedding. That's what she did, the devious cow.'

Realising that her mouth was hanging open, Theresa snapped it shut. 'I don't believe you.'

'You'd better believe me. It was a shotgun wedding all right, and no two ways about it. Dan has already admitted it,' Tess assured her.

'And he never had an inkling? Not even the slightest clue? No doubts whatsoever, all these years?'

'So it would appear.'

'You sound as if you don't believe him.'

'So do you, for that matter. I just don't know what to believe any more. I know you only ever saw photographs of Jack, but did you think he looked like Dan? If you had been in Dan's position, would you have believed Anne?'

Theresa sent her mind hurtling back in time. 'No, I remember saying to myself at the time that Dan certainly hadn't passed on his handsome looks, but I didn't think anything of it. It happens all the time you know, Tess. Children not inheriting their fathers' looks, and old biddies nudge-nudging each other when they pass them on the street, and their mothers innocent as newborn lambs. Still, there surely must have been some snide remarks regarding the milkman or the coalman to give Dan cause for thought. You know what people are like.'

'Exactly! That's what I think. People being as they are,

368

tongues must have wagged. But apparently Dan never doubted her.' Tess gestured with her hands as if to imply that that said it all. 'But no matter what, Dan loved Jack and devoted himself to the lad's welfare.'

'Maybe he was so much in love with Anne at the time he just didn't want to see the truth for fear of losing her,' Theresa suggested.

'Maybe! But that's neither here nor there. We now know the reason why Jack didn't resemble Dan. And if Anne's new boyfriend *is* Jack's father, Dan can't possibly be Jackie's grandad, now can he?' Tess sat back and watched Theresa closely as she digested these words, waiting for the penny to drop. She was not disappointed. Theresa's eyes suddenly lit up and her mouth dropped open again and she clapped a hand over it as comprehension sank in.

'That's going to put the cat among the pigeons, isn't it?'

'It certainly is.'

Theresa's mind was still working overtime. 'Does that mean that this guy can get custody of wee Jackie?'

'Who knows? Only time will tell. Whichever way it goes there's going to be an awful lot of muck-raking. I dread to think about the outcome. I never slept a wink last night worrying about it.'

'Poor Dan, he must be in an awful state.'

'It's my mam I'm worried about. This will kill her.'

'But why? Why should it affect her all that much? Oh, I know she'll be sad and angry if they lose Jackie, but she'll still have Dan. He's more important to her than anything else. Even you, if I may say so.'

Tess was disappointed that her friend hadn't caught on who Jackie looked like. It would have given her the opening she was seeking to blurt out all her secrets. It would be wonderful to get a second opinion, be able to share the burden; get things into perspective as it were. For a moment Tess wondered if she should point out the obvious to Theresa. Common sense prevailed and drawing a deep breath she curbed the impulse. Better not jump the gun; best to wait and see how things progressed. Theresa wasn't stupid. Next time she saw Jackie she would probably twig. Tess contented herself with saying, 'Come what may, one way or the other Mam is bound to get hurt.'

Unconvinced, Theresa gave a slight snort and returned to her sewing. In her opinion the world could crumble around Alice's ears and she wouldn't notice so long as she had Dan Thompson there beside her.

They sewed in silence for some time, each enveloped in their thoughts. Then Theresa's mind turned to her own affairs and she blurted out, 'I phoned Bob last night at his digs. He was working late but his landlady took a message and he rang me back later on.'

Tess was immediately attentive, glad to shelve her own worries for a while. 'Oh . . . and I presume you told him about Les's offer?'

'Yes. He wasn't as supportive as I would have liked but he said it was up to me what I did and he wouldn't hold it against me if I chose to go.'

Tess smiled at her in delight. 'So you're going to Canada?'

'I don't know what to do for the best.' She choked back a sob and Tess left her chair and, pulling her friend upright, gathered her close.

'You'll go! That's what you'll do. Have you by any chance got Les's phone number?' Theresa nodded. 'Here . . . with you?' Another nod and Tess said, 'Right! Phone him now and tell him you would like to take him up on his very generous offer.'

'On the shop phone, this early in the day? Why, it would cost a fortune, so it would. Besides, I don't know what time it will be over there but I'm sure it'll still be in the wee small hours.'

'I think in this instance we can afford a few minutes' air time. Les is very considerate, he won't keep you talking unnecessarily, and I don't think for one second he'll mind about the time. It will show him how pleased you are.' Tess gestured towards the phone. 'Go on, phone him now before you change your mind,' she urged.

Theresa still hesitated and Tess bundled her towards the phone. 'We need some postage stamps. I'll leave you to it while I nip round to the post office.' Grabbing her coat she left her friend to make the call in private before she had time to change her mind.

Theresa was still standing by the phone looking stunned when Tess returned. 'What do you think?' she whispered in awe. 'Les was delighted. He even asked me if I could be ready this weekend.'

'And what did you say?'

'I foolishly said yes, and he is going to try and book a flight for me, but how can I just take off in five days' time? Bob will be furious.'

'Is Les phoning you back?'

Theresa nodded, still in a daze. 'As soon as he knows the time and flight he'll be in touch.'

'Right! Let's make a list of all the things you need to take with you.' Struck by a sudden thought Tess gripped her friend's arm. 'You do have a valid passport, I take it?'

'Yes, I had to get one the year I took Mam to Lourdes.'

'Thank God for that. Don't look so worried. You're going to have the time of your life.'

'I'm worried about Bob.'

371

'Forget Bob! If Les gets you on a flight and Bob doesn't make a point of coming up to see you off, I'll attend to him when I see him.'

Theresa threw her arms round Tess and hugged her close, almost strangling her in the process. 'Tess, you're the best friend a girl could ever have. Thanks for making me phone. Les sounded so pleased to hear from me.'

Embarrassed, Tess cried, 'Hey! Lay off, you're strangling me. Don't worry, we'll have you ready to fly at the drop of a hat. We'll even drive you up to the airport.' There were tears in her eyes as she returned Theresa's hug.

After Alfie had left, Anne moved restlessly about the house. No matter what Alfie had implied she couldn't believe that Dan could have had it off with his son's girlfriend. He was a decent man through and through! If something had taken place between him and Colette, the minute Colette had confessed to him that she was pregnant he would have done the honourable thing and insisted that she marry him. Of that she was dead certain.

Thoughts of Alice Maguire brought her abruptly to a standstill in the middle of the kitchen floor. What about Alice? Would his love for her have made Dan turn a blind eye to Colette's dilemma? Was that why Colette had run off to Carlingford? Had Dan refused to acknowledge the child was his? Oh, surely not!

No! No, there was something not quite right here. Shortly after the baby was born she had learned that Colette had stayed in Carlingford with a friend of Alice's brother Malachy during the last months of her pregnancy and confinement. If Malachy was in the know, and he must have been, there was no way that he would have kept his sister in the dark if the child's father was Dan!

Again Anne stopped in her prowling. Or would he? Had Malachy, with the best of intentions, thought he was doing the right thing because his sister was so much in love with Dan Thompson?

Feeling the need to clear her fuddled brain, she shrugged into her coat, covered her hair with a scarf and left the house. It was bitterly cold outside, the sky once again blotted out by gathering dark clouds. A slight drizzle was beginning to fall but she was glad of the cold rain on her face and the wind that moulded her clothes to the contours of her body. She felt as if she was in a fever as she made her way up the Falls Road past Dunville Park and the children's hospital. She had no particular destination in mind but soon found herself at the corner of La Salle Drive.

She squinted down through the drizzle and could see that Alfie's house was in darkness. Undecided, she walked slowly down the street, past his driveway, trying to pluck up the courage to go up and knock on his door and announce herself. Many a time in the past she had felt bereft and in need of sympathy, but never so much as now. Her feet faltered. She badly needed company; someone to talk to. Surely he wouldn't turn her away? But after all the bad things he had learned about her tonight, she was afraid that he might do just that. Maybe even slam the door in her face, and then what would she do? Her heart plummeted to the very soles of her feet at the idea of his rejection, and afraid to risk it she quickly turned on her heel and started the journey back to her empty house.

Dinner that night was a quiet affair. Knowing Dan's penchant for keeping abreast of current affairs, Alice and Tess tried to draw him into the conversation by discussing the Vietnam War. When that didn't work, and not wanting to discuss anything of significance in front of Jackie, Tess even brought up the Cod War between Britain and Iceland. Ignoring their endeavours Dan stayed locked in his own troubled thoughts, rising in panic from his chair when the telephone rang; dreading the call from Alfie that could change his life for ever.

As they cleared up the dishes afterwards, Alice confided to Tess in whispers, as she glanced furtively over her shoulder every so often, 'He has no intention of going in to work until this is all settled, you know. He said it wouldn't be worthwhile as he wouldn't be able to concentrate on the job. I phoned in and told them he had a tummy upset, but this business could go on for a very long time. I can't keep on making excuses for him, you know. What if he loses his job? What will we do then, eh?'

'He's a fool, that man. He'd be better off at work, so he would. It would take his mind off all this.'

'I told him that, but he paid no heed. I honestly don't know what will happen if he loses Jackie.'

'You'll still have each other! Surely that's what matters most.'

'Hmm.'

Tess drew back and frowned at her mother. 'What do you mean?'

'If he keeps on like this he won't be worth living under the same roof with. I just can't get through to him any more.'

The doorbell pealed and glad of the diversion Tess said, 'That'll be Tony. I've a bit of a headache coming on so I think I'll go out for a walk with him. See if the cold air will do me any good. We won't be too long. That's if you don't mind me leaving you for a while.'

'Away you go, love. I'll prise Jackie away from in front of the telly and give him a bath. It'll pass the time till you get back.'

Tony was surprised when Tess came out on to the step struggling into her coat. 'Are you going out? Is anything wrong, love?'

Quickly Tess made up her mind. She needed advice and Tony was the obvious one to confide in. Anything she told him would go no further. 'I need to talk to you in private, Tony. Where can we go?'

He hesitated a moment before saying, 'Mam and Dad are out at the moment but I've no idea for how long. Shall we risk going over to my house?'

'No. What I have to talk to you about is very private and I don't want any interruptions. Let's go down and sit in Dunville Park.'

Unable to fathom what could be so wrong as to affect her like this, why she was quite literally shaking, he asked with some concern, 'Will you be warm enough, love?'

'I'm not likely to perish. Especially if you put your arms around me.'

Slipping her arm through his she managed to control the shakes and walked briskly down Springfield Road by his side, her long, slender legs matching him stride for stride. Crossing the Falls Road they went into the park. A few lads were playing football at the bottom end, while they were still able to see the ball, and Tony led her to a bench near the top that was sheltered by one of the summerhouses. When they were seated he waited impatiently for her to speak.

Tess dithered. Was she doing the right thing? Once the truth was out there would be no going back. Tony's voice interrupted her muddled reasoning.

Knowing that Anne and her friend had been invited

to Tess's home the evening before, he now enquired, 'Has this anything to do with last night?' He put an arm round her and gratefully she snuggled against the warmth of his body.

'Yes, Tony, it has everything to do with last night,' she confirmed.

'Can you tell me about it?'

'If I tell you everything, it will have to be in the strictest confidence. You must understand that, love. Okay?' Tony nodded his understanding and she continued, 'I'll be breaking a promise that I made to Colette Burns just after she gave birth to Jackie. Correction! I'll not really be breaking my word, because she left a note with her solicitors releasing me from my promise if I thought it was in the best interests of all concerned, especially her son. Of course I only found out about the note after she died. But how will I know what's for the best, eh? I'm biased! I've my own mother's interests at heart. However, if I speak out she's the very one likely to suffer the most, and I don't know what to do. I'm at the end of my tether, so I am.'

Tony rubbed his cheek against hers and gave her a gentle kiss, then said, 'I haven't the slightest clue what you're going on about, love. Just relax and tell me slowly and precisely what's happened to upset you so much, and we'll decide between ourselves what to do for the best.'

Tess thought she had never loved Tony more than at this moment when he was here with his unwavering support, ready to share her worries. In a voice that shook but soon gained in strength as her confidence that she was doing the right thing grew, Tess told her story.

Tony heard her out in silence. Then, 'Phew! Who else knows about this?'

'Just me, and now you.'

'No one else at all? Not even Malachy or Rose?'

'They were under the impression that Jack was the baby's father and we didn't disillusion them. As I've already said, Colette entrusted her solicitor with the information and left a note with him that he was, in the event of her death, to give to me.'

'I see.'

'That's why I decided to confide in you. I need your advice. I'm distracted. What am I going to do, love?'

Tess had told him who Jackie's father was without going into any details of how the conception came about, and now he said, 'If Dan was carrying on with Colette before Jack died in that crash, don't you think that your mother would be better off without him? Surely if she had known the truth then, that he was having an affair with a young girl, his own future daughter-in-law to boot, she would have had nothing more to do with him? Your mother doesn't strike me as a woman who'd turn a blind eye to anything as unsavoury as this.'

Tess gazed at him for some seconds, completely taken aback by his reply. Then realising her mistake she said, 'Oh, I'm sorry, love. I should have explained. They weren't carrying on! It happened just the once. On the day that Jack died, well that very night in fact. Understandably Dan was drunk at the time. When the mourners had all left, Colette stayed to keep him company and forced herself to have a couple of Jameson's to deaden the terrible pain she was feeling for the loss of Jack. She had never drunk spirits before and she said that after a couple of large ones she was well beyond self-control. They comforted each other and one thing led to another and Jackie was the result of their comforting.'

'He couldn't have been all that drunk, surely!' Tony ground out scornfully. 'That he didn't know what he was doing.'

'Colette said he had been drinking all day but he was able to hold his liquor, and she didn't realise just how drunk he was until it was too late.'

'It's still no excuse for him neglecting her afterwards. Surely he guessed when he heard that she was pregnant that he was the culprit?' He shook his head in disgust. 'He must have!'

'That's just it! She didn't tell him. That's what all the secrecy was about. After it happened, Colette dreaded facing Dan and she was mortified when he acted as if it had never happened, so she decided the best thing to do was take a leaf out of his book and ignore it too and keep out of his way. Then when her grannie died shortly afterwards and left her a considerable sum of money, she jumped at the chance to get away from it all, to join a friend in Canada and start a new life out there. Do you remember when we started going out as a threesome?' He frowned but nodded. 'That's when she inherited the money from her grannie.'

'I recall thinking that you were trying to throw Colette and me together.'

'I thought I was doing the right thing. You were nursing a broken heart because of Agnes Quinn and Colette was mourning the loss of Jack. I thought you might fall for each other.'

'That was a waste of time. I should have pulled *you* that night at the Ulster Hall when we met at the Rolling Stones concert. I was such a fool not to have realised then that you were the one for me.'

Tess gnawed on her bottom lip and admitted sheepishly, 'Since we are being completely honest with each other, when Colette confessed that Jack wasn't the baby's father I asked her if it was you.'

He was scandalised. 'Tess! How could you even think such a thing?'

'You can't blame me. As far as I could see there was no one else on the scene, unless maybe it was someone from her work.'

'The only reason I went out with Colette was to stay close to you.'

'I know. Colette told me. Thank you for caring so much, Tony.' She gently touched his cheek with her fingertips by way of apology. 'Well, anyway, the wheels were already set in motion for Colette to go to Canada when she discovered she was pregnant. She was devastated and confided in me. I assumed the baby was Jack's and she didn't enlighten me any. I couldn't believe her when she said she didn't want to keep it. A part of the man she loved? She intended going over to England for the last few months of her pregnancy and having the baby adopted, and then going to Canada a little later than planned. She swore me to secrecy. I was in a terrible dilemma.'

Tess could see that Tony was flabbergasted and continued quietly, 'To cut a long story short, Rose, Malachy's wife – though at that time she was just a close friend of Uncle Mal's – well, she guessed that Colette was pregnant and between us we managed to persuade her to stay in Carlingford with Rose until the baby was born. We hoped that once she saw the infant and held it in her arms, Colette wouldn't be able to let it go and be reared by strangers. And we were right. She couldn't! That's why she sent for me when Jackie was born and confessed everything.'

Tess was sobbing softly against Tony's chest and he

pressed her closer still. 'Hush, love. Don't let it get to you so.'

'I was shocked! I couldn't believe that the man my mam had brought into our home, the man I had come to look up to and respect, could be guilty of such deception. I was all for bringing it out into the open, exposing him. In fact I wanted Colette to cry rape, I felt so strongly about it. But she assured me it wasn't anything like that, that she had been more than a willing party. She said that the grief of Jack's death had made them both vulnerable, and they had got carried away.'

'Dan should have been more responsible,' Tony insisted. 'My God, he must have been twice her age.'

'That's what I said, but she pointed out how it would affect my mam. She said if Dan was left to think the baby was his grandson, he would still rear it and no one would be any the wiser.' Tess wiped her nose and added bitterly, 'Except for me!'

'She never once considered staying at home and rearing the baby herself?'

A sad shake of the head confirmed this. 'Rose and I tried to persuade her but she was adamant and determined to make a new start in Canada. She told me that every time she'd look at the child she'd be reminded of how she had betrayed Jack, and she couldn't live with that. I wanted her to tell Dan that he was the baby's father, but she wouldn't hear of it, so I let myself be persuaded to cover up the truth and keep my mouth shut. She said the finger would be pointed and my mother wouldn't be able to hold her head up in public. She would become a prisoner in her own home because it would soon become common knowledge that Dan had betrayed her. Not that he had done so deliberately, mind you, but who would believe him? I eventually came round to her way of thinking. You know what I'm like where my mam is concerned. I'd do anything to save her suffering any pain. And look where it's got me. I don't know what to do for the best. Now you know why I had to talk to you in complete privacy.'

Tony was silent for some moments, going over Tess's revelations in his mind. Then he said tentatively, 'Does the truth have to come out?'

'I honestly can't see any other way round it. If Alfie Higgins believes all Anne tells him he's sure to want custody of his grandson. And who can blame him? He has no close family ties of his own according to Anne.'

'What's this Alfie fellow like? Is he gullible? Is he naive enough to believe everything Anne tells him?'

'Far from it, I'd say. He seems a very shrewd but nice, down-to-earth person.'

'In that case he's bound to notice that Jackie is Dan's double. So I can't see him pressing for custody of a child he has no claim to. I mean, Dan wouldn't just sit on his backside and take their word for it, no matter what he thinks. He'd want proof and I mean concrete proof and it would then go to court. Tests would soon prove that Alfie wasn't the grandfather and a lot of time and good money would be wasted unnecessarily.'

Tess sat mesmerised by Tony's reasoning. 'And what about Anne? If she learns the truth she won't give up so easily.'

'We could go and have a word with this man at his home and see how the land lies.'

For the first time Tess saw light at the end of the tunnel. 'Oh, Tony, wouldn't it be great if it could all be hushed up without any scandal coming out?'

'Personally, I think it would be better all round to have it all brought out into the open,' he admitted ruefully.

'Think of the scandal! It would break my mam's heart. She'd never forgive me.'

'She'd have to. She'd have no one else to turn to.'

'No. She would never forgive me. Oh, she'd pretend to, but she'd make my life hell on earth. Not intentionally, but that's how it would be. Can't you see? I'm still being selfish. I'm only thinking of myself as usual. How could I move out and marry you if Mam was left on her own nursing a broken heart? She might do something stupid, you know what I mean? I would be blaming myself and I'd feel obliged to stay at home. It took me so long to realise how much I love you, Tony Burke. I couldn't bear to lose you now. And I want us to start married life in a home of our own.'

Tony eased her away from him so that he could look into her eyes. 'You really mean that, Tess?'

'Of course I mean it. How can you doubt me?'

'Well, you're usually a bit more reticent when it comes to revealing your feelings for me.'

'Tony, we are engaged to be married! Remember? Does that not prove how much I love you?'

He grimaced slightly. 'Remembering how often you had turned me down, I was inclined to think that something else prompted you to at last accept my offer of marriage, but I didn't care as long as you did accept it.'

'What! What do you mean, something prompted me to accept?'

He hesitated, then shrugged. 'It doesn't matter. Forget I spoke. I was probably letting my imagination run away with me.'

'Tell me, Tony.'

'I was afraid to say anything in case I was right and maybe you were interested in someone else. Someone you wanted to make jealous by becoming engaged to me.'

Fear was a tight ball in her chest, leaving her breathless. Feigning innocence she gasped, 'Who did you think I might be attracted to?'

'I hope I'm wrong . . . but for a while I worried that Bob Dempsey might be trying to get off his mark with you, and I was devoured with jealousy.'

His gaze was fixed on her face and Tess prayed that any change of colour would not be noticed in the failing light. It was so true. Bob Dempsey had been one of the reasons she had at last let Tony put a ring on her finger. She had been so stupid and blind, thinking only of herself as usual. He must never learn just how deceitful she had been. God, she loved him so much! She wasn't the most fortunate of girls when it came to boyfriends, but this was one she couldn't bear to lose. If she lost him now how would she cope? She had to make him understand her need for him.

She gulped as if in surprise but in reality to give herself time to gather her wits about her. 'Bob Dempsey? Why, Bob couldn't hold a candle to you. I just wish I could make Theresa see that he's not worthy of her. I think she's wasting her time on him.'

His eyes narrowed and she was sure that he must see right through her. After a pause during which he examined her face closely he said, 'You mean that?'

'With all my heart. I love you, Tony, and I hope to spend the rest of my life proving to you just how much. I've wasted so much precious time by my own stupidity.'

Their lips met and Tony thanked God for the silver lining to this very dark cloud that hung over them. It didn't matter that Bob Dempsey might have held sway for a while so long as it was Tony she loved.

When they came down to earth again Tess gasped, 'Oh, I forgot to mention, Les O'Malley has invited

Theresa to visit him in Canada before she marries Bob. Isn't that a turn-up for the books?'

'You're not kidding. They got on like a house on fire when he was over here. She would have a great time over there. Is she taking him up on his invitation?'

'She already has and he's trying to book a flight for this weekend.'

Tony threw back his head and laughed aloud. 'I'll say this for him, he certainly doesn't let the grass grow under his feet. What has Bob got to say about it?'

'From what I gather he's not exactly over the moon, but he says he won't hold it against her if she goes. Imagine! Isn't that so gallant of him? Of course Theresa was in a tizzy. It took all my persuasive powers to convince her to go ahead and phone Les and accept his offer.'

'Good for you. Will you be able to manage on your own in the shop?'

'If Theresa goes out to see Les, I'll make it my business to manage on my own. Besides, it will only be for a couple of weeks.'

'What if she decides to stay in Vancouver?'

'And leave her precious Bob? No way. Besides, she has the shop to consider too.'

'Away from Bob and in the company of a man who is so charming and attentive to her? Who knows, they might even fall in love. Stranger things have been known to happen, you know.'

Tess pondered on this. 'You're right. She does like Les, and he seemed to like her. Wouldn't it be great if they did fall for each other? It would serve Bob Dempsey right for taking her so much for granted. As for the shop . . . I'll manage somehow.'

'I'll help in any way I can. You know that.'

'I know I can always depend on you, Tony. That's one of the reasons I love you so much. Now I've got all that off my chest, let's head back and see how things are faring on the home front. And thank you, darling, for being so understanding and supportive.'

'If nothing's changed, we'll fish around and find out just where Alfie Higgins lives and then we can arrange to go and see him. Test the waters as it were. Okay?'

'That would be great, Tony.'

Again their lips met, and it was some time later when they eventually got home.

While the debate between Tess and Tony was going on, Alfie was visiting Anne. He had arrived at half past seven and Anne was still in a dither. She couldn't bring herself to believe that Dan would do anything so dishonourable. She knew the man only too well.

Pushing a bottle of Black Bush into her hand, Alfie said, 'Here, pour us two big helpings of that. We must talk.'

Anne poured two glasses of whiskey, thinking it strange that Alfie should need Dutch courage to say goodbye to her. You'd imagine he'd be glad to be shot of her, with only a few sarky parting remarks. They sat facing each other by the fireside and sipped at their strong drinks in silence for many moments, Anne putting on a brave front, dreading what she was about to hear, and Alfie trying to decide how to put to her a proposition he had in mind.

Eventually he asked, 'Well, Anne, have you given any more thought to what we were discussing last night?'

'Given it any more thought? For God's sake, Alfie, I didn't get a wink of sleep all night for thinking about it. I've tried and tried but I just can't see Dan as the villain

385

of the piece. I know him through and through. He just wouldn't do anything like that. I tell you, he's too decent a bloke for his own good.'

'Who do you think could be the suspect, then?'

'I've no idea. I've relived the past in my mind over and over again but I can't recall anyone who looked anything like Dan Thompson.'

'Can you think of anyone who could help us solve this enigma?'

Anne started to shake her head, then, pausing for thought, said firmly, 'Tess Maguire! If anyone knows who the father is, it's her. If I remember correctly, she was in the midst of everything that was going on. It was her who brought the baby home to Dan and Alice. And I have heard that Colette left her some money in her will and also named her one of the trustees of the child's legacy. So if anyone knows anything, it's Tess, but I can't see her talking to you. She's very protective of anything to do with her mother, so she's more likely to send you away with a flea in your ear.'

Alfie sat sifting this information about in his head while Anne watched him fretfully. Did he intend breaking off with her or what? She wished he would get it over with. Let her know where she stood, one way or the other.

Setting his drink carefully down on the hearth, Alfie leaned towards Anne. 'Tell me, is there any way that we could meet with Tess without anyone else being the wiser?'

She gave this some thought. 'I'm not sure. I suppose I could approach her in the shop and ask her to meet us. But don't count on it. As I've already said, she's very touchy where her family is concerned, and she's not exactly kindly disposed towards me.'

386

'Tomorrow, give it a try . . . please. Tell her we'll meet her wherever she likes. Any time, any place, but the sooner the better for all concerned. Okay?'

Anne wasn't in the least hopeful but she muttered, 'I'll do my best.'

'Thank you. Now there is something I want to get straightened out between you and me.'

Anne's heart thumped against her ribcage and tears started to her eyes as she sat bolt upright in her chair expecting the worst. Here it comes. The fond farewell; the not so golden handshake. Pride held her head high, and willing herself not to break down she nodded.

He smiled and she bridled with resentment. He didn't have to look so bloody smug about it. 'First let's get everything else out of the way. We might never know the truth, but I believe with all my heart that Dan Thompson is Jackie's father. I really do, Anne.'

Her head shook from side to side. 'No . . . no . . . I've told you . . .'

He reached across and took the glass from her shaking hands. Placing it to one side he pulled her up from the chair and over to the settee, where he pushed her down none too gently and sat close to her. Bewildered by this sudden twist of events and overcome by his proximity, she could only gaze at him in wide-eyed surprise.

'Listen, Anne, I don't know all the ins and outs of it and I don't think I want to know. It's just a gut feeling I've got, but I'm totally convinced that Dan *is* Jackie's father.' She opened her mouth to object again and he put a finger to her lips. 'Please bear with me. I imagine that Alice has never known the truth and now Dan is in a dilemma. He must be out of his mind with worry on account of his love for Alice, but believe you me, if I appear to be a threat to him, Dan will own up to being the father rather than lose that boy. I'd do exactly the same in his position. Think of all the misery it would cause if I were to try and get custody. I couldn't do it. Especially as I don't believe for one second that I've any right whatsoever to him. I just want you to know that I don't intend making any claim regarding the child.'

Turning towards him she grabbed his hands and clung to them. 'Alfie, I'm telling you the truth. I swear as God is my witness that you're Jack's father. You've got to believe me. You saw the photographs. I swear I wasn't trying to pull a fast one on you.'

'I believe you.'

She blinked in bewilderment. 'Then why—'

He quickly interrupted her. 'You're right! You've convinced me that Jack was my son, and I admit I would dearly love to have a grandson, but I'm not Jackie's grandfather. It would be wrong for me to stir up the dirt when I know I haven't any rights to the boy. Obviously Dan's wife is completely in the dark regarding all this and it would surely break up their marriage were she to find out. Despite this apparent bit of deception on his part, I happen to like what I've seen and heard of Dan Thompson and I don't want to ruin his life when there's no need to. If he made a mistake years ago and between us we've managed to cast doubts on his integrity, I would like to help get him off the hook. We know he dearly loves that boy, so let him get on with his life in peace.'

'But why? Why should you worry about *him*?'

'Aren't you forgetting the most important point in this sad saga? He has paid for my sin all these years. He reared my boy, even when you apparently deserted him. Also, I've been there. I can remember how hard it is to walk away when your blood is on fire. I wasn't able to do it that night, when you were concerned about the state I was in, and look what happened. Both you and Dan suffered because I lost all my self-control. So I can identify with whatever happened between him and Colette. It can't have been any worse than my betraying the woman I was about to marry.'

'Putting it like that, I can see your point of view. But why not let things be? No one would be any the wiser. Just let sleeping dogs lie.'

'Dan must guess that I know the truth of the matter and his wife would always wonder why I backed down over my custody claim. It could cause all kinds of misery for them. I want to sort things out my way and to my satisfaction. So will you set up a meeting with Tess?'

She still looked unconvinced. 'I'll try. But she is a very strong-willed person.'

'Tell her it's imperative that I speak with her.'

Anne's eyes clung to his. She had been reprieved for another day at least. He smiled kindly at her. 'Don't look so worried, Anne. In spite of all the unkind things I've heard about you lately, I believe you've turned over a new leaf. At least I sincerely hope so.' She opened her mouth to eagerly assure him that indeed she had, but he forestalled her. 'When we get this mess cleared up I'm going to take you away from here for a while. Let things settle down. Go on a long holiday abroad maybe. And then we'll move a long way from Belfast. That is if you'll accept my proposal of marriage. I don't want a bit on the side, Anne. I want a wife. Someone to share the rest of my life with.'

Her head moved up and down and her mouth opened and closed like a beached fish in her efforts to speak, but the words stuck in her throat. 'You . . . you . . .' At last her tongue unfurled. 'Am I hearing you right?'

He cupped her face in his hands and kissed her long

and hard on the lips. 'You're hearing me right, sweet-heart. Now let's go and see if we can rekindle the passion we shared all those years ago. You've been holding me at arm's length long enough, madam, but the ice is now well and truly broken, so can we go upstairs and discuss this further in more comfortable surroundings?'

She scrambled eagerly to her feet and grabbing his hand literally dragged him towards the stairs. Spluttering in her excitement she gasped, 'Oh yes, yes, please let's.'

Happiness radiated from every pore of Anne's body as she made her way to the shop. She had never in all her life felt so fulfilled. Alfie had dropped her off at Springfield Road junction and she had had great diffi-culty leaving him in case it was all a wonderful dream from which she would soon awaken.

At the tinkle of the doorbell, Tess came from the back of the shop and her brows rose in surprise. 'What's happened to you? You look like you've just won the pools.'

'Oh, much better than that! Alfie still wants to marry me.'

'Congratulations.' Tess's lips twisted in a wry smile. 'Aren't you the lucky one. What can I do for you?'

'I'm here on a matter of business, on behalf of Alfie Higgins.' She peered over Tess's shoulder into the back room. 'Are you alone?' Tess nodded. 'He wants to know if you would kindly agree to meet him somewhere you and he can have a talk in private. You choose the time and place.'

'It's Dan Thompson he should be talking to, not me.'

'He has a proposition concerning Dan and Jackie, but he would like to speak with you first.' Seeing that Tess was about to refuse, Anne quickly stressed, 'It's imper-ative that he talks to you. Please meet him, Tess.'

Gloom and despondency had still permeated the air inside the house when Tess and Tony had eventually returned the night before. It had been so depressing. Later, while saying his farewells at the door, Tony had told her to stop worrying. He assured her that he would find out where Alfie Higgins lived, and both of them would pay him a visit, but they had been beaten to the punch. Here was Anne offering her the chance to meet and talk with the man. Could she trust this woman? Was Anne cooking up one of her devious little plans?

She was silent so long, Anne urged, 'It can't do you any harm, surely. Alfie says he will meet you wherever and whenever you like,' she reiterated.

'Who would be present at this meeting?'

'Whoever you like. It's up to you.'

'I would like Tony Burke to be there. Just him and me and this man of yours. I don't want you there. If you put in an appearance, Tony and I walk. Is that fully understood?'

Glad that she was managing to carry out Alfie's wishes, Anne hurriedly agreed. 'Yes, I understand. When and where?'

Where? That was the question. It had to be somewhere private. She cast her eyes vaguely round the shop, seeking inspiration. Why not here? 'Tonight. Here in this shop. Tony's coming over to the house about seven, so ask your friend to come here at eight o'clock. Okay?'

'That will be fine.' Anne quickly scuttled out of the shop before Tess could have second thoughts. She was overjoyed that she had succeeded in setting up a meeting between Tess and Alfie. He would be delighted with her.

Tess was ready and waiting and when she answered Tony's knock on the door she joined him on the doorstep.

'Hey, this is getting to be a habit.'

She kissed him tenderly on the lips. 'We have a business appointment to meet Alfie Higgins in the shop at eight o'clock tonight, so I thought we could dander down a bit early to talk it over. You know, decide just how much we should tell him. Plan our strategy.'

'That shouldn't take very long. The less that man knows the better. We just listen to what he has to say and take it from there. How did you manage to set up the meeting? I thought I was great just getting his address.'

Tess led the way and he fell into step beside her down the Springfield Road. 'He approached me. Sent Anne to ask me to meet him as soon as possible.'

'Did she say why he wanted to meet with you?'

'No, she didn't go into any detail, only to say that he wanted to talk to me about Dan and Jackie. I told her it was Dan he should be talking to, but she said he has a proposition to make. I told her I wanted you to be present and made arrangements to meet at the shop.'

Tony unlocked the security grille and the door and entered the shop. Tess left the door on the latch and turned to him. 'There's no way I can tell him who Jackie's father is. You do realise that, don't you, love?'

'That goes without saying. I can't think why he wants to talk with you. But remember, whatever he says, don't you go rushing in with a reply. Pretend you're thinking it over and I'll step in if necessary.'

'That's a good idea. I haven't a clue what he's after. I did warn Anne that I didn't want her present at the meeting, and she said that was okay so long as I meet Alfie. If she accompanies him I'm leading them straight out the door again and that will be the end of the meeting before it even gets off the ground. I've already told her.'

Tony smiled. 'Hush, love. Don't let's get excited, eh? It might be all plain sailing. Let's just play it by ear. Come over here. We may as well pass the time more pleasantly than worrying about what might or might not happen.'

She willingly fell into his arms and they exchanged words of endearment and kissed and cuddled until a silhouette on the frosted-glass window of the shop door heralded the arrival of Alfie. Tess jumped up, smoothing her hair back into place and straightening her skirt. 'Do I look presentable?'

'You look gorgeous.'

Alfie tapped lightly on the door and Tess called for him to come in. Glad that he was alone, she greeted him cordially. 'Good evening, Mr Higgins. This is my fiancé, Tony Burke.'

The two men took stock of each other and liking what they saw, warmly shook hands. Tess locked the door and motioned Alfie into the back, where she turned to face him. She didn't invite him to sit; this was no wee tête-à-tête but a serious meeting, and she wanted it over as soon as possible. 'Anne seemed to think that it was imperative that I meet you, so here I am.' She was annoyed with herself for sounding nervous.

Alfie looked her straight in the eye. Where to start, that was the question. These two would be on their guard and would have probably discussed a game plan already. They wouldn't want to admit anything regarding Dan Thompson. Perhaps he was on a fool's errand but he would give it his best shot while he had the opportunity.

Well, here goes, he thought, in for a penny ... 'It's hard for me to put into words as to where to begin, without going into a long-drawn-out dialogue, so I'll come straight to the point and be as brief as possible. Perhaps you know who Jackie's father is, perhaps you don't. I'm certainly not his grandfather! That's quite obvious. But I can hazard a guess as to who the father *is*.' He looked squarely at Tess as if willing some sort of reaction from her.

Her head rose defiantly. 'Oh. Can you indeed?'

'You'll probably deny it even if it is true, and, mind you, I wouldn't blame you in the slightest. But I'd put my last penny on Dan Thompson being the boy's father.'

Tess felt the colour drain from her face and gave an involuntary gasp. He certainly didn't pull his punches! She had mentioned to Tony that he was a shrewd customer, but not this perceptive. Recovering her poise, she asked, 'What on earth makes you think such a preposterous thing?'

'I'm right, aren't I?'

Tess turned to Tony for guidance. 'You had better be very careful what you're implying here, mate,' he advised. 'That's a very slanderous statement to come out with.'

Alfie gave them one of his little smiles. 'Look, let's get something straight. I'm not here to cause trouble. I just want you to tell Dan that his secret is safe with me and that's the God's honest truth. Many a lad is the image of his grandfather so no one else will be any the wiser. I can't go to his house to reassure him, on account of his wife. I'm sure you'll understand. I assume that's why he's in such a dither, because she doesn't know. He certainly seemed to me to be on the verge of a breakdown. Am I right so far?'

Tony voiced Tess's thoughts. 'Just supposing what you say is true . . . mind you, I'm not saying that it is, but if it were, do you for one minute think that Anne would be capable of keeping her mouth shut? I'm sure you've already discussed this with her.'

'Yes, she knows, but believe it or not, she won't hear

a word said against Dan where this business is concerned. She says I must be wrong. In her estimation Dan is too decent a gentleman to do anything like that and leave Colette holding the baby, if you'll pardon the pun.'

'But you hardly know the man, so why should you think differently?'

Alfie gave a little sigh. 'For a start, you've only got to look at him and the boy together. I've seen photographs and I believe Anne is telling the truth when she says that Jack was my son, therefore Dan can't possibly be Jackie's grandfather, now can he?' He spread his hands wide and gave that little smile again. 'I rest my case!'

Tess was speechless and just stood there staring at this man as if he were psychic. Every word he had uttered so far was absolutely true. It was as if he could read her very innermost thoughts. She was racking her brains trying to find a positive response without admitting anything. It was Tony who broke the silence.

'Tess, I think we can trust Alfie.'

'No! No, we can't, Tony. He could be trying to trick us into admitting something.'

Tony gave a negative shrug of his shoulders and turned aside. It was up to Tess to make her own decision. In a voice that shook she ventured to suggest, 'Since you say you're not going to seek custody of Jackie, that will be the end of it, right? Then it won't matter who the father is.' She turned hopefully to Tony. 'Will it?'

Alfie answered before Tony could utter a sound. 'I think you're wrong. Dan is bound to know his secret is out when I don't press for custody, which I would do if there was the remotest chance that Jack was the father. He will always be waiting for me to come knocking on his door. Just tell him that I know the truth but I also know how these things can happen. I let myself get carried away with

Anne all those years ago. It was actually on my stag night. I was quite tipsy at the time and Jack was the result.'

Tess grimaced. 'And I didn't believe Anne when she told me it was a one-night stand,' she said apologetically.

'She spoke the truth. Mind you, I knew nothing about her being pregnant until a few weeks ago. But because of me, Dan Thompson was left to rear my son and for that I'm most grateful. I don't want to be the cause of him being worried and distressed, now or in the future. I want him to have peace of mind as far as Anne and I are concerned. It's the least I can do for him.'

'Thanks for your thoughtfulness, but just leave it, Alfie. We'll take it from here.' How could Tess ever make this stranger believe that Dan didn't know that he was Jackie's father? He'd think he'd wandered into a madhouse.

Alfie frowned. 'You're quite sure? What about your mother? Won't she be curious and want to know why I backed down?'

'To tell you the truth, I don't know how I'm going to go about it. I'll have to give this a lot of consideration before I decide what to do for the best. Someone will get hurt if it all comes out. It's Mam I'm most concerned about. The truth will kill her.'

'That's why I wanted to talk with you. It needn't come out! I give you my word that I will never say anything that might be harmful to Dan Thompson. And I'm a man of my word, even if I say so. Also, I'm taking Anne on a long holiday as soon as I can arrange it. She's had a raw deal over the years and basically it all stems from my drunken behaviour. Because of me she rushed Dan into a shotgun wedding. If I hadn't seduced her that night, they might have married different people and lived happily to this day. See what I mean? I hope you understand all I'm saying, and trust me.'

Tess grunted. 'Look. I'm not admitting any of this, but I know from past experience that Anne can't keep her big trap shut. Especially if there's the slightest bit of scandal involved.'

'She will this time, I guarantee it! I'm putting my house up for sale while we're away on holiday and we'll get married as soon as possible. I intend to settle down south somewhere and I'll make sure that Anne, should she ever come back here for any reason, keeps her mouth shut.' He shrugged. 'I can do no more than that, but you can trust me. I can handle her.'

Tony waited to see what Tess would say or do. When she remained in a stunned silence, he thrust his hand out towards Alfie. 'Thank you for all the trouble you've taken. I personally think you're one decent bloke, going to all this bother. Anne's very lucky to have you give her a second chance. Goodbye, and may God go with you, Alfie.'

Tess came to with a start and going to Alfie kissed his proffered cheek. 'Thank you. Thank you very much . . . and congratulations. Give our best regards to Anne. As Tony said, she's a lucky woman and I pray you'll have many happy years together.'

Tony closed and locked the door behind Alfie and gave Tess a big hug. 'That's a relief. What do you think of that then?'

'I don't know what to think. Where do we go from here? Do you think that we should just let it drop? Say nothing? It's a very delicate situation we have on our hands.'

'I know, but it's like Alfie says, Dan is going to worry about repercussions. Every time a man knocks on his door will be another nail in his coffin. He's half out of his mind already. If he's really in the dark he'll worry about the real father showing up and laying claim to Jackie.'

'But we know the real father won't show up, don't we!'

'Unless Dan has been very successfully stringing us along all this time, he can't be sure about it, though. There lies the problem. I personally think he should be made aware of his part in this conspiracy. For that's what it's turning out to be, a bloody great conspiracy.'

Tess looked aghast. 'And just how would we go about telling him, eh?'

Taking her in his arms Tony hugged her close. 'For a start we'll have to get him alone.'

'Fat chance of that happening! Mam's always hovering over him like he had a terminal illness. We don't stand a chance of getting him on his own.'

'Listen, love, so far we've been playing it by ear and we haven't done too badly. Let's continue to do so, and see where it gets us.'

Wonders never cease. Dan *was* alone in the house when they got back. Tess stood listening and looking around as if unable to believe her senses. 'Where's Mam?'

'God knows. I think she's fed up listening to me whingeing. The minute Jackie fell asleep she grabbed her coat and almost flew out the door. She's probably up in the monastery now lighting candles. You know what she's like when anything upsets her.'

'Had you an argument, then?'

'Yes,' he confessed, looking ashamed.

Tess glanced at Tony, an unspoken question in her eyes. He nodded to show he understood and she took the plunge. This was too good an opportunity to pass up. 'Dan?'

Her demeanour must have alerted him that something was going down and he became wary. 'Yes?'

'Alfie Higgins asked us to meet him earlier on. We've just left him.'

Dan straightened up in his chair, instantly alert, and she imagined that she could detect a glimmer of fear in his eyes. 'What did *he* want?'

'He sent you a message. He says to tell you that he knows your secret and that he will never reveal it to anyone.'

Dan looked dazed. 'What secret? I've no secrets.'

'The name of Jackie's father.'

He almost jumped from his chair. 'The name of Jackie's father?'

'He knows who Jackie's father is.' Tess nodded, watching him closely.

He asked quickly, 'Well, did he tell you?'

'He didn't have to. I already knew, and you see, Alfie thinks you also know, hence the message.'

'You know?' Dan had now risen to his feet. 'How long have you known?'

'I've always known . . . at least—'

Dan moved to face Tess in a threatening manner and bellowed, 'You've always known? And you let me wallow in the depths of despair, fearing the loss of my grandson, and never once said? In the name of God, what were you thinking of, girl? Have you lost your marbles or something?'

His stance was so menacing that Tony quickly insinuated himself between them. 'Now take it easy, Dan. Tess wasn't sure whether you knew the truth and have been putting on a big act all these years for everyone's benefit.'

Dan growled at him. 'Know the truth? Putting on an act? What the hell are you talking about? Are you out of your mind too?'

'Dan, sit down and listen to me. Mam can't be much longer and we have to thrash this out before she comes back.' Tess was becoming agitated.

At once Tony offered, 'I'll go outside and watch for her and try to stall her for a while if you like, Tess.'

'Thanks, Tony. That's a good idea.'

'Will you be all right on your own?' He nodded towards a glowering Dan.

'I think so. You're not likely to hit me or do anything stupid, are you, Dan?'

'Don't talk nonsense. I never hit a woman in my life and I'm certainly not about to start now.'

'Away you go, Tony. Give me a bit of notice when you see Mam coming down the road.'

'Right, love.' With another warning look at Dan, Tony left the house.

'Sit down, Dan. And no more theatricals! Either you're very good at hiding the truth or you haven't a clue what I'm on about, and that's what I have to find out before Mam comes back.'

Dan sank down on the settee and spread his hands wide. 'I'm all ears. I haven't the slightest clue what you're talking about, so tell me, please.'

He was too innocent-looking, too much at ease, and doubts began to niggle at Tess. 'You know, don't you? You've known all along,' she accused.

'Know what, for heaven's sake?'

'You've been putting on one great big act all these years. Playing on Mam's goodness and sympathy, making a mug of her. And me as well!'

All the nonchalance fell from Dan, and rubbing his hands over his haggard face he confessed wearily, 'No, Tess, if you're referring to young Jackie, I truly believed I was his grandfather. When Anne said Jack wasn't my

400

son and brought Alfie Higgins along to prove it, I was gobsmacked. If you had hit me over the head with a sledgehammer I couldn't have been more shocked. Since then every time I look at Jackie I've been racking my brains trying to think who the father could be. It was staring me in the face the whole time and I couldn't see it. Perhaps my inner self didn't want to know. I can't remember anything about it, anything at all. But it became apparent to me that *I'm* Jackie's father. For the life of me I don't know how or when it happened. I didn't think it possible that I could sink so low as to seduce Colette. I'm really not that sort of person, Tess. You must believe that,' he implored.

Tess sank down on the chair facing him. His confession had taken the wind out of her sails. 'What about Mam? What are you going to tell her?'

He astounded her even further. 'She knows! I told her what I considered might have happened. At first she thought I was having her on; pulling her leg. She just wouldn't believe me. However, after giving it some thought she actually slapped my face and called me a lot of unmentionable names.' He grimaced at the memory and unconsciously rubbed his cheek where Tess could now see the shadow of a bruise. Mam must have hit him very hard, Tess thought with satisfaction. Serves him right! Dan continued, 'Next thing she's storming out of the house. She's finished with me, I'm sure of it. She'll never be able to forgive my being with Colette. But I swear, Tess, it wasn't planned. I honestly can't remember a thing about it.'

'That's hard to believe. You can't really blame Mam for doubting you. Any woman in her right mind would have done the same.'

'Honestly! Once the truth hit me in the face, I could

remember how Colette seemed to go off me after Jack's death. She wouldn't have anything to do with me. Scorned any attempt I made to help her. I couldn't understand it. Why on earth didn't she tell me about the baby? I'd have stood by her.'

'She only found out she was pregnant after she had made all the arrangements to go to Canada.' Tess rubbed salt in the wound. 'She couldn't even bear the sight of you. She said it was far too late to tell you. You were obviously in love with my mother and you wouldn't have believed her.'

'Does that mean she knew that I didn't remember a thing about what happened?'

'Yes, actually she did, and she managed to convince me . . . eventually. Now I'm not so sure.'

'I swear to you, Tess, I remember nothing. I was very drunk the day that Jack died. More drunk than I've ever been in my whole life. I don't know how I got through that day. The memory of it is a complete blank. That's the only time it could have happened. She should have told me. I had every right to know.'

'What right, Dan? The right to seduce a girl young enough to be your daughter? No, you had no rights whatsoever. Colette only told me because when she saw the child she couldn't bear to give him up for adoption. Right up until he was born I thought she was carrying Jack's baby. How that poor girl kept her mouth shut I'll never know. If it had been me, you'd still be rotting in Crumlin Road jail because I'd have shouted rape.'

Dan looked devastated. 'Did she say I raped her?' he wailed.

'No, she didn't! You're a very lucky man, Dan Thompson.'

'I can understand your anger, Tess,' he acknowledged.

'I'd have felt the same in your position. But please believe me when I say I really can't remember. I know it's a very feeble excuse, but it is the truth. Does anyone else know?'

'Only Tony and myself know the truth. Alfie guessed, but we didn't confirm it so he's still very much in the dark. He thinks you knew all along and were just covering it up so Mam wouldn't find out. Of course he confided his suspicions to Anne . . .'

A harsh laugh escaped Dan's lips. 'I'll put it in the *Irish News* tomorrow, save her the bother of spreading it about.'

'Alfie says he'll make sure she keeps her mouth shut.'

'And do you think he can? His hand isn't big enough. Can anybody, for that matter? You'd do a better job trying to stop the wind by holding up your hand, than preventing Anne blabbering on about something as tasteless as this whole saga.'

Tess couldn't help but smile at his sarky remarks. 'Alfie thinks he can and so do I. She's very much in love with him and he has asked her to marry him. He intends moving far away from Belfast, so I don't think she'll do anything to upset the apple-cart. It's Mam I'm worried about. What's going to become of her?'

Tony's urgent tap, tap on the door was a signal that her mother was approaching the house.

Dan gripped her hand. 'Tess, I love your mother more than life itself. You believe that, don't you?'

'Yes, but . . .'

'Bear with me . . . please.'

They heard Tony talking to Alice in the hall. Dan anxiously rose to his feet to face the music and implored, 'Please, Tess?'

She nodded as Alice surged in like a whirlwind. Coming to a halt in the middle of the room, her face a mask of revulsion, she berated Dan. 'You conniving, filthy bastard.' She glared at Tess. 'Has he told you then? Is he trying to win your sympathy like he tried to do with me?'

'He didn't have to. I already knew.'

Alice couldn't believe her ears. 'You mean you've known all these years and let me live in a fool's paradise with that dirty swine?'

'Colette confided in me a long time ago and I promised I wouldn't break her confidence.'

'You betrayed me? You put a mere wee chit of a girl – who by the way seduced him on the very night his son died – in front of your own mother? And you've the cheek to sit there and call yourself my daughter. Dear God, is there no end to all this deception?'

Wasn't that just like her mother, to lay the blame at Colette's door. 'Here! Hold on a minute. Colette Burns was the injured party in all this deception.' Tess threw a look of pure venom at Dan and stabbed a finger at him. '*He* was twice her age. *He* should have known better. *He* is the guilty party, not poor Colette.'

Ignoring her, Alice swung to face Dan. 'And as for you . . . you can pack your friggin' bags and get the hell out of my house. That's what you can do. I never want to see your ugly face in my house ever again.'

Dan swayed on unsteady legs, grasping at his chest. 'Alice,' he croaked, uttering her name as if asking for help.

Immediately Alice was at his side, taking him by the elbow. 'Sit down, love.' When he obediently slumped down on the armchair, she knelt beside him and loosened his tie. 'Take a deep breath,' she ordered, and threw a command over her shoulder to Tess. 'Send for an ambulance, quickly.' All her animosity and profanities were forgotten in the face of his immediate plight.

With Alice's head turned from him, Dan winked at Tess and Tony to let them know an ambulance wasn't necessary.

'I don't think he needs one,' Tess ground out through clenched teeth, and grabbing a bemused Tony by the arm pulled him towards the door.

On the pavement Tess turned to Tony and he gathered her close.

Seething with anger she asked, 'What did you make of all that, eh?'

He smiled slightly. 'An Oscar-winning performance, I'd say.'

'Do you think he knew all the time?'

'Perhaps, but that is something we'll never be certain of. So long as your mother knows the truth, that's all that matters. And it looks like she's going to forgive him. Love is blind, that's surely one true saying where she's concerned.'

'Oh aye. You can be sure everyone will be in the wrong but Dan Thompson, as far as she's concerned. She'll make my life hell, so she will. I'll get the blame for everything. Even bringing on Dan's staged heart attack. That was a laugh, wasn't it? I'll say this much, that man's one bloody good actor. He's wasting his time pulling pints, he should be on at the Palladium.'

Tony cupped her face in his hands. 'Listen to me, Tess. The way your mother's fawning all over him in there, she wouldn't have the cheek to find fault with you.'

Tess drew a deep breath and relaxed. 'I suppose you're right. What time is it, love?'

Tony glanced at his watch. 'Would you believe it's only half past nine. It has been a long two hours, so it has.

More like a week. Shall we walk over and fetch my car and go down to Johnny's for a fish supper?'

Bearing in mind the fate of Tess's Mini, Tony now kept his car in a lock-up garage over on Beechmount Avenue, near where he lived.

'No, it's not a bad night. Let's just take a slow stroll down and we can talk over our wedding plans as we go.'

'Sounds good enough to me.'

As they made their way down the Grosvenor Road, Tess suddenly remembered. 'Oh, by the way, love, in all the excitement I forgot to tell you. Les got back to Theresa. He's booked a flight from Aldergrove to Shannon on Friday and then on to Canada. Isn't that wonderful?'

'As I said before, he's keen as mustard, that bloke. I for one won't be surprised if Theresa finds him more attractive than Bob Dempsey.'

'Me too. I told her we would drive her up to the airport, so everything else rests with Les.'

Tess clung to Tony's arm. She'd never been happier. It was as if a great weight had been lifted from her shoulders, leaving her free to wallow in the glory of her love for Tony. 'Now that I don't have to worry about Mam any more, do you think we could bring our wedding forward a bit?'

Tony gave a delighted laugh. It was true indeed that every cloud had a silver lining. 'Any time you like, love.'

They were passing Dunville Park and he drew her into the shadows. They did eventually get their fish suppers, which they appreciated very much, having worked up quite an appetite, and were now looking happily forward to a spring wedding.

Mary A. Larkin would like to hear from her readers.
You are very welcome to visit her at:
www.marylarkin.co.uk